Praise for Jack L. Chalker:

"Stunning . . . The ingenious Jack L. Chalker is back with . . . another intriguing series. . . . Mr. Chalker has outdone himself!" —*Rave Reviews*

"His work is distinguished by imagination, a fascination with political and social orders, [and] satisfying, suspenseful, action-oriented plots . . ."
—*The New Encyclopedia of Science Fiction*

"An entertaining storyteller of alien beings and worlds." —*The Science Fiction Source Book*

". . . exhilarating and innovative. . . . Jack L. Chalker is a novelist of considerable flair, with an ear acutely attuned to the secret dreams of freedom mortals tend to dream. . . ."
—John Clute, *The Science Fiction Encyclopedia*

THE CHANGEWINDS

JACK L. CHALKER

THE CHANGEWINDS

This is a work of fiction. All the characters and events portrayed in this book are fictional, and any resemblance to real people or incidents is purely coincidental.

A Baen Book

Baen Publishing Enterprises
P.O. Box 1403
Riverdale, N.Y. 10471

ISBN: 0-671-87734-8

Cover art by Stephen Hickman

First printing, August 1996

Distributed by
SIMON & SCHUSTER
1230 Avenue of the Americas
New York, N.Y. 10020

Printed in the United States of America

PART I

WHEN THE CHANGEWINDS BLOW

For Eva

1
The Girl Who Was Afraid of Thunderstorms

There is something almost other-worldly about a huge shopping mall; enter it and you leave heat or cold, night and day behind, and enter a futuristic Disney-like vision of a future world which is all antiseptic, insulated, and artificial yet somehow it caters to all your basic modern needs. It is the synthesis of the ancient bazaar, the communal marketplace, the soda fountain, the drive-in, and the town square and more. Its vast interiors with their wasted space, careful fountains, phony waterfalls, plastic park benches and canned music which may be *The 1001 Strings Play the Best of the Rolling Stones* but somehow sounds like the same elevator music the parents and grandparents of those denizens of malls heard in their day. To many of the youth who are too young to be allowed in the adult bars and clubs and too old to be in by eight o'clock it is a massive singles bar as well.

Wednesday night wasn't the best night out, even in the mall, and it was tough on a school night to figure out an excuse to get there that parents might accept, but teens have had many centuries of evolution to get to a point where they instinctively know how to manage such urgencies when they have to, and Sharlene "Charley" Sharkin certainly felt like she had to.

It wasn't anything to do with the mall itself, but rather what it filled in her life. She was seventeen and due to graduate in five months, an occasion she was looking forward to with great anticipation. She was bright, athletic, and had good grades for the most part, but she hated school and all it stood for. Her parents had all sorts of plans for her, all of which included college and perhaps beyond, but the thought of four or more years of additional school was just *gruesome,* that was all. She could see herself putting up with some secretarial school—she was already a lightning typist and did some word processing on the school computer for office brownie points—or maybe even a medical technician's course, or paralegal, or something like that, but nothing more. College wasn't like regular school in one way: if you didn't get it and later regretted it there was nothing that said you had to be eighteen and not twenty or even older to get in.

She had a nice, round face with just a bit of an overbite set off by mid-length Clairol brown perm-curled hair, no beauty but cute and she knew it. She was slightly chubby and thought she was fat and hated it but not enough to really work at dieting or giving up all the nice foods that made life worthwhile. She'd been a skinny, athletic kid but it had just started to come on and stay there, particularly in the past year or two, but at five foot three and a hundred and thirty-six pounds she didn't *feel* out of whack. She'd really let herself go since—well, since Tommy.

She had just turned sixteen, and was real popular with the boys, and the night of the junior prom Tommy Meyers had brought out this bottle of high-proof whiskey he'd gotten someplace and before she knew it Tommy had popped her cherry for good in his brother's borrowed conversion van, and while nothing had come of it she'd gone through *months* of nervous fear wondering if she was pregnant, or had caught something, or who knew what, and it'd scared her far more than all that blood. The experience made her something of a leader among her friends, of course, but it'd also given her a reputation among the boys as an easy girl and she'd had more than her share of troubles from *that*.

She'd let herself go after that, giving up most of the athletics and pigging out on whatever she wanted, particularly chocolate. If it hadn't been for Sam moving into the city she might have gotten really depressed, but even though Sam was a real straight arrow she didn't care and there was no closer friendship.

And now Sam was gone.

Samantha Buell was certainly her best friend in the whole world and the only person she felt she could confide in. Sam had needed a friend when she'd moved here with her mother a little over a year ago and they'd hit it off, the original thing they had in common being that they both went by nicknames that sounded more boy than girl—although Sam just called it "unisex." They liked the same rock bands, the same TV shows, they swapped romance novels—although Sam was more of a reader than she was—and they both *loved* roaming the mall and trying on all sorts of outrageous fashions. They spent a lot of free time together and talking on the phone and all that. They were the same height, and while Sam had a better figure she had a little bit of extra weight herself. Still, they looked enough alike to be mistaken more than once for sisters, and they were both also the only children of well-off professionals, spoiled without really realizing it.

Not that there weren't real differences, the least of which was Sam's slight but noticeable New England accent contrasted with Charley's southwestern twang. Sam's folks were divorced, and she lived here now with her mother who was a lawyer who worked for some federal agency or another. Environment, she thought, but she'd never really gone into it. Sam's dad was a contractor in Boston and they still got along pretty good—Sam would fly out to stay with him part of the summer and some of the long holidays and he called a lot—but maybe three thousand miles was a lot of distance for so-called "joint custody."

But Sam's voice was, well, unique. She had one of the deepest, most asexual voices Charley had ever heard in a girl, although not unpleasant or irritating. It was just, well, *asexual*, the kind of tonal voice that was stuck between the half octaves and could easily belong to a boy her age although it didn't sound wrong in her, either. Sam said that her grandmother—her dad's mother—had the same kind of voice. She could actually shift that voice even lower a bit and you'd swear she was all male, too, or higher a bit and sound feminine and sassy. Sam had hoped that this odd ability might get her into acting one day.

She'd always been something of a tomboy type, fooling around in Dad's workshop as a kid. She particularly liked carpentry and was really good at it, but her Dad had always tried to steer her away with some ingrained sexist ideas about what was properly boys' work and girls' work while her mother, who wanted her to be like the first female President or a great doctor or something was appalled by Sam's taste for manual skills. Charley, on the other hand, wouldn't be caught *dead* if not dressed in the latest style. Until she'd met Charley the only real concession she'd made to unmistakable femininity was long, almost waist-length straight black hair.

Still, under Charley's skilled eye and guidance, Sam had lately taken to trying all sorts of new and feminine fashions, taken a real interest suddenly in perfume and cosmetics and stuff like that, which somewhat pleased her mother and also started getting her all sorts of attention from the boys. So far she hadn't done much, though; Sam had some real hangups of her own. Back in Boston she'd gone to this private all-girls' school, and two of her classmates had done it before they were past sixteen that Sam knew about. It was sheer stupid bad luck, but one of them had gotten pregnant the first time out and the other one had come down with VD. The odds against both of 'em, or even either of 'em, having anything like that happen was small, and maybe that was only the two Sam found out about, but it had scared the hell out of her. She was still a virgin and not real inclined to changing that in the immediate future. That was why a best girlfriend was an essential. They protected and supported each other. Together, somehow, they were safe.

And now Sam was gone.

At first she hadn't thought anything of it, when Sam hadn't shown up for school on Monday. Charley had been away visiting relatives all weekend, and had been too damned tired to feel sociable on Monday. On Tuesday she'd called over to the house and gotten Sam's mother's answering machine and left a message. No big deal. Maybe somebody got sick back east or something. Later, she heard it had been in the news over the weekend and in the Sunday paper, but they'd thrown out everything but the comics.

But today, in school, she'd been called out of first period English to Mr. Dunteman's office—he was the administrative vice principal—and waiting there had been this strange man who introduced himself as Detective O'Donnell of the Juvenile Division and said he wanted to know if Charley had heard from Sam in the last few days.

"Huh? No. Why? Has something happened?"

"We—don't really know. When was the last time you saw or spoke to her?"

"Uh—Friday. Here. I went away that night for the weekend and didn't get back 'til Sunday night."

"Uh-huh. And did she seem—different? I mean, did she seem out of the ordinary in any way? Nervous? Irritable? Depressed? Anything like that?"

She thought a moment. The fact was, there *had* been something wrong. She'd sensed it rather than been told it, but it was noticeable enough that she'd asked Sam if there were any problems.

"She seemed—you know, tense. Yeah, maybe nervous. I figured at first it was just her period or something but it wasn't like that, really. She looked, well, kinda *scared.* But she said everything was okay when I asked her about it. She just sorta' shrugged it off and said she was havin' some problems and that she'd tell me when I got back. I *did* kinda get the idea that she wanted to say more but when she found out I was goin' away, well, she just tried to laugh it off. Why? What's happened to her?"

O'Donnell had sighed. He was big and craggy and built like a cement block, with curly red hair and real pale blue eyes. If you'd been ordered to build an Irishman he was about what you'd come up with.

"She left school normally—we know that much," he told her. "She caught the first bus home, got a few things—her mother wasn't back from work yet—and then left. We don't know anything beyond that. She simply—vanished." He paused as he watched her look of horror grow. "These things *do* happen, Miss. All the time. It's my job to piece everything together and see if we can find her before something very bad happens to her."

"You think she—*ran away?* Not Sam! The only one she could run to would be her Dad and he'd send her right back here. I *know!*"

"We don't honestly know. She certainly hadn't made any long-range plans to bolt; there's no sign of it. Everything points to a sudden decision to just take off. She went home, packed a small suitcase, went down to the Front Street Bank's automated teller with the backup of her mother's card and withdrew the maximum three hundred dollars allowed by the machine."

"Yeah, her mom gave her the card just in case she needed money when her mom wasn't around but I don't think she ever used it for more'n twenty bucks. Three hundred . . ."

"That's really not that much when you consider it," the detective had pointed out. "Enough to buy a ticket to most places but only if you had money or people at the other end. We checked the airlines and bus stations—no sign, although that doesn't always mean much. She didn't have a driver's license?"

Charley shook her head. "Nope. Flunked the test three times. She was just too scared behind the wheel."

"And no boyfriends? Particularly new ones? No major infatuations? You're positive?"

"Positive! She's not gay or nothin' like that—she liked boys and all, but if she had anything going she'd'a told me. No way there was anybody she'd do *this* for, not unless it happened between Friday morning and Friday afternoon."

"Stranger things have happened, but I admit it's unlikely unless it involved someone in school and we can account for everyone but her. Very well—if she contacts you let me know *immediately*. I'll give you a card, here, with my name and number. It looks very likely that something scared her very badly. Something she couldn't or wouldn't confide for any of a thousand reasons to either her best friend or her mother. She panicked. She ran. No note, nothing. But her resources are quite limited. If she uses any of her mother's charge cards we'll find her and I think she's bright enough to know that. Her cash will be running low if it isn't gone already. She'll only have a few choices, and they're crime, or falling prey to the seamier side of society, or she'll have to contact somebody she trusts. You're a likely candidate for that. If she does, try and get her what she needs and find out where she's staying and then call me. And, if you can, find out what in the world could scare her so much that this was the only way out."

She had promised it all, but the truth was that if Sam called she didn't know *what* she would do, and she suspected O'Donnell knew that, too. What the hell could have *scared* her like that? Caused her to run rather than go to her mom or best friend? Had Sam been less honest than she seemed? Had she, like, gotten knocked up? No, that wouldn't do it. Hell, she might get grounded for six months but her mom would still have worked it all out and Sam would know that. Her mom was pretty busy but she was all right deep down—much more modern than Charley's parents, anyway.

Sam always said she wanted to be an actress; she'd been in the drama club and was set for a pretty good part in the class play coming up in April, but she had few other real interests. Setting off for Hollywood on impulse just wasn't her style.

It was hard for Charley to imagine Sam out there on her own in any event. Hell, she was scared to go out alone most times. Like, she was even scared of thunderstorms. Well, maybe she'd find out now.

Charley had gone through the day confused and depressed and then went straight home. She'd gotten the mail and found a small envelope addressed to her and postmarked locally with very familiar handwriting and she'd torn it open. Inside, on a piece of notepaper in Sam's handwriting, had been a nervously scrawled message.

Dear Charley—Sorry to get you into this but I got noplace else to go. Can you meet me at the mall at seven o'clock? Just go browse at Sears. Look normal, then at seven go back to credit like you was going to the ladies room. Don't tell nobody or let them see this note. Don't let nobody follow you. I'm OK so long as you don't bring nobody. Love and kisses, Sam.

Charley was afraid at first that she wouldn't make it in time. Her Dad had a bunch of stuff to talk about and wasn't in any mood to let her out, but she'd convinced him it wouldn't be long and that she really needed to pick up something for school tomorrow. She barely had time to change into an outfit more appropriate for the mall—the satiny blue pantsuit and the midcalf boots with the fold-down leather fringes. And it'd been like six-thirty when she'd gotten the okay, and while it was only a ten-minute drive to the mall she had to park and go to Sears and spend some time browsing, too, so it'd look natural when she went to the jane. There was also the level of paranoia the note induced.

"Don't let nobody follow you. . . ."

Like, who would be following *her?* Well, okay, the cops, maybe—if they figured one runaway teen was worth a stakeout. Or, maybe, whoever scared Sam so bad. They might figure it like O'Donnell and keep an eye on her best friend, right?

Damn it, she's got me seein' cars and mysterious people in trenchcoats!

The worst part of it was, she had to wear her glasses and she hated that. Made her look like some dumb librarian. But she was fairly nearsighted and needed them to drive, and she'd had her contacts in all day at school. Not like Sam—Sam only needed glasses to read close up, and she'd look like an idiot, face at arm's length from a book, rather than wear them in school.

The mall was pretty crowded for a winter Wednesday, maybe because it was unusually warm tonight for this time of year, and Charley saw one or two kids she knew, but the time didn't allow for her to be anything but single-minded. If somebody was following they'd just have to follow, that's all. What the hell could happen in a place crowded like *this,* anyway?

She made her way to Sears, then went and looked at some of the clothes there. She knew she didn't have Sam's acting talent and she probably was giving the most unconvincing show of her life, but she had to try. She glanced at her watch—five after seven! Past time to go to the bathroom.

Had she delayed long enough? Had she delayed too long? She went on back to the business office and then around the corner toward the restrooms. You sure knew where *they* were in a big mall. Most times the biggest department stores had the only bathrooms in the place.

The restrooms were near the end of a corridor that wound up at an "Employees Only" door to the warehouse part, and there was a branch corridor just before them leading to some offices. She went into the bathroom expecting Sam to be there, but it was empty. She wasn't sure if she should just stay there or not, but she sure as hell wasn't gonna stay there all night. She really did have to go—this Jane Bond shit didn't really make it at all—and so she decided to just do everything normal. Maybe Sam wasn't there tonight. Maybe something happened, or Sam figured the note would come earlier, or maybe this was just a way for Sam to check and see that she wasn't being followed.

She gave it fifteen minutes, during which one pregnant lady came in and nobody else, and then decided to get out of there. She opened the door and heard, behind her, in a loud whisper, "Charley! In here—quick!"

She turned and saw a small, chunky figure in boys' blue denim jeans and matching jacket holding the employee door open. She hesitated a moment, then went to the door and out just before the pregnant lady exited.

Charley stared at the other. "Christ, Sam—is that really *you?*"

"Yeah! Come on! I want to get us out of here and someplace where we can talk. Hurry up!"

As close as she'd been to Sam she wouldn't have recognized her from any distance. Gone was the long, straight black hair, replaced with a slightly curly sandy brown cut, extremely short, like a boy's, and combed straight back with a side part. She was also wearing a man's style rose-tinted pair of glasses and dressed in the stiff denim that completely concealed her figure and some cheap sneakers and high black socks. It was a fairly simple disguise but by its subtlety very effective. No fake beard or shit like that that would never be convincing. The fact that Sam was one of those people whose face by itself could be either male or female depending on the hair and body and the like helped, too. It was also a natural disguise—her voice was already unusually low, and it didn't take much effort to get it low and raspy enough to sound like maybe a thirteen- or fourteen-year-old boy.

They wound up outside, then walked across the parking lot to the theater entrance. Sam bought two tickets to the newest Disney cartoon, knowing that for the late show there'd be very few people there and none they would know. Not with a "G" rating.

Sam was right. There were like a dozen people in there for the Wednesday late show. They took seats on a side aisle near the back, away from the rest. Sam put her arm around Charley. "Just act like we don't care about the movie, which we don't," she said. "Nobody ever notices much about a boy and a girl makin' out in the back of a theater."

"Okay, I'll play along," Charley whispered back, "but what the hell is this all *about?* Why'd you run? Where you *been?* Everybody's worried sick. . . ."

"Long story," Sam responded. "I'll tell you as much as I can. Some of it'll sound crazy and maybe I am, but it's damned *real.*"

It hadn't been all that sudden, only the final act. For months, almost since moving out west, she had been having strange experiences. First it was the dreams—lots of them, long and elaborate, sometimes several nights in a row with no break, and always involving the same things although never quite the same.

Charley knew about the dreams. The most frequent one involved the demon and Sam, who was always driving a red sports car around a twisting mountain road along a coast, although Sam couldn't drive and they were hundreds of miles from any coast.

It always began with a dark figure, sitting alone in a comfortable-looking room that none the less resembled more a medieval castle than anything modern. There was a low fire in the fireplace and a few goblets about, but everything was indistinct, as if in a dream. She saw his form, but not really his face, masked in shadow, but it was a strange form of a fairly large man in flowing robes and wearing what might have been a helmet with two large, crooked horns emerging from each side. She saw him, though, not as a vision, or a completed scene, but as if she were there as well, sitting opposite him in a chair of her own, looking at his dark form with her own eyes. Somehow, she was aware that the goblet near her on a small table had until recently contained some kind of drug, and that the dark figure's mysterious, hazy, dark presence was partly due to that.

Suddenly there was a rumble and crackling, more like an electrical short circuit than anything else, but it seemed to overwhelm them, to carry them, not physically but mentally, through a dizzying, blinding, multicolored ride like an out of control carousel, although the dark form in the chair was still there, silhouetted against the swirling maelstrom.

And then there had been darkness, with scenes illuminated now by flashes of lightning and accompanying clashes of thunder, and a view from a great height down to a frothing ocean below beating itself against black rocks, and a low range of mountains forming a jagged and serpentine coastline, and, in the distance, two small lights approaching along that coast. They were not the storm, but they were of and with the storm, and they moved swiftly inland to a point where storm and lights must meet.

And now she saw herself driving that red sports car, but not from the point of view of the driver. Rather, she saw herself from the height during the flashes of lightning, and now they were nearly on top of it, and the dark, horned figure whispered fearsomely in a tone that somehow still cut through the noise of storm and surf, "Now! I was correct. The equations are perfectly in balance. She is the one we seek and she sleeps in the stupors of overindulgence. Minimum resistance, maximum flow, calculated odds of success in the ninety-plus percentile. . . . Now!"

And from the cloud a great bolt of lightning shot out, and while it struck just ahead and on the ocean side of the road the car suddenly slammed on its brakes and spun, aided by the sudden rain, and . . .

All then was blackness.

That had been the first of them, repeated many times with little or no variation, but it had not been the last. At first she put them down as mere fantasies, as nightmares, maybe, or possibly even a sign of a good imagination, but then the dreams progressed and she began to see a pattern both in when the dreams came and in their progression.

Always in the night. Always when thunderstorms approached and then raged around her.

But during this season of the year she felt she'd almost licked it. No thunderstorms, no really bad dreams. Not until last Thursday night, when this freak warm front had moved in and clashed with the very chilly winter air and set off a rare winter one.

Charley frowned. "I don't remember a thunderstorm last Thursday."

"It was real early in the morning. Like two or three. You'd sleep through an atomic bomb anyway. You can check it in the papers, though. We had it—and I had another real mean one."

"You mean you're running from a *dream?*"

"Not—exactly."

She had awakened to the sound and fury of the freak storm, and lay there, eyes wide open, feeling wide awake and afraid to go back to sleep, but even though the storm raged and she was fully conscious, through the thunder, through the roar of rain and hail on the roof and the rattling of windows by heavy winds, the voices intruded and the room seemed to fade. It was also quite dark, but she was seeing through another's eyes, a visitor without influence or control; an interloper who should not have been there, wherever "there" was.

It was the hall of a medieval-like castle, damp and somewhat dark, illuminated by torches and by a fire in the great fireplace. She sat in a large, lushly upholstered chair at the head of a long table, an elegant if greasy and overcooked meal in front of her. She knew it was a woman's body, and probably royalty; long, feminine arms reached out for food and wine, with long, delicate fingers unblemished by any sign of work or wear, with crimson, perfectly trimmed and shaped nails so long they could not have withstood doing anything serious.

There were others at the table. A large man with a full beard and shoulder-length hair, stocky and rough but dressed in fine clothing including a cape. Several others, mostly rough-looking men, some accompanied by young women dressed in satin and gold, were also there—and a few others.

One was a tiny, gnarled man who must have been no more than three feet high, dressed in gray and brown with a rich black beard that seemed to go down almost to his feet, sitting there on a very high stool to be at equal height to the others. Another wore a crimson cloak and hood but seemed to have a frog-like snout extending from it and two round, yellow eyes that never blinked but, cat-like, reflected the torchlight. Yet another had a long, distorted, puffy kind of face, huge round blue eyes, and a rhinoceros-like horn rising up from the center of his forehead, and a woman whose hairless head seemed covered by a bony gray plate and whose arms ended not in hands but in claw-like mandibles. There may have been more, but the onlooker did not focus on them but rather on eating.

Finally the hairy man closest to her asked, "Highness, has the problem of the simulacra been disposed of?"

From behind her a voice, that *voice, responded, "My Lord Klewa, we all know that nothing is certain except that the unthinkable must be thought, but there was little danger. So far we have found only a very few in all our months of searching that even slightly posed a danger and we are dealing with each in turn. The odds of that ever being a factor were always slim—the enemy would have to find a simulacrum and somehow transport before we could find and destroy them, and we had the only model for such loci searching anyway. You have no idea how many levels up we have gone and continue to go. Just when we believe it is no longer possible my storms find another, but so far away. . . . Even so, I shall deal with each.*

"If you wish certainties, then kill yourself," the strange one continued, "for that will produce a certainty in this *world, at least. If you desire minimum risk, we have gone far further in that regard then anyone could imagine. But risk there will always be, and should be, for gain without risk would make a prize meaningless. So vast is our enterprise that we risk disrupting the fragile fabric of our reality and might cause the changewinds to increase and turn on us as well, but consider the goals and the alternatives. Be at ease."*

And then she *spoke, with a voice not unlike her own voice, strangely deep, although the tongue was strange and musical and not at all like English or any other language she had known, and the tone was softer, gentler, maybe sexier than she'd ever used.*

"My Lord, why these questions now? You know my talents, and you know the skills of Protector Klittichorn. None of you entered into this alliance blindly, and our ideals and goals are of the highest order. The small brains who blindly struck down your own son to preserve their evil statist values would also have at me. We unite and triumph or die, or we do nothing and thus only die ever so slowly but no less certainly. But if we die, let it not be from faint hearts when all goes well. Speak your mind freely here, for we are equals at this table."

"Equals, aye, except for him,*" muttered the gnome-like man in a surprisingly deep, gruff voice. "We would follow you and your ideals to the death, My Lady, but not to deliver ourselves into the hands of another oppressor."*

"The Protector is a brilliant man who has the same dreams as we," she responded. "I have complete confidence in him, and, of course, there is no real chance of true victory without his tremendous skills. I regret that he has not the pleasing personality of court and politics, but I do not doubt his motives. He has always served me faithfully and well, and if you have any doubts then you must discard them. All of us must trust one another and give our bond; it is the only true thing of value between us."

Suddenly the scene began to fade, jumping in and out, becoming disjointed and impossible to follow, like hearing three seconds out of every ten in a conversation. Another voice seemed to be cutting out the connection, with intermittent words here and there in a totally different tone and appearing to come from much farther away.

. . . bee . . . kow . . . low . . . bap . . .

There was a sudden dizziness, first one way, then the other, as if someone were tuning a radio and she was the dial. It stopped almost as quickly as it began, and again there was a sense of contact with someone or something far away, but with a difference. This time she was lying there in the dark, fully aware of herself and her surroundings, her skin tingling oddly, and there was a sense that now the situation was reversed and that someone, or something, was looking at her or through her to the room beyond.

"There is darkness. She is awake and her eyes are open but there is darkness." There was a sudden slight tickling sensation as if cobwebs had been run up and down her body. *"Hmmm . . . Nothing*

really wrong. I was afraid for a moment she was blind or something."

"It's nighttime, you idiot, and she's in bed in a trance," came *another voice.*

"Who are you?" she called aloud to the voice in her head. "What do you want with me?"

The voice either did not or could not hear, and ignored her. It was inside her head, yet distanced. A man's voice, but not any of the men at the court dinner she had witnessed. Someone new, someone different, almost clinical-sounding, like some of her doctors. More interesting, if a bit more frightening, the words were certainly American English.

"I have her construct now. It is identical in every detail. Astonishing. There must not be one point of similarity in background or origin yet there is an identical genetic code." A sigh. *"Too late. The storm is passing and the lock of hair is not sufficient for more. But—does he know of her? He must—the storms are passing through and she's next. Still alive, Cromil! The first one we've found before he's killed her!"*

"The one in the red car was barely dead," the other noted optimistically. *"At least we're catching up."*

The man ignored the comment. "Too late to do more now, damn it! Time for preparations. We must not let him kill her if we can. In our hands, she would be a great weapon. One test, no more. It already fades. . . ."

Suddenly, eerily, she was entirely back in the room, the storm already going away, her senses abnormally keen and sharp.

And then someone began to run his fingers through her hair!

It was terrifying, horrible. She wanted to scream, but dared not. The sensation faded in a moment but it was some time before she could move, dared to sit up, to turn—and find no one there.

Charley didn't know what to believe but she could understand her friend's terror. "Jeez! That's why you looked like hell and were so shook up at school Friday."

Sam nodded. "Yeah—but what could I do? You were goin' away for the weekend, and my mom would have all kinds of pop psychology bullshit. I mean, I didn't have any proof or nothin'. Hell, maybe I *was* nuts. I didn't know. But when we got out of school, well, something else happened. Just comin' out the door, kids all around, I thought I saw this big guy out of the corner of my eye, all black and stuff, maybe ten feet away. I turned, but there was nobody there. I got spooked. I got on the bus and sat up front, almost behind Miss Everett. I was lookin' out, and I know it's nuts, but I saw him again. Out of the corner of my eye, like before—standin' on the street. In a crowd. But when I looked around, he was gone."

"Just nerves."

"Yeah, that's what I told myself, but then I looked up for some reason straight into the rear view mirror. You know what I mean—shows the aisle and seats? And he was there, sittin' in the back, and he didn't disappear. I turned, and there was nothin' where he should'a been but empty seats. I turned back to the mirror and there he was."

"What—what did he look like?" Like, was this a loony tune or was this strait jacket city?

"He—he didn't have any real features. He was all black, kinda like a cardboard cutout of black paper, but he moved. He breathed. He was *alive!* And, I mean, I had to get off that bus. I walked the last three blocks, and when the bus passed I kinda saw him on it still. I got into the house, I didn't know what to do, but I knew it'd be dark in an hour and Mom wouldn't be home for three. Besides, they'd got me in my own room in my own bed. All she'd do would be to get me off to the funny farm where I'd be cooped up, and I figured he'd find me easy there. I looked out the front windows and I saw him, across the street, by the mailbox, just standin' there. I didn't know what he was doin', but I figured he was either just keepin' an eye on me for somebody else or he was waitin' til dark and I just wasn't gonna give him no chance. I panicked. I stuffed one of Mom's overnight bags with whatever I could find quick, grabbed the cash card, and got out the cellar window and out through the backyard. I snuck six blocks to Central Avenue, hit the automatic teller—I forgot you couldn't get much from one—and then caught the bus to the mall. I knew I'd given him the slip—no sign of him, not in the mirror of the bus, not anywhere. All I wanted was to shake him—and I did."

She blew a hundred and ten bucks on the boy's denims and shoes and another forty in the Hair Palace, a unisex hair salon. "I told them it was for a school play," she said. "That I had to look like a boy 'cause the role was a girl pretending to be a boy. The glasses were fifteen bucks. Plain lenses. I washed the stuff at the little coin-op at the motel over on Figuroa. I finally dumped most everything I brought with me in the dumpster. Then I started hidin' out here in the mall. There's all sorts of places if you really want to, and don't mind gettin' locked in. They got a couple of security guards but they're easy to dodge and they only go to midnight, eight on Sundays, then they just lock up tight and go. The water fountains work and the employee rest rooms in the mall security area ain't never locked. Durin' the day I been hustlin'. You know—carrying groceries to cars down at the Food Mart, helpin' little old ladies with shit, that kind of thing. I been doin' maybe twenty, thirty bucks a day in tips."

"And, like nobody's *recognized* you?"

She grinned. "Nope. I even been real close to some of the gang from school, mostly by accident—no use in pushin' things—and they never gave me a glance. You'd be surprised how many kids are around durin' school days, too. Nobody ever says nothin' unless they're at the arcade or like that. And everybody's been treatin' me like a boy. I even use the men's room. I always wondered what a urinal looks like. No wonder they can be in and out so fast. Only thing wrong is the mice." She shivered. "You'd think a classy place like this wouldn't have things like them hiding around. At least they should get a cat or something. And I'm *dying* for a shower!"

Charley stared at Sam in the darkness as an evil cartoon cat was chortling over plans to do in a very strange-looking duck in France or someplace on the screen. "You nuts? You gone stark raving mad? Sam, you can't keep going on like this! Your mom's probably worried sick by now, the cops are all over looking for you, and sooner or later somebody's gonna notice."

The fugitive sighed. "I know. I know. But I can't go home yet—I'll never feel real comfortable there again, and what if this character doesn't care who he hurts? I know it sounds nuts, like spook city, but it's for *real*. When I get out of this and have some breathing time I'll call Mom and tell her I'm okay. It won't stop her worryin' but at least she'll know I'm not kidnapped or dead or somethin'." She paused, sensing that it wasn't getting through. "Charley—I'm scared. I've never been more scared in my whole life. I'm—doing this—'cause I don't know what else to do."

"Sam—you just gotta come home. You just *gotta*. You're not cut out for this. Sooner or later somebody's gonna find you out anyway, or somebody else will spot you for what you are and you'll wind up in some strange city all doped up and turnin' tricks or somethin' like that. Jesus, there must be a hundred rapes a year just in *this* town! This ain't TV and you're no karate queen!"

"I made out so far. It's different when they think you're a boy. I found out how different just around here. But—you think I *like* this? I never thought ahead. I had to run and hide. Whoever it is, though—they haven't found me here. Not yet, anyway."

"Look—your mom and the cops can help."

"How? From a black figure who's only visible when he wants to be seen? From fucking thunderstorms that can put *something* in my own bedroom with me? You're sayin' go back and stand in front of the guys with guns who want to kill ya 'cause if you run through the door and get away from 'em you just *might* run into a guy with a gun someplace who wants to kill ya."

"They're just *dreams,* Sam! Just *dreams.* They're just all in your head. And a black figure who's seen only in mirrors and once in a while when you're alone—that's creepy but it's right out of a horror movie. Those things just don't *exist* in the real world. I may not be a real brain but I know better than to believe in elves and fairies and Santa Claus and the Boogeyman."

Sam sighed. "I kinda thought you'd say that. I *know* that's what Mom and Dad and the cops would say—what almost *anybody'd* say. Okay, forget the dreams, forget the Boogeyman, forget everything I told you. Just promise me that you won't give me away here. Not until I can get clear and get settled someplace. A day. Two days tops. Will you promise me that?" She stared at her friend in the darkness of the movie house. "Charley—if I have to go home now, or to the funny farm, I'll kill myself. You can't *know* what it was like. Don't force me to do that. *Please!*"

Charley didn't really know what to do. Sam needed help—a lot of it. That was for sure. Help she couldn't give. She needed a really good psychiatrist and a lot of time. On the other hand, Sam was still Sam and she was still her friend, and there was such a note of desperation there that Charley felt Sam might well kill herself at this point. She needed advice on what to do and there was no way she could get it. Anybody she told about this would be hell-bent to recapture Sam, and if anything happened to Sam as a result of what she did she'd never forgive herself.

"Okay, okay, keep cool," Charley responded, trying to think. "Look, there's not much I can do tonight, and I got school tomorrow and Friday. I was supposed to go to a movie with Harry Friday night, but I can break that without my folks knowing. Look, I'll pick you up here. We'll do this boyfriend-girlfriend bit so it'll look right. I'll pick you up in front of the Food Mart say . . . seven-thirty. We'll go someplace and try and really figure it out. If anything happens before then, call me and I'll see what I can do. I *swear* I won't tell nobody nothin'. All right?"

Sam seemed somewhat relieved. "All right. Friday night, then. You better get home now—I'll get by."

Charley kissed Sam and squeezed her hand and then, hesitantly, got up and walked out of the theater. The mall was already mostly closed down, and she had no trouble finding her car. She got in, started it, and pulled out toward the exit light, trying to think, to figure things out, and not paying any attention to the rock blaring from the car radio.

"And here's the latest from Action Weather. Cool tonight, lows about thirty-five in the city and lower than that in the suburbs, with light snow possible above the six thousand foot mark. In spite of this, unseasonable freak thunderstorms continue in the area due to an unsettled mix of very cold air aloft and relatively warmer air near the surface. High tomorrow around fifty. This is Doctor Ruben Miller with Action Weather. . . ."

A car's lights turned on behind her and slowly pulled out toward the exit traffic light. *Just nerves,* she told herself. *Most people would be leaving now who hadn't already left.*

She turned onto the street and couldn't help but see the lights of the other car turn the same way. She began feeling very paranoid, very silly. Sam was, well, *sick,* that's all. It'd take a shrink to figure it out, but Sam never really liked it out here in the southwestern boonies or being this far from her dad, she was too straight arrow to even date in the usual ways, and she was hemmed in by her lack of wheels to get out and enjoy things. She'd gone so far into that fantasy life she couldn't quite get out anymore, Charley decided.

Still, she couldn't shake some of the paranoia that rubbed off Sam like dirt. Was that the same car still following? What if she made a turn?

Feeling stupid, she turned onto a side street well before hers just to get a little peace of mind. She went about a block and then saw headlights turn in from the main street. She made a left, then another right before the other car could possibly see her, then pulled over and parked just ahead of a big black car that would partially shield her from view.

A car passed on the cross street; a dark blue Ford. It was impossible to see who was driving, but that was certainly the car. She pulled back out, then threaded her way through the development and back toward her house again. She chided herself for being so spooked and came up to the stop sign on her street, then forward to the middle of the block where her house was. She almost panicked when she passed a blue Ford—*the* blue Ford—parked at the corner across the street from her house. It looked like there was somebody in it, but she couldn't really make him out.

Unnerved now, she parked in the driveway and got out, wanting to be inside as quickly as possible. It was probably a cop—all the cops on TV seemed to drive big, dark cars like that. O'Donnell or his boss had decided to bet a couple of men that Sam was still in town and would be likely to contact her best friend, that was all. It was scary, but it sure as hell wasn't no mysterious dark figure you could see only in mirrors or any magic princesses.

A mall is a strange place at night, full of half-lit halls and ghostly stores and vast, deserted airspace. There were bars or roll-down security fronts on the stores, of course, and after Security left at midnight all of the entrances and exits also were wired, although, of course, a few key doors had safety bars just in case someone got trapped inside. Some malls had twenty-four-hour security inside, but, fortunately, this wasn't exactly a major crime area and the place was pretty secure against burglars and vandals. All the stores closed at nine; only the theaters were open later, usually until eleven or so, and they had a separate outside exit allowing them to have their final show without disturbing the mall routine.

By ten the merchants were gone and the cleaning crews were out in force. It was pretty impressive to see them work a whole mall in such a short time, but everything was on such an impressive system that they almost never stayed past midnight. The theaters had their own crew that came in at seven in the morning; their first features were the matinees and it was more efficient to clean them during the unused morning time than pay overtime to a night crew.

The first security personnel arrived about seven, give or take a couple of minutes. They checked the locks and made the rounds once to make certain that all was well. Around seven-thirty some mall personnel showed up, checking all the settings and turning on the lights, fountains, and the rest, and soon after the early merchants would begin to show, starting with the food stall people and then the rest. By nine it was all ready to go once again. Only on Sundays, when the mall was only open noon to six, did anything vary. Then, starting at six, a veritable army of cleaning and maintenance personnel moved in and it was often after midnight when they left.

Behind the facade, however, were miles of service corridors, storerooms, and other areas that were the nuts and bolts of running such a place. There were even some classroom-sized rooms and a small complex of offices. By now Sam had explored them all and discovered the areas where virtually no one went on a regular basis, and there, well hidden from even the most chance encounter, she'd made something of a nest using some removable seat cushions from stored chairs and other things picked up along the way that nobody would miss. Saturday night she'd made a valuable find, in fact, although she hadn't yet had to use it, where the day cleaning crew who picked up while all was open changed. It was a nice red security badge with a male name on it—George Trask, whoever he was—and a number but no photo. She always wore it when getting in or out of here, though, just in case.

She had run in terror and run to the only place she could think of, but when it became clear that she had not been seen or followed and she had, at least temporarily, some safety, the focus had changed. The more nights she got away with it, the more confident she became, now often staying awake late and sleeping late, sneaking out into the mall itself well after it was alive and going. By Monday it had become something of an adventure, although she knew full well it couldn't last. She also had to know what was going on, what was being said about her, how large the hue and cry, and that was the reason for the note to Charley. She wasn't sure what Charley could do. if anything, but it was better than being alone.

She also felt frustrated. She didn't want her mom to worry, or her dad, either. He was probably flying out now if he wasn't already here yelling and screaming at her mom and the cops and everybody else. Better they should worry than find her dead, though.

She would have liked to have reassured them, but what the hell could she say? She'd tried the truth with Charley and Charley had reacted like it was psycho city, so explaining this to her parents was just impossible. She needed to get away for a while, far from here, and sort it all out. Maybe north or east into the real cold where they didn't have thunderstorms this time of year. Someplace where she could get some kind of menial job that would keep her going. Damn it, she knew carpentry and construction. There had to be something out there someplace. Not much chance for a girl, but she played a mighty convincing boy if she did say so herself. She had the walk and the moves and the vocabulary down pat. Hell, she had it down so pat she'd gone right past some people she'd been in school with for a year and they never noticed, and she'd even gotten friendly with a couple of fifteen-year-old girls who hung out here.

She'd kind of fantasized being a boy off and on and she had to admit it had its points. Boys didn't have to spend an hour and a half just getting ready to go out in public; they didn't have to suffer lewd comments from passing pickup trucks or worry much about being alone on the bus or why a guy was being nice. In a sense, they were just more invisible in everyday life.

She acted the part well enough but she wasn't a boy, and on Thursday evening that was driven home to her hard. Everything was closed, she was getting her damned period, and there wasn't a reachable tampon in sight. Some blood had seeped through, soaking her panties and getting on the jeans. She had spare panties but she knew she had to work on that jeans stain before it set. The one small washroom that was open had some soap but the basin wasn't big enough for that. *Okay, Sam, you figured out the rest up to now—what the hell do you do about this?*

And so she found herself, at two in the morning, stark naked in the middle of the main concourse of the mall, sitting on the edge of the fountain and soaking her pants and underwear. The fountain was turned off for the night, but there was a pool of water there maybe two feet deep. It was also surprisingly warm—well, tepid, anyway—and quite clear. At the bottom she saw what seemed to be hundreds of coins thrown in by people over the week—they generally fished out the stuff on Sundays. Mostly pennies, but there was occasional silver in there and she found herself slipping into the fountain and combing the bottom. She came up in the end with only three dollars and fifty-five cents in non-pennies but it was okay.

She finally decided to hell with it and gave herself something of a rinse and she felt a lot better for it. Her flow was still intermittent; by tomorrow she'd buy something that would keep it from betraying her.

When she got out, rinsed out the clothes and laid them out to dry as much as possible, she found herself feeling a lot cheerier but not at all sleepy, even though she should have been dead tired. She looked out at the silent mall and felt a kind of kinky thrill. In a few hours this place would be jammed with people, but here she was, stark naked in the middle of it all. She decided to have a stroll around the mall. She'd once had a dream about touring a mall stark naked, although, of course, all the stores were open in the dream. Even so, it was sort of like living a brief fantasy and it was kind of funny.

Most of the stores kept lights on at low levels, but a few were completely dark, and their display windows reflected her form. She stopped at one and stared at herself. She sure didn't look like a boy now, and for the moment she didn't want to. She'd never been thrilled with her face—her ears were too big and her nose was wrong and her teeth were too big and prominent and she had a kind of chubbette face, or so she thought, but there was nothing wrong with her body. It amazed her that breasts like hers could be so effectively concealed by that stiff denim jacket, although she'd paid a price for it in rubbing and chafing. Nice body curve, too, and pretty good hips if she did say so herself. Her ass looked fatter than it should be, but that was about it. She struck a few sexy poses and kind of liked it. She was getting turned on by all this and she didn't fight it. She tried to imagine herself as a boy now, though, and couldn't. No, she could play one all right, but she didn't want to give up what she was seeing now.

She passed close to one of the security cameras monitoring the staff exit and suppressed a giggle. Couldn't *she* give 'em something to really look at! Not that she would. If anybody saw her like this now, she'd just *die.* Suddenly the thrill was gone. What if somebody *did* show up now? What if some merchant or security man or mall supervisor had to come in real early for something? They hadn't yet, but suddenly the possibility loomed like a certainty in her mind.

She went back down to the fountain where her clothes were. In the dry mall air the undies were almost dry although they looked like veterans of a chainsaw massacre; the jeans, however, seemed as wet as ever. They generally took an hour on high in the dryer at home. Hell, it might be a long time before they were dry enough to wear, damn it. Still, scrubbing the fresh stain with some hand soap and water had done wonders. It was still there but wasn't much and certainly didn't look like blood anymore.

Outside, as if very far away, she heard a faint rumble. *Oh, God! Not a thunderstorm! Not now!* To be heard much at all inside *here* it must be right on top of her! *They* were still looking for her, that was for sure. They'd lost her once but they wouldn't give up if they thought she was still around the town. She knew that. If the cops were still looking, then *they* were sure as hell not gonna give up.

She felt sudden panic. What would she do if *they* found her in here right now? Visions of mad slasher movies started running through her head. The jeans were still so wet they'd be more a hindrance than a help. Being chased, naked, through a deserted mall by *him* . . .

What was that? Some kind of noise over by the bookstore . . .

She grabbed up everything and made for the staff exit, being careful to avoid the camera and other more actual traps and back to her hiding place. She could hear the storm a bit more here, closer to the outer walls, but she could do nothing but huddle, shivering in the dark, eyes glued to the door of the storeroom.

Oh, God! Please, God! Steer them away from me! I'll do anything, anything, but please don't let them find me tonight! Just send the storm away from here, away from me!

And, although wide awake and terrified, she seemed to hear the Horned One's voice, as if in a whisper far away.

"Damn it, I almost had her, but something is deflecting the storms, interfering with the focus. I can't seem to get a fix. This requires too much energy; I am drained. But we will find her, never fear. If not this night, another night. This one must be dealt with. She has tapped the Power. Potentially she is the most dangerous one we have yet encountered. . . .

And all the while the object of this ghostly conversation sat crouched against the wall in the corner of the storeroom, naked, helpless, and terrified in the dark.

2
The Maelstrom

Morning dawned bright if a little crisp over the valley. Inside the insulated mall the canned music was turned on and a chorus of massed violins was playing a soft, melodic version of *Beast of Burden.* In the storeroom, Sam had gone to sleep after several hours in spite of herself but her real gain was perhaps two hours of rest and she felt like she'd been run over by a truck.

Even so, she felt some elation. Once again, somehow, she'd beaten them, if only for a night. One thing was sure, though—she had to get out of here now. *They* knew, or at least suspected, that she was here. They'd be back, again and again, until they found her. She wanted to meet no dark figure in this mall at two the next morning.

Still, it was now Friday. If Charley hadn't decided to stay out of it and if she really wanted to help she'd be there tonight, maybe with a car.

The jeans were still damp and badly wrinkled, but they would do. The socks might as well be abandoned. After days in them they were beyond the help of merely soaking. She never liked the feel of them anyway.

First things first. She'd have to get out of here and find enough light to count her money and see just what she did and didn't have. She didn't feel much like eating right now, but she needed tea or a Coke or something with a jolt in it to get her going and keep her moving today. It was gonna be one damned long day.

She managed to dress and slip out and into the mall proper. She had to pass a few people in back as she always did, but so long as you looked like you belonged nobody ever said much, particularly if you were going out. She headed first for the now open public restrooms. Nothing like a well-lighted stall for privacy, although the men's rooms weren't as nice as the ladies' rooms and had far fewer stalls.

She sat down and pulled out the crumpled mass of coins and bills and flattened and counted them. A hundred twenty-seven sixty-five. Not much. She still had her mother's bank card but the odds were they changed that just in case she was kidnapped or something. Still, it might be worth a try tonight. Friday night—if the number hadn't been changed it'd be Monday before anybody'd find out it was used again and by that time she really would be gone while they searched here. Not bad. Nothing to lose, anyway.

A pocket-sized pack of maxi-pads solved the immediate problem and just in time, too. That and some Panadol for the cramps, although it only helped a little. She was one of those unlucky ones who got it bad, at least for a day or so. Charley was luckier in that regard; she hardly ever had it bad. Sam always wondered if it was because she was oversexed or something or if it was easier once your cherry was popped or if the combination would turn her into a nymphomaniac or something. Hustling much was out today; her lack of sleep, period, and nerves combined to make her unfit for much of anything. She picked up a couple of donuts and a Coke and managed to get them down. It helped only in that it was an improvement over no donuts and no Coke.

It was tough to stay awake and kill a whole day without doing much. She browsed a lot, but the fact was that time really crawled and she was feeling just miserable. Worse was seeing all the things she'd like to buy, things she really needed—like more clothes and a jacket at least—but didn't dare pick up. By the time Charley was due she was in pretty bad shape. Still, she spotted the little red Subaru wagon cruise by the entrance slowly, then stop by the curb, and she practically ran to it and jumped in. Charley pulled away almost immediately.

"Jeez! You look like warmed over shit," her friend commented. Charley was dressed like she was going on a real heavy date—lipstick, makeup, perfume, fake fur jacket, nice satiny blouse and short skirt, even pantihose and heels. She even had her contacts in—at least, Sam *hoped* she did.

"This has been one of the worst days of my whole life," Sam responded honestly. "No sleep, cramps, you name it. Glad to see you dressed up for me, though."

Charley laughed. "I had a couple of days to work this out and some of the gang at school were willing to help out, too."

Sam had closed her eyes but one opened. "You didn't tell nobody else about me, did you?"

"No, relax. There's a group going up to Taos to ski this weekend and I just begged my folks to be included, since the weather's been so weird and we have a four-wheel-drive wagon. I think they're happy to get me out of town and someplace safe for the weekend. It's not the first time—you know that—and Monday's a school holiday. The cops seem to have given up on you but my folks are still real paranoid about me since you vanished. It was almost World War Three just to go to the bathroom alone after they found out about you yesterday."

"Yeah? And what's the group gonna say when you don't show up?"

Charley laughed. "Oh, if necessary they'll cover for me. They think I'm sneaking out this weekend to spend it with a new and secret boyfriend. Remember my reputation at school. I'm a woman of *experience,* remember. I'll give my folks a call later on tonight and again tomorrow night and lie and that gives me until Monday night before I have to be back."

Sam leaned back in the seat, too exhausted to even be concerned anymore. "I just need someplace to sleep and get myself together if you know what I mean," she sighed. "A hot bath and a bed."

"I've got some money for the weekend and I got my own Visa, remember. When the bill comes in next month I'll just kinda tear off the bottom of the form and lose it and stick it in the pile to be paid. We'll get you a motel tonight but tomorrow I think we'll go up to my folks' cabin by the lake. Dad bought it years ago but we hardly ever use it. I think there've been more relatives stay there than us. Nobody'll be up there now and maybe not for miles. I figure it's as good a place as any to start. We got all Saturday to work something out."

Charley was still a little paranoid from Wednesday night and decided to see if anybody was following. Not that she could do much if they were, but it would give her something of an edge. She took a number of turns and spent a good fifteen minutes at it until she felt sure she wasn't being tailed. Then she headed out to the freeway and headed north, out and away from the city. Only then did she look over and see that Sam was out cold, dead to the world. She looked so damned—*helpless* out like that.

For Charley, it was just helping out a friend and a little touch of adventure that broke the boredom of day to day routine. She found a small motel off the highway and registered as "Mr. and Mrs. Sam Sharkin." She had to use her last name since it was on the credit card. She didn't know why she put that down instead of passing Sam off as a more credible little brother or something, but it kind of added to the adventure, to the sense of doing something naughty.

Sam was still out cold and it took some doing just to get her awake enough to get her inside. The room was small but comfortable, with a full bath and a queen-sized bed. Charley went back out to get her suitcase and lock the car, and found that Sam had gotten awake enough to strip and was running a hot bath. She certainly needed it, so Charley took the opportunity to call her parents and lie enthusiastically. They seemed satisfied, relieved that she was out of town and with a group and told her to have a good time. She felt much better afterward, and turned on the TV. She was a woman now, damn it, and a bit too old to be towing her parents' line all the time. What they didn't know wouldn't hurt them.

Sam was in the tub so long Charley got worried that maybe she'd gone to sleep in there, but then her friend struggled in, dried herself with a towel, and flopped down on the bed. "You bring any tampons?" she asked.

"Yeah, sure." Charley got one from her suitcase. "Don't leave home without it. How are you feeling?"

"Dead. Like a pool of warm shit and my head's poundin' something fierce. Dead—but *clean.*" She said the word like a religious fanatic talking about heaven. "You?"

"I'm okay. A little tired but not like you. What happened to you? You looked so good on Wednesday." She got up and turned off the TV—nothing much on anyway—and the lights and crawled back into bed. She'd brought pajamas with her but somehow they just didn't seem right.

Sam sighed. "Just my nuttiness screwin' me up again."

"Tell me—if you want." It might be easier if she could get it out of her system.

Slowly, Sam described the previous night in the mall, sparing nothing.

"You *actually* walked nude around the *mall?*" The image had an erotic kinkiness to it that appealed to her, although she was sure she couldn't have done it.

"Yeah. It was kinda fun, but then the thunder came and I panicked and then the voices in my head started again and that was the end of that. The worst part was being all alone." She shivered.

Almost instinctively Charley put her arms around Sam and drew her close. "Well, Charley's here now. You're not alone tonight."

Sam clung to her tightly, and Charley, a bit embarrassed, realized that her friend was softly crying.

It was a small, very dark cloud in the night sky, nearly impossible to see, yet if it could have been seen from the ground it would resemble a swirling, seething mass that pulsed almost as if it were alive. It flowed like an amoeba across the dark sky, faintly pulsing with electrical energy that made it appear almost to have a broad, comic, if still demonic face, the internal flashes of lightning illuminating two small areas almost as if they were eyes.

It settled first over the mall and remained there for quite some time, drifting a bit this way and that as if trying to catch a scent. Then, finally, catching a hint of something, it began to move out, away from the mall, stopping again over a residential neighborhood where it swirled in sudden confusion for almost an hour. Then it seemed to find its direction again and slowly moved northward. It was tenacious but ponderously slow. It headed northward now, following a road below, but it was no longer going with the prevailing winds and the energy drain was enormous. Even as it moved, it shrank, losing little bits and pieces of itself to the atmosphere. With single-minded determination it ignored this, but the effect was to slow it even more. The fight against the other elements was too great, its dissipation too fast. Even as the scent grew stronger the cloud grew weaker and weaker, until, perhaps just short of its goal, it weakened sufficiently that it could no longer maintain its structural integrity.

For a brief moment, the swirling mass gone, only two bright, terrible spots of light remained suspended in the air, and then suddenly they were shattered by the prevailing winds.

Saturday dawned bright if a bit crisp and cool, and the brightness was reflected in Sam's attitude as well. She had slept for eleven straight hours and she felt hung over, but she also felt a tremendous lessening of the tension she'd been under for a week. Charley checked out and then they went over to MacDonalds and had what was essentially a brunch. Charley was never very hungry and nibbled on a cheeseburger and fries, but Sam was ravenous, putting away two quarter-pound burgers, a fish sandwich, fries, and a shake. It was as if she hadn't eaten in a week. Still, by the time they were off again it was almost like the old Sam was back and it was the two of them out for a lark.

In Amarillo they found a mall and made good use of Charley's credit card. Sam declared the old denim outfit unfit for further human consumption and hit a western-wear store for a new if similar outfit in a young boy's size, cowboy boots, leather belt with antique copper buckle, and even a Stetson. Considering the season, the addition of an imitation sheepskin jacket was welcome. She also got a small overnight case of fake leather, with a shoulder strap, which looked pretty masculine but could double as a purse, and some boys' underwear. She also hit a barber and got a haircut so short it was called "the military cut" in the style book—very short and flat on top and almost shaved on the sides. She still looked fourteen but, dressed that way and with that cut, just about every outward trace of femininity was erased. In fact, with her cool, tough, male act, Charley thought Sam was kind of cool and cute and sexy, not butch but convincing.

It was a bit over two hours more on back roads before they reached the cabin. It had been so long since Charley herself had been there that she had to check all sorts of landmarks and even then missed the dirt road turnoff twice. The cabin itself was a single-room log affair about a mile and a half off the main road and sheltered from view by both the land and the trees. Fortunately, it was locked with combination locks the numbers for which were in Dad's address book, so they were able to enter and look around.

"It's not much," Charley admitted. "It was supposed to be hot shit when we bought it but they never developed the so-called getaway wilderness resort they were selling in the brochures. Some folks camp around here in summer but I think we're the only ones that ever built anything within miles of here. Dad sued the hell out of them and got the cabin in a settlement. This was used as the sales office years ago and it's the only one with a well and septic system. You still gotta pump it up by hand over there, though, and add water to the toilet to flush it. They powered the place in the old days with a generator and they took that with 'em. No electricity."

There were, however, kerosene lamps, a wood stove built out of a fireplace, a sink with an old-fashioned handle pump where the faucets should be, a bare toilet that once had a curtain around it, some cabinets, pots, pans, and an old and squeaky but serviceable double bed. "Used to be my folks' but it either got too squeaky or too small for 'em so they moved it here," Charley explained.

Sam looked around. "Real country primitive, that's for sure. Matches the outfit, though. How long's it been since anybody was here?"

"Oh, a couple of cousins used it like for a week last year, I think—there's wood in the woodpile out there that we can use that I guess is from them. I don't think my folks have been here since the one and only time I was, which was like *years* ago. The river out back's supposed to have good fish in it, leastwise in the summer and fall. I don't know why Dad hangs on to it 'cept I guess you can't get much for it. Ain't exactly the great vacation spot of the universe or even Texas. I guess maybe he like figures he fought for it and it cost him, so he's keepin' it on principle or something."

They took turns trying to make the pump work. It took several minutes to get any water up, all the time screeching like the wail of the dead, and when it did come it was very rusty, but after pumping what seemed to be gallons it cleared enough so neither felt nervous about drinking or using it.

Charley had prepared for many of the cabin's obvious lacks. They'd stopped at a grocery store and picked up a pretty good assortment of stuff, although very little in the way of meat and nothing frozen since there was no refrigerator. Still, with the kind of stuff you could buy freeze-dried or boil-in-bag these days you could get by pretty good without it for a while.

They spent the day cleaning up and more or less playing house for real, and it struck Charley after a while that even out here and with the act down they had just sort of naturally assumed sexual roles, with Sam doing the logs and heavy stuff and she doing the cooking and making the bed with the linen she'd brought along. It was almost like they were acting like—well, her mom and dad—and it hadn't been deliberate. It was kind of fun, really; if Sam had really been a boy it might be different, but this was like a pleasant fantasy game and far preferable to making the hard choices ahead.

Sam came in from the car with a small brown bag which she'd obviously already opened, then pulled out a fifth of vodka. It was open, but still three-fourths full. "And what's this? Lighter fluid?"

"It's from home. There's so many bottles in the club room they'll never miss it. At the time I kinda figured you might need it, but to tell you the truth I forgot about it. I could'a got some grass from Louisa but I knew you couldn't stand the smell of the stuff."

Sam sighed. "I never really touched much of any of that. Too scared, I guess. What's it taste like?"

"Not much of anything, really. You just mix it with juice or pop. It just makes me real silly and it makes you feel good for a while. Too much can make you sick in the morning, though."

Sam looked back outside. "Well, we got a nice fire in here, it's hot as hell inside, dark and cold outside; we got no TV, no radio 'less we want to sit in the car, and not much else. Maybe I can stand bein' silly once."

And they *did* get silly, partly because they had no real way to measure the stuff and partly because the early attempts caused no real effect quickly and by the time they had enough to really feel it it was pretty cumulative. They sang and they danced to the songs they sang and they laughed at really stupid things and Charley got up on the table and did a silly striptease and just like the last time she'd gotten drunk she got real turned on. She had no inhibitions at all and it was all impulse, all feel, now, not thinking. Sam, too, seemed real vacant and giggly and pretty unsteady.

They were both pretty giddy and helped each other to blow out the lamps and make it to bed. Charley snuggled up close to Sam and started gently rubbing the other. She sensed Sam stiffen. "What's wrong?"

"I—I dunno. I have these funny feelings inside and I'm all mixed up. It's all *wrong.*"

"You want me to stop?"

"That's just it—I *don't* want you to stop. I—I had *other* dreams, not just the bad ones. Ones I never told about. You dream about boys. I know you do. Mine had you and me in bed, like this, only in my dreams I was a boy and you was you and that made it all right. . . ."

In any other circumstances Charley would have reacted differently, but she was high as a kite and horny as hell. "Okay, just for tonight, then, let's do a fantasy. You're the boy and I'm the girl and we're here all alone. Jus' relax and pretend and ol' Charley'll show you just what to do."

It wasn't clear how long it went on in the darkness before they both passed out from the booze, but it was day when Charley awoke with a splitting headache to the sounds of Sam throwing up into the toilet. Charley didn't feel that sick, but her head was throbbing and the room was slightly spinning and she could do nothing but lie there and try not to move.

She didn't remember much about the night but she remembered—enough, and it started her thinking and worrying. She was slightly troubled about herself, wondering if this was anything much inside her head or not. She sure as hell fantasized about boys, but she'd gotten turned on by looking at a girl or two and it hadn't bothered her much. Hell, when she'd been fourteen she'd had a real, if short, adolescent crush on Mrs. Santiago, her English teacher at the time. Months later Mrs. Santiago had been replaced with Mr. Horvath. Sam, though—she was such a damned straight arrow it must be killing her inside, or would when she stopped being sick and really sobered up. She and Sam were physically only a month apart in age, but emotionally Sam was closer to fourteen than seventeen going on eighteen, and she'd had that split home and since being separated so long and so far from her dad Sam had turned him into almost Superman in her mind so no boy could ever compare or measure up.

Boy, Dr. Joan Herwitz—she was the phone-in psychologist on the radio—had lots of cases like this. Sam got a crush on Charley but it went against everything her straight arrow upbringing and church groups believed. So she couldn't handle it, and finally invented this weird fantasy world and dark mysterious ghosts and talking thunderstorms. Man! These were *heavy* thoughts! Sam was running, all right, but not from the darker dreams and fantasies but rather *to* them. The solution startled Charley but it also cheered her. It explained *everything!* The trouble was, would *Sam* buy it now and deal with it? It was Sunday. There was only one day left.

Still, they had to survive a rough morning first. Charley had one of those awful problems—she *desperately* needed to take some industrial-strength Tylenol she had with her but to do so involved pumping some water and the screeching of the pump was unendurable. It was also very cold in the cabin; Sam was covered with goosebumps but first things came first and upchucking had a way of forcing itself to the head of the line. Even so, once her stomach was empty she felt much better if dizzy and lightheaded. Still, she had enough sense to know that building a fire was essential and she managed to throw some wood in the stove, light some paper with a cheap lighter, and toss it in. It would take a few minutes but at least things would be livable.

She found an unopened bottle of orange juice that was slightly cold because of the cabin's temperature and got the pills from Charley's purse and brought them to her. It was only then that they both discovered that Sam, the bed, and even Charley were something of a bloody mess and Sam felt bruised and scratched up inside. It confused her. "Jeez—my period's pretty well over and I never had flow like *that*."

Charley had to laugh even though it hurt to do so. "Long fingernails," she muttered. "Sam, I popped your cherry last night. Don't worry—it'll never happen again. Hurt a little inside?"

"Uh-huh."

"That'll go away, too, and shouldn't ever come back." She sighed. "I guess if we can heat a little water we can wash ourselves off but I didn't bring but one set of bedding. I figured it was only a couple of days. Best we can do I guess is wash 'em in the sink when my head slows down. They'll still look awful but at least they can be used."

By the early afternoon both were feeling much better, although the after-effects lingered on in upset stomachs and generally feeling drained. Sam, perhaps because she'd cleared her stomach, seemed to get over it faster than Charley, much to Charley's chagrin, although the mental effects of the binge were dwelling inside the fugitive.

"So what do I do now? Go to San Francisco or Greenwich Village or somethin'?" Sam muttered unhappily. " 'Cept I don't wanna go to any of them places."

"Oh, come on, Sam. Like, you never even *tried* it with a boy. Hell, I been pretty straight lately myself but I'm no saint. I got all sorts of urges and attractions and most of 'em I don't let out unless I'm high or drunk or whatever, but some I do. Don't you see? That's what's happened to you. You been so scared of letting go, lettin' your hair down when you had it and, well, *sinning* a little. You're scared you won't be the Virgin Mary and you're not. Nobody is. You're almost scared of makin' friends or gettin' into a little hell raisin' and that's got it all bottled up inside. I don't know if you really swing that way exclusive or not and I don't think you do, neither. You don't have the experience yet to know."

Sam sighed. "I always felt I should'a been a boy, that somebody screwed up someplace. I never felt comfortable around boys, 'cept my dad, of course. Even my *voice* wasn't no girl's voice. But when I was naked in front of that store window I kinda liked what I saw there, too. Fact was, for the first time in my life I liked me as I was, if that don't sound crazy."

Charley shook her head. "I understand."

"But it didn't change nothin'. I still felt the same towards you, and when you not only didn't turn me in but picked me up and went to all this trouble it was like, well, you felt somethin' for me, too. And since we been together I felt, well, *safe*."

Charley hesitantly chewed on her lower lip, thinking hard, then said, "And you don't see the connection? It's been buildin' up inside you and it scared you, that's all. When I went away for the whole weekend leavin' you alone around the house you had your shadow man. When you looked at yourself in the mall and turned yourself on you got panicky and had another dream. I bet almost all of 'em happened after something stuck in your mind about your own feelings or me. And since we been together there's been nothin'. Don't you see, Sam? Them dreams, them voices, they're not real. They come for you when you get hung up and feelin' guilty and all. They're in your *head*, that's all. They're scarier even than what you're really 'fraid of so you don't think about that no more."

Sam thought it over. "They're so *real*. And the thunderstorms—

they're real, too. Thunderstorms at high altitude here in the middle of winter."

"Yeah, I guess the storms are real, but they're real with you or without you. It's not like they never happened before—I heard the weather guy on the radio. Come on, Sam! Lotsa folks are scared by things that don't make no sense. Me, I'm terrified of spiders and I ain't too fond of tall buildings, neither, even when I'm inside 'em. You step on spiders and leave 'em outside to catch flies and I bet back in Boston you went in lots of tall buildings and never thought 'bout it. You got thunderstorms which I always thought were kinda neat and exciting so long as you was lookin' at 'em from inside someplace. You just put your storms and your fears together and it *still* wasn't enough. Your shadow man didn't come durin' no thunderstorm, did he?"

For the first time there was a glimmer of doubt in Sam's mind. "You really think so? That this was all for *nothin'?* But everything was so *real.*"

"I guess it can be. But it's out in the open now, at least between the two of us, and I don't *care.* You told me and showed me and I didn't run screamin' away or nothin'. Look, you go home, you see a shrink. Your mom's into all that liberal cause shit; you'll wind up gettin' one that'll say just what I'm sayin', I'll bet you. We won't tell anybody else about it." She was thinking furiously now. She'd hooked the fish and didn't want to let it slip away. "Maybe we'll go off to college together. How's that sound? We'll room together and raise a little hell ourselves."

"But you hate the idea of college!"

"Well, like maybe I can stand it with a good friend, huh'? It'll freak out our parents but they'll love it. Come on—what do you say?"

Sam thought hard about it. "I really want to believe it, Charley. But what if I go back and it all starts again anyway? *They'll* get me sure, then, and you better believe I'll be grounded for months."

"And if you don't? Where you gonna run, Sam? Sure, you look and can act like a fifteen- or sixteen-year-old boy, but ten years from now you're *still* gonna look fifteen or sixteen Nobody'll hire a kid that young with no ID, no background, no experience, no family. Nobody you could ever trust workin' for, anyways. You can't even get a job for the minimum at *MacDonalds*, for Christ's sake, without a Social Security card, home address, parental permission, you name it. Only thing you could do would be to turn yourself back into a girl with everything hangin' out and sell yourself."

"I—I couldn't do that."

"You get hungry enough or fall into the wrong hands and you damn well will, or you'll die—and what's the difference if your shadow man kills you or you freeze to death hitchin' or starve to death in Denver? Hell, you can't even *drive.* There's bastards out there pickin' up *boys* for the last ride, you know, and if they find out you're a *girl* they'll find your body in a ditch someplace years from now if ever."

"But what if my dreams are *real?*"

"They're *not,* damn it, but real or not they'll follow you and you know it. You don't face it, it'll get you. I can just see you hitchin' on some warm day in the middle of nowhere when a thunderstorm comes up. *There* you face it alone. Back we face it together."

"Charley, I—I really want to believe you but I *have* to *know.* Before I can go back, I just have to."

Charley looked out the window. It was a clear sky, only a few high wispy clouds, but the winter sun was coming close to the horizon. "Then let's face them now, huh? All night if necessary, or until we freeze our tits off. Together."

Sam looked suddenly nervous as Charley pulled on designer jeans, a lavender cashmere sweater, her calf-length boots with high, thick heels, then got her fur coat. "Put on your boots, coat, and hat and we'll see just how nasty this all is. If they're so hot to find you, then they should accept a call."

"*What?*"

"If you love me, or *think* you love me, then you'll do it. For me."

"But—what if they come?"

Charley sighed. "Well, if you can conjure up a storm it'll show there's some ESP or that kind of stuff and if you can do it here you sure as hell can convince other folks. Besides, didn't you tell me that you thought you sent it away from the mall? If anything really shows up, push it back."

She didn't really believe any of this, but clearly Sam did. It was better to play the game out.

"Come on," said Charley. "Prove to me that you can screw up this pretty day."

They walked down the dirt road until they cleared the trees, Charley leading. She wanted as unobstructed a view of the sky as possible, convinced that there was no way to imagine storms or demons in a sky like this. There was a chill in the air but it wasn't unbearable, partly because there was almost a dead calm; the sky pale blue with only those high, thin, wispy clouds and nothing else visible as far as they could see.

"Here. This is far enough," Charley said firmly. She stopped and looked around. "Well, I don't see no shadow man and I don't see no storm clouds. If you can conjure up anything in the here and now then you got a hell of a power."

Sam looked uncomfortable, feeling vulnerable, but she was unable to back out at this point. "So what do you want me to do?"

"Call 'em. Just look up in the sky or towards the horizon and just sort of like *think* them to come. Just tell 'em, 'Here's Sam Buell! If you want me come and get me!' Do it over and over for a few minutes and see if anything develops. Either it works or it don't. If it don't you're home free."

Sam looked up at the very pale sky with perhaps no more than an hour's light left in it. She had real problems with this because she was not at all convinced that it was all in her head, but, damn it, Charley was right. She had to *know,* and this time somebody else was watching, too.

She stared at the clouds, took a deep breath, then closed her eyes and thought, hard, *Who are you? What do you want with me? I'm sick of running from you! If you want me come here, now, and have it out, or get away forever and let me alone!*

She tensed, then after a few moments opened her eyes. It all looked the same. Nothing had changed. She felt, suddenly, very emotional, even angry, and tears welled up inside her. "*You bastards!*" she screamed at the sky. "*You storms and shadow men! Come and get me! Now! Or the hell with you!*"

Very slowly, the wind began to pick up. The temperature was certainly dropping, at least in wind chill, and what had felt pleasant at the start now began to feel pretty cold. Still, nothing else had changed and the wind was more natural than the calm had been.

"Come on," Charley muttered. "My fingers are turnin' blue. Let's get back up to the cabin and thaw out."

Sam nodded, and they started back up the road toward the cabin. "I dunno if I feel happy or sad," Sam muttered. "On the one hand, this proves nothin'. *They* always picked the time and nine out of ten times it was after dark. Only the shadow man was daytime, and he only scared the shit outta me, followin', waitin'—until dark, maybe. Still and all, it's lookin' more and more like I'm really a nut case and that don't 'zactly make me wanna shout 'Hallaluja.' "

"Yeah, well, it proves *something,* anyways. Look, we'll do one more night even if we have to sleep on them sheets. If nothin' happens, then you come home with me tomorrow. Man! That wind is really pickin' up." She looked over her shoulder and up at the sky. "*Ohmygod!*"

Sam froze just before the door of the cabin and turned to look and saw immediately what Charley was seeing.

The sky was alive!

The thin, wispy clouds were now suddenly in motion, rapid motion, and they were moving in a circular pattern around a broad arc of sky, moving outward to form a circular collection barrier around an invisible blue center, thickening every second, growing dense and ugly with every increase in speed. It was as if they were at the point where the eye of a hurricane formed, the motion violent and building all around them.

The circle of thick clouds now began to grow inward, toward the center, in a spiral pattern. Charley stared at it in sheer terror, for the first time experiencing what Sam surely must have felt. "Sam! Send it away!" she screamed as the noise grew and the ominous, distant rumbling of thunder sounded. "*Send it away!*"

"Back off!" Sam screamed at the sky. "Get away! I called you, I send you back! *Get away from me!*"

For a second the entire sky seemed to freeze and there was a momentary stillness that was almost as frightening as the spectacle, but then enormous claps of thunder answered the frightened girl and it started up again. "It's too strong! Damn you, Charley! Why didn't you *believe* me?"

Charley was too stunned and frightened for any rational response. Sam took her hard by the hand and pulled her. "Come on! Get inside the cabin! It'll give us *some* protection!"

They got inside as the storm continued to build. Charley was shaking and Sam wasn't much better, but she was more accepting of what was happening and trying to think fast.

"The car!" Charley muttered. "I'll get the keys! We can try and outrun it—"

"*No!* That's how they killed that—other—girl!"

"We can't stay *here!* It'll suck up this whole cabin and make pieces out of it and us!"

Even now the cabin was shaking and things were rattling and falling all over the place, and Sam realized that Charley was right. They had no damned chance at all in here. "*Under* the car!" she shouted. "Ain't that where you hide if you get into a big storm? No storm cellar!"

Charley finally got some wits about her and grabbed her purse. "Not *under!* Inside! It's grounded!" There were sheets of rain coming down now, and wind so great it felt like the cabin was going to shake apart, yet they both hesitated. Suddenly there was a horrible, gut-wrenching, tearing sound near the bed and a small section of roof just broke off like ripped by some giant hand.

It took both of them to get the door even open, and then they ran for the car. The storm itself had only a superficial resemblance to a natural storm now; it contained not only the grays of its violence but seemed to seethe with electrical power, pulsing like a living beast, each pulse a different color—crimson, violet, emerald green, yellow—there was no end to it.

Outside it was a sea of mud in a tropical storm; even the air temperature had warmed incredibly and it felt now like a muggy summer day. Sam made it to the car and had her hand on the door when she heard Charley scream and turned and saw her friend fall forward into the mud. Sam rushed back to her fallen friend and pulled her up. They both just made it to the car when a strong finger of lightning came down and struck the very area where Charley had fallen, sending up a short burst of smoke and mud.

They got inside the car and automatically locked the doors. Charley was a mass of mud and Sam was drenched. Charley had lost her purse in the fall and she disregarded the mud and pushed open the glove compartment knob. "There's a spare key in there! We gotta get out of here!"

"No! Don't touch nothin' metal, not even the keys! Lightning strikes the car and you'll fry even if me and the car don't! You think it won't follow us no matter where we go anyways? If it can't get the wind to blow us over . . ."

"Damn it, we got to do *something!*" Lightning was striking all around them with the regularity of a piston engine and the car was being rocked by the wind as if it were under assault by some powerful yet invisible monster.

"We hang on if we can! I had the dreams, remember! They can't keep this up real long! If they could they'd' a had me long ago! They ain't God—just the next thing to it!"

They both suddenly shrieked as a bolt hit the car and they could feel the electricity crackling in the air and even see it dancing around the hood of the car. A few loose metal objects—keys, an old film can, a loose part of a seat—flew up to the roof and stuck there as if magnetized.

The radio crackled and buzzed, although there was no automobile power being fed to it. Suddenly a clear voice in American English said, somewhat tinnily out of the speaker, "If you want to live, then calm down, shut up, and listen to me!"

"It's *him!*"

"Who? The one with the horns?"

"No! The other one! The one that thinks I'm a lab animal!"

"I'm moving the damned magnets on this thing by external force but I can't maintain it for long with all this damned storm interference, so listen up!" snapped the man on the radio through numerous and loud snaps, crackles, and pops.

"You called him. He'll never have you as exposed as this again," the voice noted. "He can't keep this up for long but he can hurl trees at you and smash in that car and overturn it and get you exposed before he runs out of steam. I want to save your life. You must believe that, and it's him or me. The other girl—I don't know who you are but he can't tell you apart in this mess so you're in this, too. Now, listen up! Hold hands, close your eyes! Lean back! Clear your minds as much as you can and will yourself to come to me! You'll feel the pull. Don't resist it—and don't let go of each other if you both want to wind up alive and in the same place!"

The car shook so violently that the entire left side rose a few inches and came crashing back down. There was a sudden, violent pounding all around and they saw the front and back windshields begin to crack under hail the size of oranges. Even the roof seemed ready to cave in, and the hailstones were like iron balls against the hood.

Charley looked at Sam in fear and anguish. Sam grabbed her hand tightly and shouted above the roar, "Let's do it! I don't know about him but it's better than any chance we got here!"

It was impossible to ignore the terrors being visited on the car or suppress the fear, but, somehow, through it all, they both seemed to see something in their minds, a tiny point of bright light that grew larger and larger by the second. There was the sound of shattered glass and Sam felt pain in her leg, but at that moment the light, which seemed to be enormous and approaching them, somehow, reached and engulfed them.

The sound abruptly ceased with a silence so deafening that it was in many ways as scary as the storm had been. Sam couldn't stand it; she opened her eyes, and almost immediately shut them again.

They were floating in air, in the center of the storm, with the swirling, charged, multicolored clouds of violent energy all around them as far as the eye could see, not only on all sides and above them but also below. There had been nothing, no place at all.

Sam opened her eyes again, and after a few moments of vertigo got used to it. She looked over at Charley and saw her friend's eyes tightly shut, lips quivering. "*Charleeeee. . . .!*" she called, the sound thin and echoing into infinity.

Charley was in the grips of total, unreasoned terror, the only rational thought in her head, going 'round and 'round in a never-ending loop, was *God damn all fucking radio psychologists!*

"*Charleee . . . Open your eyes! It's*—beautiful!"

"*I—I can't!*" But after a moment she did so, since she was suddenly hearing nothing but Sam's voice and did not feel any other sensations, not even wind. When she saw the maelstrom it almost took her breath away. She tightened her already solid grip on Sam's hand. "*Are we—are we dead?*"

"*You're too damned filthy to be dead and I'm too wet!*" Charley responded, the eerie echoes of their voices almost mixing in the distance. "*I think we're moving, though. Down!*"

It was true. The storm was no storm anymore, if it had ever been, but rather it seemed to be a long tube, or perhaps a giant funnel would be a better term for it. It had such a uniformity of broad bands of lighter cloud, or whatever it was, separated by thin bands of darker stuff that it was hard to really tell movement. Charley looked down once and decided she didn't want to anymore, but she could look straight ahead, at the bands, and when she had looked long enough she began to see, or thought she saw, a scene, a picture, that flipped every second or so to become slightly different, like viewing a movie one frame at a time.

Woods . . . clearing . . . paved road beyond . . . even telephone poles, all against a stormy-looking sky. It was looking out from the car's position—it was the cabin land! But there was no car and no cabin and the image was ghostly, two dimensional, not at all real.

Dark band. Same scene, but suddenly the telephone poles were gone. *Dark band.* A few differences in trees, subtle differences as each band came floating by. Slowly, ever so slowly, the road was dirt now, then a track, a mere trail. Trees changed subtly, not only in number and position but in shape and kind. And now it was a true winter scene, with snow suspended in air while the ground was getting progressively covered.

"*Stare straight ahead and watch!*" Charley called, pointing but not taking her eyes off the scene.

There was something now in and among the trees. It emerged after a while—time had no meaning in this long descent but it seemed to be going on forever—as some sort of deer, maybe an elk, clear in the stormy twilight and making tracks, one snapshot at a time, in the snow. They watched it walk, but as it did, with each still frame, it, too, subtly changed. The antlers became horns and then bony plates, the dark brown skin changed to tough and leathery, the short tail grew long and thick, the legs thickened and became three-toed and clawed rather than hooved. All this took time—hundreds, maybe thousands of snapshots—and each time the creature looked complete and whole, not in the midst of any transformation.

Now it was no elk nor anything like an elk, but rather a creature like a dragon, larger and meaner looking than anything they had ever seen, and it was no longer walking in snow at all but across a swampy region, the trees now more Amazonian jungle than west Texas woodland and hills. Now it, too, was gone from view and the land continued to change. Unfortunately it also continued to darken, and soon there was nothing left of the scene but a few fleeting impressions of things that stood out in the storm clouds and the night.

The storm itself had now grown dark and ominous once more, the walls closing in on them where at the start the thing had seemed a mile across. But the storm was still alive; red, pupilless eyes like burning coals started suddenly out at them from below, then leaped out into the maelstrom itself, floating as they were floating but maneuvering toward them.

They were ugly, horrible beasts, three in number; monstrous creatures, resembling dogs, that seemed almost as big as they were, with gaping mouths dripping something yellow. They were still well below, but they were coming, charging toward them as they fell to meet the things. Both girls screamed and tried to flee in horror, but there was no way to break this fall. The creatures had to be even larger than they appeared; *huge* in fact, because they were growing as they approached yet there was still some distance between the three beasts and their obvious prey.

Both of them stopped screaming only when they saw the others emerge from the walls, closer to them, between them and the beasts. Shadow people, with no features, like two-dimensional black cardboard cutouts, but *alive,* and, from their looks, not unarmed. The beasts tried to dodge the newcomers, and Charley had the strangest feeling that those six terrible eyes were fixed not on Sam but on *her* and on her alone.

The three shadow humans worked quickly, one drawing a shadow sword, another placing an arrow in a shadow box, a third with a great, long, sharp spear. All three struck their dog monsters almost simultaneously and with great accuracy, but the beasts, while wounded and suddenly howling in agony a strange, supernatural howl that echoed forever down the spout, kept coming, kept staring not at Sam but at Charley. She could practically smell their breath, but the three shadow hunters were not done turning the tables on the fearsome hunters, falling upon the beasts, stabbing, spearing, gripping their foes and dragging them down and away. One beast let out a great scream and suddenly vanished, dissipating like smoke in the wind, while the other two were now being dragged down, away from the girls, at an accelerating rate until they were just tiny dots, then gone.

All returned to normalcy for a moment, but then below them at the point on the storm wall they were facing, another figure seemed to grow, a figure that was anything but cardboard and two-dimensional or even black. It was the figure of a large man, imposing, well built, wearing flowing robes of crimson and gold, his face sporting a full snow-white beard that was trimmed oddly as if an inverted V-shaped notch was cut from it, and on his head was a crown from which arose two long, sharp, slightly curved horns.

Sam gasped, knowing that this was the one she feared the most, her tormentor and would-be murderer. They were falling—or he was rising—at a rate that would bring them face to face in a matter of seconds.

Suddenly there was an odd sound like a giant spring suddenly uncoiled at great speed, and between them and the horned figure there appeared a thin, transparent pink barrier.

"*That will hold him only for a minute or so,*" said a familiar voice nearby. They turned and saw another figure, this of a small man with long, unkempt white hair, a bulbous nose and oddly chubby cheeks, like a doll's, dressed in similar fashion to the Horned One, only in robes of silver and emerald green. This, then, was the voice from the car radio. "*I'm going to have to face him down,*" he told them. "*I don't think he wants a full calling out right now, so I can stall him long enough to get you down to someplace neutral and out of the way. Trust Zenchur. He's a scoundrel but he stays bought and he'll be expecting you and know what to do, and he speaks English.*"

Both of them were beyond shock at this point and it brought a curious clarity of mind, almost like this was normal. "*But what's this all about?* " Sam called to him. "*And where are we going?*"

"*What's the difference? You're going there anyway,*" the man in green responded pragmatically. "*He's through the barrier already. Stand by. When I divert him you'll get a real sudden push.*"

The Horned One raised a hand and the barrier vanished, and he continued until he was level with them, perhaps ten feet away from the girls. The one in green, however, stood suspended in the maelstrom between them and their immediate nemesis.

"*Enough!*" said the Horned One impatiently in that sinister, terribly cold voice Sam had heard in the dreams. "*This is not your affair, Boolean. You are out of your league here. Stand aside. She is mine,"* he said emphatically, holding out a thin, almost skeletal hand and pointing, clearly, not to Sam but to Charley!

This is nuts, Sam thought, thoroughly confused. *This is* my *nightmare, not Charley's!* And, just as suddenly, she realized what was going on. There *was* a fair resemblance between the two of them, and Horned One knew he was seeking a girl. Whatever power or sense he used to track his prey, the two of them, together, touching hands, confused it. Charley was also still pretty well covered with mud, but her hair and dress made it very clear she was female, but Sam looked like a boy and with the very short hair . . .

He thinks Charley is me!

The man in green, who clearly knew different, did nothing to correct the impression. Instead he said, *"I am making it my business. Do you want to have it out now over her? You think you're ready for me? You think you can finally beat me in something?"*

The comments clearly infuriated the Horned One, but he hesitated. *"You would fight me for* her? *Risk everything?"*

For an answer, the small man in green raised his hands and there was a pyrotechnic light show that was almost blinding in its brilliance. At the same moment, both Charley and Sam felt a tremendous push on them, forcing them suddenly and very quickly down and away from the duo. It was so sudden and forceful that it took their breaths away in spite of the green one's warnings, and it was no longer an eternal floating sensation but more the feeling of going down the biggest hill on the roller coaster.

The walls continued to close in until there was no more space between and they were inside the clouds themselves.

Lightly but very suddenly and unexpectedly they hit the ground and rolled, letting go of one another's hand in spite of themselves, tumbling to a stop.

Wherever they had been going, they had now arrived.

3
The Mother of Universes

Wherever it was, it was dark and hot and incredibly humid; a layer of gray mist so thick you couldn't see a thing in it lay over the land and extended perhaps two feet up from the ground it clung to. Sam groaned and managed to get first to her knees and then to her feet and look around. The night sky appeared totally clouded over; at least, there were no stars visible, nor any moon, although it wasn't pitch black. She could see the thick carpet of mist well enough, although it seemed that it was not from any light source on high but rather that the mist itself was faintly glowing.

"Charley?" she shouted worriedly. "Are you anywhere in this gook?"

For a moment she was worried that they had not landed together, that the last moment when they'd lost their grip on each other it had sent them to different places and left them both alone. Sam's hand hurt like hell from what seemed like *hours* gripping Charley's hand—and it might well have been that long.

She heard something moving not far from her. *"Oh! Jeez! That you, Sam?"*

Sam frowned. "That you, Charley?" The voice just didn't sound right, but then she saw a familiar form, still caked with mud, rise eerily from the mist.

"Yeah, I *think* so. Damn! My voice sounds funny. Are my ears stopped up or what? *You* sound okay."

Sam frowned, but went over to her friend and helped her to her feet. "Your voice sounds as deep as mine! I don't know. Maybe I—shit!"

"What's the matter?"

"That chubby-cheeked bastard! He saw that Old Horny mistook you for me. He looked, saw a boy and a girl, and since he was after a girl he made the obvious mistake. Old Greenie, then, figured he'd keep it up I bet. He wants old Stick Head to keep goin' after you, that's what! Both of 'em don't give a damn about *you*—it's me they both want for some reason. So Greenie, he cast a spell or something to make you sound like me. Keep it up as long as possible. You don't sound to me like I sound to me, but I bet to anybody else your voice and my voice now sound pretty much the same. You still got the accent but who's gonna know the difference *here?* If I keep my voice on low and keep dressin' and actin' like a boy then anybody sent out lookin' for me'll go for *you.*"

Charley didn't like any of this. She was scared, confused, and totally off-balance, but what Sam said made sense considering the crazy low voice she was hearing in herself and the fact that those *things*—she shivered at the memory even though it already seemed like a dream—only had eyes for *her* and even that fancy wizard with the horns had pointed to her. It wasn't at all comforting; she was nothing to them, a sacrificial lamb, no more, no less. She had become the target and it wasn't even her nightmare.

"I'm dreaming this. Somehow this is all a dream and I'm back home or in the cabin or something sound asleep," she muttered in that strange-sounding voice. The whole thing *did* have a dreamlike, nightmarish quality about it, and to think otherwise was to believe in monster storms called at will and shadow people and wizards and magic spells, none of which she'd believed in for many, many years. She believed in Halston and Gucci and I. Magnum's and they seemed very far from here.

"Sam," she said very softly, "I'm scared. I'm filthy, wet, miserable, and scared to death."

"Yeah. Me, too," sighed the other. She looked around. "*Now* what are we supposed to do, I wonder? Wait here to be picked up or move someplace or what? And if we're supposed to go someplace, where in hell *is* it?"

"I don't know. If this is a dream, why can't we conjure up a bath tub? Talk about gettin' mixed up. I dunno if I'm in *Alice in Wonderland* or *The Wizard of Oz.* A storm sucks you down the rabbit hole. . . . Can't even get our damn fairy tales straight."

Sam knelt down and felt the ground. They had landed relatively gently for the apparent speed, but it felt like pretty hard rock down there, covered perhaps with moss most places. It was firm, but her hand was wet when she ran it around on the surface.

Off in the distance there was the sudden sound of thunder and an area of the sky was illuminated, briefly. Charley started, then turned quickly back to Sam. "Don't you *dare* call it!"

Sam looked out at it. For some odd reason it hadn't the unreasoned fear she had always felt when seeing or hearing such things; instead, it inspired wary caution, as if it were a person, directed by an intelligence, that she had to avoid. Somehow that made it easier to take—particularly since she'd evaded or fooled that intelligence more than once now. But that had been on essentially home turf. This place—wherever this place was—was something else again. Still, she was thinking fast and surprisingly clear considering her experience and how tired she was feeling.

"I don't think it's the same here as back home," she mused.

"No shit. Tell me something else that's brilliant."

"No, no! I don't mean *that.* You don't have to worry 'bout me callin' no storms, 'cause I bet that's one of the few easy ways Old Horny can find me here. If he could find me here the same way he could back home, then what's the use of sendin' us down here, changin' your voice, and all the rest? Here's got to be different. If I don't call him he's got no more chance of findin' me than if he was lookin' for anybody else. He don't know where Chubby Cheeks plopped us 'cause he was kinda busy. Now he's gotta find me the hard way. The same way somebody normal would try'n find somebody else back home."

"Yeah, that makes sense. But your Chubby Cheeks knows where he dropped us and even which is which. That's okay for you—he wants you alive for something—but it sure as hell paints a target on me. I'm stickin' to you like glue, girl, 'cause if I'm ever separated, your savior there could just let some of Horny's agents bump me off and then he thinks he's home free and you're off the hook."

Sam sighed. "I'm sorry I dragged you into this, Charley, I really am. But it was *your* idea to call that damned storm."

"Yeah, but how was I to know it'd actually show up? This isn't *real!* It *can't* be! It just *can't* be!" And then Charley dissolved into tears.

Sam didn't know what to do except try and comfort her friend. Common sense said to stay the night right here. Charley was right about one thing—old Chubby Cheeks knew just where he dropped them and they were supposed to be met by somebody. Move too far and they might not meet—and *then* where would they be? Lost in some damned weird world where they didn't know the rules, that's where. And Charley was worried she couldn't cope with Denver!

Still, staying here, in this crap, wasn't too comforting. She was dead tired—they both were—but what lived around here, hidden by this glowing fog? Damn it, what the hell were they supposed to *do?*

Ultimately, it was decided by practical matters. They were too tired, still too much in shock, and it was too damned dark to make a try for someplace better than they were in now, if in fact that place existed. Still, it was not hard to sit there, just your head and shoulders above the mist, and imagine monsters moving underneath. They clung to each other and comforted each other and, eventually, they went to sleep in spite of themselves, so exhausted that not even fear could hold it back.

Sam awoke suddenly with a start and sat up. It was still quite dark and still, and the mist was still there—in fact, it seemed to have risen some. She was soaked through again by the mist, and it was clammy and uncomfortable, but she put it from her mind. Charley still slept, protected beneath it, but Sam had always been a lighter sleeper and she had been on the run and under tension for more than a week. There was something—an odd noise—coming across the dark to her, approaching.

It was somebody whistling. It was a casual but firm and loud whistle, and whoever it was was whistling a bright, fast tune.

It was *Yankee Doodle!*

She tensed, alert, and used the mist as a cover so that only her eyes and the top of her head were visible. Protecting Charley and herself became the only purpose in her mind. She reached down and shook the sleeping girl, who mumbled and murmured but suddenly came awake and sat up. "It wasn't a dream," she said, more amazed than anything else.

"*Shhhh!*" Sam hissed the warning. "Listen and stay low."

The whistler continued to approach, and now, too, she could hear the sound of hoofbeats as well on the rocky ground, as if a horse was progressing ever so slowly through this stuff. Now she saw them—two people eerily illuminated by the glowing mist, only their upper torsos showing because of it. One was a woman and she wasn't wearing any clothes! She was a light brown color, and there was something odd about her face and hair, and although it was hard to tell it looked like she had the biggest tits Sam had ever seen.

At first Sam thought that the other was a woman, too; the clean-shaven face was set off by what looked like a *mane* of hair cascading up and then around the head and down to and below the shoulders. This was the whistler, who suddenly stopped and looked around, appearing very unconcerned about anything lurking in the mists, and called out softly in a voice that was unmistakably a pretty fair male baritone.

"Come out, come out, wherever you are," called the man with all the hair. He had a thick, somewhat gutteral accent that sounded vaguely east European, but his English was clear. "I do not have eyes to see in this mess. I know you are around, watching us. Do not be afraid—I am Zenchur and this is Ladai. We were told you would be expecting us."

"Can we trust him?" Charley whispered nervously to Sam.

"No, but what other choice we got?" Sam stood and was instantly spotted by the newcomers. "Hey! You from the green guy with the chubby cheeks?"

The man started, then looked a little confused. "What is 'chubby cheeks' meaning? I am hired to get you to someplace safe and to help you. Or would you rather stay here?"

Charley got up, and the sight of her also seemed to surprise the man, while the woman just looked suspiciously at both of them. The man frowned. "*Two* of you! I was only told of one. This will double the price. Well, come on—we must be away from here by dawn. There will be others looking for you that you do not want to meet, I think."

They moved hesitantly forward, wary but knowing they were helpless in this situation to do more. Suddenly, both girls stopped and just stared at the female member of the duo. Now, up close, they could see that it wasn't a woman at all.

Her hair flared out in front, then seemed to be pinched back to the back of her head, becoming a thick mane of dark brown hair running completely down her upper back. Her ears, their exteriors covered in brown fur, were pointed and seemed to move independently of one another, rising up stiffly from the side of her head in animal fashion. Her eyes were extremely large and bulged slightly outward, and were like two huge black orbs floating in a brown rather than white sea. Her nose was somewhat flattened, but the nostrils seemed to move slightly in and out as she breathed. Her hands had three thick, very long fingers and an even thicker thumb, and seemed to be all fingernail from just beyond the knuckle joints; her breasts hung down huge and fat—although she seemed quite thin otherwise—to or below where her navel would have been, if she'd had a navel. And at the hips, and beyond, she merged into a long body whose top they could barely see but which seemed to reach out in back of her as long as her torso was tall, yet she stood shorter than the man who was of no more than average height and only five or six inches taller than the two girls.

"Is that—is *she* a centaur?" Charley breathed softly.

"Ah!" responded the man. "*That* is the word. Yes, centaur in English, They call themselves *ba'ahdon,* which sort of means human being. It all depends on how you look at it, yes?" He paused. "She speaks no English, but she is good people. They do not understand why we do not fall over when we walk."

The speaker was himself certainly what *they* would call a human being, but he, too, was decidedly unusual in appearance. For one thing, his huge head of curly reddish blond hair ballooned out as if permed and framed his face as it dropped below his shoulders. He had no sideburns nor any trace that he ever had to shave; his face was smooth as a woman's although it had clearly seen a lot of exposure as its lines and wrinkles around the eyes demonstrated. It was a large, squared-off face with steel gray eyes and frankly androgynous, a fact emphasized by his twin earrings which hung down from pierced earlobes, each ending in a copper oval in which there was a maltese cross. He had an olive brown complexion that was most certainly dark even without exposure to the sun but now was deeply tanned. He wore frontier buckskins with fringe ornamentation, the jacket ties not fully done and revealing a surprisingly hairy chest for one with no noticeable facial hair. It was almost as if somebody had stuck Farah Fawcett's head on the body of Davy Crockett, Sam thought crazily.

Zenchur turned to the centauress and said something in a singsong tongue that sounded sort of Chinese or something, and she nodded. Then he turned back to them. "Come. Follow us. We have not too far to go but it is best that we go there. It is very unlikely that you can be traced to this spot, but one does not live long by not taking the unlikely into account."

They began walking, the centauress leading the way and the three of them following.

"If you please, sir," Charley said as they walked, "can you tell us just where we are?"

Zenchur chuckled. "You are in Akahlar. That is the name of the world in the dominant language and it is used generally. There are more than six thousand languages, you see, so there had to be some standards."

"Yes, but—where is Akahlar? Is it another world than ours or what?"

"Another world, yes—and no. You come from the Out-planes and it is hard to explain things to you since I do not understand them myself. You are almost where you left yet you are as far away from your home as if you were on a distant star. It is—how you say?—a layer cake. Many layers. Hundreds. Thousands. You fall from somewhere near the top of the cake or in the middle or like that through to the bottom. Is the asshole of creation. People, things, falling down here all the time and stick here because there is no farther place to fall. Well, there is, but this is last layer where people can live. Every once in a while, when big storms come, some more drop through, but not like the old days."

"But you—you're a native? You're from here?"

"From here, yes. Native—there are no natives of Akahlar. All our ancestors come here from someplace else long ago. Used to be giant storms all the time go far Outplane before they stop, but no more. Oh, we still get big storms, but there is too much out there now. They break up, get weak. We still get some—one here, another there—like you two, but not big groups, whole tribes, towns, like ancient times."

"You speak English quite well," Sam put in, feeling left out of this. "Is it spoken around this place?"

"Some places, yes. Not many. I learn it because Akhbreed sorcerers use it. Is good to know the tongues they use. They like it because it is so hard to learn, so confusing. I am good at languages and I buy this one not long ago. I know sixteen very well and another ten or so enough to get along. Ladai, she is also good. Knows ten or more, I forget. Fortunately, we both know one the same so can talk. She can do ones I can not handle. The throat will not make the sounds. You understand? That is why we work so well together."

Sam thought she had enough problems with English. "Are we gonna hav'ta know all those languages to get by here?"

Zenchur laughed. "Oh, no, but the more you know the better it is. I get this job because I know English. Ladai and me, we need them in our work."

"Just what is it you do?" Charley asked him.

"Sort of—what is the term? Mercenary, I think. No, that is not quite it. They are paid soldiers. I fight, when I have to, but I do not like it if I can keep away from having to do it. People pay me to do these things they need to have done that they cannot or will not do themselves. When no one pays me I think up my own little jobs to get pay. Free some extra valuables from ones who will not miss them, that sort of thing. Better working for someone else, though. Same danger, same trouble, but if you get caught you are not alone."

Sam thought about it and saw just what he was. "And Ladai—she does the same? You are partners?"

Zenchur chuckled. "Partners. Yes, I think that might be the right term. You see, our sort of work—requires—that we live away from most, from civilization. When we go to cities, to lands, it is to either spend money or on the job. Then go, usually run, sometime chased, back to the wastes. You never know where you might have to go. I am Akhbreed. You are Akhbreed. Akhbreed not very welcome in lots of places. If you are not Akhbreed—Ladai, for example—you are not welcome in Akhbreed places. I can do little about Akhbreed law. It stinks. But I can go where few Akhbreed can follow. Akhbreed have the power. Akhbreed sorcerers have the greatest power of all. Like gods. Akhbreed does not see any of the other races as human. They take what they want, all the best, leave the garbage to the rest. Akhbreed have massacred whole races here for petty reasons, for greed. Enslaved others. That is why I do not mind stealing from them or causing them problems."

"But you said you were an Akhbreed," Charley pointed out. She was getting very tired and the short distance was turning into a very long hike in the dark.

"I am sometimes ashamed of it. If one race tortured and enslaved your people and drove them off your lands would you not hate that race? Yet I was trapped, with a storm coming, many years ago out in the wastes. I had no chance. Two *ba'ahdon* found me, wounded, half dead. They took me to their camp, brought me back to health. I lived with them long time. Got to know them. How could I go back and be Akhbreed again?"

"But couldn't you go back and tell 'em that these are good people? Work to bring everybody together?" Charley couldn't help thinking this sounded a lot like the Indians and the white man in her own southwest in the frontier days.

Zenchur looked at her strangely. "You must have interesting Outplane. If anyone were to go back and say that, they would be called traitors to their kind. If they kept it up, they would be publicly tortured, mutilated, then killed or given to the sorcerers to be made monsters. The kings and queens of Akhbreed do not permit disagreements."

Suddenly the mist ended, at least just ahead of them, and a grassy hill came out of it and went up and then out. There were some trees and bushes there and what seemed like a rock wall rising imposingly into the darkness. They walked along the bottom of the cliff side for a bit, then entered an area that really could not be seen from outside and which, even in daylight, would betray no hint that it was there. It led to a fissure in the rock that zigzagged back underneath and either led to or became a cave. Well inside the mountain it opened up into a large cavern lit by torches. There was a definite airflow here, and in the center of the cave there was a pool of clear water.

To one side, in a natural depression, was a rather basic camp, with two tents, an obvious fire pit, atop which sat a cold cauldron, all of which sat upon a thick layer of straw with many rugs in front of the tent to add insulation from the cold and damp cave floor. It looked pretty damned primitive but at least it was *someplace.*

Ladai's full form was visible from the moment they entered the torchlit area. The lower body was not really all that much like a horse's; the legs were far thicker than a horse's legs and ended in large hooved feet that, while proportionately small, reminded them more of an elephant's feet than a horse's. The lower body was relatively short—certainly not much longer than the upper, more human body—and sloped slightly down, terminating in massive hind legs that none the less were shorter than the forelegs by several inches. The mane continued along the back all the way and merged with the tail at the base of the spine where it became rather like a straight, thick head of human-looking hair reaching almost but not quite to the ground. She was not just the old idea of a human upper mated to a horse's lower; in fact, she was an entirely separate creature that seemed to be less hybrid than something new and different but a single whole. Nor was she massive like the centaurs of legend; on the whole, she was about the size of a Shetland pony.

Zenchur and Ladai exchanged more conversation, and she went and started up the fire in the fire pit using one of the torches. Soon it was burning quite well, the smoke rising in a steady diagonal to the roof of the cave and then vanishing somewhere. It had certainly been well thought out; Charley bet that no smoke ever was visible from outside.

Ladai went and brought a loaf of thick, black bread and an amphora and some hand-fashioned but sturdy-looking cups. She poured some of the contents of the amphora into each of the cups, handing one to each girl, then broke the bread.

Both *were* hungry, and the bread was fresh and with an odd but very sweet flavor to it. The liquid in the cups was thin and refreshing, more like white grape juice than wine although they both knew it probably *was* wine of some sort. It had an aftertaste almost like honey, and in their condition it was irresistible.

When they had finished, Charley went over to the side of the pool, knelt down, and stuck her hand in the water. It was quite warm but not hot.

"You wish to wash off the grime," Zenchur said. "By all means. Just stay close to the sides of the pool. It is mostly safe but there is a sharp drop perhaps six paces in. Plenty of room for bath. Ladai bathes in it, and if it is safe for her it is certainly safe enough for you."

She wanted to very much, and so did Sam, but here, in front of Zenchur . . . Neither of them wanted to bring it up, but it seemed to occur to Ladai even though she obviously had no problems with exposure and the centauress said something to Zenchur. He chuckled. "Ah—modesty. You will have to get cured of that out here, although it is an Akhbreed trait. You go ahead—I will go into the tent here. I have—how you say it?—I have to make a long-distance call."

And with that cryptic remark, and with something of a flourish, he turned and entered the nearest tent.

There wasn't much to use for soap—Ladai offered them a rough, shapeless white mass that didn't smell like much and didn't work all that well, either—but the water was warm and they both needed it badly. Ladai collected their clothing and took them off toward the cauldron. The clothes were in as bad shape as they were, so they didn't protest too much, although Charley figured it was goodbye to the fake fur jacket. They were a hell of a long way from a dry cleaner's, she figured, although it was warm enough around here that maybe she wouldn't need it. After all, it wasn't like mink or anything, anyway.

With the neutral, bland soap or whatever it was and no washcloths, they generally had to help one another scrub and get off the grime, particularly Charley's. She longed for her herbal shampoo and rinse but rubbing the soap stuff in and then ducking under and kneading the hair out took out the dried-in mud fairly well. Sam, at least, had less of a problem, with her very short hair, and what mud she'd encountered was mostly on her clothes.

They finally pulled themselves out, feeling clean and *much* better. Ladai, who seemed to be cooking or burning something very hot and bulky—the black smoke was billowing up from the fire pit and even tainting the air away from it—came away from her activities and brought them two thick towels the size of good hand towels which Charley suspected might have been cheap rugs, as well as a rather primitive brush and comb for Charley's thick, wet hair. They worked, anyway, at least for the basics, although Charley was going to have a time getting her hair completely dry and right.

"I guess we ought'a get our clothes and wash 'em as best we can, too," Sam suggested. "They might hav'ta last awhile."

Charley looked around and frowned. "Where *are* our clothes?" She stood up and went over to Ladai, who looked up at her from stirring the fire and smiled. "Our clothes," Charley said slowly, then remembered that the centauress couldn't understand them. She made as if to put on pants and a sweater and repeated, "Where—are—our—clothes?"

Ladai smiled sweetly and pointed to the fire pit. Charley looked down and could see the remains of a jacket and boots being charred to bits. "*Sam!*" she screamed. "*She's just burned all our clothes!*"

Sam was up and over there in a flash and saw the unmistakable remains. It was no use reaching in there to get them—the fire was incredibly hot, far too hot to get close to, and what was left in there was beyond help anyway.

Zenchur came out of his tent, frowning. "What is going on out here?"

Both girls instantly reacted with a shriek and covered as much of themselves as possible with their hands and arms. "She burned all our clothes!" Sam complained.

Zenchur sighed. "Yes. Sorry, but it was necessary. The appearance of any clothing or artifacts which you could not get here would be like standing up in the middle of town and saying, 'Here we are!' Even a fragment could be taken and any competent alchemist could indentify it as coming from the Outplane."

"But what do you expect us to do? Parade around stark naked?" Charlie asked, feeling terribly embarrassed.

"No, we will find other clothing for you. Do not worry so. It must be a very strange world you come from. One in which you can openly try to overthrow the king but where the sight of a naked body arouses anyone and incites instant attack. I hope you will not be incited to attack me if you see me naked on this trip." He seemed genuinely bemused by their reaction, yet irritated by its inconvenience.

"Look," he sighed, impatient now. "If I wanted either or both of you I could take you. I would not do so for—many reasons. Not that you are unattractive or undesirable, mind you, but this is business. I am your protector, not your attacker."

When neither of them moved a muscle but just stood there with their arms doing a bad job of covering what they wanted to cover, he got impatient. "I cannot afford such foolishness. I am tempted to let you stand there indefinitely until you get hungry or thirsty or have to go to the bathroom, but I cannot. I have no schedule to keep but something must be done and it must be done yet tonight. If you fight me or fail to trust me from this point you may yet die. I had not thought to need this so soon, but, very well." He reached into a leather pouch hanging from his belt and pulled out a small box. He opened it, and immediately there was a golden glow from it. They watched, not knowing what to do.

He removed the thing from the box, a glowing opaque, oval-shaped jewel perhaps the size of a half dollar, then held it out, waist high. He stared at them, not at the jewel, and if they had bothered to notice even Ladai was looking away.

Although there was no light source for the thing, a pencil-thin ray of the same golden color shot from it and made a small spot of light on the floor of the cave. He suddenly brought it up and let it shine for a moment on Sam's forehead. Charley frowned and looked for a likely place to run, but then he shifted the locus from Sam's forehead to hers.

She felt a sudden shock, then very strange and tingly, but it was another moment before she realized that she could not move a muscle. She was frozen, a statue, in this absurd and embarrassing position.

"The difference between common magic and sorcerer's magic is that common magic comes from an outside source, and belongs to the one who owns the source and knows how to use it. I have no magic powers, but this does. It has gotten me out of many scrapes and at times saved my skin. It was payment by a magician and alchemist for a particularly ugly and dirty piece of work I had to do for him, but it is the most priceless payment I have ever received. It debases it, almost, to use it for so silly a reason. Now—look upon it, both of you."

They did, compelled to in spite of themselves, and felt a numbness come over them. They could see only the gem, could not take their eyes off it.

"Come," he commanded, and they stood up and followed, eyes staring ahead, walking right into his tent.

The tent was larger on the inside than it looked; the floor was covered with rugs, there was a large chest to one side with an ornate gold dragon design on it, an enormous, mattresslike layering of rugs covered with silk, and, off to one side, a disk of polished wood with an intricate design carved in it, raised up on four ornate wooden legs. Five small incense sticks burned around it, each relating to a point on the disk's design.

"Stand before the disk, one on each side," he commanded, and they did so. "Now," he said, sounding somewhat relieved, "when I put this away you will have your wits back, but I want no more hysterics. Were I to focus this once more on your faces and tell you that down is up, black is white, and we are mice in a giant cheese you would believe it and try to eat the ceiling. If I said you both worshiped me like a god and wanted only to be ravished by me you would plead for my favors. I will demonstrate if I have to but at your peril. Such things have been known to permanently damage the mind." And, with that, he placed the jewel back in its case and slipped it back in his pouch.

Instantly they felt some release and both had a slight headache, but they were terrified. Right now, either one of them would do whatever he said rather than be subjected to that thing again, although Sam, in particular, felt disgusted. Not even in the midst of the storm had she ever felt as weak and small and helpless as she did here. And *this* was supposed to be the *good* guy!

"Hold hands, do not look at me, and stare at the center of the disk," Zenchur told them. "Just keep stating. He might not be immediately available."

Not all the fight was out of Sam. "Who's *he?*"

"My employer."

Sam took Charley's right hand in her left and squeezed it and they both stared at the center of the funny diagram carved into the wood. *He* was apparently on hold; things happened almost immediately.

There was a sudden shimmering just above the center of the disk but no touching it, and then it thickened and took on a definite shape outlined first in golden sparklies, but it soon became the form of a man, slightly transparent but in full, realistic three dimensions. The image was a living hologram of the green-robed wizard from the maelstrom, perhaps ten inches high.

"About time," the sorcerer snapped, the voice a bit thin and proportionate to the image, yet very clear. "I dare not risk keeping this open any longer than I have to. Ladies, we have several problems and we must deal with them quickly. I know you have a lot of questions but the answers to most will have to wait, perhaps until we can meet in person. All you need know is that you, with the short hair and the deep voice, are a target here just like you were. The fellow with the horns is very powerful both in magic and in temporal power. I'm also powerful—maybe his superior in magical power but I don't have much of a temporal base. In this case Satan has the army and the Pope has none. Nevermind. He was too gutless to try me back there, so he's lost track of you and unlike on the old world he can't just whip up a spell of location. If he tried that in Akahlar he'd risk whipping up a changewind even he couldn't handle.

"He knows I've got you, so he'll put all sorts of temporal and magical tails and shadows on me. I can probably get to you and protect you but then we'll be back where we started because he can follow. If he finds you, Short Hair, he'll kill you without hesitation or mercy. Believe that. Oddly, that's an advantage since he has strict orders to his minions that they are not to harm you but merely to capture and summon him. That's because only he can tell if it's really you. I could run some interference in the tunnel but that wouldn't have fooled him for long if I hadn't been there in person. As such, he's put out a very high reward for you, alive only and held until he can come to you. Every damned crook and politician in the business will be drooling over it, even his enemies. Trust only Zenchur. He is the only one who knows that the greatness of his reward will be matched only by the horror if he sells me out. What *is* your name, anyway? I can't keep calling you Short Hair."

"S—Sam, Samantha Buell," she managed. "And this is my friend Charley—Sharlene."

"You're not even related? Remarkable. Sam and Charley. Huh! Who'd have thought it?" He sighed. "All right, Charley, I don't know if you are here by accident or choice but you are here and you are stuck and as such you are going to be useful to me and to your friend. You might have noticed old Horn Head and his beasties both got confused, a common occurrence with them. That's why I had to alter your voice. I was afraid you'd say something and give the show away. The fact is, he doesn't know a damn thing more about you than I do and only what he saw. He knows what Sam looks like if Sam's looking like a young woman. I need Sam alive. Not only for now but for the far distant future. Alive and physically unchanged by magic or any other forces. He thinks Sam was a boy, possibly your brother. He'll be looking for an attractive young lady with a deep and distinctive voice. They all will. Sam must continue to be a boy to all outward appearance and that leaves you, Charley."

"You're gonna make her the Judas goat! They'll *kill* her!" Sam protested.

"Perhaps—but remember that everyone hunting for you knows there is no reward and perhaps some punishment for killing you, and if Horn Head comes without me running interference he'll know it's not. That gives you a chance, which is more than you have on your own. I can't fill the countryside with Sam clones. For one thing, it takes a small part of Sam to do it right and there's only so much of her. Understand, though, I don't want him to catch you, Charley. If he does he'll catch on fast to who the real one must be. We will protect you all the way as if you were the real quarry. In the end, not only your friend's life and future but your own as well will depend on you carrying it off. I can help a little now. Interlock the fingers of the hands you are now holding. Go on—do it."

They did so, although it was a bit awkward.

"There is feminine in the most brutish male, and there is masculine in the most gentle and beauteous female. Sam, I can't change you physically—I wish I could but I cannot and he knows it—but I can make some temporary mental adjustments and Charley stands right next to you now. Put your clasped hands into the center of my image. Go ahead—I'm not going to turn anybody into a toad."

Hesitantly, they both did as instructed. There was a sudden tingle and the image of the sorcerer seemed to mix with and grow out of the two hands clasped together. There was suddenly a sharp and painful shock through both hands that made them cry out but they could not pull their hands away from his image. Sam felt a wave of nausea and dizziness and would have fallen to the floor if not frozen there; Charley felt the same sensation but in addition a thin, burning sensation that started at the top of her head and went slowly and methodically down through every part of her.

"Okay," the sorcerer said with satisfaction. "You're probably both going to pass out when I break the contact, so I'll say the rest of my piece here. I've been able to get away with this because Horn Head doesn't know where I am yet or where you are at all, but since I have to be public shortly that will end. Within a few days he will have narrowed down and figured out the rough area where you had to land, so you will have to move. Zenchur will take you to a place where you can be safe and be taught something about this world and trained in what might be needed of you in the future. Horny can't touch you there but if he learns of your presence there he sure as hell can make it hard to get out again. When it blows over and the hue and cry is yesterday's news to all but your enemy and us, then we must meet. We must do what he fears most. I do not understate this. If we fail, it is entirely possible, even likely, that it will mean the destruction or total domination not only of this world but every world—your old world, too—by the blackest of evil. The odds of our survival, let alone success, are quite small, but the alternative is far worse than death. But if we succeed the prize, *your* prize, will also be great, and Charley will share.

"Zenchur—one last thing. I have now done the calculations and the clumsy and heavy-handed attempt on this pair by my adversary has triggered the largest and deepest changewind in a decade. I have calculated it will penetrate the Malabar District just beyond the Brothers. It might well proceed a great distance before going Outplane—it's that bad. Sit tight a full day and night more before moving and take its aftermath into account when you go. I go to alert those I can—or care to. Farewell, and may the winds be with you."

The image flickered out, the hold was released, and, as the sorcerer had predicted, both of them fell unconscious to the floor. With Ladai's help he got them apart and to the other tent, where they were laid side by side on silk-covered rugs and silk pillows. Looking down at the pair, Ladai could only shake her head in wonder. "It is incredible. And at such a distance! What power he must have!"

Zenchur nodded. "And that is why we must do as he says even though our hearts are not in it. I *knew* I should never have done that job for him, Jewel of Omak or no Jewel of Omak. It was payment for services rendered but the bastard now owns my soul. He *knew* about this! He *knew* even then! That is why he threw in the spell that allowed me to learn his accursed tongue."

Ladai nodded sadly. "Still, they seem quite nice, if very shy and very frightened girls. In a sense, they are more victimized than we. Their shyness in front of you was actually quite touching. They took me as an equal, yet were embarrassed and frightened by you. It would be well if they continued to fear the Akhbreed and showed no hatred or fear toward the other races. It shows what this world *might* become. See them now. They look so tiny—so helpless. What in the name of the Five Netherworlds would cause two such powers to go to such lengths to have them?"

"Just the one," Zenchur told her. She had understood none of the English conversations and was very curious. "That one. The other is the decoy. I have no idea what this could be about, but I am not certain which I envy least—the one they want or the decoy." He sighed. "At least they won't need the Jewel of Omak with us anymore. Our employer has seen to that."

The pair left them to their dreams, and they were vastly different dreams, many in number and vivid in their realism.

For Sam, the dreams were adventure stories with, for her, an odd perspective. Time and again, through many variations, she was the hero; a small but handsome man in sword and cape, battling various monsters both human and inhuman, saving the innocent and the helpless and rescuing the fair damsel in distress who then threw herself at "him" in gratitude and love. They were a boy's dreams, romantic dreams, of brave knights and muscled warriors vanquished by power and skill and guts.

And through it all ran a thread that somehow her mind sorted out, and she understood and she believed. You are a man, born heir to a kingdom that only males can rule, but a great sorcerer stole your soul one day to advance the cause of a greedy rival to the throne and placed it far away, in another world, in the body of a girl. Now you are back in the land of your origins but still in that alien female body but your soul rebels. Henceforth you will let your soul guide you; you will look, act, talk, think like a man and all things womanly you must put aside or you will remain trapped in that body forever. None who do not now know your secret must ever know. You must put aside all womanly things and convince everyone, even yourself, that you are male. Only that way is redemption.

But for Charley, the message was quite radically different, as were the dreams.

For Charley, the dreams were exotic and erotic, almost a 1001 Nights *scenario, in which she was the beautiful slave girl coveted by all, or an exotic and mysterious* femme fatale *desired by all men and using her charms to twist them to her will. They were romantic fantasies of the power of beauty, of being so alluring that men would risk their lives and their honor over her and for her while she risked very little. They were curiously mixed, with dreams of power intermingling with dreams of subjugation and domination, but they were all intensely erotic.*

And, deep inside, she knew that this was what she wanted. To be glamorous, sexy, uninhibited, erotic, in all ways totally feminine, totally female.

Charley awoke first to find herself extremely turned on. She had awakened turned on quite a few times since puberty, but never this intense. She just lay there and felt herself up, mentally pretty well switched out. The same girl who was so shy and terrified the night before of even revealing her naked self would at that specific moment have been unable to resist the ugliest nerd who might have walked in.

Charley's active moaning awakened Sam, who for a brief moment had that flash of utter confusion when, opening your eyes and seeing strange surroundings instead of a familiar room, you did not immediately remember where you were.

Then, abruptly, it all came back and she sat up, and as she supported herself on her hands she felt a slight dull hurt on the left palm. She looked at it and saw a tiny, odd-looking cross-shaped cut just below her thumb. It wasn't very much, but it was slightly bruised and not yet quite scabbed over.

She looked down at her body and hated it. It was a prison, a shell that kept her trapped. Still, a rush of hope and possible power went through her. She was a *man,* damn it. She would behave that way and let no one know the secret shame. She heard Charley moaning and chuckled. The new Sam could give her what relief was possible, but somehow the thought was no longer attractive but seemed rather like kissing your sister. Well, time to get her up, anyway. But when Sam turned and looked at her companion all such thoughts drained from her along with some of her color. It wasn't Charley there beside her! It wasn't Charley it was—Sam!

"Wake up!" Sam snapped. "What's going on here, anyway?"

Charley opened her eyes and smiled. "What's the problem?"

"Charley—that *is* you, isn't it?"

"Yeah, sure. What . . . ?" Sensing that something was definitely very wrong, she jumped to her feet. "What's happened, Sam? What *now?*"

"Your face—your hair, your eyes, your build . . . We always kinda looked like sisters, but, Charley—you're *me!*" Sam pointed to a scar on Charley's abdomen. "That's even my appendix scar, and my birthmarks. A few of the freckles. Holy shit!"

Charley grabbed her hair, which was uncharacteristically trailing down her back, and brought it forward. It was nice, thick hair but it was straight and black and down almost to her waist—like Sam's had been before she'd cut it and run.

Hearing them, Ladai entered carrying a fairly large but manageable hand mirror. She had anticipated the problem again, as usual. Charley almost grabbed for it and looked at herself in the mirror, then all the way down. She stared in the mirror, then at Sam, back and forth, unable to believe it. Other than hair, they were absolutely identical, twins in every way except that one. Body hair was similarly missing; Charley's underarms were smooth and her legs even smoother, while Sam's underarms were fairly bushy and she had never shaved her legs.

"Well," she sighed at last, "he *said* I was the decoy, didn't he?" She looked at her right palm and saw the small cross-shaped cut similiar to the one on Sam's left hand. Something—something had been exchanged. Blood or whatever from Sam had gone to Charley and triggered the marching orders. "At least I got your figure, and it's the easiest diet I ever been on. I wonder if it's permanent?"

"Well, at least we still talk different," Sam noted. "You got my voice but you still got your accent."

"And you have yours," she retorted. "But you are talking at your low end normally, in your most male voice. Are you doing that deliberately?"

"No. I hadn't noticed until you said something. But it's—convenient. Charley, once we get some proper clothes and get moving I'm staying a man. You're gonna have to think of me that way, too. From this point on I'm Sam and I'm your brother. Okay?"

"Uh—sure. If I got to look like you I guess one of us ought'a be safe."

"You know you're talkin' high and a little whispery. I never knew it sounded that way. It's still real low but it's kind'a sexy and definitely female. You suddenly got the moves, too. Just standin' there. Jeez—I never knew I could look that sexy in the old days. Well, that's the old days." She shivered. "It's kinda damp in here. I wonder if we're ever gonna get any clothes?"

Zenchur took the cue to enter as Ladai left. He had pants and boots on but no shirt, and did he *ever* have hairy arms and legs! Somehow his presence no longer elicited in them any embarrassment at all. It wasn't that something had changed that they recognized; they simply didn't even give it a thought.

"I see you have found what your sorcerer has done," the mercenary noted. "I will not ask you how you like it because it makes no difference. Charley, you can still be Charley—the enemy knows only the looks, not the name and family history. I received explicit instructions before you had your encounter. Ladai is fixing a light breakfast; while she does, come in to my tent and we will find you suitable clothes and adornments."

They followed him and again were in the larger tent, this time at the two trunks. "The one on the left has typical Akhbreed male garb. The one on the right is similar but female. Select what you like—there is a large mirror over there in the back. Dress comfortably—we cannot leave today."

Sam looked through her trunk and found it an odd assortment. She wasn't sure what she expected—Peter Pan outfits or whatever—but the pants were mostly loose but leather, the shirts very thick wool or cotton with large wooden fasteners, the boots mostly high-top range-type or chukka boot height. Clearly whoever assembled the grouping had in mind disguising the female figure; much of it was stiff and reinforced in the places that would conceal the breasts and blur the body shape while still looking natural. Most if it looked fairly worn, although it all smelled clean and new. An interesting touch, actually—anybody out looking for her would naturally look for brand-new looking outfits. All the stuff had a handmade look.

Several things were immediately obvious when sorting through the pile as well. There was no real mass production of clothes, no big machines to make them, and nobody here had invented zippers, underwear—at least for the men—or opposing shoes. There were no left and right boots, for example. The harder fabrics had some cotton or wool lining in the seat to cushion extremities on leather, but it was still gonna take some getting used to. She picked a cotton outfit and low chukka boots to start—no socks, either, but they had a soft fur lining. It was clear, though, that if she couldn't tolerate the stiff stuff or it wasn't appropriate she was going to have to create a makeshift minimizer to tie around her breasts, and as for pissing—well, she doubted they had stalls around here so it was gonna have to be real circumspect.

Charley's trunk contained a far different assortment. It was quite a bit tighter, for one thing, and maximized what Sam's assortment minimized. The pullovers were mostly cotton and cleverly stitched to give some breast support, and the lone pair of pants was of similar material and would never be in danger of falling off her hips no matter what she did.

There were a few gorgeous skirts, mostly slit to mid-thigh, made of silk or satin, with tie-on matching halters that supported but stretched just enough that you could see her nipples through them. There was an outfit that looked for all the world like a mink bikini. There were several bottoms with no obvious tops, suggesting that often here, if the weather permitted, women went topless. She knew she couldn't do it on her own, but if *everybody* was doing it, well . . .

They did seem to go in for capes here. There were quite a number of matching capes even for outfits that had no tops. There were no clearcut bras or an equivalent to pantihose or any other sort of underwear. Footware seemed to consist of sandals, sandals with thick heels, and a kind of high-top boot that laced up almost to the knee. As with the male shoes, there was no right or left.

There were also three smaller boxes in the trunk. One, to her surprise, contained cosmetics—recognizable cosmetics in the generic sense at that. The two lipsticks were in copper cylinders, true, but they weren't bad. There was also a kind of rouge, eye shadow, a nail file made out of some dull, heavy metal, even two small baked ceramic jars of what proved to be nail polish. The brushes were independent and not the sort you'd buy in stores, but they were there. She had a sudden urge to really do herself up, to see just how sexy she could make this Sam body and how much she could erase any traces of maleness from the face and distract the rest with the other parts of the body. But first she decided to see what the other, larger boxes contained. The other contained ceramic jars with a funny kind of writing on each, but they proved to be perfumes, a couple not to her liking but the others seemed great. There was also a pad, powder, and a couple of jars of nice smelling but mysterious paste-like stuff. There was also a brush, a comb, and a small polished surface that made a decent mirror.

The third and final box contained an odd assortment of jewelry. There were bracelets and anklets and necklaces and earrings that hung down as teardrops like quartz almost to or maybe below her jaw line. None of it was fancy, no jewel-encrusted stuff—but it was mostly bronze or yellow-gold and not at all bad.

Sam was comfortably dressed and ready to eat while she was still deciding and trying on several of the outfits. She loved trying on outfits anyway, always had. Finally Sam asked, "You noticed anything odd about this stuff?"

"Huh? No. I think I'm gonna be *dying* for a bra and panties under some of this before too long, and I'd *kill* for some pantihose, but it's not that bad."

"It all fits. Perfectly. I—we—got crazy wide feet. Always drove me nuts findin' shoes that I could get into. These fit. Perfect. All my stuff minimizes me just like they had my measurements. All that stuff you been tryin' on fits you, too. Even the stuff with built-in cups are perfect."

"So? Old Greenie hoped he could get you here, right? You got to figure he prepared. Like, that burnin' of the clothes."

"Yeah, but there's one for each of us—and Zenchur said he only expected me. He was real surprised when you popped up—that wasn't faked."

Charley shrugged. "Maybe he thought of the boy disguise, too. He didn't know your name or nothin' 'bout you. So he fixed up this for a real *femme fatale* type and he fixed the other as a disguise just in case. No big mystery."

"Okay, I'll give ya that. He just sorta thought of everything. But, Charley—*how'd he know my size?* In everything, too. Far enough in advance to age this shit so it don't look new and get even the shoe width and breast sizes right. He didn't know my name—or says he didn't. If he didn't know my name or nothin' at all about me, how come he knew my shape and size and all better than *I* did? Hell, better even than my mother?"

Charley shrugged. "Beats the hell outta me, but I still ain't sure I believe I'm *here* yet. We got a lot of answers to get, that's for sure. Let me just use the pullover here and slip on this skirt and sandals—they clash but I'm not goin' noplace—and we'll get something to eat and try'n make sense of all this. Maybe Zenchur can give some of the answers. I think he knows a lot more than he's lettin' on."

Charley let her go and set about choosing an outfit. It was all sort of fun, like a Flintstones makeup kit, but when she sat in front of the mirror it was not her face that stared back and it jolted her. *This isn't any game,* she thought, feeling suddenly chilled. *Somehow this is really happening!* Images suddenly arose, of her Mom and Dad, her home, her other friends at school. What would they think when she didn't show up again? When they finally found the cabin demolished and the bloodstains and the Subaru all smashed and crushed? And now, here, in this God-forsaken hole, she sat and it wasn't herself she saw in the mirror.

My God! she thought, suddenly a frightened and nervous girl even younger than her years. *What have I done?* She wanted her Mom and Dad very badly then, and her own face and lousy figure back, too. God, how she just wanted to go home!

She started crying softly. She'd never been the crying sort, but she'd never been in a situation like this before or felt so completely helpless and alone. It didn't last very long, but she needed it. Finally, she wiped away the tears and took stock of herself. She was stuck, and she could either give up or just go along for the ride and make the best of it. The body wasn't half bad; if only Sam didn't have such a boyish-looking face. Well—the long hair helped. Maybe she could use this and see just what she could make out of it all.

She had no idea what kind of a world they were in, but if there were men like Zenchur around there were certain universal things you could assume as well. If she was gonna see that world, then that world was gonna see her looking *right.*

4

A Hard Wind's Caress

There was no day or night inside the cave, only a certain eternal quality that insulated you from the world. Sam felt a sense of safety here such as she hadn't known in a very long time. Even the storms did not seem able to penetrate this spot, where there was only the water and the rock and the flickering brightness of the torches. She wanted to know about this world, this place that had brought her to it against her will for reasons still unclear. She wanted to know, but she felt no impulse to leave.

"This world is not like your world," Zenchur told Sam as they sipped strong, black tea and nibbled on sweet rolls. "It is, in fact, like *all* the worlds."

"You said you never left this world," Sam responded. "So how can you know much about mine?"

"I know about many of them because so many like you fall from them here. Not like it used to be, but regularly enough to get some pictures. Yours is a stable world. The rules are known and are always the same. Nothing ever falls up, rain is always wet, snow is always cold—yes?"

She nodded. "Yeah, I'll grant you that. But you gotta have some rules here, too. I mean, we're stuck on the ground here, the fire's hot, and it all looks real normal."

"Here, yes, because we are on the lip of a hub. But when we move out it might not always be so. It is hard for me to explain and it will be harder for you to believe until you witness it. Tell me—if you had a map showing your world, its nations and peoples and mountains and seas, would that map not be true many years later?"

"Sure. I guess some of the nations and people might change or move around, and the names seem to change a lot in places, but the maps I started out in elementary school with are still pretty good."

"Well, that is not possible here. The maps, and more than the maps, change. You see, long ago there was nothing but a single tiny block containing everything that ever was and ever will be. It grew heavier and heavier and heavier until it was too heavy to remain together and too—unstable I think the word is. It exploded and created everything else. Can you grasp that?"

She nodded. "Yeah. I wasn't too good in school but I seem to remember that the one thing the church and science agreed on was this big bang that started it all. It created the universe, whether by God or something else."

"Good, good! But it did not create the universe. It was far too powerful for that. It created the *universes,* in layers, like the layers in a fancy cake. One on top of the other." He picked up a charred stick and drew a funnel shape on the cave floor. "See—this little bottom point is where it all started." He drew a series of lines bisecting the funnel from top to bottom. "Each of these—thousands, millions, who knows how many?—is a universe. Yours is up towards the top someplace. Mine is down here, not at the bottom but as far down as you can get and still live and breathe and have our kind of life. Up near the top the distance between them is great and you are rarely aware of any others except perhaps in dreams, but down here we have a smaller universe and things are packed more closely together. Here many universes lie almost on top of each other—layers with no cake, as it were. Akahlar is not one world, it is many."

She stared and shook her head. This was getting too much like school. "But if you got all them universes on top of each other like this, then what keeps it all from gettin' to be a jumbled mess?"

"No two can occupy the same wedge at the same time. That would be chaos. But the forces still coming from the core, from the place where it all began, keep things in motion here. Whole sections of Akahlar drop out and are replaced by others." He drew a circle, then an inner hub, then drew spokes out from the hub to the sides. "There are forty-eight of these. They are not true circles but close enough. Each two spokes creates a wedge and that wedge is *someplace.* The forces that strike us from below, at the tiny point, cause the circles not to turn but to change. One land drops out of a wedge, another drops in. If you are there you do not notice it. If you are *not* there you do not notice it. But where a city by a sea was the last time you were through there might now be a mountain lair for dragons. Twelve wedges to a wheel, as it were. Hundreds of combinations. Such changes keep us in constant turmoil. The weather changes, there are always storms and changes in most everything."

"Jeez! How do you ever keep anything straight?"

He smiled. "Never underestimate intelligence, my young friend. The races who think and build and create are the ones who can adapt. Tell me—on your world, do not people live where it is freezing cold all year, and others where it is an eternal steaming jungle, and still others where it is a hot and near lifeless desert?"

"Uh—yeah, I guess so. Sure."

"That is why they survive. There are literally thousands of races, not all even close to our kind as are the ba'ahdon. All fell to this point in ancient times when the changewinds blew strong through the whole of creation, before everything stabilized and got built up and solidified. Each is a little slice of a real universe, and each universe has exacting rules—but they are not necessarily the same rules."

"Seems to me everybody'd get lost or all mixed up or somethin'. Couldn't tell nobody from nobody else."

"Well, most races cannot breed with most others. It is possible that even you and I are different enough that we could never produce offspring, although we appear close enough that it is possible that we could, too. It is rather—what is the word?—*insular*. Everyone sticks to their own kind and their own ways and defends their land against the others. There is some trade, of course, but how can you even have a lot of trade when you do not know if your trading partner will be there next week or next month? Many races believe themselves superior, higher than the others, and so would not consider the others human or worthy of respect. Some may even delight in *eating* other races. For thousands upon thousands of years there was just a lot of little worlds. That is, until the Akhbreed conquest."

She frowned. "How the hell could you conquer something like *that?*"

"You don't. What you conquer are *these*," he replied, pointing his stick at the hub of the wheel. "The loci—the hub. These do not change. They are constant always no matter what wedge you come from. They coexist in all our universes. They were mostly uninhabitable messes, however, until the Akhbreed came with their powerful sorcery the likes of which none had ever seen before. Many of the other races possess magic, some have great power within their own wedges, but this was different. These people could do *all* the magic, and they could do it anywhere. They created order in the hubs and established kingdoms for the Akhbreed. Because all hubs coexist in all universes that are down here, they could step away into any wedge they chose. They are brutal, ruthless, powerful, and they believe themselves the anointed superiors to all other races who exist for their benefit. They alone can trade. They alone have stability. They alone can force their will by sending armies against the wedges that resist them. The forty-eight kings and queens of Akhbreed rule Akahlar because of it and keep the rest down, their power based in their god-like sorcerers. That one whom you saw last night—he is an Akhbreed sorcerer. You have just a small taste of his power."

Sam's head was spinning a bit at this. "I sure don't understand this and I ain't sure I believe what I do understand, but *him* I understand. And the one with the horns and the thunderstorms? He's another one?"

Zenchur stiffened. "Do not even speak of him so. Yes, he is of the same kind, but he is not in the service of the Akhbreed. He is what the Akhbreed call a rogue. He serves no Akhbreed kingdom. If they could locate him and gang up on him to destroy him—you do not kill Akhbreed sorcerers, you destroy them—they would. This one of whom we speak is very powerful but rebels at the Akhbreed dominance, as do I. He is their sworn enemy, and he plots to destroy the Akhbreed kingdoms and end their dominance. He offers liberation from Akhbreed tyranny to those who follow his cause, and as he is the first of that rank of sorcerer to offer his power to them he is a formidable foe, since the forty-eight Akhbreed kingdoms are bound together only by their common belief of racial superiority and their power. Otherwise, they hate each other, and the sorcerers of one are jealous and not at all cordial towards others of their kind from other kingdoms."

Sam shook her head. "Jeez! Lemme get this straight now. You got tons of races and they're all kinda bossed around and made to work for the ones who look like us 'cause the ones that look like us got the power. But our kind don't like each other, neither. They kick around all the others but they don't like the fact that all them other kings and sorcerers got the same kinda power they got. Is that about right?"

"Yes. Very good. But because they hate each other they are vulnerable—if a sorcerer of high enough power could combine with the magic of many other races as well as building a physical army that could outnumber and outfight the Akhbreed troopers, they might well fall one hub at a time. This one of whom we speak is the first of his class to offer such power to the other races. All hate the Akhbreed; some will be convinced to support him. He builds to strike at the heart of the tyranny. He has some command of a weapon that could even weaken or possibly destroy the Akhbreed hubs—if he could control it. Until he can he dares not risk it, for it is as dangerous to him and to his followers as to the Akhbreed. He is the master of the storms and can summon the changewind of old, the sort that can alter or destroy even the hubs. We get a few every now and then, randomly, in different parts of Akahlar, every year, but he can cause them. If he ever learns to control them he will smash all the tyrants of Akhbreed."

Sam frowned. "This is nuts. The way you're talkin', the guy who's tryin' to kill me is somebody doin' a good thing, and the guy who's tryin' to save me is defendin' a real evil system. This is nuts! Kinda like discoverin' that the Russians are your friends and protectors and the Americans wanna string you up when you're an American who likes the American way." She paused a moment. "I can see where some might be scared, but seems to me that this guy would have the support of everybody who ain't us. But he don't, right?"

Zenchur nodded. "Right. It is partly because he is Akhbreed, and the other races have learned through bitter experience never to trust one, and it is also that it is known that such tremendous power, like the gods, is impossible to have without corrupting your very soul. Every Akhbreed sorcerer is in some way insane. You can see the problem. Do you trade in a tyrant for a god? Which is worse—to be dominated, or to be owned? Every Akhbreed kingdom overthrown will make his domain greater and greatly increase his already unbelievable power. It is the ultimate dilemma. Without one such as him there is no hope of ever breaking the bonds that enslave countless millions of other races, but with one such as him one might long for the good old days of Akhbreed rule. It is dividing many races and many leaders. This last business will not win him many converts, either. Just to get at you he expended enormous power and that power has created a hole, a vacuum, in Akahlar. Such vacuums do not remain unfilled for long. He has of necessity created conditions that will bring a changewind to us. We must wait until it passes and hope it does not come this way."

Charley stepped out of the tent, hearing only the tail end of the conversation. She was wearing some of the jewelry and a colorful slit skirt and sandals but was topless. Sam couldn't figure just what Charley had done, but she looked *damned* good. "What's a changewind?" she asked curiously.

Zenchur looked at her and frowned. "A changewind is the random wrath of God. It is a storm. It is every storm that you have ever seen and more. It destroys worse than the worst kind of storm imaginable, yet it does what no other storm does. It also *creates*."

"Wow!" breathed Sam. "I was in a hurricane once and I seen a coupl've tornadoes. I don't wanna be in any of 'em, but I'd sure like to see one of these things—from a safe distance, of course."

"Not even an Akhbreed sorcerer will look at one of these storms," Zenchur responded. "One who looks upon the change-winds too closely gets some of its curse. Only the freaks and the monsters have looked upon the changewinds and survived in the wastes, belonging only to each other, to tell the tale. Believe me, you do not want to see a changewind—ever!"

Charley shrugged and shook her head. "What the hell is a changewind?" she repeated.

"A random force that does the one thing everyone fears every-where," the mercenary responded. "It changes the rules."

Ladai suddenly made a sharp comment in her strange tongue and he nodded. "It has come," he said softly. "Not close, but close enough. To Malabar, the hub to the southeast, and its attendant wedges. A bad one."

Charley looked at him strangely, then at Ladai. "How does she know?"

"No traveler though this world is ever completely untouched by the changewind, and, once touched, you *know*."

Suddenly Sam felt a tremendous throbbing in her temples, her ears stopped up and the cave and those in it seemed to vanish. Charley, Zenchur, and Ladai saw her suddenly get straight to her feet, looking not at anything they could see but somewhere else, and then Sam cried out—and fainted.

Zenchur was fast enough to break her fall, but even as Sam was lowered to the cave floor she seemed to come to, in a sense, her eyes opening wide, still staring at something none of the others could see and hearing things that none of the others could hear. Inside her, she felt awake, alert, the scenes she was now seeing clear and vivid to her as if she stood there with them. She knew somehow that she was not really there, but as much as she wished that it was a dream she also knew with absolute certainty that it was no dream but reality she was witnessing. Somehow, in some way, she was getting her wish whether she wanted it or not.

The coming of the changewind.

Terror wafted in on a nice spring breeze, filling the air with intangible charged particles of fear. As always, the animals felt it first, stopping whatever they were doing and then raising their heads to the northeast, almost as one, looking for what could not be seen.

The horses froze in the fields and turned to took, as did the cows. The dogs did more, emitting after a while a low growl, and the barn cats turned their ears back and arched their spines as if facing some immediate and tangible threat. Even the chickens, ordinarily too dumb to get out of the summer hail, stopped their incessant cackling and darting about and turned to look; turned to look at the northeastern horizon.

It was a clear, warm day, the kind of day that comes but once in a while in early spring but which lifts the spirits and tells all that the majesty and life of summer is approaching. The sun shone brightly down on the small village and its farms and fields and illuminated the golden coating on the great castle that seemed carved out of the hills in back of the settlement, making the greatest and grandest of the buildings shine like some majestic fairyland jewel. The sky was a pale blue, broken here and there by fluffy cumulus clouds too white to hold the threat of moisture. It was the kind of day that wouldn't dare be rained on, yet it was suddenly bathed in silence.

The lands of the hub were places of pure magic yet also places where such magic should never intrude.

People, of course, were the last to notice, as usual. Still, eventually, they noticed the silence, and the animals, and soon they, too, began looking fearfully to the northeast.

Perhaps it's nothing, they told themselves, trying to gain some measure of confidence and fight back the fear that was growing inside them. *Perhaps it's not coming our way. There hasn't been one through here in generations. This is a charmed village, a safe place, in the solidity of the hub, protected from all harm by the sorcery of the Akhbreed and even from the changewinds by the great Mountains of Morning.* So they had told themselves and each other for generations.

The changewind blew down from its far north origin, though, ignorant and uncaring of such things. It had been riding well high in the weather patterns and had not touched ground or near ground, making it more a fearsome sight than something of lasting effect that might be seen and felt and known by those over which it passed. So far it had a pretty clear run along the air currents across the plains, but now it was caught in the twisting currents at the base of the Mountains of Morning and sucked in toward them. They were ancient, massive peaks, all purple in the distance and snow-clad, and they stood as a formidable barrier to all save the changewind. It was too dense to rise over the mountains, and too stubborn and powerful to allow them to get in its way.

Nothing really could be seen from the castle or the village as yet; it was still too far away. Yet it could be felt, and sensed, even by those inside the castle who had grown fat and complacent over the decades of stability, and on Akahlar stability was everything. Even they could not ignore the behavior of their animals, or some of the signs from their instruments.

The Royal Sorcerer made his way to the forward battlement, his blue robe flapping in the breeze, a tiny green monkey remaining expertly perched on his shoulder in spite of the sudden movement. The sorcerer had a large bronze telescope mounted there, pointing to the north and east, and he swung the thing but did not look in it himself. Rather, it was the small green monkey who looked in it, as the sorcerer moved the telescope, scanning the horizon, yet from the sorcerer's head movements one would swear that he was indeed peering in and looking hard, not for anything direct or obvious, but just for the signs he knew would be there.

In the valley between the twin peaks they called the Two Brothers he found his signs, although they would have meant little to the untrained eye. Just a bit of a glow, pale crimson, beyond the peaks, and the peaks themselves framed slightly with a blue borderline, as if superimposed upon another scene beyond. It was enough. It was more than enough.

"Captain of the Guard!" the little man yelled, and a soldier came running. "There is a changewind coming. A high probability, too, given the wind patterns aloft, that it will come straight down the valley. Alert His Majesty and Colonel Fristanna at once. Waste no time in preparing the shelters and sounding the alarm to the people."

This was bad; a lot worse than either he or the king had originally thought. This was going to be the storm of the century for this old place.

The Guardsman did nothing right away. Finally, licking his lips, he said, "Are you sure?" Ordinarily questioning or in any way failing to immediately carry out the order of an Akhbreed sorcerer would be unthinkable, but the sorcerer had just introduced the unthinkable and forced consideration of it.

The little man in blue fumed. "Why do you hesitate? Time is of the essence! If you don't do as I say now you will see the changewind close up, from down there, outside the castle and Keep!"

Galvanized, the Guardsman turned and ran off. Within two minutes the sound that all dreaded, highborn and low, rang out from the same battlements as Guardsmen turned the cranks on the howler boxes sounding a terrible siren call that reached for miles and penetrated the very soul.

The man in blue looked down to see the castle's company springing into action. One, an officer, already mounted and ready to move, looked up and saw him. "How long, wizard?" he shouted. "Do we have a time frame?"

"Hard to say," the little man shouted back. "Certainly an hour, most certainly not two. Keep an eye on the Brothers. If they change, then you have at best five to ten minutes. Understand? Watch the Brothers!"

The officer nodded, turned, and began shouting orders.

The sorcerer himself could do little. He of all the people was most vulnerable to the changewind; it might well be attracted to him like a magnet, and he knew his only real duty was to get inside and behind proper insulation until it passed. He sighed and looked out on the peaceful valley and the town below. A simple place, with rolling green fields newly fertilized and planted with summer maize, oats, corn, and other grains, the vegetable regions newly tilled. Off to the west were the groves of grapes, hardly ready as yet for the harvest but promising a very good year. He sincerely hoped that they, at least, would be spared.

The low stone buildings of the town with their thatched roofs newly repaired after a harder than usual winter looked somehow unreal, like a painting in the Great Hall.

There would be little time to gather much in the way of personal belongings; those who dallied might well be caught outside, for when the howlers howled again it would signal the closing of the refuges and the closing of hope for anyone and anything left outside.

Below the Golden Castle, at the base of the hill that supported it, great teams of men and oxen turned massive gears that had been moved only in drills for the past fourteen years. Below, great doors slowly swung outward, revealing a massive cavity that went not only into the hill but down below it. Not even hills were safe in a changewind; not even mountains.

With the aid and none too gentle encouragement of the cavalry, the village began to move toward that cavity. The women and children first, of course; they were the least expendable. Then the men, some pulling hastily filled carts, others not bothering, while the farmers themselves herded cows and horses and as many sheep as they could quickly round up from the nearby meadows.

Malachan was only fourteen, but that was old enough to make him a man in the village. He had been still in his mother's womb the last time and knew of such things only in legends and tales told by his elders, but now one was coming and he was of age, subject to his father's orders, and it was partially his responsibility to see that all living things that could be saved be protected. The rest could be replaced or rebuilt, if need be. He was aware of the tales and legends of the change-winds and knew it might not be needed, that in fact they might gain better than they lost, if they but protected what could not be risked.

Up on the battlement, the Captain of the Guard stared at the Two Brothers, which no longer seemed so distant or so permanent, and then he gasped and his heart leaped to his throat. For a brief moment he was paralyzed, this man who had fought a hundred battles and faced a hundred foes, by what he now saw.

The Brothers were melting, melting down like ice on a hot summer's day, turning purple and white to a burnt orange color and revealing suddenly a huge pass through the Mountains of Morning, and beyond that pass the sky turned an ominous, yet beautiful cyan, a massive violet that was moving and twisting and writhing like something alive, and which flashed with bright sparks as it did so. Beyond it, on its fringes, the regular clouds coalesced into a dark, nasty storm that rumbled lightning and thunder and accompanied the swirling mass.

He broke free and ran to the far end, shouting as he did so. "It's through! It's through! Sound the alarm and take cover!"

A wind came suddenly up from nowhere, rustling through the grasses and causing the trees to sway and speak the roaring tongue. And from the ground and the houses and the trees and the very air there seemed to come shapes; indistinct, wraithlike shapes large and small, gentle and fierce, and they rushed through the air as well, beating the wind to the great enclosure, going over the heads of the people and animals still going in.

The siren call of the howlers wailed. *Ten minutes! Last warning!* But ten minutes was not ten at all, but five, for they had to be closed and all well below in the insulated, packed shelters by the time that mass got here, if indeed it was coming. Men dropped carts and abandoned what they had been carrying and ran for the great opening, and even the animals seemed to quicken and run for that last place of escape.

Malachan prepared to run as well, when he heard a plaintive wailing cry off to his right. He stopped and then made for it, quickly spotting a very frightened small cat hunched up against the side of a house and mewing in terror. He picked it up and it clung to him, and he petted it for a moment, then turned, aware now that the howling had stopped. Clutching the kitten, he made as fast as he could for the doors which were even now beginning to close.

It was not much distance; it was designed that way, but the usually clear and easy path to it was now littered with carts and dropped and spilled goods. Here a treasured picture, there an old clock, and over there bottles, some smashed. It was like running an obstacle course, and on top of that the kitten's claws were dug through his clothing to his skin.

Still, he was going to make it. Perhaps at the last moment, but he was going to make it. The doors were only three-quarters shut, and he was small. At the same moment he made to leap a smashed basket of what looked like bowls and dishes, the kitten decided it had had enough and launched itself away toward the closing great doors. The action was enough to disorient him briefly, and he tripped over the box and fell hard on the ground. It didn't take him long to recover, although he was scraped and skinned up a bit, but it had cost him precious seconds and all his momentum. He looked at the doors and saw they were almost closed, and took off again on a run, screaming, "Wait! Wait! Just a few seconds more!"

But the forces turning the great gears that controlled the gate ignored him, as was their duty, if, indeed, they had heard him at all.

He was but three steps from the doors when they closed tight with a mighty clang and echoing roar that seemed to rebound across the entire valley. Malachan hurled himself at the doors and beat upon them with all his might, shouting loudly, but it did no good at all.

He wasted little time once he realized this, running back and then over toward the road leading up to the Golden Castle. There would still be someone there, probably until the last minute. There were ways in and down from there, he knew. The Stormholders and Guardsmen would have their own privileges.

The wind was picking up, reaching almost gale force, however, and it drove him back. The air was full of dust and debris, and everything loose began to shake and shimmer and take on a life of its own. He knew now it was no use; the storm would be upon him before he could reach the top gates, and by that time no one would be left. He tried to think.

If you are caught by a changewind, and have any warning, go as low as you can, below ground if possible, and cover yourself with earth, they'd taught him. *Let no part of your body be exposed to the air and wind.*

He looked around. That was easy to say, but hardly useful right now. The defense of the village was predicated on and dependent on the Refuge carefully built below and lined with the best of insulators. Even the golden coating on the castle was an insulating substance that might work if it were not directly hit, but it would do him little good. He knew that you had to stay away from such substances if you were on the outside, since any forces that were repelled would build up and concentrate there.

And so he found what shelter he could against the conventional winds behind a stone wall and peered out at the coming great storm. It was both beautiful and awesome. It was preceded by a rolling bank of black clouds that seemed to advance like some great carpet, a carpet fit for a king or a god. Lightning flared out from this leading edge, dancing along the ground and sounding mighty reverberant thunderclaps throughout the valley.

The changewind also had its attendants; more clouds, racing with a speed he had never seen before, giving off not only lightning but darker shapes, funnel-like clouds marching beside the changewind and sucking up whatever they trod upon.

In the center of it all was the changewind, most beautiful and awesome of all. Everyone was properly frightened to death of it, but none had ever spoken of its great beauty and majesty. Swirling clouds like violet oil in a sky full of clear water; that's what it looked like at first. The closer it got, though, the less color it seemed to have and it became paradoxically more and less complex. A sea of infinite stars, blinking and wavering, in a vaguely violet universe unlike any known to any people of his own world. It was a vastness that covered, engulfed, all that it rolled across. The air was thick and heavy, drawing the great wind down until nothing but it could be seen in the center of the valley. The changewind, finally, rode only a hundred feet or so above the ground and influenced all that was below it. Had it reached the ground it would have been grabbed by enormous friction, slowed, and absorbed, its effect major but localized, and it would have quickly died.

This one would not oblige.

Malachan knew nothing of its physics, which was just as well, for in truth the learned wizard who had first spied it had vastly more questions than answers, but he understood well that it was coming and that there was no way really for him to get out of its way.

Strangely, he found himself suddenly drained of fear, taken up only in the awesome beauty and wonder of that force he could neither comprehend nor do anything at all about. He knew he was going to die, and he only hoped that his reincarnation would be swift and his judgment fair, for he had been a good boy. For a brief moment he thought of his family, all safe inside and huddled there in the torchlit darkness, and knew that his loss, when discovered, would bring them grief. He hoped it would not be too much or too long. He would get his experiences in the next life; this was almost worth the price.

The changewind advanced into the valley and did what it always did. All below its pulsing form took on an eerie glow and became outlined in brilliant, electric blue. Grass, trees, everything—even the very air seemed altered and illuminated with a glow. The grape vines shimmered and writhed and changed, becoming strange, gnarled trees with dark, huge blossoms unlike anything he'd ever seen before. The maize field shimmered and melted and part of it became water, pushed by the storms. The rest became taller, wilder grasses in spots, and yellow and sand in others.

The changewind began to pass over the thatched cottages and stables of the village. They glowed and flowed and changed as well, becoming blocky, multi-story structures made of some reddish-brown material, a form totally alien to him. He could already see beneath and beyond the changewind to a fierce rainstorm on the back side, while over on the edges there seemed to be clearing and even the start of breaks in the clouds.

And then it was over and upon him. Curiously, there was no sensation, no pain, nothing. Just a light tingling sensation, nothing more. He held out his arms and saw that he was bathed in the changewind glow. He grew, and his clothing burst and then seemed to melt away within him. His arms became thick and muscular, his fingers long and powerful, with steel-like claws as nails. His skin turned thick and brown as he watched, then was covered down to the wrists and even on the backs of his huge hands with very short thick brown hair like an animal's.

Below his waist the hair changed, becoming thick and wooly, and his legs throbbed and twisted and changed as well. They were animal legs, although not exactly like any animal he had ever known, and they terminated in great, cloven hooves which would be fine for running but provided less than the best balance standing still. He went backward a bit, but found himself well supported on his long, thick brown tail.

Malachan was less terrified than horrified at what he had become. Death he could accept, and had been willing to, but he had not died. He had become some sort of monster.

The changewind was past now, and proceeding far up the valley, losing force as it did so. It was already rising, and losing some of its consistency. It would not travel on much farther. Malachan stood there, stunned, as the torrential rain came down upon him, masking and taking with them his very real tears.

The backwash of the storm was quickly through, though, and the clouds grew thinner and then began to break up. Sunlight dared peer down on a vastly different scene. It would be quite some time, perhaps months, before the climatological changes stabilized and it was possible to really see what the changewind had made of this wonderful place, but it certainly was no longer the paradise that a previous changewind helped create.

The Golden Castle still stood, its golden sheen now a metallic blue-black, but it would be quite some time, perhaps days, before the assembled populace could free itself from the Refuge the way they got in. The great doors had held, but in the process they had melted a bit and been fused into a solid metallic wall.

The place was not without some familiarity. The Two Brothers no longer stood out in the distance, but the vast wall of the Mountains of Morning otherwise remained pretty much as it was. There was now a vast lake leading from just in front of the village back almost as far as the eye could see, yet it was not wide; patches of real green could be seen in the distance.

This side, however, had not fared so well. The soil was sandy, and rocky as well, and the vegetation was wild grasses, some waist high, and nasty and twisted plants unlike any known here before. Over where the grape vines were, intermixed with the trees, were strange looking bushes bearing large and beautiful pink and crimson flowers that looked like giant roses.

Hesitantly, Malachan moved toward them, and as he got within five or six feet of the first it barked at him. All of the flowers barked at him, and snarled, like a pack of angry dogs, and the beautiful bushes shook and flailed out blindly. He backed off quickly, very confused.

He looked down at himself and then at the vicious plants and shook his now massive head. He simply did not know what to do. He was still Malachan—at least, he *thought* that at least that part of him remained unchanged. Changewinds could alter anything, inside and out, even the very soul, but this one seemed to have limited itself to the physical.

He looked at the lake, and the menacing plants, and knew he could not go there. He looked back at the transformed village, so alien now, and beyond it. The last of the storm was leaving, but where the two lines of hills had once come together there was now unbroken plain littered with tall grasses and equally tall bright, huge flowers. *Everything* had changed, everything but the castle itself, and it would never be the same again any more than he would. He just wished he knew what to do.

He was still trying to determine this when the laborers and cutters up at the castle broke through and managed to peel away the remains of the armored doors at the top. Within minutes, a large troop of cavalry rode out, stopping just outside to survey the new scene and take it all in. The real survey, however, had to come later. Theirs was a different mission that had to come first.

The leader peered through field glasses, panning the scene, looking for what his duty required, and he finally found it. It wasn't hard, not against this new landscape and being the size and shape it was. He put down his glasses and pointed. "Down there, to the left and behind the village. See it?"

His sergeant squinted, then nodded. "Yes, sir. I had hoped we had gotten them all this time. Pray the gods this is the only one."

"We don't know if it was human or animal," the lieutenant: shouted to his men, "or whether it will attack or flee. Weapons ready, then move down. Shoot first and study the thing later!"

Malachan saw and heard them, too, and for a moment didn't know whether to stand there or flee. When he saw that they had their weapons out, though, he turned and began to run at full speed through the tall grass.

He was fast, very fast, as if made for this sort of country, but the skilled men and superbly trained horses were faster and smarter and more experienced. He quickly realized that he could not outrun them and stopped, marveling that he was hardly breathing hard at all, and waited, his massive hands raised in a gesture of surrender. They were all around him in a minute, but none too close.

"Please!" he bellowed as they stared nervously and uncomfortably at him. "I am Malachan of the old village! The doors closed on me just a few steps before I could enter! Have mercy! I am hideous, but I am just a fourteen-year-old peasant boy!"

That startled some of the newer men, but not the officer and the sergeant who were more experienced. It was usually kids.

"I know, son," sighed the lieutenant in a sad, almost tragic-sounding voice. "I just hope you're old enough to understand. Understand that what we must—do—now *is* out of mercy."

"*No!*" wailed Malachan as the missiles struck and penetrated even his powerful body, again and again, with great pain, until he was so helpless that the officer had no problem administering the *coup de grace.*

Up on the charred battlements, the sorcerer Boolean examined his old area. The telescope was gone, of course—sort of. What stood in its place was a very odd sort of weapon mounted on a similar tripod, a weapon not known in this land before, but one the Akhbreed sorcerer understood full well.

"Well I'll be damned," the wizard said under his breath. "Have to melt *that* one down for scrap pretty damned fast. Can't have 'em getting too many ideas of *that* sort around here. Things are rotten enough already." He turned and looked out at the changed landscape, the new lake, the missing hills, the strange trees and grass, and shook his head.

"Well," he sighed, again talking to himself, "there goes the neighborhood."

Sam awoke, sweat dripping from her, the scene fading gradually and being replaced by fuzzy images that resolved into the concerned faces of Charley and Zenchur.

"They killed him!" she shouted, slightly in shock. "They hunted him down and killed him! Just a kid who got caught in some bad luck! The bastards! The dirty bastards!"

"What did you see?" Zenchur asked curtly. "Tell me all of it—now!"

Ladai spoke to him a bit sharply and then brought some dry wine for Sam to drink. Once she had a bit of it down, she felt more and more in control of herself, and with a little prompting she told them the entire story.

Zenchur nodded. "It sounds right, although I can't understand how or why you would have such a vision, particularly of Malabar where neither of the ones involved in your own affairs here have much interest or influence. The Akhbreed tolerate no one not of their own kind to live in any of the kingdoms, and none may remain overnight except right on the edge, as we are here."

"But—but it changed *everything!* The houses, the plants, the dirt, the water, even that poor boy. Even if he was a victim, why'd they hav'ta *kill* him? Why not just send him off someplace?"

Zenchur sighed. "It is complicated. The Akhbreed believe themselves the superior race to all others. Therefore, it is unthinkable to them that any of their kind would even wish to live as some sort of—well, monster. They killed him as a mercy—to keep him from suffering in an inferior form. He was also probably one of a kind in Akahlar—that happens a lot with the big ones. He would be a freak, an outcast, and none would take him or accept him."

That was not an answer either girl could accept, and they were beginning to like this place less and less with each passing discovery. Still, Sam wanted to understand. "Where did those changes come from? His form, the houses, the barking bushes . . . ?"

Zenchur shrugged. "Practically everything is possible, you know. If one little thing went differently, if your ancestors had arisen from different stock than they did, our whole race might have looked like that. The houses, the land, everything was probably consistent with beings of his kind. They may even exist somewhere on an Outplane—there are far too many to know. They call it probability theory. Sorcerer's mathematics. Ask one sometime about it if you get the chance—and somehow I suspect you will meet one or more sooner or later. More to the point now is why you had this spell, this vision, and how."

She shrugged helplessly. "In my dreams—back home. The dreams always brought visions—I guess of this place—and always when it stormed. I guess even this far away and buried this deep a storm like that triggered it off again."

Zenchur robbed his chin thoughtfully, then muttered to himself in the singsong tongue of the Akhbreed, "The Horned One, and a girl from the Outplane who is linked to storms. Of course! Why did I not think of this from the start? By the gods—what do I do now?" He paused a moment more, then sighed.

"All right," he said in English. "You saw the Chief Sorcerer of Malabar there. Did he seem to be aware of you? Did anyone give the slightest hint that they were aware of your presence? Any? Think! It is important!"

"It was like I was a ghost, not seen and not being able to say or do anything. I was just *there,* that's all. Besides, they were a little too busy to bother much with me."

"And you sensed no one else there? No other presence, or guiding force?"

She shook her head. "Nope. It just—*happened,* is all."

"Very well. That is some consolation, anyway. Just relax here. I must discuss this with Ladai." He walked over to the centauress who was relaxing by the pool. The distance between them and Sam was a good twenty feet or more but the cave made it fairly easy to hear everything in the mercenary's low conversation with his strange companion.

"I don't like this," Charley commented sourly. "I wish I could make out that language of theirs."

"*Shhhh* . . . ," Sam responded. When Charley seemed not inclined to shut up, her friend mouthed, *I can understand it.*

And she could, just as she had understood the comments in the Akhbreed tongue that Zenchur had muttered to himself. She had not understood many of the conversations between Zenchur and Ladai before, since they had been in some other, less formal, tongue, but now the mercenary was using Akhbreed, the same language of Sam's dreams of the past, the language which, somehow, she instantly understood.

"We cannot go on with this." Zenchur told Ladai. "Our distrust for that horned bastard kept us neutral in this so far, but we no longer have that luxury. If we deliver her to Boolean it is more than possible that the entire rebellion will be crushed and Akhbreed dominance assured for another thousand years or more. *We*—you and I—will be the instruments of perpetuating this foulness! This I cannot accept!"

Ladai understood him, apparently used to him speaking in his native tongue when he was angry or upset, but she answered in their common speech and Sam could not make out any of it.

Zenchur nodded. "I agree. We cannot just kill them—Boolean would know and there would be no place to hide from his wrath, for one thing. And, no, I can't have either of us leaking the facts to others because that would destroy our reputations for never betraying a commission. We would be finished. Yet, somehow, they must die."

Again Ladai said something unintelligible.

"Yes," he responded, sounding somewhat pleased by whatever suggestion she'd given. "You're right. If they are placed in a position where they are certain to be exposed, and the odds are overwhelming, then what can we do? Besides, they are ignorant of all of this. If the name Klittichorn should be spoken rather regularly it might well attract just the wrong attention on its own." He kissed her. "My dear, I believe we will have another of our honorable failures."

Charley thought the unintelligible scene a bit charming if very kinky, but Sam's expression told her that it was far more than that. Still, she knew better than to press it right now; if the odd couple's conversation could carry, so could any other.

Zenchur came back over to them, ever the friendly protector. "I will have to leave here for a while in order to make arrangements for mounts and the like to get us into Tubikosa, the capital city of this hub. Because of the changewind we will need up-to-date information on just what damage it did and where. I am a competent navigator but we will have to engage a trustworthy pilot who is also up-to-date. That means the city, although I detest it and had hoped we would not have to travel there. The changewind makes it essential that we do so. Ladai will stand guard and you will be all right. Take some time to look through the trunks and choose a selection that could fit in no more than two of the saddlebags in my tent. Um—you can both ride horses, can't you?"

"Never been on one in my life," Sam responded, " 'cept the pony rides at the fair when I was little. But I'll make do."

"I'm a pretty good horsewoman," Charley told him. "We'll have to teach Sam what she needs to know."

Zenchur shrugged. "Very well. I will secure a particularly gentle horse for Sam, a first rider type. Now—farewell." And, with that, he walked to the cave entrance and was gone.

"I don't like that," Sam muttered, almost to herself. "Come on—let's go look through the trunks."

Charley frowned. "But it's okay. He's gone, and she don't speak English."

"Yeah, maybe, but I'm not about to make the same mistake he did. Come on."

They walked into the tent and Sam stood there for a minute or so, as Charley watched in frustration. Then Sam peered out of the tent flap and looked back. "It's okay," she whispered, "so long as we keep our voices down. She's still just lyin' there playin' with her reflection in the water." Quickly she told Charley of the conversation in low tones.

"Damn! What the hell do we do *now?* I mean, if you're new on a horse you're a sittin' duck and you know it. All he has to do is get one that's got a mean streak or is easily spooked and it can look real natural. Horse bolts or panics, you fall and break your neck, and he's off the hook, right? And I'm all alone and stuck here as witness to the terrible accident." Charley sighed. "But how come you understood him at all?"

"Lucky break. He don't speak it like I know it but it was close enough. Sort'a like hearin' an English farmer instead of American. It's the same language I heard in my dreams and I understood it then. I guess I still do. Maybe I can talk it, too, but I ain't gonna try until I hav'ta give away the fact I know it. Couldn't make out Ladai's speech for nothin', though."

Charley sighed. "Well, that's a break, sort of, for what it's worth. Too bad we can't talk to Ladai. I know they're partners and all, but she seems so sweet and understanding. . . ."

"Bullshit! She was givin' him the ideas on how to knock us off without gettin' caught at it. Look, I was out there talkin' to Zenchur long before you got there. The guy's *weird.* Got some sort'a guilt complex or somethin'. His family's rich—maybe nobles, I dunno. Lots of money and power, though, that they got partly from the sweat of labor by the nonhumans. He got to know and like some of 'em, found out they was regular folks and all, and got a real heavy conscience. When he could he just ran away rather than keep livin' under that system. Tried to live with some of the other races but they didn't trust him none, run him out. He was on the run when he nearly died and got rescued by the—whatchamacallit?—horse people?"

"Centaurs."

"Yeah, that's right. They took him in 'cause they can look deep inside you and read your feelin's. Not your mind, but whether you're happy or sad, in love or whatever, that kind of shit. They just know, somehow, who their friends are. He lived with 'em a long time and just real flipped out. Went native Ladai—she ain't his business partner. She's his wife."

"Wow! *Kinkee* . . ."

"You bet. He thinks he's one of *them.* They believe in that reincarnation stuff, and he thinks he's one of them horse types reborn by accident or whatever as a human. He believes it so strong I think she believes it, too. She's got a few screws loose herself 'cause she went for him in a big way, too, but their marriage wasn't all that popular with her folks or tribe or whatever it is. So they got kicked out, and they been workin' the dirty job and mercenary racket all over ever since. So now they got in over their head and they're gonna try and shake it so's they can get back to ignorin' the world and its problems. And I'm what they gotta shake."

Charley sat down on top of the trunk and tried to think. "So what can we do? We stay with them, we're dead. We sneak out and, like, we're alone and friendless in some crazy world where we don't know a damned thing and where I can't even speak nobody's language, we don't know the rules, and everybody wants our heads."

"Yeah, well, maybe so, but I got to figure we got a better chance on our own, small as it is, than we do stickin' with *this* pair. At least we're Akhbreed—the bosses—and we're in a land of Akhbreed where I can probably get by in the language and we won't get tossed out or strung up 'cause we ain't got four legs or six arms or whatever. Trouble is, our disguises ain't gonna help much if these two know about them. Damn it!"

Charley looked suddenly horror-struck. "Sam! I—I couldn't kill them! Even if I thought we could get away with it, and they're pros, I just *couldn't!*"

It was Sam's turn to sigh. "Yeah, I know. I mean, maybe if he was in the *act* of tryin' to kill me and I had a gun or somethin' maybe I could, but not cold."

"Not at all! I just don't think I could kill another human being, or even one with a horse's body."

"Then we're gonna hav'ta run from them all the time, too. That's just the way it's gotta be."

"Yeah, but—where to? We can't run forever without gettin' in real trouble and you know it. This ain't Texas or Denver, you know."

"I know. The only thing we got is that we know the names of both the one who wants us live and the one who wants me dead." She suddenly stopped, an idea coming into her head. "Say! It's crazy but it don't cost nothin'!"

"Huh? What?"

"Well—Zenchur said that if he could get us and maybe him, too, sayin' the name of Old Horny that somehow that crud would hear his name and maybe find us."

"Yeah. I remember him tellin' us not to even *talk* about that guy."

"Uh-huh. Don't you see? Maybe it works for the other one, too. The green guy. Zenchur called him Boolean. Maybe if we say it enough times he'll hear us and figure somethin's wrong."

Charley shrugged. "Makes as much sense as anything else has so far,"

"Well, let's give it a try. Just over and over while we go through the trunks and do the packin' and all."

"And if he don't hear us and do something?"

"Then we get the hell out of here tonight. Grab what food and water we can and just go. If he's got the horses we'll use 'em, I guess. If not, it's on foot."

Charley got up and opened her trunk, then looked into it. "I dunno even what I should *wear,* let alone pack."

"Well, I got a look at that Malabar and that's supposed to be the next Akhbreed kingdom to this one, so I know kind'a what they wear. You ain't gonna like it, though."

"Huh? What'd'ya mean?"

"Well, you ever see pictures of them strict Moslem countries on TV or in school? It ain't that bad, but it's bad enough. Lemme look through your trunk. I bet there's a couple of outfits right there someplace. Yeah—here's one down here. Thought so."

"Oh, *no!*"

"Just try it on and start chantin' 'Boolean' over and over. I'll show you how it goes on."

5
The Road to Tubikosa

The chanting of the name didn't seem to have much effect except to bore both of them fairly quickly. The outfits Sam picked for Charley quickly took over the latter's attention. They were basically one-piece outfits, kind of like Indian saris, but they were made of some very thin, ultra-light material that conformed well to the body's shape and were tied off at the waist to bring it into shape there. The wrap started below the arms leaving the shoulders bare but went down almost to the ground and, without slitting or pleating, gave little play. You could walk in it fairly well and there was enough stretch in the material to allow comfortable sitting so long as you didn't cross your legs, but it would be hell if she had to run for it. Still, it was relatively easy to get on and the fasteners, while snug, were carefully and invisibly built in with the material somehow adjusting to whatever body shape it needed.

It felt like fine silk, but was so lightweight it was almost like having nothing on more formidable than a negligee, although when you tried to move in a way it wasn't designed to let you, it won. The stuff was *tough,* which was somewhat reassuring. The material was plain, but the three in the trunk were lavender, crimson, and emerald green and were quite attractive. There was also a long, wispy black transparent scarf, more gossamer than anything, that was worn on the head and tied off under the chin. "I think that's important," Sam told her. "At least, the women I saw in that—vision—all had their heads covered. 'Course, their dresses were plainer material—mostly cotton, I think—and the scarfs more the usual type, but I think this is what we got that'll be okay. Beats the other type which were kind'a Mother Hubbard dresses all to hell, anyways."

"The sandals, I suppose?"

"Most all the women had bare feet where I saw, but I didn't

see inside that castle or any of the higher class people 'cept the wizard and some soldiers so I can't really tell. Up to you but I'd pack the sandals til we needed 'em for protection. You slip and fall in that outfit and you'll hav'ta be helped back up."

"I'll go along with that. Who knows? Maybe bare feet are sexy here. At least we'll have a chance for Zenchur to see it and make comments before we have to split. What about you?"

"Well, since I'm the brother, one of these Robin Hood outfits in brown ought'a do okay. The top's loose and everything's kind'a bloused, so it should give me the look. Black's strictly for soldiers, from the looks of it. The high-ups might wear fancy stuff but the common folk mostly wore this kind of outfit in earth tones, with a wide belt and these short boots. Wonder what this sucker is?"

Charley looked at it, thought for a moment, then gave a slight laugh. "I think I remember that one from last year's drama class. You didn't take that, did you? We all dressed up in those old Elizabethan outfits to do scenes from Shakespeare. If I remember right, that's a codpiece."

"A what?"

"Think of it as a boy's bra. It holds and protects your prick. Hmmm . . . Pretty stiff at that. You don't have anything to protect there, but if you wear it it'll sure look like you do if those pants are as tight as they look. Tie it off above the hips, then—yeah, okay. Now pull on the pants."

"It feels like I got a rubber ball between my legs."

"Well, you'll get used to it. It's *perfect!* With a bulge like that and the rest disguisin' your other parts it kind'a advertises your sex like a good padded bra. Take a look in the mirror."

"Uh—yeah, okay. I see what you mean. I hope it stays in place when I walk or run, though. Be kind'a embarrassin' seein' there's nothin' there to hold it."

"You'll manage, and I'll keep an eye out. I wish I knew some of the language, though. I can't play deaf and dumb—the first time somebody shouts a warning or a pot drops I'll jump. I know English and Spanish 'cause half the neighborhood spoke it when I grew up, but that stuff you and Zenchar talk—that's like Chinese or something."

"Yeah, I know. I thought I only knew English til this came along. But you'll just hav'ta keep your mouth shut and let me do the talkin', I guess. I been tryin' to go through my head and teach you some words and phrases, but it just don't come out right. It's a whole different kind of talkin' that just don't work like 'good-bye' means 'adios'. Seems like they got a hundred ways of sayin' 'goodbye' dependin' on the situation or the words before and after. And lots of our words they don't have words for at all. It's like, well, you say somethin' that takes a sentence with us and then there's one big word that puts all the sounds together just right to make, like, well, a song, and it says it all. How in hell do I teach *that?* There ain't no way I could learn this sucker by myself."

"I know, I know, but it's like driving me *nuts.* Not so bad now, but when we get out in the world here I won't know like 'There's the ladies' room' from 'There's robbers and rapists back there.' I—"

Sam held up a hand. "I hear somethin' in the cave. Maybe Zenchur's back. I'll go out and stall; you get yourself the way you want and we'll see what he says."

Zenchur *was* back, looking all business. He may have been crazy but he wasn't dumb. When he saw Sam he nodded approvingly and said, "You really *did* see it all, didn't you? That is precisely the right outfit for Tubikosa and most of the surrounding hubs. Other kingdoms have far different rulers and so far different rules and dress, but that one is good everywhere, just marking you as being a southerner. All right—I have secured a horse and wagon as well as a spare from a farmer nearby who is quite blind to anything if money is produced. The wagon will allow us to move most of the supplies we have and will need so we can take both trunks, and it should allow for your lack of expertise with horses. The city is a good day's ride from here, so get a good night's sleep."

"If I can," Sam responded.

Zenchur went over to Ladai and began talking in that language they both used that she couldn't understand. Sam had to regret that the mercenary wasn't upset or agitated again. She would love to have known what was being said.

Finally Zenchur came back over and sat down, looking a bit tired. "Ladai cannot accompany us, of course. It is forbidden for any not of the Akhbreed to be inside the city or any town after sundown, and the kind of pigsties that they have for such people are below any standards of decency. She will close up here and join us on the road out from the kingdom."

Charley emerged and immediately caught Zenchur's eye dressed as she was. "Ah! More accuracy!" he exclaimed. "It is perfect for the city, although I'm not certain that something plainer but looser might not be appropriate for the trip. Still—we have the wagon. Ah! I see you have the scarf as well. That is good. It is considered something of a sacrilege in these more conservative kingdoms if a woman ever appears in public with her head uncovered—or a man with his head covered. The makeup, the jewelry, gives the correct impression, too, I think, although I suspect you hit upon it by accident."

"I could'a used some press-on nails but like I did my best with that Stone Age Emery board and file set," she responded. "I just feel so damned *helpless* not speakin' anything but English, though."

"A good point," he agreed. "That is where you are both vulnerable, I fear. More than likely him who seeks you will have supplied some English phrases to the rogues and scoundrels who are looking for you to claim the reward. Do not feel too hesitant about using English when you must, since they will not understand it or recognize it—they are merely being taught sounds—but some will undoubtedly come up to you and whisper an English phrase, possibly a question requiring a response. If you *do* respond you give yourself away, see? Both of you should remember that. Hopefully we can find some second-rate magician down on his luck with some language spells there that can give the two of you working knowledge of something useful, but until then you must depend on my translations and do *not* react to any English spoken to you by any not now present. Do not drop your guard! The price is most certainly good enough that they will kidnap you and ask questions later."

"Thanks a lot," Charley responded sourly.

"I should warn you, though, that the way you are gives you a good cover but at something of a price. Women in these conservative kingdoms do not wear jewelry or makeup and dress rather plainly in public, you see. To do otherwise marks you as an—what would be the word?—*entertainer.* That is, I am afraid, not a position of respect."

"Well, that's not so bad. I can't sing or dance much, but I can fake it."

"Uh—Charley," Sam said slowly, "I don't think that's exactly what he meant. I think he means like an entertainer of men—one at a time."

Charley looked blank for a minute, then said, "Oh. You mean—*you mean I'm dressed like a two-bit whore?*"

"No, that is not the word," Zenchur said, unfazed by her reaction. "I am trying—*courtesan* is too much of the noble sort—prostitute? I do not know what this two-bit means."

"Cheap," Sam told him. "As cheap and common as you can get."

"Yes, that is about it. Oh, I see your reaction, but here it is something of an honorable profession, you see, for those who are, pardon, too slow and unskilled to do much of anything else. It is, in fact, one of the few businesses here run by women, since when one is too old or loses one's looks she becomes a manager of younger ones or a housekeeper for them or something like that. You see, true basic unskilled labor is something that Akhbreed just do not do. Young girls who are ignorant or orphaned or who refuse arranged marriages or the like do not have the menial jobs to fill and all must contribute. Unless you are very old or disabled you must have a function, a job. Few are natives. Most come from distant hubs or from some of the Akhbreed settlements in the wedges. Many of the wedge settlements come from different Akhbreed stock than the ruling race, as is obvious to look at you. Many do not even know the Akhbreed tongue and if you are not raised with it you do not learn it more than a little to get by. It is a very difficult language. So it would not be unusual if you did not know Akhbreed. In some circles it is considered an advantage."

"Oh, great! A great cover, huh? But every damned man I meet is gonna figure he only has to wave some money around and I'll sleep with him. Oh, no! I draw the line at that!"

Zenchur grinned. "It is not a big problem. You see, it is improper to make a direct offer, as it were. As you are passing through, they will think you are along with us for serving business clients, as it were. The offers would be made to either your brother or to me."

"My *what?* Oh—I see. Yeah. It's hard to remember how much alike we look now."

"Yes, and since the brother cannot speak Akhbreed, either, then they would come to me. You look quite lovely. I am certain to get offers not only to lie with you but to purchase rights to you. I shall, of course, refuse."

"You better! What's that about purchasing rights?"

"Akhbreed are all free by definition and cannot be bought or sold. However, you would be under a contract if it were for real and someone else could purchase that contract. An employment contract, essentially. Without it you would be illegal to sell your services and that is a crime with very hard punishments."

"Sounds like slavery after some lawyers got done changin' the words," Sam noted.

"No, no. You do not have to agree to such a contract and you do not have to agree to its reassignment. Of course, then you would have two weeks to find some other form of work or you would be arrested."

"Are there any male—*entertainers?*" Charley asked him sarcastically.

The sarcasm was lost on him. "Why yes, there are, certainly."

"That what you're gonna make me?" Sam asked, not liking this a bit. She could see a scenario where Charley was sold into a brothel, helpless without friends or language, while she was somehow compromised and taken away.

"No, no. One is enough. I will make you an apprentice for their purposes. An apprentice—trader. Basically a hired hand, a helper. With my type of business and my wanderings it will draw no attention." He paused a moment. "Come. We have some light left. Would you like to see what this place really looks like?"

Charley looked a bit anxiously at Sam and saw that Sam was suddenly tense as well, but then the object of all this said, "Sure. Why not? You sure we won't be spotted?"

"It will make no difference, as no one likely to see us is likely to have anything to do with us. Come—follow me."

"It'll have to be damned slow in this dress," Charley grumped, but went along.

Sam was genuinely curious after all this time cooped up in a cave but she was also wary. Zenchur had more than enough time to betray them and perhaps have people lying in wait for them outside. She decided to go along partly because it really didn't matter—better to know now than be kidnapped sneaking out later and let the bastard completely off the hook. If this Boolean was half as powerful and half as devious as they'd pictured his kind to be then *something* would happen in their favor. If not, then there really wasn't much hope anyway.

It was hot and very humid just beyond the cave entrance; they were sweating in no time.

The eerie mist was still there; maybe it was *always* there, for some reason or other. It stretched out for miles from the rocky outcrop, featureless, with nothing seeming to grow up from it or in any way disturb it, but it was not endless. Off in the distance rose low hills of green and what looked like pleasant pasture land. For all Charley could tell, it might well be right out of Lincoln County in northern New Mexico, with perhaps the high mountains just beyond the horizon. It appeared overcast almost everywhere.

"The mist is a natural phenomenon," Zenchur told them, sounding not at all tense or threatening. Maybe he was having second thoughts about double-crossing a sorcerer. "It surrounds the hubs and in a sense insulates them from the wedges. That green region you see beyond is a wedge. It looks like Habanadur, although it's been awhile since I was there. The people are herders, primarily—impossible to describe unless you have seen one, I am afraid, but not particularly pleasant to our eyes. They herd large, hairy herbivores called *blauns*, and exist entirely by drinking the blauns' blood and milk."

Charley shivered, and saw that Sam wasn't reacting too well to that one, either.

"They are a rather fierce race when provoked, and quite tough," the mercenary went on, apparently not taking notice. "The Akhbreed kings treat them with some respect and they act as soldiers and enforcers for much of the region. They consider it pragmatic; they still hate the Akhbreed but fear the magic too much. Of course, most of the other races identify them as tools of the king and hate them as much or more than they hate the Akhbreed. You can see why unifying such people seems impossible."

They made it up a trail—Charley needing some helping hands—to the top of the bluff and looked inland. This land was quite rocky, with thick forests and probably rushing streams. It looked lush but wild, yet, looking in toward the mountains and forests, it seemed like the overcast thinned and there were hints of sun.

"Is it always this cloudy?" Sam asked him, remembering his comment about frequent storms and bad weather.

"No, not always, although it is cloudy more than clear most places outside of the hubs, except in desert regions and places like that. This is part of the after-effect of the changewind. You saw it. It will influence the weather for vast regions."

Sam nodded, then turned to look back out over the mist. "Hey—wait a minute!"

The other two turned and looked out as well. The green, rolling hills in the distance were gone; now there was an enormous wall of snow-capped peaks reaching into the clouds and beyond, reflecting back a hazy purple cast to them.

"What happened to the hills?" Charley asked. "There were no mountains there a minute ago!" She turned and looked back at the forest as if to reassure herself that she was still somehow at the same location, then back. The forest was still there, and so were the mountains.

Zenchur chuckled. "That is Maksut, or so the Akhbreed call it. Those people produce among the finest furs of Akahlar. I know it well."

"Yeah, but where the hell did the *hills* go?" Sam wanted to know.

"They're still there. Both of the lands you saw are not mere slices of things but entire worlds of which only a small portion overlaps here at any time. If you wait—perhaps a few minutes, perhaps hours, or even days, it will be a portion of another land that you see. That is the ever-changing nature of Akahlar. They appear, and disappear, around the hubs—sometimes here, sometimes elsewhere, sometimes not at all. My trade is navigator. I know the ways to tell where I am physically in Akahlar at any given time—with some work, of course. I can plot a course between two definite points on the globe, short or long, and get you there. I do not, however, know what will occupy that point at any given time, or the points in between. Maksut, or Habanadur, or a hundred others. Only the Akhbreed with their Pilots can choose their path and their destination exactly, and the Pilots do not tell how they do it. I can get to the exact same spot—but I may be worlds away. That is why one cannot travel long out there without Pilots. They are Akhbreed who work with the locals, each Pilot guild assigned to a particular wedge. When I fled my homeland I was without a Pilot and without navigational skills and only sheer luck and the hand of the gods kept me from death."

That's why he's taken us out here, Sam thought to herself. *He suspects we might not fully trust him and he wants to show us just how impossible it would be to even survive on our own. And he's making a good case for it, damn his soul!*

"In the morning we shall go inland—that way," he told them, pointing to the forest behind them. "The hub is large, but it is not as primitive as it looks. There is a major road just beyond that hill, and in a hub all roads tend to lead either to the capital city or to the border. Come—we will be hot and wet enough tomorrow. Let us enjoy the coolness of the cave while we still can."

They went back down and inside, and Charley in particular felt frustrated that she and Sam couldn't immediately get together. That time would come much later.

It was quite late when that opportunity came with some certainty, and all of them were supposed to be asleep. Charley and Sam felt tired, too, but there was much to think over and, perhaps, to do.

"Okay, is he crooked or square with us?" Charley asked.

"Crooked," Sam responded flatly. "That little show today was to show us just how at his mercy we are. To tell you the truth, I'm not real sure just what to do now, damn him! If we take off in the woods in the middle of the night we'll probably break our fool necks, and if we go in towards the city we'll be pretty easy to track—and he'll have horses and lots of practice trackin', I bet. If we go out there we'll be in that creepy mist for miles and then wind up God knows where."

"You think those vampires he talked about are real?"

Sam shrugged. "Maybe not where he said, but all you got to do is look at Ladai to know they're probably around someplace, and maybe worse. One thing's sure—we go out there without somebody who knows what he's doin' and we ain't got much chance."

"Yeah, but if we stick with him he'll stab us in the back first chance he gets. You said it yourself. The only reason we're not already dead or worse is 'cause he's gotta make it look like it's an accident to keep Boolean from turning him into live sausage or something. I tell you, I don't see why he just don't hypnotize us with that jewel of his like he did last night and command us to betray ourselves. He flashes that thing and commands us to parade naked down the main street of that city saying 'Here we are—the ones the Horned One wants. *Please* take us to him!' And we'd hav'ta *do* it!"

"I dunno. He acts like he's scared of that thing himself. But if we got centaurs and magic jewels and storms that can change a boy into a monster then the jewel ain't the only possible thing he can use. There's all sorts of drugs—would *we* know a bad drug from one of Ladai's sweetrolls here?—and once he's in the city he'll have magic types he can probably pay off cheap. I figure he don't want to do it here 'cause there's just us and the two of them. Pretty easy to get a full treatment from Boolean, huh? Lots more chances to make a play in the big city, maybe even hope we get nailed by accident and he don't hav'ta lift a finger."

"The only thing we can do is figure our odds, then," Charley said thoughtfully. "If we run, there's no chance now and he's off the hook. if we stick with him, maybe we got a chance to at least duck. I mean, this country's this Akhbreed, right?"

"Yeah? So?"

"So they talk Akhbreed. Once we're off, no Ladai, there's only humans like us, right? He'll have to do all the talkin' for us to them in their language—and he still don't know *you* know it. At least we'll know what he's planning before he does it, right? That's a chance."

Sam nodded. "I never thought of that. Yeah. sure. Okay. So I guess we figure we're safe for now, huh? Might as well get some sleep. We got to be damned sharp tomorrow."

"Yeah. Sam—one other thing. You're gonna hav'ta clue me in on what's goin' on without him catching on that you know yourself. I wish you knew Spanish—he sure don't—but I been tryin' to think of some edge someplace that'll keep our talk as crazy to him as theirs is to me. It's pretty far out, but I don't think he learned English any more than you learned that other stuff. He thinks in this Akhbreed—that's why he spoke it when he got upset. I think he sorta *wills* it to be translated both ways, to and from Akhbreed."

"Yeah, so?"

"Well, I been thinking about how you said, like, it wasn't like any language you ever heard of. If that's what his brain's actually hearing, and not English, then there's no way in *hell* he'll ever handle pig latin."

Sam thought it over and gave a wry smile. "You know, it ightmay ustjay orkway," she muttered aloud.

The "wagon" was sure different. It resembled a Roman chariot, with two big side wheels and an oval-shaped center, but it had a third, smaller wheel in front of the carriage giving it some stability. Inside, the driver had to stand, although there was a kind of bar that allowed him to relax against it, then a bench seat more reminiscent of a rowboat, and some cargo area in back. It wasn't fancy or ornate; it was old, hadn't been painted in years, and had both dirt and splinters. But it held the two trunks and a sack resembling a duffel which was Zenchur's traveling things, and they climbed in and held on for dear life as the navigator climbed in, lowered and latched the wooden safety bar on the side, leaned against the back rest bar, and jerked the reins forward. Two horses, side by side, seemed to have little trouble in pulling it and them, but *man* was that ride *rough* on those wooden wheels! After a while both Charley and Sam's bottoms hurt so bad that they actually envied Zenchur's standing position.

The horses looked pretty much like horses. They seemed a little large, more like the kind of horses that pulled the beer wagon in all those ads, and they looked a lot hairier than the horses they were used to—you could have styled the hair between their ears, in fact—but they were still basically the same sort of animal.

The same went for the countryside. The trees were tall but basically trees, although some had odd colors to their bark, and the grass seemed more blue than green, and every once in a while they'd pass a patch of strange flowers like the bunch of pink ones that looked like roses but grew on separate stalks maybe six feet high and thicker than most people's legs with flowers the size of Zenchur's head, but it was no Alice in Wonderful world—just exotic, sort of like being in another country like Brazil or one of the African ones.

There were birds, many quite colorful, and one fairly large one that might have been some kind of falcon but who seemed to change color and become almost invisible in the trees until spooked by the passing of the wagons. Then you suddenly had what looked like giant leaves taking flight and eventually becoming nearly invisible again as they changed to the gray of clouds or the blue of open sky.

It was good to see the sun again, first in breaks in the clouds and then as time went on more regularly, although the sky was never completely clear. Still, it was damned hot and getting hotter the more sun they got. This was a climate for loin cloths or bikinis, not full dress. The Arabs got away with theirs because their land was so dry their clothes kept in the moisture and that made sense. It was far too humid for that here. The Akhbreed were not only arrogant, they were hung-up assholes, Charley decided.

The road Zenchur had told them about was there, wide and well maintained, but it didn't really help the comfort much. Packed dirt roads truly added to the sensation of being on a rolling ship at sea and made the bumps ever harder. Still, the horses needed to rest once in a while and they had to eat and drink, and about a three hours' ride in from the cave they came to a small village that looked with its red slate roofs and white stucco and brick façade like it had been plucked out of some European movie. The thing seemed to be built around a broad, central square with a marketplace all around it. It was not crowded, however; clearly this was a sleepy weekday afternoon and not a main market day.

Zenchur made some preliminary warnings to them. "Remember—say as little as possible, only to each other, and whisper. I doubt if there would be anyone here who would even know about you but be on your guard anyway."

It looked different than the one in Sam's vision, but not any more different than she would have expected going between, say, France and maybe Germany. While there weren't many people about, those they could see seemed to mostly be women, all wearing long, loose, baggy dresses tied off at the waist, the dresses going down to their ankles and looking to be made of cotton or some similar material. All had matching scarves on their heads. The colors were mainly muted reds, browns, or blues, but here and there a woman wore white. What set the white-clad ones apart was that they alone wore not the scarves but rather light white headpieces which covered their entire head and formed almost a hood, and they looked for all the world to be wearing white masks over their faces with only the eyes cut out. They also did not use a tie at the waist, making the dresses so shapeless and sack-like it was impossible to tell anything about them.

"The ones in white are unmarried—virgins of age, or in some

cases past it," Zenchur told them. "They are forbidden to show any more of themselves in public or to anyone outside their immediate household than you see after they undergo a rite of passage on their tenth birthday. They are also forbidden to speak to or even show they hear the speech of any man save their father and brothers. They live like that until they are married and then, as you see, things loosen up a lot."

"I can't see how any of 'em would ever *get* married, considerin' them rules," Sam responded.

Zenchur laughed. "All marriages are arranged—by the mothers, by the way, talking to the groom's father or, if orphaned, the male guardian. Oh, there are stories of romantic trysts and separated lovers, of course, but almost nobody does it. Actually, the girl has some power the man does not, since she can see *him* without his ever really knowing it's her and can make a real case for certain boys and against others with her mother. All the boy gets is a sketch by an artisan known as a Wedding Broker, although in villages such as these he can usually get some information from relatives and friends of relatives."

"The same old story. Women as cattle again, though," Charley noted sourly.

"No, no! The women have rights here. They are given what education they need or can handle, although separately from the boys of course, and they can inherit and have definite rights in courts of law. It is not as bad as it sounds. Most of these shops are run by women and some are even owned by women. This is because, in these conservative societies, the man is the boss but inheritance is through the female line, not the male. I am not saying it is perfect, only that it is not as bad as it looks."

"Still, neither one knows what they're gettin' until they're stuck with it," Sam noted.

"And is it any worse than other ways? Marrying for lust of the moment and then one day you discover you have nothing else in common, or marrying one for supposed wealth or position? I am not defending this system, I am only saying that I have not found the number of successful and happy marriages here any different than other societies' ways."

"Still, with the slim pickings in a village like this and kept apart, I can see why some of 'em would run for the city and sell their bodies rather than take it, particularly if the guy's awful and she can't talk her mom out of it," Charley commented.

Sam looked around. "Somehow, with all them worlds to steal

from, I kinda thought this'd be a little more modern than the Dark Ages."

There was a service which unhitched and cared for the horses while you were in town, and they were more than grateful to be out of that box and on their feet again, although both were so sore they had some initial trouble walking. Sam was together enough in a minute or two, though, to note the various signs around the square that all seemed to be filled with little squares and circles and squiggles and realize that her knowledge of the language did not extend to literacy. The letters or symbols or whatever they were seemed to not even have a lot of organizational sense; they were scattered all over and didn't look very consistent at all in their shapes and forms. It reminded her of something that might come out of a kindergarten art class back home.

The one they went into turned out to be a tavern, and a somewhat peculiar one at that. It had the look on the inside you expected going in—round wooden tables, rough, well-worn wooden chairs, sawdust over the wooden, creaky floor, and a long bar with a big polished mirror behind it that just about reflected the whole place. But there were anachronisms as well, things that just didn't make sense.

For example, there were the three Casablanca-style ceiling fans turning slowly above them, keeping the hot air circulating. And the lights, both behind the bar and, subdued, along the side walls, looked, well—not at all primitive. The bottles behind the bar seemed to be of clear glass with fancy labels on them, not the crude stuff of the cave, and when someone yelled to the barman he nodded and drew a tankard of what might have been beer or ale from a *tap* and brought it over. The customers—the only ones other than themselves—were also obviously from somewhere else. One fellow had a loud and ugly voice and a face and body that looked more like a Neanderthal than a modern human, accentuated by the fact that he was wearing a worn fur breech clout and a somewhat matching fur vest over his incredibly hairy chest. His companion was dressed in a fancy bloused top and tights, with fancy pointed boots, and had features far different from those seen in the village—lighter, sharper, with long hair, a black goatee. and a moustache that must have been half wax.

"Don't look now," Charley whispered to Sam, "but I'd swear Conan the Barbarian over there is wearing a wristwatch."

"I noticed," Sam whispered back. "And I think that fugitive from a playing card is smoking a filter-tipped cigarette. This is nuts."

Zenchur gave them a sour look and they shut up. Sam was curious to know what the strange pair was discussing, but the cave man had such lousy command of the language it was hard to make him out most of the time. In a language where a shift of a mere quarter tone could make "I am going to kill you" sound like "I want to make love to a fig tree" she was definitely at a disadvantage only slightly less than Charley's.

"But, my friend, I need five," said the fop, clearly but in a very strange accent. You knew what he was saying but only barely and with some concentration. The people in the changewind vision had also seemed to have odd accents to her, but not this extreme.

"You ask my ass be cake-baked," the Neanderthal seemed to reply. The conversation, thanks to his horrible lack of subtleties, seemed almost comic to Sam, although Moustache seemed to make the right sense out of it.

"But, be reasonable, my friend. Fewer will simply not work."

"I want to lick my pig-sucker," replied the barbarian.

"But there's the watch, the grappler, the—"

"Our names be pudding Daisy loops!"

Sam had to stop listening. The thing made no sense, but if she kept on with it then Zenchur would surely know that she could understand—more or less—if only because she would no longer be able to keep from cracking up.

The barman came over to them. "Yes, sir. How may we serve you?"

"You have food, I take it? You did the last times I was through."

"We do, sir, but there is no kitchen between lunch and dinner and this is off-hours. I could bring a bread, meat, and cheese tray and some fruits or vegetables, though."

"That will do fine. Make it large enough for my companions and bring three cold drafts,"

"At once, sir." The barman turned and went back to the bar, drew three very large beers, and brought them over, then went back through a doorway to the right of the bar to get the food. Charley noted that both Zenchur and Sam had the beer set in front of them while the third was simply placed to one side, as if a refill rather than for her.

"Oh, all the respectable types of both sexes will absolutely ignore your existence," he whispered to her. "To them you are to be treated as if you do not exist. But, do not worry—if that old man wanted a fling he'd pull me aside discretely and try and make a deal for an assignation." He paused a moment. "But—please, no more talk for now. I do not like the look of those two."

Charley had never heard of an assignation, but she got the meaning. The usual high moral hypocrites. She did have to wonder what kind of dictionary they'd used to teach him English, though.

The platter that the barman brought out looked like it'd been arranged by a caterer; it had mounds of sliced meats, as well as what appeared to be lettuce, tomatoes, cucumbers—you name it—along with a *very* long loaf of French-type bread and a bread knife. Small canisters with spreaders contained something that looked a lot like mayonnaise, a type of mustard, soft white butter, and two others, one of which seemed a lot like very thin peanut butter. Cutting off a piece of the bread and slicing it, then filling it, was no trouble at all; watching Zenchur eat what looked for all the world like a peanut butter, radish, and roast beef sandwich was harder to take.

Again, as with the plants and birds, the tastes and textures of the sandwich material were slightly off what they would have suspected—the tomatoes, for example, tasted very tomatoey but also had a kick like mild peppers—but nothing was all that exotic and it was pretty good.

Zenchur was a pretty big drinker; he finished off two large steins and was working on his third before he completed his first sandwich. Sam, too, had a big thirst although she was unused to beer or other alcoholic beverages and Charley worried about that. Charley also worried about her own reactions; alcohol always brought out the worst in her, and she just sipped it and tried to eat what she could of her own sandwich concoction. She found to her surprise that her eyes were far bigger than her stomach; what she would have normally packed away with no trouble back home was far too much for her now and she felt stuffed.

Sam had no such limits. Clearly in spite of Boolean's look-alike magic, they were very different beyond outward appearances, something that made Charley actually feel a bit better. Still, it was amazing to see Sam pack away almost as much as the big, muscular Zenchur.

"You are beans! I *will* seduce the governor!" proclaimed the barbarian at the far table in a loud voice, pounding his fist on the table. They all looked at him, a man clearly with too much to drink in the middle of the afternoon, and the fancy dressed man looked nervous.

"This is not the place for more talk," he said. "You are drunk. Can you ride some more?"

"I can sail a fish to the moon!" responded the barbarian confidently. Sam dearly would have liked to have seen *that,* but she was relieved that the pair got up, threw some coins on the table, and made their way out of the tavern. She was having great problems stifling the giggles and stuffed some more sandwich in her mouth to cover it.

"How far are we from this city?" Charley asked Zenchur.

"Not far," the navigator responded. "A few hours. We should be in by nightfall."

Charley groaned. "More hours on that hard seat! Well," she sighed, "I don't think my rear end can get any more bruises. It's tough sitting here now on this chair."

"I think I want a bathroom," Sam said. "They got one or is it out the back?"

"Oh, there's one off the kitchen. Through there. Come—I should go, too."

Charley didn't really have to go but she had this sudden fear of sitting there alone while her two links to this world were both out of sight. "If they have separate rooms I guess I should, too."

"They do. Even in the home there are two bathrooms."

The men's room was surprisingly clean, with two bowl-shaped toilets in two door-less stalls. They looked a lot like pinched oval toilets without seats, and on either wall of the stall were grip handles. Apparently you didn't sit down—you just squatted and held on to the handles. Zenchur was appalled by the idea of a toilet seat. "It would be so—unclean," he said, shaking his head.

Still, he didn't have the problem. He just stood there and pissed into it, while she had to take down her pants, remove the codpiece, and hold on for dear life. You sure as hell wouldn't spend any time reading in *these* johns. She envied him the convenience but couldn't help but stare a bit. My god, it was so–*large!* How did they *walk* with those things between their legs?

Zenchur would have been far more startled had he known that this was the first time Sam had ever seen a male organ except in a picture.

If Sam was having trouble, Charley had to practically undress to be able to go. The toilet was the same sort of hold-on affair but shaped very differently. Still, this was gonna take some getting used to.

Even so, here was another thing that seemed oddly different. Flush toilets—inside plumbing. A small, basic sink with running cold water. And while the toilet paper looked more like Kleenex and came out that way, and was *rough,* it was none the less a manufactured product. Clearly, for all its looks, this was not any Dark Ages civilization.

There was a full-length mirror that was a big aid in rewrapping the dress, but which also gave her a real look at herself. She looked *thin,* thinner than Sam ever looked, and the skin was really smooth. It was a hell of a body, better than she remembered Sam's as being. Even the boyish face looked not at all boyish now but, well, *sexy.* It was more than just the look, though; it was the way you moved and carried yourself and even the way you used your face. She would have preferred a better face than Sam's, but it was, overall, the kind of body she would have *killed* for.

Maybe it was the beer again, but, God! Was she *horny!*

She got ready, then left the bathroom and rejoined the pair already back at the table. She was relieved to see them both; she had this paranoid fear that they would somehow disappear and leave her alone in this world.

As they made their way back to the stable she saw two of the white-robed girls walking hand in hand across the street, their white masks impassive, their features—frankly, even their sex or humanity—impossible to tell. She didn't think she ever could've stood that, although you never know what you'll accept if you grow up thinking that's normal. The sad thing was that little girls probably dreamed of the time when they'd wear the white robes and masks. It was being grown up.

Still, she had to wonder how easy to get those outfits were. They all looked manufactured, that was for sure, but fitted, probably. They'd make one hell of a disguise in a pinch, though—and in this kind of society who would dare pull off the mask and hood and risk being wrong? She bet that such an act would be tantamount to rape for these people.

Before leaving they went into an odd little store and Zenchur purchased a small device that looked something like a spout from the top of a gas can with a long, narrow and bendable base. It wasn't until they were back on the road, however, that he explained it.

"Learn how to use it," he told Sam. "If you learn the proper positioning and get it just right you will not have to sit to pee. It is very handy out in the wilderness where there are few or no bathrooms."

"Yeah—what about those bathrooms?" Sam asked. "Modern plumbing, and I swear those lights and fans were electric!"

"They were. The town is rather modern, as are most. There is a small generating plant at a waterfall not far from here."

"But there were no wires anyplace!"

"So? Your world is so primitive it runs its wires openly? And do your plumbing pipes run atop your streets? How ugly that would be!"

It was time to change the subject. "Those two men back there—who were they? They sure didn't look like nobody 'round *that* town," Sam pointed out.

"I do not know who they were but, you are correct, they are not from anywhere around here. The big hairy one might barely be considered Akhbreed at all, I think. Certainly from some primitive wedge far away from here to the north. The other—I am not sure. He was wealthy but no noble and his speech marked him as coming from elsewhere. Such men hire men like the barbarian to do dirty work they do not wish done themselves. Such men are the sort who usually hire me, in fact."

The countryside grew less wild; the farms seemed smaller and more specialized, the towns a bit larger although still in that European provincial style, and traffic built up, not just on foot or horseback but wagons and carriages of every shape and kind. They made good time, reaching the city before sundown, and it *was* a city—one hell of a city. Sam had expected something on the order of the primitive farming village and castle she'd seen in her vision, but this was something else.

Densely populated and stretching out along the shores of a lake or sea, its central core rose up in great buildings like shining cathedral spires, and out from it spread the rest of the city, smaller buildings to be sure, certainly much lower, but it was sure a big city all the same.

"Tubikosa contains about a half a million people, all Akhbreed," Zenchur told them. "It is one of the largest cities on the planet, and one of the grandest, although it is also one of the most dangerous. If a changewind ever got this far in, there would be no place to really run and hide from it."

Charley frowned. "What's the chances of something like that happening?"

The navigator shrugged. "Who knows? Perhaps tonight, perhaps in a week, perhaps in a hundred years. There has been none through here in more than a century and a half, that is known, and the people are complacent. They choose to ignore the risk, perhaps even the inevitable, just to live and work here."

Charley couldn't get a handle on all this. A civilization great enough to build maybe forty-story buildings, crazy as they looked, with electricity, indoor plumbing, and all the comforts of home, yet one that still used the horse and wagon as a primary means of getting around, with no buses, cars, trains, or anything else, and maybe no TV or even radio, and where swords, spears, and armor were still the rule, and who had a city of half a million people with mostly dirt streets where the women dressed in robes and saris and scarves on their heads and the men dressed like Shakespeare or Robin Hood. It didn't make much sense at all.

It *did* have mass transportation, though, of an old-fashioned sort. Horses pulled big double-decker stagecoaches that looked like buses and acted like them, too, and all over the place fancy-looking three-wheeled enclosed black carriages went about, picking up people and letting them off, and were clearly cabs.

Zenchur took them eventually to an area just off the waterfront and well away from those gleaming spires. It was clearly a low district, with narrow streets and grimy buildings. As darkness overtook the city the lights came on, including many for signs that looked just like home even if you couldn't read them, and the main streets were lit not by lamp posts but by long strips of indirect lighting running along the top of the first floor of buildings on both sides. The secondary streets and back alleys weren't lit at all and looked for that all the more menacing. They went through a district whose nature seemed no different than any back on their own Earth and very easy to spot. In the midst of joints and painted pictures of semi-naked women and muscle men were basically store fronts, lit from within, most having several young and heavily made up women in them, lounging and looking back out at the street, and here and there one with some well-built and well-oiled muscle men wearing only tights doing much the same thing. No white robes and masks around *here.*

Just off this district, Zenchur pulled up to a creaky old place of brick and stone that might have been whitewashed regularly once upon a time, and stopped. It was five stories high and looked and smelled older inside than outside. The reception area was quite small, hardly a lobby and more just a registration desk behind which was a tough-looking middle-aged woman wearing a colorful if threadbare green flower print sack dress and scarf.

"Hello, handsome," she said upon seeing Zenchur. "Been a while since you was through here."

"I just need a room on the street for maybe two nights," the navigator responded. "One that sleeps three. And we have some baggage that's heavy."

She nodded. "Fourth floor, second on the left. Here's the key." She looked at Charley and smiled sweetly. "You know the house gets ten percent if you run anything for profit in the room."

"Nothing like that. Long story not worth the telling, but if you must know she ran away from one of the wedge villages far to the northwest and quickly regretted it, her young and impulsive brother went to find her—and did—and now I am helping them work things out if I can."

"Old story," the woman commented. "She's got all the nice moves and looks like a real nice body. The boy got much potential for anything useful?"

"He's bright but unskilled and neither of them knows the language."

"Well, if you want a quick turnover, you take 'em over to Boday. A little of Boday's universal love potion and some lessons and she'll be broke in perfect. The boy—without the language best he can do is get much the same treatment. There's a small bunch that likes 'em real young."

"I'm not quite sure what I'm going to do yet with them," Zenchur told her, possibly truthfully. "At any rate I'm going to need to find a good Pilot heading southwest." He took out two large, golden square coins and passed them to her. "This should cover it."

She nodded, picked up, then bit the coins, then stuck them in a slot in the desk, then turned to the back where there was a curtained-off doorway. "Zum!" she shouted. "Haul ass!"

The curtains parted and a huge man entered. He was close to seven feet and had to stoop to get through the doorway, but he was also enormously broad, the kind of man whose muscles had muscles. He was getting on, though; his hair was gray, his face was lined and wrinkled, the skin on his hands was tight, but most unsettling was the expression in his eyes and on his face, that of a rather childlike confusion.

The woman said something to him in an unintelligible tongue, and he grunted and gave an equally unintelligible reply and went immediately past them and out the doors.

Zenchur looked at Sam and Charley and cocked his finger, and after a moment they followed. He led them down a hall, then up four flights of creaky, narrow stairway. The key was one of those massive types, and he fitted it in a lock and opened the door to the room.

It was not exactly the Regency Plaza. A bare, round bulb burned when a button was pressed on an old wall plate illuminating a smelly room with two large windows covered by tattered drapes. There was a sink with a single long, curved pipe for a faucet, a worn bowl, and two porcelain cups both of which were chipped. There were also two beds the size of double beds, more or less, next to each other opposite the sink. Both had twin sets of small, round pillows, a bedspread that looked clean, and, under it, some dark sheets. Charley hoped that they hadn't been dyed to match the stains.

"The toilets are down the hall," Zenchur told them, "and I do mean just that. If you want a bath it's at a commercial bath house down here, and it's public, so I think Sam will have to wait and I wouldn't like to send Charley in alone. Don't worry—as you probably already know, bathing is not something done often here, even by the nobility."

Charley sat on the bed. It sank down unevenly, was lumpy, and creaked something awful. It definitely was both too old and not built like beds back home. She wasn't sure she wanted to find out how it was, or was not, put together, though.

There was a knock, and Zenchur opened it and found the huge man there carrying one of the heavy trunks in each hand and the duffel on his back. The navigator pointed and the man put them down, then took each one in one at a time and set them near the windows. Zenchur nodded, the man looked pleased, and left.

"*What* is *that?*" Charley had to ask.

"Oh, that is Zum. At least he answers to that name. He has been here longer than anyone now at this hotel. He's from some Outland wedge, and he never was very bright and knows none of the language. You might have noticed that the woman downstairs used a different tongue for him if you have a good enough ear. Because of the language problems with such as him there is a straight and simple language—short, nonsense, perhaps a few hundred real words—that is used by folks to communicate with such as him. He was probably taken here or wound up here as a boy, fell into selling his body—you saw the men in the windows—and then grew too old or perhaps impotent or both. Now he serves out his days doing the basics for this old hotel, just like the woman downstairs, Argua, who was once young and beautiful and had a thousand lovers before she grew old and fat. Zum will see to the horses and wagon, too."

"Speaking of fat, when do we eat? Or do we?" Sam asked.

"Yes, we do, and we might as well. As you might guess the service here is not that great, but there is a not very fancy tavern a few minutes' walk from here that serves some decent food and asks no questions. Come, if you are not too tired—but remain mute, particularly around here, when out of this room. No slips. Here the word will be getting around about you."

Sam glanced at Charley, knowing that her friend must be as dead as she was, but Charley said, "We'll go. I don't think I want to be alone in this place."

"Oh—you may change if you wish now, Charley," Zenchur told her. "In this neighborhood at this time of day a slit skirt, top, and scarf are appropriate, and it might make you more comfortable. Here—I will show you in the trunk."

Charley was of two minds about this. She didn't like the idea of his suggesting such a radical change—they would still be completely at his mercy and who knew what he might do with her?—but the outfit she'd been wearing was now so tight and uncomfortable she was dying to get out of it. She finally accepted his suggestion, choosing a long pattern skirt slit right up to the thigh and a pullover that matched, sort of, but was so clingy it left nothing to the imagination. Still, she had a freedom of movement in her legs that was more than welcome, and the stuff was dry and clean even if she was not.

"One more thing," Zenchur said warningly to Charley. "For your own safety, be solicitous of us. Open the doors ahead of us, pull our chairs out at the tavern before sitting, and when food and drink comes it will be on a serving tray and you will be expected to serve always with a smile and no comments."

"Huh?"

"It isn't just sex people want down here. It would be best if it appeared that we were your clients and not merely your companions. That way it seems as if you are already working for someone and, therefore, no one else will make any moves on you. Understand?"

"Yeah," she sighed and looked at Sam. "You got all the luck."

6
Backup System

"Wait here just a couple of minutes. I will be right back," said Zenchur.

Sam's eyebrows rose. "Where you goin'?" she asked suspiciously.

"It has been a long day. Do you need such constant protection that I cannot go to the toilet?"

Sam shrugged, and Zenchur left.

"Think he's pulling anything?" Charley whispered.

"Maybe. He put us in this sleaze bucket in the worst part of town. I heard that woman down there suggest that he send you over to some bastard called Boday to get 'broken in.' They give ya some kind'a potion and you just sort'a love everybody and then they teach you all the right moves and that's it, sounds like."

Charley didn't like that. "Potions are just strong drugs in liquid form. He could slip either or both of us one any time and we wouldn't know. I don't like this, Sam. The way he was talkin' I really don't think he's made up his mind yet, but he's gettin' ideas. What a place! All them respectable folks wearin' fancy clothes and the women all wearin' them robes and virgins them white bags and masks and here we got a district where *anything* goes and no cops show. It's like they took everything bad in them and put it all in these few blocks and said, 'Okay, here's the place of sin. Stay here and we don't bother you.' "

"We got to figure something before he does," Sam said firmly, "and soon, 'cause it's pretty damned clear he's thinkin' real good. Damn it, I don't care *what* his reputation is, he's a flake and a whacko. I can't say I think too much of these wizards if they trust people like him."

She paused a moment and continued, "I dunno. It's kind'a funny, really. I think he was all set to do it, no real problems, and then, well, somethin' happened. He suddenly figured out what all this was about even though he wasn't supposed to. Figured it and changed. I wish we could get him to tell us what it was."

Charley frowned. "You know, he's taking an awful long time in the john, for a man. Damn! I don't like this! We *got* to eat and I got no place to run around here, but it's like in a slasher movie where you're huddled in the closet hoping against hope the slasher won't find you while all the time knowing he will. I wish we could grab that hypnotic jewel he's got. Then *he'd* dance *our* tune! Or at least something we could use as a weapon—just in case."

"I know what you mean. But I don't think he's gonna pull nothin' tonight. He's thinkin', and he's got a problem with us, too, remember. He wants to force *us* into a goof so he won't get the blame."

"You know, I kind of wonder why he just doesn't use that jewel of his on us," Charley mused. "I mean, we'd go out obediently stark naked in these streets and scream, 'Here we are! We're the ones the horned guy's looking for!' until somebody nabbed us. Or just keep mumbling the bad guy's name over and over until he came for us. I wonder why he hasn't'? Or has he and we just don't remember or notice. Now *there's* a mean thought."

"I don't think he did. He might if he has to, but for some reason he doesn't want to use that thing on us. Huh! Maybe it's from Boolean! Yeah, that'd explain it. Maybe he's scared that Boolean would know if he used it against us or something. It's a thought."

"Yeah, well I—oops! Here he comes—I hope."

It *was* Zenchur. "Sorry to have taken so long," he told them, "but it was occupied and I had a fair wait. Now, Charley—you remember. Open the doors for us, serve us, speak only when spoken to. Best docile behavior. You might get some propositions, but nobody will think beyond that."

"Seems to me I'm being told to be a sweet little old slave and I don't like it."

"Consider—what you do is not important. But if you do *not* do it, then many will wonder why and start to ask questions. They will start to compare your features to those out on the wanted contract, and they all know that I have done work for the Akhbreed sorcerers before. They may not be positive, but if the reward is large enough then they will ask questions later."

It was a good point. She opened the door for them and they walked out, her following. She definitely didn't like this stinking world, though, not one bit.

The big city was a bit eerie at night. Oh, the "adult entertainment district" was just what you'd expect, all lit up and very active, but beyond, only a few lights in some of the taller buildings gave a hint that any big city was even there. The contrast was odd but also somehow reassuring; the mere existence of a thriving "adult" district indicated that this place was not as lockjaw fundamentalist conservative as it had seemed to be.

The customers on this three-block walk were equally interesting. The men, mostly dressed in those fancy Robin Hood outfits, you expected, but in just the couple of blocks they saw at least two of the three-wheeled, horse-drawn cabs pull up and, inside, heavily robed women waited alone until the cabbie went to the door, knocked, and someone came out to open the cab door for the woman and usher her inside. Clearly for all the outward appearances to the contrary, women had a fair amount of freedom here and, in a society of anonymous, arranged marriages they took advantage of the services of some of those muscular and well-endowed males to get what their own husbands weren't giving them. Charley found the sight oddly satisfying. The men had been doing it for years; it was about time the women could, too, without falling into disastrous affairs with the postman or some neighbor.

This district, then, was the safety valve for a society that was simply too closed in and structured every place else. In this small area the rules were off; in this small area sin and pleasure were the norm, and frustrations and social claustrophobia could be relieved as needed. It wasn't a nice place; it was merely necessary.

Somehow it seemed to make the role she was told to play less degrading; just another service industry, like butlers, maids, housekeepers, and gardeners. It was a new way to look at this sort of thing, but it was clearly flawed. If such "services" were voluntary, it was one thing—an essential job, perhaps. But one only had to look at the dazed faces in the windows and the eyes of the street procurers to know that many of those who performed the services did so because they were trapped or drugged beyond caring. The trouble with a sin district was that it was inevitably run by people who considered sin simply a commodity and the people just objects, like hammers and nails were to a carpenter. Disposable, replaceable, and they had to be cost effective.

Charley opened the door to the tavern and let the other two enter, then followed. It was fairly late and apparently midweek and so not all that crowded; they found a table with little trouble, and Charley acted like a waitress, pulling the chairs out and getting everything just so before taking her own seat.

The place reeked of food, mostly steaks of some kind on a specially designed long charcoal-style grill in the back. The few waiters and the cooks and barkeeper in the back were all men, but there were a few women in the place, all with groups of men, all acting pretty much like Charley was acting—although these women had a different look to them. For one thing, they had oddly painted faces and bodies, with remarkable designs in bright colors on them. One had eye makeup that surrounded the eye with a design that made great orange catlike shapes, almost a mask, and most wore very skimpy clothing that revealed intricate body designs as well. Sam, too, could hardly fail to notice them as they jumped up to light cigarettes or cigars or get something for their clientele, always with a smile, always their minds totally on anticipating needs.

Sam leaned over to Zenchur and whispered, "What are they?"

"The top of the class," he responded in a very low tone. "They are neither common whores nor servants but experts. Only the smartest and the prettiest get that position. For a very high fee, for an evening, they will try and fulfill any reasonable wish. *Shhhh! Waiter!*"

A man wearing an apron that was probably white when he'd started work came over. "What do you wish?" he asked in Akhbreed.

"Full steak for the two of us, medium, and give the lady the lady's plate and house wine. We'll take drafts."

The waiter nodded and went back to the cooking area, told the order to the man there, then brought a tray with a huge pitcher of thick, dark beer, two stoneware mugs that must have held a quart each, and a carafe and tall-stemmed glass. He placed it on the table but did not serve it, instead going back to the counter.

Charley had been watching the other women. She got up, poured the beer into the two mugs with some expertise, showing that she'd poured beer somewhere before. The pitcher was well balanced, which was a good thing because it was close to being too heavy for her. She served each from the left, then went back, poured some of the dark red wine into the glass, took it, and resumed her seat, smiling with some satisfaction as Zenchur approved with a nod. Charley thought it was kind of fun; play-acting a fantasy, more or less, while knowing it wasn't real. Besides, those other women were so damned *glamorous* and perfect she instantly felt a sense of competition.

She was a bit nervous about the wine on a mostly empty stomach, but she sipped it and found it surprisingly sweet and very good. In the time it took for the food to come she had mostly finished it and was feeling a rosy glow that made it easy to just put everything out of her mind and pretend she was one of those sexy ladies over there.

The steaks came sizzling on the platter, which the waiter put in front of the other two so Charley didn't have to do much there, and he even put a plate in front of her—on oval-shaped dish which was mostly filled with fruits and salad combined with small cubes of cold meat and cheese. It was, in fact, just what she might have ordered rather than the heavy and greasy steaks, and she was both pleased and amazed at it.

Not that there weren't some mysteries there. What were the blue leaves, for example? She tried one and it didn't taste all that bad. Some of the fruit had odd colors and unfamiliar textures as well—light brown, for example, and almost snow white with little red grains—but nothing looked threatening or repulsive and she tried it, keeping an eye on the other two. You apparently ate it with a little spoon and with your hands. Twice she stopped and refilled their mugs, as well as her own glass, but the more she drank of the sweet wine the easier it was to be this courtesan, the more able she was to tune out all the fears and anxieties and the noise and smells of the surroundings and just *become* this character. She even started trying to imitate the sexy moves of the painted women at the other tables.

Sam was starving and ate heavily, once she'd picked up the system from Zenchur. It had been a little unsettling to discover that the silverware consisted of a very sharp pointed knife, a thin. serrated blade second knife, and a very small spoon, like a demitasse spoon, and nothing else. Clearly nobody had invented forks around here, and you cut the meat by holding it with the sharp knife, cutting with the serrated one, then spearing it with either. The little spoon was used for not just the drippings but also to scoop out the potato—it sort of looked and tasted like a potato although it was kind of purplish inside. Some slicked stalked vegetables were in a small container and proved raw, but tasted all right and gave it whatever balance it might have. Once she'd filled the emptiness inside, though, she also began to observe and to think.

Charley was doing a hell of a job, but she was nothing compared to those others. She wasn't dressed or made up like they were—that eye and body stuff was particularly erotic—and was clearly not in their class. She was good, but she wouldn't fool anybody that she was one of *them.* Then why go through this charade? Was Zenchur just playing games, or what? It seemed to her that Charley would've been less conspicuous wearing the sari and being a new girl in town.

Not that Charley, usually the more suspicious and the brains of the outfit, seemed to mind or question it. She was really getting into, and off on, this stuff.

A man who'd been sitting alone in a corner booth now got up and came over as they finished their meals. "Zenchur! How have you been? Long time," said the newcomer in Akhbreed.

"Well, Kligos. You received my message, then?"

Sam froze. Because Zenchur didn't know she knew the language he was speaking freely. When did the son of a bitch have a chance to send a message? So the toilet was occupied and a long wait, huh?"

"I need Pilots. One for the seven o'clock sector and one again for the five o'clock in the next cluster."

"Malabar, eh? Rough that way, you know. Changewind came through just yesterday and screwed up the hub and a few sectors something fierce. It'll be several more days before we have any accurate information on just what the damage is."

"It did not touch this cluster. I could be halfway there in several more days and closer to the source of the information. By the time I crossed clusters to Malabar the Pilots should have it well in hand. I need ones that keep their mouths shut and know the back ways."

"Woof! You're talking money for security there, my friend. At least a thousand just for services."

Zenchur nodded. "I know. I have full credit in Malabar and I have word that the Palace survived, so that won't be a real problem once I get there. I'm under budget for Tubikosa, though—my employer gave me an extra burden I hadn't counted on, and I had to make it over here fast and on short notice."

"I see. You want to relieve your unexpected burden and enrich your coffers more than enough to make it. Well, you contacted the right organization, old friend. I have been watching and I am impressed. I'll go your five hundred right here and now."

Zenchur chuckled. "I was thinking more about fifteen hundred. You and I know the profit potential from a rare good one. I would be guilty of allowing theft even at that price."

"You take advantage of an old friendship. Seven fifty tops. There is overhead, must preparation and break-in, and I still take a risk. It might not work out and then what do I have?"

"You know what you have, you old thief. This is difficult and risky for me as it is. A sorcerer is involved. Twelve fifty."

"Who you want to work for is your affair and your funeral. We all have our problems. I'm short-handed now because half the low-life in the kingdom is out looking for two Outplane girls dropped by storm here. You want money, go find them. The word on the street says fifty thousand, but only for both. Seems only one is wanted but they don't know which one. For that kind of money I am almost tempted to go look under every scarf myself—except that I know the odds of their showing up here are less than winning the royal lottery. Knowing you, though, if it wasn't for this bit of business I'd be very suspicious of you, too. All right—final offer. A thousand, flat, cash. Take it or leave it."

"Done." They clasped hands, apparently the local form of handshake. "You are aware of the subtleties of the problem?"

"I don't need diagrams. You just go along. Well—good seeing you and a pleasure doing business with you." The man waved, then walked out the door and away from the tavern.

"Who's that?" Sam whispered, not liking this a bit.

"An old friend, but one you cannot turn your back on. He was friendly enough but I do not like the way he was looking at you two. He brought up the price on your heads and it was enormous. Let us pay the bill and get back to the hotel before he starts looking a bit too closely at you and starts figuring out what sort of girl you might make with longer hair and fewer clothes, if you know what I mean."

Sam nodded, suspicious but still not quite sure what the hell was going on. Zenchur wasn't playing it straight—they had made a deal, and for good money if you could hire somebody skilled and closed-mouthed for five hundred. He hadn't mentioned either the bargaining or the deal, yet he'd pegged the fellow as a bad one and accurately reported the search and reward information and suggested just what Sam was feeling. She wished she knew more about this place.

Zenchur called over the waiter and paid the bill from the coin purse, and Charley then led them out, properly opening the doors and the rest, all with a big smile. She was certainly drunk but it was hard to tell more than that. They began walking back up the street to the hotel, and for a block or so Sam was keyed up. The next block was the darkest, without real street lighting, and she hadn't liked it much on the way down. She just had an uneasy feeling about all this, and with Charley high as a kite she felt very much alone and on her own.

At the end of the second block, three large men turned the corner together and started walking toward them. They were *huge,* but they were no male whores. These guys were dressed in the dark tunics and leggings of Tubikosa but they looked like they'd come straight from Al Capone.

Sam suddenly had an impulse to look over her shoulder and saw three more like these only a few steps in back of them. Where had they come from? One thing was for sure—Sam was scared to death. Zenchur stopped the two girls and grew tense. "Watch it. I don't like this."

"You're the damned protector. *Do* something," Sam said in a low, tense voice.

"With three on either side and two across the street? What do you want me to do—die gloriously? All I can do is try and talk our way through."

They had all stopped now, and the men seemed to be waiting for Zenchur to say something, so he did.

"Hello, my friends. Nice night. Do you wish us to let you pass?"

"Can the crap," said the middle one in front of them. "Just give us the girl and we're gone."

"*Arleychay . . . Aythey antway ouyay,*" Sam said out of the corner of her mouth. *Etgay eadyray ootay unray ikelay ellhay. . . .*"

Charley was already aware that this was no chance encounter and the color started draining from her cheeks. She was sobering up real fast.

"When I move, you run," Zenchur told them in English while keeping a smiling face at the trio. "Meet back at the hotel when you can . . . . *Now!*"

With that the navigator lowered his head and rushed straight at the three men. Sam grabbed Charley's arm and almost pulled her at a dead run diagonally across the street. The pair Zenchur had seen but she hadn't moved equally fast, and the trio in back were right behind them. It was no contest; strong arms, impossible to get out of, grabbed Sam and lifted her right up, one arm pinning her own arms while the other covered her mouth. A second man got to Charley and picked her up like she weighed nothing at all. She yelled and beat at him, struggling to break free, but the man holding her seemed more amused than troubled by it.

Sam managed to get her mouth open and chomped down hard on the hand holding her head. It sunk deep and the man yelled, "Ow! You little brat!" He dropped her, and she started to turn but something hit her head that felt like a ton of cement; there was a roaring in her ears and then blackness.

Sam came to slowly and with great agony. Her head was splitting and she felt dizzy and sick, but she remembered immediately what had happened and opened her eyes. She was back in the hotel room, on the bed, and she could see Zenchur at the sink, washing off what might have been some blood from his mouth.

She moaned. "Charley! Where's Charley?"

Zenchur turned and looked at her. "So you survived that blow. You are tougher than I thought. Your hard head may come in handy many more times before this is over."

"Where's Charley?"

"They got her. I took a couple of good punches but then the three of them pinned me against a wall. I could do nothing. I saw them hit you with the truncheon, but did not know if you were dead or alive. When they took her away, the three gave me a farewell set of punches and then fled themselves. When I could, I got to you and saw that you were still breathing. I thought it best to bring you here as quickly as possible. I hoped you were not seriously hurt. If I had called the medical alchemist it would have been impossible to hide the fact that you were female, and then a lot of people would get ideas about two similar girls, you see."

She managed to get to her feet and felt her head. There was a lump there. With Zenchur's aid she made it to the sink and looked at herself in the mirror. There was a large knot on her head near the back, and some dried blood. She had to admit she looked like she felt, but she couldn't afford to feel sorry for herself now. She dashed some water on her face, then took one of the towels, wet it, and carefully applied it to the lump. It hurt, but it also helped. She turned back to him, leaning against the sink. "Who were they? Why'd they take Charley?"

"Common thugs. I recognized two of them—the ones across the street trying to keep out of my sight. They work for Kligos, the man I spoke to at the tavern. The others I hadn't seen before, but the odds are very good they are Kligos muscle, too. He never travels far without bodyguards. I should have known it—him in the tavern alone. Kligos does not travel, he embarks with full entourage."

"But why Charley?"

"He—he is the largest supplier of full courtesans in the district. Those in the tavern tonight were all his, I think. They are not like common prostitutes, as I said. They require beauty and intelligence and are a special breed. The only thing I can guess is that Kligos decided Charley was one of the rare ones, and he knew his muscle men were outside, and he did not figure he had to pay me to take her. I once did him a disservice in the employ of one of his competitors, although he has also hired me. I guess he was getting even for that other time."

"Yeah, that's all well and good, but how do we get her back?"

They really had punched Zenchur out—that was clear—and she wasn't yet ready to give in to her suspicions. Not just yet.

"We do not get her back. She is gone, Sam. Vanished into Kligos's territory in the district."

"But—we *got* to get her back!"

"It would cost much, and we would probably still die. Do you think it would be that easy to go into his territory and just snatch her back? It might take days just to locate her, never mind actually rescuing her, and by that time she will not be worth rescuing."

Sam froze. "What do you mean by that?"

"You saw the others. First they will drug her and send her to an alchemist to be made to look that good. Then they will give her a potion that will drain her personality, so that she would no longer remember who or what she was and where she came from. Others would then make her mind malleable to remolding as she was trained to be the perfect courtesan. You see? Hopeless."

Sam was appalled. "We have to *do* something! I don't care about the risks—we can't let that happen to *Charley!*"

"Perhaps you cannot. I can."

"But you need both of us for Boolean! He won't be pleased at this!"

"He won't care, really. There was not supposed to be anyone but you. It is *you* they are all interested in, not Charley. She just came along for the ride. Even the two trunks—they were both for you, so we could disguise you as male or female, any way we saw fit or useful. She means nothing to me except someone else to worry about, someone else to drain our finances, which were, by the way, doled out on the basis of my having to protect you alone."

It was all too clear now, and the realization only added to his cold and callous manner. "She was just an extra burden to you, wasn't she? You could find her. You could use that hypnotic jewel of yours and get right to her—but you won't. You won't because *you sold Charley to those men, you son of a bitch!*"

His eyebrows rose and he looked somewhat offended. "You were there. This cut, these bruises. Does it look like a cold business transaction? There were gentler ways."

"I wanted to believe that. That's why I kept hoping. . . . But let's skip *all* the pretendin', you bastard." She switched suddenly to Akhbreed. "I heard and understood your whole conversation, you horse fucker!"

That got him. His mouth dropped and for a second he really didn't seem to know what to do.

"Yeah," she pressed. "I speak and understand it completely.

What was to be next for me? A horse that bolts and kills me, or runs away, or something like that? Maybe something Ladai is arrangin' that you don't even know nothin' about so when you go in front of Boolean you can honestly say you tried, right? Well it won't work now."

He sighed and put down his towel. "You are quite right. This does change everything." He stood a few feet directly in front of her, and his hand went to his belt pouch. "I had hoped to avoid using this because it came from Boolean, but now it is the only logical approach. First you, then a good cover story, then I will use it on Ladai and myself so that even we will believe it. In a moment you will feel *very* girlish yourself, you will go over and put on the sexiest outfit in the female trunk, go down, and introduce yourself to someone who will be very lucky getting that reward from Klittichorn."

She hadn't known what was coming the first time he'd pulled out the Jewel of Omak, and so she hadn't paid much attention. Now, though, she saw that it did not shine its nasty light right off, but that the surface, a swirl of white and tan and black like polished onyx, slowly opened, like a camera lens. She weighed rushing him but knew that would be futile; the only hope she had was the oldest, stupidest trick in the book.

At the instant the full glory of the jewel's interior shone forth, she dropped to the floor. The beam struck the bottom part of the mirror behind her and reflected back, striking Zenchur, because of the angle, in the neck. It was unexpected and apparently painful. He cried out, dropped the jewel on the floor, and his hand went to his neck while his face contorted in pain.

Sam's head still hurt like hell but somehow it didn't matter anymore. She lunged for the jewel that was only a few feet from her now on the floor, came up with it, and rolled over with the gem in her hand as Zenchur recovered and whirled to come at her. She held it up in front of her without bothering to get up, and the beam shone and struck his face.

Zenchur froze, the expression of mixed anger and pain also frozen on his face. She whistled some relief. *Just like the freeze-frame on the VCR,* she thought, amazed. She didn't dare move, though. Not yet.

"Okay, lover boy," she said in English. "You will relax, go over and sit on the bed, and you will obey me and answer all my questions. Understand?"

His facial expression softened. "Yes," he mumbled tonelessly, then loosed up, went over, and sat obediently on the side of the bed as told.

Now she could get up. "How long do the effects of this jewel last?" she asked him.

"Six to eight hours," he responded dully.

"All right—you sold Charley to that man, didn't you? The whole kidnapping was a put-up job, wasn't it?"

"Yes."

"You had her actually *auditioning* in there for the courtesan role, and then you sold her for a thousand.

"What you told me about what they'd do to her—was that true?"

"Yes."

That was bad. "How long have I got before they give her the potions that make her forget everything?"

"They do the physical first and that takes a full day and night. They save the rest for after because the potions to do that are far rarer and more expensive than the physical ones. After a full day she would invite Kligos over to give her a love potion. Then she would do anything Kligos said. It makes the rest go very easily."

"All right—so who would they take her to? If you *had* to find her in secret, where would you look?"

"First I would look at Boday's studio," he responded, still in that dull monotone. "The two women in the tavern tonight were Boday's work and Kligos would want the best."

That name again. "Who is this Boday and where would I find him?"

"Boday is a woman. She lives and works out of a studio loft in the warehouse district. She is an expert in artistic alchemy."

Sam frowned. "What the hell is artistic alchemy?"

"She feels she is an artist. She used to be a sculptor but when she came down here she changed. The courtesans are her creations. She thinks of each as a unique work of art."

Well, that explained all the body painting. Kind of sick, though, not just that somebody would think of poor, helpless girls as nothing more than raw material like clay or paint. Even worse that it was a woman. She had—how long?

"How long has it been since I was knocked out?"

"About three hours," Zenchur replied.

Okay, that was something. "So they can't mess with her mind until after dark tomorrow, right?"

"That is the usual way. With Boday it often takes longer. She considers herself an artist and will not be rushed."

"Where is this Boday's place? Exactly—from the hotel?"

Zenchur told her. It wasn't all that complicated, since the warehouse was on the lake, but she made very sure she got it right. Twenty, maybe twenty-four hours. Oops! There was a thought.

"How many hours are in a day, Zenchur?"

"Twenty-four," he responded.

Okay, at least some things were still the same. "This place of Boday's—have you ever been there?"

"Not inside. I have been past it many times."

"Is it guarded?"

"The warehouse is owned by Attum Merchandising. It has many guards there at all hours. Since the only stairs up to Boday's loft are well inside, it is all the protection she needs."

"Uh-huh. And if you wanted to get inside Boday's place without those guards knowing, what would you do? Use the jewel?"

"No. It might not get all the guards and might activate some protective spells. I would hire a thief, small and strong, and get up the outside of the building under cover of darkness, then secure a rope for me. There are large windows like skylights up there, most open to the breezes."

"Huh. It's a wonder thieves don't get up there all the time, then. Or is there something else?"

"Not that I know of, but I have never been inside. Boday would be well protected in any case from such things. She does work for Kligos and for a dozen others, including some procurers for the royal family, yet she has no taste for money or jewelry or anything of major value. Anyone breaking into Boday's would have the instant and total wrath of both the lords of this district and the nobility on their heads, yet probably such a crime would net little. It would not be worth it."

Now *that* made a lot of sense. And most, if not all, of Boday's human raw material would be from the elements where nobody would be looking for them, anyway. It sounded easy—if you had a professional thief.

She clenched the Jewel of Omak tightly in her hand. "I wish I knew how to do it myself," she said aloud.

Immediately, clearly, in her mind, an eerie and inhuman voice responded silently, *Awaiting input/action command.*

She jumped and almost dropped the jewel. "Who said that?"

The hypnotized Zenchur took that as a question directed at him. "You said the last thing."

"No, no! There was a voice—sort of. Like inside my head. Or is this bump doing it?"

"I do not understand."

"Neither do I. I . . ." She looked suddenly down at the jewel in her hand. Was it possible. "Was that you, Jewel of Omak?"

Yes. You stated the activating command. Awaiting input/action.

"Holy shit. Zenchur—did this jewel ever talk to you'?"

"Talk? No."

Well it was sure as hell talking now. And in English, too! She had stated the activating command, it said. What had she said? Just "I wish I knew how to do it myself." Hey! Maybe that was it. This was a land of magic. Maybe you had to wish.

"Jewel—is that it? Do you do something except hypnotize people?"

Yes.

"I wish I knew how to use you properly," she said, hoping it could take a hint.

Operation. Standard feature. Direct mental manipulation of remote subjects by carrier beam centered on forehead. Undocumented features. Manipulation of mind and body of operator as willed subject to energy limits. Access to data information files per specific request. Various protective measures available to bearer. Language used must be English as protective feature. Command must be phrased as wish. End operation guide.

God. Sounded like a computer. "So how come you never talked to Zenchur?"

Zenchur used only standard feature. Never used English until you appeared in speech or thought. Zenchur does not think in English, cannot therefore command access this mode.

"You're from—Boolean?"

Yes. I am backup system in case Zenchur failed. Any attempt by Zenchur to use jewel against Boolean's predetermined interests would have resulted in his destruction.

She grinned and looked at Zenchur. "You don't know it, but I just saved your miserable life." She thought a moment. "I guess the wishes aren't like magic lamps, huh? I can't just wish Charley here and lots of money and all that?"

Impossible. Wishes limited to mind manipulation of others and mind and body manipulation of bearer.

She knew it wasn't gonna be *that* easy. "Zenchur said the effect lasts six to eight hours. Any way to make it longer? Like forever?"

Yes. Aim beam at forehead, express input/action command as wish.

She could command Zenchur to help her, but Zenchur said the only way he could manage it was to hire a thief and she'd had enough of others in this for now.

She stood back, held up the jewel, and put the spot on the navigator's forehead. He stiffened.

"I wish Zenchur would never recognize Charley or me again. Even if we went up to him stark naked and told him he would never recognize us or believe us."

Done.

"I wish that Zenchur would never see me as other than a man, even if he saw me naked or in a slinky dress and everybody else knew what I was. I also wish he would forget he ever knew English, or even what English was, and be unable to ever learn a word of it again."

Done.

She was on a roll now. Power corrupted, particularly when it was on the other side.

"I wish Zenchur would forget about the Jewel of Omak, or that there ever *was* such a thing, and that he could never touch it again, even by accident. And I wish that he would forget Boolean and everything he ever did for Boolean. I wish he would forget everything for the past five days forever."

Done.

"Zenchur—stand up."

The navigator obeyed.

"First, get and give me all your money. Anything of value that could be spent in this crazy world."

Zenchur gave her the change purse, which was fairly heavy, then went over to the trunk with the female dress inside and pulled out a small secret compartment. He removed a second bag and brought it to her. It seemed a lot heavier than the change purse. She managed to cram it all into the small leather change purse that was part of her own outfit, although empty.

"So you were gonna have me put on a bikini and go down and wander around offering myself until somebody took me up on it, huh? You bastard. I ought'a just order you to go down and become one of those storefront muscle men, but I won't. Uh-uh. Too easy. But for what you did to Charley, what I might not be able to undo, you deserve something real mean." She aimed the jewel.

"I wish that you only loved men," she said to him, her voice firm. "I also wish that you loved to wear women's clothing and jewelry and cosmetics all the time if you can, and that you had the manner and tongue of one of these courtesans—very swishy and real feminine. And I wish you were scared, terrified, of a lot of things. Scared of all women, for example, Akhbreed or not, and the dark, and lonely streets. I wish you felt completely powerless most of the time, and scared. And I wish female centaurs were the scariest thing to you of all."

Done, said the jewel.

"Okay, get over there and go to sleep, you bastard," she ordered, "Dream nightmares, and when you wake up you'll be a new man."

It felt good, really satisfying, to do in somebody like that. It wasn't until she had done it, though, that she realized she had blown it. He'd already forgotten her and Charley and everything. He could no longer answer the one big question: why she was wanted by so many people.

"Shit," she muttered, dismissing it as a lost opportunity. The real problem was what to do next.

"Boy, I wish I could wish that *everybody* see me as a hundred percent man," she muttered. "That would protect me around here."

Done, said the jewel.

She was startled. "You mean I can really do that?"

You are the bearer. Nothing has changed, but optically and aurally they will see someone male and different. I said I was a protector. Limitations: I can do only physical self: not clothing or inanimate objects. Illusion will also be transparent to higher classes of sorcerers, some non-Akhbreed races.

"Huh. So I can't slip into something of Charley's without lookin' like a man in a dress. Still, it's good enough. It means I won't hav'ta worry 'bout this as much. I'm still real amazed that *anybody* bought it. When that guy looked at Charley and me in the tavern and said that 'bout the two girls I figured I was nailed." She sighed again. "Okay, jewel. I talk to you in English but the one I zap don't hav'ta know it?"

Correct. I will provide the interfaces needed.

"But it'll work on the others, too. Not Akhbreed. Like Ladai."

Yes, but not all. I may also be unable to affect halflings, the accursed, and others of that ilk. Also certain races with intrinsic powers or whose memory and emotive patterns are too different from your own.

She thought a minute. "You can make most folks see a man when they see me. What else can you do to me?"

Question oddly phrased. I can maximize use of anything that is actually a part of the animate bearer. I can give pleasure, dampen fear, speed some types of damage repair, direct energy where it will do the most good, and provide some needed survival reactions and data within the limits of the information available to me. Warning: use me sparingly. I must recharge my energy or my abilities diminish.

She nodded absently. "Yeah, but what I need now is to save Charley and I don't know how. I wish I had the strength, stamina, ability and sheer guts to go after her myself, but . . ."

Done, said the jewel. *Warning: your body will pay a physical price for this later.*

Suddenly there simply was no question in her mind as to what she had to do. Her head stopped its aching, her mind became remarkably clear, although the knot was still there and it was still ugly. She felt strong, confident, wide awake, and cautious, not afraid. She searched Zenchur's bag and the trunks for anything else of use. Not much, and she had no patience to search for secret compartments, not now. Still, in his bag was something solid wrapped in soft crimson cloth, and she took it out and unwrapped it.

It was a knife—no, bigger than a knife. The handle looked more like a sword handle, but the blade was maybe a foot long, perfectly proportioned. She picked it up, felt it, made a few slash and jab moves. It was as if she'd always had the thing and practiced every day.

She took the time to change. There was a soft pullover top of near jet black in there, a pair of black male tights, and a loose but sturdy black leather belt. She tried on the outfit and it fit pretty well, although the top was lifted up a little by her breasts. The body was all girl, though; she searched and found a loose leather jerkin that went over it and concealed a bit. She knew she didn't really need it with the power of the jewel working for her, but you never knew if you were coming back. Her soft leather boots would continue to be fine. The short sword's scabbard fit on the belt, so that was added. She was reasonably satisfied—it was men's clothing, although she didn't look very mannish in it. That jewel's spell had better work. She kind of liked the look, though.

She was almost ready to go when she realized she'd almost forgotten the money purse. That, too, went on the belt, and she hoped it wouldn't jingle much.

Next was finding a way out. She considered risking the stairs, but the less seen the better. She went to the window, stood on the trunk, and with a real effort got it open and looked out. It was four stories down to the street below, but there were ledges and cornices all the way. The fact that she had always been scared of heights and never even climbed trees well as a kid was forgotten; her mind plotted the whole thing carefully, then she let herself out of the window and lowered herself down onto the four-inch ledge. She worked her way along it, carefully but confidently, until she reached the corner of the building, then eased herself down and let her body flow over the side until only her hands were on or held the ledge. The cornices and brickwork at points gave her only an inch to work with, but, very carefully and in fair darkness, she made her way down the side of the building without aids.

The darkness which had been a fearsome enemy was now a friend to her, and she stepped into it and drew the short sword, then allowed her eyes to grow accustomed to the murkiness and made her way along the back streets. She had made Zenchur be very precise; within ten minutes and with no real incidents except a few rats or rat-like creatures, which she ignored contemptuously, she made it to the waterfront itself and looked back on a row of warehouses, one of which in particular interested her.

She made her way completely around it, unobserved in the darkness, studying it with a professional's eye. It was bound on all sides by streets, the smallest of which was maybe fifteen feet. So much for roof to roof; without equipment it was just physically out of reach. That left the warehouse itself. It was about the same distance to the roof as it had been down from the hotel room window, but this was stone and cement block. The only possibility was the rain channels and gutter pipe, which was more of a rounded pipe than the aluminum rectangles back home. The lowest channels that were useful were a good ten or twelve feet from the street level, more than twice her height, and it wasn't clear just how they were set in. She was five-two, a hundred five—okay, a hundred and twenty. Why quibble? The gutters and mounts back home wouldn't take either weight. If these didn't, then she was screwed and there'd be a lot of banging. If these did—then what?

To hell with it, she told herself. *Charley's in there and I don't see another way.*

She removed her boots in an alley that separated two warehouses in back of her target, then used the sword to cut away the bottoms of the tights up to the ankles. She knew she'd be better off if she left the sword and maybe the money as well—even though the money bag also had the Jewel of Omak—but she wasn't about to leave her only weapon behind and certainly not the money or the jewel.

She sized it up from every angle, calculated the timing, speed, and place, then, without considering things further, she took off, hit her mark, and leaped, arms outstretched.

Both hands grabbed the gutter pipe, but then the rest of her body slammed into the stone wall. It hurt and she almost lost her grip, but she held on. Damn! Wasn't she gonna be a sight if she lived through this?

The pipe was solid and held, and seemed to be mounted on thick steel rods embedded in the concrete of the building itself. With supreme effort and contorting more than she ever thought possible she got a leg up, then rolled into the building letting the two inches of clearance between the rods and the side of the building hold her. It took her some more time and much care and breath control as well as strength, but she managed to get up so she was standing on the two-inch pipe. She worked her way down to where the vertical pipe from the roof met and merged with the horizontal one and studied it. It went all the way, right up the corner, but there wasn't much to hold on to except pipe and support pins.

Taking a deep breath and willing away the pain, she used the same arms that could not have possibly lifted one of the trunks, let alone Charley, and pulled herself up the side of the building.

The roof was a sloping affair of dirty green copper. Cautiously she moved along it, until she reached the corner and a scary turn to cling to the side facing the water. She hoped Zenchur knew what he was talking about. It would be unendurable to find at this point that this was the wrong warehouse—or that Charley wasn't inside.

There *were* windows, at least—a long string of very large ones, only on this side. Some had been propped open several inches to catch the breeze, which was definitely there, although mostly blowing from the land to the water. She made her way to the nearest window and looked in, praying she was not going to find herself looking down into the warehouse.

She wasn't. It was a room—a big room, with a polished wood floor and tons of stuff all over the place. It definitely looked like an artist's studio—there were even sculptures around on stools and stuff like that. It was definitely what was advertised. Now the only question remaining was whether or not Charley was inside. Zenchur had said that Boday wasn't the only one doing this filthy business, only the biggest name.

Further on down and out of her direct line of sight some lights were certainly on. She had come this far; she had to find out one way or the other. At least, damn it, she made the effort.

It wasn't easy opening the window more than the pins allowed without them falling back, but she managed it, wondering how the hell Boday opened them in the first place. She managed to get under, just barely squeezing through, until she was hanging, suspended inside, but still a good six or eight feet from the floor.

There was no way around it. She would have to drop and roll, and hope that the sound wouldn't be heard or would be dismissed by any who did.

She let go, falling immediately to all fours and then freezing as the short sword went *thunk* against the wood. Holding it up, she crawled into a dark corner and waited to see if anyone would come to investigate.

Someone did. The figure silhouetted in the far doorway was imposing, but, backlit, it was impossible to tell much more than that she was *very* tall and *very* thin and she wore very high heels.

"Hello! Anybody there, darlings?" she called out in a voice that was deep and rich and very female. The Akhbreed dialect was also heavily accented. She walked into the darkened studio without showing any real fear, and in the darkness various forms and colors seemed to glow, although she was barely visible. It didn't take much imagination to see that the glowing parts were shapes and highlights of her body that made the whole show obscene. In a few steps, she stopped again and was slightly illuminated by a shaft of reflected light from the lakefront outside.

The most obvious thing about her was that she was wearing tall, high-heeled leather boots and matching panties or bikini or whatever. What was anything but apparent for quite a moment was that she wasn't wearing anything else, although that realization restored Sam's confidence in fashion design. The fully lit version of the woman did not have the very obscene shapes, but it was a whole new category of obscenity.

From the top of her small, firm breasts to the top of her boots, the woman was a walking art show. It was like she was tattooed all over, yet it wasn't like that—these were no skin-dulled designs, but bright, flashy colors, and lots of them. Dozens, maybe more, all in loops, swirls, waves, and every sort of shape possible. She looked like a walking modern art sculpture. Even her face had some starburst design exploding from her eyes. Only her arms and hands and shoulders seemed free of paint.

After pausing a moment more, she walked out of the slim light and again there were those glowing patterns, although now Sam realized that it was part of the designs on her body. Like day-glo or something, they glowed softly in the dark. Jeez! Those spirals around the breast and nipples moved when she did and could almost hypnotize you! And the hair. It was long, but she'd never seen spikes that thick or that perfect, going out in all directions maybe a foot from her head—and each a different color, too.

Even without the boots she'd be a tall woman, though. Sam guessed her at well over six feet. Neither she nor Charley would come up much higher than Boday's breasts.

She went to the far part of the studio, unlatched a lock, and opened the door. "Amswaq! Are you there, darling?" she called down into the warehouse.

"Yeah, Boday," came a man's voice from far off. "Problems?"

"Boday thought she heard someone knock. Did anyone come in?"

"No, nobody and I been sitting here all night. Not since them big bruisers hours ago. You want I should come up and check the place out?"

"No, it's all right, darling! Boday must have simply put something where it was sure to fall over later. She will find it in the light of day. Good night."

"G'night, Boday," the man responded, and the woman closed and relocked the door, then turned and walked briskly back to the lighted doorway and through.

What kind of whacko paints herself like that and then talks about herself like she's somebody else? Sam wondered. *I guess the kind that would think of people as things.* Everybody in this damned world seemed to think about people that way. Weren't there any *good* people in this world?

After waiting to make sure Boday wasn't setting a trap, Sam crept out, keeping low and in the shadows, until, silently, she made it to the doorway. She could hear Boday's voice in there, clearly talking to somebody, although if she had somebody in there why hadn't they come with her to investigate the noise?

The next room was still a large one, although nothing like the studio, but it was a mess. Walls were covered with shelves containing old and musty-looking books, some intermixed with jars and other containers, and one whole wall had only the small jars on it. There was also an old, beat-up looking marble-topped counter in front of the wall full of jars, on which were the odd-looking, Akahlarian equivalents to bunsen burners, holders and stands, and even several mortars and pestles. The whole counter was covered in multi-colored crud. There was also trash and even some ancient garbage on the floor and counters and shelves. Boday was something of a pig.

Boday was clearly working on something—or someone. With a little maneuvering, Sam could see that it was a girl with very long hair standing there, still as a statue, stark naked, on a pedestal. It *could* be Charley, but the hair was colored wrong, and there were designs or markings on the girl's rear end. Boday circled around her, stopping to study or think now and then, a palette balanced professionally on one shoulder and arm, a long, brush instrument in the other. Boday was talking, now and again, to the girl, who gave no reply, no reaction at all.

"Ah, darling, Boday is tempted to create from you a whole pattern of color and design, but that would not be artistically true. No, understated is best with you, my little butterfly. Boday knows best, including when to fight her impulses and excesses. Oh, those potions have done their work *perfectly!* You are simply *gorgeous*. Boday shall hate to give you away, but that would be selfish, cheating the world of Boday's genius. You must be displayed to be appreciated. How Boday wishes you could speak to her and sing her praises. Ah, but not to worry. Boday could have created this in plaster or clay. Tomorrow comes the true art. Living art." She turned, put down the palette and brush or whatever it was, and looked on the counter, then picked up a black bottle.

"Here, precious one, is Boday's special essence of love which will bind you to your master so you will be protected as Boday's works should be and not get in any trouble." She picked up a green bottle. "But first this, which will sponge away all those memories, all that guilt, all those things you were before Boday remade you. Then you will be a blank slate on which Boday will create the rest of you. The simple tongue—only a few hundred words but all you will ever need. A wonderful creation of times past in which you will only be able to *think* as my creation. You will want for nothing, think of nothing, live for nothing save the *tableau* Boday's living art will teach you, and you will be eager to learn and know nothing else so none will ever spoil the creation. Now—some proper adornments to insure the perfect symmetry, then Boday can rest and you, my sweet, can rest as well and let the potions complete their work."

Sam thought quickly. What the hell could she *do?* Getting here was tough enough, but if that was Charley—should she take on Boday or wait? The multi-colored woman was a big woman, thin or not, and in her own element. She had done a lot already considering it'd been maybe six hours—dawn was breaking fast through the studio windows—and the jewelry and stuff Boday was putting on her was finished off with little dabs of something that caused tiny puffs of smoke and hurt to watch. Still, Zenchur had been right. No love potions or amnesia juices yet. If Boday couldn't give them until all the other stuff had set and taken, then there was no reason to jump the gun and take a big risk. If Charley was "setting" then Boday had to sleep *sometime.*

It was tempting to use the Jewel of Omak and be done, but that might come later. It suddenly occurred to Sam that she had no idea what the range of the thing was—and no way right now to ask the question.

The sun was shining brilliantly by the time Boday finished with her "proper adornments" and seemed willing to let things go. It had been at least two, maybe three more hours; the sounds of the warehouse starting up work for the day came muffled through the floor while other voices and noises came in from the windows as the studio, in particular, heated up.

Finally Boday put out her hands and took the girl's and brought her gently forward off the pedestal, then led her around and out of Sam's sight. But before she did, Sam got a look at the face and felt a thrill. It was Charley, all right! But, boy! If she snapped out of this okay, she was sure gonna be in for a shock when she looked in the mirror.

It would be best, Sam decided, to wait a couple of hours more before going any further. She wanted Boday very solidly asleep and the full din of business outside and below to cover her. She was feeling damned tired, that was for sure. All the aches and pains of the previous night were catching up with her, including a new and growing sensation that every inch of skin was bruised and every bone in her body was broken. She barely made it into a corner where she'd be well hidden behind some boxes. She was just in time, too; Boday came suddenly out of the door, went somewhere in the studio, messed about with something for a little while, then turned and walked back in the other room and perhaps beyond.

God, I'm so damned dizzy and sore I can't move! Sam thought miserably. She was incredulous at what she'd done, but it was wearing off quite rapidly now. The jewel had warned that she would pay a price. She didn't want to rest long, though, certainly not sleep. It would be horrible if she fell asleep and let the worst happen when she'd come this far. It was a plaintive thought, and she wasn't aware of sinking into slumber.

But when she next jerked her head up to stay awake, the studio was no longer lit by sun and the shadows were long and darkening. She was suddenly wide awake, although still feeling some pain.

She was awake—but was Boday? And, if so, had the crazy artist gone too far?

7
Personality Changes

Sam removed the Jewel of Omak and gripped it tightly. "What is your range for hypnotism?" she whispered. "Tell me."

Normal power three meters, the gem responded in her brain. *I am now under severe power down, however. Perhaps one meter. I believe I can maintain your protective disguise for up to two more days without time to recharge, but no other functions fully operative. Last night was a heavy drain. You were warned.*

A meter! That was like three feet! She'd almost have to be kissing Boday to get it to work. "How long will it take you to recharge?" she barely breathed.

If I am not used at all, thirty-six hours should be sufficient.

She put it away. Thirty-six hours! Christ—Charley would be dead meat by then. Not to mention the fact that she herself was feeling pretty drained and achy as hell—and there was no way she was getting down the same way she got up. She was also hungry and thirsty as hell and she was going to burst if she didn't piss pretty soon. This was *great.* Just *great.*

Boday was up and about in there, too. She could hear the artist now moving around, humming an inane tune, and smell some pretty wild smells, a few of which were helpful in making Sam forget how hungry she was.

Sam sat there trying to figure out what to do. Damn it, if she didn't do anything at all Charley was gonna be history, but what could she do? The jewel was no good, and Boday was bigger and from the looks of those arms a lot stronger than she was. Sam went to the short sword which the previous night had felt so light and easy to use and found it so heavy she could hardly manage it. This wasn't *fair,* damn it! It just wasn't *fair!*

But what she had done last night, as incredible, as unbelievable, as it now seemed, was only partly magic. The gem had given her nothing but confidence and some background knowledge skills; she had done nothing she was not capable of doing, only things she would not have dreamed possible for her to do. It was getting dark and she was about to piss on the floor. The hell with it. Without Charley she just didn't want to see what this armpit world looked like, and to hell with Boolean.

Grasping the short sword for all it was worth, she crept around the corner, through the doorway, and into the laboratory, keeping behind a mound of piled up stuff on a table. She could see Charley lying kind of diagonal on a bed with an X-type adjustable frame. Boday was over at the lab counter checking on something. The two little bottles were still on the counter, too, but it was hard to say whether or not they'd been used. Sam had to believe they had not; it was just dark, and it was still not quite twenty-four hours.

Boday was in her usual state of colorful undress, although she was wearing a pair of sparkling pink panties and open-toed sandals now, and she had a bib around her to shield her in case something bubbling on her countertop might splash.

The artistic alchemist had her back to Sam, but she still looked *huge.* Sam felt like David and Goliath—only David had God and a slingshot. Both would be very useful right now.

Boday suddenly dropped something on the floor. "Moon-stones and little fishes," she cursed a bit colorfully. She got up slightly from her work stool and leaned down to pick up whatever it was. Sam decided it was now or never.

She summoned every bit of strength she had, leaped suddenly out with sword drawn and rushed the big woman, saying "Yaaaa!"

Boday was so completely surprised she jerked up just in time to see what was coming but not to do anything about it. Sam hit her full force with her body, and Boday, bent over and just in the process of straightening up, went back sharply when hit and her head struck against the marble side of the lab table. Her eyes opened wide, her eyeballs went up toward her eyebrows, and she sank down onto the floor in a heap.

Sam rolled off and managed to pull herself up. It was so quick and impulsive she hadn't even thought beyond the rush, but now she suddenly was aware that the big woman was lying there in a heap, like some discarded giant colorful rag doll. She stared incredulously at the sight, then thought, *Oh, my God, I've killed her!*

But then Boday moved and Sam realized she had only a minute, perhaps seconds, before things got different. She grabbed one of the bottles off the counter—the black one—and kneeled down beside the artist, who was just returning to consciousness, if not sense. "Here—drink this. It'll make you feel better," Sam said, sounding concerned, and put the bottle to Boday's lips.

The big woman tasted it, coughed a bit, then almost greedily drank the rest of it down. Her big eyes opened hazily and she looked at Sam, then saw the bottle, and the eyes grew suddenly wide.

"Apple cider," she mumbled. "Boday always wondered what it tasted like. How about that . . . !" She sighed, gave a sweet smile, then passed out again on the floor.

Sam had deliberately grabbed one of the potions, of course; it was the only sure way to make sure the big woman didn't come to and turn the tables fast. Now she looked at the bottle and tried to remember what it might have been.

Well, whatever it was, it had knocked the artist out again and that was plenty of breathing space. She wanted to rush to Charley, but first she spied a door at one end of the lab and a somewhat familiar object and headed to it. The piss was almost as sweet as the victory.

That done, she was able to see to Charley, and what she saw amazed her. Boday had been *very* busy with Charley, and if they could do this sort of thing with potions, who knew what magic might accomplish?

Charley had had Sam's old very long straight black hair, but Boday had changed that to strawberry blond with streaks of black and brown, and somehow managed to really fluff it up and thicken it, at least so it appeared. There were differences in the face, too. The lashes seemed extraordinarily long, like the most extreme false ones, and the pronounced overbite was gone, the lips a little turned out more, fuller and thicker like an almost permanent pucker, and colored a deep, rich, solid red. But most noticeable was the face painting around the eyes themselves, each a separate, delicate drawing and a mirror image of the other although they did not connect across the bridge. They were delicate, pale blue butterfly wings, one per side, coming out from the eye and curving gracefully away, yet in the solid color were small, fine lines of white and black that gave it a fascinating look, and from the tops of the "wings" came fine black lines that curved as well and ended in small black dots.

Boday went in for eye painting. She had it on herself and the pair in the tavern had it, too. But it was so intricate, so nicely balanced, that Sam had to admit that the tall woman might be a lot of nasty things, but she was a hell of an artist.

Setting it off were large pierced earrings that would hang down to the jaw line were she standing; thick, more brass than gold but impressive all the same, they were in fact stylized butterflies flying toward the front of Charley's face.

The motif continued on the body painting, although it was, as Boday had said, "understated." The butterfly, mostly in outline but subtly shaded so that it still gave the effect of a solid drawing with gossamer thin wings, used the breasts as the upper wing foundation, blue lines coming off from the wing tips and onto the breasts, circling the nipples and making them appear perfectly round. The wings, outlined in the blue of the eyes, curved down to the navel in which was mounted a matching blue gem, then back out along the hips and back in. The "head" was the pubic hair, dyed to match the new hair color. While it seemed almost an outline, the faint solidity of the wings actually contained hints of many colors, perhaps a very complex pattern depending on how the light caught it or the angle from which it was viewed. The complexion of all the skin, even that untouched by the design, seemed almost wet, glisteny and soft and perfectly smooth. The breasts were the same *C* cup size, but they seemed rock hard, incredibly firm, and far more prominent. Sam's sagged and drooped, which helped with the boy disguise. There was no way to disguise these, though. They were as firm as a—statue's.

There wasn't a sign of body hair anywhere except pubic hair and even that seemed manicured, and even the duplicate of Sam's old appendix scar was gone. There wasn't a blemish on this body. Not any of Sam's freckles, not a mole or anything.

The fingernails were so smooth and long and perfect they had to be artificial; they had been painted to match the blue of the eyes and the butterfly and had to be an inch or more long. The toenails were also smooth and painted to match, although trimmed.

More jewelry had been added, to match the earrings. Bracelets and anklets of a twisted braid design, loose but firmly on, and with no sign of any seam showing, and a matching, loose-fitting collar.

Sam knew from seeing her back earlier in the morning that there was another butterfly, same color but different style, cape-like on her back, perfectly following the natural curves and folds of the body as did the one on the front. The colors were bright, vibrant, not at all like tattoos, but Sam had to wonder if this stuff came off.

One thing was for sure. Sam had always had a kind of androgynous look to her, very male in the face and female in the body. Charley had not one trace, one hint, of anything masculine remaining in her looks.

Charley was gonna shit bricks when she saw herself.

"Charley," she called, gently shaking her friend. "Charley—wake up! It's me—Sam."

Charley smiled sweetly and moved a little but did not wake up. It had to be some kind of drug. They'd passed some drugs in the wine last night—that was for sure. Probably more here to make her cooperative and not prone to waking up inconveniently and maybe trying to run away.

Sam heard a sigh behind her and whirled. Boday was stirring again, pulling her legs up and rubbing her temples with her long fingers. She stopped suddenly, looked up across the room, and saw Sam.

Instantly a look spread over her face that could only be described as ecstasy. It was the kind of look one might give when seeing God face to face. "Boday loves you," she whispered in a soft, throaty, sexy voice. "Boday worships you. She grovels at your feet. Whip her, chain her, beat her, but she will always worship you."

Well, that settled that. The black bottle was the love potion.

"Command her! Take her! You are her world, her life. Nothing matters but you! The world revolves about you!" Boday continued in that tone. She got on her hands and knees and crossed to where Sam stood, not knowing quite what to do next, and, without any warning, the artistic alchemist started kissing Sam's feet.

Sam felt embarrassed and pushed her away. "Stop that!"

"Yes, yes, Master. Command me! I instantly obey!" The alchemist scurried back and seemed to be almost whimpering with delight.

Holy shit! That was some potion! was all Sam could think of right off, but then she suddenly began to understand the possibilities. "What about my friend? What have you done to her?" Sam asked.

"Made her beautiful. That is what Boday does. Creates beauty. She was easier than most. I can see why one of Master's greatness would seek her."

"The way you made her look—that is permanent?"

"Oh, yes, Master, kind Master whom Boday loves. She is beautiful, exotic. One gets so few with fair skin in this region. Do you approve?"

The way the alchemist was speaking and acting Sam thought she was going to have an orgasm all by herself.

"What about—the inside? Have you given any potions to change her brain?"

"No. Well, a few little things to make sure it all remains true to the artistic vision, but not thought, not memory, not personality.

The art must be fixed first. See." She rolled and pointed to a small line of bottles. "These change the body chemistry so the body renews itself in my design. Only then, after twelve hours with nothing else ingested, are the potions for love, obedience, and the rest given. Boday was preparing to do it when you came into her life. The girl is still a work in progress."

Well, *that* was a relief. Charley might not like the work of art Boday made from her—but maybe she would—but at least nothing important had been screwed up. She'd been in time! Just barely—from the looks of that potion's effect on Boday.

"Do you remember why you feel the way you do towards me? Do you remember?"

"Oh, yes, Master. Boday drank her wonderful potion—as *you* commanded."

"It don't make no difference that it was that?"

"Oh, *no,* lover, God in the flesh. It can never matter how."

"And it's permanent?"

For the first time she showed a bit of her old pride. "Of *course,* my sweets. When Boday creates, it is *forever!* Isn't it *wonderful?*"

Sam gestured toward Charley. "Can you wake her up—now?" She desperately needed Charley right now to help figure out what to do next.

Boday was on her feet, cat-like, engulfing Sam and kissing her, then over to the workbench. "I obey, Master. Boday lives only for you. Whip her, beat her, she will worship you all the more." She picked up a small jar and uncorked it, then held it under Charley's nose. The unconscious girl made a face, tried to turn away, then suddenly came awake, looking terrified and a little in shock. She stifled a scream.

"Charley! It's me—Sam! It's okay! It's over!"

Charley frowned for a moment, then stared at Sam. "Sam? My God, Sam!" And then she was off the table and hugging and kissing her rescuer like she couldn't believe it and crying all the time. "They were gonna—turn me—into one of *them,*" she sobbed, and Charley let it all come out. Suddenly Charley seemed to see Boday and froze. *"Her!"*

"It's all right, Charley." Quickly Sam told her all that had happened up to that point, with one exception. "Uh—I think you better look at yourself in the mirror, Charley, if you're up to it, before we go any further."

Charley froze, then with Sam's help managed to get up and go cautiously over to the three-way mirror as if afraid to look in. The hair tumbled down as she got up and showed not only was it full and colored but it was somehow *longer,* going down to below her ass. Sam couldn't help but think that this was the first hairdresser she'd ever seen who could truly work miracles.

When she did, what she saw took her breath away. "Oh, *man!*" she breathed. "*She* did this?" She wet a finger and rubbed at the thin but colorful design. "It doesn't come off!"

"No. She thinks she's an artist. She says her creations last a lifetime." Sam paused for a moment. "For what it's worth, you are the prettiest, sexiest damned girl I ever saw. It's not really bad at all."

Charley whirled. "That's easy for *you* to say! You don't have a damned butterfly on your body!" She frowned, then approached Sam. "They did something to you, too. Your voice, your manner, even your hair . . . Sam—you're a *guy!*"

"Huh? What the hell do you mean?" She pulled up the shirt revealing her breasts which were still there and, although a bit misshapen and flabbier, every bit the size of Charley's. "Does this look like a guy?"

But Charley wasn't buying. "Your breasts—they're gone! And there's even a little hair on your chest!"

"Such a magnificent chest, my love. So clean and manly," said Boday in Akhbreed.

Sam was so confused she looked down and saw the same old things she'd always seen. "What the hell . . . ?" She pulled the shirt back down and reached into her pouch and pulled out the Jewel of Omak. Sure! The disguise! It worked! Curious, she put down the jewel on the floor and stepped away.

Charley frowned again. "Huh? What the hell . . . ? You're back to normal!"

Sam nodded, reached down, picked up the jewel, and stuck. it back in her pouch. "At least I know I'm not the one who's nuts. Man again, right?"

"Uh—yeah. That's like *weird.*"

"It's an illusion, a fake. The jewel is causing it. Charley—I figured I been real lucky up to now and this is part of it. At least I think it was luck. Nobody could be *that* smart. Zenchur did a job for Boolean and got this thing in payment. For hypnotizing folks for getaways and stuff like that. But he *really* hired Zenchur for that first one just to give him *this.* It's a lot more than Zenchur thought it was. It's kind'a like, well, like a computer for magic. So long as I have this thing I look like a guy—to everybody, even you. It has lots of other tricks, too; ones that Zenchur never knew. It hypnotized me into thinkin' I was the world's greatest thief and I did things I never would'a dreamed and got here. I just *knew* everything—includin' how to use it. It—*talks* to me, sort of. In my mind."

"Boolean," Charley said flatly. "That's why he didn't answer us. He already had a backup system in place—for you, anyways. And it was in something so handy, so valuable to Zenchur that he'd never let it out of his sight, never sell it, trade it, or get rid of it in any way. Maybe these sorcerers *are* what they're cracked up to be after all."

Charley looked at Boday, who was just sitting there giving Sam the kind of look Sam had only seen girls give to hunks and rock stars. "What about Boday?" she asked. "Is she kidding? Is that love potion really permanent?"

"I think so, considerin' what it was invented for." She looked ruefully at the admiring Boday, who couldn't understand a word of the English conversation, of course. "I just don't know how I'm gonna handle this."

Charley sniffed. "You got a nutty lover, but I get to go through life looking like a member of a fucking freak rock band!" She turned and looked at herself again in the mirror. "Actually, it's not that bad—except I can't take it off!"

"Yeah, well, you got my body by magic 'cause Boolean thought it'd be useful. He was improvisin'. What he can do he can undo, I bet. You got to figure that magic is stronger than chemicals and potions, right? Me—damn it, can't I ever be *normal?*"

Charley lost a little of her self-pity. "Maybe not, Sam. I dunno. What did you do with Zenchur?"

"I used the jewel to turn him into the fairy queen," Sam said, chuckling, "with a fear of women in general and a real terror of female centaurs. After what he tried to pull, he deserved it."

"Yeah, maybe he did, but you blew it. You should have ordered him to go back and kill Ladai and then forget everything."

"Charley! I couldn't do that!"

"Well, maybe it's about time we started getting a little ruthless here. Don't you see, Sam? It's them or us. Period. Sure, you took Zenchur out of it, but you also took away her husband, lover, and only friend. She was outcast from her own people, too. You also took away her access to the ruling class, and, really, her only livelihood. You took away every reason she had for living. Now, put yourself in her place. What would *you* do?"

Sam hadn't considered that angle, but she still wasn't convinced that ordering a killing was the way. "Everybody's tryin' to do us in anyways. Why should we be like them?"

"Because now she's the only one who knows us and can finger us. She'll get in touch with the horned guy—bet on it. She'll tell him we came down near here, that we went into the city with Zenchur. She'll tell what we look like, and that you're disguised as a boy. The heat is gonna be on something fierce around here, and she won't rest until she finds us."

"Um, yeah. But—damn it, I just can't be that cold-blooded. And neither could you."

"Well, I changed a lot more than a nicer bod and butterfly eyes in the past day and a half. You don't know what those bastards are like. Pawing at me, making faces, feeling me up while I was strung up stark naked. They was setting me up for an eight-way gang bang. Only that boss of theirs showing up and ordering them to bring me here immediately, I guess, stopped it—but you don't know how close it was. They all had their goddamned pants down! You better believe if I had *them* and that sword I'd have your nutty friend here bronze eight sets of balls. I have had it with this shit. I may be stuck, but I am sick and tired of being a victim."

Sam sighed and couldn't think of anything else to say. Her eyes went around the room and focused on the now empty bottle of love potion and something else clicked. "Kligos! Holy shit, we forgot about him!"

"Huh?"

"The boss. He was supposed to come tonight so you could take that love juice and fall in love with *him* so he could own you. 'Scuse me." She turned to Boday and switched to Akhbreed.

"Boday—Kligos is coming tonight, right?"

Boday frowned, then nodded. "Yes. That's right. It had slipped Boday's mind. It is no longer of importance to her."

"Well, I don't want him to have this girl. I went to a lot of trouble to rescue her. He's a very powerful man, I know, but we have to stall him, or get him no longer interested in Charley. Is there any way to do that convincingly?"

The alchemist thought for a moment. "Well, we could always use a placebo, but that would buy only a few days. Let Boday think. She is a genius. She can solve any disputes." She paced for a minute, then snapped her fingers. "Yes! Of course! Royal prerogative!"

"I beg your pardon?"

"Never beg Boday's pardon, my love. You can do no wrong. Royal prerogative. It has happened before. Boday does work for the royal family at times in matters like these. A noble drops by, sees a work in progress, and takes a fancy to it. Even Kligos will not interfere in such a matter. They could shut him down here in hours and fillet him alive on a number of charges if they chose. Boday will simply tell him that the girl was so perfect—and she *is*—that the royal prerogative was invoked. Bad luck. Kligos will be pissed but he will not question it. After all, what does he lose? He just cancels the payment to the procurer, that's all."

"That's great! But won't the warehouse guards be able to tell him that no such royal visitor showed up?"

"No problem, darling! They are three shifts. He will believe. Why should he *not*?"

"Well, do it, then. But that doesn't solve any problems now." She told the alchemical artist about the problem of Ladai. "You see—if Ladai's tale gets back to here, then Kligos is gonna remember the boy and the girl with Zenchur and put two and two together and he'll be back here fast figuring you're just stiffing him for the fifty thousand." She did a quick translation for Charley's benefit.

Charley was also thinking. "I wonder if we're ever gonna get out of the frying pan or the fire? Well, you're right. We can't stay here, but we can't go, either. Once that story gets out they'll be looking for us. They'll have the city and this little country bottled up, maybe for weeks. You're not so bad off, so long as you got that jewel and you aren't around me. Kligos saw you close up but without the magic. That—spell—or whatever it is takes you and cancels out everything, and I mean everything, feminine, and it tightens you up a lot and makes you seem taller. Not real tall, but taller'n me, anyway. I think you can get away with walkin' right past this Kligos, so long as that spell holds, and if not you can zap him with the jewel. Now, he also saw me, and he knows what Boday does, so I think he'd still make me, though. And where can I go in this straight society, like *this*, and without the language?"

Sam explained the problem to Boday, who thought for a moment. "First, then, my love, you must get your little bauble attached, so to speak. That way the spell holds. Once Boday's genius solves your problem we can think about your friend's, yes?"

She went over to the lab counter, reached down, pulled open a big drawer, and started rummaging through the largest collection of baubles, bangles, and beads Sam had ever seen. She would stop every once in a while, pulling out a wound roll of thin gold chain at one point, then a starburst backing. She reached for a bubbling chemical beaker, then said, "Remove all from the waist up. Let Boday see what she can do."

First a length of thin gold chain was measured so it would fit comfortably around Sam's neck but not with enough play that it could be taken off over the face. "Now your pretty bauble," said the alchemist.

Sam was reluctant to hand it over, even to Boday. "But I will change back into a girl," she noted. "Will you still love me anyway?"

"Not to worry, darling! Boday always has played both sides of the street. She saw you briefly when you proved yourself to your friend. Nice body. Much like hers, I think. Boday could do *wonders* with you."

Sam had forgotten that lapse. So it didn't matter. Whatever bond that potion created was more than just appearance. Or, perhaps, because Boday saw the change there was now no difference in her altered mind between the illusory male vision and Sam's real self.

Expertly, and in very short order, the Jewel of Omak was mounted on a strong backing and held there with folds in the setting and some kind of alchemical bonding. Sam hoped she didn't have it on backward. Then the gem and setting, on a slightly longer chain, was bonded to the neck chain. Again, the fusion appeared seamless, but that thing was *on.* It might be cut off, but never would it fall off.

But the other problems would be tougher to solve. It seemed like every fix they'd gotten into had been resolved more by dumb luck than brains, and there was a limit to how much you could count on that, but that wasn't the real depressing thought. It was that every time a super grade problem had been solved it had created new ones that looked just as or even more formidable.

"Ask her if she's got something to eat," Charley said to Sam. "I'm *starved.*"

Suddenly Sam's own hunger and thirst came back full force. "You have anything we can eat? It's been a long time."

Boday brightened. "Anything and everything for you, my darling! Wait, and Boday shall create a *masterpiece!*"

They settled initially, though, for some wine, fresh bread, and cheese, which helped the two of them from getting more nauseous. Boday, however, was in her kitchen making a great racket, but soon the smells coming into the lab were pleasant, overwhelming the chemicals still on the boil.

"It's too bad we can't just stay here," Charlie sighed. "This is the first time I've felt reasonably comfortable in a long time. It would be nice if it'd last, but I keep sitting here expecting eight big bruisers to crash through the door any minute."

"I know. I been tryin' to figure something but nothing's coming. We just don't know this *town,* let alone this world, well enough, and I keep remembering that sight from the cliffs—the green hills changing like that into tall mountains. Even if we could get out of this place we'd be screwed without somebody to take us. Navigators and Pilots, they call 'em. Like ships. And Kligos told Zenchur that just to get a Pilot who don't talk or ask questions would be five hundred or whatever they call their money here. If we also needed a navigator, it might cost a *fortune,* and we don't even know how far it is we're supposed to go."

To Boday the entire world existed for most people to go about drab, colorless, irrelevant lives while she existed to put artistry there. It extended to her cooking, too, even when doing something essentially quick and dirty in the kitchen. Admittedly some of the colors of some of the items looked more than a bit artificial and odd, but the arrangement, the preparation and look of each item, and, frankly, the smells and taste were really good. They already knew that the food in this part of this world was either basic meat and potatoes or very spicy, even hot, but they had never had things that tasted this uniformly different and good. Neither Sam nor Charley, however, had the guts to ask what any of it was.

Kligos's arrival a bit later, however, forced some improvising. Charley was kept out of sight, but Sam decided it was time to test just what good this magic spell might be before an expert in phoniness. She had gotten this far on guts and she was beginning to learn confidence in a big way. She was prepared, though, to use the jewel at close range if she had to.

"Oh, darling! Boday has the most wonderful news and the most terrible news!" Boday gushed to the tough but slick-looking gangster. "The wonderful first. She is in *love!* This is Sandwir! Isn't he *cute?*"

"Adorable," the big man grumbled, nodding to but barely giving a second glance otherwise to Sam. Test passed. "He looks like he might take awhile for you to wear out. What's the terrible news?"

"Ah! Boday is crestfallen! She is desolate! Pamquis—he's the ratty little fellow from the Chancellor's Office—came by today to see about something for the regency celebration and he saw your little darling!"

Kligos's face froze into a hard and mean look. "I don't want to hear what I think you're gonna tell me, do I?"

Boday threw an arm up to her forehead in mock despair. "Darling! What can Boday say but what happened? Those two terrible words—'royal prerogative.' He asked who had brought her and I told him, of course, and all he did was grin evilly and—oh, it is confiscation! What must Boday do to atone, but what could she do in the face of those words?"

"Sons of bitches," Kligos grumbled. "She was a lot of trouble to get, too. I wish I'd let my men have at her. *Then* there wouldn't be no 'royal prerogative' with my property! Well, at least no money's been paid yet. Damn! She was worth a hundred a night minimum!"

"Boday *knows,* darling! And she, too, is out much investment. She is as blackmailed as any. What can she say? He insisted on the potion right then and there as usual. Apparently they hold a grudge for that switch we pulled last year. Can you ever forgive this?"

Kligos sighed. "Forgive, yeah. Forget, no. Those highborn royal bastards. It's not enough that we got to pay 'em a percentage just to operate in this town. No, they steal, too, and smile about it. All right, couldn't be helped. But cut rate on the next one, you hear?"

"Boday will create a *masterpiece* for you! She promises!"

The gangster had a look of total disgust, but he turned around and left, slamming the door behind him. He looked in a foul enough mood to go out and torture a few women and children just to get it out of his system.

"*That* is a dangerous man," Sam noted worriedly. "Right now, he's our biggest worry, too. At least he didn't recognize me, I'm sure of that. But he's dangerous and smart or he wouldn't be where he is."

Boday shrugged. Such things were beneath her notice. "Still, we have a few days. He does not connect you and her, my sweet. Come. Let us go back and you can tell your worries to Boday and she will try and solve them."

"It's simple. There's an Akhbreed sorcerer trying to kill me by any means he can, and there's another who wants me alive and in his company, maybe just because he hates the other sorcerer so bad he wants something to hold over him. I don't know the reason. *Our* sorcerer can't come to us because he's real powerful, but maybe not powerful enough to match this guy on his home turf. Maybe he's got friends here that can outnumber our man, so our man can't come to us. If we can sneak in and get to him, though, then we're under his power and protection and he can help us. Zenchur was supposed to get us someplace where we could be taught the ropes in this world, then to the sorcerer, but that's out now. I don't even know where this guy is in relation to where we are. I wish I did."

Boolean is chief sorcerer of Masalur, said a familiar voice in her head. *Masalur is two hubs northwest and two hubs due west of that. Add in the seven sectors, or wedges, required for traversal and the nulls as well as the hub traversals and the distance would be approximately four thousand five hundred and six kilometers.*

She had forgotten that the jewel was now against her chest and that a wish was a wish.

"Darling! Lover! What is the matter? Do you feel ill?"

"Yeah, maybe," Sam responded. "I just got the answers to my questions from my magic jewel and now I'm like Kligos. I didn't really want to know. Four hubs, seven sectors—it says the distance is . . ." Suddenly in her mind some measures appeared but they were meaningless. "How big's a leeg?"

"Oh, how can it be put? From here near the water to the tall buildings in the center of town is a bit less than two leegs, my love."

From her rooftop vantage point she'd seen some lights in the spires of those buildings and she now guessed them to be about a mile in. A leeg, then, was about half a mile, and a kilometer wasn't much more than that.

"Would you believe about five thousand leegs, maybe a little less?" *Well over two thousand miles and eleven countries with God knew what!*

"Boday believes all that you tell her, love. That sounds about right. Sectors average about six hundred leegs, give or take, and hubs about four hundred across. This one is four hundred fifteen across."

Then they weren't that standard. Still, it was pretty depressing, and Charley wasn't exactly cheered when clued in, either.

"We can't do that distance on our own." Sam told Boday.

The artist nodded. "No one could, not even Boday. You would need a navigator just to start with. Such a one could arrange for the proper Pilots as well as plot the routes and outfit the trip, but this is not cheap. A navigator for such a distance would easily cost two thousand sarkis. Particularly one who would be basically loyal and might defend his client against attack. Say twenty-five hundred just to be sure. Pilots who will just do their jobs and not ask questions are easily five hundred each, and you need—what?—seven of them. No pilots necessary for the hubs. They're all *our* kind, darling, and they stay the same most of the time. Now we are at six thousand. Then there are supplies. One would not wish to walk if it can be avoided. yes? Two thousand more. And then there will be expenses on the trails, and in both sectors and hubs. The more money the merrier but two thousand minimum. Let's see—that is ten thousand sarkis. I think I know where Zenchur was supposed to take you. It is where Boday was perfected! But it is southwest—

add six more, you see. Another three or four thousand and another three thousand or more leegs."

"Yeah? What's so special about that place, anyway?"

"It is—university. You go there, whatever you need to learn, they teach you."

"Not whatever you want, whatever you need," Sam noted. "And who decides what you need?"

"Oh, *they* do, darling! And they *know*. Those who decide are all Akhbreed sorcerers. Those without positions, those studying further, those who have retired or do not wish positions. They know, lover. They know. Boday was an artist. A good artist. They did not teach her design. No, they teach her alchemy. The secrets of arts and potions. it is where sorcerers learn to be sorcerers, and heroes and heroines learn how to be heroes and heroines, or navigators, or Pilots, or any other great skills."

"Yeah, and what does it cost to go there?"

"Cost? Precious, it does not *cost!* Only a graduate or a fully ranked sorcerer can send you. Then you must do him service if and when he or she needs it."

"She? There are female sorcerers?"

"Oh, of *course,* darling! Not many in the hubs thanks to this foul male-dominated system, but many indeed. But why talk about it? It would take probably five thousand to get there at all. How much money do you have now?"

Sam removed the change purse and handed it to Boday, then gave a running translation of what was going on. "So how much we got?" Charley asked.

"That's what I'm finding out."

"Find out how much *she's* worth, too."

"You have four hundred and twelve sarkis, two ilium and seven pillux. A nice sum but it would not even get a Pilot. All that is Boday's is yours, dear one, but money has never been something she has been terribly good at keeping. The filthy pigs of art critics have always insulted her sculptures. The ones here are priceless, of course, but they would bring little money so long as Boday lives. When she dies they will discover her though, and then they will be priceless treasures. This place is leased, paid up in advance for a year, but no refunds, and subletting a place like this would be very difficult. I have, perhaps, two thousand cash, and another thousand in jewelry and chemicals, but those would bring little if sold in haste or desperation, perhaps a quarter of their worth."

"So we're only halfway if we went to this university or whatever it is," Charley noted after hearing the translation. "And it's south and Boolean's north. So whatever they teach us, if it isn't how to fly we'll wind up dead broke with most of the distance yet to go."

"So you think we shouldn't head there? I mean, that's where Boolean wanted us but it's also not only out of the way but where Ladai might be watchin' and waitin'."

Charley sighed. "We probably *should* go. Somehow I feel it's bound up in all this. And he said we'd be safe there from all enemies, which would be real neat. But we don't dare go broke. Without that extra thousand then when they kick us outta there we're like up shit's creek."

Sam nodded and turned back to Boday. "Stuck again. Not enough money to go most anywhere, it seems. Five thousand for this university, ten thousand to get to Boolean, and fifteen thousand for both. It's a *huge* amount of money, I know. We can't go, and we can't stay here."

Boday looked at Charley. "Boday gets perhaps two, three commissions a month. Kligos is not likely to use us again for a while, so there would be at most two. Even if she is frugal, that is at best a thousand a month less two hundred or so for expenses." She sighed and looked at Charley. "It is a pity that Boday cannot complete her creation on this one. Kligos was right—a hundred a night easily, perhaps more. Satisfied customers have been known to double or triple the payment, and clients of Boday creations are *always* satisfied."

Charley looked at Sam. "What did she say? Come on—I want it all. I saw her looking at me."

"She said at the rate she's doing her girls it'd be one to two years before we'd have enough. She said—well, she said it's too bad you can't be put to work, you might say. Kligos said you was worth a hundred a night minimum, and Boday says, well, there's tips."

Charley looked amazed. "A hundred a *night? Me?*"

"I guess it's true. I mean, Kligos was willin' to shell out a thousand to Zenchur for you and another five hundred or so to Boday. He don't do that 'less he figures you'll make back lots more."

Charley was incredulous. "A thousand to Zenchur and five hundred to Boday? You mean I'd be worth fifteen hundred of these *sarkis* just on my *potential* as a *whore?* That's ten percent of all the money we'd need?"

"Damn it all, you're lookin' *pleased!* We're talking men paying money and you sellin' your damn *body!*"

"Yeah," she responded, still sounding more amazed than shocked. She realized how terrible she sounded, but she had never been considered pretty or glamorous before, and she had always thought of herself as something of the Ugly Duckling that grew up and turned into the Ugly Duck. The last time she'd gone to bed with a guy she'd gotten a Big Mac, fries, Coke, and mountains of fear and guilt the guy didn't have to deal with at all. The idea that men would pay her, and big, was too ego-boosting for her to dismiss even though she knew it was wrong. Jeez! Klogos shells out fifteen hundred and makes it back in—what?—fifteen days? Impossible. Then he has her for, like, *years*.

Boday couldn't help but interpret Charley's reactions, and smiled. "She is impressed, yes?"

"Yeah," Sam growled, feeling *very* uncomfortable. Damn it, she thought she *knew* Charley, and first this thing about killing and now she's actually impressed by her price. "But to just sell your body . . ."

"Oh, it's not merely *that*. Sex is cheap!" Boday noted "Boday's creations are no common *tramps*. Not *her* creations! It is an *evening*, with men, perhaps one, perhaps several. Impressing and entertaining business clients, you see. You receive them, prepare and serve a meal that they pay for additionally, then you might entertain—sing, dance, whatever. Make them feel good, feel important. Your client might wish to be bathed, or massaged. Whatever. If he wants sex, you give it to him, whichever way he wants it. He might not even want it. He might just want a sympathetic ear to tell his problems to who'll treat him with sympathy and respect. In the end, he pays you the hundred, maybe more—sometimes much more—if you gave him just what he wanted. It is never quite the same."

"Sounds like Japanese geisha girls," Sam noted. "Still, it's a form of slavery, damn it. Selling your *body* and mind and soul, doing whatever they ask. . . . It's *degrading*. It's bad enough with all them damned potions but at least they don't know what they're doing. Charley would."

But when she translated it all for Charley, the girl with the butterfly eyes nodded, lips pulled in, thinking. "Two hundred days," she said, more to herself than to Sam. "Eight months, tops, and we'd have more than enough without starving—if this guy Boolean's in no hurry."

"*Charley!* Stop thinkin' like that, damn it! You gone completely nuts? Did she give you some of that brain potion anyway?"

Charley stared at Sam. "So what do we do? Hide out in some miserable safe place for two years waiting for your girlfriend there to turn enough new innocent young girls into love slaves so we can go on their blood money?"

"Yeah, if we have to. I mean, they're lost balls anyway."

It was Charley's turn to be appalled. "Listen to you! And *you* called *me* hard!" She took a breath and calmed down. "Look. I'm not sure deep down that I like the idea, either, but you got a better one? If it could be done without this Kligos getting involved . . ."

"Charley! Do you know what you're *saying?* You, the big feminist? Do you know what it'd *mean?* Are you really thinking about that? You're talkin' 'bout servin' and scrapin' and bowin' and maybe *fucking* up to sixty different guys! Maybe gettin' gang banged or worse!"

"Yeah, I know. But it's no feminist thing. I mean, it's a service industry and the money I earned would be for me—for us, not for some corporate pimp. And it's not like getting raped or anything. I mean, it's *my choice.* Maybe I'll hate it. Maybe I'll regret it to the end of my days. Maybe I'll come back and beg for the drug that makes you forget you're even human. But you got a better solution?"

"It's out of the question! It's—*indecent!*"

"Hah! Look who's talking! You just figured on letting *her* turn like a couple dozen girls into this against their will and for life! Sam—she's nuts but she'll do anything you say. You can save lives with a word, but if you do—then what?"

That stopped Sam for a moment. Finally she said, "But you don't know how. Or have a place. Or a wardrobe, or whatever."

"I have a feeling Boday could mix up potions to do temporarily what the others do permanently, and she can teach me. If it came down to it, you could use that thing to hypnotize me, so I'd be just right, and it'd be willing so there'd be no problems with my head gettin' permanently screwed up. And if ten thousand will buy all that, I bet your two or three hundred would buy all the wardrobe I needed."

"I think your brain's pretty screwed up now. Damn it, do you realize what you're almost *begging* me to let you do?"

"Yeah," she sighed. "I do. And I can't believe I'm actually arguing it this way. But—what other way is there? You gonna rob a bank with your magic jewel? I bet they have spells you wouldn't believe on those banks, and it's sure a neat way not to draw attention to yourself. What kind of job you gonna get honest? You may look like a real strong boy but you ain't. I know what you can do. Look at me. *Look at me!* What the hell else can I do in this crazy place? I can't ever play 'respectable' in this burg. Even if one of them robes or dresses or saris covers my body my butterfly eyes and permanent jewelry mark me. I saw the way they looked at me and treated me just in that small town we stopped at. And even if I could somehow mask it, I don't speak the language! I don't speak any language around here. I'm like stuck in ancient times, and the only way I can be a plus and not a minus is like those early ancient women did in the mighty hunter, male-dominated societies. Charge 'em for the only thing I got that has any value."

"I—I can get some kind of job. Anything's better'n that."

"Yeah? What kind of job? We already agree you can't do heavy work, and while you can speak the language you can't read or write it. This may look like a cross between Shakespeare and Robin Hood but it ain't, pal. It's as modern in many ways as where we came from. You don't read or write or have a skill you're up the creek. What's the next idea? Have Boday make up some real strong drugs you can sell to kids?"

"Charley, I—"

"You can go anyplace in this big city. I'm 'beauteous property' wherever I go, and just one look says it. Face it, Sam! We ain't going nowhere without the money and I'm the only one in this group who can get it without exploiting innocent people or stealing it. Maybe I'll be disgusted. Maybe I won't be able to go through with it. I don't know. But right now it's the only thing we got."

Sam, appalled and confused, appealed to Boday for help and alternatives, but she wasn't much good.

"Face it, lover. Why fight it? If she wants to pull in the money then there is more time for *us.* Boday can manage it. It would be nice to see the complete work, too. But if you say no, then it's no."

Sam didn't know what to do but she was still looking for excuses. "She couldn't work out of *here,* or even this district! Kligos would be bound to find out!"

"Oh, piss on Kligos. Boday has many friends and art lovers among the merchant and even noble classes. Many of them would *love* this sort of thing but don't want to be seen down here or are just too scared to come. So we set her up in a nice apartment in a good neighborhood. Boday will decorate it just so. She has often been pressed by people who know her who are upset at enriching the likes of Kligos and his ilk to do something like this but up until now she was not interested in money or business, only art. I will teach her the Short Speech which anyone can learn. It is all they expect a courtesan to know—in speech. Kligos will probably never know, but even if he finds out he will think it is someone at the

Palace's doing. And you will stay here with me and we will check on her."

Sam, grudgingly, told all this to Charley, adding, "But you'd be a prisoner in this place. You'd be there, night and day, for months, and I don't think they invented TV here even if you could understand it. And we can check on you and keep you supplied but for safety's sake we'd have to be here, not there. You'd be alone and not even able to call me for help."

"I'll survive," Charley responded. "It's better if we separate. No ideas putting us together. And the time we need should work out, too. Nobody keeps a roadblock and teams of searchers on for months. They'll figure we got out by them somehow and the search will be elsewhere. It's the only way, Sam, considering the circumstances."

Sam sighed. "All right, but I got a bad feeling about all this. Damn it, it's *me* they want. I feel like it should be *me* doin' this if anybody does. Go back to bein' a woman and let Boday do her thing on me."

Charley smiled. "You're just jealous. No, Sam, it's because they want you that it's gotta be me. And if I'm ever gonna get home again, or even back to me again, then I got to get to that sorcerer, too. This isn't just for you, Sam. It's my only way out."

The next few days seemed more unreal than real to Sam, although she spent much of it sleeping and regaining strength. The knot on the head went down, until there was only a slight scar from the sapping on the street, and the Jewel of Omak reported that its power was back up to strength, which gave her a real sense of security. Just where it was getting its power from she never thought to ask.

Boday continually attempted to seduce her as well, and she was a pretty easy mark for it considering how she felt. The mad alchemical artist was in fact an artist in all things, including that, although some of the things Boday came up with were more bizarre than anything Sam had imagined. She simply gave up and gave in, partly out of guilt over Charley and partly because she just needed *somebody*. She was getting to be fairly experienced in sex, though, and she still had never had a man and had no idea what it was like. She wondered if she might be gay, but she reserved judgment until the opportunity arose, if ever, to find out if she was or not. She certainly hadn't met very many sexy or attractive men so far.

Watching Boday work was also fascinating. The range of miracles that she could either lay her hands on or concoct in her lab seemed beyond belief, but it wasn't hard after a while to understand how she could make hair grow and change color and even self-streak in a matter of hours, or create an environment where the very bone structure could be expertly manipulated and altered—such as she'd done in altering Charley's overbite to make it sexy rather than intrusive.

Sam had instructed Boday specifically to do nothing more to Charley that was irreversible. That is, that couldn't be undone and Charley brought back to her normal old self. Boday noted that all of the commercially available formulas had absolute antidotes; it was only her special blends that conferred permanency by altering the standard formulas. Thus Sam watched, fascinated, as Boday did to Charley exactly what Sam had gone to so much trouble to prevent, only this time with antidotes available. The result was the same, of course: failing those antidotes, Charley would remain Boday's remade creation.

First was the potion that wiped out all memory, anxiety, inhibition, and fear. She became a wide-eyed, staring, baby-like blank, but she was eager to learn and all that she was taught she grasped quickly. Boday began by teaching her the Short Speech, which was actually a soft and very primitive subset of Akhbreed with certain clever alterations and a lack of any tonalities or subtleties. More interesting, it had only the present tense and mostly second person at that, so that one who thought only in it would have an ego that was always the reflection of another. Charley learned what she was taught while under the potion's influence, but exhibited no curiosity to learn any more than she was given. Without a conscious, repetitive effort to teach, she simply did not learn at all no matter how obvious something was.

By the end of three long days it seemed impossible to Sam that Charley would ever become more than a wooden, childlike puppet. Sam couldn't stand it much anymore, and, following Boday's leads and contacts and with Boday's money, she spent some time exploring the city and ultimately finding an apartment in one of the tall downtown towers with a fine view of the palace, Government House, Royal Gardens, and the rest. As a male, she had considerable freedom to roam and see what the place really looked like, and it was impressive.

There were shops, large stores, bazaars, you name it, there, including many specializing in things from the sectors, the "nonhuman" regions of Akahlar. Many were practical items, some were particular kinds of clothing and materials, perfumes, luxury items of all kinds. The shopping district was divided into single product neighborhoods where everyone sold much the same thing in hot competition. Sam bought a great deal of material at Boday's request to form Charley's outfits, and also discovered that there was a whole industry devoted to very sexy and risque women's fashions—"for home and husband," of course. There was even a small street selling magical things—amulets, charms, potions, you name it. Some magicians advertised that they could weave practical spells "for business and industry alike," or so the pitchmen proclaimed.

Remembering the jewel's caution about the illusion and magical powers, she had shopped for and bought several comfortable but concealing male outfits before venturing onto *that* street.

By now she was known to the watchmen as "Boday's new sex interest" and had no problems going in or out, even with bundles, although she discovered that men do not help other men who are overburdened with packages like they help women. Men, in fact, treated each other far differently than they had treated her even back home, and she also found by discussions with the guards that men's talk covered a very different range than the sort when women got together, most of it very boring and of no interest to the listener.

Charley had still been mostly a dull-eyed automaton by the end of the third day, so it was a shock to see her near dark at the end of the fourth day. She stood there in the studio, a vision of ethereal beauty, dressed in a flowing blue dress of wispy material that showed her entire perfect body through the gauze. She seemed alive—full of life, and almost supernaturally gorgeous, the eyes lively and attentive, all of the moves so damned sexy it was turning Sam on just to watch her.

Charley gave Sam a sexy smile and bowed slightly, hands in the prayer position. "We greet you, our lord," she said in a soft, seductive whisper. "How may Shari serve?"

Sam dropped the whole bundle of stuff and then heard Boday's joyous cackle. "Darling!" she cried and ran to Sam, hugging and kissing her and picking her up almost off the floor. "Isn't she *wonderful?* Isn't she just simply *marvelous?* Boday knew she would be good but even she had no idea how simply *stunning* it would turn out! Tomorrow she will learn the technical fine points and then she will be ready! Boday took the liberty of giving a decorator her sketches, so the day after tomorrow we can be in *business!*"

Sam just stared at Charley, all sorts of thoughts and emotions jumbled up together inside her, many in conflict with each other. One, however, was very personal and more than a little jealous. *That's my body she did that with!* I *could look like that!*

Still, another part, from the guilt corner, snuck in and snapped her back a bit. She was both fascinated and awed by the process, but there was still a strong part of her deep down that made her feel like a common pimp and degrader of women.

"You're gonna keep her like that? So she don't even remember she's Charley?"

"Oh, darling, but of course! Any other way would be a *crime,* not only because it would of necessity spoil the creation but also because it would not be a mercy to *her.* Right now, she will do what she must do willingly, with no guilt, no regrets, no afterthoughts, no reservations. All of her day will be spent preparing for her evenings, and she will get better as she goes along. The more clients, the more perfect she will become, and single-mindedly, to the exclusion of everything else. Look at her now—she barely exists. She exists only through interacting with another. She exists to give pleasure, whatever is required. We will move her in and complete the training there—a few days at best. Then we will look for art lovers."

Sam was feeling pretty queasy about all this, even though Charley had asked for it and she'd argued against it. "You're sure it can be reversed? That we can bring her mind back?"

"But, of course! Do not worry, Boday's sweet flower! Did you not command it? Did we not discuss it with her? It is arranged. In a month it wears off and she will remember everything. Then she decides. To take the potion some more or to come running back here. Every month after she will decide again. It is a pity if she ruins it, though. She is so *perfect.* Well, no matter what, Boday owes you even more for kicking her into this. Never before has she also designed the *setting* as well as the jewel. It is a new challenge!"

Sam just stared at Charley and licked her lips. *And will you be sickened when it wears off?* she wondered. *And will you hate me and yourself for it?*

With the year-long apartment lease, the decorating, the clothes for Charley and for Sam, and the supplies, they'd blown all of Boday's two thousand, and most of the change purse as well. If this unpleasant idea did not make money, they were in a hell of a fix. Charley, damn it all, had to start earning their keep.

8

Of Decadence, Demons, and Brassieres

The problem with decadence is that it is based on decay.

The last of the money went to set up a payment mechanism that would distance both Sam and Boday from Charley just in case anybody in the district thought to check on the new competition, and to arrange for various supplies and services—Charley might well be expected to cook for clients (Boday had taught her three meals which she did exceptionally well), which meant food and beverage had to be provided and there would be the laundry and cleaning bill. The services were easy to arrange but they could only scrape up enough to prepay ten days' worth. If more money wasn't coming in by then, it would be all for nothing.

Boday did manage to use her contacts to start the ball rolling, but there were only three customers the first week, then five the second. As word of mouth spread, though, and Charley gained practice, things picked up. Still, most of the income was plowed back into the services, leaving tittle for Sam and Boday. Neither of them had any real business sense. and they had underestimated the start-up costs of even this sort of business and with all the intermediaries doing the work it left them broke and with nothing at all to do for a solid month. Not that they starved, but they wound up buying food that was cheap and easily spiced to disguise its cheapness and they ate a lot of fat and starch.

Sam literally had nothing to do and no place to go. The city offered plenty of diversions but almost none of it was free and Boday was rather limited in the circles she could travel in. With no TV, no radio, no money to go out, no reading material she could read, Sam found herself basically trapped in the loft with Boday who similarly had nothing to do, since Sam, honoring Charley's wishes, had forbade the artist to take any more live commissions and Boday wasn't much interested in the old forms which she dismissed as "dull" and "passé." Not that Boday minded; anything she did was fine so long as it was near Sam. That potion was potent.

By the end of a week Sam was willing to do most anything for a diversion, if only to keep from thinking of Charley over there in that apartment, and Boday had an almost infinite mind for diversions. Sam resisted, though, figuring that if Charley could make this kind of sacrifice she owed it to tough it out for a month after which she was convinced that Charley would be coming back. That left baking and eating the sweet breads and confections that were the easiest to make from their limited grocery budget, and, eventually, letting Boday play out her perversities, which seemed infinite. Boday, after all, was a master teacher of courtesans—and consorts, too—and she knew *everything*. At first Sam was nervous, then repelled, but eventually she found herself drawn to it by sheer boredom and Boday's persistence.

And, after a while, Sam just didn't have reservations anymore.

It was Boday who'd taken the love potion, but that did nothing to dim her dominant personality or to change any of her ways. In the hands of a love object who was equally strong she could have been curbed, restrained, even radically changed, but in this case her love object was a confused, lost, lonely, bored seventeen-year-old girl with little experience and waning self-confidence while the potion-obsessed lover was strong, domineering, experienced in many ways, including the manipulation of others. It wasn't like the fairy tales where the taker of the potion became the submissive love-slave of another; in this case, the tables were turned as the single-minded lover more and more dominated the object of that artificial love.

It wasn't quick; it was a slow, bit by bit breakdown of Sam's old morality, her self-image, her attitudes and behavior. Charley could have stopped it, but when the month passed and the runner informed them that the little vial had been accepted and later picked up empty and that Charley was still there and still the same, it all crumbled. Sam had hoped at least that Charley would have sent word before taking the potion again, that they could have seen each other, talked. When that didn't happen, and she faced months of unremitting boredom in the loft with Boday, all resistance crumbled. She even gave in to Boday's pleas and allowed the artistic alchemist to begin doing commissions again, even eventually helping out.

But now the money rolled in. Boday was delighted to get an accounting, and drew some of it for fine food and new fashions and a bit of celebration. Their standard of living improved and they even went out a bit, although Boday was clever enough to understand that Sam was best kept on a tight leash, with bright little magical toys a nice reward and diversion, and new clothes for both in the loft and outside for Sam, who no longer even cared what she looked like or how much she ate. At the start she'd tried some diversions like asking Boday to teach her to read the Akhbreed language, but after only a couple of weeks she'd given up. It was like ancient Chinese—almost a character for every word in the rich and colorful language—and she'd never been much good at memorizing anything. She tried art and sculpture but she was awful and she knew it and again quickly lost heart, and any attempt to figure out more than the bottom line basics of alchemy just made her dizzy. She finally simply gave up, and it was the last crushing blow to her ego.

With one day looking much like another and one week looking much like another, Sam lost track of time completely. There was supposed to be an end to it, but the end never seemed to come, one day looking exactly like the next. Boday, quite satisfied, was arranging things, and Sam, so that such an ending might never come and this could go on indefinitely.

Only the nightmares and visions remained uncontrolled. They were infrequent and came at odd times, but they were particularly virulent during times of storms on the waterfront. Twice more she saw the horror of the changewind in remote places far different from Tubikosa, and many more times she was back with the Horned One again, this time watching dark armies grow secretly composed of hordes of mostly nonhuman creatures, some of which were horrible indeed just to look upon. They were secretive, training in small groups all over Akahlar, but for what she did not know.

But every time she had such dreams Boday would be there, soothing, calming, often with a dram of elixir that induced sweet dreams without thought.

It was late one night when Sam awoke and struggled sleepily into the bathroom. She was having a very bad period, with the worst cramps and heaviest flow she could remember, in spite of Boday's potions that were supposed to keep it from noticeably happening. She made her way to the sink and turned on the small light, then looked at herself in the mirror as something twinkling caught her eye.

It was the Jewel of Omak, and it was shining. It was such a startling, unexpected thing that she frowned and stared at its reflection—and was caught by its beam. Suddenly she was immobile, unable to move or react, and the magic jewel spoke to her mind.

You are now pursuing a course contrary to the interests of Boolean as well as yourself, the jewel told her. *As per my instructions in this eventuality, I must take independent rectification actions. Henceforth you will see yourself clearly as you have made yourself. Henceforth, the drug action will be negated. I will take the appropriate biochemical measures to insure that this brings clear thinking and not suicidal depression but you will not like yourself. What you do for your own appearance and self is not my concern, but I will now intervene. You now have the means. You have had the means for some time. You will proceed to carry out Boolean's wishes. The trip to the university is optional, but you will no longer be permitted to act in a manner not calculated to bring you eventually to Boolean's presence. If you do not do this then I will take command. Boolean requires only your body, not your soul. Protection of the body and its delivery to Boolean alive is the only directive. Demonstration.*

She suddenly felt as if she were falling down a deep well, swirling around in the water, falling, falling. . . .

And then she saw again, but not as she had ever seen before. The image was low, somehow, and it was two-dimensional, slightly distorted, with the middle of things seeming close up and then everything else going away in the distance on both sides. It was a washed-out, strange-looking, ugly vision of herself in the mirror, but she could still see her face, distorted by the contorted lens, if she looked up. It was all she could do. She felt disembodied, a mind without a body, only a single, imperfect eye. There was no pain, no pleasure, no sensation at all.

"Now you see," said a strange, horrible, lifeless voice from her own lips. "My energy comes from the soul and the spirit of the bearer. I do not take much; you never miss it, but it bonds us together. The jewel and the bearer are one."

There was a dizzying sensation as her body turned and the single image whirled for a moment before stabilizing, although it was a bit shaky an image. Now they were in the apartment, now the lab. She turned and walked up to the three-way mirror and her entire body was reflected back to her.

Seeing herself clearly and objectively for the first time in a long while was a shock. Not that she didn't know; until now, it somehow hadn't been something she cared about. Her hair had grown back in well; it was still short but it was now substantial and more or less at an asexual length for this culture. Still, it seemed a lot longer than it should have considering how long it took hair to grow out.

But, lord! Was she *fat!* She hadn't really looked in this mirror in a very long time. Mostly, she hadn't wanted to. Her grossly fat-swollen breasts hung down over a massive beer belly; her arms and legs were very thick, and she had an ass the size of Chicago. Her face, too, showed the weight, and she didn't have to look down much to show a double chin. And this had started with the same body that had created Charley.

It was as if everything within her that was pretty and gentle and nice had gone with Charley, leaving her with the grotesque remains.

"See what you have made of yourself," her body said in that same inhuman whisper. "The same body that your friend has kept beauteous beyond compare. The same body that made three-meter jumps to sneak in here that night and was agile and strong enough to climb drains and move silently across a sloped roof. You are the same one hundred and fifty-seven centimeters, but you weigh one hundred and eleven kilograms. This body grows weary climbing the stairs."

The figures were a shock. *One hundred and eleven kilograms—let's see, each was two point two pounds. . . . My God! I weigh over two hundred and forty pounds and I'm just five-two!*

"No, I weigh that. You weigh under four hundred grams," said her body.

I—I'm in the Jewel of Omak! she suddenly realized. *I'm in the jewel, and whatever thing that dwelled here is now in my body!*

"Yes, quite correct," responded the image. "You thought of me as a computer, which was all right, so long as everything went well. I influenced you and your friends as needed to accomplish the primary mission. I am no computer, Samantha Buell. That is of your world, not of mine or my master's. I am what you would call a demon."

Oh, God! A demon! Visions of Hell and creatures with horns appeared in her mind from her old upbringing. *What have I done? Have I lost my soul?* Suddenly she felt anger. *You! You convinced Charley to do what she did—because it was the only way to get the money!*

"She might have done it anyway. She was inclined that way. I think you know your friend less well than you think. I merely made it easier for her to decide. Just as I used what little strength I had for your charge at Boday, so it would strike perfectly to knock her down. Just as I put the idea in your head for the love potion, since we needed an ally. Just as I put how to do it in Boday's mind. I did not mind your lapse into decadence so long as there was nothing else to do, so long as resources were building up. I fear we demons have rather a taste for decadence. But I am bound to enforce my master's will. That is why I am in the jewel and he is sitting comfortably in Masalur. I do not even particularly like him, but greater power always commands lesser power in all things. I am a lesser power to him and so must obey. You are a lesser power to me. Just as I find being in a human body but with such restrictions repugnant—but if I must possess you, then I must. But I would rather we had an understanding."

You—you have been controlling all of this?

"Naturally, up to a point. Did you think under the circumstances that you could have even survived unaided here for long? I made certain that, when he discussed betraying you, Zenchur spoke Akhbreed, to warn you. When you proved too immature and nervous to act or even plan a course of action, I waited. Do you really believe that one of Zenchur's experience would use the jewel while facing a mirror unless he somehow was prevented from considering that possibility? Do you think you would have had the presence of mind to duck?"

But you let him betray Charley and kidnap her! You could have stopped it!

"Yes, but I have no interest or instructions on Charley. She was not anticipated. Zenchur was a sincere hope, and so long as he did not betray *you* there was no reason to act. When he did, I intervened. Now I must intervene again. Do you like your body now?"

You know I don't! I'm huge! Ugly!

"The outside merely manifests the inside. You have let Boday take over and dominate your mind. You have become complacent with perversity, you have lost your sense of self and purpose. You have betrayed your friend who sacrificed for you. You did not lose your soul. You gave it away."

It was Boday!

"Boday can do nothing that you do not allow her to do. This time could have been put to productive use. You started to do so, but you did not really want to, and at the first sign that learning was work or the first mistake in learning you seized as an excuse to give it up. It was incomprehensible to me that one who would risk everything and sacrifice all to save a friend would have so little sense of self-worth. Your friend was willing to voluntarily lie and be servile to a hundred men or more because she understood that it was the only way to her own goal, to reach Boolean, to get out. To attain something worth attaining, one must sacrifice, do whatever is necessary. She understands that. But you! You never had any goals. You never really succeeded in anything. Charley was the only backbone you ever had, and you used her and wound up dragging her here. Without her, you switched to Boday. Only one thing keeps me from taking complete command, imprisoning you in that bauble and remaining here, possessing your body. Just once, in your whole life, did you have a real goal that did not concern yourself. Just once, you put aside all thoughts of self and risked everything for someone else. I provided the physical stamina and the knowledge and skills needed, but it was your will that used it. I did not send you to save Charley from Boday. That is not my affair. I provided the resources, but you provided the will."

Sam felt very ashamed of herself right then and there. She wanted to cry, but jewels don't cry, or feel any sensations at all. *What would you have me do?* she asked the demon.

"The object was to gain the financial resources to undertake the journey and perhaps acquire some of the skills needed. You have it. In spite of Boday's lavish attempts at spending it down. How long do you think it has been since you abandoned your friend?"

Total confusion. *I—I don't know. Four or five months, I guess. I suppose the way you talk it's a year.*

"It *has* been a year. *Exactly a year today.* Boday in fact is in the process of renewing the lease and taking more rooms for more girls. *You* may not be able to read those papers, but I can read Boday. She has plans to make this permanent. She is the one whose elixirs kept you pleasant but which also induce a massive appetite for sweets. At this weight you will take no other lovers, nor have much energy for ambition. You sleep half the time and the rest you lie around eating and doing whatever she desires. You do not vegetate, you have become a vegetable. You have not left this loft in five weeks, partly because, deep down, you do not want others to see you this way. Boday prepares now for her final coup. She is signing the final papers and leasing a grandiose suite near the Palace into which she will move Charley and the last two girls she did here, which were procured for her use, not as commissions. She is confident now. Then your friend's position will be made—permanent. *She* will teach the others and all the ones who come after her. Soon there will be so much money and power she will be able to eliminate Kligos and the rest."

No! She can't! I wouldn't permit it! I told her about Charley!

"Indeed, you have been very naive. What do you think a love potion does? It directs all of the emotional needs, primitive lusts, whatever, toward a single individual. You fall madly in love with that person—but nothing else changes unless that person changes *her*. You, instead, have given her a free hand. She is protecting you, even from yourself. Do not lovers lie to one another? Do not lovers do something against the other's wishes for what they really believe is the good of the other? That is why I must step in. She must not be allowed to do this thing. This must end now. Either you must end it, or I will. The enemy gathers strength. It builds in secret now, so as not to frighten and unite the Kings of Akahlar, but it builds. When it is strong enough it will move, and millions will suffer, and the fate of all worlds will be decided. You are a player in this matter no matter if you wish to be or not. Many of the soldiers and victims in wars are unwilling and even uncomprehending or uncaring, but they still fight and suffer and die. You are a chess piece in this game. Whether pawn or queen I do not know, but you are none the less important, for even a pawn may capture a king."

I will handle it! I will stop it! I swear to you! I'll kill that bitch!

"No. If you handle it, if you stop it and redirect it, it must be with thought, not emotion. How will you bring Charley back without Boday? How will you access the funds and find the personnel needed and chart the course? She is corrupt. Use her, and prevent her from using you." The demon sighed. "I sense you need some incentives of your own to match your friend's. If you do not act now, your friend is lost. That is the first incentive. Once you recover her you must not be turned again from the objective." Her own brown eyes surveyed her body in the mirror.

"It is fitting, even useful," the demon said, mostly to itself. "The male illusion was for the purposes of disguise but it would not have held up on the trail in any event. It has taken some of my intervention to hold *this* long. But no one, absolutely no one, would recognize you now. I give you back your body, until such time as you give me cause to seize it again. But I also give you my curse. I cannot in any way alter your true body and part of my charge is to prevent that from happening, but *this is* your body, and so it will stay, regardless of spell or potion or three weeks in the wastes without food. If need be the fat will be useful in an emergency to convert to muscle, say, but it will return when not needed. This is the way you will see Akahlar, and this is the way Akahlar will see you. A perfect disguise without illusion. Oh, I will give you strength when needed and undo some of the effects on your mind that keep it dull and sleepy, but this is the way you will look—until you stand face to face with Boolean. And you can look at Charley and think of what might yet be, but only if that meeting comes."

No! she cried from her prison. "Wait!" she finished aloud, in the body. She was back, staring at her reflection in full command of it all, her mind clear. She hated that reflection. She felt the weight, the pressure on her back and ankles. Those huge, sagging, floppy breasts hanging down to a stomach that looked nine months pregnant and wasn't, and a lower body that seemed all rear end. My God, she looked old, too. A lot older. Still, her mind was clear and the body obeyed. She wasn't gonna be running any races but she felt new strength inside her.

Still, she looked—*gross.* In more ways than one. It would *take* a love potion for anybody to love *this* body. But the demon was correct—she hardly recognized herself. And yet, the demon had been absolutely right. She *deserved* this. Without that damned demon it would have all gone on as scheduled, irreversibly. She was ungainly, obese, ugly—she would have to earn redemption.

She walked to the door of the studio and looked out. Dawn looked to be just breaking. There wasn't a lot of time, and whatever was to be done had to be done quickly. First Boday had to be stopped and brought to heel. Charley had to be sprung, everything then redirected to the journey. This was no time for a test of wills with Boday, although that would surely come.

She fingered the jewel. "All right, demon," she said, "let's put your powers to emergency use." She walked into the bedroom where Boday was sleeping, stood beside the bed, and took the jewel in one hand, aiming its growing light at Boday's head. It struck, and there was that sudden slight stiffening, but Boday was still asleep.

"Boday, can you hear me?"

"Yes, darling! Boday hears," came the sleepy reply.

"Is it true? Were you going to give the permanent potion to Charley and set up your own business? Answer me!"

"Yes, darling."

"Why?"

"Because Boday lives only for you and fears only that you will desert her. This way you will never leave Boday. This way Boday can have you to herself forever."

"No, Boday. If you did that I would never forgive you. I would leave. I would kill myself rather than live with that. I wish you would believe that."

Done.

Boday's eyes opened. "But she has already *done* it!" she, exclaimed, sounding horrified. "Boday sent the potion over today so that she would be ready for the move."

"What! Oh, my God! Demon, your clock's off, damn it all!

Boday—get up! Put on some clothes that will get you to Charley's place and then wait for me." She turned on the lights and searched through the drawers. Damn! Would *nothing* fit any more? She found some stretch tights that threatened to strangle her lower half or fall down but they had to do. The top was a joke, barely reaching her navel, but the hell with it. Boday had several wraparound capes that might help. Fitted properly they barely covered her back and went down to the floor, but turned sideways and pinned, a black cape made a sort of poncho. It would do. With some difficulty she managed to pull on a pair of the short, soft leather boots, but they pinched like hell. The hell with it!

Boday pulled on a robe with hood and her long leather high-heeled boots. She put up the hood, which covered her head as per regulations and also shaded her face.

"Get some money!" Sam snapped at her. "Then get me to Charley as fast as possible at this time of the morning!"

Dawn was just breaking, but there was always some business in the District. Boday spotted and hailed down one of the horse-drawn three-wheeled cabs and they got in. "Sikobo Royal Tower." Boday ordered, "and quickly!"

The driver was used to picking up strange-looking people here and taking them at top speed back to higher neighborhoods. They also usually tipped real well. He made damned good time, but Sam used it for questions she didn't like the answers to.

"When did you send it over?"

"In the morning. When Boday went to the market."

"Then she's had it most of a day. Did she have any clients today?"

"No. There are never clients on potion day, and none tomorrow, either."

"Then we might be in time. She might not have decided to take it yet."

"No, darling," Boday sighed. "We are too late. In the past she has always had a day to think it over, but the potion she had last time is not due to wear off until next week. She was still Shari, and the bottle had Boday's seal on it and the messenger was told to tell her in Short Speech that her mistress wanted her to take it. Boday did not want her to choose this time. The new set-up would already be in place and she might balk. She took it. There is only 'now' to such as her. She would obey immediately."

"Damn it! *Nothing* is a hundred percent permanent except death. You made the stuff. Somehow you can make a way to undo it!"

"Darling, there is not. The brain is like Boday's file cabinet. The top drawer is Charley. The next drawer is Shari. The soul is the person going to the cabinet. With no potion she can go to either one with ease. With the regular potion she is able only to open the Shari drawer, but the other drawer is still there. With *this* potion all of the files in the Charley drawer are taken out and burned. Erased. They are no longer there. Only Shari remains. She will remember every bit of being Shari from waking up blank, so to speak, in the studio, but nothing else, not even the in-betweens."

"If that's true I'll kill you."

"Boday will willingly die for you at your command."

And that was the trouble, damn it! There was no satisfaction in this. No satisfaction at all. There was absolutely no way Boday could be punished, not really.

There was a doorman at the Towers, but Boday knew the password. He looked at Sam with gruff disapproval but he let them in. There were two elevators of sorts, but they were of a very odd type, with no doors. They ran all the time, very slowly, and you just waited, stepped on when a floor presented itself, and rode it up until you stepped out fairly quickly onto your floor of choice.

Boday jumped off and Sam followed, falling slightly and hearing a nasty tearing sound. The tights collapsed around her thighs, but she didn't care any more. It was the second door on the right. No key would be needed—the door was always open for the service people.

"How long does it take to work completely?" Sam asked Boday.

"You skip into a beautiful, dreamy sleep for twelve hours, darling. Then the new you wakes up."

It *was* a gorgeous apartment and quite luxurious. Each room was different but all was styled to match Charley's own features and design. They passed through the living room, dining room. Sam stopped at the entrance to the small kitchen, reached in, and picked up a bottle next to the sink. A little gold bottle with Boday's seal—and it was opened and empty! She threw it against the wall and rushed back to the bedroom, which was dominated by an overlarge heart-shaped bed.

Charley lay asleep on the silk sheets, naked, and Sam was struck once again by how absolutely beautiful she was. Even her sleeping position, and the expression on her sleeping face, was sensual and erotic.

"Charley! Wake up!" Sam shouted. The sleeper shifted slightly but did not respond. Sam turned to Boday. "Wake her up!"

Boday threw back her hood and knelt before the sleeping figure. "Shari. Shari, love. Awake. Thy mistress commands."

Charley frowned, moaned a bit, then opened those big eyes and saw Boday. She smiled. "Shari greets thee, Mistress," she said sweetly if a bit sleepily, and sat up on the bed.

"Oh, my God! We're too late!" Sam cried and started sobbing uncontrollably. Charley looked at this stranger and her eyes widened a bit at the sight, but she remained passive and blank. "Mistress want Shari give comfort?" she asked innocently.

But Boday was still hypnotized by the jewel and couldn't respond to anyone but Sam. "Oh, God! I'm sorry, Charley!" Sam sobbed in English. "Everything I do turns out wrong! All I do is hurt people! I'm not fit to live!"

Charley looked at the stranger and frowned. "Jesus Christ. Sam! Is that *you?*" she exclaimed in perfectly understandable English.

"Yeah, it's me," Sam sobbed. "Big and fat and—*what did you just say?*"

"It *is* you! Jeez! I didn't recognize you! How the hell did you get to look like *that?*"

Sam was in shock. "But—but—you're talkin' normal plain English! You sound like yourself! The potion—it was there! It was empty! I—"

Charley yawned. "Sam, if I'd known it was you I wouldn't have put on Shari. What's the big deal about the potion?"

Still shaking and sobbing, Sam managed to tell her the story.

"Shit! Good thing things turned out the way they did, then." She looked at Boday. "She's hypnotized, huh? Well, leave her. Come on up on the bed and get hold of yourself. Jeez! I been wondering if you'd *ever* show up!"

It took some time for Sam to get a grip on herself, and when she did it was true confession time. She told Charley everything—all of it, right down to the demon and the curse. Charley just nodded and shook her head. *God! She was beautiful!*

"Sam, you can't completely blame yourself. You can't. Damn it, you just weren't prepared to grow up so quick." She sighed. "I guess I was."

"But the potion—how did you . . . ?"

"Sam, I didn't trust her from the start, but I knew it had to be done. I figured she was too loopy yet to pull anything, so I went along with all that back in the loft. But when it wore off, I sat there and I thought about it. I thought real hard about the life I lived for those first weeks. Then this nice girl, maybe all of fourteen, dressed all in white, you know, with the mask and all. came by and delivered the little jar of potion, I looked at it and then I came back here and I lay down right here and I went over every single day of 'Shari's' life and every one of the clients. It was easy to do—there isn't a whole lot there, you know, in memories, but there's more otherwise than you think. A lot more. My first impulse was to send the bottle back when the cleaning people showed up, which would be the signal to come pick me up, but I couldn't bring myself to do that. Then I opened it and looked at it and knew I couldn't bring myself to take it, either. I left it there in front of me and thought some more."

"Why didn't you just get out of here?"

She sighed. "Sam—that was the thing. I didn't *want* to go back there. I—this may be hard to understand—didn't want to give this life up. I'm sure it wasn't any of Boday's tricks. I *liked* being Shari. I used to lie in bed some nights and fantasize about this. Being beautiful, glamorous, sexy. So beautiful that men would pay a fortune for just my company. It was more of an Arabian Nights meet Las Vegas kind of fantasy, but this was it."

"But all those *men* . . ."

She smiled. "Yeah. I always figured if I ever did wind up like this I'd get the bottom of the barrel types—ugly, middle-aged, stinking breath and drooling, the whips and chains types. But they weren't like that. It was more like my fantasy. Some were middle-aged, sure, and some were younger, but they were mostly nice-looking men with good jobs from their looks and manner. Successful types with something missing in their lives. All of 'em probably had those forced blind marriages. Hell, some of 'em were so inept in bed you kind'a wonder they had *any* sex life before. Some wanted a few things—oral stuff, mostly—I guess they just couldn't get. A couple of the young ones, I think, wanted some experience before they got married so they wouldn't seem fools. More than one just wanted to be babied, or hold someone. It didn't go all the way every night. One guy just clung to me on the sofa out there and talked and talked and finally cried his eyes out. That's all he wanted. Didn't make no difference I couldn't understand but three words he said."

"Jeez! That's *weird!*"

"No, just a little sad. They had no place else to go, nobody to unload on, to get the tensions out. Oh, I'm not saying there weren't a couple with odd wants in sex, but I kind'a liked that, too. I sat here and I realized that I really liked the sex. But the main thing was I was doing something these guys needed and they were willing to pay top money for me. *Me!* I knew I should feel real guilty about it all, but I just didn't. I still don't. So, finally, I poured the potion down the sink and washed it away and decided I'd try it cold. I just wanted to see if I was really nuts."

"Yeah?"

"It was better. With a little practice I discovered I could shift to Shari, actually thinking in that language, and just tune out and go along for the ride. But it was easier with the whole me there. I could figure out the clients better, give them more of what they wanted and maybe some new things, too. In a way, I turned the tables just like Boday did with you. I was in control. I could handle the bad ones cleverly without pissing them off and I could give the good ones extra. And when I got off, I *really* got off! Weeks went by and I still wasn't tired of it. I'm still not. But it was kind'a dull on the off days and in the days. I wanted a way to get out, to be *completely* in control of my destiny, and I figured it out. It wasn't that hard. They paid the money to the account, right? I never saw that. But they also left tips—bigger tips after I stopped the damned potion, if you want to know. Every day the White Virgin would show to collect, but I knew she wasn't no unmarried virgin. In fact, I ain't even a hundred percent sure 'she' was a 'she,' and that gave me an idea. So I started holding out on the tips. Didn't take long to build up a nice little nest egg. I knew the golden ones were the sarkis and I could count."

She got up and walked to a closet, opened it, then went in. Sam followed, not quite over the shock yet and not knowing what to say.

In the closet, a walk-in type, were lots of sexy outfits all designed for Shari, but well in the back and hidden was another, which she revealed and brought out. It was a white robe, white hood, and face mask.

"I knew that my collector couldn't be real. No self-respecting girl of that status would be seen *near* the docks or the District. I didn't know much of the language, but it wasn't hard to get the message across with gestures. If she or he or whatever would get me an outfit like that and not tell Boday or anybody, I'd give her a small fortune. She didn't even wait til the next day. She had the outfit back that afternoon. The first day off I had I put it on and walked out and went down and walked around the block. It was a *wonderful* sense of freedom and total anonymity. I was a little worried at first that the bracelets on my arms would give me away or that somebody would notice the earrings under the hood but nobody ever said a thing. The hair was a bigger problem. I had to let it go down under the hood and then down so it was completely out of sight, but then I had troubles sitting down. You learn."

Sam listened, feeling more ashamed than ever that she'd allowed herself to, well, vegetate was the right term, while Charley was figuring.

"After maybe three months," Charley continued, "I had lots of money, freedom of movement, and with a lot of concentration I picked up enough of the language to make my wants known. I don't speak it, really, but I can understand a lot of what's said if I really concentrate. I always was good at languages and I didn't have much else to do. Reading's different—they have like *thousands* of characters—but I know the most common ones, like which is the ladies' room and 'store,' 'restaurant,' and stuff like that. I bought different foods to try, got a bunch of nice other things, and after I spotted a couple of the goons who'd mugged us staking out this building I bought a knife and a blow gun. The blow gun's neat. But they never came in. I figured, though, that was why you never looked in. I didn't *dream* you were having such a bad time. When the time passed and there was a tenth little bottle—I kept careful count—I figured the heat was still on or maybe expenses were high. I really didn't care. This was the best time I had since getting sucked into this place." She paused, and added, in a slightly more distant tone, "It's the best time overall I ever had in my life."

She looked at Sam and then kissed her gently on the cheek. "Poor Sam! Well, your demon's right. I kind'a think that neither one of us come close to the descriptions. You know, I wonder what Boday could do with you as you are?"

"Huh? Charley—look at me!"

"I know, I know. I don't mean body painting, and I don't mean me, but maybe she can make the best of a bad situation. We have a ways to go."

Sam stared at her. "Charlie—you just finished soundin' to me like you don't wanna go, don't wanna give this up."

"I don't," she admitted, "but you need me. You don't *know* what this has done for me, Sam. But, anyway, a girl can't operate independently in this society, and you need Boday. Don't hate her too much for this, Sam. She did it for you, but she also was kind'a being a secret revolutionary. Women would control all the vice in this town, top to bottom. That's power, Sam. And influence, if you know the names of the ones who use it most. Come on—get out of that ridiculous set of tatters and tell Boday to go to sleep in the corner, then get some rest yourself. Order her to wake us up if she wakes up first. Once we're rested we can find out how much we're worth and go from there."

Sam stripped, which wasn't hard and gave great relief, but she didn't just sit Boday in a corner. She used the jewel.

"Boday—I wish that you would be totally obedient to my needs and wishes," she said. "I also wish that from this point on you will be incapable of lying to me or to Charley, of doing anything concerning me or Charley without telling me first, and that you will obey any order that either of us gives to you. I wish that from now on your sole interest in me will be satisfying my desires, not anticipating them."

Done! said the demon, and there was a bit of satisfaction in its usual cold tone.

Boday was not exactly a changed woman when they awoke, and had no regrets, but now she wanted only to be cooperative and promised that she would never *think* of doing something like that again.

She had a perfect eye for figures, even bad ones, so they sent her out that afternoon to find out just how much money they had, to cancel her deals, and to buy some appropriate clothing for Sam while Charley cooked breakfast. Sam did more than clean her plate. In fact, she ate most everything that was left in the kitchen.

Charley watched, fascinated in spite of herself. "How much *do* you weigh, anyway?"

"The demon says about two forty-five. Don't say it. I'm a walking bowling ball with two huge fingers and I know it. I'm gonna eat compulsively and I got to live with it. At least I don't hav'ta worry 'bout my figure."

Charley smiled, but she knew it was killing Sam. It was the perfect demonic punishment. Sam would get to Boolean or die now: Her friend just hoped that the near perfection that would accompany that journey would inspire rather than breed envy and resentment.

Charley had a couple of saris she'd bought in case she had to make a run for it. They were kind of pretty but her eyes and jewelry would mark her, of course, as one of *those* kind of women. She didn't care anymore. Boday returned with a cotton robe with hood that fit loosely and a pair of sandals and a lot of material. "Darling—much more in your size Boday will have to make," she said apologetically. Shari's costumes and few personal belongings were packed in two black bags. The bags were there anyway; Shari, after all, had been set to move. Where they moved was back to Boday's loft.

The account information was not bad, less than great. Between fees and tips Charley had earned in the year more than thirty thousand sarkis, and Boday, with her "art" for others, had brought in another ten thousand and still had two of her creations. Charley didn't like it, but it was too late to do much for them. They would bring perhaps two thousand five hundred more. That was forty-two thousand, and Charley had held out about a thousand, of which she had something like five hundred now. Forty-two five in sounded good. But almost six thousand had gone for Charley's support services, and their initial money had covered only the first and last month on Charley's apartment, and there went another six thousand. The loft had been renewed for another two thousand. Another eight had gone for Sam and Boday's food, clothing, living expenses, Boday's materials, and close to five for a deposit and decorating on the new place. The cash on hand actually amounted to a bit under fourteen thousand two hundred sarkis.

"I can't believe it!" Sam exclaimed. "One whole fucking year and we're still *short?* Not just short—*way* short! Can't we at least get the deposit back on the new place? That'd add another two thousand."

Boday shook her head. "Sorry, darling. Once the decoration and furnishings were done there was no way out."

"I could always take the two girls in there and run them with me in the new place for a little while," Charley suggested. "If we ran seven days and all got booked we'd have it in another month. After a year, what's another month?"

Sam sighed. "Yeah, and so we take in eight grand and we spend three on expenses. That makes it two months. But in two months we owe two more grand in rent. Three months. My demon will have shit fits by then, and so will I."

More delay is unacceptable, the demon agreed. *Money or not, you have enough to start. I will give you thirty days to do so. Every day you are in Tubikosa beyond that you will gain another kilogram. With your height, weight, and frame, another thirty kilograms and you will be unable to walk or get up on your own.*

She was close to tears. "But, damn it, we don't have enough! Besides, it's counterproductive. What does it gain *you* if Boday has to pull me in a rickshaw or whatever if she could? Besides, I bet I eat fifty sarkis a day worth. That adds to the cost."

You eat whatever would otherwise be spoilage, but your weight will be maintained if you eat relatively normally. I will suppress hunger until necessary. You are giving up again. Giving up before you even try.

Sam tried to repeat the conversation but gave up and just broke down and sobbed. "I'm so *miserable!*" she cried. "I'd kill myself if they'd let me!"

Charley sat back and thought. Finally she said, "Look, we can probably scrounge up enough stuff by liquidating the new place's furnishings and what has value here. And we can't afford to be fussy about this navigator and these Pilots. We take what we can get for the money, that's all. Calm down and ask Boday what ways we can do this on the cheap."

The artist thought it over. "The old price was for our own navigator and secure Pilots. If we just sign on with someone else's trip and take it as far as it is going, then found another and so on, and were not fussy about the company or the accommodations, it would be much cheaper."

"I understood her," Charley said, quieting Sam's translation. "I'm getting pretty good at it. Can't speak it worth a damn, though, except some single words and the Short Speech. I just play mute and communicate real fine. Okay, that's a lot, and we got your demon jewel to help out, too. If it's the one in the all-fired hurry, it should be ready and willing to help pull the weight. So will we, wherever we can. And if we get stuck and broke real close to the goal line, then we can find some kind of work or other. Hell, Boday's an alchemist and you could stomp grapes if you had to, and as for me, I kind'a think that if we're in human territory my special skills are universal. Maybe old Boolean will get antsy and break his tails and come get us or send help if he really wants you, particularly if we get close and no cigar. Cheer up. We may still be on the wanted list but ain't nobody gonna finger us as the ones, and after this long they probably wrote us off."

Sam stared at her. "You make it sound so *easy*."

"No. It's gonna be hard and nasty and probably real unpleasant, but if it wasn't possible Boolean wouldn't'a stuck you with that demon. Too bad we can't afford to go to that university, though. I bet they could figure out a thing or two and tell us what all this is about, too. I figure I just been to graduate school. I think maybe I want to see a little bit of this world and what's out there."

Sam sighed. "You're not only beautiful, you got the guts I wish I had and the brains to use 'em. God, I feel miserable."

"Hey! I'm scared shitless by this. That apartment—that was *safe* after one hell of a series of scares nobody should have to go through. But I grew up a whole lot this past year and I know you can't keep hiding and feeling miserable for yourself all the time and do anything worthwhile." She looked at both of them. "Three women against a whole world. One fat broad, one lovesick painted loony, and one high-class call girl. It's the stuff of which legends are born. But, first things first. I looked at the material and at

Boday's sewing stuff and I got an idea that'll help you a whole lot. I think it's about time somebody in this shitty burg invented the bra."

Boday was actually thunderstruck by the design and the concept. She was built so she'd never need one, and Charley had been designed never to need one, but it wasn't just Sara who did. Charley managed the basic sketch and, with gestures, pretty much described the thing and how it worked. It took some help from Sam, but once Boday got the idea her designer's mind was off in a tear. The first few tries didn't really work—not stiff enough, not enough support stitching—but after a while she got it. It wasn't Playtex or Maidenform, but it worked, relieving a lot of back stress and balance difficulties and revealing inevitable irritating chafing under Sam's pair.

Boday worked like she, too, had a demon pushing her, and after she explained they didn't stop her.

"But, darlings, don't you see? This is *revolutionary!* Think of the market for this in large women in Tubikosa alone! Tomorrow Sam and Boday go back into the shopping district again. She needs more stuff anyway. Only she wears *this* and we take these design sketches and patterns. We show these to the wear-at-home bosses and bluff that we have applied for a Royal Patent. If we can find one run by a big-breasted woman we are home free. Even if it is a man, he will buy it—if only to make certain his competitors do not. Strictly cash."

Sam was open-mouthed at that. Finally she asked, "What could we get for it, do you think? Five hundred?"

Boday laughed. "Boday intends to ask for ten thousand and perhaps get argued down to five or six."

"But—these courtesans are only going for a thousand! You mean the idea for a *bra* is worth more than *human beings?*"

Boday smiled. "Girls are cheap and in good supply. Original ideas that fit a need are very rare. They will be robbing us blind at the price!"

"Wow!" said Charley. "I wonder what they'd pay for tampons?"

9
The Long Road to Boolean

Ideas turned out to be worth a fair amount at that. Because they insisted on cash or convertibles, they had to take a beating, but they still got more than five thousand sarkis for the bra idea even though it was hard bargaining and Sam for one didn't think anybody was really interested. They got a fair amount of material thrown in, including some nice, stiff, reinforced stuff and heavy-duty threads, and with that Boday, using her strange kind of manual sewing machine and with Charley's help, was able to come up with several pairs that would help Sam.

Sam had never paid a lot of attention to her clothes, even back home, but Charley, it appeared, was something of a would-be designer, although she had to defer in the end to Boday both to make proper patterns and to put them together correctly. The fact was, those super-long glamour nails made much that required manual dexterity not all that practical. That was okay, but it was hard to convince the artist to leave out her own outrageous embellishments.

What they came up with, over a period of a couple of weeks, was an ensemble of clothing not just for Sam but for them as well, since much of what could be gotten off the rack in Tubikosa was pretty dull stuff. The buyer of the bra idea even offered to loan them a couple of seamstresses at low cost and gave them some access to the small sewing sweatshop, an offer they accepted in spite of the fact that they knew the real motive of the generosity was probably to steal designs and ideas for nothing. That was all right with Charley; she thought this place could use a little flair.

They concentrated most on stretch fabrics that would protect but would breathe. The lack of the invention of the zipper hampered them somewhat, but since neither Sam nor Charley, when they thought about it, understood just how a zipper worked well enough to show how to make it, they forgot about it and concentrated on more solid fasteners. With this they were able to make Sam a series of fitted outfits that gave when she did but didn't pinch. Boday's talents were prodigious when doing a fitting; they had the look of one-piece outfits that exactly clung to the contours of the body. That was of little comfort to Sam, whose body definitely didn't need the clingy approach, but it was comfortable, it worked, and, somehow, dressed all in a black or brown outfit, it looked at least reasonable. Charley wasn't satisfied, though, and came up with the idea of a Mexican *serape*—basically a cape-like garment with a hole in the center through which you poked your head. The effect was about as good as you could do with Sam's figure.

Charley was delighted to find that there was an equivalent of jeans here, but, of course, it was men only. It was asking too much even for the seamstresses to come up with custom jeans, but she found some boys' pairs that she was able to have shaped and modified. Those, some tops made out of the same sort of clingy material they'd used for Sam only in brighter colors, and a couple of body suits of the same material for her and she felt she was ready for the trip, too. Nothing she made for herself left much to the imagination of an onlooker, though.

Boday went with her custom leather outfits and long capes. With those on her long, lanky, six-foot-two-inch frame and in the high-topped leather boots with the thick high heels she looked, well, imposing. Charley learned not to be too flip around her, though. When she remarked that all Boday needed was a leather whip, Boday produced one.

The busy whirl of getting ready to go helped Sam somewhat, but not completely. She was still depressed, particularly about herself, and she had such ambivalent feelings around Charley she felt pulled this way and that. On the one hand, she needed Charley badly to see her through all this. Her old friend's take-charge attitude and confident, sympathetic ways were essential. But Charley had changed. She was no longer the schoolgirl chum; she was suddenly wise, mature, very adult, very strong. Sam still felt very much a kid. Charley was beautiful and sexy without even having to work at it much. Sam felt ugly, clumsy, and she had to work at it constantly just to keep doing things. The fact that her looks and weight were not the result of any magic spells or evil potions but were largely self-inflicted didn't help matters a bit.

To top it all off, Charley was a whole lot smarter than she was. It hadn't been obvious when they were just pals together, but Sam had been working at high capacity and Charley had her brains in coast. Now she had learned a language, pretty much on her own, that even Zenchur had said you almost had to be born with to speak. That might have been true to speak it, but Charley rarely needed help in translations to understand what was being said now. The plain fact was she was *smart,* and no magic spell made her that way. Back in junior high, when Sam was trying to get into a special course she really wanted, one of the guidance counselors had looked at her record with her mom there and all and said, "I'm afraid that course load just might be too much for her. I know she reads all right and her grades are good, but she's at her maximum capacity now and it wouldn't be good to frustrate her when she's doing so well. Her IQ is a hundred and she's doing exceptional for all that where she is. Don't be upset—it's average, just not exceptional." And she'd looked it up and discovered that "average" was a hundred to a hundred and ten, so she was just *barely* average. And she'd just sorta quit after that, because what was the use of knocking yourself out when you were damned stupid? And what the hell did straight *B*s mean if it was in a class of stupid kids?

She didn't *feel* stupid, but maybe stupid people didn't feel stupid. So what was the use of trying? Mom was a lawyer and Dad was a contractor, but maybe she just didn't get the brain part. Charley had seemed a kindred spirit at a time when her folks had split and she'd moved. Hell, they'd liked the same things and really hit it off. But now she realized she never really knew Charley. Maybe Charley hadn't really known Charley, but she sure as hell wasn't "barely average."

She loved and needed Charley, but it was impossible not to hate somebody like that, too.

And she'd been afraid *Charley* would hate *her!*

At first, Sam was pretty self-conscious when going out. She wondered what the warehouse people would think when they saw a girl instead of the guy but nobody seemed to bat an eyelash. Sex changes weren't exactly the rule in Tubikosa, but these guys had been around the place so long they just weren't surprised by anything that came out of Boday's place.

On the street, even dressed in the conventional, "respectable" ways, she felt everybody would be staring at her, that they'd be thinking "Look at the tub of lard," but the fact was nobody gave her much notice and people she had to deal with treated her as a normal person. After a while the worries simply faded. It was true that no guys were whistling her way or putting the make on her but they never had before, either. Her self-consciousness vanished quickly and she felt much better. In fact, with that out of the way, it was a relief. No more play-acting; just be what you were and the hell with it. Somehow, some of the tension she'd lived under since running away to the mall seemed to vanish with that acceptance.

Arranging for transport was done through halls of the Royal Guilds, no matter what your class or status. Instead of trying to hire a navigator for a special trip, though, they looked over the list of trips to see who was going where. Even though Sam couldn't read the lists, she knew each squiggle beside a number squiggle was a trip and there were *hundreds.* Boday *could* read them but they didn't help much. Nobody was going all the way through to Masalur and most of the destinations meant little. Boday was a native of Tubikosa; her odd accent was mostly put on while she studied at the university and just stuck, and that trip had been her only one outside her homeland. Maps appeared useless on Akahlar; they had to see a Guild dispatcher.

It was decided that they wouldn't ask for a direct trip to Masalur; the odds were if Boolean were really dangerous to this enemy, whoever and whatever it was, they'd be specially interested in *anybody* out of the ordinary who booked to there. It made more sense to book to Covanti, the halfway point more or less, and then take stock from there. The university was out of the question; they were now reasonably flush but not that flush, and they had wasted too much time. The demon was uncharacteristically neutral on that, but Sam wanted this *over* with and the distance was still huge.

Although class and social rules meant nothing to navigators, who'd seen and done it all and disdained most local customs, Sam found it fascinating that even the dispatcher basically addressed *her* as the leader or spokeswoman. Perhaps it was because she was wearing one of those stock sack dresses and a scarf and had on no makeup or jewelry and thus she had to be the leader because she was "normal." If only they knew!

"I can't get you to Covanti directly for another six weeks," the dispatcher told her. "Tubikosa only does some seasonal business with them, and a minor flurry of changewinds have made the direct route too risky anyway." He showed them a map that showed the hemisphere with Tubikosa in the middle, but showed only the hubs in detail. The rest were blank, the hubs looking like the center of flowers surrounded by petals.

"Now, then," he went on, "the only reasonable route is southwest to Mashtopol, even though it's a little out of your way, then northwest to Quodac, then up to Covanti. I can get you to Quodac with no troubles, and I'm sure you can get something from the Guildhall there to get up to Covanti. That bypasses the unstable regions. You say it's three women traveling in a group?"

Sam nodded. "Just the three of us. But I don't like it. We're adding a lot of distance and extra expense that way."

"Well, I can get you a break on the Tubikosa to Quodac leg since it's related to poor conditions, but your supply budget and time will be greater. If you wanted to change navigators at Mashto-pol and were willing to have as much as a week's layover there, we have something going tomorrow. If you want it through to Quo-dac it'll be leaving sixteen days from today. Your share of the navi-gator's fees plus the Pilot's charges would be—thirty-five hundred sarkis for all three, plus supplies. That's to Quodac. You are advised that this particular route may be hazardous."

Buddy, you don't know what hazardous is, Sam thought sourly. "How long is it to Quodac?" she asked. "As opposed to direct to Covanti?"

"It varies," the dispatcher told her honestly. "but the average straight through, before the troubles, was fifty days direct, give or take a few and depending on local conditions. Now it's about sixty. Quodac should be about the same—closer to fifty than sixty, I'd say. Another thirty or so to Covanti depending on how long you would have to wait in Quodac for a trip. It's not great, but it is a safer route these days anyway. You get stuck in a sudden changew-ind and you wouldn't ever be able to come back to a hub."

It was a good enough argument. "All right, then. The one sixteen days from now is best, I guess. How do we work it?"

"You fill this out. If you cannot read I'll fill it out for you and take your mark. Then you pay me fifteen hundred cash now, with the balance due to the navigator directly when you start your trip. I'll give you a list of basic supplies you'll need to buy and your routing when you pay me."

She nodded. "This woman will pay you and fill out the form," she said, nodding to Boday, who took the paper and an inkwell-style pen and started in on it. Another of Sam's discoveries made her feel less inadequate about this. The damned written language was so complicated that very few people could read any old book, including Boday. You learned what you needed for your profession and for functional literacy. That was Charley's discovery as well. The practical vocabulary of most people in day to day life was at best a few thousand words; the rest were used only for more spe-cialized things. There were lots of people who never could manage much reading even in Akhbreed society, and deliberately so. Out-side of royalty, the better you read and the more you could read the higher you could rise. That meant that even the lowest might rise close to the top if they were smart enough. That was one reason women, even low in status, ran a lot of the stores.

Boday read the form to them. "Names, ages, sex—Boday always wants to write 'yes' in there—spouse, clan, and occupation. Nosy, aren't they? Well—Boday is easy enough. She is thirty-one, female, artist-alchemist, she has renounced her clan before they could renounce her—*peasants!*—and what is your real name, my love?"

"Samantha Rose Buell, but do we hav'ta put that? It's kind'a a giveaway of me bein' from someplace not usual."

Boday thought a moment. "Then why not Susama? An odd name but not a bad one. Boday has met someone of that name before and it will let you keep using 'Sam.' We will make you of the clan Pua'hoca. It's a big sector clan, so big the name is used if one does not wish to give a real one."

"Like Smith or Brown back home," Sam understood, nodding. "I once knew a guy really named John Smith and nobody ever believed it." Good. That gave her some legitimacy—if she could remember the damned name.

Charley looked over their shoulders. "Uh—I can't read this stuff, but the mark under 'spouse' is different for the two of you. What did you put?"

"Why, darling, Boday puts Susama as her spouse and Boday as Susama's. Her legal name would then be Boday Susama, and Sam would be Susama Boday."

"Hmmm . . . Won't that cause some problems or raise some eyebrows?"

"Not at all. Is the law of Akhbreed. If you cohabit in all ways with one partner only for a year and a day you are legally married under the law. In fact, we should register it."

Sam didn't like that. "What are you trying to pull now, Boday?"

"Boday is serious. You are a woman. Your age is eighteen. You do not wear the white nor live with family and you are listed as apprentice to Boday but you have no husband and there is no records on you except cohabiting with Boday. Marriage to a citizen is the only way to get travel documents unless you are *sent* someplace by authority as Boday was sent to university. You are obviously no courtesan. It is the easiest way out without getting into a lot of very fictional stories that might betray you."

"Yeah, but—in this straight a society, what will they say if you registered two women?"

"The law was designed for foreigners, but with an address in the District it will not be disallowed. And once we are on the trail it will not be questioned. Things are different out there. Trust me, darling! This happens more than they want to admit, particularly with men."

Sam looked at Charley, who shrugged. "I don't know. I keep feeling she's pulling something again, but she's also right. If they allow it, then you're suddenly a somebody instead of a nobody and that'll keep things even less suspicious."

This time Sam decided to take no chances. She turned away from the busy hall and pressed the jewel against her. "Demon, is what she says correct?"

She cannot lie to you. Yes. It is legal and the easiest way to get total legitimacy as if you were a native. It completes the disguise.

"I'm not gonna be stuck limited to just her by this, am I?"

Question interpreted and understood. If married people could not and did not cheat here there would be no District and no business for those like Charley.

It was a good enough point that she decided to do it. The hell with it. After the last year it was nothing more than the truth, and, considering her looks, it was Boday or nothing anyway.

For Charley they put down "Shari, 18, female, no clan, Beauteous Property under contract to Susama and Boday." There wasn't, after all, much way to hide what she was.

They paid the money and got the supply list. Boday read it over as they walked from the Guildhall to the Royal Ministry of Records. They got a lot of stares from the city crowd, with Charley getting the most from both sexes, but aside from treating them like they had leprosy the others gave them no problems. Sam was glad they were blowing this kind of place.

"Boday thinks we should get a wagon rather than horses and pack animals," the artist said. "You are not much good riding horses, you say, and this will be just as good. Besides, a decent one will provide some cover in bad weather. No sleeping out under the stars, either. The basic foods list is manageable and we can take more than that if we pay a bit for preservative spells. It is worth it—you never know what you might have to eat out there. Clothing—jackets. We will have to pick up some jackets. And perhaps hats and gloves. Tubikosa is always very warm but there are cold places out there. And Boday will take an alchemical kit. Not bad. Ah—here we are. Here we will register and then use the certificate to get the documents. 'Shari' is already registered, of course."

The marriage registrar looked more bored than shocked, although perhaps it was because of the looks of the women in there. "You swear that you have cohabited for a year and a day or more and that you have during that period been intimate with each other and with nobody else?"

"Yes," they both answered. Sam felt uncomfortable with this but she could see the practical reasons if they allowed it. This sure as hell wouldn't be allowed back home, but here it was actually a law!

"Dip all five fingers in this solution and then place them where I point on the document," the registrar instructed. The stuff tingled, and when Sam pressed her fingers on the paper there was a hot sensation. It made a nice embossed set of prints, though.

"You understand that this pairing is unorthodox and by registering it the Kingdom does not imply that it condones or approves such unions but that it allows this only to ratify an existing fact so that legal adjudication of disputes, property, powers of attorney, and so forth can be maintained in an orderly manner," said the registrar in a tone so routine and bored it sounded even more soulless than the demon.

"Yes," they both answered.

"Dip both palms completely in the solution and then place palm against the palm of the other," the registrar instructed. "If you have sworn falsely to this you will feel a painful shock at the end of this."

Some kind of truth stuff, Sam thought. They really wanted to make sure of this. Of course, it protected the pair, since if they'd cheated it would tell, but it also forced a somewhat embarrassing admission in public and on the record that indeed you had had sex with another woman. She and Boday pressed palms.

"Say aloud your given name and then the given name of the other," the registrar said. "Be exact, for from that point on that will be your only legal and true name."

"Susama Boday," she said, and Boday said, "Boday Susama." There was a sudden but not unpleasant shock and their palms were stuck together for a period. Sam felt a little dizzy and seemed to black out for a moment, then it was gone except for a slight headache. They let go, and the registrar stamped the document and then gave them a certified true copy.

They left and went out into the main hall. Sam was mad and Charley saw it. "Got you *again*?"

"I don't know. Damn it all. Oh, I don't *feel* much different, even about her, but—it's hard to explain. I'm *really* married to her. It's a spell or something. I can't shut her out, I can't really act without considering her. It's not sex. Nothing like that, although I can't deny her her rights in that. But, somehow, a tiny part of her is inside me and I guess the other way around. I could fool around all I wanted to but I couldn't be not married to her as long as she lives. I can't dump her, run away from her, or shut her out. And I'm Susama Boday. Everything inside me says that that's me. Damn it, demon! You said she wasn't pullin' nothin'!"

She wasn't. As I said, it was the easiest and best way. You need her to survive, to read, to protect. From my point of view it completes the disguise in an almost iron-clad manner so long as no one runs a skin or hair sample or something like that—and why would they? Even under truth potions and spells you will say that you are Susama Boday, legal consort of Boday Susama, and she the same. You cannot slip anymore. All you need is to take care to use English sparingly and you are beyond suspicion. She now has a tiny bit of your soul and you have a tiny bit of hers. Since it is your body, not your mind or soul that is required, this was a permissible deviation. You will never miss it, but it is vital. Even some magics will be fooled. Do not worry. I assured you that you could cheat, didn't I? And thanks to the potion, she won't.

She growled but said nothing. This damned demon was her master, and that was the most galling part of all.

The marriage document smoothed the way for her to get whatever legal documents she needed, though, just as promised. Boday showed her how her name was written in Akhbreed script and it wasn't all that complicated, but it saved a lot of time. The full documents would have to be picked up in ten day's time, the usual bureaucratic thing, but they issued her a citizenship and identity card. For the first time she could open or close an account, sign or make contracts, and have all the legal rights of a citizen. Socially and religiously, of course, she was an outcast, but legally she was a real person in this world. The most unsettling thing of all was the near reversal when clerks and others dealt with them. *She* became "Madame Boday" and Boday became "Madame Susama." Sam was still Sam, of course, but the trouble was she had no problems knowing which one they were speaking to, and it was aggravated by Boday's new use of "Madame Susama" to refer to herself—still in the third person, of course. That got to her and she blew her stack.

"Boday! You're still Boday and I'm still Sam, okay? Now cut out the Madame crap!"

And to her surprise Boday responded meekly, "Yes, Sam."

Sam thought long and hard about herself over the next few weeks, and about the other two as well. After all her fantasies and play-acting at being a man, here she had a chance to be legitimately butch and she found she didn't want it anymore. It hadn't been the fun of her fantasies at all. Maybe it was the spark of Boday inside her that got all the right things in balance, but she wanted to be all woman now. She shaved her arms and legs, took some time styling her hair, and applied a little perfume and makeup.

The link with Boday also gave her an odd sense of security and identity that somehow hadn't been there before. She no longer cared what other people thought; the vision in the mirror no longer repulsed her, it just *was* her. The reflection became her identity. She had no illusions that the shape with the monster tits and ass and the two spare tires was gonna knock 'em dead and drive men wild, but she didn't dwell on it anymore, either. It was sure as hell a body that *two* men wanted on this world, two big and powerful ones. And even some of her resentment of Charley faded as she stumbled into facts she simply hadn't considered. It had come out of a very simple situation.

"Hey—the bags and trunks for the trip are in," Sam said to Charley. Boday was off pricing other stuff and shutting down her interests, such as they were, and without her Sam was stuck with a splitting headache and no alchemical remedies. "I just can't make it now."

"You kidding?" Charley replied. "Sam, I can't go out alone. Not unless I pull my virgin trick and around here that's a sure way to get yourself snatched or arrested."

"Huh? Why not?"

Charley sighed. "Sam, *think.* Both you and Boday are full citizens of the master race here. You have rights and separate identities and can come and go as you please. Sam, I'm *property.* Legally I belong to you and Boday. Oh, they go through this contract business because they don't allow slavery, but that's just a sham. Legally and officially I have no rights at all. In fact, under this law I'm treated as if I were a baby, mentally incompetent to make any decisions for myself. It's illegal for me to own anything—even the dresses and stuff. It's illegal for me to have money, let alone spend it. It's even illegal to give me anything, or even to talk to me or me talk to them, without your permission. In fact, it's illegal for me to be out of my quarters unaccompanied by a responsible citizen who's either you, Boday, or somebody delegated by either of you. It's even illegal for me to use anything but the Short Speech, although in your company and outside the earshot of strangers they can't do much. My prints and documents are on file this way and have to go with me. Didn't you *know* that?"

"Uh—no, I didn't. Jeez, Charley—that's the pits. No *wonder* you didn't want to stay here."

"Well, it would just have been a matter of transferring my contract to somebody else, but I couldn't be on my own. In fact, if I fail to act within the law, even to the slightest degree, then the punishment must be a public whipping by my—contractors. You or Boday. A real one, too."

"Come on! I could never allow that!"

"Then if you couldn't you forfeit your contract and I'm either sold to the highest bidder around who has to do it or I must be put to death. I like being taken around to all these places but I got to be on my best Shari behavior. Didn't you even notice how I opened the doors and stuff like that?"

The truth was, Sam hadn't. "Charlie—the only way anybody'd know is if somebody told them, right? I mean, Boday has the eye makeup and more body painting than ten of you."

"And she has to show her citizen's card a lot, too, and she doesn't even look the part of a courtesan. I do. Boday also reads, writes, and speaks the language and I think she's a known character in this town. I'm not supposed to—and I don't. Oh, maybe I could get away with it once, but if I got caught the penalty is too much for the risk. I kind'a hope that once we blow this country the laws won't be all that strict but, face it. Those other places aren't our kind of people, and the Akhbreed system, I think, is pretty consistent in its basics. Oh, I understand there are some places where the girls are loose and high fashion and maybe even some where they run the place, but there are men of my status, too, remember. I think there's a certain—standardization—in the basic system no matter how different they are. I'm resigned to it. I envy you your freedom here but we have to take what we're dealt and make the best of it."

Sam looked at the stunningly beautiful woman who none the less was an alternate version of herself and couldn't believe it. "*You* envy *me?*"

It was inconceivable, yet, the more she thought about it, the more obvious what her friend said was true. Charley liked being a courtesan, it was true, but if Sam was as smart and pretty as Charley and had the kind of adventurous spirit Charley had and found that the price of being a courtesan was irretrievable slavery . . . Well, maybe. Damn, this was a lot more complicated than it looked.

All of the documents came through, and they went shopping for things on the list to take with them—other than food, of course. That would come last, as it must. Somehow neither Sam nor Charley had envisioned this trip as Wagon Train, but that's pretty much the way it looked. Oh, the wagon was oddly styled and had fancy suspension and a comfortable driver's seat, but it was still a covered wagon. It was not pulled by horses, either, but by odd-looking animals called *nargas,* which looked like a cross between a big mule and a humpless camel but tan and white striped like a zebra. They were strong if not swift, could survive on almost any known grasses alone, and if need be could go without water for up to ten days. They were tough, muscular bastards not native to any of the hubs but an import from one of the sectors, but they were highly recommended for wagon travel. They had long, skinny, snake-like tails with big tufts of tan hair at the ends that they carried looped up on top of their bodies most of the time—but you found that those tails were *very* prehensile and that a favorite narga sport was to swat you hard in the behind if you had your back turned to them. Apparently they thought it was funny.

The wagon was cleverly designed. You carried most of your stuff in compartments underneath, putting only what you needed every day inside. The area behind the seat was lined with a soft, thick material like a mattress, and another compartment came off the back end when stopped and turned into a kitchen-like area, although, of course, you had to build your fire on the ground away from the wagon. It had compartments for carrying water and two more for wine, and it also had a small box with a cut-out that was sort of a toilet, although it appeared that whatever you did in it just dropped down onto the road.

"More like an early American Winnebago," Charley commented.

They also bought a sleeping bag—it was as roomy as it could be but kind of cramped sleeping for three, although in really bad conditions it would do in a pinch—and some cold and foul-weather clothing, giving in to Charley's pleas in her case to buy her a fur jacket. It looked like mink and was pretty well styled, but if it was, then mink were cheap and common around here. Sam finally found a sheepskin coat, man's type, that fit even if it did come down to her knees, and Boday, of course, stuck with leather.

Charley was pretty good at helping them hitch up the team and showing them how to drive the thing. She'd driven buckboards and hay wagons when still a kid at her relatives' ranch where she often spent the summers, and she knew most of the tricks that also proved true for nargas. "By rights and status I should be the driver," she told them, "but I don't dare. It's not possible for beauteous property to get or wear glasses and they never invented contacts here. Neither Boolean nor Boday was able to change my nearsightedness. It's not awful—I can see to the lead narga, but beyond it's just a blur."

Sam hadn't considered how little change had really been necessary in Charley to make her look a twin. "I'm still farsighted," she told Charley. "I guess I figured you were, too. Since I can't read this stuff I haven't really thought about it much. I know Boday's got decent vision so I guess you teach us to drive this thing. At least you know how to hitch 'em up and unhitch 'em, and the care and feedin' and all. They seem to like you, too."

"Yeah, we got things in common. We both got the same owner, we're kind'a pretty, we go where we're told and we don't own nothin'."

Buying the food was the last thing, and it was a real expedition, although there were a couple of companies specializing in this sort of outfitting who even had magicians in their employ giving preservative spells, then packing it all nice and neat and stowing it in the wagon. Counting what they would have to give the navigator the next day, their fortune was already down almost seven thousand. They did a final check to make sure the expedition was really kicking off the next day—delays were the rule—and found it on schedule. The navigator had been vacationing here and so was starting fresh.

All three of them were excited by the idea, if a little apprehensive. They were setting off in near total ignorance of their destinations on a trip few generally took who were not in trade, finance, politics, or the military and diplomatic corps, and they hadn't the slightest idea why or what might await them at their destination.

The square in front of the Guildhall looked like a scene from an old western movie in spite of the alienness of the buildings and setting. People scurried here and there, there were a number of wagons laden with who knew what, and men on horseback looking like they were out of an old cowboy movie, hats and all. Somehow, both Sam and Charley had thought of the navigator as a single individual, a guide or something like that, but clearly this was part of a company. The actual navigator was a middle-aged man with thick, long gray hair and a white, neatly trimmed beard dressed in buckskins with fringes and, of all things, a buckskin tan top hat! He gathered all of the people around who would be making the trip other than his "crew"—all apprentices only a few of whom would ever make navigator.

He went around to each in turn, introduced himself as Gallo Jahoort, although his crew and most others addressed him as "Master Jahoort" in respect for his position, checking travel documents, and collecting and counting the money. He didn't blink an eye at Sam and Boday, although he certainly spared one for Charley. She gave him the shy, sweet smile and he almost forgot his count. Charley, for her part, appreciated the reaction. She had learned that power came in a lot of unexpected forms and it was nice to see she had it.

That finished, Jahoort gathered everyone around. "All right—first things first," he bellowed in a loud, booming baritone that could probably be heard through a thunderstorm. "How many folks we got here who never been in the bush before?"

Several, other than just Sam and Boday, raised their hands. Charley, who wasn't supposed to understand this, just kept smiling sweetly.

"All right. Today we're gonna start gettin' some practice and see where the weak links lie," the navigator went on. "It's a hundred ninety-two leegs to our jumping off point but it'll still be country riding for the most part. We want to average sixty leegs a day minimum, but we should do much better while still in Tubikosa. In three days we'll be at the border, and the next mornin' we're gonna cross into buffer null and make the first sector. I'll tell you more about that when we get there. For now, we have three days for breakdowns, for findin' out you got clipped, your horses or nargas are all geriatric cases or psychopaths, your food's spoiled, you don't know how to build a campfire, and you forgot to buy toilet paper. Once we cross, it's too late to learn that. Me and my crew will be checking on everything, seeing that it's all in shape for the trip, teaching you what you don't know, and all that. But once we start this mornin' we ain't gonna stop. If we can't fix it and you can't get it on the way, we're gonna just give you a refund and leave you here."

He paused to let that sink in. Charley found she couldn't follow much of what the man was saying, so she surveyed the others who would be coming along. They were mostly men but there were a few women, too, none it appeared unaccompanied by men. She made it as four wagons and six on horses with pack nargas. The half dozen or so tarp-covered flat wagons were obviously some kind of trade goods going from here to somewhere else on consignment. This was after all a shipping company. There were even a couple of kids in one of the wagons. The boy looked to be thirteen or fourteen, the girl maybe nine or ten—getting close to the time when she'd be putting on white and being segregated. Tubikosans had a certain look about them and most of these people and most of the crew didn't have it. There were almond-eyed Oriental-looking men, although a lot bigger than she thought of Orientals as being, some with brown skin, some with olive skin, all sorts of hair, and lots of different features. Clearly the Akhbreed encompassed a lot more than one race as she understood race.

The crew of about a dozen men looked rather young and even dressed in their cowboy outfits they almost seemed to be boys playing at cowboys rather than the genuine article. Some smoked and a few had beards but that didn't change the impression. Apparently the buckskins were the uniform of navigators; only Jahoort wore them, as Zenchur had.

One fellow who was making the trip on horseback with pack narga looked familiar. For a while she wondered if he hadn't at one time been one of her clients, but it didn't seem like it. She would have remembered that outrageous moustache.

And then she had it. It was a long time ago and almost a lifetime away, or so it seemed. In the tavern in that little town they'd stopped at with Zenchur. He hadn't been wearing a black trail outfit then; he'd been dressed like some kind of rich Shakespearean character, and he'd been talking to Conan the Barbarian with the wristwatch. It had been a short period of time and long ago, but she was dead certain it was the same guy. Both Sam and Zenchur had thought he was making some kind of shady deal with the big Neanderthal in skins. She wondered what he was doing here—and if it was a coincidence. The odds of them ever meeting again, let alone under these circumstances, were pretty damned slim. Of course, if it *was* him it just *had* to be coincidence, no matter how remote. They looked nothing like they did then and if he knew or even suspected that they were the two girls old Horned Head was looking for and knew it well enough to make this wagon train, then he would have known where they were all along and turned them in long before.

Still, he would bear watching.

The train was organized by the crew, and they moved out slowly and carefully, taking the lake front route right past Boday's old loft warehouse and continuing on even as they began to leave the city. Sam looked at the warehouse a bit wistfully and saw that Boday had a slight tear, the first she'd ever shown. "Regrets?" Boday asked, looking at Sam. "Boday can still cut that damned thing off your neck and we can go back, you know."

Sam shook her head. "No. I already had that once. All I got was boredom and two and a half times my weight. Any future I have is straight ahead."

She knew that what she said was true, but there still wasn't much enthusiasm in her for this. After all, Charley really just wanted to stay here and keep at her—trade. She had done it initially because, as the demon had said, it was the only way possible to get home, but now Sam wasn't all that sure Charley wanted to get home. As for her—what was so big about getting to this sorcerer, anyway? Seeing how this world worked, it was just as likely he wanted to use her body in some kind of human sacrifice or something as anything else. She sure wasn't vital enough for him to take no risks. All the risks had been theirs. Back there she had rights now and a name and place, somebody who loved and watched over her while making few demands, and, now, a friend to talk to when need be. The only thing was, she didn't love Boday, although she'd gotten to know the crazy artist so well that she had a lot of affection for her in spite of her treachery and her numerous faults. All she really needed was to take some of Boday's love potion herself and they'd live blissfully ever after.

And she'd been tempted, too, particularly during those terrible months of sloth and drifting. She wondered why Boday hadn't figured that one and slipped her some potion during that time. The demon, probably. Protecting her by putting the thought out of Boday's mind every time it surfaced.

The pace was slow, stately, but deliberate, and men rode up and down keeping everyone and everything at the proper distance and pace. There were a few problems, mostly with the wagons or with improperly tightened cinches or unbalanced loads, but these were quickly and professionally solved.

That night they camped in a farmer's field by prior arrangement. Charley built the campfire expertly and did the cooking and serving and it was probably the best in the train by far. Charley, as was custom, ate apart from them and by herself.

While camped the crew dug a pit toilet that had little modesty but some remoteness. The hole-in-the-wagon approach just wasn't that practical while standing still. It was while Boday was over waiting her turn after dinner that one of the crew came by. He was a good-looking guy, at most in his early twenties, with a full but short-cropped brown beard, long, trimmed curly hair, and built a bit burly but not at all bad. Charley, watching from the other side of the fire, thought he had a cute ass.

"Hello—Madame Boday, isn't it? I'm Crindil. I wanted to check and see if there were any problems today we missed." His voice was a pleasant middle tenor, and his accent was sort of folksy, although not so much as Jahoort's.

Sam smiled at him. "*Sam,* please. It's so much better than Susama or Madame Boday. No, no real problems that I know of, but it's early yet and I'm always the one for problems. Will you have some of this? Shari is a superb cook and if somebody doesn't eat it I will and the last thing I need is more food."

He looked at the dish and smelled it. "Oh, I don't know. I always liked women with some extra paddin'. There's more to look at and like." But he took the rest and started in on it.

Sam knew a line when she heard it but it didn't make it any less effective, being exactly what she wanted to be told. She knew he was probably angling for a crack at Charley but she found herself instantly attracted to the man anyway. "You're kind to say it, anyway."

"No, I mean it," he responded between bites. "Uh! That girl of yours is one fine cook and a pretty good rigger, too. That was the best-rigged team we had today and it was taken down just as good. But, gettin' back to the subject. I never met a lady with weight who didn't think she was ugly, and I never met a woman without a weight problem who didn't think she had one. But, uh—you really married to the tall woman? I mean, *married?*"

"Yes," she admitted. "But it's not quite how it looks. I was lost, penniless, stuck, in the city through circumstances I'd rather not describe, and I wasn't exactly built for *her* line of work." She gestured to Charley. "Anyway, there was a kind'a freak happening—Boday's both an artist and an alchemist—and Boday accidentally swallowed some love potion she was making for a client. I was the only one around when she came to, and you can guess the rest. I had no place else to go and no other alternatives."

Crindil looked at her with an amused expression on his face. "Well that's the damnedest story I ever heard. Love potion, huh? So you sorta got trapped into it. And you married her to get a new citizenship, a new start. I can see that." He put down the now empty dish and got up and sighed. "Well, that's real interesting. I'd like to talk more but I got more rounds to make and duties to perform. Maybe we'll have a chance to talk again on this trip. How far you goin'?"

"Well, we're supposed to be going to Covanti. Your guild recommended this route as safer, if longer."

"Yeah, well, it's sure longer. Then you'll be with us all the way to Quodac. Well, we'll have plenty of time then. Nice talking to you, and my regards to your—wife? Maybe I'll talk to her, too. We often got use for an alchemist out there. And don't you listen to nobody else on your looks. For the record you're kind'a cute."

She smiled and got up and was startled when he took her hand and kissed it. She felt almost an electric shock at the gesture, and her eyes followed him off to the next campfire. God! He was charming! Ten minutes and he'd bummed a good meal and had her swooning over him like she never did with a man before.

Charley came over to collect the dirty plates. "Real Romeo," she whispered to Sam as she cleaned up. "Three women alone and he's drawn like bees to honey the first night. You watch out for his type or you'll wind up givin' him the money and me in the bargain."

"You're just jealous 'cause he came on to me and not you." She paused a moment. "I never had a guy come on to me before."

"Oh, he was lookin' at me. He'll seduce you to get to me, if you let him, though."

Sam felt a flush of anger. "Just do the dishes and shut up!"

"Yes, Mistress. Y'm," Charley said mockingly, but she didn't press it.

Boday returned and sat down. "Sorry to be so long, darling, but while waiting over there at least three men came to Boday wanting to know if they could have a bit of Charley. Peasants, mostly. They offered little. The first one, the big fellow with the beard, Boday deferred to you."

Sam suddenly felt angry and betrayed. Deep down she'd known all along that Charley was right but she didn't really want to have it proved to her. She got up and walked to the side of the wagon, out of view of the other two, and felt the Jewel of Omak against her breast, and she thought of its power so seldom used by her. The demon *owed* her for what it had done to her. She had the power to have any man she wanted no matter how she looked or sounded. Up to now all her sexual experiences had been with women. Maybe she *was* one of "them," and if so, that was okay—she certainly enjoyed it. But there would certainly be differences with a man. Big ones. Hell, Charley had done it with her in the shack and Charley was a real man-lover. Charley's power was beauty, but she had power, too. She was through being a patsy. It was time for Sam to take a little.

From Zenchur's cave to the city had been only forty miles or so; the trip to the border where the train would leave Tubikosa was maybe a hundred in the other direction, counting having to go around part of the big lake. The trip was already just starting to settle into a big and potentially boring routine when they reached that border.

Tubikosa ended in a flat plain here, but it still gently sloped down into that glowing mist. It had been so long since they had seen it that it was almost like seeing it for the first time. Tubikosa was a mixture of the primitive and the modern but it was still a large, cosmopolitan city. It was easy to forget that it was such a small part of a new and very alien world rather than just a remote part of their home.

Across the mists another land could be seen, one not very appetizing to look at. A mass of tall, green trees that seemed to cover virtually everything in sight. From their distance it looked just plain green, but with the aid of strong binoculars borrowed from one of the crew it looked like a pretty creepy and dark jungle.

There was a large staging area at the border and a large building for officials, sort of like a customs and immigration station, although it was pretty large and included barracks in back and seemed to be run by the black-clad professional army troops. Sam didn't remember any such things where they'd come in and suspected that, like most borders, you could get in and out of this one secretly if you knew the territory and if you really had to.

There wasn't much incoming traffic, but waiting at the border post was another wagon, this one guarded by four heavily armed men wearing uniforms of a different sort. Private security. Mercenaries. Sam was startled by the sight of both the private and national troops; it was the first time she had seen guns here. They were sleek and oddly curved and shaped yet, oddly, they appeared to be single-shot short rifles, and even the pistols had no barrels—you put in one bullet and that was it. Charley, from the conservative southwest and no stranger to firearms, figured they had to be pretty good shots, since you might not have the time to reload.

"I sure hope so," Sam responded worriedly. That jungle looked pretty mean, and on top of that it looked like it was raining buckets over there. The weather here was cloudy, with the clouds in rapid motion in that somewhat circular pattern, but it wasn't really bad.

That night they had a campfire meeting with Jahoort, this time around the new and still guarded wagon.

"All right, we shook you down and we didn't lose nobody," the navigator commented. "That's pretty good. Now the easy part's out of the way. Tomorrow it gets tough, and we'll have to go through that ground fog you see. Now, we'll all be sittin' high enough up that we'll be able to see each other, but fix cold sandwiches for tomorrow 'cause we won't be stoppin' in it unless we have to. The area extends about forty leegs"—that was a little under twenty miles, Sam knew—"and then we're out of the hub completely. The weather will likely take some real turns for the worse, too. Lots of overcast at least in the region closest to the hub and probably some nasty weather. Be prepared for it but don't let it get you down. It don't last a long ways in and then the weather gets more like normal—which means unpredictable. Normal weather we can handle, I think. Your first mud bath will try your strength and your patience but you'll soon take it in stride. The only kind of storm you really have to worry about you probably won't meet—and pray you don't. But you better know what to do just in case you meet one."

He got up, walked over to the wagon, and pulled back the tarp, then pulled out what looked like a large blanket or rug made of woven wool the color of dull gold.

"This is Mandan gold, and it's fairly heavy although not as heavy as regular gold. Some of you may have seen it before and know all this but listen anyway. Self-confidence gets more folks killed or worse than any other cause. Each of you is gonna get one of these blankets about this size and we'll stow it for you. You don't own it—Mandan's worth more than all of us put together, particularly in this form—and we'll take it back when you leave us, but for the duration it's yours. If we get much changewind warning, we will stop, the crew will handle your things, and we'll all pitch in and dig a series of bunkers—holes in the ground, really—and get in, lying as flat as possible, with these blankets covering the entire hole. Don't worry—you won't suffocate, you'll just feel like you will. Air passes through the blanket, but Mandan is the only known substance that insulates against the effects of a changewind. You stay down and under it no matter how long it takes until I, personally, or one of my crew comes and tells you it's all clear. Understand. No peeking out, no feeling to see if it's still going, nothing like that. Any exposed area of your body will be permanently affected by the changewind."

Sam shivered at the vision, remembering her own changewind nightmare. So *that* was why all the villagers crowded into the underground bunker! And why that castle and even the big door looked golden. It was Mandan coated, inside and out. Inside, they were protected. All but that poor boy. . . .

"Now, changewinds could blow any time—even here," Jahoort warned. "At least two hubs have been hit in the last five years. Both had a great deal of warning, although ones like Tubikosa with large cities simply like to play with the fates. But the odds of a changewind hitting here, or hitting us, are slim—but not as slim as they used to be. There's been a dramatic upsurge in the number of them, mostly very small and localized, in the past year and a half. The unique conditions of a hub prevent many of these small local ones from happening here, but they are not that uncommon in the sectors and can come without much real warning at all.

"If you hear this," he continued, blowing a sharp, shrill, unpleasant air-powered horn that startled them and the animals alike, "then don't even *think.* Grab the Mandan blankets, get on the ground, and under them. If you're caught in the open and can't get to the blankets quickly enough, take cover in any enclosed or depressed area you could, particularly one that's sheltered from the wind. It might not save you, but it's the only chance you got. Now, we'll practice and drill and drill and practice as we go along. Don't grumble at the drills. It might save more than your life."

Charley stared at the big, heavy golden mats and shivered a bit. She had trouble following Jahoort's rapid-fire and dialect-tinted speech, but she understood the basics: the mat was the only protection against the changewind. She had never seen a changewind and knew of them only from Sam's terrified account of her vision, but she wondered very much if she had the strength to lift or carry one of those things.

"Now we'll distribute these tonight, before you go to sleep," Jahoort went on. "Hopefully we won't need them. I've plotted a course that should take us away from where any changewind activity has been seen for a fair amount of time. Be ready for a changewind, but don't worry about them. We have far more probable things goin' wrong than that. Our route is gonna take us first through a land called Bi'ihqua, which has some dangerous terrain we'll try and steer clear of but is peaceful, friendly, and pretty rich in agriculture. Just stick to the trail and the train and don't sight-see and you'll be fine. The trouble will come when we leave this cluster and cross into the Kudaan Wastes. Right at the start is a sort of no man's land, a refuge for bandits, escaped prisoners, changelings, and the accursed. That will be the dangerous time, but we have to go there. I have cargo to be picked up at the mining stations. If we pass the close end of the Wastes we'll be fine. If all goes well, we'll have you safe and snug in Mashtopol in twenty-two days. That's all for now. Wakeup is zero five-thirty, push off is at six-thirty sharp. Be ready."

They walked off a ways back toward the wagon. "Boday does not like this Wastes with bandits," the artist commented. "Still, it might give inspiration. Perhaps she will paint a bit on this trip, make a record of it."

"Not a bad idea," Sam replied. "But I think I'm scareder of the changewind."

"Do not fear, my little flower! Boday tells you that lightning and meteors falling on your head are as common as changewinds. She has lived here her whole life and traveled as far as this leg and never seen one. The journey will be dangerous enough without worrying about something that is strictly fate. Did you think about tonight?"

Boday and Sam had both been approached by a fair number of the crew about spending an evening with Charley. Boday thought that a few careful favors might pay off on the trail in extra protection and service. Sam knew it probably would, but she felt uneasy about it. "Charley? What do you think?"

"Hell, Sam, I been horny as hell around all these nice-looking guys who are seducing me with their eyes and I haven't been able to do a thing about it. I'd love to do it."

She sighed. "All right, then, but I can't stomach it. Boday, you set it up. I have some other worries about it, though. Can you make up some potion to make her just Shari just for the night?"

"Not with the kit we brought, no. Why do you wish this?"

"Just in case somebody notices that Charley's a little brighter and more talkative than the usual girl of her kind. I don't want any slips right away. Of course, I could always use the Jewel. I'm sure His Demonic Highness wouldn't have any objections to that. Charley?"

"Just so long as you bring me back and I remember it all. No problems. It can work both ways, you know. I can overhear things they don't think I can understand."

It was getting quite dark now, but they walked right past Crindil, who gave them a smile and a nod. He'd continued to be friendly but he'd been a bit busy for much conversation. Sam thought it over. Charley was gonna be away and Crindil was now winding up his duties, looked like. Tomorrow onward they'd be in alien lands and under who knew what pressure? Tonight was the best night.

She reached under her tunic, brought the locket out, and aimed it at Charley. The "eye" opened and the usual stiffening occurred. "Jewel, I wish that when I say 'Charley be gone' that only Shari will be in that body, and that she will continue to be Shari until I say 'Charley return.' Then Charley will be back in charge but will remember all that happened as Shari."

Done. I will make it a standing command so you may do this whenever you like.

She hadn't even considered that, but the power of it gave her a slight thrill. She judged distance, then made a sudden move and shined the light on to Boday's head. "Jewel, I wish that when I snap my fingers Boday will be back to normal, such as that is, but that she will still be under my power and not know it. She will make the arrangements for Charley, then return here and go to sleep in the sleeping bag out here and not be awakened until I wake her up."

Done.

"You know what I mean to do?"

Yes.

"And you have no objections?"

No. I never object to such things so long as they do not interfere with my charge. I am a demon, after all. Like you, I am trapped. I may only find freedom by fulfilling my commission.

Oh, wow! She hadn't ever considered that. She snapped her fingers and Boday was as if she'd just finished with Charley. "Boday, go set it up."

"At once, darling." The tall artist left, leaving Sam with Charley who was still in a sort of trance and would be until one of the commands was given. "Charley, be gone," she said, and her friend was once again animated, but not like usual. The brightness, the spark, was gone from her eyes, and there was little thought behind them.

"Wait here for Mistress Boday," she ordered, and Shari nodded. "Yes, Mistress."

Sam then left to find Crindil, who was checking on the riders' horses before the start tomorrow and was pretty well by himself. He turned, smiled, and nodded to her and she returned it. "Hello, there! Any problems?" he asked nicely.

"You all finished for the night?"

"Just about. I should get some sleep, though. Long day tomorrow."

"I just wanted to show you this," Sam said, pulling out the jewel. He frowned, stared down at it, and it caught him.

"I wish," Sam said, "that when I say, 'Crindil love,' you will find yourself suddenly very horny and attracted to me, to the point of lust. You will want to have sex with me. From that point on you will treat me as the most beautiful, desirable, sexy woman you have ever made love to and you will make mad, passionate love to me until I tell you to stop. Then, when you leave my presence, you will forget it ever happened and go to bed."

Done, said the demon.

"Now show me what normal is, Crindil love," she said softly, feeling the power.

10

Power and Privilege in Akahlar

Sam had all sorts of things to do fast when the navigator's blast woke her up at five-thirty. For one thing, she needed several more hours of sleep; for another, she was alone in the wagon. Well, not quite—Charley was curled up asleep on the seat and now stirred and looked up sleepy and confused. Sam spotted her and yelled, "Charley! Get up and get going! I got a lot to tell you later on!"

But Charley just stared blankly and said, in Short Speech, "Pardon, Mistress. Shari not understand."

"Oh, shit," Sam growled. "Charley—come back!" And Charley was back—quickly, but no less sleepy. She shook her head as if to clear it then looked in. "Jeez, Sam! Where's Boday?"

"Nuts," Sam growled, and jumped out of the back of the wagon. Everybody was stirring and running around and there was Boday in the sleeping bag dead to everything. "Boday! Wake up! Time to get up and go!"

Boday stirred, opened her eyes, then frowned and looked around. "What in—how did Boday come to sleep here?"

"Nevermind! Just get out of there now and let's get packed up! You sleep okay?"

Boday slithered out of the bag, still fully dressed from the previous night. "Yes. The best sleep Boday has had in weeks. Odd. Perhaps she should consider this more often."

"Good. Then you're gonna drive 'cause I feel like I got no sleep at all."

Charley came around with a tray with a steaming pot and two mugs. The Akhbreed had excellent if very strong coffee and in the year with Boday Sam had gotten hooked on it, with a fair amount of sugar. Boday drank it black and only in the mornings. A huge amount, almost a cauldron, was always on when the train camped for the night and all were welcome to it. Charley couldn't stand the stuff—never could—and somewhere in the process of her becoming what she was she'd lost her taste for almost all stimulants, as well as her taste for meat, although she prepared it well. She did like wine and fruit juices, though, and although there weren't any juices along and the concept of sipping wine in the morning to wake up was incredible to both Sam and Boday, that's what she had. She went back and brought the last of the sweet breads, noting that somebody was going to have to bake in primitive style or they would be eating dried preserved hard biscuits.

"The woman with the kids seems to be doin' pretty good," Sam noted. "I'll have to ask her just how to do it and when I learn I can teach you. I know we got the equipment, anyway."

Boday and Sam went into the wagon and closed the flaps and used some of the water to sponge each other off before they changed. It was going to be a long trip. By the time they'd finished, Charley had found the narga team and was in the process of rigging it. Even so, almost nobody seemed quite ready an hour later to get going except the crew.

They lined up in formation, a rider checking each horse, pack horse, and wagon to see that all was there and secure, and then they waited for Master Jahoort. Across and beyond the customs station was the mist in the first light of dawn, and beyond . . . Well, it was hard to tell without binoculars but it sure as hell looked like a pretty bleak sandy desert, and a dry one at that. It sure wasn't any green jungle.

Jahoort came by them on his huge tan horse—Charley suspected he'd bought it because it matched his outfit—as he circled the train. And then—they waited. Now each and every rider in the group was checked by the black-clad soldiers, and identity papers were inspected.

Charley, knowing that Boday could understand no English, took advantage of the delay, coming up in back of Sam. "You did it last night, didn't you? That's why all the rush and Boday out in the sleeping bag."

Sam nodded but didn't look back at her. "Yeah, I did. I used the jewel. He don't remember nothin'. I figured, hell, we don't know what's out there but why should you have all the fun?"

"And? And?" Charley prompted.

"It was—interesting. Not bad. Not what I thought it would be, either. So much of it was the same, 'though I liked that beard. That was neat. He was rougher, though. Not gentle where he should be. I'm sore in places. Messier, too, but it felt good goin' in. That was something new. And it was quicker. A lot quicker. I wanted more than he had. I just don't know. I'm glad I did it, glad I've done it, but it's an itch that got scratched. I know this much: women's bodies are a whole hell of a lot prettier to look at than men's. I dunno. I wouldn't *not* do it again, but only if it's for real. I won't force it ever again. You?"

"Well, maybe all that with Boday just jaded you. I know she knows things that have *never* been in books. Maybe he wasn't much good. A lot of men aren't, you know. Sometimes I wonder how people have kids. I had—fun. It was kind of a group thing, which was neat, and it was on the grass, which was fun. I sure as hell wouldn't mind doing it regular on this trip. Anybody except Mister Moustache, that is. There's just something about him that just gives me the creeps."

"Yeah, well, it was so long ago. Your memory's better than mine. All I remember is that big guy in skins with the speech impediment. I had my back to 'em, anyway."

Boday asked about the conversation, and Sam told her about the fellow with the fancy waxed moustache and Charley's suspicions.

She frowned. "Boday, too, has seen him somewhere. She had been trying for three days." She snapped her fingers. "Now, suddenly, it comes to her! She has seen him several times with Kligos!"

"Kligos! Then he *is* a scoundrel! He works for Kligos?"

"No, no. It was as if they were friends. Equals. Boday does not know more, but perhaps our little Butterfly is correct. We should keep an eye on him, particularly if he continues on with us. Ah! Here come the inspectors."

Boday handed them the passport, which covered both her and Sam, and which contained the clearance stamps, as well as the small document that certified that one Shari was contracted to them for life as beauteous property. They looked at them, gave a few looks like "We're glad to get rid of the likes of you," then went on. Charley pointed to the little fold-over card that was her only ID. "Don't lose that," she cautioned. "That is the only identity I have here. Lose that and I'm fair game."

It took a few more minutes for them to clear everybody, and Sam stared out ahead at the mist beyond. She was nervous and confused and didn't know quite what to think about herself. Instead, everything came around in circles to Charley's comment on her little card. This wagon was *her* card. Not just all she had, but everybody who loved her and cared about her. Both of them. Charley was her true friend and confidante, her trusted companion who was both big and little sister. That had never changed. But

Boday—it was crazy, but she was fond of the tall woman's outrageousness and often awed by the talent there. Boday's devotion, whether chemically induced or not, was real down to the core of her heart and soul, even if it was kind'a like making a deal with the devil sometimes. You had to be real careful around Boday or she could smother you. That had finally been worked out now. She suddenly looked at the slim body, long fingers, strong but attractive face, and saw Boday in a new way. Okay, so it wasn't "normal," wasn't accepted, but it was real. More real than what Charley had—or maybe needed—and more real than what Crindil had, too. Maybe more than most people.

She'd been around men, lived for a time with men and kept company with them as one of them, and now she'd had one, and, on the whole, she liked the company of women better. So be it. The hell with fantasies. Like Charley said, you take what you got and you make the most of it.

The border soldiers rode back past and Master Jahoort gave a cry of "*Hooooo!*" and they started to move.

"Oh boy," Charley muttered nervously to herself, "here we go."

By the time they passed the border station and descended into the mist Jahoort was already well ahead. They were the first of the high, covered wagons but were in about the middle of the train. The desert landscape still held, and all looked normal as the sun rose, although behind them the clouds were gathering and it looked like a possible storm at the exit point.

They were above the mist, but it came up to about the center of the wagon wheels and up to about the middle of the nargas, making a pretty weird sight. Jahoort, leading the way on his big horse and unmistakable with his top hat and buckskins, seemed to know just exactly where he was going, and the crew, those not driving the cargo wagons but on horseback, moved up and back along the train, keeping it tight but not congested. All Sam could think of was the old song *Ghost Riders in the Sky.* That's sure what it looked and felt like as they went back and forth, their animals' legs lost in cloud.

It took a couple of hours to cross the region, and then the riders began to direct traffic much like mounted traffic police, putting many of the wagons side by side and stopping them. with all the passengers on horseback with pack animals behind. They were now no more than a hundred yards from that fearsome-looking desert, and they could even feel some of the dry heat.

Jahoort rode out so that he was about in the middle of the parked train, and just ten feet or so in front of them, and he just sat there, looking like some Old West painting, staring at the desert for enough time for Boday to sketch him. She was really good, too.

And then, in front of them, the desertscape started to change, and not subtly like the visions Sam and Charley had seen while "falling" down that storm-created tunnel to Akahlar. No, it was more like slides, like one slide fading out as another faded in, only in full three-dimensions and brilliant, lifelike color. Slowly, at first, then faster, until they were going by at a good clip and it was hard to categorize them as more than types before they were gone. Several different colored deserts with wildly different landforms, certainly; a number of jungles, one of which had purple and pink trees and no green in sight; rolling hills manicured like a golf course that looked complete with water hazards and sand traps—everything but a hole, flag, and putting green; a shore looking out on a vast ocean-like body of blue-green water; tall mountains, short mountains, green mountains, white mountains. . . . It just went on and on.

Still, while there were infinite variations in color and placement and in some of the vegetation, the fact was that there were only a few basic landscapes. There were mountains, valleys, hills, deserts, plains, jungles, and seashores both sandy and rocky. The variety of them, however, startled and impressed even Boday, who'd seen it before. In most, it was overcast; in some, it was raining—or even snowing, although they knew this was the equatorial region of the planet.

"Are *we* moving or is *that?*" Sam asked.

"Neither, darling," Boday responded. "All of it is in the same place at the same time."

"Well—which one's Akahlar?"

"Darling—they are *all* Akahlar!"

"She's right about one thing," Charley said, coming back forward. "I just got dizzy looking at that and checked out the back. It still looks just the same."

Sam translated and Boday nodded. "Of *course,* because it *is* the same. All sectors intersect with the hub, but none with each other. That is why they can all be there but all are Akahlar. What you are seeing, though, is something that only a master navigator like Jahoort can do. He is flipping through all of the wedges intersecting this point for the one he wants. This Bi'ihqua, which is not an Akhbreed name. You can expect to see a native race, my darlings. It will be the first time, yes?"

"Second," Sam responded. "We met one before that we sure as hell don't want to meet again."

"Yeah," Charley agreed. "Tell her if we're ever near Ba'ahdon to give it a wide miss."

The end came very suddenly, when a view simply locked in before them. It was a very pretty view, but not one of the most friendly looking.

A valley and well-traveled dirt road opened before them, but on all sides were high mountains dotted maybe two-thirds of the way with lush greenery but with barren peaks, some with large patches of snow showing just how high they were. Thick gray clouds were overhead, cutting off the tops of some of the mountains from view, but it wasn't the mountains that was most impressive. Even on their greenest sides, there were dark, black, ugly scars, some quite wide and imposing, a few coming down into the valley and looking like blobs of oozing black rock suddenly frozen in mid-ooze. At various points around the valley and even near the trail the ground seemed to be on fire. At least, there was constant smoke and steam rising there.

"Looks like a cross between Yellowstone and Hawaii. I hope those bubbling places smell better here than there."

Now Jahoort motioned with his hand and gave his cry, and the mounted crew reformed the train and had it start to move out after Master Jahoort. There was no question as to where to aim for; there was only that road.

As they got to the edge of the land and came up out of the mist they discovered that Charley's wish did not come true. While the air was mostly decent and humid, now and again they would get a whiff of sulphur and even the telltale rotten egg smell of hydrogen sulfide. Even the nargas snorted their disgust.

They pulled onto the road that seemed to come right out of the mist, and Charley looked back. The mist was there, and she could see around the next wagon and beyond, but there was a darkness of sorts at the other end of the mist. All view of the hub seemed to have gone. In a few minutes all sight of the mist was gone, and they were in the volcanic landscape.

The temperature was down but it still wasn't all that chilly; Sam guessed it was maybe high sixties or low seventies, but after just leaving ten or more degrees warmer you really knew it.

Charley was trying to figure out how the hell the world was put together. "Like a crazy kind of flower, maybe," she suggested. "You know—the hub is the middle of the flower, and then there are the petals all around, like on the maps. Only the maps just show a view from the top, seeing the top petal. Suppose there were a hundred or a thousand petals all stuck to the middle of the flower at one point—that mist—but leaning away from each other, drooping down and giving a little space between? And each petal was one of those places. I dunno how the hell that's possible, but it's gotta be something like that."

Sam suggested the analogy to Boday, who liked it. "Yes, Boday has heard that before. It is very much like that, in fact. Is it not wonderful to have such variety? And there are forty-eight flowers, each with twelve series of petals. Darlings, only in Akahlar can every place and everything be possible!"

Conversation stopped as they heard what sounded like a very large group of barbershop quartet singers sounding off one note at a time at random—and very loudly.

They were passing a pretty but ugly-smelling area very near the road that seemed to be boiling colored mud. Sam looked at it, fascinated, but she wasn't sure what variety she wanted. The singing notes were coming from it; as each bubble burst, it gave off a noxious-smelling gas and a note that sounded just like a tenor or a baritone in one of those groups singing "ah Ah AH AHH!" only not in any ascending or descending order. It was kind of funny and a little neat, but she preferred her mud unboiled and she wasn't too keen on the ground singing to her.

She also wondered if there were any alto and contralto and soprano mud boils about. As it turned out, there were, and it sounded just awful as the sounds of one blended in with the sounds of others.

Charley just couldn't resist, even though she realized how precarious her position was. "The hills are alive with the sound of music," she said, giggling.

Sam turned and gave her a look and for a moment was tempted to turn her into just Shari.

They stopped just a half mile or so into the valley, but were not given much of a break or told to form a camp. Instead, Jahoort seemed to be waiting for somebody, and that somebody showed up fairly promptly. He was a rather dashing figure dressed all in khaki, with a small, upturned matching hat with brim, atop a chestnut brown horse. He had a large and comfortable-looking saddle and two large saddlebags mounted just in back of it, as well as what might have been a bedroll rolled up between the two bags. It was hard to tell detail at this distance, but he appeared to be ruddy brown from the sun and younger than Jahoort, although perhaps as experienced. It wasn't just the newcomer that caused attention, however, but his two companions.

"My God! What are *those?*" Sam asked.

Boday frowned. "Most likely the man is the Pilot," she answered. "The other two are probably natives of some sort. Odd little ones, are they not?"

Odd was not the word. The pair on either side of the Pilot were hardly half his height and seemed little more than brown humanoid blobs, but they were riding in tiny saddles atop what looked like the largest mice in all creation, and mice that not only had saddles on their backs but stood on their hind legs and hopped like kangaroos.

The Pilot shook hands with Jahoort, then looked back at the train, nodded, then turned to look ahead. He barked some orders to the little creatures, and they whirled their strange mounts and went forward, hopping rapidly, until they were perhaps a hundred feet ahead of the lead. Then Jahoort gave the cry, and they started forward once again.

The valley twisted and turned before it opened up into an enormous expanse flanked by high volcanic peaks. The valley had several large rivers and streams running through it, and seemed about as lush and green as it was possible to imagine. It seemed to go off in the distance forever.

The road dipped down into it and then followed a broad and fairly straight river. At the road's junction with the water there was a—well, a village. There seemed to be hundreds of conical grass huts of varying shapes and sizes, all built atop stilts at least ten feet in the air and some far higher. There were no ladders, no stairs, but there were small porches in front of the oval-shaped door openings, and there were people on some of them, as well as below on the ground.

Well, not people, exactly.

They were small, all between three and four feet high, and they all seemed to have broad, muscular brown bodies that seemed hard and tough as leather or maybe rock, with small, thick legs and short, stubby arms and heads that were very round and hairless, with enormous bulging brown eyes, thick, flat noses that ran half the distance of their face, and mouths that ran the entire distance. They were ugly as sin and they all looked kind of alike, although you could tell the males from the females. The females had small, round, hard breasts and were also, it seemed, a few inches taller on the average than the males. Most wore brightly colored loincloths and nothing else; the younger ones wore nothing at all.

They ran by the dozens out to greet the train as it passed, all yelling and gibbering in some odd-sounding language that was high-pitched and totally unintelligible. Others popped out of the stilt huts to join them, simply jumping out off the little porches and sliding down the not very smooth-looking stilts like firemen answering an alarm. When they got real close to the slow-moving wagon and seemed to be shouting up at her and grinning with those incredibly wide mouths, Sam felt repulsed and tried to shrink away lest they jump up or try and touch her. Charley, looking out from behind the seat, was finally able to see them as well. They *were* ugly, even repulsive in a way, but she felt no particular fear of them. This was, after all, probably *their* land.

Their fellow Bi'ihquans who were working with the Pilot whirled on their mounts and hopped back, coming down either side of the train and shouting at the natives and pushing them away with whip-like tools that looked like giant wicker dusters. They weren't hurting anybody, but the crowd moved back.

Giant brown and gray tailless mice were the best description for those mounts, too, although the creatures were clearly bipedal, with very large and powerful rear legs oriented that way and very small forelegs mounted on thin, short arms. Charley was less tolerant of their sight when she could finally see them; she had never been very fond of mice.

"Boy, I'd hate to be a cat in this place," she remarked, still being flip, but not really feeling funny right now.

Those creatures could *hop,* though. There wasn't a horse that could move that fast or turn that much on a dime. For the little people who could ride them, they were an amazingly versatile form of transportation.

They were past the village in no time, but others could now be seen popping up in the distance. In fact, they seemed to be scattered, yet pretty numerous; in between were lush fields that were obviously carefully cultivated. In one they could see lots of the little people walking down neat rows of plants taller than they were, carrying baskets and picking something or other. From the plants nearest the road Sam guessed it was the local Tubikosan style of banana. It tasted like one, but it was green on the outside all the time *and* green on the inside as well.

There were still occasional thermal areas but they weren't as pervasive as at the entrance to the land. Some steaming blue pools here and there, and off in the distance there could be seen an occasional geyser spouting off, sending its plume high into the air.

The banana seemed to be the main crop of the land, but every once in a while they would see a large amount of acreage planted with other fruit trees, or bushes bearing large, almond-colored nuts, and here and there what might have been a purplish relative of sugar cane. Mostly the small villages dominated, but here and there in the distance they saw some very large if conventional-looking houses with massive barns and other outbuildings that looked entirely out of place here, and areas that were cleared of all but thick grass and which had horses and monstrous-sized longhorn cows grazing.

About four hours in they pulled off the trail and toward one of those large houses, stopping just short of it in a large grassy field. Charley looked at the house—it was almost a mansion—and then around at the fields. "Kind'a looks like *Gone With the Wind,*" she noted. "Sure looks more like plantations than farms or ranches."

They set up in the field, allowing the horses and nargas to get water and do a little grazing, and allowing themselves to stretch and fix something to eat. The crew warned them that this would be just a ninety-minute stop, so they ate as fast and light as possible in order to have some time to look around.

Master Jahoort and the Pilot had gone into the big house and emerged only about forty minutes later, along with a young-looking couple and their four children, all Akhbreed. The woman and two of her daughters wore the long saris of the Tubikosans, and scarves, but clearly the business of young unmarried girls going in white and masked was out the window here. This was less formal.

Work was going on around the place; dozens of the little people were scurrying this way and that, carrying large things on their heads with balanced ease and hauling and repairing and cutting and sawing and all the rest. Two females attended the Akhbreed family.

Sam had Boday point out a couple of the train crew who had been part of the company Charley kept the previous night and walked over to them. She was curious. One of them, called Hude, a tall, lanky guy who always had a cigarette in the corner of his mouth but never seemed to light or smoke it, felt talkative.

"Yeah, most of these are big places," he told her. "It's the usual thing. Most of the produce here will be shipped by a train goin' where we just come from back to Tubikosa's markets. Them, they're the relatives of rich or powerful folks back in Tubikosa but they got the life out here. Hell, I bet they live as good as some kings and queens, only they don't got all the politics and shit you do if you're royalty."

Sam nodded. "But it's the land of these little people, right? I mean, they look so poor and primitive."

"Yeah, but they're ugly little brutes. All this volcanic stuff makes some of the richest farmland anywhere. Just drop anything at random here and it grows. They never did nothin' with it, though. Just squatted in their little huts and went out and picked wild fruit to eat back in ancient times. The Akhbreed come in, they made it a science. Growin' ten times as much, gave the little buggers medicine and sanitation and stuff like that. Taught 'em the work ethic. They never had it so good."

"Yeah, maybe," Sam responded, but she wondered if Charley's first impression of the old slave-owning South might not be a better example, or maybe some of the colonies in the old days when the English and French and others went all over the place "civilizing" the world. These little people didn't seem much better off than Hude said they were before the Akhbreed "made it a science." It was real clear to see who was bringing the tea to who, and who was dressing good and living in mansions and who was living in primitive huts, carrying water back to their places on their heads, and begging wagon trains.

Charley thought so, too, but she wasn't all that surprised. "It's like we were told at the start, remember? The Akhbreed run all this. 'Sectors!' 'Wedges!' They should call 'em what they really are—colonies!"

The Pilot and the navigator, along with the plantation owner, walked toward the rest, still talking, and their conversation now could be overheard.

". . . Much real trouble?" Jahoort was asking.

"Only out near the nulls," the Pilot, who kind of looked to Sam and Charley like a shaved Mark Twain in a bush outfit, responded. "We're getting some cross banditry whenever the synchronicity is right. We've asked for more troops but it's the usual story, you know. Things are pretty good here, you should see what some of the others are facing, we're spread thin, that sort of crap."

Jahoort shrugged. "Yeah, well, I've been talking to some of the other navigators at the Hall and they say there's been scattered outbreaks of outright resistance in some of the wedges, particularly in the more permissive kingdoms. Would you believe it? *Resistance! Natives* killing Akhbreed! And it's spreading. Mark my words, we're going to have a nasty mess on our hands if we don't stop it now, but the damned monarchs and their asshole advisors can't even agree on when to go to the bathroom, let alone unite."

"Laxity, that's the root of it," said the young plantation owner. "We've gotten too gentle and too permissive as a race over the years. Keep a tight rein and a whip and treat them fair and you'll have no trouble, I say. You don't see any of that rot seeping in *here!* Fairness and toughness, that's the answer. You talk as if it was some sort of worldwide conspiracy afoot."

As he said that Charley noticed a little native behind them pick up a melon and make as if to throw it at the owner. He didn't, but the thought was there. Charley smiled at him and he grinned. If they were bold enough to even show off like that, she thought, this idiot was in for a lot of trouble and couldn't see it if it was right in front of him. This place was grand, but it was dependent on native labor and the next Akhbreed plantation was a good ways from here. They were very vulnerable; only the threat of reprisal kept them alive and in this arrogant and ignorant state of wealth.

"Some think it *is* a conspiracy," the Pilot remarked. "I take trains through from all over. There's lots of talk about whole villages of natives disappearing in some sectors, and there's been more changewinds reported in the past year than in any one year in my entire memory. None here, yet, thank the gods, but you never know."

"You really think there's some dark conspiracy that might overthrow the Akhbreed?" the plantation owner asked in a very skeptical tone.

"I can't see how they could actually overthrow us," the Pilot admitted, "but if somebody was mean and powerful enough they could cost massive loss of lives and property and break the system. The hubs have gotten too damned soft and dependent. Jahoort can tell you. You stop the imports from the sectors and you'll have starvation, unemployment, maybe revolution."

The plantation owner chuckled. "Oh, come on! I can't take you two seriously! Revolution indeed. So one king and clan is traded for another. The army and the sorcerers still suppress things and that's that. Besides, it would be an inconvenience, nothing more. Why, it would take the revolt by a majority of sectors to more than irritate the hub. Besides, nobody in their right mind would foment such a disastrous and doomed uprising. There would be no gain in the end, only losses all around. Even the unhappiest of natives wouldn't follow such a course when it meant defeat and possible genocide for their people. I can see some power mad madmen dreaming of it—there are always psychotics—but actually getting a following? Come on, gentlemen! When the gods gave the Akhbreed the power, this system was *ordained*. One can scratch it, but hardly alter it."

It was an interesting debate, and one neither Sam nor Charley wanted any part of. In the end, the owner was right. The Akhbreed were in power because they *had* the power. Their sorcerers were demi-gods, the navigators alone could go where they liked and bring troops to bear on any problem area while any revolt would have to trust to luck for help from anywhere else. But you had to wonder . . .

Boolean had said that whatever it was about Sam involved the fate of everybody, and not just Akahlar, either. Suppose somebody like the horned wizard *had* figured out a way to solve the problems? Suppose his biggest problem was convincing enough sectors to support and go along with him? It'd take lots of time, but these sorcerers had that time and the natives of all these worlds would be offered hope for the first time.

Suppose, just suppose, you could lock up the Akhbreed in their hubs so only the ones out here were around. If the sorcerers and the troops couldn't get out for some reason, then these Akhbreed would be outnumbered by a whole lot. And all sectors led to the hub. . . . What if most of the natives from most of the sectors all decided to attack the hubs at the same time?

"Impossible, darlings," Boday assured them. "Such a thing could not be. Only Akhbreed has sorcerers of such general and unlimited magic. No other race could do it but we against ourselves and that was settled in wars long ago. It is like everything, darlings. We have the power. There is no way to take that power away and we alone have it. You worry about everything, I think."

Sam remembered her strange visions and the horned sorcerer. "Yeah, but suppose some of the sorcerers went real bad? A lot of 'em?"

Boday laughed. "They are all insane, my love. Such power does that to the best of them. And some do go rogue, as it is called, and can be very, very dangerous. But to get two rogues with all that power to agree to do *anything* together—that is against nature."

But both Sam and Charley wondered about such confidence. Neither of them understood enough of this world to either accept or contradict the prevailing view, and neither had enough experience or education to compare it to their own world—if it could be compared—but it smelled. Something sure smelled.

When they were back on the trail, though, they couldn't stop discussing it. "Suppose Horny *did* figure a way," Charley theorized. "And suppose Boolean caught on? Remember—even Zenchur kind'a said that was up."

"Yeah, and the demon said the armies were gathering and the enemy gainin' strength," Sam responded. "I wish it would say more but it can't or won't about that. I don't think it really cares 'cept it wants to deliver me before all hell breaks loose. It's just trapped and wants out."

Charley nodded. "So in the tunnel this horned guy is blocked for the first time by somebody. Boolean had to come out of hiding to save us from him. Remember how surprised the Horned One was? So now Boolean's an enemy to the horned guy, right? He's too strong to take on, but I bet you Boolean's run into the same kind'a guff that plantation guy and Boday are giving. It ain't possible. It don't make no sense. Go away and stop with your conspiracies. Only Boolean's got something up to either prove it or give Horny fits. You. Only Horny knows it and he wants you out of the way. He now knows Boolean's his enemy so he has him covered. If Boolean reveals where you are, Horny pulls out all the stops. Maybe he can't zap Boolean, but he sure as hell could zap you. So *you* got to sneak in to *him.* It all makes sense. Zenchur's supposed to be the old dependable native to get us through with me as decoy, but Zenchur catches on and plays us dirty 'cause he hates his own kind. So the backup, the demon, comes in. It ain't human and it don't really give a damn about us, so it gives you Boday as a Zenchur replacement and makes you too fat to be recognized. Yeah, it really hangs together, except . . ."

"Yeah, 'cept why the hell would a girl from another world who don't know much 'bout nothin' and sure as hell don't know sorcery or Akahlar or nothin' be the key to stoppin' all this? Why *me?* What in hell could I do against a sorcerer like *that?*" she sighed. "And the worst part is, from what I seen so far, I ain't even sure I like the game. It's the same feelin' I had when Zenchur first explained it all. I kept thinkin' that I went along more with the guy who was tryin' to kill me than the one tryin' to save me."

"I noticed you didn't get real fond around these natives," Charley noted.

"Well, yeah, but this is *their* place. I don't think I could ever kiss one of 'em but that don't mean they aren't *people.* I saw that bit with the melon, too. I don't like it, Charley. I don't like it at all. It seems like if we make it, somehow, and I do whatever it is Boolean wants, I'll keep thousands, maybe millions of people enslaved forever even if I get a gold star and fame and beauty and money and whatever. It'd be blood money. But it seems that if I don't, I *die,* and I don't wanna die right now. I ain't the hero type but I'm not smart enough to figure out a way out of this."

"I don't know who is," Charley sighed. "We don't know enough. Like, why do these sorcerers speak English with American accents yet? Your demon, too."

"Actually the demon sounds kind'a English. I don't know. But I sure don't like bein' pushed and that's all I've been since I got here. So pushed around that I almost gave up everything. It's nuts.

I'm goin' where I don't wanna go—to do, if I get there, something that'll keep all these people from freein' themselves from their masters and lock in the Akhbreed for another ten thousand years or whatever, which I hate. That or die."

Charley sighed. "Well, we just play it by ear and try and figure it out. It's a long trip yet. Maybe we'll learn enough to figure it all out before we hav'ta make a decision. Or maybe we'll find some people who are smart enough to figure it out." She shook her head. "I dunno. Maybe we should spring for that university place. They *got* to know, and somebody there has got to be smart enough to figure it all out."

"Well, I can't do nothin' but play it by ear," Sam noted sourly. "But I don't think that university would help us figure out a way to beat the system. I mean, it's Akhbreed run, right? They *invented* the system. They might know what it's all about, but they sure wouldn't be no help to me."

Boday's sketches were getting very good and very elaborate as they went along, although she was running out of paper fast. She hoped that Jahoort would have some, or that there would be some available at one of the stops.

The days and nights went by with little change in the routine and little worry. The scenery changed a bit, but only occasionally, and they would pass from one valley up and through a pass and into another that might be growing some different things but was still pretty much the same plantation system. At least they could get fresh fruit and fresh fruit juices as they went along.

There were surprisingly few Akhbreed, all in plantations, and no non-native towns in evidence. The plantations were supplied by and supported by the trains that came through and dependent upon them not only to get the luxury goods and materials in, even importing skilled workmen when needed, but also to get their products out. Special trains just for this were employed using junior navigators; the long-haul trains generally dealt only with inter-kingdom commerce.

Sam eventually broke down and bargained for a pair of binoculars just for them, since most of what was worth seeing was well away from the roads and the "host" plantations were all ready for them.

One thing was obvious, particularly through the binoculars. The farther away they got from the hub, the looser the Akhbreed living in Bi'ihqua were as well. On their farms and generally secure, there was little sign of robes or saris on the plantation women around the places they were not set to stop at. Practical work clothes, even pants, were the rule and not the exception, and Boday once caught an excited look at a couple of women reclining by a pool about a half mile back who seemed to be wearing nothing at all, and twice Sam thought she saw a couple of women wearing work pants but topless. The men, too, seemed more casual but they had less distance to go to be that way.

The natives began to fascinate them as well. It was the first time either Charley or Sam had ever seen or heard of a race more advanced than spiders where the women were bigger and stronger than the men, on the whole—and clearly the bosses in their society. Both decided that they liked the idea. Boday couldn't care less. At six two and with her personality the concept was irrelevant.

The seventh day was notable because it rained torrentially and was one of the most miserable experiences any of them could remember. The wagon was in fact waterproof, but when you had to sit in the seat and drive it wasn't much help, and with poor visibility and several wagons getting stuck and having to be pushed out, including theirs, it was a really rotten time. It was not, however, a thunderstorm, and for that much Sam was thankful. The last thing she needed that day was more visions and nightmares.

Still, it took Boday to put it into perspective. "Look at it this way, darlings. Suppose you were one of those on horseback?"

On the eighth day in, they saw a strange and scary sight that brought the reason for the repeated changewind drills home to them no matter how they griped about them. They sat atop another mountain pass looking down on yet another valley, but it was not the same as before. Well, it *was* for part of the way, but right through the middle, visible from the heights, was a vast and strange scar that seemed several miles long and a mile wide. It was gray and yellow and when they reached it there were in it the remains of what had once apparently been a dense forest. The change was so sudden and dramatic and the result so creepy they had to ask about it. Charley thought it was volcanoes; her folks had taken her to Volcanoes National Park in Hawaii when she was thirteen and she'd never forgotten the sight.

"Volcanoes, yeah," they were told, "but not directly. Oh, them things do pop their corks now and again and it can look real ugly for a while and cover the place in ash a krill deep"—a *krill* was roughly five or six feet—"but that's just how the land stays so rich. Nothin's growin' again here 'cause the soil's all wrong. Poison for these plants. This was a changewind come in maybe twenty years ago. You can see where there were eruptions around that time and it's already grown back. Not here. The land's wrong. It was some kind of nasty forest that didn't belong here, but the effect also opened up a hot crack and set the whole thing on fire. Nothin's grown here since or will, and the tree remains just stay there, mostly petrified."

The Pilot, who was old enough to remember, agreed. "Used to be a native village over there," he told them. "Just like all the rest. Only when the wind was done they was stone huts and the natives were foul-lookin' red buggers with lots of teeth and tails like reptiles who just started off tryin' to eat anything and anybody they could. Took months to root 'em all out and kill the last of them. They was just startin' to breed." He shuddered.

At that Sam's mind went back to that horrible vision of the boy turned monstrous by the changewind. He'd looked horrible, but he'd been the same scared little boy inside. That was why it was so awful, them killing him. But turning these pleasant little natives into demonic killers—maybe there was a reason why they killed them. Maybe it could change you inside sometimes, too. Or maybe the natives just found themselves about to be hunted anyway but now with a form able to do some damage, so they did. Hard to tell.

Still and all, the Akhbreed killed all changewind victims they could catch as policy because they no longer fit. Everything and everybody had its place here, and those changewind victims had the least power of all.

They all felt better when they were through the desolation.

Late on the afternoon of the ninth day in Bi'ihqua, they met the soldiers. They were a tough-looking bunch of men who'd obviously been out in the field a long time. They weren't all sharp and spiffy and totally clean-shaven like the ones back in Tubikosa, but they looked like the kind of men you'd want on your side in a fight. It was only a patrol, a dozen or so men under a junior officer and an old sergeant, but they were doing their business and it was something everybody learned soon enough.

"There's been some banditry off and on for months along the border," the officer told them. "They're a special kind of bandit and we've been hunting them for half a year to no avail, although we don't know how they could hide in this land for that long. They're ruthless when they have to be but they're only after one thing, or so it seems. They take the Mandan gold and leave most of the rest. Oh, they'll take something if it strikes their fancy, but that's their target. Been a rash of these things at or near the borders. We're escorting all trains through to the Null from here, though."

"Hard to believe that few enough bandits to be able to hide in this country could take a train," Jahoort noted. "Ain't like the old days, I'll tell you."

"Yeah, we've had the natives out looking into every nook and cranny and we can't come up with 'em. Can't figure out why they're so hot just for the Mandan, too. It's valuable enough, sure, and rare enough, but it's not characteristic of bandits."

". . . *We've had the natives out looking* . . ." Sam couldn't help but wonder if maybe the natives were deliberately not looking in the right places. These people were so used to running the show and also so used to thinking of the natives as primitive children it just might not ever occur to them that the natives could be in cahoots with the robbers. They'd dismiss it. What's the motive? The natives would be wiped out if it were discovered, but couldn't profit without being obvious, right? Maybe it was just the satisfaction of doing something, however small, against their arrogant bastard masters.

"Where'd they come from?" Jahoort asked.

"Probably when the Kudaan Wastes synchronized with here. The timing's about right. But we figure it wasn't any impulse thing. They had their hiding places prepared in advance for sure. They don't hit every train, just a few, but it's best not to take chances. Could be they got a deal in collusion with some of *our* bad ones. Might be partly an inside job. There'd be big money in exporting Mandan."

The Pilot sighed. "Yeah, some people will do anything for a sarkis. Glad to have you, officer. I was arguing for this policy for months."

Charley frowned. She'd gotten the gist of it and whispered to Sam, "Aren't we going to this Kudaan Wastes? Jeez! We're goin' where they *came* from!"

"Kudaan Wastes," Boday repeated. "It is not even a pleasant name. You wanted something real to worry about, darlings. Boday thinks this is it."

As if in confirmation, Jahoort said, "Well, I'm goin' right into the Wastes. I'm supposed to have a patrol from the Mashtopol Forces meet me at the border there. Until I talked to Ganny, here, I hadn't expected much trouble til I got there. I'll order all my men armed from this point anyway."

The officer spat. "The Mashtopol Forces. That motley lot might be more dangerous to you than the bandits." When they left Bi'ihqua they would also leave the Kingdom of Tubikosa and enter the Kingdom of Mashtopol; it would be another country's jurisdiction.

"I can't say I ain't worried," Jahoort responded rather casually, "but I been through the Wastes many times and I got a few surprises if anybody makes a try on me there. You just get me to the border and we'll be fine."

Although it had seemed a long trip already, and they had far to go, in many ways Sam and her companions were sorry to reach the end of this place, with its spectacular geysers, singing mud pots, colorful mountains and rich land. It had been an education in how things worked on Akahlar, but it had not been unpleasant until the patrol showed up. After then, every time they reached a point where the road went through thick growth or sloped down, presenting rocky outcrops on either side, their eyes combed for any signs of movement and the friendly land seemed filled with potential menace.

Charley was positive that Mister Moustache was the inside man and that he would somehow signal and bring down a horde of fierce bandits on them at any moment, but while the odd little man kept to himself pretty much he did nothing of a really suspicious nature. Perhaps he just decided that this one wasn't worth it; there'd be easier pickings on later trains.

Along the way, too, Sam had gotten to know a number of the people, both travelers and crew, including Madame Serkosh, the married woman traveling with husband and kids. Rini, as she insisted she be called, had the art of trail cooking and packing down pat. "You have to, with five along," she said practically. Her husband seemed somewhat withdrawn and aloof, but she and the kids were outgoing types, delighted to show a newcomer the art of baking on the trail and lots of other practical things, and seemingly not at all put off by the unusual nature of the female trio Sam represented. They were headed home after showing off the kids to her brother-in-law, who managed a luxury hotel in Tubikosa. They lived in a Mashtopol sector off the southwest of that hub, and would change there for the final few days home.

"You'll like Mashtopol after Tubikosa," she told Sam. "Things are a lot more fun and a lot less strict there. The capital's not very big compared to Tubikosa, but it's a nice little city that minds its own business and lets you mind yours. I wish it had the markets and bazaars of Tubikosa, though. Seeing the variety there compared to what we're used to was just amazing."

Their own sector, which was called Shadimoc, apparently was involved in some kind of manufacturing, although just what it produced—and what sort of inhabitants really produced it—wasn't all that clear. Sam didn't press it; with all the possibilities of this world it didn't seem worth it, and besides she was still getting used to the little Bi'ihquans.

Neither of Rini's boys—Tan, eleven, and Jom, seven—would have much to do with Sam; she suspected their father feared those weird women would infect them with some kind of debauched ideas. Apparently he didn't care about his daughters getting corrupted, though, or thought they were too smart to be corrupted, since he seemed to have no objection to their talking not only with Sam but even with Boday, who showed an unexpected soft side for kids. Charley, at first, had felt stuck, since she really wanted some company, but felt she had to play Shari at all times around them so they wouldn't be going back to their parents with news that the pretty girl was smart and clever. After a couple of days, though, it was clear that while Charley could fool adults, she had little chance of fooling kids. The language barrier, at least, kept things at what seemed to be a safe level. Both dressed in long pullovers and pants, apparently the standard garb for Akhbreed colonials where they came from. It wasn't all that fashionable, but it was practical; they had all clearly left the strict codes of Tubikosa, or at least had exchanged them for looser ones.

Rani was thirteen and already pubescent, only just so, and still trying to deal a bit with what that all meant and what her body was doing to her. She was thin, with her parents' dark olive complexion and her father's rather prominent nose, with thick black curly hair and eyes that seemed just as dark, and she was already about five feet tall, almost to Sam and Charley's height. She looked like somebody from the Middle East, as did her parents. She wasn't all that pretty, with a mouth too large and a nose too prominent, but she wasn't ugly, either, but to Sam, at least, the girl seemed both ordinary and exotic. She was a rather quiet child, but she warmed Boday's heart by looking at the eccentric artist's sketches with awe and wonder. Boday instantly decided that this was the most tasteful and intuitively brilliant child she'd ever met.

Sheka was nine, and had that same mouth, but her nose was a bit better proportioned, her eyes large, and her hair straight, and she was chubby—not fat like Sam, but chubby. She was also more outgoing and inquisitive, and seemed fascinated by Charley. She was also capable of asking embarrassing questions in total innocence like why Charley waited on them like a *serk*—apparently the name of the natives of Shamidoc—and if the butterfly eyes came off and how much of Boday's body was covered with designs and pictures—and why. With the aid of Rani, who seemed constantly embarrassed by her sister's questions, they managed to deflect the hardest to answer.

Both were allowed to come over now and then, usually together, when they stopped for the evenings, and even though their stays were brief they were welcome ones.

The last day's journey was through rough, less developed country and rugged, volcanic terrain, and it was easy to see why this place would be ideal for bandits, but when they reached the end of the road nothing had happened. It seemed almost anticlimactic, but neither Sam nor Charley nor Boday could say they felt disappointed. So far so good. Over four hundred miles and the worst that had happened overall was a good drenching.

The end of Bi'ihqua was not like the beginning. The road did not just end; only the land changed just beyond the border posts. The change was dramatic, but there was nothing to suggest anything odd or magical here. The road did not end; it continued on past a border control post and fort, and a few hundred yards beyond, the volcanic terrain simply ceased and was replaced by a thick, northern-style forest. The road changed at that point, too, from the rich black hard-packed earth of Bi'ihqua to a hard, unrutted red clay. The road seemed better maintained on the other side for all the soldier's remarks about Mashtopol, even to having drainage cuts on either side. There was a small border post there, too, with far fewer soldiers wearing blue, not black, uniforms and colored epaulets on their shoulders.

They disembarked and set up for the night on the Tubikosan side, just outside the border fort. Sam couldn't help noticing that while the Tubikosa border was heavily double-fenced as far as you could see in both directions, the Mashtopol one was not. After getting set up, she wandered over to the Serkosh family wagon and found Rini. "*That* is the Kudaan Wastes?" she asked them. "It looks pretty nice to me!"

Rini laughed. "Oh, no! That's Kwei, I think. It's hard to keep track but I thought I heard the Pilot say so. I wish we *were* going that way, but few trains do. Kwei wood goes almost entirely to the rest of Mashtopol; little is exported. Unfortunately, the international trains coming back almost always go through the worst and ugliest sectors. That's because it's cheaper to get *them* to pick up the dangerous or heavy cargo and bring it in for free in lieu of transit fees. If we'd known someplace like Kwei would be up when we got here we would have arranged a special transfer through to it, but there's no way of knowing what you'll get when you come here and it's too late now." She sighed. "Too bad, too. I'd much rather pick up some nice wood furnishings cheap than go through a damned desert."

Sam felt disappointed. The land in front of her looked so *pleasant.* "Then that's why they call it the Wastes? Because it's a desert?"

Rini nodded. "They'll take on a water wagon here, I bet, and maybe more. I've heard the Wastes are pretty, though. It's just that down this end they're pretty dangerous. The land is so rugged it's a perfect hideout for anyone who, well, needs to hide out and can somehow get there. Ten armies wouldn't blast you out of there if you didn't want to be blasted out, so they don't try. There's a *wonderful* lot of books written set in the Kudaan Wastes. It's very romantic. They just quarantine the area and have a military escort the first hundred and fifty leegs. Nobody usually bothers the inbound trains anyway, though; not much to steal. So they only pick up the ores inbound. See? Oh, it'll be exotic but I don't think we'll be molested. If we thought there was a real danger we'd never go through there with the kids. There's a number of spots like Kudaan, and most of these navigators have deals, anyway. We might even see some of the accursed or changelings."

Sam wasn't sure she was too excited about seeing anybody called accursed or a changeling but she let that pass. Charley seemed genuinely excited by the description; it sounded much like her own native desert southwest. Boday seemed interested only in the artistic possibilities, but she did explain two terms.

"Changelings are those poor unfortunates caught in a changewind who manage to make it to such places," she told them. "They are often horrible or grotesque, and not all were Akhbreed to begin with. Some are partly changed—only a part of them received exposure and the result was able to live—and they are the halflings. The accursed—they may look similar or look ordinary, but their troubles are due to more deliberate magic. The changewinds are random; the accursed are truly that. Often they change in the dark or under special conditions from normal to quite mad, or from man or woman to beast. The others—criminals, malcontents, political refugees, zealots. Boday thinks most will keep well out of sight, particularly if we have troops with us. Most are there because they do not *wish* to be seen."

The next morning dawned bleak and dreary. Kwei was gone; in its place was a slimy, creepy-looking swamp that was being wet down by a light, misty rain. The road still continued on; this one, however, was not in nearly as good shape as the one into Kwei; it was hard-packed and looked paved and slightly elevated and it had potholes in it that looked mean enough to bounce a wagon to the moon. There was a tiny border post there but it appeared unmanned. Boday read the sign on it that said, "Mashtopol Entry Point. All entrants should report to Customs Office in the Village of Muur, one hundred and six leegs."

"They're real worried about their border, aren't they?" Charley noted sarcastically.

"About as much as they are about road maintenance," Sam responded, eyeing those potholes. "This is one I'm glad we *don't* have to go through."

Jahoort got them all assembled as if it were just another day's journey, but this was different. For one thing, all of the crew, including Jahoort, were now packing weapons. Sam saw pistols, rifles, shotguns, even fancy crossbows. They looked loaded for bear, that was for sure. Some of the people traveling with them also now were armed, a few with swords, fewer with guns which were generally prohibited to the public in Tubikosa.

The navigator stood a moment with the Pilot who'd brought them through with no trouble. "I'll be picking up an inbound sometime tomorrow if he's on schedule," the Pilot was saying. He offered his hand. "Well, good luck. It's been a pleasure, as usual. Take care through that armpit you're going into and shoot anything that don't shoot you first."

Jahoort took the Pilot's hand. "Well, can't say I'm fond of taking paying passengers this route, but in a choice between saving money and risking lives the Company always chooses the money. I been that way dozens of times, though. It's not as bad as it's cracked up to be." He pointed to the swamp across the way. "Now, *that* just shouldn't be allowed. I'd rather go through Kudaan than risk horses, nargas, and wagons on that kind of road."

With that, he stepped out, mounted his horse, then rode right up to the gate at the border, and stared out at the swamp.

Again the scenes changed, first slowly, then more rapidly. Again infinite variations flashed before them, and again it suddenly stopped and there before them now the road led into the Kudaan Wastes.

"Bleak," said Sam.

"Beautiful," said Boday.

"Oh, wow!" exclaimed Charley.

11
When the Desert Storms

The misty rain and the humid feel suddenly vanished and they were hit by a sudden blast of incredibly dry, superheated air.

Charley had not been far off in her guess. The Kudaan Wastes resembled the Four Corners area of New Mexico, Arizona, Colorado, and Utah; the land where most western movies had been made, the land so pretty but so bleak nobody had even *wanted* to take it away from the Indians.

It was a broad, flat plain punctuated with tall mesas and buttes of multicolored rock, twisted spires and places where the land ended in great gashes revealing more rock layers as you looked down into canyons. The colors were red, purple, black, white, tan, orange, even blue, in all sorts of shades and hues. The road was little more than a worn dirt track on the parched and cracked desert floor and it seemed to go off into the distance forever.

Jahoort didn't immediately signal a forward advance and it was fairly clear why. He had said that troops were to meet them here and escort them beyond the no man's land before them, but there was not a living thing in sight and sight extended a fair ways. No military also meant no Pilot, and that meant they were on their own with no warnings of what was ahead. He gave a hand signal and all members of the crew went forward to meet with him, the ones driving the wagons jumping down and walking over there or doubling up with the horsemen and riggers.

"Gentlemen, the safety of this train is our responsibility," Jahoort told his men, "and particularly mine. As you can see, no troops, no nothing, and I cannot maintain this synchronicity for very long, certainly no more than an hour. Any thoughts?"

Donnah, one of the older hands and the cargomaster, spat, then said, "Hell, boss, if we could drop the passengers I'd say go for it, but I wouldn't go in *there* with paying customers for nothin' if I could avoid it. 'Course, I'll do what you order."

"You know better, Donnah. We drop the passengers and make it, we're goona have to refund their whole damned passage and send a safe special back for 'em. Might be penalties, too. I ain't old enough to retire yet, let alone get kicked out on that account. Either we all stay or we all go. How say you?"

It was Crindil who spoke for most of them. "You know we're game for it, boss. Been kind'a dull lately. I haven't been through here in six, seven months, but I didn't have much trouble with Sanglar and I don't expect none with you. Seems to me we go and we got a real club to hold to Mashtopol's head. Still, there's too many women and children this trip for me to just bravo it. I say we ask them."

Everybody else gave their advice as well, but much of it was conflicting and contradictory. Still, the consensus was to go.

Jahoort was asking for advice, though, not a vote. He was an absolute monarch in the end and the final choice was his. "No," he said. "I'll not have the blood of a child on my hands because her father was a damn fool." He took out a pocket watch and looked at it. "Forty-nine minutes. If them troopers get here within that time we'll move in. If not, we'll try again tomorrow and the day after that until we get sick and tired of it and go someplace civilized."

He would have liked the option of simply defaulting to a better sector, but he really didn't have it. Those border posts that were staffed would not let them through if their papers said otherwise, and those that were not staffed were as bad as this one.

They held in position, as instructed by the outriders, waiting for Jahoort to signal go ahead or abort. Sam waited impatiently, the reins in her hands, and scanned the terrain with her binoculars. Nothing much to see. Time dragged, and even the nargas grew bored and restless.

Jahoort, too, sat atop his horse scanning the road, as immobile as a statue, except that every once in a while he'd take out his watch again and look at it. He was just about to give up and tell everybody to return to camp formation when he gave one last look down the road. There, in the distance, he could see riders coming toward them, kicking up a bit of dust, definitely in formation. They had four minutes really to cross, and he had a split second to decide. He turned and made the call of "Ahead at full speed," and they began very suddenly and quickly to move, the outriders screaming at them to hurry up and cross and never mind the formation or the road. They'd fix it later.

They were through the border before anyone even had time to wonder what would happen if they didn't make it—or, worse, made it halfway. Later they were reassured to learn that that simply did not happen, although the shift could occur the instant you were across.

Jahoort wasted no time in reforming the train, and everyone was so busy that they could pay attention only to themselves. It was Charley, looking out of the back of the wagon, who wondered idly where some of the riders had gone and worried for a moment that some of the crew might have missed the crossing, but she dismissed the thought. She could not, after all, see everything, and nobody else seemed concerned. As soon as everyone was formed up and ready to go another reality hit them that began to occupy their attention.

It was hotter than hell here, and so dry that perspiration seemed to evaporate as it formed on the skin. It bothered them all almost immediately, but it didn't seem to concern Jahoort, who had to be broiling in those buckskins. His attention was entirely on the oncoming riders.

In back of them, the landscape was now tall, seemingly impenetrable mountains rising up through clouds. It was as barren a landscape as this one, but it looked a lot cooler. Wherever Bi'ihqua now was, it wasn't connected to them anymore.

Jahoort waited for the riders, letting them come to him. There were ten men, in the blue uniforms of the Mashtopol Forces, but wearing white headdresses that sheltered their faces and left their dark, brown features to peer from folds of cooling white. Considering the dark blue uniforms had to soak up the sun, nobody could figure out how the hell they stood it.

The man leading the ten-man patrol approached Jahoort and saluted. "Pilot Captain Yonan, sir. Sorry we were delayed. I hope we didn't inconvenience you."

"Quite all right, Captain," Jahoort responded, looking over the men. They were a motley lot, and a couple looked like they had beards beneath those burnooses. "I'm most anxious to clear the Furnace Region by nightfall. If you like, I can have the water wagon release some into the portable trough so your horses can replenish. Then we'd best be off."

The officer thought a moment. "Kind of you, sir. I believe we will."

The navigator gave one of his signals and the water wagon driver lowered the trough and then turned a valve releasing water into it to a depth of perhaps six inches. Enough for all of them, three or four at a time.

"That's the filthiest, motleyest crew of soldiers Boday has ever seen," the artist commented as they went past. "Look at that. Dirt all over, and even rips in their uniforms."

Charley scurried back to get a good look, then went over and opened one of the trunks. "Sam—warn Boday. Here's that short sword of yours. Be ready for it. I'm getting my knife and blow gun."

"Wha—what's the matter."

"Sam, those aren't tears in some of those coats, and they're dirty for a reason. Hides the blood stains, but not completely. I guess the lead ones had the most intact uniforms." She saw that Sam still didn't get it. "Sam—they're not soldiers, and in that condition they can't play-act being soldiers real long."

"Jesus!" Sam turned to Boday. "Charley says they're not soldiers. They're a gang in soldier's uniforms."

Boday did not have an emotional reaction, but simply responded, "Good."

"Good?"

"Yes. Boday would hate to think any so mangy could be real soldiers. Tell Charley to hand her the whip."

Jahoort maneuvered around on his horse just to one side of the gang as they went for the precious water, then drew his two pistols. "Pilot Captain!" he yelled. "You should tell your men to shave. And uniform means uniform—including bullet holes!"

They turned and drew their own weapons, but as they did the navigator fired and the top of the water wagon suddenly swung out on hinges and four rifles fired simultaneously. The maneuver was obviously carefully planned and perhaps a standard for the crew; as five raiders fell without firing an accurate shot, one jumped to the water wagon and the other four turned to run before there was a reload. They didn't make it; the three remaining mounted riders of the crew opened up, cutting two down, then took off after the other two.

The one who'd jumped on the water wagon, however, struggled with the driver and then managed to sock him hard on the chin and push him over. The raider then grabbed the reins and started off, yelling at the narga team to make speed.

Boday stood on the running board of her wagon and waited. When the water wagon came close to pass, her whip snaked out and actually caught the driver, who was not hurt but was so startled he dropped the reins. The nargas weren't all that fast, but they were fast enough and now had no control. The top-heavy wagon overturned, breaking the hitch and crashing to the hard ground, while the team continued on. The huge, keg-like wagon cracked a bit, and water began spilling out of one of its seams even as the men in the compartment up top struggled to get out.

Jahoort made for the water wagon and got there just as the raider was picking himself off the ground. He stared into a reloaded pistol and raised his hands, palms out.

The three outriders were even then returning—empty-handed. "Two got away, boss," Hude told Jahoort. "They made it into the rocks over there and it could be all day catchin' 'em. We figured it was better to get back here."

"Help the men out of there and tend to any injuries," the navigator ordered. "This scumbag is going to talk if I have to get that alchemist woman to make him fall in love with a narga."

The wagon drivers checked on the rest of the fallen band of pseudo-soldiers. A couple were still alive, but they were badly wounded and needed attention they did not get.

Jahoort and Crindil stripped the one surviving raider stark naked and staked him down face up on the desert floor. He looked better with the uniform on, Sam decided. He was an ugly, hairy brute whose body seemed full of scars. He looked mean as hell, though.

The navigator took a sword from its saddle scabbard and then stood over the man. As he did there was a series of yells from the area of the overturned water wagon, and everyone looked to see what was happening there. The water had almost completely seeped out, wetting down the immediate area heavily enough that it should have been soaked through, yet it was drying even as they watched. Then, suddenly, they saw what the yelling was all about.

From everywhere under and around the overturned water wagon thick, green shoots like tentacles shot up—hundreds of them, growing, or oozing from the hard rock, whichever—with lightning speed and in a matter of a minute completely engulfed the wagon. One of the crew from the top, injured, had been pulled away just in time before the long green fingers came up right where he'd laid.

Boday turned to Sam. "Get Boday her kit. Some of those men might need help!"

Sam idly turned and picked up the small alchemical kit and handed it to Boday, at no time taking her eyes off the wagon which was now engulfed in the long, waving tendrils. Boday jumped off and went to see to the injured crew.

"My God, Sam! They're *alive!*" Charley breathed, watching the spectacle. "They're *moving!* Crushing the wagon!"

And that was exactly what they were doing to the entire wagon. Enfolding it, grasping it, then crushing it, tearing it slowly and methodically to shreds.

Sam frowned. "Are they plants—or what?"

Charley shook her head. "I think they are. I guess out here everything's below the ground and when water activates them or wakes them up they do all their living in a few moments. They're tearing that thing to pieces looking for the smallest extra drop of water still left, Sam!" She looked nervously down at the ground on which their wagon sat. "Do me a favor, Sam—don't spill anything. *Please* don't spill anything!"

On the other side of the still immobile wagons, Jahoort was fairly free with his sword over the captive.

"I'd like to pour some water slowly over you, but I can't spare none," the navigator said matter-of-factly. " 'Course, if I was to prick an artery along here and let the blood flow down it'd come to the same thing, wouldn't it? Only a lot slower." He kicked the man in the side. "What do you say, friend? Or do I maybe cut your balls off and let the blood make the *sippiqua* rise? That'd be a pretty neat entry into the body, wouldn't it, friend? They'd slowly drink you dry from the inside."

The man glared at him, but looking in Jahoort's eyes he saw immediately a reflection that scared the hell out of him. He saw himself.

"What do you want to know, you old fart?"

Jahoort smiled sweetly. "What happened to the troops? What's this raid all about, anyway? We don't have nothin' worth this kind'a risk."

"All I know is this changeling's got hold of some kind of repeater gun. Mowed all ten of them Whiteheads down in nothin' flat. Never saw nothin' like it. Neither did they. We was picked up, recruited for odd jobs. Good money. They told us to pretend to be the soldiers and make sure we met you soon enough for you to see us and too late to backtrack. Whatever we found was ours. Only thing *they* want's the Mandan cloaks. If you was too tough, we was to blow the water and scram. I'd'a got away, too, if that bitch hadn't got me with that fucking whip! All your horsemen were off chasin' the others."

"Mandan gold again! *Why?* Folks out here don't need no Mandan gold cloaks. They already been touched by the changewind. They can smell 'em so far away they can warn all Creation to keep out of its way."

"I dunno."

The sword moved; sharp as a razor at its tip, it traced a thin, bloody line on his thigh.

"I don't know, I tell you!" the man screamed. "I swear it! You don't ask no questions in this business, Cap. You just do it and take your reward or your lumps!"

The answer seemed to satisfy the navigator. "This changeling—what's it like? He or she? How's its shape and form? How would we know it?"

"All I can tell you is that it's a woman," the raider replied. "Wore a dark purple cloak that covered her up good. Sharp, nasty voice. Sounded like my ex-wife. Caught a glimpse of the face—not a bad looker, but you see them arms and the shape of that cloak and you know. Black, nasty arms. Devil hands with claws. I can't tell you no more. I swear it!"

"Oh, I believe that, son," said Master Jahoort, and slit the man's throat with the sword. He turned and walked away as the man still struggled, strangling on his own blood, which was seeping into the ground. . . . "Shoot any survivors in the head!" Jahoort ordered his crew who were looking over the wounded raiders. "I know everything I need to know and I don't like it! Circle for camp! Crew conference in twenty minutes!"

Three shots rang out. Eight of the ten raiders were dead, but they weren't very competent or clever enemies. They had merely been sent by competent and clever enemies. It had been an easy victory overall, and that bothered Jahoort as much as a tough fight.

Of the four men in the ambush compartment atop the water wagon, two had mainly bruises and a few cuts, one had a broken arm and rib, and the other was in worse shape. Boday was doing what she could, but without her full lab she could only set and treat and ease the pain; she couldn't do much in the way of repairs.

"All right, boys, they cut us down to size on this one," the navigator told his men. "I got suckered even though I'm an old pro at this. Somebody banked on even the most experienced pro's weakness for the schedule. They cut us down to size, that's for sure. I got to hand it to that crazy alchemist, though. Without her that bastard would'a disengaged the wagon and crashed it and got away with four good nargas. We couldn't chase him and save the boys up top and he knew it. Smart one. He should'a been leadin'. 'Course, if he had we'd be taken now and all of us'd be dead. Crin, how's the remaining water?"

"Not too bad," Crindil responded. "Everybody filled up like they were told to at the fort. I'd like more but I don't think anybody's gonna die of thirst."

Jahoort nodded. "All right. Whoever sent those ten men with the collective IQ of a narga probably didn't figure they'd take us. They probably just wanted to slow us down. Men like that are cheap, and, who knows, they might'a got lucky. But now we know. We got a changeling with some kind of repeater gun up ahead and I don't figure she's even trusting to that. I'll bet you a thousand sarkis that band that was raidin' in Bi'ihqua was just sittin' there well away from the fort waiting for either Kudaan to come up or somebody like me to bring it up." He looked in back in both directions, ignoring the majestic mountains of the other sector that also blocked any retreat for a short time.

"I figure they'd cross south, maybe thirty, forty leegs or more just to be on the safe side," Jahoort continued. "Cut that fence and come on through. It's fairly flat down there, an easy cross with no surprises but far enough down we couldn't see 'em. We go forward, we got the changeling with the repeater in front and them in back of us. They know we can't stay here 'cause the risk is almost certain somebody's gonna spill things and then the sippiqua'll cause us more problems than they could. From the looks of them mountains somebody involved has got navigator skill and I bet there won't be nothin' useful come up to retreat to before they close on us. I could go in a test of wills but that might take hours and I still might not win. You never know with these changeling types. If they didn't think they could at least hold me they wouldn't have tried this. And without a Pilot we're up shit's creek if we go off this road."

"I don't see where we got a choice," Hude commented. "I been through here myself once before. You go much this way or that without a guide and you'll be in a canyon or chasm or worse. Let's just get on that road and depend on some decent scouting ahead. I'd rather risk that repeater, now that we know it's there, than who knows how many pushin' us in back? Ain't but so many places you can put and hide a repeater, and we know they can't be more than maybe two hours ahead allowing for horse speed rather than wagon speed. Keep on both sides, never bunch, and if anything opens up go like hell!"

It wasn't a very satisfactory plan, but considering the alternatives it was the best available. At least they knew now what they were dealing with, if not the location and exact numbers. The train was formed up yet again, the people were briefed and, if they could handle them, given arms. Then they pulled out.

A little over an hour later they all saw where the ambush had to be. The open desert area was growing wilder and nastier as they went, and in a few miles more the road would descend from the cracked desert with the tendril-like lurking plants and into a canyon formed by a now dry riverbed that, either in the past or on rare occasions now, had lots of rushing water in it. The canyon narrowed around the road in at least two places, either one of which had perches that seemed impossible to reach but, if they could be reached, would be ideal spots for ambushers. For now, though, they were still on the sippiqua flats, a fact that made everyone a bit nervous.

Jahoort stopped the train with the intention of sending men forward on either side with binoculars and rifles, with the hope of spotting the ambush and, if not taking them out, at least making it very hot for whoever sat there. If there was enough of a crossfire from enough rifles and pistols, one bullet at a time or not, then the wagons might be able to haul ass through the narrows before they could be cut down. The road was also very well defined through the area; Jahoort, if he knew the location of the gun, might risk running the thing at night.

From the rear of the train came the sudden shout of "Dust behind!" which put an end to such thoughts. The raiders from Bi'ihqua, as the navigator had figured, had closed on the train and were now riding full in to force them forward into the slaughter.

Jahoort quickly rode back to the rear of the train. "How many you make it, Dal?"

"Shit! Must be a dozen at least. Maybe more. Remember, they been hittin' *trains* in Bi'ihqua and gettin' away with it!"

Sam and Boday had jumped down to see what was going on, just like some of the others. The dust cloud approaching told the story, and they knew as well as the crew what had to be ahead.

Boday let loose her whip. "Well, little flower, we die together!" she sighed. "They shall never take you unless it is over the body of Boday! Do not be downcast! It was meant to be! And the heroic death of Boday will awaken the critics who will proclaim her a legend and the greatest artist who ever lived!"

Even Charley was pretty glum right now. "All this for nothin'. Damn! Wish I had a couple of guns right now!"

Sam had just stared at the cloud, not believing that it could really be happening. Not now. Not to her, and Charley, and Boday. Not to those nice kids. . . . She clutched the Jewel of Omak. "Demon, get us the hell *out* of this!"

You expect miracles or something? asked the demon. *I'll save you if I can but you know my limitations.*

"Damn it! You forced me into this!" she screamed, suddenly terrified.

Charley sighed behind her. "I sure wish we had one of your damned thunderstorms *now,*" she sighed.

"What?" Sam was hardly even sane anymore as she continued to stare.

"One of your damned thunderstorms. Can't you see what would happen if it rained on them? Especially *here?*"

My God! Why not? Sam thought crazily. *They came every time before!*

Distances were deceiving on the flats; the crew was circling and setting up the train for defense methodically, with no sense of hurry.

Sam looked up at the sky. A few wispy, white clouds in a pale blue field, nothing more. Just like back at the cabin long ago. . . .

"Okay!" she screamed up to the heavens, loud and forcefully. "You blood-sucking nightmare storms! You been huntin' me and huntin' me! Well *here I am!* Come and get me!"

The wispy clouds started to move. The fact that they actually did both awed and startled her, and at first she didn't believe it, but *they were actually moving!* Thickening. Drawing moisture from behind them—from whatever sector of Tubikosa was now along the border maybe ten miles back!

Now there was a near solid wall of clouds in the distance, going from horizon to horizon, a weather front so straight you could have drawn it with a ruler. On their side it was sunny and blue, sucked of any clouds, but at that line it was dark and rumbling. . . .

"Holy shit! You *did* it!" Charley exclaimed, a little awed herself.

No, not *quite* ruler straight. Centered perhaps right over the road there was a prominence coming out from the front, forming . . .

A head. A clearly defined picture of a face in the clouds sharp as a cheap photograph and just as solid. A face and a neck going down to the shoulders, with arms out, infinite arms, that were the front itself. . . .

A face she knew.

Charley might have been awed but she was more scared than that and she had a sudden horrible thought. "Sam! Boday! *Get in the wagon! Get us the hell off this mesa or we're gonna be sucked up, too!*"

Sam just continued to stare and Boday did not understand, so Charley went up and actually shook Sam and repeated her panicked warning.

"Charley—the clouds! There's a face in the clouds!"

"I don't give a fuck if there's God Himself in the clouds! We gotta move and you got to warn the rest!" Charley was nearsighted. She could see the storm as an approaching line of darkness but could not make out even so huge a detail.

Jahoort and the others weren't so oblivious, either. They yelled and screamed and told people to forget anything and just do a firm hitch and get into the canyon and stop. They had to beat that rain.

That Boday heard and understood as well, and she practically yanked Sam away and back into the wagon, which they'd never even gotten into defensive position. Charley needed no persuading—she was back inside quicker than they could get on the seat and jiggle the reins.

Nargas weren't very fast animals even when pushed, and the dip down into the canyon was narrow, really no wider than two wagons' worth if that, and a bit more than a mile away at the start. It was going to be a very near thing for most of them as the front with the strange head came ever on.

Sam peered back nervously. "But it's gonna catch me this time!"

"One damned problem at a time!" Charley yelled, wondering if they *would* make it. Some of the professional and veteran drivers, sure, and maybe all the ones on horseback, but she was dependent on two citified novices doing all the driving.

But Sam suddenly snapped out of it and took the reins like a pro, getting the nargas into a rhythm and making the best possible time without becoming unbalanced. The demon of the jewel couldn't handle ambushes and small armies, but it sure as hell knew how to drive a wagon.

They drew abreast of a cargo wagon going at top speed and the nargas, seeing the competition, matched pace, but they were mere inches apart. A mistake on the part of either driver or the nargas themselves would bring the two into a side collision at speed.

Then they *did* bump—once, twice! It was all Sam could do to control the nargas and keep them straight but she managed. Charley was holding on for dear life and looking back out the back flap. She couldn't see any horses or wagons and figured they had to be last, but she sure as hell could see that dark approaching mass. "It's gonna *catch* us!" she muttered, teeth tightly clenched.

The edge of the rain shield raced after them, darkening the parched desert and causing in its wake a veritable jungle of thin, waving tentacles to rise all across the plain, turning it from a sun-baked nightmare into an instant sea of living, active plants.

And then they were down, down into the canyon, the walls rising up, as rain suddenly overtook and then enveloped them. Sam started to pull up but Charley yelled, "No! Keep going if you can see!"

"But the ambusher!"

"The hell with the bushwhacker! If he can see to shoot anything in this shit he *deserves* to get us!"

This thought had not occurred to everybody, and there was almost a traffic jam at the bottom for a moment. Jahoort and his crew, though, were there, drenched by the rain, screaming at people to keep going. They no longer cared about the bushwhacker; this much rain would cause a flash flood of this dry riverbed very quickly, and that narrow ambush spot would be like target zero when the dam burst in a very short time.

Sam needed no urging. Demon-driven, she made her way expertly around those too scared or dense to move and made it full speed for the opening ahead. Already the dry riverbed was starting to fill, and there was almost a waterfall behind them.

Something went *smash! ping!* inside the wagon but she didn't stop and was soon on the other side and pulling to the side, off the road, where it was higher ground. Still she didn't want to stop, though; others would come through and would need room as well.

The highest point available wasn't very high, particularly with the crush and in the near-blinding rain, so she picked the best spot she could and stopped, then turned around. "Charley? You okay?"

"Yeah. I *think* so," her friend muttered. "Jesus, Sam! There's a line of fucking *bullet holes* through the wagon and half our stuff! That's no repeater—that's a damned *machine gun!*"

"Take the reins, Boday," Sam said, handing it off to the artist, and went back where at least it was nominally dry. There were holes in the canvas top, though, through which rain was coming, and wood was splintered in a neat diagonal line. Charley had taken a small knife and was busily trying to pry one of the spent bullets out. After a while she exposed part of it, enough to see what it was.

"Thirty caliber, copper jacket," she said, shaking her head. "That gun's regular Army issue. With guns and ammo like that it's no *wonder* those soldiers got mowed down. Without that rain there was no way to keep that sucker from taking out the whole train easy. They got nothing to fight *this* kind'a stuff." She stopped a moment, thinking. "You know, with enough of these just a few could really hold off a whole damned Akhbreed army. Son of a bitch! I think maybe they really got a chance to pull their revolution off! Imagine a couple of these in the hands of a couple of little Bi'ihquans instead of melons!"

Sam nodded absently. "Charley—there was a face, a head, in the clouds."

"Yeah? So? What's got you so hung up? Never seen faces in clouds before?"

"Charley—it was *your* face. It was your face in the clouds, bringing on the storm like a cape."

For a moment Charley was taken aback, then she got it. "Uh-uh, Sam. Not *my* face. *Your* face. I'm the gal with the big nose and the chubby cheekbones, remember? This is *your* face, only prettied up a bit and still thin."

Sam shook her head slowly from side to side. "Uh-uh. I always had a boy's face. This face was real feminine-lookin' even though it had short hair. That's how clear it was. And it had somethin' on its head or around it—a headband or crown or tiara or somethin'."

"Sam, there's a lot more that goes into a face than that. It was yours—and, even though I know it sounds crazy, if there *was* a face in there it *should'a* been yours. All this time you been running from those storms and you *call* 'em. You called this one, crazy as it sounds."

"I didn't call those other storms. They were *hunting* for me." But, dimly, she remembered that last one at the mall, the one that had scared her half to death. She had told it to go away—and it had.

"You gotta think magic around this place," her friend reminded her. "If you can call a storm and make it do tricks, then so can other people. So now we know there can be good and bad storms, right? Sam—this is important! Not just now; 'though Lord knows if you hadn't done it the rest wouldn't make no difference, but in general. Sam—*you can do magic.* Not Boday's potions, and maybe stronger than your pet demon's tricks."

The storm was letting up; it had almost passed now, with just some light rain and dreary mist on its back side. Suddenly the wagon started to jerk and lurch, and both women moved forward.

"Darlings! The nargas will not hold still! There is some kind of noise—you hear? The ground seems to be shaking. . . ."

Charley was born and raised in the southwestern desert and it didn't take her long to figure it out. "Cut the team loose!" she said sharply. "Cut 'em loose!" She stood on the seat and looked around. Damn! It was near sheer cliffs around here. There might be a few holds here and there but there wasn't much time.

"What d'ya mean, 'cut 'em loose'?" Sam responded.

"For God's sake cut 'em loose and climb up as high and fast as you can for dear life!" she screamed. "Sam—*it's a flash flood!* Any second now!"

Sam didn't have to hear any more. "Boday—cut loose the team and climb the walls! Flash flood!"

Boday jumped down, knocked loose the pin, then made sure Sam was down and made for the walls. In back of them, they could see remnants of the train scattered all over the canyon floor, some still inside that narrow stretch that would be flushed like a toilet any minute. There was no way to do more than scream warnings as they got up as high as they could. Charley was way ahead of them, her hands holding onto a very narrow rocky outcrop. She intended to pull herself up if she could, but she turned and saw the wall of water coming and could hardly believe her eyes. The surge looked like some dam had busted.

As if in slow motion she watched the narrow end of the canyon as horses reared and started to run while others, just stick figures, turned and watched what was coming in sheer panic.

The water hit her like a brick wall and instantly she, who had gotten the highest up, was nonetheless in the water and being carried at high speed toward the rock wall of the narrows, back where she'd come from.

She kicked off her boots, took a deep breath, and went under, hoping to ride the center surge.

Charley came to in what seemed to be dense brush. For a moment she didn't know what had happened or where she might be, but after she'd coughed up a little water and taken several deep breaths she suddenly thought, *I'm alive! I made it!*

But—to where? The top of the canyon? Not likely. Somewhere high up in that narrows section where there were lots of ledges. She got up, feeling a bit bruised in the ribs but otherwise surprisingly good. Her long hair was waterlogged and it took a lot of wringing out before it was manageable enough to forget for the time being.

It was only a few yards to the edge and she saw she was just where she thought—on some fairly wide and lengthy ledge about two thirds of the way up the canyon wall. At least the bushes here didn't drink your blood—although it probably wouldn't matter if they did right now. After that drink *they'd* had, there was no way they could take any more for a while.

The water was already receding and, frankly, gave little hint of what it had been not long before. The clouds were breaking and the sun was actually coming out. It seemed good at first, but as soon as the heat and tremendous evaporation hit she began to wonder if clouds weren't better.

She couldn't see well enough at this distance to make out details, but it looked like loads of debris scattered all over the canyon floor, maybe even the bodies of drowned horses and nargas. Maybe the bodies of people, too, she thought suddenly. Sam, Boday, those really nice kids . . .

She had survived, although it looked mostly like luck. Maybe others had as well, although she wasn't at all sure how good a swimmer Sam was. Maybe that demon knew all the swimming tricks, though. It was a hope. The water level had been high enough but not so high as to wash anybody up out of the canyon, that was for sure, except maybe right at the end—and that would have washed them right into those creepy crawlies that lived there. Of course, they were so saturated that somebody might have a chance if they weren't so full of water they couldn't come around in time to get back.

Still, she knew she had to face facts. She could *hope* they survived, hope that *everybody* survived, but from a practical point of view she was alone and it was one hell of a long way down without a rope.

She examined herself. A few scratches, probably from the bushes, and the bruises, nothing more. She was oddly undressed, though. She'd been wearing one of the stretch pullover tops and that had come through fairly well, but when she'd contorted to get the boots off she'd also slipped off the pair of work pants that threatened to drag her down with their extra waterlogged weight. She was naked from the waist down, a rather odd feeling. She slipped off the top and wrung it out as best she could, then went over to lay it out on one of the bushes to dry. Better something than nothing with this sun. She was about to stretch it out when she suddenly saw a hand and gasped. She cleared away as much as she could and found a man there.

He was dead; no question about that. It was Fromick, one of the quieter crew, who had been one of the men who'd set out after the two surviving raiders. His clothes were bloodstained and ripped to shreds—he must have hit the rocks and not much use, but, oddly, his gunbelt was still on and the twin pistols still in their holsters. She didn't like touching dead men, but if she could have made use of the shirt or pants she'd have done so. She undid the belt and managed to get it off him. Most crew kept their personal stuff in the crew wagon, but these belts often had compartments, pouches, whatever, for practical stuff.

It was well worn; a veteran's gunbelt, but it was also very well made. She examined it, felt it—it felt heavy and looked a bit too thick. There were also some pouches which she opened and checked, knowing that they were supposedly waterproof.

Some money—the hell with that. What good would it be here, anyway? A silver-plated cigarette case containing fifteen cigarettes and a small flint-activated lighting stick. That might come in handy. The cigarettes were dry; the odds were she could build a fire if she had to. A partly eaten bar of dark chocolate—*that* was a godsend. A tiny, toy-like penknife. And, all along the lining in a clever series of folds, bullets.

She examined the pistols. They were nicely balanced, if a bit strange to look at. No barrel. Somebody could make machine guns with thirty-caliber copper-clad ammunition, but nobody official had more than a single-shot weapon. Weird. Surely these people could figure out the principles involved. It was like there was a law against repeaters or something.

And, of course, she realized that this must be it. It must be, in fact, the explanation for a lot of crazy things like people with flush toilets, electric ranges, and elevators, who *didn't* have cars or trains or telephones or even telegraphs and whose guns had single shots so their swords wouldn't be obsolete. It was like a code. If the Akhbreed controlled everything, they also controlled what knowledge was permitted to get out and what could be made in the colonial factories. No repeaters. Not honorable or something.

But you didn't make fancy machine guns and the kind of ammunition they used without big factories, machine tools, standardized parts, lots of supplies. Either some king himself was with the opposition, which seemed improbable, or else that gun came from the same kind of place she did—somewhere else. If people dropped down now and again, then maybe machine guns did, too. But with bullets? Enough to make it worth toting around and using? It was still not making sense.

She ejected the bullet in the chamber, then stuck a dry one in and snapped it closed. Not bad, she thought. The shells were man-stoppers, more like forty-fours than police specials, but it *was* nicely balanced. She had—let's see—twenty-four bullets now. When the leather dried out, she had at least a weapon and one she felt she could shoot. Just like on Cousin Harry's ranch back home.

That sun was really mean, so she went back a bit until she had some shade from the canyon wall itself. The evaporation was so intense she felt like she was trapped in a steamer, but there was nothing to do except wait it out and try not to cook. She settled back in the shade, put the pistols beside her, and worked with the penknife on the gunbelt until she had a little if not very neat-looking hole where she wanted it. She tried it with the belt buckle—one of those fancy green stones that looked like a design cut to oval shape and mounted in a big, fancy brass setting sort of like the truck drivers wore back home—and it fit and seemed to hold. She got up and tried it on and it worked, although, of course, the belt was *way* too long after the hole and it was still a bit wide, although it hung nicely at an angle on her hips.

She was suddenly struck by how she must look, stark naked with a wide gunbelt and holsters with twin pearl-handled single-shot pistols and nothing else. It seemed at one and the same time the most erotic and damned stupid silly vision she could think of. *Watch out, Akahlar!* she thought crazily. *Here comes the Butterfly Kid and she's hot to prowl!* She needed something silly to think about right now, and she laughed about the vision, then took off the belt, cut some of the extra length off, removed the pistols and kept them with her, then stretched it all out to dry just beyond the shadow where the sun would be right on it. Then she sat against the rock wall and just tried to get some rest and eventually, in spite of herself, she did nod off.

She awoke what had to be hours later because the shadow was now very thin and even her legs were in sunlight; she started, and looked around. There was a strong wind up now, and a dry, hot one. It no longer felt all that humid but it still felt like an oven. She'd simply traded the steamer for the bakery. She was hungry and thirsty but there wasn't much she could do about the thirst right now and she didn't want to eat the chocolate for fear the extra dryness it might bring would drive her mad for a drink.

The gunbelt had flipped over and actually been blown several feet; the wind up here was pretty good as the climate returned to its former state with all deliberate speed. She retrieved the belt and then went over to the swaying bushes to discover that Fromick was getting very gruesome and very smelly and her top had blown away someplace. *Great,* she thought. *My only protection, such as it was, from this damned sun.* She briefly considered undressing Fromick and making what she could from his tattered clothing, but the look and the smell were just too much. She couldn't bear to touch that body, not for anything.

The noise the wind made blowing through the narrows made it next to impossible to hear anything else; no use listening for people or cries or whatever now, and she was too damned nearsighted to tell even if there had been an ice cream wagon in the canyon.

She checked the sun. Might not be long until it was beyond the other wall, and when it was it would get dark real fast around here. If she had any chance of getting off this place without help, now was the time to explore. The Butterfly Kid was on the prowl for sure.

The ledge or whatever it was was larger than she thought, and followed a curve around the rocky wall. Just beyond there was another bushy outcrop and it looked recently occupied. She drew one of her pistols and walked cautiously to it, then knelt down. Shells. Hundreds of them. And several spent cartridge belts as well. She suddenly tensed. *This was the ambush spot!* But there was no mysterious lady changeling, whatever that was, around now, and no machine gun, either. The fact that the assassin wasn't there was not unusual, since somebody from these parts could be expected to have some abilities to get around here. She got *up* here, after all. But machine guns—this wasn't the Al Capone type, this was the Army type. They were bulky and heavy. If this mystery bushwhacker could have levitated a machine gun she wouldn't have needed one. And she and it hadn't washed off—not if the shells were still on the ground. That meant there might be some way off this place!

She followed the rock wall along very closely and it didn't take long to find it. You don't expect to find a wide, flat piece of wood around this area. Two ropes secured it, nicely tied off to make an effective scaffold. *Hot damn!* She didn't even consider that there might be danger at the top; if she didn't get off here it didn't matter, and if they came back later and took this all away she'd be stuck anyway. She holstered the pistols as tight as she could, grabbed on to one of the ropes, and with a lot of effort started up the cliff.

She was amazed when she made it to the top. She never would have believed that her arms had the strength for it, but, then, she had a lot of motivation as well. The arm muscles hurt like hell and she felt exhausted, but she was up and out.

It was a crude wooden winch at the top, anchored by steel pins driven hard into the rock, but it was more than enough to haul up a machine gun, maybe all in one piece, and definitely pull up a person, too. That meant at least one, probably two people up here as well, most likely very big and very strong. Of course, it may have been the pair who escaped come back to rescue their boss, but Charley doubted that the brain behind this would trust to ones like them.

She surveyed the terrain. It was pretty jagged and some of the connections between sheer drops were pretty damned narrow, but she would have no trouble with it—if the light held. At least she had more of it up here, maybe an hour or more additional. It was like following a maze to get all the way to some safety, but aside from being pretty hot on the feet it was also easy. The right route wasn't that hard, either. They apparently hadn't taken or risked horses or other pack animals in here, but tracks of a small, narrow, wheeled cart or something were easy to make out wherever the rain had softened fill or dirt. It wasn't a continuous track, but it wasn't hard to spot, either. Probably the mount for the machine gun. And there *was* a trail of sorts, worn right into the rock. Clearly this was a favorite vantage point to look down on the road and not be seen.

Here and there, too, were hard natural rock depressions in which there was still collected rainwater. The rock was too solid for seepage and the depressions just a bit too deep to be evaporated in one day. She eagerly went to one, then carefully tasted it. It tasted like rocky rainwater, so she drank, and even took some and rubbed it on her body. The wind evaporated it quickly, but it felt good and at least she wasn't gonna die right off of thirst. She celebrated with two bites of the now nearly liquid candy, then reluctantly continued on. Light was failing and you couldn't afford a misstep in *this* country.

It apparently ended in a sheer rock wall, but when you got right to it you could see that the trail veered sharply to the left and continued on up. It was real nasty badlands, all right, but clearly *somebody* lived around here.

The trail reached the top, then followed it for a bit, then continued on part way down the other side. There was no way to get much farther today, and nobody, but nobody, human walked the badlands at night. She found a rock-ringed depression that gave some shelter from the wind and wasn't *too* uncomfortable and settled in. Both pistols were loaded with dry bullets; it was *some* comfort, but not much. Sooner or later she'd have to find somebody or starve or die of thirst or exposure. If that person were Akhbreed she'd be his or her slave instantly under the law—or else. If it was somebody else, it would most likely be somebody allied with the woman with the machine gun and that wasn't too thrilling an idea, either. One day at a time, one problem at a time. At least she was still alive and in one piece.

When it got dark out here, it got *very* dark *very* fast. The wind died down to nothing, though, causing for a while an eerie stillness. She slept for a while, never very long and never very deep, and then she'd wake up for periods, during some of which she would be unable to keep from dwelling on her fears. She'd been brave and tough long enough; she couldn't hold it back anymore, and during more than one waking period she couldn't help crying until she was just more or less cried out.

Then she'd just sit there, trying to see *anything* in the blackness. The stars overhead were pretty thick but blurry, and what moon there'd been went down not long after the sun. So she sat there, staring into the blackness, and after a while she swore she heard voices. Imagination? Wish fulfillment? She strained again to hear. Definitely somebody, maybe a lot of people, and some animals, too. Where? She carefully made her way back onto the trail and tried to look down and around. *There!* A sort of blurry glow like a big campfire or something. She wished she had better vision or glasses, but that was the best she could do. Now the question was, what to do about it?

There was nothing to do but try and make for it. Even if it was the bushwhackers, it might be the only chance she had. She'd be going down the trail blind and in the dark, so take it slow and easy girl, but the trail up had always had one side against solid rock. The trick would be figuring the curves. Slow and easy . . .

It took her quite some time, perhaps two hours or more, to get down, but finally she was close enough to really see where she was going. It was a big, mostly level area just off the main trail, set into a huge natural stone arch. There were horses there, and a few small wagons, and some people, too. She needed to get closer. It looked like a couple of guards down there, with rifles, but they weren't looking *her* way. Who could come from *this* direction, after all?

That allowed her to get in very close, close enough to see just what was what in the encampment. What she saw both excited and repulsed her.

There were two men with rifles all right, one at the head of the trail and the other by the fire. The one closest to the fire was wearing a dirty blue uniform; definitely one of the pair that escaped. The other might have been the other one; it was hard to tell for sure. There was also somebody asleep in the arch, maybe two. There were also four horses and a pair of nargas tied up there docilely.

Laid out to her right and the right of the fire was a grisly scene. There were bodies, lots of bodies there, all stripped naked, all terribly mutilated. Maybe five or more. All looked to be men, although it was hard to tell from that distance and in their condition.

To the left and nearest her were more bodies stretched out, but some of these, at least, were definitely alive. They were all lying naked on their backs, spread-eagled, their arms and legs apparently tied down with rock bolts securing heavy rope. All were female, and all appeared to have gags or something stuck in their mouths. She counted four and she knew them all. Boday was easiest to spot—long and looking like an abstract painting. Sam, too, was there, in all her corpulent glory, and the other two . . .

Sweet Jesus! The Serkosh girls! Rani and Sheka! Those *bastards!* It didn't take Sherlock Holmes to figure this out.

After it was safe, these men and their confederates had gone hunting for loot and maybe survivors. They'd found both, from the looks of it. They might even have saved a few lives—but not out of the goodness of their black hearts. The loot was piled up in front of the fire, with the Mandan gold blankets neatly separated off to one side. Sam—it was hard to tell but it didn't look like she had anything around her neck. Ten to one the Jewel of Omak was in that pile as well, the demon helpless with Sam probably unconscious and maybe half-drowned, while they cut the neck chain off her and tossed it in their loot sacks. Helpless now because there was nobody to aim the damned thing.

The male survivors had been brought here and then apparently tortured to death, either for revenge over the morning's work or just for fun. The women had been stretched out and, well, it didn't take much of a leap of imagination to figure out how they'd been used. Sheka—she was only nine years old, her sister just thirteen! *Damn* these monsters!

But what could she do about it? Two guards, and at least two more in the arch, probably with weapons nearby. She spotted the machine gun on its little cart, but it was well on the other side from her and looked packed down, anyway. Useless. She had two single-shot pistols. She had always been a good shot, and even with the distance she thought she could take the far guard, which would alert the one by the fire but wouldn't give him anyplace to hide or a clear target to shoot at. She might take both of them—but then she'd be at the mercy of the ones in the cleft until she reloaded, and that would take precious seconds. During that time those others could take cover—and use the stretched out and helpless women in between as a bargaining chip. Sam had twice come to her rescue. There was no question of not doing something, only what to do without getting her and them killed?

She had maybe an hour til dawn to figure that out.

12
A Choice of Evils

It took Charley several minutes to realize that the guard by the fire was asleep. It figured; he'd had a long day, although not as long as she had. Let *him* survive a raid, a chase, an ambush, and a flash flood and wind up in fairly good shape! Still, she'd experienced nothing like those prisoners there, and nothing like what they might experience if she couldn't figure this one out. She had no demons or magic jewels to help her, no special powers, but she *did* have weapons she knew and superb control of her body and whatever brains she'd been born with. They would have to do.

The real question was the other guard. If he was the other raider and he was asleep as well, then there was a chance. He had a rifle, perhaps other guns, and a very good field of fire for the whole area. If she had *his* position, then she might not be able to rescue the prisoners but she sure as hell would have a point-blank field of fire into the arch. Her long vision was poor enough that she might not be able to hit still forms in there, but she sure as hell could detect and hit moving ones, while she would be in darkness and behind some cover. She also wondered what a few rifle shots rattling around inside that arch might hit.

But first she had to get over there.

The fire was down but it still gave off pretty good illumination; there was maybe a twenty-foot section of trail that was lit, if dimly, by the flickering fire and its reflections against the deep rust red of the rock arch. If the trail guard had either nodded off or was concentrating entirely on the trail in the other direction, and if she was quiet enough, she had a chance. She just hoped there weren't two trail guards there; she would have to shoot the bastard from the start and then try and nail the other one before he reacted to the first shot. If there was somebody else up there or farther down the trail she was dead meat.

She had no reservations about shooting these men, though. In fact, if it hadn't been for her courtesan life where she'd met some pretty decent guys and had seen a slice of normal life, she might have had the impression that, here in Akahlar at least, all the men were vicious, brutish monsters, even the good ones. Even Jahoort and his crew had butchered those wounded raiders without a qualm; the only real deep down difference between them seemed to be that one was official and the other criminal. Just like in the Old West, where the only way most times to tell the difference between the psychopathic killer and the marshal was that the marshal wore a star.

No matter what, though, nobody with any guts at all could have any feeling for these men, not with the grisly sights laid out right here in front of them. The problem was, could she do it alone? Everything she saw told her that all she'd be doing would be adding another victim to these bastards' scalp belt even if she got one or two of them. Still, she would have to try.

She looked at the looming cliff wall that followed the trail opposite the camp; that went up who knew how far into the darkness and she wondered if there was any possibility of another route over to the other side. She backed off and decided to see if there was any way short of a direct walk down the trail where either of the guards might, if he wasn't really asleep, pick her off with ease.

Still, she didn't relish the climb. It might end in a sheer drop for all she knew, and it'd be pretty close to pitch dark up there. If it had been easy or a real threat to them they'd have put a guard up there, too.

That was a nasty thought. Maybe they did. Looking at the potential field of observation and fire such a post would present such a guard, she knew she damned well had to find out.

It wasn't an easy climb, but the rock was mostly layered shale on the far side and there were footholds, if tenuous at times. Still, it was very slow going in the darkness; for all she knew a single misstep might send her plunging a mile or two down into some nameless canyon.

After twenty minutes or so it began to level out, but just as she felt she had a real chance she sensed something in the darkness ahead and froze.

"*Shhhh!*" somebody whispered in Akhbreed. Then it added, in the lowest of whispers, "Come ahead, girl. I won't hurt you. I'm from the train as well."

She wasn't sure if it was a trick or not, but considering her position there wasn't much she could do but act as if it was not.

She hauled herself up and sat, breathing hard. She could see the figure of a man now propped against a rock outcrop, but it was impossible to tell more about him.

"You are the courtesan," he said softly. "The butterfly girl. I always thought you were a lot smarter than you were supposed to be. Can you understand me?"

She groped for the words and hoped they came out all right. The trouble with the language wasn't learning the words but duplicating the complex intonations. "Saa," she whispered back. "Ducadol, nar prucadol." *Yes. Understand. No speak.*

He gave a low chuckle. "You just told me you want to speak to my ass, not blow it, but I think I get the meaning. I saw you down there with the two pistols trying to work it out. I know how you feel. I was a mess when I crawled out of that damned ravine after hiding from them scavengers, but I made it after 'em. I was already busted up somethin' fierce; this just about's done me in. Kind'a hoped you'd try this route, though. I thought I could get the drop on 'em but wasn't much I could do. Might plug one or two of 'em but the rest would get me or hold them women hostage. They's bloody monsters, they are. Don't worry 'bout them hearin' me. Wind's wrong at this low pitch."

"Who?" Charley managed.

He coughed and seemed to shake a bit but got hold of himself. "Who, you mean? Them two guards is the ones who hit us and got away. There's four more in the cleft. One's Zamofir, the little fellow with the moustache from the train. He's banged up bad and wasn't with them but they knew him and took him in. He's a bad 'un. Two more are big suckers, maybe changelings. Hard to say. Their leader's mighty strange. Changeling sure. Woman in purple cloak and robes, real sharp tongue, but there's a lot more movin' under them robes than should be. She was the gunner—and the leader."

"Who?" Charley repeated, somewhat impatiently. She didn't like the idea of fighting six of them, not one bit—and if one or more were inhuman . . .

The man seemed to grope for a moment, then understood. "Oh—you mean me. I'm Rawl Serkosh. The two young ones down there are my daughters. It's why I had to follow and why I haven't been able to act." He shook again, this time in rage. "You don't know what it's been like, or how long I been wonderin' if causin' their deaths wouldn't be a mercy." He sighed. "Rini's dead. So's Jom. I don't know about Tan. Right now, though, them girls is all I got left."

She crawled slowly over to him. He had a gun—maybe more

than one. One was a rifle, anyway, and maybe there was ammunition. He saw her feel it and sighed. "Yeah. Took it off a dead narga. One of the pack animals. Rifle, couple'a pistols, even a crossbow. What good does it do me? I'm busted up bad inside. Bleedin' inside, too, I think. I ain't goin' nowheres now."

Her mind raced as she thought of how to use this poor man to best advantage. She struggled, then came up with a few words she needed. "Knife?"

"Yeah. Still got mine. Why?"

"Me cut girls loose. You—protect. Up here."

For a moment there was no response, and she was afraid that he was dead, but suddenly he said, "Maybe. If they ain't been drugged or magicked or somethin'." Again a slight cough. "Been thinkin', though, what I could do if I was able to move right. That big repeater of theirs. See them boxes right there? That's the bullets. Somebody stick a fire under that, all hell would break loose. Might blow up, might shoot all over. Yeah, I know, might kill the women, but they're better off dead if they can't be rescued. Go down, toss a fire under that gun wagon, then get back and cut 'em loose—I'll cover. Get 'em to the rocks on this side if they can move, otherwise leave 'em. When it goes, we shoot the guards under the cover of the bangs and booms. The ones in the cleft will stay put til its over, then come rushin' out, not knowin' we're here. By that time we'll have reloads. We have to nail 'em before they know they're bein' nailed." He paused a moment, as if expecting a reply, then sighed when none came.

"Yeah, I know," he sighed. "Odds are they'll spot you first thing. I'm sure both them guards are out cold—the one down by the fire ain't moved in two hours—but who knows how hard they sleep? One little thing goes wrong and it's all over. It was just the best I could do."

"Give crossbow, knife. Load guns." It was the craziest plan she'd ever heard and sure to get her killed or worse, but damn it it was worth a try!

"You know how to use a crossbow?"

"Saa," she responded confidently. She was ready to do this now, before she thought about it too much and realized how insane it was. The truth was, she really *didn't* know the crossbow, but the thing resembled a rifle with a bow and arrow set on top. She figured she could use it at the distances she'd be dealing with—and maybe without waking people up.

"You keep live. Shoot straight," she told him, knowing it sounded all wrong but that he'd get the idea. If nature didn't crush him at the critical moment, in which case she was at least no worse off than before, there was a glimmer of a chance. "That way safe?" she asked him, thinking that this would be better from the go-around position.

"Yeah. *Now* it is. Good luck, little beauty. May the gods bless you with success or death."

She made her way past him and for the first time saw why this was a safe route. There was a body next to Serkosh; a dead, rumpled heap that was all that remained of the guard who'd been posted up here.

"Arrow or knife right in the throat," he told her. "Slow death but they can't yell for nothin'."

Getting down was not all that much easier on the other side than getting up, and now she had extra things to carry. She was nervous that the crossbow might hit against the side of the rock and awaken the guard below, but she was loath to give up any added weapon.

The snores she heard from below gave her the first feeling of optimism she had. If the fellow by the fire was asleep, and this one was as well, then they were a pretty confident, complacent bunch—or stupid. They had, after all, depended on sheer numbers and brute force against the train. Effective, but not exactly subtle plotting.

This one was certainly dead to the world. She managed to get almost all the way down, and not as silently as she would have wished, without his breaking his snoring rhythm. He had a shotgun in his lap and a pistol on his hip, but neither had moved.

She carefully threaded the arrow into the crossbow and pulled it back until it latched, then crept toward the guard. For the first time she wondered if she could really do it. Kill somebody in cold blood, that is, rather than in a fight. She knew she could shoot him if he were awake or even became aware of her, but, like this, she wasn't so damned sure anymore. Easy enough to tell Sam to do it, but this was her and this was now.

She stood up, barely two yards from him, and raised and aimed the crossbow. If it had been loaded right, if she figured it out and it worked, she could hardly miss. She stood there a moment, frozen, all thought really gone, then she pulled the trigger—or tried to. It was jammed, somehow. It wouldn't fire! She realized instantly that there had to be a safety catch, fumbled for it, and found it, sliding it forward. She raised the crossbow again and took aim through its sights when suddenly the man jerked awake and turned and started to stand up!

It was almost as if the world had turned to slow motion, but she adjusted with a proficiency that only danger gave her and pulled the trigger. The arrow went off and went straight into his head, missing the neck and throat. He fell back from its force, then to her horror twitched, then started to pull himself up again! The force of the arrow had split his skull wide open; blood was pouring from his head, yet he still moved! She dropped the crossbow and went instinctively for her pistol, but then the man stood up absolutely straight, froze for a moment, then toppled back down atop his rocky perch.

Shaken, she dropped the crossbow—no more arrows anyway—and approached his body. She reached out and pulled the shotgun, a double-barreled type, from under his body as if he might turn and rise again at any moment. *That* was one tough son of a bitch!

The other one was asleep at the dwindling fire. That fire was beginning to die now from not having been stoked or fueled once again, and it was the only source she had for her own little bonfire. There wasn't any way around it; she'd have to quietly but boldly go right to that fire, get something useful and still burning, and torch the ammunition wagon, then make it all the way back to the captives before it went off. The hell with it; either she had cover or she didn't. She wasn't sure about Serkosh's long-term prospects, but as long as his daughters were down there she felt he'd keep alive on sheer will alone.

She gripped the shotgun, took a deep breath, then walked out into the exposed flat, keeping to the back of the guard at the fire, and alert for any signs of movement from him. Serkosh was certainly right, though; even if she had to blow this guy's head off and wake up the others, the first and only real priority—and hope—was torching that ammo.

A horse snorted and shifted slightly over to one side, and a couple of nargas echoed the sounds, which reverberated eerily in the camp, but the man remained still and there was no sign of real movement from the arch-like cleft. She circled around before going to the fire, so that it was between her and the sleeper, then knelt down. There weren't many trees in these parts; they had been burning the remnants of a wagon, and there were curved wooden pieces of ribbing there. She hauled one up, thankful that she'd been good at pick-up sticks as a kid, and got it free—but it wasn't actually aflame, just glowing red. She gingerly put its glowing tip back in the small remaining flame and caught it again, then slowly withdrew it, all the time looking up at the man on the other side of the fire.

Now it was slow going, guarding that flame, as she went back to the ammunition wagon. She reached it, but just as she did her flame went out again. She put down the shotgun and tried blowing on it, then swinging it in the air to get some oxygen to it. It glowed brightly, but wouldn't keep a flame. The hell with it, she decided, and touched it to a rope, then blew on it with all her lung power until the rope began to char and then smolder and then, with more blowing, she got a flame in the rope. It was tenuous, but it might work. She waited, oblivious to the danger, until it caught fairly well, then finally used it to re-light the stake. She touched off the covering over the ammunition crates and, when she felt she had enough small fires going, she threw the stake on top.

So far so good. She crossed back to the other side as if she owned the place, always with one eye on the sleeping man, and reached the staked out prisoners. She went to Sam, knelt down, and shook her. Sam stirred, then began to say, loudly, without opening her eyes, "No! *No!*" Charley put her hand over Sam's mouth and stifled any further outburst, and Sam seemed to settle back down. Serkosh had been right; they were drugged or something. That complicated things.

Charley took the knife from her gunbelt and sawed away at Sam's ropes. It wasn't easy; the ropes were fairly thick. Finally she got one, then a second, then the feet. By the fourth and final rope she was getting good at it; she knew by now where to cut for maximum speed and efficiency. Sam did not move even when less restrained; Charley hadn't expected her to.

She had freed Boday's arms when she suddenly stopped and froze. There was a sound from the arch, and she retreated back into the shadows and watched, glancing over at the ammunition wagon with the machine gun. It was smoking pretty damned good now but there wasn't any visible open flame.

A man emerged from the arch. He was big and covered with thick black body hair as well as a full beard and very long hair in back, and he was stark naked. The smoke was really pouring from the wagon now; Charley was certain that the man had to see it and got ready, but he went to a break in the rock near where the nargas were tethered and pissed.

When he was done he returned, but he was awake enough now to look at the man by the fire. He stopped, swore, then stalked to the sleeper, reached down, carefully got the guard's rifle, then pointed it at the sleeping man's head. "Sarnoc! Wake up you sleeping son of a bitch!" he snarled, and pushed at the man.

The guard stirred, then reached instinctively for his rifle and found it not in front of him but rather a few inches from his head. He whirled, saw who it was, and seemed to relax a bit. "Don't *do* that to me!" he exclaimed, more in relief than anger.

"I should blow your stupid lazy brains out," the hairy man responded. He looked out at the trail. "By the condition of the fire and the first slight lightening of the horizon I'd say it was only an hour to dawn. Did you ever relieve Potokir?"

The guard frowned. "He—he never come and got me. Never yelled or nothin'. Hell, Halot, he must'a gone fast asleep, too." They both turned in the direction of the guard and then suddenly spotted the near volcanic smoke coming from the vicinity of the machine gun. "*Holy shit! The ammo!* Hey! Everybody! The ammo's on fire!"

There was some stirring in the cleft, and just about that time the nicest little set of flames Charley ever saw popped up right in the center of the covering on the wagon.

"Get some water!" Halot yelled. "We got to get that thing out before it goes!"

Charley wondered if the thing would *ever* "go." It might not be very worthwhile to wait and find out; if the mere threat of it could bring out the others, and if Serkosh were still alive and capable of shooting up there, then between them they might well be able to take them out. There had been six, Serkosh had said; now there were five, and if one of them was Moustache he wasn't in any great shape himself.

Another man came from the cleft; a big, dark, ugly sucker pulling up a pair of pants. He had a shaved head and looked more like a professional wrestler than a gangster, but he sure looked mean. "Where are Potokir and Tatoche?" he thundered. "Halot! Fetch Potokir! I don't like the looks of this!"

That was too much. Praying that she was as good a shot with these things as she was with her dad's pistols back home and also praying that Serkosh took the hint, she took steady aim with the first pistol and fired. Halot cried out and pitched forward, a small wound in his back. Immediately she saw her mistake; she should have shot Baldy first, since he was closest to shelter, then Sleepy, and finally Halot. She aimed at the bald man who was starting to duck down and look around suspiciously and fired again, but this time she missed as the man dropped and rolled back toward the arch.

There was a sudden extra sharp report from overhead and to her right, and the bald man suddenly cried out and fell back. He wasn't dead, but he was hit pretty bad.

Charley reloaded, leaving any targets of opportunity to the man above them, and she heard another shot—and then several. Sleepy seemed to have figured out where the sniper had to be and gotten his guns; using the nargas for cover, he was shooting up into the darkness at Serkosh—but he was shooting blind.

Charley had to wait. The distance was too great for accuracy with these pistols—hitting a big man walking away was one thing, but this was an armed man behind cover and wary, and almost at the limits of her vision's resolution. It was a standoff, though; neither Sleepy nor Serkosh could move and neither could hit the other from where they were at. It was a Mexican standoff, and since those in the camp didn't and couldn't know just how badly hurt Serkosh was or even who or what he was, they were very much at a disadvantage. That had to occur to Sleepy and the pair still in the cleft; they would have to make a move or stand an indefinite siege, and daylight would give a potential sniper a clear view of everyone and everything.

Sleepy might have been sloppy and a sound snorer, but he was definitely a survivor in a hard life, once it was him or them. He startled both Serkosh and Charley by suddenly breaking free and into the open, using the shadows of the near dead fire and firing two shots wild up at his unseen assailant to cover his movements. Serkosh fired three times at him and missed, closely, all three times. It wasn't easy when you were dying and you also had to pick up a new gun each time.

Sleepy made it to the darkest shadows near where the captives lay. He took time first to reload his pistol and rifle, then looked around and spotted the cut bonds on Sam and Boday.

"You up there!" he cried out, his voice reverberating around the rock walls. "You throw down your guns and you come down—*now!* I'll count five, then I'm gonna start blowin' some beauties' brains out!"

He paused a moment, then shouted, "One! Two! Three! Four! Fi—"

That was as far as he got. Charley stepped out not ten feet from him and fired both pistols into his hulking black form. He screamed and fell back from the shock of being hit, and both his guns fired harmlessly in the air, the bullets ricocheting dangerously around the almost amphitheater-like camp. The effect gave her an idea and she cursed again her inability to really speak this tongue as she reloaded.

Serkosh, however, had the same idea, but when he spoke he sounded like someone already dead and rotting, a living corpse somehow alive and dangerous. "You in there! Come out with your hands up!" he yelled, his hollow, ghostly voice, amplified by the reverberations, sounding even more ghastly. "I wonder if you thought about how it would be if I pumped bullets into that arch cave of yours? Got lots of bullets. They'll make a nice *ping! ping! ping! ping!* sound, I bet. Might even hit somebody. Let's see."

He fired three shots at two-second intervals, about the best speed he could make with three guns. He was right about the sounds; being in there must be scary as hell. Charley liked that; these people should suffer a bit. She wondered why he should have all the fun. It was still just a dark hole in spite of the rapidly lightening sky, but she only had to fire into that dark hole. Two shots, then a reload even as the bullets continued to *ping* around inside. She was about to do it again when, at last, the ammunition wagon went up.

There was a tremendous explosion and a plume of fire, and then all sorts of small explosions and now the effect was not just on those in the cave, but on Charley and the captives as well. Horses and nargas reared and panicked, trying to pull away from their tethers and in some cases succeeding; in others falling to the sudden hail of random bullets.

Suddenly a tall, looming shape took form out of the sudden illumination of the cave, and the fire and small explosions and everything suddenly seemed to freeze and then be drawn—*sucked* was more appropriate—toward the dark form who seemed to absorb the energy and take on an unnatural blue glow.

A shrouded arm went out and up, and a stream of fire and bullets sped like a solid thing to the top of the cliff overlooking the camp, right at Serkosh, landing there with a flare and the sound of a hundred bullet reports. Charley heard a last, pitiable scream from on high and knew suddenly that she was alone once again.

She was also stunned by the incredible power that action had demonstrated. Damn it, if their boss was some kind of wizard why the hell hadn't she or he or it saved her men? Maybe, just maybe, the creature had only so much magic to use and saved it for self-preservation.

And now it came forward, a female figure in a dark, shimmering blue robe and hood. This, then, was the machine gunner and the mistress of all that had happened. What was it Serkosh had said? There was something odd about her, not quite human, as if she were hiding far more than a female form under that blue wrapping? Charley could see what he meant. The creature was large, menacing, and moved very oddly.

"Well done, well done indeed, my dear," said a sharp, crisp female voice from inside the hood. "You must realize that your bullets have no effect on me, and I know you must be over *there*. That trail is a dead end, as you must know. Come—I will make it easy on you. You saw how much I absorbed from the explosion. There were thousands of rounds in those cases and I used barely half to finish off your friend. Shall I, then, use the rest of them on your friends over there? Shall you watch them be ripped apart, into bloody messes, before I still come for you?"

Charley figured on this, but it didn't make much difference. What would be the fate of Sam and the others if she *did* surrender?

When there was no immediate surrender this also occurred to the blue-robed woman. She thought for a moment, trying to decide whether or not to go through with her threat or not. Charley hoped, even suspected, she would not; if she killed them all there would be nothing left to bargain with, and she couldn't be that selective. Those bullets went in a stream. There were clearly strong limits to this one's magic, but it sure as hell was better than no magic at all.

The blue-robed woman sighed, then reached a hand into a hidden pocket in her robe and pulled out something. "Jewel," she said—in perfect English, although in a *very* English accent, "who is this one I am facing and how do I deal with whoever it may be?"

Charley realized with a start that the villainness had the Jewel of Omak! But what would that damned demon tell her?

The woman in blue laughed. "So!" she said loudly in Akhbreed, "your name is Charley. How quaint. And I need but say a simple phrase in your native English to banish all but the courtesan in you. Did you even know that?" She paused, then said, in English, "Charley be gone!"

It was sudden and absolute. Charley no longer existed in a practical sense; only a very scared and very confused Shari.

"Come here, girl!" the woman in blue ordered, and she obeyed, totally bewildered and terrified. "Ah!" The woman in blue saw her now as she approached and knelt before her. "So! *You* are the one! I saw your face in the clouds you summoned that cleverly dispatched my men—at the cost of dispatching your train. What fun to have you in this state! How . . . *tempting* to keep you that way."

She put out a long, slender finger and pointed at the kneeling courtesan.

"Take off that ridiculous gunbelt with the guns in it and throw it as far away as you can, dear," said the woman in blue. Shari, who hadn't even realized she had such a thing on, immediately obeyed. The throw was pretty far for someone like her.

"This is such *delightful* fun," said the witch, adding, in English, "Charley return!"

Charley immediately came back to consciousness, now well aware of her complete vulnerability. *Damn* Sam! These little power trips were gonna kill them all!

"Ah, now the return. *Fascinating!* You may speak, my dear. I'm afraid that all of this complicates my plans a great deal, and your unexpected appearance after so long raises possibilities long discarded. I must think of this."

The blue cloak and hood effectively covered the strange witch from any real view, but Charley got a glimpse of a dark, beautiful face inside that cowl, and long, slender fingers with dark, long nails emerged from the sleeves.

"Who are you?" she asked the witch. "How do you know English? And how could you permit—*this?*"

The blue witch laughed. "I am Asterial," she responded, "and I am of no place but this wasted land. Once I was of the Akhbreed, like yourself, and a building sorceress, but then I was kissed by a changewind, forced to flee here, forced to seek my revenge on those who cast me out. Most had given you up for dead, you know, even myself. Only Klittichorn remained convinced that you lived and were not in Boolean's hands or his control. Now you are in mine, although I never expected it. A fascinating new set of possibilities unfolds."

Suddenly Charley realized why she was still alive. Ironically, Boolean's little trick had worked. The woman in blue thought that she, Charley, and not Sam, was the woman the Horned One sought. Not that it was doing much good, considering Sam's state at that moment. The demon inside the jewel apparently had gone along with Asterial so far because it did not threaten Sam, only Charley. The most practical thing probably seemed to the demon to let the witch kill Charley and believe the deed done, then handle Sam's own rescue in a less obvious way. It was an unsettling thought, but whatever worth it had to the demon was now negated. Clearly this powerful and ambitious sorceress was not going to kill her; at least not for some time.

"At least you could tell me what all this is about," Charley prompted, feeling a bit more secure and hoping that conversation would keep those damned words away and keep her mind whole. "I've been snatched from my own world after many attempts to kill me, tracked all over, and I really don't know what this is about."

"Ambition, my dear, and power, as usual," replied Asterial. "A great wizard has turned against his own kind and works to bring an end to Akhbreed rule. Quite naturally he couches this in liberation terms, but his true aim is to rule—first here, then everywhere. We all know it and even his allies suspect it, deep down, but they go along dealing with the devil in the knowledge that he is the only hope, perhaps for thousands of years, to overthrow this wicked system. They join him with prayers that perhaps they can find some way to stop him as well. You, my dear, represent a dagger at his throat. You see, whosoever defeats the Akhbreed will need the changewind as his weapon. Even Klittichorn cannot control the changewind, but the Storm Princess can influence, call, direct, nudge *any* storm."

"You mean—I'm the Storm Princess?"

Asterial laughed. "Of course not, my dear! How *could* you be? You are of the Outplane, not a native of Akahlar. No, my dear, you are her double, her parallel. Genetically identical in spite of different worlds, different ancestry, everything. The Outplanes contain all things that might have ever been, and certainly they include a few parallels of most everyone. But the forces of Probability have no way of telling one from the other except location. Here, on Akahlar, you have access to the same powers as she. You are identical, unless touched by the changewind or otherwise altered in your basic makeup. Here, her powers and your powers are indistinguishable. Here, you may, with the proper training, cancel the other out, and with it Klittichorn's ambition."

So that was it! She remembered when they fell through the great tunnel or whatever it was; the scene of the cabin region where the deer had changed, bit by bit, into something totally different. All those worlds. . . . And by sheer probability, on a few of them would be ones like Sam, perfect doubles, which an enemy of Klittichorn could turn. One by one the sorcerer had been seeking them out and killing them off. Sam's girl in the red car . . . Not Sam, but Sam all the same. Boolean hadn't been kidding them. Right now, Sam was probably the most important person on Akahlar.

Charley looked over at the captives, relieved to see no sign of wounds. They hadn't moved during the whole thing. "What have you done to them?"

"A bit of a test. I recognized this gem around the fat one's neck as an amulet of power. I simply put them under with it. The restraints were earlier, and remained on because I did not and do not know the limits of this amulet's spell. I am told that the painted one is an alchemist. When we get back to my lair I shall have her create potions that will create the perfect slaves. You have cost me most of my organization; it is therefore fitting that you all should become my obedient slaves and rebuild. But no potions for you, my dear. A few words are all it takes for you to become my willing and obedient slave—with your full self about as insurance against Klittichorn. After he wins it all, you will be there to give *him* a taste of the changewind. With the greater sorcerers gone and you at my side I shall exterminate the Akhbreed and myself rule."

"Good plan," Charley muttered dryly. She now knew the basics of it all and she didn't like the position they were in. It sure was gonna be a hell of a shock to this witch, though, when she trotted out Charley to do old Horny in and discovered she had somebody whose magic powers were less than nothing. Boolean must have much the same plan, but after revealing himself to Klittichorn it was impossible for him to act—if, in fact, he knew just where they were all this time. "And when's this war supposed to break out?"

"Ah! It will be a complex affair. Great armies as well as great magic will be required, and as for the magic it will not get two chances. Klittichorn may be destroyed but not aged, although the withering old fart is bad enough now. He has time to build and train and practice—and teach his little Storm Princess. In the meantime, he pays well for the Mandan gold cloaks we steal from the trains and whose manufacture is limited and very tightly controlled. One cannot use the changewind unless one's army is protected from it. Oh, we shall have a long, long time together before this all comes about, my sweet. Why, it might be many *years* before you are needed."

Charley thought fast. She'd come this far on bluff and bravado and sheer luck; this time it might well run out, but it was worth the chance.

She looked around. "Your gang's pretty well wiped out," she noted, "and the horses and nargas that didn't spook are dead or soon will be. You ain't gonna be able to move this shit, and you don't know who else survived with a gun and is sittin' around someplace waitin' for sitting ducks. Me, I don't wanna be Shari for the next ten years, but I got no axe to grind. I don't like what you and your boys did, but they paid for it. Now I got to think of me. Boolean or you is all the same to me since you got reason to keep me alive and kicking, but I don't owe old Green Robes anything. He sure dumped me in a vat of shit and left me there to sink or swim. I'm stark naked, marked for life, and I got nowhere to go. You, and this place, is as good as any. Seems to me, though, that I'm no match for my twin sister or whatever she is. Sure, I called the storm, and I sent one or two away, but strictly out of emotion or fear. Your horned boy is teachin' her the fine points and he's got years to do it in. You keep me around as some servile little ass-licker and when it comes time for the showdown they're gonna wipe the floor up with me."

Asterial paused. "Go on. Just what are you proposing?"

"Not exactly what you got in mind. More the same kind of relationship your big boy has with my twin sister. We get a sort of partnership. You teach me the magic and I'll handle the guns and work with you. You got nothin' to lose, after all. Like, all you do is say the words and I'm gone even if I got ten storms comin' in on you and five guns aimed at your head."

The proposition was really tempting to the sorceress, but she simply could not be sure. "I would *like* to trust you. Anyone who can pull this off is someone quite exceptional. You have done to me what armies could not. But seeing all this, even knowing those words, how could I ever be certain? You have not truly seen me. You are repulsed by what I permitted here tonight, even though it was merely payment to those men who were all I really had left. I believe you are from too moral a background to be trusted."

"I'll show you how valuable and trusted I can be—and how trusting," Charley responded, feeling her stomach tighten and hoping her nerves didn't show. "Use that jewel and bring one of the captives over here. The fat one—I already cut her bonds so she's the logical choice. I'll show you how to make a devoted, obedient slave without potions or new spells."

"But I was told she was your friend and companion."

"She is—but she also stuck that go away and come back on me, and I stuck out my neck once too often. She can still be my friend, she just will also be your slave. That's fair enough."

Asterial thought a moment, then said, "I will do it." She held up the jewel and let it open and its tiny beam fall on Sam, who stiffened when it hit her forehead. "Arise and walk to me," the sorceress commanded.

Sam got up, with some difficulty, and walked rather wobbily over to them, still in a trance state.

"Now," Charley continued, "you just shine that jewel on her and say, in English, 'I wish that you will forget all about Boolean and will instead become my obedient and abject slave for life beyond the ability of any spell or potion to change.' Don't forget the 'I wish' part and make sure it's in English."

"This grows interesting," the sorceress muttered to herself, too interested in the potential new powers of this thing to think beyond it at the moment. "I wish that you will forget Boolean or even that he exists and will instead become by abject and obedient slave, willingly and joyfully serving me as your only reason for living, and that this will be so permanent that no spell or potion may change it."

Suddenly there was a strange, hollow voice in Asterial's head, one she neither expected nor was able to cope with.

Command inconsistent with prime directive. I am not going to stay forever sealed in this fucking thing until the end of time!

Suddenly the jewel seemed to transform, growing in an instant from a tiny bauble to a huge, amorphous, sinister shape that was dripping both power and evil. It was unlike anything Charley had ever dreamed even in her wildest nightmares and she felt repulsed, unclean; she wanted to turn away, to run, but she could not. She had to watch.

Waves of amber-colored energy both enveloped and outlined the thing, and it reached out with a horrible, monstrous roar and took hold of the blue-clad sorceress, the energy waves growing to envelop her as well.

Asterial screamed and threw off her blue cloak, and Charley's mouth dropped. The sorceress *was* beautiful, but it was the beauty of the new dawn against the millions of tiny scales over her body reflecting every color and hue. The head and upper torso were human, but the rest of the body was like a giant insect, the two human arms the forelegs and the other six thin and spiny, and from her back suddenly emerged great sets of wings which began to unfold and begin a terrible buzzing.

My God! She's a six-foot-tall dragonfly! was all Charley could think.

Both figures rose into the air now, several feet off the ground, and the sounds from the two of them were horrible, the energy flowing through, around, and out from them like some fantastic lightning show.

There was a sudden great roar as Asterial expended the last of her acquired energy and all those bullets into the *thing* that had sprung from nowhere, but to no effect. It simply absorbed them and roared with a horrible ferocity and enclosed the insect woman in an ever-tightening embrace. There was a sudden brilliant, blinding flash, and both figures shimmered a moment and seemed to blend, then they simply faded out.

Quite suddenly there was a dead silence in the amphitheater, and, a moment later, something small dropped from a height and clattered against the rock floor, rolling near Sam's feet. It was the Jewel of Omak.

Sam began to sway a bit, then collapsed on her knees and went down on all fours, shaking her head as if waking up from a deep sleep. The others began to groan and shift, the two girls still bound and Boday's feet still held by the rope and stakes.

Sam looked up, appearing both haunted and confused, and suddenly saw Charley standing there looking at her. "Charley?" she called weakly. "My God! Charley!" And then she suddenly started to cry hysterically.

Charley rushed over to her and just held her and rocked her back and forth for a while. Boday, seeing the scene and having her hands free, managed to undo the knots around her ankles and then retrieve Charley's knife and free the two girls. For a while they were all stunned, all in shock of one kind or another, but suddenly Sheka, the cute nine-year-old, spotted the body of Halot, grabbed the knife where Boday had put it down, rushed over to the body with a cry and started stabbing Halot's still form again and again and again.

Sam got hold of herself, and Charley was able to get free enough to reach down and pick up the Jewel of Omak. "It must'a been tough," she said as calmly and sympathetically as possible. "Maybe you should use this to give her a little bit of peace."

Sam stared at the incessant stab, stab, stab, as the child cried and cried, and she shook her head negatively. "No. One day, yes. She'll need more help than this stupid demon can give anyway. Maybe we all will. But, right now, she should hate. If she hates, she might yet survive."

Charley started to respond, but she couldn't think of anything to say. Finally she managed, "You okay—otherwise?"

"I'll live." Sam was starting to think clearly again for the first time in the whole day of terror. She suddenly looked around at the dead bodies, the jewel back in her hand, the new carnage, and she was acutely aware that only she and the four others seemed to still be alive. "My God, Charley! All this—how'd you do it? Where's your army? And that—thing. That bitch. She was *evil,* Charley. I've seen a lot of bad people, but I never before saw pure evil." She was suddenly awed. "You did all this—yourself?"

"I had a little help. He's dead now. I—" But Charley could say no more. Suddenly she felt land and sky heave and she passed out cold on the rocky floor.

Things were different when Charley came to, not the least difference being she herself. She ached all over and she felt more tired than she ever had in her life. She was also incredibly thirsty, and everything was so damned blurry. She made out a figure sitting nearby and tried to call to her but only a croak came out.

Boday jumped at the sound, then rushed to her with a canteen. "Drink slowly," the alchemist cautioned. "There is plenty of water but too much at once will make you sick."

In fact she had to be forced to stop, then had a fit of coughing and dizziness, but her voice loosened a bit and she felt a slight bit better. "What—what happened?" she managed.

"We have been near dying to ask *you* that question. Even Boday had her doubts, it must be admitted. Captured, a night of horror, then put out by the jewel in the midst of a powerful and evil changeling and her cohorts, and suddenly—they are all dead or gone and here you are. But rest, relax now. Boday will not press you. We have been waiting almost two days for the story; it will wait a bit longer."

Charley felt her mind reel. "*Two days!* You mean I've been out for two days?"

Boday nodded. "You performed miraculously, my beauty, but you were not designed for this. Climbing, hiking, shooting, and who knows what else, with no rest and nothing to eat or drink from the looks of it. Boday wishes she had her kit to give you some help but it is all gone. You will feel this for some time. You pushed yourself well beyond your limits, and we are all blessed that you are not dead because of it."

She *felt* half dead, anyway, and sank back on the cot. How the hell *had* she done all that? My God, it was like some kind of weird dream. She couldn't believe it herself.

Using the canteen some more she splashed water on her face and rubbed her eyes. God, she needed a bath! A nice, warm, extra-long bath. . . .

By the time she was in reasonable shape to talk and feel some degree of normalcy returning, Sam was there, and they hugged and talked until morning and filled each other in on just what had gone on.

The flash flood had been more devastating, more likely, than Asterial's machine gun might have been to the train. It wasn't like an old-fashioned Earth flood which would have taken far longer to build, but it might well have been typical of what to expect in the Kudaan Wastes. Still, even with little warning, there had been some time to get ready for it and a fair number of survivors managed to swim to dryer high areas. It wasn't until later, when the waters receded, that the gang went into real action.

With Asterial as a spotter from her high perch, the quartet of henchmen was easily able to spot a number of living and dead and they had the expertise and equipment to get to them. The dead were stripped and left to rot; five male survivors in varying degrees of shock and injury were hauled out along with the four of them. Boday had clutched Sam with tremendous force and even the action of the flood hadn't separated them, but by the time they made it to a rocky butte they were all in and simply collapsed until found and taken captive. The other two girls had an even more miraculous escape, being washed straight through the narrows and onto the sides of the bowl-shaped canyon. All the captives had been stripped and tied with their arms behind them linked to a rope collar. If they struggled or failed to keep up, they might well have strangled themselves.

But they had some time to recover because their rescuers, Halot and the one called Tatoche who'd been later killed by Serkosh, had gone scavenging over miles of valley terrain, foraging for everything they could find. Some of the discoveries were astonishing—two wagons intact, although their covers had been torn off, and even some live horses and nargas. They put all the loot they could find in the wagons, then began their march around to the camp at the arch. Waiting there for them were Asterial and the two others who'd helped get her gun and equipment out of the ambush spot. It was unlikely that Asterial needed any help herself; Charley, from what she saw, was convinced that somehow the changeling could fly, at least for short distances.

Then, well after dark, when they had stowed away all they really wanted to keep and broken down and burned the rest, the night of horror had begun. Asterial encouraged it like some demonic queen; she seemed to take a perverse pleasure in torture and mutilation, although she did not participate—she presided.

The men—two paying passengers, three trail crew—were brutally questioned about almost everything they knew, then tortured, mutilated for sheer fun, and eventually killed. One man took a very long time to die. The women expected much the same, but while they were horribly brutalized, tied up, made to do most anything imaginable, and ultimately repeatedly raped, they were by Asterial's express command not mutilated or killed. She was a creature of some magic and so felt the magic in the jewel taken from Sam; she had experimented with it and in the process, of course, knocked them all mercifully out cold.

"What about Moustache?" Charley asked. "Zamofir, I think his name is."

"He was here and in pretty good shape," Sam told her. "He

seemed to know them and they seemed to know him and he sure wasn't treated bad, but he looked real uncomfortable at their blood orgy and stayed back in the cave. You didn't see him?"

"No, not at all, but Serkosh said he was there and he hadn't seen him leave, either. He didn't even come out when the fire started. He's not there now? You looked?"

"Nowhere. Some signs that he was there but nothin' else. I guess you were right about him, but he didn't seem to have nothin' to do with *this.* I'm pretty sure he had nothin' to do with the trap and didn't even figure on it."

"No difference. He works for the same master as they do. He's just the more genteel, brainy, sly kind of monster. The kind that don't care how many folks get murdered or raped or enslaved or anything like that but who can't stand the sight of it themselves. Instead they pay somebody else and order it done out of their sight and mind. I don't like the fact that he's disappeared so well here, either. He could'a answered a ton of questions for us and given us the lay of the land. More, I sure as hell would like to know *when* he split. He could paint a big target right on my butterfly eyes, you know. And if he knows any English he might know how to turn me off and on at will. Say—will you do me a favor? Use that damned thing and get rid of that? It's like a sword over my head. If Asterial hadn't been so damned arrogant in bringin' me back we'd all be slaves now."

Sam sighed. "I can't. I tried the jewel—it doesn't answer. There's not even any little beam of light. It stays closed and silent, like so much junk jewelry. That—*thing* you saw come out of it—could it have been the demon?"

Charley shuddered. "Could be. I hadn't thought of that. If it is we're well rid of it even if it was powerful and on our side. The damned thing—you said Asterial was pure evil, but she wasn't. She was just an evil creature, like a lot of others we've met this trip. This thing was. Pure, unadulterated, undiluted evil of a form and kind I just can't describe to you. I dunno. Maybe it figured a way to spring itself on its own. Maybe Asterial drew it out. Maybe they're both still alive." That gave her another chill. "If so, my neck's had it. Asterial will spend all eternity hunting me down and she knows just how to nail me, damn it."

Sam sighed. "I'm sorry. It was the demon who suggested it. Did it almost on its own, really, although I went along. All that power . . . You just can't not use it."

Charley sighed. "Well, it's done. At least we showed we're no pushovers. You looked for any more survivors?"

"Yeah. The girls went out. We couldn't stop 'em, so one of us would stay here with you and the other would go with them. Not much left even now down there, but well up the canyon past where we got—and we was the leaders, I thought—I swear there were wagon tracks. And somebody'd dug several graves. It could be that some of the train not only managed to escape Asterial's boys but actually put together enough to push on. Hard to say. They sure as hell pushed on without *us*. Trouble was, they wasn't much useful to us, neither."

"What have you got?"

"Well, we got five horses, if that's anything. I guess it is. All the wagons pretty much burned or blew up. Nothin' that could be done about that. We got lots of guns but only a few boxes of ammo that were in the arch. Plus some assorted knives, swords, spears—that kind of shit. Nothin' much for clothes. A few blankets, maybe, that kind of thing, and a couple of bedrolls. Saddles, too, if we can manage to get 'em on the horses. They're *heavy* sons of bitches. Took all of us to saddle up and go back down there today. The kids ride good, though, and I'll manage. Also six or seven of them Mandan gold blankets. Talk about *heavy*. They looked like dyed wool but they ain't, I'll tell you. Plenty of water here—there's a natural spring back there—and lots of these rock-hard biscuits. Could be worse."

Charley nodded. Daylight had broken by the time they'd finished, and she struggled up and insisted on getting to her feet. She still felt like every bone in her body was broken, but she knew it wasn't. In the end, it would go away, and she'd return to some semblance of normalcy. What worried her most was that the sun was up now and it was quite bright, but everything was still pretty damned blurry to her. Real clarity lasted only inches beyond her outstretched arm; after that the world just dissolved into blurry, indistinct shapes that, after ten or fifteen feet at best, became a nothingness. That one frantic night she'd seen with a clarity she hadn't remembered for years, but this was far worse than her usual nearsightedness now. It could be that her eyes were just like the rest of her—pushed by will beyond their limits, overused, overstrained, and that this would pass. She hoped it was so, but she had to wonder if that supernatural bout she had witnessed on top of it all hadn't given off more damage than it seemed. Right now, from maybe ten or twelve feet, she couldn't tell short, fat Sam from tall, painted Boday. They were just blurry, indistinct shapes.

She decided not to tell them, not just yet, but to wait and hope that vision returned. She could fake it for a while, considering her condition. They all had enough problems without her going blind.

The crazy thing was, a good eye doctor and a decent pair of glasses would probably restore her vision to better than theirs, but the only eye doctors were in places where girls like her couldn't wear them, and there seemed a real lack of medical help in the Kudaan Wastes.

Later, when all were awake, they held a council to decide what to do. The kids were a bit withdrawn but not nearly as much as Charley thought she might have been at their age going through what they'd gone through. It was also sort of embarrassing to discover that, to them, she was some sort of incarnate superwoman. She could easily have had the default leadership role if only she spoke the language. It fell to Sam to coordinate, with Charley kibbitzing.

"We should all turn 'round and go back," Boday suggested. "The loft is still ours."

"Yeah, and Kligos ready to take us all out," Sam noted sourly.

"Kligos!" The artist spat. "After Asterial, what is such a pimple to us? Boday is in her element there in any event. We have papers there. We are recognized, known."

"Yeah, but we'd have to get back through that damned desert with the creepy crawlies all alone," Sam pointed out, "and after that we'd have to cross who knows what land to get back to Tubikosa. No navigator, no Pilot, no choice."

"Oh, we might have to wait a dangerous day," Boday admitted, "but all we would need is one with a proper border post. The tickets, the passage, included insurance, darling! We make contact with a company train and we get a new wagon, new provisions, all of it. Or a free ride home on the first train going that way and a settlement."

"Yeah," Sam sighed. "And we're right back where we started from again. Maybe I don't have no demon pushin' me, but I didn't get fat and lazy 'cause of no demon. I did it to myself. This insurance works both ways, don't it? I mean, if we can make it farther on to some outpost it's one and the same. Maybe a little wait for the documents to be sent and catch up but that's all."

"It may be more complicated than that," Boday responded. "Besides, it would be hundreds of leegs yet to anything approaching civilization. We are no army and these are dangerous lands. Many days we would have to go without so much as clothes to protect us or anyone to guide us or warn us of the dangers."

"Yeah, there's never a mall around when you really need one," Charley commented sourly. Sam did not bother to translate.

"And who knows the level of corruption?" Boday pressed. "Two women, two children, and a courtesan, naked and without means but with large claims on a powerful company liable for those claims. Far cheaper to delay, stall, misdirect those papers, let us rot at some isolated army post. And have you not forgotten that we were raped by men with near magical capacities? What if one or more of us is with a rapist's child, stuck there in the middle of nowhere without resources snared in bureaucrat's tape? We must go back, Sam! It is the only reasonable thing to do."

Sam looked at Rani, the oldest girl and one of those who might well have that problem on top of being orphaned and brutalized. "Rani—what do you and your sister want to do now? What can we possibly do for you?"

"We want to stay with you," the girl responded unhesitatingly. "If we go back, you see, we will be—unclean. Our families will disown us. We would have nothing and no one."

Sam was appalled. "But you were attacked and *raped* through no fault of your own, damn it! Surely they can't hold that against you!"

Boday broke in, conscious that while Rani had grown up a great deal in forty-eight hours she still wasn't adult. "They are colonials, but they are all that is left of the colonial branch where they were," she tried to explain. "From what I gather their parents became colonials because their clan is strictly Traditionalist. Their bad fortune would be considered then the wrath or curse of the clan gods. Desecrated as they were, they would be expected to commit ritual suicide so that they could be cleansed and then be reborn pure. Not all clans are that strict but the ones that are have a lot of volunteers to be colonials."

Sam looked at Rani. "That right?"

The girl nodded somberly. "We have no family now, and no clan. If we were to get out of this hellish place we would be forced to sell ourselves or die."

"Die," said little Sheka firmly. "Ain't no *man* ever gonna touch me 'gain. I hate 'em! I hate 'em all!"

Charley stepped in. "Remind her that her father was a man. And one hell of a man, too. He gave more than he imagined he could give for them. Tell her to remember that."

Sam did. It didn't immediately illicit a response, but after a while it was clear that Sheka was softly crying.

Sam sighed. "For what it's worth, you have one, maybe three new mommies as of this moment and I have two daughters."

Rani gave a slight gasp, then got up and practically threw herself at Sam, hugging her, and Sam returned it. Finally the new mom asked, "But there's some things you got to know, too. About Boday and me, for instance."

"We know," Rani replied. "Mom—our real mom—sort'a told us. It don't matter. You want us and we want and need you."

Well, that settled that part of it, and it was up to Sam, with some help from Boday, to explain exactly who they were and what was going on as best they could, at least on the level of one wizard bringing them here and then losing them, the other trying to kill them. She also spared nothing in explaining what Boday had done for a living and what sort of underworld they'd lived in and which Boday was urging a return to. It wasn't clear just how naive they might be, but they seemed to get the general picture.

"And if we get to this Boolean, what then?" Rani asked her.

"I don't know. All I know is that we'd be among rich and powerful people who have a stake in keeping me alive and maybe the power to really do it."

"I think I know, Sam," Charley said, forgetting until now that she was the only one. "I think he wants to train you. Make you a sorceress, a mistress of the storms. This horned guy that they all worked for, the same one who tried to get you—he has this sorceress he's trained who can do what nobody else can. Control or influence the storms, maybe even the changewinds. He's gonna use her to try and take over, first here, then every place. Become like a god. The only other one with that kind of power is you, Sam—but it's raw, untrained. This Boolean wants to train you like the other guy trained *her*, and when the war comes set you against her. Asterial told me—when she thought I was you."

Sam thought it over. "Well, it's something, anyway. Now I know the power's real and why this all happened. Don't do much good, though, 'less I can figure what to do about it. I figure we got three options, no more. We can go back—but that might make us sittin' ducks if Zamofir's around or Asterial's still alive and maybe even if they're not. It'd also turn these two kids into the bastard daughters of a pair of dykes. You and I know how they'd wind up in a culture like that. And I'd wind up a fat, corrupt, brainless vegetable. And that's if Zamofir and Kligos and Asterial and all the rest would leave us alone."

"I know," Charley replied, nodding.

"Or we can keep on going to Boolean and probably get the girls and maybe the rest of us killed or worse—now I know there *is* worse. Or we can say the hell with all of 'em and try'n find some quiet place where nobody knows us or cares and where we can live our own lives."

"Until Horny launches his war," Charley pointed out. "And we—all of us—will be targets just because we're Akhbreed. And you'll be sittin' there watching him make himself a god, the kind of guy so evil that things like these guys here and Asterial actually *work* for him, and know maybe, just maybe, you could'a stopped it."

"But this whole fucking system's so *evil* right now," Sam noted. "It's a different kind of evil—nicer, maybe, and quieter, 'cause we're all on the ruling side, but evil just the same. And if I *could* stop this thing, I'd be cementin' this evil in place for many lifetimes. Charley—what do I do? It ain't fair to be offered a choice of evils. You're tellin' me that if we get out of here and if we live through all this and if it all comes out right I get to choose between killin' millions or permanently enslavin' like *billions.* It just ain't fair, Charley."

"I know it isn't, kid, but that's what there is. Five naked broads stuck in the wilderness and we got to decide it for 'em no matter what. Me, I'd just like to find out why all the damned magicians here speak English. Why not French or Chinese or Hindu or something we never heard of? It's been drivin' me nuts. So I guess I got a stake in this, sort of. And there's tons of little worlds out there filled with people and things we never would guess. We've seen so little of this crazy world I think I want to see more before I give up on it. Besides, until you're secure someplace I'll never be. I'm target number one."

Sam gave her an odd half-smile. "We've come such a long way already," she noted.

Charley nodded. "And we got such a long way to go. . . ."

Sam got up and turned and looked out at the trail and the sun-parched but colorful landscape beyond. "Well, everybody, it's time we got going," she said.

"Where?" asked Boday.

Sam pointed. "Out there. Someplace. Until we find a mall, or a good motel, or Boolean. Whichever comes first."

Somewhere, far in the distance, something shimmered and changed, and the changewinds shifted and bounced and flew about in new and unexpected patterns as if a new randomness had been introduced that they were keen to follow.

Far away, in his spacious Palace tower quarters overlooking an exotic and beautiful city, a man wearing a green robe who also had a strange, pea-green monkey-like creature perched on his left shoulder, sensed it, and gave a slight smile.

"Well, Cromil, it might work after all," he said softly to the little creature. "It just might work out in spite of the odds."

"More likely she'll just get her ass blown off or worse," responded the green creature in a shrill, nasal voice. "She'll never make it here and you know it. Look how long it's been already!"

He sighed. "If she cannot make it here then she has no hope against the powers of Klittichorn and no prayer of countering the Storm Princess. We take what we can get and make of it what we must, my friend. When she started she was a frightened, ignorant, vacuous schoolgirl with the active intelligence and self-confidence and ego of a carrot. If she makes it here, then she will already have developed the confidence and skills and toughness required to make her one of the most dangerous survivors on this planet. That *is someone I can take and revolutionize the world. If she does not—well, she is not the only one, as you know. Relax, Cromil. We will still all probably lose out and die I know, but, just for now, just this once, let* Klittichorn *do a little bit of stomach-churning."*

And, half a world away, inside a great castle set into and partially cut from a towering purplish snow-capped mountain peak, a tall, gaunt figure in a crimson cloak was walking down a hall when he suddenly felt a sudden and mysterious chill. He stopped, frowned, and tried to figure out what it was, but failed. He didn't like it, though. He didn't like it at all. He continued walking and went into the Council chamber, unable to shake this new and, for now, merely unpleasant chill. "Alert all agents and commands," he ordered crisply. "Something very odd just happened and I don't know what. Until I do and we remedy it, spare no effort in finding and isolating it. And triple the magical guard on Boolean. If he scratches his ass I want to know it."

"At once, sir," responded the Captain General. "Uh-sir? Any idea what we are looking for?"

He shook his head. "A random equation seeking a definite solution. It floats, seeking its own answer. I prefer not to solve it." He went over to a blackboard and picked up a small object. "The easiest path is to erase it. Find it, Captain General. Find it and erase it before we all catch our death of cold."

PART II

RIDERS OF THE WINDS

For Ted Cogswell, and Polly Freas, and Bea Mahaffey, and Alice "Tip" Sheldon, and too many other old friends who left this outplane while I was writing this. I owe you all, but too many of you are missing when I return to this reality, and contrary to natural law, there are far too many vacuums where once special brightness dwelt.

1
A Choice of Bad Roads

Clouds were rare in Kudaan Wastes; its blasted appearance, orange, furrowed hills, and deep ravines and lack of much that was the green color of life attested to that. To have two storms in a matter of days was not only unheard of, it was a prescription for disaster, since such parched lands had ground baked so hard it would run off and the flash flood might ensnare anyone or anything anywhere.

This was a small storm, forming with suddenness as such storms usually do, perhaps over some cool spot where sufficient moisture from the last rain had collected and begged to be evaporated by the harsh sun. The clouds swirled and thickened and seemed to take on a life of their own. Small flashes of energy built up within, and from the darkest part of the building thunderhead shone two tiny, deep depressions that illuminated a crimson red from the charges within, as if the cloud indeed was the protective shield or shroud of some dark and loathsome monster.

The Sudog drew its strength from the storm and took control of it, blazing eyes looking down, scouring the land. There was little wind that it did not create and little variation in the heat of the day except where its shadow fell, and so it had a relatively free hand.

It swung first west, until it found the main road leading into the Wastes, taking care not to get too close to the border where the interaction between wedges could cause unpredictable and perhaps fatal weather effects. The desert floor that was usually so flat and featureless was in full bloom, with great blood-red flowers hanging from strong green vines that shot out of the soil and into the air and tried to do all that they had to do in the days, perhaps even hours, before the moisture dried and they were forced once again into dormancy.

The Sudog wasted none of its energy on them, nor any of the water that kept it cohesive. If floated well over the growths and towards where the road went down deep into a canyon with steep walls and isolated bluffs, its dull red and yellow and purple rock layers thus exposed leaving part of its depth forever in shadow.

There were the clear signs of a disaster here: broken wagons, half-eaten and rotting corpses of animals and some people, partly crumbled rock walls and ledges, showing what a true heavy rain on the down-sloping plain above could do to anyone unlucky enough to be trapped here.

The Sudog floated overhead and looked down for a distance, until the wreckage and remains ceased, then it floated back, away and to the north, back out again over the Wastes themselves where roads were mere trails through colorful desolation.

Twisting, turning, following the trail it discovered a great rock arch on the downward side and there the remains of more violence, this of a far different kind. A new grave on the rim opposite the arch and overlooking it, and much scorching of the very rock itself. Below, some animals, both nargas and horses, and the remains of burnt-out wagons, and a number of bodies of more recent vintage than those in the canyon had been, bodies not drowned but bloodied and mutilated by shot and shell.

It began to follow the trail, but its energy was nearly spent; it was next to impossible to withstand the low humidity of the surrounding air and the scorching heat of the desert sun for long. It felt itself first weakened, then almost coming apart. The eyes faded, the sliver of crimson that might have been a mouth grew dull, then merged with the clouds, which were already turning from dark to white. Its last impression was the mere hint of life farther on, of horses, possibly, and riders, but no details. It was sufficient, however, for the Sudog's master.

There were four horses farther on, had it been able to get just a little bit closer, four horses but with five very different riders. Also along was a narga, a four-footed beast of burden that somewhat resembled a cross between a no-humped camel and a mule, laden with packs.

One was a very fat young woman, looking because of her weight older than her years but still with youth in her face and complexion, with short black hair. The second was a strikingly beautiful young woman in possibly her late teens with long strawberry blond hair and a perfect figure, her eyes painted or possibly tattooed with the flowing lines of sapphire blue butterfly's wings, and a similar, if much more grandiose, design on her chest from her breasts down to her crotch. The effect was neither grotesque nor overdone, but rather exotic.

The third was an older woman but in very good condition, extremely thin and very tall, certainly over six feet in bare feet. Her hair was black, her facial complexion very dark, but little more could be said, since almost all of her body was covered with colorful and exotic designs that seemed to flow into one another and made her appear outlandishly dressed even if she were nude, which in fact she basically was. In fact, they all were.

The final pair sharing a horse were very young, one in her early teens who was thin and fairly plain, the other, no more than nine or ten, almost insufferably cute. They looked grim and tired, though, as did the others, and their faces reflected experiences that had aged them as none of their tender years should have aged, inside.

They had clearly made what they could out of what they had. The two youngest wore what were obviously pieces of blankets with crude holes cut in their middles to give them basic serapelike protection from the sun. Much the same had been done with a full blanket for the fat woman, while the butterfly woman wore a shorter length tied at the neck like a cape. The tall one with the tattoos wore nothing at all save double pistols on a cut-down gunbelt. Both the big woman and the butterfly girl also were similarly armed.

There was some thunder in the background and the big woman stopped and turned to look back. "They're looking for us," she said tensely. "I can feel it. We have to put as much distance as possible between ourselves and this place as fast as we can." Her voice was very low and gravelly, almost a distinctive and not very melodic young man's voice, straddling the octaves between male and female. She spoke in the nonetheless melodic language of the Akhbreed, but the butterfly girl answered in American English.

"Sam, we're all dead tired, and the girls most of all. We've been through a *lot,* and there's maybe only a couple of more hours of sun left. We can only push ourselves so far and God knows where the next water is. If they find us then they'll find us, no matter what kind of distance we make today. Best if we're all at our best. I say we look for a campsite that seems safe." She sighed. "What a mess. No guides, can't use the main trail, and, considering the horses, maybe two days' worth of water tops. And we can't go back to the border 'cause all of those *things* are blooming."

The plants now flowering on the plain were not placid creatures. They had crushed and eaten people, horses, even wagons that had the bad luck to spill some moisture on the plot of ground above them, and who knew what they were like thick, aboveground, and in full bloom?

Samantha Buell, the large woman, did not bother to translate for the others. Charley could understand the Akhbreed language, or enough to get by, but speaking it was beyond her. There was no need to translate; why get the others more depressed than they already were?

"All right," Sam said, "we'll look for a safe place to camp. I think tomorrow, though, we have to track north until we can find some clear way back to the border. With all those wedges changing all the time if we can get someplace else, anyplace, they'll have a real tough time finding us then."

"Do you think those who seek you won't also have that in mind?" the tall, tattooed woman asked sharply. "Even now they will be sending their minions to patrol the length and will use their pet monsters to deter or discourage us from trying it until they can get there. There are always storms on a border, even one such as this, to breed them. Were Boday your enemy she would keep you in the Wastes and off the roads, running, jumping, and hiding, until the water ran out and the horses died; and, afoot and thirsty, all would be as easy to pick as flowers in a garden."

Sam sighed. "You're right, Boday, and that's probably exactly what they *will* do. Damn it, they're not after you, Charley, or the girls. They're only after *me.* The rest of you are in danger only because of me. They couldn't care less about the rest of you."

"Yeah, but they think I'm you," Sharlene "Charley" Sharkin, the butterfly girl, responded. "Even that sorceress or whatever she was thought so. You're the quarry but I'm the target!"

The Akhbreed sorcerer Boolean had arranged it so that Charley, who bore a superficial resemblance to Sam before the weight gain, had come to look, *sans* butterfly tattoos, precisely like her friend. And a combination of a long wait, depression, and Boolean's pet demon had caused Sam to become more than merely fat, so that one would have to be a very good observer and look very close to take Sam and Charley as virtual twins. The idea, to make everyone chase Charley instead of Sam, had worked well—to Charley's dismay. They didn't know if Boolean's demon and the monstrously beautiful but evil sorceress who had vanished while in combat with one another were still alive somewhere else or in another plane or had destroyed one another. If not, then the enemy for whom that sorceress worked had given a pretty accurate description of Charley to her master, and with Boday's butterfly tattoos Charley wasn't exactly easy to disguise.

Charley knew, too, that the others were still somewhat in shock and that the day's labors had helped put off the inevitable horror within the others. Sam, Boday, and the two girls, Rani and Sheka, had been tied down by a marauding gang of animals in the shape of men and brutally raped; the two girls had further been subjected to the loss of both their parents and probably their two brothers in the flood. Charley, with some help from the girls' dying father, had managed to rescue them and eliminate the gang, but she couldn't know just what they had been through and because of the language barrier she couldn't lead them. She could only lead Sam, and then only to a point.

The two girls had barely spoken all day, and Sam was clearly on the edge. Boday seemed normal for Boday, but the artist and alchemist was more than eccentric, and even rape and torture might not have affected *that* very bizarre mind; but for the same reason Boday was the last person Charley wanted in charge of anything. The only control now was that love potion Boday had accidentally consumed that had caused her to fall madly in love with Sam, the first person she saw after coming around, but even that wasn't as absolute as it always seemed in the fairy tales. When somebody who was both mad and dangerous was passionately in love with you, you had to watch yourself even more than otherwise, as they had discovered more than once.

Boday called a halt and pointed to their left. "Up in the rocks there, darlings! Looks like enough room for us and the animals, at least, and there's high ground overlooking the only trail in these parts."

Sam looked up at it. "Might be rough getting all the animals up there," she said worriedly.

"Perhaps. But it will be just as difficult for anyone else to get to us."

It *wasn't* easy, and the final solution was to walk each of the animals up by leading them and not falling down themselves. All of them were exhausted, all had pushed themselves beyond their limits, and as soon as the horse blankets were converted to beds by laying them out on the hard, uneven ground most wanted only to sleep, although they did have hardtack-type biscuits and invaluable canteens and small casks filled with water and wine.

Charley got out the single-shot shotgun and a box of shells. "I'll take the first watch," she told them. "You get some sleep. When I can't take it anymore I'll wake you up, Sam, and then Boday can finish off the night."

"No," Sam told her. "I'll go first. I don't think I can sleep right now. We at least got some rest thanks to that damned spell or whatever that *thing* put on us. I'll be okay. I got to do some thinking anyway."

The sun was still up and casting long shadows against the forbidding landscape when most dropped off into states more approaching unconsciousness than sleep, but for Charley sleep just wouldn't come. She was overtired; she knew that. She also ached in every muscle in her body including some she had never even suspected before, but that only made it harder. She lay there, looking over at Sam, who was just sitting there staring vacantly into the distance towards the setting sun. She finally gave up, got up, and went over and sat beside her friend.

"I can't get off to sleep," she told Sam. "Maybe I should take the watch anyway."

Sam shook her head negatively. "Uh-uh. Take some of the wine. It's not great but it's pretty strong."

"Maybe. The way the animals went at that keg of water, though, I think we should save any liquid until we just have to have it." She sighed. "It's been rough so far, hasn't it? And we only just started."

Sam nodded. "I been thinking about that, and a lot of other things. I just don't know how much more of this I can stand, Charley. Right now I feel—*dirty.* Those filthy, murdering scum playing with my body, getting *inside* of me, getting off inside me, and there was nothing I could do! Nothing! I'm still matted up down there with dried prick juice. And *her*—that—that *thing*—laughing and cheerin' 'em on. I think she was gettin' off on it herself just watchin' 'em."

Charley sighed. "Yeah, I can imagine how you must feel. At least, though, we learned one thing from it all. We learned just what kind of people and creatures work for this bastard out to get you. Somehow I just can't picture this Boolean being real cozy with that dragonfly queen. You didn't get to see her full, I guess, like I did. Half beautiful woman, half some monstrous insect. Nobody's born like that, not even here. You remember your changewind vision? Of the boy changed into a monster by one of those winds?"

Sam nodded absently.

"Well, I think this one was another like that, only maybe only part way, like part of her was covered and part wasn't and somehow it made a new whole. You can almost see how somebody like that is made. A pretty woman like that, changed into half what she was and half monster. Maybe that *is* the only way she can get satisfaction herself now—by watching it. Maybe she's just gettin' even with everybody, 'specially girls, who can still have what she can't. Even so, she worked for the guy with the horns. She told me so. He might look human, but inside he's gotta be an inhuman bastard, worse than she was. Imagine this whole place, all of it, dominated and run by ones like the dragonfly queen."

Sam shook her head in wonderment. "Maybe. I think I could have stood it for me, but those *children!* How could *anyone* defile kids like that? I wanted to do much worse than kill them. I wanted to roast them, live, over a fire and take 'em apart piece by piece."

Charley looked over at the sleeping girls. "Yeah, and they been so quiet. The little one is so full of hate, though, you can feel it, and the big one—you can't tell about her at all. And while I'm glad we saved 'em, I wish I knew what we'd saved them for. They're gonna slow us down and we'll have to have extra supplies for them and protect them in a fight. It's not good, Sam."

The large woman nodded. "I know, I know. You don't know how I want to give in to Boday, find someplace away from it all and just rot there in peace. But, you're right—we've now seen what the enemy looks like and it's not pretty. If stopping them means I got to reach Boolean, then I got to reach Boolean. Bad as this Akhbreed rule over all these colonies is, when I think of guys like the ones we killed rulin' over all the little kids . . ."

Darkness fell quickly as they sat and talked, bringing a hot, dry wind with it as the temperature cooled down to merely intolerable.

"It's a long way from the mall," Charley sighed.

"You ever think about home?"

"Lots. Particularly Mom and Dad and what my disappearance has to have put them through. I think I could take this better if there was some way to contact them, tell them I'm still alive. And I dream of warm showers in comfortable homes and cars and mall hopping and all the rest. God! For high school dropouts we sure dropped out farther and lower than anybody else."

Sam gave a dry chuckle. "I guess that's right. The funny thing is, though, I don't think of home too much. Oh, yeah, I'd like Mom and Dad to both know I'm still alive, too, and I kind'a have this crazy hope that maybe my vanishing act brought 'em back together or something, but every time I think of home I also think of here. Where the hell was I heading? I can see myself as some butch dyke on the make with some job sellin' shoes or maybe a waitress. I dunno. I kind'a think I was on my way to poppin' a ton of pills one night or drinkin' myself to death. So here I am a really gross fat girl hooked up with a flaky nutso cross between an artist, a madam, and a pharmacist, stuck out in the middle of nowhere and bein' chased by who knows what—and no matter what I feel like I'd pick here over there. I guess I *am* nuts."

"No, I think I can see it," Charley told her. "You got a few things here you never had back home. Thanks to that potion you not only have somebody who cares about you but one you know isn't gonna back stab you later on or hurt you. And you don't hav'ta get anorexia or do anything to attract other people. And you got a purpose here. No matter what, you're important. In a way, all the powers of Akahlar are tryin' to get you to Boolean or keep you away from him. That may not be safe or comfortable, but it sure as hell is a big deal."

"Maybe," Sam responded. "But, deep down, I really wish you were really the one that was important, the one they wanted. I really don't want this. It's too heavy for me. I think I could'a been happy just stayin' with Boday in Tubikosa, cookin' the meals, doin' the laundry and cleaning, and running the studio and household. It's crazy. What most girls won't have no part of anymore back home was all I really ever wanted. Only trouble was, I never wanted to do it with a guy. I didn't want to admit that, even to myself. It'd kill my mom. Hell, even I thought it was evil, one of the big sins. It ain't until you're tied down and stretched out naked while a bunch of dirty, slimy bastards play with your body that you see how dumb that is, what real evil and sin is all about."

"Poor Sam," Charley sympathized. "No matter where you wind up there's something you can't control lousing things up."

"Well, at least likin' girls don't bother me no more. I'm comfortable with it. That's one thing last night did for me. No more lies, not to nobody, not even to myself. If other folks can't handle it that's their tough luck. And if I'm okay with myself as a fat slob, then that's all right, too. Hell, all them fantasies about me bein' a glamour queen and what the hell would it get me, huh? I ain't never gonna be my mom, so I might as well just be me."

"I guess that's the best way to think about it," Charley told her, "Me, I never figured on any of this, but I *do* like the men. Jeez! Could I use a good fuck right now! Not like what you had," she hastened to add. "I mean a good one."

"I still need you, Charley," Sam said seriously. "Not as a lover but for your strength. Maybe that's why I was so attracted to you all that time. You're more like my more than I could ever be. Supermom. Lawyer, activist, mother, church deacon—you name it, she's it. Maybe we had the wrong parents. Maybe they switched us when we were babies or something."

Charley chuckled. "Good trick since we were born two thousand miles apart. I'm not sure I ever wanted to be superwoman, but I sure had ambition, that was for sure. I was gonna be a businesswoman, that was for sure. M.B.A. and all. Maybe create a chain of stores or some kind of design business. Maybe even an architect. I spent so much time in malls I could design the perfect one in my sleep. So I wind up a painted courtesan selling myself for money here. No citizenship, no rights, no nothin'. Can't even speak the cockamamie language except in words and gestures. And chased around while everybody thinks I'm you. At this point all I'm interested in is getting you to the big boy so I can get the heat off me. I can't think beyond that right now."

Sam sighed. "Boy, are we screwed up!" She reached down and started scratching her inner thigh. "Tell you one thing I'd kill for from home, though. Some kind of lotion. I've got chafing like mad from thighs to crotch and under my tits. I sure wish Boday had her kit at least." She looked out in the darkness. "That's odd," she said suddenly in a tone quite different than the one she'd been taking.

"Huh? What?"

"It's glowing over there. Many miles away. Like towns glow on the horizon in the dark anyplace. But there ain't supposed to be no towns in this hole! See it?"

Charley shook her head. "Sam, I was trying to keep this from everybody, but I can't see well at all. I've never had perfect eyes—you remember I needed glasses or contacts to drive—but after watching that magic duel it got suddenly worse. I can't say if it's a little better, a little worse, or just the same now, but with you riding just in front of me today I could see you, only blurry. I could tell it was somebody on a horse but if you paid me I couldn't say if it was really you or a total stranger. After you was nothing but a blurry fog. Maybe six or eight feet clearly, then double that very blurrily, and after that I'm blind as a bat."

Sam gave a low whistle. "I didn't need to hear that. You're in the best shape and you're the only decent shot we got. Damn!"

"You're telling me? Without company I'd be dead meat out here now. Of course, now that it's black as pitch it doesn't make much difference. Maybe when we can get to some civilization it can be fixed, maybe with glasses or something. In the meantime, I'll take the shotgun. You don't need to see much to hit with a shotgun."

Sam turned back and looked at the glow on the horizon. "I'd sure like to know what that is," she said at last. "If it's some kind of small town or mining camp we might be able to contact the authorities. If it's an enemy encampment I'd like to know just what we're facing."

"Most likely some bandit camp," Charley replied. "That's who supposedly lives out here, isn't it? Refugees, exiles, and changelings. At least we have some bargaining if it's bandits. The jewelry and stuff from the train they looted plus we know where a bunch of Mandan gold blankets are hidden. They seem to be worth lives around here."

It was for the Mandan gold blankets that the marauding bands of the enemy was stalking and attacking trains, for they were rare and valuable and the only things that could protect you in a changewind. Why Klittichorn and his minions wanted and needed so many was unknown, but clearly it was a high priority. They would have liked to bring the cloaks in the rock arch with them, if only for protection for themselves, but they were far too heavy to carry on horses that also needed to carry riders, and with all wagons broken or destroyed and only one narga healthy and untouched enough to carry a load, they had to sacrifice the blankets for more water and wine casks. They had managed to haul them a ways, though, and more or less bury them under rock and debris away from the main camp.

"Yeah, but most of that type of person or thing or whatever would be just as likely to enslave us and turn it all over to the enemy," Sam pointed out. "After all, he's playing it as the champion of the colonials and the outcasts. No, let's try and slip by 'em and get to someplace where we can slip across the border into someplace cool and rainy where they never heard of you or me."

"Maybe. But if I could see better I'd sure as hell like to take a peek at them. If they're off a ways, then it's even money we'll be camping tomorrow pretty near them if we keep going that way."

"We'll see. We can't go back—they're sure to be sniffin' all around there by now. We can't go to the border—that's a sure way to get caught out in the open. And if we go inland we don't know where we're goin' or what the hell we're doin' and we run out of water fast. Boday's in pretty good shape. Maybe she'll be our scout."

Charley suddenly felt dizzy. "I think it's finally caught up to me. I'm going to try and get some rest. You remember to wake somebody up when you feel it yourself."

"I promise. Get some rest now. We got another day of that sun tomorrow."

Charley went off and Sam turned back to the lookout. The glow was small and subdued, but it remained constant, not like someone or a body of people on the move and certainly larger than a camp. They had money, but no place to spend it, and little else. She scratched again. God! How she could use a long, hours long, bath! A real soak. They were all dirty, sweaty, itchy, and smelled like warmed-over turds. Right about now they needed some allies more than anything in the world.

"I still don't like the idea of that camp or whatever it was over there," Sam said over what passed for breakfast. She was still dead tired, ached like hell, and felt like she hadn't slept at all—but she knew that she didn't feel any different than the others. "If there's no fork later on, this road seems to be heading right for it."

"Boday is for cutting back a bit and making for the border now," the mad alchemist put in. "There will not have been enough time to bring up a force capable of covering the whole border area and we are certainly beyond the rain and bloom period of those *ghastly* plants. If we continue south, on this trail, we might or might not run into whoever is over there, but we would certainly be easy to find from above, either by something flying or even sentries on the high points. To go by night is suicide. To go by day is suicide. To go in any direction is suicide. To stay here is suicide. Let us make for the border!"

Charley listened to the arguments and finally said, "Well, it's clear we can't stay here but we don't dare go back. Somebody's sure to be hot on our trail. I say we go on, now, as soon as possible, before the sun's full up and there's maximum heat, but if there's a fork or anything that takes us towards the border we go that way. I'd rather know what I was facing and shoot my way through than keep *this* up and die of thirst or worse."

Rani looked up at them and spoke in a dry, soft voice. "I know we don't have much say in all this, but I got to tell you that we won't let nobody, no men, no freaks, take us again. We can shoot. I never was sure I *could* shoot nobody before, but I'm sure now."

Charley didn't feel comfortable, particularly with that comment about "freaks." It was hard to remember these were Akhbreed children, born and raised to be masters of the colonial empires. "Just don't you both go shooting *everybody* you see, and everything," she warned. "The odds are most folks we'll meet are not our friends, but not all will be enemies, either. Wait for one of us before firing."

The girls stared at her sullenly, but said nothing.

"All right, then," Sam said firmly. "We go both ways. North and towards the border first chance if it's a trail that looks like it has even half a chance of being able to take horses. Let's pack up and get moving. No matter what, I think we got to stop at midday and find some shade, for our sake and the horses', so the earlier the start the better."

As they rode along, Charley eased up close to Sam. "Sam—just in case, I think we oughta make clear that we're all heading for Boolean. If, somehow, we get split up and can't find each other, that's where we head."

Sam nodded. "Okay by me. I'm not so sure, though, that we're likely to get split up. Killed, maybe, but not split."

After only a few hours it was as if someone had turned up the thermostat to "broil." If anything, it seemed worse than before, and shade more nebulous and not much help when they could find it. Still, they covered quite a good distance before it was clearly time to stop and take some kind of a break. It was hard even to think under these conditions.

Suddenly Boday called out, "Look, loves! The trail splits, and one of it goes down into a canyon. We dare not hope for water but it looks deep enough for cool shade."

They made for it, feeling in no condition to argue, although Sam noticed almost casually that the fork into the shade was going in the wrong direction. Anything right now for relief, she decided.

It was clear very quickly that this was no ordinary canyon, but a long and relatively straight side break to a much larger formation. The ground seemed to drop away to their left, leaving them with a very narrow trail to navigate through many switchbacks on their somewhat nervous and very tired and thirsty horses. Charley couldn't see much past the edge but she could see to it, and what she saw made her almost glad she couldn't see just how far a drop it was.

But it was all in the shade, at least for now, and as they descended it really did seem to be getting just a little bit cooler, with a slight breeze hitting them from the side.

"This trail's well maintained," Sam noted. "There's a spot we went over a few minutes ago that you can now see up and in back of us. Some kind of rock slide took it out and now it's back, reinforced with rocks and timber. And there have been animal turds, maybe horses', on and off along the path. They aren't fresh, but they don't look all that old, either."

"We approach the main canyon," Boday announced. "See? It looks almost like a river down there. Small, yes, but water! We shall live if but briefly! There are even some trees and bushes along it."

The horses and narga seemed to smell it, too, and gained some confidence and quickness. Charley decided just to hang on loosely and let the horse do the work, and hoped that the others had the sense to do the same.

It took perhaps two hours to fully descend, and the canyon floor was surprisingly narrow, but there was no mistaking the feel and smell of life and the water that brought it.

The animals had no hesitation in heading straight for the river and drinking from it, and neither did the riders. The river was fairly wide, perhaps a few hundred yards right here, and it was *fast.* This was white water, and treacherous, but there were points at which it slowed as it was forced to turn and at one such place they just let loose.

The water felt cool but not cold, and it was *wonderful.* They took off their gunbelts and blankets and just waded in, sitting in it, splashing it on both themselves and each other, and generally acting like little kids at the beach. They finally got out, in ones and twos, exhausted but happy, and settled on the sandy silt bar caused by the river's bend. "God! All I need is a comb and I can feel almost human again!" Charley exclaimed. "Wow! Did we pick the right turn!"

Boday's head suddenly jerked up and she grew serious, intent. "Perhaps. Perhaps not. Boday thinks she hears thunder far off, and she remembers the last time we were in a canyon in the rain in this cursed land."

The hilarity suddenly stopped and they all strained to hear. "That's not thunder," Sam muttered at last. "That's—horses, or something like 'em. A fair number, too. Too fast to be comin' down the mountain one at a time. They got to be already down here! *Shit!* And us trapped in a squeeze like this!"

"I knew it was too good to last," Charley responded. "At least we never unsaddled the animals. Get the weapons and horses and let's move ahead as fast as we can. Maybe there's someplace up ahead we can make a better stand than here!"

Boday looked around. "They have moved too far upstream in their grazing! Boday can barely see them, and the riders come from that direction! Get the guns and run downstream as fast as you can! Perhaps we will see places to hide out there! The sight of the horses may stop them and buy us some time!"

The sounds left no room for argument. They grabbed their guns and began running as fast as possible along the river trail. They were quickly out of sight around the bend from the silt bar, but things didn't look much better up ahead and there seemed no choice but to keep running for the next bend well ahead and hope they made it before the riders.

It wasn't until they had made it, and stopped, gasping for breath, that they realized that the rumble of horses had ceased, leaving only the loud river noise.

"I'd say they found the horses," Charley managed. "What's it look like ahead?"

"Not good," Sam managed. Her weight was really telling on her now and she was gasping and coughing and sounding almost like she was going to die. Clearly she wasn't going to be able to take this for much longer.

"Sheer rock walls and darker and deeper," Sam told her, through coughs and gags. "And what do we have? Four pistols and the shotgun. Maybe enough if every shot counted and we were under cover, but let's not kid ourselves."

Charley thought furiously. "Everybody can swim or we wouldn't be here."

Sam managed to stop coughing for a moment. "In *that?* It's white water, Charley! There's rocks and stuff out there, too!"

"Yeah, I know it's dumb, but you got a better idea? We shoot and give up or we just give up or we jump in and try and make it to the other side. There *is* another side, isn't there?"

Sam nodded. "Yeah, but it's not like a continuous trail."

"The hell with it! If we make it over there we'll figure out how to get back when they're gone! They could be here any minute now, too! They won't be ridin' so fast lookin' for us!"

Sam told the others what Charley was suggesting.

"We'll try it," Rani responded. "I would rather drown than be caught and we made it through worse."

"All right," Sam sighed. "Then everybody throw the guns and gunbelts in the water so they won't know we went in here. The trail's hard rock, there won't be prints. Maybe I'll get dashed against a rock but with these tits I sure ain't gonna sink. Boday, you stick close to Charley. She ain't seein' so good lately. I'll try and stick close to the kids. Aim for that bar over there, but if you miss keep goin' down and hide as soon as you can. We'll regroup on the other side of the bend after they're gone."

Slipping into the water now was no longer the fun and luxury it was only a few minutes before, but at least the idea wasn't completely crazy. This was still part of a bend, where the river was forced to slow, and it was less rough and shallower than at many other parts of the canyon. Still, the water was surprisingly deep not too far out, and soon they were all floating at the mercy of the currents.

Charley felt suddenly weighted down by her waterlogged hair and swore to herself she was going to cut it shorter than Sam's if she ever lived to get the chance. She was also disoriented, and suddenly felt Boday's strong hand take her. The tall woman was much stronger than Charley and had little trouble handling her, although getting to the other side while the current picked up speed was more of a trick. Still, after what seemed like an eternity in wet semidarkness, Charley felt herself being pulled from the water onto sandy silt.

"Down and quiet!" Boday whispered firmly in her ear so she would be heard over the roar of the water. "They come."

They flattened out next to each other, and Charley thought that with their sun-darkened skins and the designs of Boday on both herself and Charley they were probably expertly camouflaged to an observer on the other side of the river. She aligned her head more closely with Boday's and whispered, "Sam? Rani? Sheka?" She cursed herself for her inability to speak this language, even though at least she could understand it.

"Can't see 'em," Boday responded tersely. "Perhaps still in the water, perhaps farther down. Boday sees the riders, though. Five of them. They have our horses, curse their souls! The narga, too. Big, tough-looking men in dark uniforms. Not the local army and not thieves. Well organized. They have the cut of those pigs we killed."

They lay there in silence for quite some time, and finally Boday sighed and sat up. "They are gone, or at least they seem to be. We shall wait here awhile before trying any more things, though. Best to be certain that they will not double back when they do not find us. Boday sits patiently and hopes that her wonderful mate is now doing what she is doing and is safe."

Yeah, safe, Charley thought glumly. *Even if we stay away from those guys and link back up, we're up this damned creek without a paddle or a stitch. Stark naked, no weapons, no food, no horses or trade goods. Nothing. Every time we think we hit bottom we fall into a damned mineshaft!*

Sam had slipped into the water and tried to stick as close as possible to the two girls. In the swift current it was impossible for them all to link together, so it was mostly a matter of using her strength to keep up with them and catch them if they lost control.

Little Sheka proved an excellent swimmer, while Rani had real problems keeping control. Allowing the smaller girl to swim free, Sam managed to grab on to Rani and keep her from being carried well away, but at the expense of losing sight of the destination on the opposite shore. By the time Sam was able to get hold of and help guide Rani, with Sheka keeping them close, they were already well past the destination and speeding up through the canyon near the center of the current.

Disoriented, Sam saw a number of rocks jutting up just to their left out of the water and at first she was afraid they would be dashed against them. Thinking fast, though, and realizing that they all had only so much strength, she managed to shout to Rani to grab on and, with a near-supreme effort, got hold of a jagged black spire and stopped both of them. She looked around and saw Sheka had managed not only to hold on but to have something of a protected spot on the other side of the larger outcrop.

It had been Sam's purpose only to slow or stop them so that she could get her bearings, but as she looked around through the white water bubbling and hissing and splashing all around she caught a glimpse of the trail side and saw the horsemen and realized that there was nothing to do now but hang on and stay where they were.

The men seemed to deliberate, looking down at the trail for signs of them and occasionally out at the water itself, but they maintained a slow and steady progress through the canyon, not seeing them and not inclined to stop. Whoever they were, they had their priorities, and perhaps if they'd taken any time at all to see what other than casks the narga was carrying they didn't really care if they found the riders or not. The lead and trailing rider had rifles ready, in case of some ambush or trap, but they didn't look too worried.

Sam let them go on until they were well out of sight down the trail and then some. Oddly, it wasn't all that bad clinging to the rocks right there, although getting safely away from them again might well be a problem. She managed to wriggle herself around so that she was facing downstream, seeing now that the narrow canyon opened up considerably a quarter mile or so farther down and that there was another river bend at that point. The shore, more like a rock ledge, opposite the trail side was closer but the way the river was running it wasn't nearly as accessible. Providing they had enough strength to keep out of the center current, it was almost certainly easier to return to the shore they'd left, and it began to look as if the men were not coming back.

"Put your arms around my neck and hold on!" she told Rani. "Sheka—do you think you can swim towards the trail?"

The girl looked, then nodded. "I will make it!"

"All right, then. Three, two, one, *now!*"

Satisfied that Rani was clinging well to her, Sam let go of the rocks and was back out into the main stream again. It was tough and awkward with the girl, but she managed with a supreme effort to get over and beyond the main current and allowed the water to take her down towards the next curve and out of the canyon. She hadn't expected the rocks and silt to have built up to such a level there and almost got hurt when she suddenly struck bottom, but she managed to grab hold of some protrusions out of the water, steady herself, and slowly make it to the shore. Sheka climbed out a few yards down, and they all collapsed for a while.

Sam suddenly was seized by fits of coughing and gagging once more and felt very sick and very sore, and it was some time before she recovered enough to think straight. She was very near total exhaustion, and knew it, but she also knew that her impulse to just stay there was impossible. Somehow they all had to make it out into the wider canyon where they could find some sort of hiding place to collapse and regroup.

Hardly able to stand but urging the two girls up, she managed to get to the trail and look around at the widened canyon. This, at least, showed promise; there were other side canyons going off here now and lots of uneven ground. Not too far off the trail was a rocky prominence that would provide some cover from the trail and shade from the sun. She urged them towards it, her mind only able to focus on getting to that spot and nothing beyond. She wasn't at all sure she could make it, but not only she but the other two did as well. It wasn't great—hard, rusty-red rock—but their spot would not be visible from the trail itself and it provided a bit of relief. They collapsed there, all of them, and Sam simply passed out.

Farther upstream, Charley was wringing the water out of her long hair as best she could while Boday was studying the land and water. Finally she said, "We cannot stay here. It looks as if this side has a narrow ledge going the length of the canyon, so we will try and use it as our trail and not slip and fall in. They must have been carried farther on. Keep your eyes and ears open, pretty butterfly, and we shall see if we can find them."

Both were in much better shape, both physically and in the amount of effort they had exerted to get to safety, and it was not as much of a struggle for them to press on. This shore, however, was not exactly the nice, wide trail area of the other. In places the ledge above the river narrowed to but a few inches, and was never more than two or three feet wide. It was slow going.

Charley was frustrated most of all by the language barrier, which kept her from even sharing her concerns with her companion. The Akhbreed tongue was complex and polytonal; the same thing said in just slightly different intonations could mean something totally different, or turn nouns into verbs and verbs into adjectives, and the rules for what type of word followed what seemed more intuitive than true rules as in English or Spanish, the two tongues she spoke well. Sam was so linked to her counterpart in this world that she had known the language from the start; Charley had no such advantages. The only version of Akhbreed she could use with confidence was the soft singsong of the Short Speech, taught to the unlucky girls who wound up in the red-light districts of the Akhbreed cities as prostitutes or worse; and its inadequate, submissive, slavelike vocabulary contained only a few hundred words at best. Still, it was better than nothing, and any Akhbreed speaker could understand it.

"Does Mistress think the men saw them?" she asked in it.

The artist shrugged. "Boday thinks slowly today, little one. For now we can but follow this shore and see what we can see. If we do not find them soon, then we might assume that they are caught and then we might have to track them." She sighed. "Boday was made to create delicate and beautiful works of art. She was not meant to be an adventurer!"

They made it out of the narrows and to the major new bend in the river where the canyon opened up. The bend was significant enough and slowed the river enough that clearly anyone swept up in the current, or even the body of such a one, would be washed up at this point. Just the lack of bodies against the silt bar on the opposite bank provided them both with some feeling of relief, but it also deepened the mystery.

Boday was thinking furiously. "We know that they could not have made it to our side, as surely we would have come across them by now or at least at this point. They are not hiding and looking for us around here or we would have been hailed. It is a good bet, then, that the children were not up to the crossing and were caught in the current, which would wash them . . . here. Sam, my darling Susama, would stick with them out of duty. Boday fears the worst, little butterfly. If they are not here, and they are not before here, then they *must* have been captured." She sighed. "We will wait a little while for them just to make certain, but if we wait too long we shall be here all night with empty bellies and a cold trail to follow."

Charley nodded. The logic was impeccable. It seemed like they were always chasing after and rescuing each other. It didn't seem fair, somehow. They were naked and defenseless, lost in a strange and hostile land, and, damn it, *they* needed rescuing.

They sat there and waited as the shadows lengthened, until finally Boday sighed and got up. "We should be able to cross here. They are not coming, that is clear. Come, little butterfly. Let us go and see what if anything we can do for them."

Charley sighed and nodded. The crossing wasn't as easy as it looked, but Boday was right; it was here or a long way farther down. They took one last look around and even risked a few shouts of the names of the missing members, but there was no response but echoes.

Sadly, they turned and started down the trail after the men and horses, not realizing that they were less than five hundred yards from those they sought, passed out in exhaustion just beyond their sight and too deep in slumber to hear their cries.

2

The Outcasts of the Kudaan

Sam awoke very slowly and groaned. She hurt all over and figured that there hadn't been a muscle not used or a square inch of surface left unbruised. The very act of attempting to sit up caused pain, but she managed it. Her eyes wouldn't focus right; it seemed pretty dark for where they'd settled in, the sky fairly light and clear but sunless, although it seemed to get a little brighter even as she watched. *What the hell . . . ?*

My god, it's morning! she suddenly realized. *It is getting brighter! The sun's coming* up, *not going down!*

Quickly she turned to check on the kids. They were there, huddled close together, still out but looking no worse than they had before. Still, they were bruised and burned by the sun and they looked, well, probably almost as bad as she did. *This can't go on,* she decided. *As much as I like them, if they stay with me they're gonna die. Somehow, if we get out of this spot, I'm gonna have to find a place for them. Maybe I'm a shit for giving my word and goin' back on it, but up to now it hasn't been my doing. If I can find 'em a spot and don't take it, though, their blood'll be on my hands.*

She sat back a moment, trying to get her mental bearings. Morning. It had been late afternoon when they'd slid into the river and crawled away from those guys up to here. *That meant they'd slept the whole damned night through!* Charley and Boday . . . Oh, god! If those guys didn't catch them, and it was a good bet they hadn't since she'd seen the riders go past, then the others had probably spent a lot of time looking for them and still missed them.

She tried to think. She'd swallowed a lot of water in and around that river yet she felt dry, her lips almost cracking. *What if we slept two days? Good god, is that possible?* It might be—there was no way to tell. She hadn't had access to a calendar or a watch in a pretty long time anyway, and they had been through so much and been so exhausted. A day and a half, anyway.

She got unsteadily to her feet and managed to go down to the water at the bend. It was shallow enough right in here that she could go in for a little, wash off whatever was on her, and get some of the water on her face and inside her. It helped, although not as much as she would have liked. She felt weak and nauseous and it was just what she didn't need to feel right now. About the only consolation was that if her stomach had anything in it she'd probably throw it up anyway, so there wasn't much loss. Well, unlike the kids, she had plenty of reserves. Considering she had water, she could probably feed off her own fat for a month. *Days without eating, lots of exercise, and I bet I lost maybe two or three pounds,* she thought grumpily. Would nothing ever go right for her here? Would she never get a lucky break?

Suddenly her depressing reverie was broken by the screams of Sheka, and she jumped up and out of the water and rushed back to the hiding place, not quite sure what the hell she could do but knowing she had to try something nevertheless.

She first saw the two girls, huddled together against the rock and staring in stark terror at something beyond. She stopped, turned, and followed their gaze.

He was about thirty feet away, standing still as stone on a rock ledge that had no obvious way up or down but was still about twenty feet up the canyon wall. He was of medium height, well built and muscular, and he was as naked as they were. He wasn't all that handsome but he had a strong face with a prominent Roman nose and maybe a mouth a little too small for its setting, and if he had any ears at all they were hidden in the weirdest-looking haircut Sam had ever seen. He also—well, it was probably the distance and an illusion, but he didn't seem to have any arms.

Sam looked around, found a couple of rocks, and picked them up. Something was better than nothing. "Who are you?" she called out to him, thankful that she'd been able to drink her fill first. "What do you want with us?"

For a moment the stranger said nothing, then he responded, in a soft, rather gentle voice that was both educated and classical in its way, "I was about to ask you that very question. This is my land, and it is not often that I discover three naked Akhbreed women in the midst of it."

Sam decided to gamble on honesty, considering that she had only two rocks and little else to play any other way.

"Look, sir, in the past few days we have been attacked, almost drowned twice, held captive by some very evil sorts who raped and abused us, lost our family and friends and all our meager possessions, hunted through here by more hard-looking men and forced into this condition."

The strange man thought it over. As the first real sunlight came into the canyon and struck him, his eyes seemed to shine, almost like a cat's, when he turned his head slightly.

"You are from the wagon train that was crushed in the flash flood over on the main highway, then," he said, nodding to himself. "You have come a long way."

She clutched the rocks tighter. "You—know about that?"

"Oh, yes. I have been surveying the region for two days now, ever since word of it came, looking for any survivors who might be in such condition as yourselves. This is not a land easy to live in in the best of conditions, and it is a killer if you do not know and love it."

You're telling me! "And have you found any survivors?"

"A few."

"And what do you do with them? Everyone we've encountered in this hell since we got here has been trying to rape, murder, or enslave us."

He sighed. "I am Medac Pasedo. My father is Duke Alon Pasedo of the Kingdom of Mashtopol, who holds the governor's position in this district. We are neither bandits nor murderers, and I am incapable of forcing anything upon you myself, but I am almost uniquely qualified to find and bring to safety any who require it."

"Yeah, I bet," Sheka sneered. "And the son of a duke forgets his pants, right? And what duke would ever be governor out *here?*"

Medac Pasedo sighed. "I am sorry if I offend your morals, but you are not exactly cloaked in modesty yourselves," he noted. "As for me, I find that any clothing that would not inhibit me would be impossible to remove when needed, such as to relieve oneself. That is for the same reason that I am no threat to you and why one such as my father would accept this sort of post." With that Medac raised what should have been his arms, but were not.

They were wings.

Not mere wings, either, but great, majestic wings, fully feathered. He looked one way, then the other, as if either testing the air or waiting for something, then suddenly jumped off the cliff and began to soar, first down a bit, then up and around, soaring and looping, and then coming down and to a running rest on the river trail.

Sam was so startled she dropped both rocks and just stared.

"By the gods, he's a freak!" Rani muttered. "We're in the hands of the freaks! They'll kill us sure, or make us into monsters!"

Sam turned and glared at the two girls who saw only horror in this man, even though she knew it was how they had been raised. She didn't necessarily trust the guy, but whether or not she did wouldn't depend on if he had arms or wings, hair or feathers.

And, in fact, he *did* have feathers, thick ones, from the top of his head back down his back and ending in a birdlike tail that almost but not quite reached the ground. It had been masked by the shadows on the cliff before but was quite obvious now.

"I cannot do you harm," he said as reassuringly as possible. "Hollow bones. Without them I could never fly. Only in the air am I among the biggest and strongest; on the ground I am fragile and easily broken."

Sam was more curious than fearful right now. The fellow just seemed too genuine to disbelieve, and he certainly was vulnerable. "A changewind did this to you?"

He nodded. "There are far worse fates the winds can mete out than this, although it has its disadvantages, not the least of which is that I would be under a death sentence anywhere in Mashtopol proper except the Kudaan Wastes. Rank and blood do have some privileges. Most of the kingdoms have places like this, refuges for the unlucky and the exiled and the sentenced. We are fortunate enough to also have a king who could not conceive of even his transfigured nephew grubbing for food like an animal. My father, who is still very much a full Akhbreed, has established a comfortable refuge in his governor's quarters for those who merely had misfortune and are not running or hiding for other reasons. I can take you to it, if you wish."

"Don't trust no freaks!" Sheka hissed, and Rani nodded nervously.

Sam whirled on them. "This will stop! *Now!* Did your father die so that you can rot in the sun of this land and your bones be eaten by animals? This is no different than catching a disease, or being crippled in an accident. The sooner you get that through your head the better. Now, I don't know if he's telling the truth or not, but I'm going with him. I'm going with him first because there's no place else to go and I'm in no condition to scrabble naked and unarmed over this land. And I'm going with him because he saw us long before we saw him, and if he meant us real harm he could have brought in anybody or anything he wanted without us even knowing until it was too late."

"You're not our real mother," Rani retorted. "You can't talk to us like that."

"Oh, so it's that way, huh? Okay, then, you're on your own, both of you. You can come, and follow orders, and behave yourselves, or you can stay here and strike off on your own. You're right—I have no call on you, but if you stick with me you behave. If you stay here, well and good, but I got a real good idea that within another day or so you'll wind up back under some bastard's thumb, tied up and used as playthings."

"She is quite correct," the bird man put in. "The canyon area is thick with every sort of dangerous type because it is the only aboveground river within hundreds of leegs. The rest are mere springs and oases that will support few and are not numerous. I know the prejudices of the Akhbreed, for I was born and raised one myself. But if I am a mere freak, this land is teeming with monsters, some physically, many more inside where you cannot see but which is far more deadly and dangerous, as well as every sort of criminal, fugitive, madman, black witch, and blacker sorcerer. They will not touch you if you are with me, as I have the protection of Malokis, High Sorcerer of Mashtopol, as a member of the governor's company; and my father's resources and troops and their knowledge of this land are enough to protect us. Here, you might escape them for a day, perhaps two, but sooner or later they will find you or you will run into them."

He said it with such casual confidence that Sam really believed him, and that made her even angrier at the kids, who were acting very irrationally considering the circumstances. The first real break in a long time and they were screwing it up. And Boolean was counting on *her* to help save this damned Akhbreed culture!

"Let's go," she told him. "They can come, or not. Is it far?"

"Not very. About an hour and a half at a regular pace. You just take the trail until it splits off, the main trail following the river and the other going into a steep-walled side canyon. The imperial seal is on a post at the trail branch to note what it is. Follow that branch and you will quickly come to the ducal residence. It is green there and quite grand, really. You can't miss it."

"You're not walking with us?" Sam asked, suddenly apprehensive about that "protection."

"I cannot possibly walk that distance. I will cover you all the way from the air, and if anyone should challenge you I will be instantly there. I am well known here, and I know most of the vermin who lurk about. There is a certain—agreement—between us. They will not break it for their own sakes."

That told volumes about how things worked around here. She would never have suspected that such a terrible place as this would have a governor, but if there really was one then he was damned sure corrupt as hell. This was not merely a refuge or hideout for unfortunate changelings and those cursed by magic, she remembered Navigator Jahoort saying, it was also a hideout and hangout for criminals and political exiles.

"Uh—you say your father has some troops?" she prompted, hoping against hope.

He nodded. "Yes. Enough."

"Do they wear dull green and black uniforms?"

He frowned. "No. Blue with gold trim, as with all Mashtopol forces. Why?"

"The men we lost everything trying to avoid were in those black uniforms. They stole everything we had."

"That is not good. There should be no foreign or irregular forces in here. My father will want to know this. And they went downstream?"

"Yes."

"I shall have a look for them from on high, if they are still anywhere in the area." He made ready to take off.

"Wait! You said you found some other refugees! Did you find any down here? A tall woman with tattoos all over and a young, pretty girl with designs like a butterfly?"

He started at that. "Um, I am quite certain that had I encountered either of the ones you mention I would have remembered. All the rest were discovered above. You are the first and only in the river canyon area."

Shit! Well, half a loaf is better than none, but where in hell could they be? "They were with us when this all started. Yesterday, maybe, or maybe the afternoon of the day before. I don't know how long we were out."

He nodded. "Well, once we have you safely at my father's, I will make certain that the word gets out. If they are anywhere in the district I am certain we will be able to locate them." And, with that, he began to run, picking up a fair amount of speed, wings outstretched; and then, suddenly, he rose into the air, perhaps only a few feet at first, but curving, swirling, and with each maneuver gaining altitude.

Sam sighed and turned to the girls. "Well? Are you coming or not?"

Rani looked at Sheka and Sheka looked at Rani and both sighed.

"Yeah, I guess so," said the older girl. And, together, they started off down the trail.

They didn't see the winged man anymore, although they occasionally looked around for him, but the trail division was pretty easy to spot. True to the instructions, right at the division was an imposing stone pillar on which were written in professional carved type some very fancy pictographs—Sam knew how to speak Akhbreed but had never learned to read and write it—and a very fancy seal of metal mounted with strong masonry bolts that had obviously been made elsewhere and brought in.

Rani looked at the words. "Well, at least he's telling this much of the truth," she said, studying the monolith. "It says 'Seat of the Royal Governor, Yatoo Canyon District, Commonwealth of Kudaan, Kingdom of Mashtopol.' That's fancier than the one *we* had."

"Well," Sam sighed, feeling a bit irritated that she had to depend on a thirteen-year-old to read her a sign, "at least we now know where we are." She looked down at herself. "Great outfit to meet a royal governor," she added sourly. A year with Boday had destroyed any sense of modesty she ever had, but she sure as hell was gonna make one great first impression.

The difference in the canyon area was apparent almost immediately. Here was the first tributary they had seen running into the main river. It wasn't much more than a creek, maybe ankle deep and six feet wide, but it was real running water and it was coming from someplace, and it appeared to be supporting a fairly large amount of vegetation. It wasn't exactly a jungle, but there were groves of tall, thin trees and other areas obviously cultivated. The trail passed over a number of irrigation canals that had the remnants of water in them, and there were actually some birds and insects about.

And there were people about in those cultivated areas, doing something that farm types might do, whatever that was. Sowing or irrigating or picking or whatever, maybe fertilizing. They were a strange crop; many of them were less human than *creatures,* at least in appearance, with all manner and variety of strangeness. Ones with saucerlike eyes and others with trunklike noses and ones with fur and tails and some too downright weird to categorize easily. They worked well together, though, and with humans. Both males and females seemed to wear only skirtlike garments, the men solid colors, the women colorful patterns, kind of Hawaiian, like before the missionaries had ruined it. There were enough bare breasts that Sam felt a little more at ease, anyway. They were loose here.

Well, how strictly religious could a governor be whose son wore feathers and nothing else.

There was something odd about most of the humans, too, though, that she only realized after they had gone a ways in towards the residence. Many bore ugly scars; others had peg legs or one leg and a crutch, or had one arm or even no arms.

"Worse than I thought," Sheka whispered loudly to Rani. "Gives me the creeps. They're all freaks or cripples or worse."

"You watch that kind of talk!" Sam warned. It *was* a little discomfiting, although she wouldn't admit it to the girls, but it was kind of like touring a hospital's worst wards. You felt sorry for the people and at the same time you were damned glad it wasn't you. That's what this place was, really—a hospital, or, more properly, a sanitarium for those with disfigurements that could never be reversed.

Most of the people seemed to live in adobe apartment blocks that reminded Sam of New Mexican pueblos. Most were three levels with those who could climb on top and those who couldn't on the bottom. Most of the changelings, except those whose very form made it impossible to climb, were at the very top. Sam was startled to see some apparently normal human kids around there playing, and there were in fact quite a few who looked like very sun-darkened but otherwise whole Akhbreed. So not everybody here was in an asylum. Perhaps they were staff.

On the side opposite the blocks of pueblo dwellings was an adobe barracks building, stables, and other signs of a small military outpost, complete with two uniformed soldiers standing guard outside the barracks building. They wore the same blue-and-gold uniforms that the wagon train had expected and was almost fooled by, only this time clean and without bloodstains and bullet holes in them. They looked a little hot to wear, but kind of comic-opera snazzy, too.

The main residence, however, was a knockout. It was *huge*—it was nearly impossible to say how huge, but Sam's old two-bedroom bungalow back home would have fit inside the main entry hall alone. Even though it, too, was the pink adobe, it looked more like a grand hotel than anybody's house.

It went up and out at all sorts of angles, with really high peaks and roofs rising at steep angles and then coming down straight. The whole thing was like a geometry lesson, with every shape represented but the triangle as king. There was lots of glass, too, whole walls or roofs of it, and what looked like greenhouses. It was an exotic yet modernist design. The magazines back home would go nuts over it, Sam thought.

Even the girls were suitably awed. "That's the biggest damned house I ever seen," Sheka said in a whisper. "This guy must be the richest grafter in the kingdom. No wonder he don't mind livin' out here."

Sam could appreciate the thought. Sanitarium or not, she'd gone from absolute bottom to this in a very short period of time—and in the nick of time, too. She felt like Dorothy suddenly at the gates of the Emerald City. She deserved one like this, one break at least. She and the girls by rights should have been captives in some criminal lair right now. Instead . . . Jeez . . .

There was a sudden dark thought. *They* were here, by luck and good fortune, but where were Charley and Boday? Who would be hosting *them* tonight, and under what conditions?

A bare-breasted young Akhbreed woman wearing a red-and-yellow flowered skirt came out from the main doors and walked down to them. She looked very normal, physically, which was a relief to the two kids, and she flashed a big smile akin to an official greeter's for the tourists.

"Hello," she said cheerily. "I am called Avala. Medac said you would be coming. The Lord Governor is busy now, but I will see to you if you will just follow me."

"I am Susama, but most call me Sam. These are Rani and Sheka."

"I am pleased to meet you all," responded the woman, sounding sincerely like she meant it. "Come this way."

They entered the house, now feeling more than a little self-conscious, although none of the people about paid them any notice to speak of. The entry hall was enormous and full of hanging plants and covered by a great angled skylight and really did seem more like a fancy hotel than any home. Of course, Sam thought, this was more than a home, it was sort of the state capitol building as well, and maybe even a bit of a hospital and hotel at that.

Rani and Sheka stuck very close as if they were afraid that some of the people going about their business around them would attack them or even touch them. Most were Akhbreed "normal," if that was the right word for it, but, here and there, there were some of the odd-looking, even bizarre changelings and some Akhbreed who were maimed or disfigured, and more than a few who looked not like victims but rather people of different racial types, some rather bizarre or exotic. Colonial races, here apparently on an equal footing. What was grotesque to the two girls was somewhat reassuring to Sam. Here, for the first time in Akahlar, were people of both the master and subject races, changelings, and people with disfiguring or debilitating deformities who would have little chance to be more than beggars in a city like Tubikosa, all mixing with apparent ease on a more or less equal basis. Maybe this duke had the negatives of royalty and the rest, but in some ways he certainly seemed a visionary, even a revolutionary. Here was the dream that Klittichorn promised to buy Akahlar with blood, only realized by a member of the established order.

That did give her a little twinge of worry, though. Duke Pasedo seemed very much the type of man who might be on the side of the horned wizard and his minions, if not openly at least secretly. Sam couldn't help but have a nagging worry that in spite of all this she might well have walked into the front door of the enemy that sought to kill her.

They were led almost immediately to a wing of the building that was obviously used as some kind of transient quarters. The rooms were fairly large and generally resembled a high-class Akahlar hotel, with large feather mattresses and pillows, a dressing table, night stand with cold running water, and what appeared to be a shared toilet. There was even a small balcony nook just out a glass door, with a table and two chairs looking out on the canyon area. The finish was adobe, as were all the buildings, but it felt sound and fairly cozy. No bathtub or shower was provided; as was the usual custom, there would be a common bathhouse for that, usually one for each sex, although as casual as they were around here it might be coed like the lower-class places she was used to.

The room next door interconnected through the shared toilet, and Sam got one room and the girls the other. The pair seemed to be delighted by the room and bed and Sam looked at her own enviously. Still, first things first. "We haven't eaten—maybe for days," she told Avala. Curiously, she felt more dizzy and weak than hungry, but she knew what had to be done to get any sense of normalcy.

The woman nodded. "I will have something sent up to you all. It is between normal mealtimes here, but I am sure we can find something filling. I will also have one of the housekeepers send up some clothing now that I have been able to see you and know what is required. Please just relax and remain here for now. All that you require will be sent up to you, and after a day or so, when you are fed and rested once again, I am sure My Lord the Duke will wish to speak with you all. If you have any needs or requests, just push the button by the door there. That will ring a bell and bring someone. Tell them to ask for Avala."

"You have been very kind," Sam told her. "Thank you."

The woman kept smiling. "It is my function," she responded enigmatically, and left.

They were as good as their word and even seemed to have anticipated their arrival. Within just a few minutes a man wearing a sarong of sorts brought in a large tray full of small sandwiches, fruits, raw vegetables, and cakes, then another appeared pushing a small cart with two carafes of wine, a pitcher of dark beer, and another pitcher of fruit juice. Sam appreciated the juice touch; she had never really gotten used to a society where the kids drank wine with meals just like the adults, although it didn't seem to do them much harm.

The two girls mostly nibbled, though, as if their systems had become unused to food, and even Sam had a tough time, although the food wasn't at all bad. Even though they'd passed out for God knew how long on the rocks, none of them felt as if they had had any real sleep in weeks. She forced them to eat what they could by badgering, but it was clear that they were still very tired and still had borderline shock, both physical and mental, and she had little trouble pressing them both to go back and get in bed. They were out in minutes, and she stood there, again looking at them and feeling guilty. She liked them—most of the time—but she had no right to drag them through this. Not anymore, if this Duke could help at all.

She went back into her room and closed the door and sat down, trying to think. The transition had just been too sudden, too great. From that horrible night to fleeing across a scorched desert landscape to losing everything including the only ones in this world that meant anything to her, and now, suddenly, this. She started nibbling again on the sandwiches and drinking some of the beer.

Maybe I'm in shock, too, she told herself. *How would I know?* It must have been *something,* since she felt oddly drained, washed out, almost distant from herself and her circumstances. Maybe one day there would come a time when she could just unbottle it all and cry it out for two or three days, but not now. The less she wanted duty and responsibility and all that the more she seemed to get. All that time she had dreamed of Akahlar back home, and many of the dreams were scary, she had still loved it because it was distant; romantic because it was just something from her imagination. Now she was here, and it was real, and it wasn't very romantic at all. Powerful people were still trying to kill her, and every time she found something at least comfortable it had been snatched away. Now even Boday and Charley were out there someplace, separated from her. She hoped they were still alive, still okay, but if Medac couldn't find them or they didn't blunder in here, what then? She would be entirely on her own.

But if they were okay, how could they have missed that big stone monolith with the imperial seal on it? Boday could read the thing, and they'd be nuts not to head for here.

So she was on her own. Now what? This place should feel comfortable, but something about it felt threatening and she couldn't pin it down. If it were a threat of some kind, what could she do about it? There was no place to run, no place to hide.

It's growing-up time, she thought nervously. *No magic demon, no Charley, no Boday. Nobody but me. And I'm not even sure who I really am or who or what I can be. Damn it, it's not fair!*

She felt a little giddy all of a sudden. Without really realizing it, she'd been drinking the beer as she sat there, munching on the contents of the tray, and then she'd had some of the wine. It was only when she tried to pour a refill and nothing came out that she realized that it was all gone. There had been a considerable amount of food and drink there and she had gone through it all without even thinking. And, the fact was, the aches had subsided, the nausea she had been feeling had gone away, and although she felt very tired and a little bit drunk she felt, physically, far better. She made her way over to the bed, plopped down, grabbed a pillow, and was out like a light.

She was out cold, but only for a couple of hours; it was just getting dark outside when she awoke, feeling remarkably clear-headed and not half-bad. Usually booze had a terrible effect on her, and quickly. Maybe after all this time in Akahlar, where they drank mostly beer, ale, or wine with meals due to suspect water, and her added weight had increased her tolerance, she thought. Well, something good had come from it.

Much of what went in got processed fast, though, and she was on the toilet for a fairly long time. After, she felt oddly famished, and decided to check on the girls and maybe find out about dinner. She was surprised, but not yet worried, to find the girls' room empty. As far as she knew, they were guests here, refugees as it were, not prisoners. She went back into her room and to the sink and looked at herself in the mirror. The sun had certainly taken its toll; she was tanned about as dark as she could ever remember, but she kind of liked the effect. If you were gonna be fat you should look Italian or something like that.

Her hair was a rat's nest, but there was an advantage to keeping her hair short, even though she knew that fat faces tended to look better with long hair. All you needed was a comb and brush, which they'd provided, a part in the middle, and you looked socially presentable. She needed a bath, or maybe a couple of hours of hot soaking, but until she found out where it was and when it was available there was no sense in wishing for what she didn't have.

Only then did she notice that someone had been and gone while she slept. The remnants of that first meal, what little she'd left, were gone, and there were clean face cloths and other things on the small dresser. There were a couple of outfits, one beige and one cinnamon, made out of the stretch-type material that seemed very common in Akahlar. They were cling-type two-piece outfits that would do nothing to disguise or support her giant jugs or mask her spare tires and blimp ass, but they would fit and they would be reasonably comfortable and, unless you had custom tailors on the premises, were about the only choice when faced with someone with a less-than-average physique. There were also sandals of the extra-large and extra-wide variety and a pair of ankle-length soft skin boots with turn-down tops. She was familiar with the type; they looked decent and would spread for wide feet, but they didn't have much give and had little support inside. They were a bit long and not comfortable, but even though the sandals would feel better they'd look tacky. She had the distinct idea that this was more casual evening wear. She decided on the beige. Considering her tan, the cinnamon would just make her appear still naked.

There was also a small pack of cosmetics and some minimal jewelry that didn't look very expensive or fancy, but she passed on them. She'd never felt any particular need to use them in the past, except when trying to humor Charley back home, and she didn't really feel any need for them now. The right earrings might have helped set off her face a little, but the first and last time she'd had her ears pierced was when she was fourteen and she wasn't about to do it herself.

At last she felt as ready as she could be—but for what? *All dressed up and no place to go,* she thought suddenly. *Well, when in doubt ring the bell.* She went over to the button just inside the door and pushed it. In about a minute there was a soft knock, and she opened it to find a tall, thin, middle-aged man there wearing the usual sarong. He didn't say anything, so she said, "I was told to ask for Avala."

He stared a moment, then pointed to his ears and his mouth. With a start, Sam realized he must be deaf. She looked up into his face and said, very exaggeratedly, "Ah-va-lah." He nodded, held up a hand that said, "Wait," and walked on down the corridor.

Lip reading must be real fun with a multitone language where how you said something was as important as what you said, she thought. For that matter, how had he heard the bell? She looked out and down the corridor and saw a small desk there, and then looked up at the outside of her own room and the other rooms on the hall. They all had lights over the doors and little switches like doorbells next to them. So that's all the "bell" did—flashed the light like a stewardess call button and kept flashing until he saw it and came and turned it out.

Avala came in another minute or two. She was still bare-breasted, but the patterned skirt she was wearing was much fancier, her long hair had been neatly combed and hung on both sides of her shoulders, she had sandals on, and wore a kind of lei around her neck made up of big, pretty pink and gold flowers with greenery linking them. Sam found the whole effect very attractive.

"Hello, how do you feel now?" the woman asked her, always with that cheery smile.

"Fine. You've been almost too good to me. I'm feeling hungry and I need a long bath, but I'll survive."

Avala gave a slight chuckle. "My Lord the Duke is very busy right now, but we can go to the staff dining room. Later on I will show you the public areas of the residence and you can bathe as long as you like. The springs that come out here are hot mineral springs, so we have many bathhouses that are much better than just tubs."

The staff dining room was a large area, nicely styled, that was basically a buffet. You got what you wanted, picked a seat along communal tables, and ate whatever you wanted and as much as you wanted. There were some areas that made special provisions for physical abnormalities, and while they weren't being used then Sam wasn't sure she wanted to see what would fit in those types of seats.

There weren't many in the dining room. While dinner was up now, the bulk of the staff ate at particular times on a schedule and the room tended to open early for "guests" like Sam and various senior staff members who did not fit the regular schedule.

"Where are the two girls that came in with me?" Sam asked as they gathered the food, which looked and smelled tremendous.

"They found you asleep when they awoke and rang for me much earlier," Avala told her. "We have a number of children here and children's facilities, and we also wanted them to be looked over by our treatment staff to make sure they had no ill effects from their exposure. You will be looked at as well, when you feel up to it."

"Any time after a bath," Sam told her, feeling somewhat at ease. The state of medicine in Akahlar wasn't all that good. There weren't any doctors as such, and a lot of trust was placed in alchemists, magicians, and a host of people who were nothing more than civilized and pretentious witch doctors—although some knew their specialties and some of their oddball charms, herbs, rituals, and potions really worked. The trick was, without real standards, finding the good from the charlatan. Still, these people had gone through a lot and seemed to be in decent health, at least as healthy as they could be considering the state of things.

She was amazed and a bit embarrassed by her appetite, and a bit disturbed that she was only partly aware of how much she was eating until it was done. She'd put on the fat herself in that year with Boday, but the demon in the Jewel of Omak had cursed her to keep it until she got to Boolean, but had assured her she would have whatever energy she required if needed. She considered that. She'd just been through several days with little or no food and had managed, in spite of her weight, to ride great distances, hike, climb rocks, swim, and in general do the sorts of things on a sustained basis that she might have expected one in far better shape to have managed. Now her body was demanding payment. The curse was insisting on being maintained.

That made it a little easier, really, since it removed the guilt. *What the hell, if I gotta be fat why not enjoy it?* she asked herself, and did not skip dessert.

The question of guilt settled, she turned her attention to why she felt leery about this place in spite of its wondrous appearance. The staff was one reason. They all seemed eternally cheery, even the ones with handicaps or disfigurements, yet from just listening in the dining room she found that they talked little among themselves and generally about inconsequential things or the events of the day. The problem was, how to get some information without seeming to.

She turned to her companion and guide. "Were you born here, Avala?"

To Sam's surprise, the young woman shrugged. "I am sorry, but I really do not know," the guide told her. "I have been here, on the household staff, doing various things as long as I can remember."

"And before? Your parents? Brothers and sisters?"

Avala shrugged. "I do not remember. They say I was found, long ago, wandering in the desert, unable to tell them anything. I do not even remember that. It does not trouble me. I am happy here and performing a useful function."

So even the "normal" humans around were actually wards. Still, the way the guide and hostess was so satisfied and apparently not even curious about her past enough to wonder about it bothered Sam. A spell, or potion, or even some Akahlarian therapy? It was impossible to say, but from the similarity of the staff it was probably one of the first two.

As Sam was shown around the palatial estate, some judicious questions brought out that Avala had no concept of the world beyond the canyon here, and no interest in it, either. She was interested only in what concerned her life here and totally uninterested in anything outside of this cloistered life. Either she was limited in her mental capacity, which didn't seem obvious or even likely, or the way she was was the way she was *supposed* to be or maybe *compelled* to be, although she was unaware of it. Of course, there was a possible innocent explanation as well, since she seemed neither overworked nor exploited in particular. Suppose she *had* been found wandering in the Wastes, and suppose she hadn't had amnesia but rather tremendous shock. Sam herself would never forget being tied down and gang raped, and she knew that the horrible scars she would have to live with inside were almost certainly magnified in Rani and Sheka no matter how they were hiding it now. Suppose that kind of fate, but sustained over a very long time until the mind just broke, had been Avala's? Suppose the choice was to leave her in a living mental hell or wipe out everything? It would fit the apparent philosophy of this place.

The Emerald Sanitarium of Oz.

The baths were quite nice; natural bubbling hot springs were allowed to flow into chambers. It was sort of like a nature-made hot tub and it really helped the aches and pains. Then clear water rinsed you, and you felt both clean and relaxed, although if you stayed in the bubbling mineral baths too long you had the muscle control of a wet noodle.

When she got back up to the rooms she found Rani and Sheka there, and she had to confess to herself that she was somewhat relieved they had indeed been out doing just what Avala said they were doing. They had seen the "examiners"—no big deal, Sheka assured Sam—and then they had been taken in tow by some girls their own age and shown around some of the outside of the place and even played and got to be kids again for just a little while. They were quite happy about it, although Rani let slip that they had thrown a fit when the first set of examiners had been men and that women were then substituted. "I just—can't—let a grown-up man *touch* me," Rani said, a little apologetically. "I knew that all the men we saw today were just being nice or polite, but I just couldn't *handle* it. Not yet. Maybe not ever. I just keep seeing those—those—*animals*."

"Me, too," Sheka agreed. "One of these days I'm gonna find a place with no boys at all, not even tomcats or stallions, and *no* freaks, neither, and *that's* where I'm gonna live!"

Sam sighed. "I know it was tough and I know it's going to take a long time to learn to live with it, but you both know that those evil men who did that to us weren't normal men. They were vicious, no better than animals, and they got what they deserved. And you're also going to have to learn that these 'freaks' are just people who had something bad happen to them, something they could no more control than catching a cold, only lots worse."

"That's all funny, comin' from *you*," Sheka said acidly.

Sam stiffened. "What do you mean by that?"

"Well, I never saw *you* makin' friends with no men, and you're something of a freak yourself. I mean, you didn't just live with a girl, you *married* her."

Now what the hell do you say? "You're a little young to explain that, but don't think I don't like some men—nice men—or won't in the future. I may not want to have a romance with them, but I don't want a romance with most women, either. It's normal to be a little afraid right now. These are all strangers, men and women alike. I admit I might be a little nervous for quite a while alone walking down a street with strange men about, but I'll do it because I *have* to. And don't forget their leader was a woman."

"A damned changeling freak!" the girl retorted. "Like the ones crawling all over this place. I don't think I'll feel better until we're out of here."

"Well, you'd better get used to it and make the best of it, because we're stuck here until they can make arrangements to get us not only away from here but safely out of Kudaan. I asked about it and they are generally supplied by a caravan that comes through every week to ten days, and one was here only a few days ago. It also suits me to stay for a bit until I can get some word on Charley and Boday. Either way we'll go with the caravan and then we'll see a certain navigation company and claim our free passage, resupply, and insurance and be on our way. All right?"

Sheka sighed. "All right, all right."

Sam looked over at Rani, who was lying on the bed face up, staring at the ceiling, a rather odd expression on her face. She looked, in fact, like she was going to cry, but was repressing the tears. "Rani—is there anything else wrong?"

"No. It's all right."

"Come on. Tell me. It might help and it can't hurt."

Rani sighed. "It—it was one of the girls we were with today. Her dad came over for her. He—for a moment—I thought he looked—well, like, Daddy." And then she did start to cry, but just a little, for Sheka's sake.

Sam shook her head and said what comforting things she could. Damn it, they didn't just have one whammy, they had two, and the loss of their parents and brothers was perhaps more devastating than even the brutalizing, since it was those very people who could have helped them over the ugliness. Sam got them into bed and turned out the light and went back to her room. She felt a little like crying herself at this point, but at least it wasn't over her own problems this time. Something like this would knock the self-pity right out of you.

The next day, Sam ate a prodigious breakfast and then was off for her own trip to the examiners. They seemed a bit gun shy after the girls; they provided a man and a woman for her, the man well up in years, gray-haired and cherubic, the woman maybe in her forties and with a real professional look and air. They introduced themselves as Halomar and Gira; he was a healing magician, she an alchemist. They gave her a surprisingly thorough physical, even using a primitive form of stethoscope, and they wanted blood and urine samples. Sam didn't like that part—she knew that body samples were useful to black magic here and that giving some of your own free will was almost putting your life in another's hands, but there was little choice.

Halomar did most of the physical, but it was the woman, Gira, who took the samples and also sat down to ask some questions while the magician took notes on a worn pad.

"Your name is Susama Boday," she said more than asked.

"Yes."

"That is a married form, but both names are feminine."

Sam shrugged. She had decided not to give excuses or long-winded explanations anymore. "Yes, I have a legally registered statement of union at Tubikosa. My wife is still missing somewhere in the Wastes."

"Hmmm ... It takes courage to do that in a strict place like Tubikosa. I can see why you were leaving. I take it that you are comfortable with it, though, and that you have no self-doubts about your nature and orientation."

Of course I have self-doubts, you asshole! And I'm decidedly not *comfortable when I'm put on the spot like this and forced on the defensive like I'm some kind of Sheka's freak!*

"Yes," said Sam. "She's also an alchemist, by the way. Want to fool around?"

The alchemist started slightly, then realized she was being baited and regained her cool composure. Still, partly to help his colleague, Halomar decided to step in.

"Were you aware that you were under some rather strange spell?" he asked.

Sam nodded. "It didn't put on this weight but it keeps it on."

"Ah! So that's the basis. It was quite complex. You should be careful, though. It is very strong, and it would take an Akhbreed sorcerer to lift it, and even then with difficulty. You can't keep any weight off at the level you were when it was imposed, but you can still gain, and what you gain if kept over any period of time will become part of the curse and will stick Your height is seventeen point four krils and your weight is a hundred and two and a fraction halg. In other circumstances we would say that was dangerous."

Sam did some quick mental calculations. She knew she was around five one—she'd always been damned short—and a halg she figured once was about two and a half pounds. Jeez—two fifty-five, and that was *after* days of starvation and exercise!

"So how am I supposed to keep it there?"

"Exercise daily and vigorously," he told her. "All you can. It is all you can do. Your heart is surprisingly strong, your lungs are moderately clean, and your blood pressure is surprisingly normal for one of your weight. Considering all you've been through, I would say that was incredible. Exercise will certainly help."

"Your periods—how are they?" the woman asked.

She shrugged. "I used to have 'em pretty bad but they've been mild and just spotty since I gained all this weight. I guess that's the one bright spot in it. My last one was two weeks ago, more or less," she added. "I haven't exactly been paying attention to the calendar." *And the demon who stuck me with the weight also shut down the egg factory, so I haven't been too concerned about it,* she added to herself.

She realized what they were asking for—she had, after all, been a victim of multiple rape—but aside from the fact that it was still a little painful down there she didn't think there were any lasting physical problems from it. It was more the extra layer of fear and anxiety it put into her in even normal, casual circumstances that was the real scar. She had never given much thought to walking alone, even in the evenings, even in the rough district of Tubikosa where they'd lived that year, but now she found it impossible to consider walking anywhere alone that wasn't brightly lit and didn't have people around.

Finally, they asked her about future plans, and there she decided to be very circumspect. She had a reasonable idea by now that these people had no idea of who she was and that she was being hunted by somebody important, but she didn't want to find out whose side they were on by letting anything slip. She had an idea that the magician could tell truth from falsehood, but limited truths would ring no bells.

"I wish to find my companions, if possible," she told them. "Whether or not they are found, though, I will continue on. This curse was a product of a magic charm, no longer any good even if I still had it, produced by a sorcerer to the northwest. I was assured that he or one of his associates could lift it if I got there."

They nodded, and the alchemist then asked, "And then what?"

"Huh? I don't understand."

"Suppose you get there and the curse is lifted—what then? Do you have family, tribe, or profession to call upon?"

It was an unexpected and somewhat disconcerting question since, indeed, she had none of those. How best to answer?

"I am told," she said carefully, "that anyone who triggers this curse can be assured of some employment by the people who can remove it."

"Hmph!" said Halomar. "The sort of way these things work, I wouldn't want to be the object of such a curse. You could well wind up being a research subject for new spells or worse. And the children? How will they be provided for?"

She shrugged. "I have always managed to fill my needs. I admit I would like to see them safe and secure someplace, but unless I was absolutely certain it was in their best interests I am prepared to do whatever it takes to raise them to adulthood."

They leaned back and whispered to one another too low for her to hear. Then Gira picked up a piece of paper—a form of some kind—and slid it to Sam. "Please read this and sign it and that will be all, I think," the alchemist said pleasantly.

Sam looked at the pictographic writing, no two characters alike, and again felt embarrassed. "I'm sorry—I know my native tongue but I never learned to read Akhbreed."

The paper was withdrawn. "That is all right." Gira paused for a moment, thinking, then said, "You are in surprisingly good health considering your ordeal. It is customary, after a physical approval, that our guests here do some work in lieu of payment, if they are up to it. Would this bother you?"

"No," Sam replied. "In fact, I was feeling kind of guilty about taking all this with no way to pay it back as it was. What sort of work?"

"We have some wide agricultural holdings here, making the desert bloom in the only part of the region where it *can* be made to bloom. In this we not only make ourselves self-sufficient in food and cloth but also experiment with new ways of growing things. This is spread out along the river and is planned so that something is always being harvested and something else planted. Now we are harvesting *enu* groves in a small valley about nine leegs from here. It is physical work but requires no special knowledge or skills."

Sam nodded. "Sounds fair, I guess." She didn't really like the idea of hard physical work but, what the hell, it was only for four or five days and she owed it.

"Very well. I will have Avala outfit you and take you there. Avala herself began with us there and she knows it well. Thank you."

Sam got up, then shook hands all around, and Gira showed her to the door where Avala was waiting outside. "Susama has volunteered for the picking crew. Will you see that she gets there and gets what she needs?"

Avala bowed slightly. "Of course. Come, it will be good to get out in the air for a while."

Gira watched them go, then shut the door and went back over to her colleague.

"She is something of a survivor, but toughness is not a good measure of her best interests," Halomar noted.

"I was thinking the same thing," Gira agreed. "She is illiterate, without family, tribe, or skills. By her own admission here she lived entirely as a housekeeper for her missing mate who is, or was, both artist and alchemist and sufficient to be a provider for both. Her sexual orientation makes it unlikely she will settle in any conventional family scheme, and she is hardly the type for courtesan work. The best she could hope for would be some sort of menial job. Otherwise, she'll be a social outcast anywhere. She certainly has a low self-image; even with her weight she seems to go out of her way to make herself look plain and unattractive. If there weren't the matter of the curse the decision would be simple."

Halomar nodded. "I agree, particularly in light of the children. Even in the best of circumstances those children would have no future with her, a fact even she tacitly acknowledges. But those children are torn up inside, as you well know, and have no anchor in family or in law. At best they would wind up of necessity being slipped some potion and working as whores to support Susama, whose background is in that seamier side of life anyway. Their hurt and prejudices are deep. I do not think Directors were wrong in fearing that eventually they might suicide without support and a stable family life. As for Susama's curse, I said that exercise will control it and she is surprisingly healthy as she is."

"Yes, that is why I thought immediately of a field worker. It is good exercise and is something constructive she can do. Avala knows enough to make certain she gets the potions that will ease the strain and aid the transition to real work."

"And precondition her as well. I believe we would be criminals if we let those children go off with her, but unless we also take in Susama it would be very difficult to do."

"Yes, I thought the same."

"If she were to have her memories and personality permanently erased and a newer, simpler one built," Halomar suggested, "she would fit in perfectly as a permanent field worker—planting, picking, and the like—and get heavy daily exercise to boot. With the aid of some careful guidance and hypnotics or spells she could almost certainly he reoriented sufficiently to be happy in a heterosexual relationship. Of course, we've already agreed that erasure is the only hope of saving those children."

The alchemist sighed. "Exactly my thinking. We have done it so many times before with poor unfortunates that it would not be at all difficult to handle gently and unobtrusively, but we would have an embarrassing, even awkward, situation if then her mate walks in. In that instance, it could he quite—*difficult*—for the Duke."

"We could cover," responded the magician, "but it is best to play it a bit cautiously. It is five days until the next caravan—Crim's, I believe, which is a good choice, since Crim won't care or ask questions one way or the other. If neither or both of the missing pair are located within that time it's safe to assume that they never will be. You and I both know this country, and the additional time will give us an opportunity to test her in this role without committing anyone. Of course, the final decision is His Grace's, but I will recommend treatment on the morning five days from today if the conditioning tests are satisfactory and nothing else develops."

"Five days seems more than safe," Gira agreed. "I'll write it up for the Directors and His Grace today."

3

Of Brigands, Scoundrels, and Slaves

Boday stepped and suddenly froze, her face a mask of revulsion. She looked down and said, disgustedly, "We are still following them. Perhaps we follow *too* closely. The horse dung is still *very* fresh."

Charley suppressed something of a giggle. She looked up and around and saw a large stone monolith with carving and a fancy seal on it. "See, Mistress—the way goes in two, and what is that?" She hated the demeaning Short Speech but it was all she had. Boday knew no English and Charley's mouth simply wouldn't form Akhbreed. She was only thankful that her ear for languages and liking for music allowed her to understand—mostly—what was being said. To be in this position and effectively mute was inconvenient; to be essentially deaf would be intolerable.

Boday finished wiping what she could against the dry grass near the river and came up to look. "It appears to be an Imperial seal," she said, marveling. "It says that there is a Governor's residence down there. Difficult to believe in this desolation that anyone would *bother* with a Governor."

"Does Mistress think they might go there?" It was a real hope.

Boday sighed and thought about it. "There is more fresh dung going straight, and we know now that it is most certainly the riders with all our belongings and horses and perhaps Susama as well. This is too far along. Why would they have come here instead of waiting for us? No, the evidence points to them being captured by the riders. They go slowly because of their extra load anyway. Boday is thinking! Ah! What we must do is follow the riders for now, while there is still daylight. If we fail to catch up with them, at least sufficient to see if they do or do not have Susama and the girls, then we will return here and beg the Governor's help."

"Might he not help now, Mistress?"

Boday shook her head. "No, any Governor of a place like this is either in deep disgrace or he is the ringleader for all the criminal bands in the area. We might well be forced to him out of sheer hunger or desperation, but until we must Boday would like to avoid it. There is no sign of any recent horses save those we follow, so it is unlikely that this Governor's people found them and took them in, but it is quite likely that they had their hands in the raiders who attacked the trains. If so, one good look at you, my little butterfly, and you will quickly meet your horned pursuer. Never mind that he will then see through the deception. That will simply make my Susama the obvious target and our own fates will be most unpleasant. No, while Boday could happily eat one of her missing horses, she is tough, she can do without for now. We know where this place is now. We can always fall back on it as a last resort."

Charley nodded, seeing her logic. This was the Kudaan *Wastes,* for Pete's sake! Who would a Governor govern, and why? But an Akhbreed noble who had both official standing and criminal connections out here, with no other authority around, would be an ideal ally for Klittichorn. Damn it, if they just didn't think she was Sam this would be all suddenly very simple!

So they continued on, moving well past the cutoff, although Boday noted that here and there breaks in the rugged landscape showed distant groves and greenery, and more than once they passed small, expertly engineered gates like the tiny locks of a miniature canal leading to under the trail culverts that obviously sent water to that far-off but lush-looking region. They were too far for Charley to see the groves, but the irrigation canals were unmistakable and she took Boday's word for the rest. Whoever that guy was, he was smart and he had smart people working for him, too. The odds were that the community over there was entirely self-supporting, but that made it doubly dangerous. They would be their own masters, paying only lip service to any central authority, and open to all sorts of influences.

After a while, Boday looked up, studying the vegetation that covered the river bank, and pointed. "Boday is *starved!*" she exclaimed. "And, look! Some of these trees and bushes have ripe fruit! They must be wild offspring of those farms, carried here by the winds!"

"Mistress, we fall more back if we eat," Charley noted in the only way she could.

"Bah! You can see that this canyon runs a very long way, and it is too late in the day for anyone to think of climbing out, so they are not going to climb out today. They, too, must eat, must make camp or reach a destination. If we do not eat ourselves we will be in no condition to do what must be done later."

There was no arguing with that logic, although Charley couldn't help but wonder what the hell they could do if they caught up to the riders. At least back at the rock arch she'd had guns and a well-armed and well-staked-out ally above, and she'd had eyesight well enough to use them. What were they going to do? Take on all those armed and dangerous guys with rocks?

Much of the fruit was overripe, but enough was still good or at least edible that they couldn't really complain. Charley managed to polish off two medium-sized *alu,* which was a lavender-colored fruit shaped like a bottle that looked inside a lot like pink apple and tasted more like a super-sweetened pear. The two of them stuffed her, although she'd eaten next to nothing for more than a day. She hadn't had much of an appetite since taking on this courtesan look, but she knew that she should be hungrier after this kind of fast and exercise than she was. Still, she felt neither sick nor particularly weak or dizzy and she was probably less tired than she should have been, so perhaps she was worrying too much. She was much more afraid of losing her eyesight than starving to death, anyway.

Boday ate well. That had been part of Sam's problem back in Tubikosa, really. Boday was the kind of person who ate all the good things in huge quantities and then complained that she could never gain any weight.

After a while, though, Boday picked up a last *alu* and got up. "Come, little butterfly! We wish to see if we can catch them before night, although Boday would *kill* to just sleep for ten or twelve hours!"

The shadows were getting long and the sun low before they got close. Boday put out a hand and stopped Charley. "*Habadus!*" she hissed. "Lots of them!"

It wasn't a word Charley knew, but the root indicated some sort of bird. She couldn't see so far, but she strained at the sky and thought she could see some kind of dark, blurry movement. "What . . .?"

"Carrion-eating birds. This is not good."

Vultures! They were some kind of vultures, these *habadus.* Giant suckers, too, if she could make out anything of them.

Following Boday's lead, they inched forward, a bit off the trail and using what cover they had, until they could see just what the big birds were feeding upon. Charley had a sudden fear that it was going to be very familiar bodies, and she almost didn't want to know for sure.

You could smell the death from here, all torn and rotting in the sun. Boday checked the whole thing out carefully, then stood up. "Come. There is nothing left living here except the birds, and even though they are as big as you are they will flee us. They have no stomach for living things." She paused a moment, then added, "Well, at least their Tubikosan relatives do not."

Thanks a lot, Charley thought sourly. There was cross-pollution, particularly of vegetation and birds, among many of the worlds of Akahlar, but there were vultures and there were vultures.

Between the flapping of enormous wings and the birdlike cries of protest, they walked among the scene of carnage and even Charley could see the very gory details and found them sickening.

Two dead horses, but no sign of the others. Lots of human bodies, though. Six, all male, stripped as naked as could be, their bodies and heads ripped open and mutilated, the blood merging into drying pools nearby. It was impossible to tell what damage had been done by the birds and what by the attackers, but it made no difference in the end.

"No bridles on the dead horses, no saddles or packs, the men stripped clean. These are the ones from whom we fled, little one. There is no doubt of that. And one of those poor horses is the very one Boday was riding! Pity. They were attacked suddenly, massacred, and stripped clean of everything of even the slightest value or use. If any had gold teeth they most certainly do not now. Boday is surprised they didn't skin them, too."

Charley felt as if she was going to be sick. "Sam . . . ?" she managed, moving out of the midst of the carnage.

"No. Rest easy, my pretty one! Boday will know if Sam dies. We are linked by potion and spell. No, since only the men died, it is probable that she and the others were taken by the attackers." Boday was suddenly very clinical and deliberative. "The blood and condition of the bodies put this at at least two hours ago. The attackers, they were very efficient, I think."

Charley was away from it. It helped, but not much. "Does Mistress think the—governor—did this?" She was beginning to have confidence enough to attempt a few needed words, as badly mauled as they might be.

"No, hardly, pretty one. They had our horses and probably their own since they would need to bring weapons and such. None of the men appears shot. Arrows, spears, that sort of thing. Not the sort that professionals would use, and if it were this governor, as Boday presumes you were attempting to say, they would have passed us on the way back. Nor were these the governor's men,

Boday would wager. They had on plain black uniforms, not blue with gold, but they were uniforms all the same and thieves and scoundrels do not wear uniforms. They were army, but not *this* army. That was why they were attacked. The attackers had license to do what they would with invaders and how could this governor complain?"

"Yes, Mistress, but—where do they go?"

"Good question," Boday admitted. "Not back or there would have been a real racket. Not east, because that would take them into this governor's domain and they would probably at least have to share the booty. West is the river—far too deep here for horses. So—we continue!"

Charley nodded sadly and they got up and left the scene of carnage, none too soon for Charley's taste. It seemed to inspire Boday, though. She kept muttering, "Boday wishes she had some charcoal and paper. Such inspiration she is getting from all this! Such violence, such suffering, such travails she has already undergone! If this keeps up much longer, Boday will ultimately be acclaimed the greatest artist of her times!"

Yeah, Charley thought dejectedly. *If the great Boday lives to paint it. At least I don't have to worry that she's one of those artists who goes crazy. She was insane before we ever met her.*

The canyon was growing dark, the shadows long, and still they hadn't come upon anything still living except for a few insects and some distant birds circling high in the ever-deepening blue sky. It was hot and quiet, so quiet that only the sounds of their own movement and the rush from the swift-flowing river broke the stillness in the land and air.

Suddenly the rocks to their right erupted with forms and fierce cries. Before either woman could even see who or what was there they were overtaken and pushed roughly to the ground. Boday gave a good struggle; as two pinned her arms she managed to twist and kick another in the groin, twist away, and start in fiercely on her attackers. Charley had no such skills and reflexes and not much strength left, either. They had her quickly pinned facedown and then her arms were roughly brought behind her and tied with some strong, tight cord, and someone else pulled on her hair to make her face come up and then slipped a noose over her head.

They had to work hard for Boday, but there were too many of them and they were too strong for her in the end, and she suffered the same fate in the end.

Charley tried to look up and see just who or what their captors were, but once she caught sight of them she didn't want to look anymore.

They were as ragtag a bunch of filth as she'd ever seen: smelly, dirty, in torn and rumpled clothing, and not a normal-looking one in the bunch. There were eight of them, all well armed and tough as nails. One was huge and hunchbacked, his face contorted, and he snorted and dribbled from his twisted lower lip. Charley instantly dubbed him the Hunchback of Notre Dame even if he didn't look much like a football player.

Another was tall, muscular, with a tremendous, flowing bright red beard and nasty, close-set eyes above a pug nose, but he walked real funny and his arms and hands—well, they weren't *normal.* Thick, blue-gray and shiny, the arms terminated in a really nasty-looking set of lobsterlike claws.

The others were no better. They had all been human once, but all now had very different and inhuman parts to them. One was a sort of cyclops with weird hands that had three thick, curved fingers like a claw machine at the fire carnival. Another had tentacles growing from his back, and still another had a face that would have looked better on a toad. In fact, after seeing them all, the hunchback looked very normal and comforting indeed.

Redbeard with the claws was obviously the leader. With both women tied and held down, he walked slowly up to them and looked each over.

"Well, now, this *is* a pretty catch, and all decorated nice and fine like they's gift-wrapped or something. Who the hell are you, girls, and what in the name of the Nine Dark Hells are you doin' out here stark naked?"

Boday managed to look up. "Do you really think the designs are pretty? You are obviously a man of good taste to appreciate the handiwork of Boday!"

Charley groaned.

Redbeard turned to her. "And who might this Boday be?"

"She who speaks with you is Boday!" the artistic alchemist responded proudly, totally disregarding her circumstances.

Redbeard looked a bit taken aback by her attitude. "All right, Boday, so who else be you and why are you here?"

"We were flooded in a wagon train disaster, then taken by brigands who had their fun with us, then escaped to here only to be split up running from those dead men back there who stole what supplies we had. We seek our companions whom the men in black captured."

"These companions be men?"

"No, of *course* not! A young woman and two small girls."

"Weren't no females with *that* crew," Redbeard responded. "Your friends probably wound up in the clutches of that bastard crazy Duke. We got your horses, though, and your booty, and now we got you. Both of you now get up and shut up! We's goin' for a little walk. Them's good nooses on your pretty necks, now, so don't make no sudden moves or you'll strangle yourselves. Now, we don't want'a kill you or damage them pretty bodies, but Hooton, there, he's an expert at the science of the noose. A little jerk just so and he can shatter your voice boxes, and we don't need your voices. And any real trouble and he's got a way of fixin' them so you don't strangle all the way but just a little, so's you don't get so much blood to the brain. I seen 'em after a few hours of his treatment. You don't have enough sense left to remember what clothes was and you might needs some help feedin' yourself, but your bodies'll be just fine. So—shut up, do what you're told, and no tricks!"

Shit!, Charley thought sourly. *Back into the fire again, and this time getting farther and farther from Sam. Damn! Damn! Damn! Why didn't we go to that governor? Damn you, Boday!*

The horses were about a half mile farther down the trail, held a bit off the track and upwind so that they hadn't made a sound. Their own horses and the lone narga were among them, still loaded with stuff. Four more ragtag and deformed nasties held them, waiting. It seemed that Redbeard simply couldn't conceive of six uniformed men with no protection just marching in here, particularly past the Imperial Governor's turnoff. He'd been convinced that more were following behind, and he wanted to make very sure what he was up against rather than risk fleeing with the loot with soldiers in hot pursuit. Now, though, he felt his wait rewarded in a different way.

Neither Charley nor Boday was allowed to ride; Redbeard didn't trust them, even naked and tied, on the backs of their own horses. They walked along at a steady pace, trying to adjust so that those strangely tied nooses didn't have much chance to tighten up. The gang made all sorts of lewd and lustful comments about them but did not try to touch them or in fact do much of anything to them. Clearly Redbeard was an authority to be feared.

They reached a point where the river bent slightly, and two riders came forward and stopped at the water's edge, checking for something unknown. Then they rode right into the river, the horses sinking only slightly into the water, and came up on the other side with their riders not even wet.

"Now you, ladies, and don't slip," Hooton said in a low, menacing tone. "Right at this point it's right shallow with just sand and mud and small rocks there at certain times of day like now. Other times it's a killer. Just go on across."

It was an unpleasant balancing act, shallow though it was. The mud and rocks were slippery, the muck just under the surface felt just awful, and while it wasn't all that bad for Boday, tall as she was, it wasn't all that shallow for Charley at just a little over five feet tall. She felt tense, and the noose pulling at her throat all the way, and when she made it to the other side she gave a gasp of relief.

The others now followed without any trouble, and then the whole group turned not farther up but rather to the left, back the way they'd come. They went back down perhaps a thousand yards, then reached a rocky outcrop that seemed so solid that it blocked passage along that shore. A rider reached up and did something that couldn't be seen in the gloom, and the rock seemed to shift and the earth to shake a bit, and when it was done there was a narrow passage revealed in the rock itself. It wasn't wide enough for more than one horse and rider at a time, single file, and it seemed to go on for an eternity in near-total darkness.

They emerged for a moment, the lack of river noise meaning that they were now well away from the river, and the last man in the gang rode through, then stopped, and again did something that caused the same rumbling and the fissure to close with a nasty-sounding finality. It was a good way to escape if you needed to block pursuit, Charley realized. Even if you were tricked and they tried to follow, they'd be crushed along the way. Still, the mere fact that Redbeard had waited showed that they didn't want to have to rely on that trick. Ignorance on the part of their enemies that the passage even existed was far better long-term protection than just using it as a means of escape.

They went down a bit into the rocky jumble of the Kudaan landscape, hurrying a bit because of the growing darkness. Here and there they shouted some strange words and were answered by others, showing that this trail was well guarded. Charley's heart sank. Even if, somehow, she escaped this crew, how the hell would she ever get away, elude all of those guardians who knew the territory perfectly, and survive? These were dangerous men; fugitives holed up in the Wastes and living a different and primitive kind of life beyond the reach of any law. Men with no place to go, nothing to lose, and with nothing at all to hold them back.

Now, at last, a great glob of total darkness loomed ahead, and they suddenly stopped. Hooton, the toad-faced one, slid off his horse and came up to them. "Now you just walk right in front of me," he told them, "and keep your neckwear slack."

It was a tunnel of some sort—no, a cave. There was a blast of cool air coming from it, and as they entered they descended, although they couldn't see a thing. Hooton, however, could, and he kept giving them quick directions.

"Turn left. That's right. Ten paces forward, then left again. Fine. Now ahead until I tell you to stop. Now—right turn."

It went on for some time, made no easier by the fact that some of the mounted horses were ahead of them and leaving the usual horse droppings.

Within several minutes, neither Charley nor Boday had any idea of where they were or how they'd gotten there. It wasn't merely one cave, it was a network of interlocking caves going off in all directions including down, and between the darkness and the differences in the dark tunnels only one who knew exactly where he or she was and, perhaps, could see or read the hidden markings, would find their way in—or out.

Suddenly all was noise and light. It was the lights of thousands of torches rather than anything in nature, and the reverberant cacophony of great numbers of people and animals. The scene seemed to go on and on below them. Charley could see only the lights but the noise and smells were overwhelming. She realized that they had now entered some grand cave on the order of the Big Room at Carlsbad Caverns or even bigger. A giant cave, far underground, that held not tourists but a town.

This, then, was the outlaw capital, the seat of the unholy of the Kudaan Wastes. No wonder the worst could hide out here! No power could find such a place except by treachery, and the system didn't really care enough to even attempt that sort of thing anymore.

They moved now down into it, into a throng of people, animals, changelings, and creatures, the discards of Akahlar. Boday was entranced by the vision, so much so that she seemed to forget her own situation. The cave was *enormous,* and it seemed to go off in the distance a tremendous way. On the floor of it were buildings, marketplaces, bazaars, a tremendous life energy that knew no day or night; a town with few laws and few limits that was a continual now, without regard for yesterday or tomorrow.

They, however, could not explore it. When they reached a central square, Hooton turned them abruptly and led them to a squared-off building that seemed made entirely of glass that was inches thick. Two guards, huge and somewhat piglike, nodded and grunted and then gave way, and a jail-like door was unlocked and opened. Hooton then carefully removed the nooses, untied their hands, and while they were still rubbing their raw wrists they were rudely shoved inside, so that both of them landed sprawling on a hay-strewn floor. The door clanged shut behind them, and the sounds of the great room became terribly muted.

"That swine!" Boday hissed, and managed to roll over and come to a sitting position. "Are you all right?"

Charley groaned, then managed to sit up and nod, feeling her neck. God! It *still* felt like she had a rope around it! She tried breathing hard through her mouth and tried to get hold of herself. Then and only then did she take stock of the cubicle.

It was small enough for her to see all of it, if a bit blurry, and beyond she could see the lights and activities of the city beneath the ground. It wasn't very big—maybe six feet by six feet, give or take, filled with a rotting straw floor that, when you dug down in it, led to an unpleasantly sticky cold stone floor. Over in one corner was a foul, rusted chamber pot, and in another a clay jug of water that had a bit of scum on top. Boday went over to it, frowned, stirred it with her finger, then tasted it.

"It *seems* all right," she said dubiously, then sighed. "And it is all we have." Still, she stared at it. "As an alchemist, Boday would suspect that this water is somewhat drugged. Still, she is *dying* of thirst, and what difference can it make now anyway?"

It was a practical, pragmatic statement and Charley couldn't disagree. They both drank it, and even though it tasted flat and mineral-heavy, it was what they needed.

The door opened, and Hooton was there again. "I've made all the arrangements," he told them, then put a basket down. "Here's some food. It ain't much but it'll keep you going. Best make yourselves comfortable. You'll be on display here until the next slave auction, and that ain't for three days yet. There's a bunch that saw you come in got real interested in you. Ain't too often we get full-blooded Akhbreed down here." And, with that, he closed the door and the noises again faded.

Charley sighed and went to one of the walls. Transparent. There were already some people out there looking at them. Sizing up the merchandise. Not just men and half-men, either. There were some women out there as well, but from the looks of them even Hooton would be an improvement. She tried to imagine the kind of woman who'd do well as an equal in a society like this. These looked the part. The one with the wrestler's muscles, purple makeup, spiked green hair, and leather outfit looked just Boday's type.

She went over to Boday, who was ignoring the outside traffic and checking the contents of the basket.

"Slightly stale bread, moldy cheese, some slabs of some sort of meat that might not poison us, if we can stand to chew it and our teeth are strong enough for it. Not much else. And the amphora . . ." She uncorked it and sniffed it. "Ugh! The cheapest wine imaginable!"

Charley had not been able to tolerate meat since she entered this life and this lookalike existence, but she was far too hungry not to eat her share of the rest, including the wine. It *was* bad, barely drinkable, but it dissolved the bread enough to make it edible. The cheese wasn't so bad—all cheese smelled yucky anyway—if you just scraped some of the mold off with your nails first.

The wine was, however, definitely alcoholic to a much higher degree than she was used to. In a little while she felt light-headed, even a bit silly, and, somehow, not so horribly down anymore.

Boday, who usually had a high tolerance for alcohol, was feeling it a little bit, too. She got up after a while and pressed herself against the wall. "Boday feels like she is at the zoo," she muttered, slurring her words a bit, "but something is wrong. The people they are on the inside of the cage and the animals are out there looking in!" She seemed to find this thought funny and began chuckling.

The chuckling was contagious. For some reason the comment struck Charley that way as well and she started laughing. Then she went over and started making very graphic obscene gestures and moves to the crowd. This kept up for a while, until, finally, both women just sank down in the straw and, within minutes of one another, passed out.

There was no telling how long they slept; there was no way of telling any sort of time in a place like this. But from the way every bone and muscle in their bodies ached when they finally awoke, they had been out a very long time. The worst part, Charley thought to herself, was that she felt like she hadn't slept at all.

There was another basket of the same just inside the door. No telling how long it'd been there, but it was clearly what they got until they ate it and needed another.

Boday made her way, crawling, to it and settled down, back against the glass, looking glassy-eyed. "Boday feels like shit," she muttered wearily. "All of the energy, the fight, has gone out of her. What is the use of fighting anymore, anyway'? She is sick of fighting, of running, of worrying. There is no escape. They can do what they want with her."

Charley was almost startled to hear Boday voice her own depression, as deep and despairing as the slight drunk had been manic. It was over for them, and something inside her just didn't care anymore. She felt so weak and small and helpless that she had no choice but to accept fate.

"It is the wine, you know, or perhaps the water," Boday noted in that still down, detached tone. "Not that what we feel is not the truth, the result of all that has gone before and all that is. It simply builds on that. Ah—Boday sees you do not fully understand. She is an alchemist. The caves here, they must grow a hundred different kinds of fungus. A minor potion, really. You drink it and for a while you have no worries or fears or inhibitions. Then it goes the other way, and the rest of the time you are passive, fatalistic, without real strength or will. Just a way to see that we perform now and then for the customers and otherwise do not fight or resist or try and make trouble."

A potion? Charley stared at the amphora. The trouble was, while Boday was making sense, somehow it didn't really matter to either of them that they knew. What could they do but accept it? She no longer cared anymore.

Hell, inside her was another, simpler personality that was probably a lot more useful here. Hell, three words in English would bring up a spell that would banish Charley from her mind and bring forth Shari, an ignorant, servile, willing slave who could only think in the few hundred words of the Short Speech. Hell, she always wondered what would happen if she herself spoke the three simple words aloud, but she'd never tried because then there'd be nobody who would know how to bring Charley back. She wondered now if that even mattered.

Still, she could bring up that part of her without any spell. She'd had long practice at it. You just relaxed, put everything out of your mind, and began to think only in the servile Short Speech. *Mistress, I be Shari. How may Shari serve Mistress . . . ?*

So easy, so tempting, so worry free.

So damned cowardly.

The hell with it. Not yet. There was plenty of time if it became really unbearable, but, until then, where there was life there had to be some hope of something. If only she had a real command of this language! At least Boday had somebody to bitch to.

They had to have slept a very long time, since there were only two more "meals" and one more, and better, sleep before they came for them. When they did, they didn't bother to truss them up or chain them or anything. Charley guessed they already had proven that, at least for now, they weren't the suicidal type, and, down here, with this crowd, what the hell were they going to do and where could they go, anyway?

The crowd was like something out of a bad horror movie, with shouting and screaming figures dressed mostly in rags or patchwork stuff and many looking and sounding only vaguely human. They were pawed and pushed as their guards made way for them to walk through to the marketplace, and it was pretty unpleasant. There was almost a sense of relief when they made this little platform in a kind of square surrounded by broken-down stalls that was clearly the center of commerce, such as it was. The crowd was jovial enough, but somehow both women felt more like the unwelcome guests of honor at an execution than the objects of an auction.

Far back in the crowd, an unassuming figure in a full brown robe, looking much like an out-of-place friar, stared at them, then did something of a double-take and stared some more. The cut of his robe marked him as a magician, but its color and design did not denote high rank. He had a pudgy, boyish face, although he was more stocky than fat, and rumpled, thin brown hair to his shoulders that compensated only slightly for his massive but natural bald spot atop his head.

He was there almost as an afterthought; captives and slaves weren't of any real interest to him unless they were somebody important. In fact, he hated this crowd and would have timed his visit differently had he remembered about this, but here he was, and as he'd needed to purchase some essential charms at the bazaar he wasn't about to go back and make a second, later trip. This would be over soon enough.

At first he'd thought the two women an odd pair. The tall one with all those tattoos over her body was at once mean-looking and singularly unattractive; the small one, though, looked so frail, a courtesan far from her element, helpless and afraid.

That courtesan looked damned familiar. That long hair and those eye tattoos took away from it somewhat, but he was knowledgeable enough to see through them and overlay the familiar on her feature and form. Yes . . . Trim the hair and restyle it, remove the tattoos, add maybe fifteen or twenty halg to the weight . . .

By the gods, they've captured one of Boolean's simulacra! Perhaps the very one Zamofir had spoken of when he was through here!

Suddenly it all made lots of sense, but what to do? He couldn't deprive this mob of their show, that was for sure. Halting the auction at this point was out of the question, and he certainly had little with which to outbid those here. Calming himself, he got control of his thoughts and knew that there was no time to do anything here and now. The best he could do was to note the buyer and then get that information back to Yobi as fast as possible.

You could tell the Grand Auctioneer in an instant. For one thing, he was clean, well groomed, and dressed in a fine togalike garment and shiny leather boots and definitely had a lot more than most of this mob. For another, he was clearly in his element in front of the crowd and very much the businessman. He was accompanied by a woman who had once been beautiful, but her face and her silver hair told of a life where fate had been less than kind, and while she was clean and well dressed herself she walked with a pronounced limp. As she came up to the platform, Charley could see that the woman had two fingers missing on her left hand, and a small brass or copper ring through her nose. She also carried a small book and stylus with her, and propped herself to one side of the platform. The Grand Auctioneer came up to her and said something that the crowd noises made it impossible to hear, and she nodded. Then the auctioneer mounted the platform.

He turned, faced the crowd, and with exaggerated hand gestures pleaded for and then finally achieved a level of quiet.

"All right, all right!" he said in a penetrating, professional voice that seemed to cut through all noise almost as if amplified, yet not shouting at all. "Now, we don't have much today, but what we do have is well worth the wait. I know most of you can't afford either of them, but you can sit there quietly and drool and pretend you can. The serious bidders and their agents to my right, please. Let them through! Thank you, thank you!"

About a dozen people made their way to the designated spot. All were better dressed and obviously more affluent than the masses in the crowd, although many were as strange in their own ways as the rest here. Most were men, but a few were women, and perhaps two-thirds of them also wore rings in their noses.

"Ah!" said the Grand Auctioneer with satisfaction. "All set? Very well, then. You've seen this pair on display now, so you know pretty well what you're getting physically." He turned to Boday. "Do you have a name and any skills to recommend yourself?."

She glared at him. Boday always expected to be recognized, even here.

"You see before you Boday, the greatest alchemical artist of the age, and one of her finest creations!" she bragged.

The crowd roared, mostly with laughter, which seemed to infuriate Boday even more. She glared at them and they seemed collectively taken aback at the glare.

"There you are!" the auctioneer told the crowd. "An alchemist and artist of the body. Two for the price of one, ladies and gentlemen! A slave such as this can be *most* useful! Can I have a starting bid, please?"

Charley stared out at the crowd in wonder. Why were they all here and making so merry at this? These were the poor, the misshapen, the dregs of this underground society. Looking at the real bidders, it was clear that even slaves of such people would be better off than most of this lot.

And then it hit her. That was it, wasn't it? These were the losers, the dregs of the lowest society of Akahlar. The accursed and misshapen, without hope, without anything much at all.

But they were still better than slaves.

So long as there were slaves in this society, they were not the lowest, not the bottom of the ladder. So long as there were slaves there was always somebody to look down on somebody so you could always say to yourself, "Well, I may be at my rock bottom but at least I'm not a slave." And if the slaves were pure Akhbreed, so much the better. She and Boday represented to these people that which had shut them out and cast them out, and just to see them sold into bondage was a sort of vicarious revenge.

The auctioneer was going well now, occasionally going fast enough to make a singsong chant in numerical units, although units of what wasn't clear. Surely money as such meant nothing to these people; there had to be some alternate value system here that was represented by the numbers.

The bidding slowed at eleven hundred and fifty, and the auctioneer began cajoling the bidders, alternately flattering and insulting them, trying to get another bid. It was now like pulling teeth, but he got another two hundred and then started his close.

"Thirteen fifty . . . once! Twice! Three times! Sold!" He pointed to a huge pale man in a white toga whose head was shaved and who looked almost like a marble monument. The man had a ring in his nose.

Boday was told to step down off the platform and stand by the woman with the ledger, and the auctioneer brought Charley front and center.

"The girl speaks no Akhbreed!" Boday shouted to the auctioneer. "She knows only the Short Speech but understands much. She is Shari, a courtesan."

"Ah! You hear?" the Grand Auctioneer asked the crowd. "No need of breaking in this one. A courtesan, schooled only in pleasure and service. A beauty if there ever was one here. Never before have we had a jewel like *this* to sell! Who needs a hub when you can have *this* one forever at your beck and call? How much am I offered?"

Charley felt a sense of unreality about it all. The whole thing had more of a dreamlike quality to it for her, and she felt a curious intellectual detachment from the proceedings. She was curious to see just how much she'd go for in whatever it was they were using to pay.

The answer was a lot. In the first minute she'd passed Boday, somewhat to Boday's clear irritation, and the bidding was still quite spirited. When it passed two thousand virtually all noise ceased except the auctioneer's chant. When she went above twenty-five hundred the auctioneer was talking about a "new record" for any individual.

She felt a curious thrill at that, even though she knew she should be ashamed of herself for feeling that way. *What's happened to me in this world?* she wondered, more amazed than upset in spite of it all. *Yeah, I wanted to be senior class president, prom queen, college coed, and then found my own cosmetics business and make a million before I was thirty. And look at me now! First a high-class hooker who finds she likes it, then, standing here, mentally charged up at how much people are paying for me! Have I changed, or didn't I just know myself before?*

"Sold! Three thousand one hundred, a new record by far!" the auctioneer declared.

She looked over, hoping to see the same buyer as Boday, but instead it was a small, ugly character in a black robe and hood standing two away from Boday's new master. It was hard to tell if the buyer was male or female or maybe something else.

She was led off the platform and placed next to Boday as the auctioneer wound up his pitch, promised big deals in affordable merchandise and booty at the auction the next day, then stepped down himself. "Make way! Make way! Coming through! Successful bidders please follow!"

Boday shrugged and looked at Charley, then the two followed the auctioneer, then the two buyers, and finally the woman with the ledger book. They went across the square, through the crowd that was now straining for one last glimpse but was also beginning to break up, then down a narrow alley between two stalls and to a door halfway through to the next block. The auctioneer took out some keys on a big ring, opened the door with one, then walked in and they followed.

"You two sit on the divan there in the anteroom," he told them in a cold, businesslike tone. "No talking or moving around."

The other three now entered, and he closed the door and went over to a desk, while his female assistant took a chair to his right. The two buyers stood in front and were not offered seats.

"You have full payment?" the autioneer asked them.

"I have a draft bill, open," said the big man with the shaved head in a surprisingly soft and high voice. "Your client may redeem it at my master's place any time after it is registered." He reached into a hidden pocket in his toga. "I also have a draft for credits at any establishment you choose in the name of yourself, so there is no problem with the fees."

The auctioneer nodded and looked at the small, hooded one. "And you?"

The little one produced similar papers. "Pretty much the same, but the amount is high enough that you will have to dun the seller for your fees."

The auctioneer sighed. "Irregular, but, then, a percentage of that . . . I'll take the bill. The seller is Lakos in both cases, as you probably know. Best he not get his hands on this until he has settled with me. I understand that won't be difficult. He made quite a score otherwise in that raid. I'm selling much of the rest tomorrow. Yes, these will do. You may claim your merchandise. Vica—give them receipts and final bills of sale."

"Yes, Master Arnos," the gray-haired woman responded, and for the first time Charley realized that all of these people except the auctioneer himself were slaves as well—the ledger woman with the limp belonging to the Grand Auctioneer, and who knew whom these two belonged to? Who—or what?

The auctioneer went back to them. "Go with these agents," he told them. "Do whatever they say. Do not mistake the fact that they are slaves as some sort of license. They are bonded to their masters and have the power to do anything with you that they wish as if they themselves had bought you."

They both nodded and got up and went back out into the alley with the two strange slaves, but they didn't go far. There was a small arcade just before the next street and they were led into it and immediately into an establishment that clearly sold unusual merchandise. From the burners and dolls and strange designs and odd bric-a-brac both knew they were in a magician's shop.

It occurred to Charley that she'd actually seen little magic in this world beyond her own change into a semblance of, or maybe an idealization of, Sam, and Sam's own summoning of the storm.

Almost everything she'd seen had been drugs and chemicals and maybe hypnosis, really. Oh, some of them did all sorts of wild things, like grow a foot of hair in minutes or make you fall in love or stuff like that, but it wasn't anything she was sure couldn't be done back home by some smart somebody. These kinds of shops with all the magic charms and incantation books she couldn't read and that kind of thing just hadn't looked like more than scams, and this junky place didn't look any different.

The proprietor, though, was something of a surprise. It was a woman, dressed in a brown magician's robe, perhaps fifty or so, with very short gray hair and deep lines in her face. There also seemed to be something odd about her eyes and her head movement, but it was hard to tell for sure.

"Yes?" she asked them.

The big man pointed to Boday. "She's enslaved to Jamonica. The other one belongs to Hodamoc. Both require bonding."

The magician nodded. "Very well. You have something I can use for each of them?"

The little one in the black hood and robe pulled out what looked to be a small, irregular stone and handed it to the magician. The big man reached in and removed a tiny box like a ring box that contained what appeared to be hairs. The magician examined both and nodded. "These will do fine. Wait here, and send the small one back first. Working from animate relics is far easier."

"I know, but Jamonica don't give no relics to nobody," the big man with the soft, high voice responded.

The magician smiled knowingly. "I understand." She pointed at Charley. "Come, little one. In back."

Charley hesitated, then followed, still in that somewhat detached state. The back of the place was a real mess, making the actual store look organized. There were all sorts of things around, making it look part chemical laboratory and part junk shop. She watched while the magician went into a drawer and took out a box containing a number of small bronze-colored rings. For the first time, Charley felt some panic. *Oh, no! You ain't putting one of* them *up my nose!*

The magician worked quickly and professionally. She took the hairs and put them into a small metal bowl, then began to add several other unknown substances, stirring and heating the mixture until it was a dull and sickly green paste. She then walked over to Charley and before the woman could say or do anything, the magician reached out, grabbed Charley's right hand, and she felt a sudden sharp sting.

"Ow!" she said, and tried to pull away, but the magician was surprisingly strong and had clearly done this a lot of times before. Charley's hand was pulled over the mixture, and her thumb squeezed enough so that two drops of blood fell into the bowl and green scum—and it sizzled. When that happened, Charley was released and stepped back, sticking her thumb in her mouth to stop the bleeding.

Now the magician took the ring and put it into the mixture, and more heat was applied, but this time the magician closed her eyes and began to wave her hands over the bowl and chant something in a low tone over it.

Suddenly there was a crackling and then a strange white light, about the size of the magician's thumb, appeared in the center of the bowl and began to pulse a bit, bulging in the center. As Charley watched, the little thing moved, going 'round and 'round the bowl in lazy circles, each one a bit smaller than the one before, and as it did the sickly liquid seemed to be pulled up into it, as if the pulsing white energy were some sort of straw bringing that crap up to some invisible mouth—and maybe it was.

In less than a minute there was nothing left in the bowl but the ring, looking good as new. The little energy thing winked out with a zapping sound, and the magician nodded to herself, turned off the heat, and removed the ring from the bowl and put it aside, perhaps to cool. She reached over, found a small gourd, uncorked it, sniffed it, then nodded and handed it to Charley. "Drink some of this. One or two swallows, anyway."

Charley hesitated and wouldn't touch it, and the magician understood.

"I am a magician, not an alchemist. Unfortunately, most magic involves pain of one sort or another, and the last step is painful. Can you understand what I am saying?"

Charley nodded, but didn't like the message.

"It will be done either with or without your drinking it. You have no abnormal auras about you. I could freeze you where you stand with a simple spell but then you would feel everything. Two swallows of this and you will feel very little pain for just a few minutes. Go ahead."

Charley drank it. It wasn't at all like the alchemical concoctions—magic potions tasted like medicine. She handed back the gourd and the magician put it back on the table, then picked up the ring. She turned and faced Charley, very close, and suddenly made a sign of something with her left hand. Charley saw the right, the one with the ring, move up to her face and she tried to step back, but she could not. She was frozen stiff as a board.

There was a sudden sharp pain, like some needle being shoved through her nose, but it was dampened down almost immediately and she felt only a numbness there.

The magician made the reverse of her previous motion and this time with her right hand. Charley could move again.

"The spell now holds you but you are not yet truly bonded," the magician told her, taking on the same clinical manner as a doctor explaining a treatment to a patient. "It is quite loose and you will soon get used to it but do not allow it to be removed. You remember that little bit of pain you felt? If you remove it, that pain will be back, in full, and it will not go away over time. The spell compels obedience. At the moment, because you are not yet bonded, it compels obedience from anyone at all, instantly. Stand on your right leg only!"

Immediately Charley found herself standing storklike on one leg. She hadn't thought about it.

"All right, put it down and stand normally. Don't worry, you're not at everyone's mercy. In a moment Hodamoc's slave will touch your ring, and since he is bonded by the same spell you will then be attuned to it and will obey only those with the same spell. Once brought before Hodamoc, he will touch the ring and it will recognize him as the controller and then you will be obedient only to him. Control is transferable, but only by a master's command. If the master dies, control passes to his or her nearest of kin. It enslaves only your body, not your mind and soul. Accept it. Even a master cannot free you. From this point on, you, and soon your companion, will be someone's property for the rest of your lives."

That was a very chilling thought.

"Stand there and do not move," the magician ordered. "I will fetch the slave."

The little one in black entered, and when he looked at her she could see an oddly oblong face, huge, round nose, and beady little recessed eyes against a small mouth and lantern jaw. On him, the ring in his nose was barely noticeable, and she could understand immediately why he liked to wear the hood all the time.

He reached out and touched the ring in her own nose, and she felt suddenly a bit dizzy. It cleared almost immediately, though, and he let go.

"Good," he said in a thin, reedy little voice. "Now hear and obey our master's commands. Until you are bonded you shall obey all who are bonded to our master as if any of us were he himself and no others. You shall harm no one, not even yourself, unless ordered to do so, nor cause another to suffer harm. You shall not be out of sight of another bonded to our master or our master himself at any time until you yourself are bonded. You shall undertake no action on your own without permission. Slaves, even those above you in rank, will always be addressed as equals. All others will be addressed with high respect as superiors no matter how low their station. But only Hodamoc shall be addressed as Master, and only Hodamoc and those bonded to him or designated by him shall be obeyed. These are the orders of our master Hodamoc. Hear and obey."

Well, she didn't *feel* any different, except that her nose felt funny, for all that.

"Now, follow me," said the little man, and she found herself turning and following him by a few steps back out to the front of the shop and then back out into the arcade, past Boday but unable to stop or signal or say a word. Charley found herself fixated on the little man, always keeping him in sight. Somewhere back there Boday would be getting the same treatment for her master, and boy! Would she ever hate *that!*

Charley didn't like the situation, but something deep down inside her liked that image of Boday. It was about time that somebody who turned lots of poor, trusting girls into mindless sex machines without a qualm got at least a taste of her own medicine. There was some small measure of justice in that.

For Boday, maybe, but what about her? Who or what was this Hodamoc, anyway? What was going to become of her now? A courtesan to the likes of Redbeard's crew, maybe? God, that was repulsive to think about! Now she was being led away to a strange place and people, severing her last link with anyone or anything in Akahlar. No more Sam, or even Boday, to fall back on. And, unlike Sam, nobody, least of all Boolean, even gave a damn about her.

Hodamoc lived well in the exile community, and he had good reason to be a major player in the underworld. It was said he'd been a general in the army of Mashtopol, assigned as commander of the Imperial Guard, one of the highest honors a soldier could attain and one of considerable political as well as military power and influence. He was of royal blood, but untitled, and those usually became either soldiers or magicians or other top secular positions of authority.

He had, however, overreached himself at last, as such people sometimes do. Imperial succession often had less to do with who was firstborn than which son of the king was the most cutthroat politician, and alliances for such things were formed early. The seven wives of the old king had borne him twenty-nine children, of whom fifteen were boys, and of whom six were well into their twenties when the old boy passed away. Hodamoc, with visions of a conferred title of Duke or Lord and perhaps a cabinet post, had picked and backed the son who appeared the strongest, and he'd chosen wrong. His boy had not taken into account just how insane Warog, the Imperial Sorcerer, was, and when promised magical support did not materialize for anyone's side, it was over.

Barely escaping the purge that inevitably followed a new ascension to the throne, but smart enough to have hedged some of his bets just in case, he had fled to the Kudaan to reorganize and perhaps, one day, return in force and teach those bastards a bit of a lesson.

In the meantime, he and some of his loyal staff had set themselves up fairly well in the Wastes, using his influence with his bleeding-heart cousin, Duke Alon Pasedo, the Governor of the region, to broker between the outlaw and legitimate elements. The outlaws laid off Pasedo's own estates and people, and in exchange the Duke, via his cousin, transferred some products he had that were worth more than gold in the Kudaan Wastes.

Hodamoc, former General of the Imperial Guard, was now the fruit-and-vegetable king of the underworld.

It was a somewhat humiliating position for him, but it gave him great power and influence. His underground estate was in a fairly large cavern of its own with its own underground water source, and by harnessing some of that power he had a water-driven elevator of sorts that could take him and his people up to the surface, where his main house was built of and into the rock but was also open to the outside.

He proved to be a tall, strikingly handsome man in his fifties, with gray-black hair, intelligent brown eyes, and a trim graying moustache and goatee, who almost always wore his full general's uniform around the place. He ran it like it was his headquarters and he was still in the army, too, and all but slaves called him "sir" or "General." He also had the military man's mania for order and cleanliness, and while his household included some who were either not quite human or very strange, in his free staff he played no favorites.

Charley wasn't sure she'd ever be comfortable with this slave business, but she was becoming accustomed to it and had accepted it. There was no use resisting, anyway, and she knew that she could be far worse off than this. She no longer even thought about the ring in her nose and was only absently aware of it. She discovered, though, that its magical properties were quite strong. Once you were given an order, it *stuck.*

She had relative freedom of movement around the place, subject to a few areas which were forbidden to her, but there was no way she could leave its clearly defined boundaries. She had to work hard to get a bunch of Akhbreed phrases correct, because she was required to ask permission of whoever was in charge of her to do most anything, including taking a bath, taking a walk, eating something, or even going to the bathroom. It soon went from being resented to being automatic, and it sure as hell kept you in your place.

She had thought that for the money he'd paid—in good credits, as it turned out—she would be his personal courtesan, but that wasn't the case. In fact, after that first brief time when he'd touched her ring and she had been bonded to his will, she'd seen him very little and always from a prostrate position as he passed. She had wondered at first why a man like him hadn't had a family, but the constant companionship of young, good-looking junior "officers" around him, some of whom were *gorgeous,* told the story.

She was not for him or his boys, but rather for various others who came and went. All were Akhbreed, many were older men, and she got the distinct impression that most of them were old friends and potential allies still within the royal structure. The General still had some power, and maybe even eventually some hope of a comeback. Kings had been known to be assassinated in these lands by brothers and cousins and the like.

Charley was ambivalent about these liaisons. In one way she looked forward to them because there was very little else for her to do, and she did mostly enjoy it, although a few of these guys were *really* kinky. But they were also active big shots in Mashtopol; as such, they could hardly be unaware of the Storm Princess and the search for ones who resembled her, and that made each new liaison a potential threat as well. She just kicked into Shari mode as much as possible and hoped that the personality obscured any sense of the familiar.

The problem was, though, it was mostly *boring.* She'd be brought out a couple of times a week to "service" VIPs, and the rest of the time she was just, well, left. Her lack of any command of the language precluded her making any close friends or confidants or even having someone reasonably friendly and secure to talk to. Her restriction to the immediate grounds made it impossible to try to contact Boday or even gain any knowledge of what was going on in this crazy world. Nor was she expected to do anything but be handy if the General needed her for a guest.

She *did* get to wear some exotic and sexy clothing for a change, play with makeup and jewelry and all that, but there was only so much of it and nobody seemed to think she required any more.

If she could just get down to that underground town once in a while she felt she'd be okay. Go through those exotic bazaars and shops and all that. She wouldn't need money; shopping was far more fun than buying anyway. The answer, though, was always the same. She was far too valuable to risk in that city of scoundrels and ruffians, and the Master wanted no harm to come to his property. The tough and the ugly went to town, but never wearing the Master's precious gems. She was a one-of-a-kind possession, and, to Hodamoc, that's all she was.

Worst of all, her vision had continued to deteriorate. She spent as much time as possible up on the surface in the open air of day because she could see there. Darkness was total for her now, and even within the house she needed a bright light source to see anything more than dimly, and then only straight ahead. Her peripheral vision was shot to hell as well. The household knew of this, but didn't much care. You didn't have to see to do what she was there to do.

She was growing more and more tempted to see if she could summon Shari and leave her permanently in place and in charge. Shari, perhaps, could handle it, empty-head that she was. Charley, though, was hanging on through force of will but it was becoming harder and harder to hope for anything.

Unable to effectively communicate with her peers, she was essentially mute, unable to really make friends or join the slave subculture. Her future was looking pretty damned bleak. She was beginning to believe that she would spend the rest of her life in this godforsaken place, lonely, mute, blind, and enslaved.

4

Some Failures to Communicate

Enu was a purplish fruit that tasted like a melon but grew on trees about ten or fifteen feet tall. The picking was tricky, since you could not pick them until they were almost ripe but if you guessed wrong and the fruit grew too large to remain on the tree and fell to the ground it was useless. It was also somewhat messy, since the trees needed a near-constant trickle of water gotten to them by a small but expertly planned network of irrigation ditches and canals and it was muddy right along the trees themselves.

The only reminder that this was not a totally normal farm or grove was the presence of armed uniformed soldiers riding back and forth. They would seem menacing but they barely paid any attention to the pickers; their concern was keeping the pickers from being rudely interrupted by denizens of the Wastes who might want anything from stealing fruit to stealing *them*.

The picking technique was to take a small wooden ladder and a basket, plant the ladder firmly, then go up it with the basket right into the tree itself and then pick the fruit. Due to both the heat and the mud, most pickers opted for what was basically a panty for the females and a jock strap for the males, a thick bandannalike headband to catch perspiration, and a pair of work gloves to protect the hands in the actual picking. Basically you walked along an irrigation ditch in the mud until you came to the first tree in a row not being picked, you planted your ladder, went up with your basket, then leaned and squirmed and picked what fruit was there, often going down to empty your basket into a collection basket—there were many spread evenly out along the work area—and then back up again, perhaps on the other side, until you picked it clean. Then you went to the next tree not being picked and did the same.

Each picker was assigned a quota of trees that he had to pick before the day was ended based upon his physical abilities or handicaps and done, from the looks of it, fairly enough. Few really *needed* a quota; the pickers all seemed quite happy doing their work and proud of it as well; they competed against each other to see who would exceed their quota and by how much.

It wasn't hard but it did wear you, and that was where the *makuda* came in. *Makuda* was some sort of potion guaranteed to do no physical harm—there were even some pregnant women out there—that was, nonetheless, a pretty good stimulant that also quenched thirst and helped retain body moisture. You could get it anytime you needed at the collection bins, and Sam definitely felt the need after less than an hour out there on that first afternoon. Living so long with Boday, she had no real qualms about such potions, not when they were obviously mixed to such a common and positive purpose.

And the stuff really worked. Not only did she feel the aches and pains vanish, but she felt very energized, willing to work, and much more comfortable. It also tended to lull the mind a bit, so grumps and complaints about working and worries of all sorts seemed to fade and you found yourself concentrating on and even enjoying the routine. She felt herself through the afternoon almost merging with the other pickers into a collective consciousness in which nothing else really mattered and there was an instant comradeship, even though the pickers were the usual settlement assortment of men, women, and, well, *whatevers.*

When she rode back in on the carts with them, she had done a reasonable afternoon's work and felt fairly satisfied as she saw the nargas pulling carts of the fruit along with them and thought, *Some of those are mine, picked by me.*

As she made her way from the worker's housing area back to the residence, however, the drug began to wear off and she began to feel her tiredness and all the aches and pains of the day. All she wanted now was a soak, some food, and sleep. Avala, however, had something different in mind.

"My Lord the Duke wants you to have dinner with him this evening," she told the tired refugee. "He always wants to meet anyone new who comes here."

She groaned. "Oh, I don't know if I *can!* I'm feeling every damned *enu* right now. I'm so tired I might fall asleep in my salad."

Avala gave a wry smile. "It *can* be a bit hard until you get used to it and your muscles get built up," she admitted, "but My Lord Duke knows this. That is why tonight, when you have worked only part of a day, and not later on. There is a potion similar to *makuda* that will give you energy and ease your aches but leave you with a clear head, and if he keeps you late you will not have to work tomorrow. Come, I will help you get clean and dressed, and then you will see."

The potion was slower to act but very effective. By the time she'd finished her bath and felt reasonably clean and presentable, she also felt very good, almost as though she'd just gotten up. She hoped that this stuff didn't wear off very quickly, either.

The outfit wasn't much—just the top from the cinnamon stretch suit and a patterned long but slit skirt that somewhat matched the boots, but it felt, well, *civilized* after spending the day mostly naked in mud that tended to bake on.

The governor's quarters were upstairs, where the administrative offices were. The whole wing was rustic-looking but very nicely appointed, and you could tell immediately that you were in an upper-class area by just looking at the quality of everything and the perfection at which it was maintained. Never before had Sam been at this social and economic level on Akahlar, and it was impressive.

Avala left her at the top of the stairs, and Sam was surprised to be met by Medac, who was actually wearing a pair of trousers and boots, which looked incongruous on a man with wings and no arms.

"Hello, there," the winged man greeted her. "I am happy to see you looking so well."

"It's drugs," she responded. "I'm dead tired, really, but I could hardly refuse."

He chuckled. "I understand they had you in the *enu* groves. Yes, I have watched them from above. I wanted to, well, caution you a bit, before we go in. I have seen how tolerant you are of changelings and I think it is most admirable, but I wish to prepare you for my mother."

Sam's eyebrows rose. "Your mother?"

He nodded. "We were returning in a caravan from one of those silly ceremonial visits, to foster goodwill and all that, that members of the royal families have to suffer through from time to time. It was in Gryatil, one of our own lands, not a day from home and safety, when a changewind hit. It was sudden, unexpected, and brutal. We had Mandan cloaks, of course, but you are supposed to have some warning and seek the lowest point, then huddle beneath them until the Navigator signals all clear. That is fine advice if you have warning and can see it coming, but we were very near the point where the wind broke through into Akahlar from wherever such winds originate. We barely had time to get on the ground and pull the cloaks over us. It was in heavy grass on uneven land, and no one had ever warned us about the true force of such a storm. The Mandan cloaks are very heavy, but they must be just so, Mine was lumpy and had an opening. The great winds came straight at us, and my cloak actually lifted up as I was facedown and the wind went through, *under*, before falling back down on top of me again. I tried to reach up without looking up and bring it down but by that time I had no arms. I was fourteen, and the mere sudden realization that the wind had gotten me caused me to scream in panic and terror."

She nodded. Although she'd only seen one changewind, and that in a vision, she could imagine the scene.

"My mother was in front of me, facing me, and she heard my terror and could not stop herself from looking out to see what terrible thing had happened. Her face, and neck, were totally exposed. Each wind is different but it tends to have its own, unique, consistency. She will be present, not only because it is duty but also because I cannot feed myself in any sort of polite surroundings. She cannot speak, but her mind is still the same. I would not like her hurt."

"Don't worry. I worked with people far more bizarre today than any I had ever dreamed about and had no trouble. The men who attacked us and committed those terrible acts on us—they were Akhbreed. Their leader was a changeling, but they were what we would call 'normal' on the outside. Inside, they were hideous, evil monsters. I do not judge people on how they look. I will not embarrass you or your mother." *I hope,* she added to herself.

He smiled. "I thank you for that. Now, come with me if you will."

They walked down a long corridor filled with portraits and antiques.

"I am curious," she said to him. "Just curious. Only part of you was exposed, and yet you were changed in more ways than just wings. Hollow bones, and apparently whatever was needed to allow you to fly and have enough energy and strength to do it."

He nodded. "That is the nature of the winds. Consistency, of sorts, is always preserved. No one is ever left who is not put together as a functioning being, no matter how much or little the exposure or where it is, although only the exposed areas are radically changed. Although my mother has no wings, internally we are consistent beings. Were it not unthinkably incestuous, we could actually mate and produce similarly structured creatures that would either be her way or mine. Impossible for us, of course, but there are actually some very small races, the products of the winds, that breed true. Ah! Here we are!"

Two guards uniformed in full military dress stood at the large wooden doors and opened them for the pair as they reached the entrance. Inside, there was a large rectangular paneled room with a long table at its center capable of seating six on a side and one at each end. There were candelabras lit on the table, and the chairs were lined with satin. It was very regal, and Sam felt decidedly underdressed, although somewhat relieved that only a few places were set.

The Duke clearly sat at the head of the table; Medac showed Sam to one chair to the Duke's left and apologized that he could not pull it out for her. She understood.

Almost immediately the Duke entered from the rear of the dining room, followed by his wife and one other man who might well have been an aide to the Duke. The Governor himself was a strikingly handsome man, the kind of man who seems to grow even more handsome and distinguished as the years go by. He had thick, curly gray hair and a bushy but perfectly groomed gray moustache, and a rugged, aristocratic face and bearing. He was the kind of man who could command attention anywhere, and in any crowd.

So would his wife, but not for the same reason. It was difficult to say what she had looked like but not a bad bet that she had been a perfect match for the Duke. Even at her age, which was probably not that much less than her husband, she had a strikingly good figure and a formal dress that fit perfectly. The fact that the head that now sat upon those slender shoulders was that of a huge, falconlike bird of prey emphasized the tragedy of the family.

Sam stood silently as they entered, and reminded herself that no matter what she must not stare at the Duchess. Idly she wondered how you greeted a Duke. Did you kiss his ring or bow or curtsy or what?

"Please, please! Be seated!" Duke Alon Pasedo said in a friendly, low baritone that matched the appearance perfectly. "We do not stand on ceremony here unless we have to. It is one of the few truly bright spots to living out here." He saw his wife to her seat and made certain that Medac was also seated. Sam realized that the chairs were all designed to allow the winged man some comfort so long as he kept his wings in. Then the Duke took his place and the other man took his next to Sam.

The stranger was fiftyish, balding, with thick glasses, and his face showed signs of weathering and wear.

"I am Alon Pasedo, and this is my wife, the Duchess Yova, and the gentleman to your left is Kano Layse, the Director of the Refuge we have established here. My son you already know. He is quite adept at spotting and guiding those lost and in need to our establishment. But, come! Let us eat, and then we will talk."

It was a hell of a meal, even if Sam didn't know what half of it was and had never tasted the variations of the half she *did* recognize before. If most of the staff were refugees, as they seemed to be called here, then one must have been a master chef. Food was served by a team of two men and two women who picked up dishes from windows into the kitchen hidden behind decorative screens and then brought them to the table. The servants had the usual evening dress of the house staff, but their skirts and sarongs seemed to be of very high quality, their flower garlands fresh and exotic, and they were both made up and immaculate.

The Duchess took no food herself, nor drink, either, but spent the time cutting and then hand-feeding her son. Medac seemed to have outgrown any embarrassment for the situation, since he was in fact helpless in such a dining room, and Sam suspected that what that falconlike head could eat, and how it ate it, would not be suitable for polite company.

The Duke controlled the talk, which was light and generally directed at her.

"You are not from an Akhbreed hub," he said casually, "although you speak the language quite well. Were you born a colonial in Tubikosa?"

"No, Your Grace," she responded, figuring out the proper form of address. "I am not native to Akahlar at all. I am one of those people who—dropped in, as it were, to my very great surprise."

"Ah! Fascinating! And yet you speak Akhbreed so well. It is a horror of a tongue, in spite of its versatility as a language. Deliberately evolved, I suspect, because even the smartest colonial can't master it on his own unless raised with it. Tell me, how did you learn it so well?"

"Sorcery, Your Grace," she responded. That was no lie, although it wasn't the complete truth.

"Ah, yes. I remember my staff saying something about an Akhbreed sorcerer's curse. That explains it. Usually the only ones from the Outplane who can learn our tongue are natural sorcerers themselves. But the better sorcerers can endow it, to their own purposes."

He very suddenly dropped that line to Sam's relief. She did not want to have to lie or admit that in fact she was allegedly some natural kind of sorcerer and that was how she knew the language and why she was such a prize.

There was more small talk, and then the Duke asked, "Is your home world like any of ours that you have seen?"

"Not really, although people are people, it seems, both good and bad and even indifferent. We had far more machines, for example. Flying machines and even personal machines that replaced the horse."

The Duke nodded. "I have heard of such worlds. That is one of the pities of Akahlar, you know. We could build flying machines, but with the kind of conditions we have and our instabilities we would never be able to get them or any other high-speed conveyance where we wanted it, or be certain that complex mechanical contraptions would obey the same minute physical and chemical laws in one place as they did in another. Even communication is a problem here. We could have a system that might work inside this building, for example, or perhaps through the whole complex, but it would always have static and interference. As for any distance—it is impossible. The shifts and constant changes in our borders cause impossible static. Still, there is much to be said for the old, tried-and-true ways. Slow and clumsy at times, perhaps, but also reassuring no matter where you are. And they keep our weapons development, our armies, on a level that does not assure total destruction."

"Where I came from they could destroy the world with a push of a button," she responded. "It always hung over us like a cloud."

"Exactly my point! Single-shot guns and cannon and swords and the like are more honorable, and far easier to control. The argument for super weapons is always that they will stop wars. But, tell me, did they stop wars and conflicts in your world?"

"No," she had to admit. "They stopped the really big wars but not all the small wars."

"Yes. And in Akahlar the big wars are impossible—the same conditions I spoke about prevent them, and the equality of the kingdoms maintains stability. We, too, have our little wars but without any threat of a global one. Who, after all, could conquer thousands and thousands of worlds? And what conqueror could be safe if he did not? No, the drawbacks here are the sorts of things that make a place like this necessary."

"Your Grace means the intolerance of the different."

"Yes, exactly. We already have to deal with thousands of races, many of them only remotely what we think of as human, but each is, after all, the natural denizen of his world. You would think that with so much variety there would be little trouble in at least tolerating the different, the unique, the ones and twos of a kind. But the sight, the existence, of one who was once Akhbreed terrifies them. It is not like one who is born different—that is natural. But the thought that one of their own could become so alien a creature, that touches a basic fear in our society. The system discriminates against anyone who does not meet the basic standards. Not everyone is that way—I was never that way—but a few rational thinkers have no way to change something which is deep in the fears of a people and their culture and society. One does not need a changewind or a curse, either. Those two girls you have with you are a fine example."

Sam nodded. "I don't know how to handle that, really, Your Grace. In my world they would get guardians, the state would provide homes, and they would inherit. Here—they are outcasts, even by their own."

"Exactly. Minors cannot inherit here, and unmarried females have fewer property rights. Your system is far more humane, or so it sounds to me, but the rigidity of this system is its true curse. They do not have to change, therefore they do not. I would not wish the suffering of my family on anyone, but I often believe there was some purpose to it. I had money, position. I could shelter them until I could arrange to move here and gain this appointment. I could afford to seek out like-minded, progressive thinkers who were frustrated by the system and bring them here. If criminals and traitors could find refuge here, then I saw no reason why good, decent unfortunates could not as well. Here there is no reason for ones like your girls to be sold to brothels or turned into chattel, or for people crippled or maimed to wind up in the gutters and back alleys. Here those afflicted with curses and those unfortunates who were caught in changewinds but not mentally deranged could find some peace and purpose."

She nodded. "It *is* nice here, and the people are very friendly and seem to not mind the differences. The feeling of security here is very reassuring, considering what I have been through."

"A refuge," he responded, sounding pleased. "We provide not only security but a decent life."

They were finally through the sumptuous meal, and the Duchess stood up and cocked her bird's head at the Duke, who said, "You may leave if you wish, my dear, or remain. Please, by all means, do what you wish."

The bird's head nodded, and the Duchess walked out that back entrance to the dining room.

"So, they tell me that you are off to get this sorcerer's curse lifted," the Duke remarked casually. "Tell me honestly—is your heart in that? Do you really want to go to a foreign Akhbreed sorcerer and beg for favor? Truthfully, now."

She sighed, and decided that honesty was still the best policy. "No," she responded. "It is just something that is forced on me. From what everyone says about these sorcerers, even though they maintain the system they are as dangerous as the changewind."

"More," the Duke replied seriously. "Far more. The changewind is terrifying mostly because it is random. It is a thief that comes in the night and steals all that you take for granted, but it is an honest, capricious, random thief with no malice and no thought, no motivation. It just is, a force of nature. One with the power of an Akhbreed sorcerer cannot help but go mad from the sheer power at his or her command. But their madness has thought, direction, and also shows no mercy. Even the best of them is dangerous, unstable, psychopathic. We are their playthings, not human beings to them, if they decide to play. Only the changewind keeps them humble. It is its place in the scheme of things, I believe. For even the greatest cannot control, deflect, or even defend himself against a changewind or its effects. There is some suspicion that the sorcerers themselves foster and promote this insane policy of destroying any people who become victims of the changewind, because they have no power over those victims. Our own sorcerers, should they be so inclined, could turn me into a frog or a maniac or a monster with a single spell. Yet they could do nothing to my wife or my son. If any Akhbreed sorcerer is ever destroyed, it is by the product of a changewind, for their power ends there and only another changewind can affect them."

That was something to think about. No *wonder* they killed them when they could! The Akhbreed ruled by the power of their sorcerers and maintained their system and their position by virtue of that power. The changelings, then, would be the only things other than the winds themselves that the Akhbreed leaders would fear.

They wrapped it up with some more small talk, mostly about her and the refuge, and she had the sense to know that it was over. The Duke stood up, and so did the Director, and so she and Medac did as well, and the Governor said good night and the two departed out the back way. It was only after they had gone that Sam realized that this Director hadn't said more than a few words the whole evening. Perhaps it was just that when the Duke wanted to talk you didn't dare not let him talk.

Medac escorted her back to the head of the stairs. "You did quite well," he told her. "I want to thank you for it."

"I did nothing at all. Your father is a charming man."

"Yes," the winged man replied with an odd tone of voice. "I often wonder if I was not fortunate to become a changeling. I cannot imagine myself taking his place or having the ability to make so many hard decisions." He sighed. "Well, good night and good luck on the work the next few days. I hope your future brings happiness and peace of mind."

She was charmed by that. "Thank *you.* I don't know where I'd be or even if I'd be alive without you and your father. But I must go now. That potion is wearing off and I want to make it to my bed before I collapse."

Medac watched her go, then sighed, turned, and walked back by a different route to the living quarters. As he expected, his father and the Director were in the study, talking animatedly over cigars and coffee. They both looked up when the winged man entered.

"Ah, Medac! Come, relax and join us," the Duke invited. "I want your input on this. First, has there been any sign of this Boday or her friend?"

"Not really. The rebel band that was ambushed and massacred just east of here shows that a strong band of marauders was in the area about the same time. The two women did not turn in here, which suggests that they were tracking the rebels, either out of fear that their companions had been taken or out of some sense of bravado that perhaps they could get back their horses and belongings. Two naked, defenseless women definitely did not do that to the rebels, and there were signs of a considerable number in the attacking band. There were no women's bodies found, and they did not double back, and they did not meet our own patrol coming from downriver. The inescapable conclusion is that the same band that hit the rebels captured them. They are probably not dead, but are almost certainly beyond caring by now."

The Duke nodded. "I feared as much. Any luck on identifying the band? I do not like anyone operating independently this close to our lands here, although they appear to have only hit the rebels and not anything or anyone of ours. That implies at least partly a political act."

"Yes, but that's probably why I can pick up nothing of importance. Oh, I have a few details. Tracking down the horses and the booty was not difficult, but it was already through many hands and they were very closedmouthed about it. They had hoped, I think, to get away without paying our 'tax,' as it were."

"I also don't like any of Klittichorn's hordes in *my* canyon without *my* knowledge or permission," the Duke growled. "They had a small army in the region. Still do, I suspect. Brazen bastards."

"They are beginning to move off and away now," Medac told him. "You know, I wonder if there isn't a connection there. They put out the word that they would pay a tremendous sum to anyone who brought them a slender young woman with a superficial resemblance to the Storm Princess. Do you suppose that perhaps this Susama's young friend might have been that one? If so, we *know* what's happened to them."

The Director stirred for the first time. "Interesting. Your Grace, that might explain a lot. A double. A living duplicate of the Storm Princess, perhaps an *exact* duplicate, born and raised on another world. Somebody like Boolean, who has been crying for years about Klittichorn's threat, might go after such a one in order to make a switch or train her as a combatant. Those powers are unique. And the great storm that did in the train but also did in the raiders—it might be!"

The Duke scratched his chin. "And this Susama?"

"Obviously a friend, probably sucked along when Klittichorn or Boolean or whoever opened a hole and dropped the double down. That would explain the interest around here, all the events, and even why an Akhbreed sorcerer would be interested in them and give them language and a curse."

"But it was Susama who was cursed, not the other," Medac pointed out.

"Yes, sir, but who knows what powers, what resistance she might have? But if she were loyal to her friend, then curse the friend."

The Duke sat back and sighed. "Logical. And the fact that Klittichorn's men are now withdrawing from the area can have but one meaning. And that means this Susama is most certainly alone and stuck here. She'd have no chance of even getting that curse removed now. She has no future, gentlemen. She's without funds, has no family or tribe or anyone to fall back on, is bright but illiterate and has no meaningful skills."

"She also has no self-esteem," the Director pointed out. "You could see that by how she presents and carries herself. She'll wind up desolate, alone—I'd say there is a better than ninety percent chance that she would do away with herself."

"I don't believe there is any reason or mercy in waiting," the Duke said. "Even if her friend should somehow miraculously come into our hands we would have different uses for her than merely a reunion with a friend. You have our permission to incorporate them into the refugee program immediately."

"I will set it up for tomorrow morning, Your Grace," the Director replied.

The Duke looked over at his son, who seemed to have a disapproving look on his face. "You still have bad feelings about this. Consider, my son—if we left it up to her she would refuse and cling to a fantasy, a dream. She is someone truly without hope or future and she is insisting on jumping into an abyss. Would you gain her permission before you saved her from jumping?"

Medac sighed. "I see your point, Father. It's just, well, she was different and likeable. Totally without any reaction to me or Mother or any of the others except curiosity."

"And that will not change. That is the nature of this place."

When she first awoke she had, quite literally, no memories at all, nor any direct means of thought, although she was curious and aware, as a small baby might be aware. Then they began talking to her, not as before but in the peasant vulgar dialect of Mashtopol Akhbreed speech. As she heard each word and phrase and thought she understood it, as if it were being written indelibly inside her mind, within a few hours she could think quite clearly in the Akhbreed tongue.

She lapped up everything they told her like a sponge, accepting it unquestioningly at face value. They had found her wandering lost and alone out in the dangerous, hot, endless desert and had taken her in. She was now a part of a great community under the leadership of Her Lord the Duke, who was kind and wise and provided all things for everyone that they would ever need or desire. All the people worked for the common good, and each had a vital role in keeping everything going. Each had a function which, when added to everyone else's functions, created a common, just society in which all were absolutely equal.

All products of the community were given to the Duke, the wisest and most just, who then redistributed them so that all received according to their needs. Beyond the community was only desolation, danger, and death. The Duke protected the community from it, and kept it safe. The community was a loving, sharing family of which the Duke was the wise, kind, and all-powerful father. All thoughts were towards the community's good; no one was above the good of the whole, and no individual should ever put him or herself above or below the group. All were brothers, all were sisters, and all were essential parts of an integrated whole.

She wanted to belong; she wanted to find her place, her function, and to contribute. She felt safe and secure within it, and wanted no part of anywhere else.

She was startled to find that she was a girl, although she would have been equally startled to discover she was anything but. It was a strange face and figure that stared back at her in the mirror, but she accepted it. Everyone told her how cute she was, how her big breasts were so desirable, how lucky she was to be so cute and look the way she did, and she accepted that as well.

They told her that her name was Misa, and although it sounded strange she answered to it afterwards because it was the only name she had. Then they told her that her function would be to work in the fields, planting and picking and tending the community's important food, and she thought that was wonderful.

Then they brought her to a long three-tier adobe complex and she climbed the ladders to the top level and then went into one of the "rooms" in the center. It was a one-room affair, with two sets of bunk beds on opposing walls, a worn but serviceable rug with pretty designs on the floor, oil lamps, and at the rear a long dresser that took up the entire back wall and contained areas for each of the occupants' clothing and personal effects plus some crude wooden stools and mirrors.

Water was rationed but there was a communal bathhouse two blocks of apartments down. There were also communal toilets there, but mostly you used a bedpan-type gadget and roommates took turns emptying it and sanitizing it each day. Human solid waste was not to be discarded; it was placed in community bins and then blended with other things and spread in the fields, so that what was needed by the land was given back to it.

Her roommates were girls near her own age, all products of the system and true believers in it, all lifelong field workers. They embraced and took to her as if she and they had known each other all their lives, and it was from them she learned the rest of what was necessary to be learned.

She made a concentrated effort to model herself after them in all things; to talk like them, act like them, *think* like them, until in a very few days it was impossible to tell the new from the old. They talked and giggled and played silly games and compared the various men around and everything was open and shared. Mostly, of course, they worked—long, hard days, but nobody minded or complained because everybody had to work to keep the community whole. Without them, the community would not be fed and the groves would die. They were vital and that made them proud.

What little they had they shared freely. There was no lying, no cheating, no stealing, no thoughts of deception or shirking work or duty. There were also no questions. None. The entire world, its rules, and your place in it were clearly defined. It was the way it was, that's all. You couldn't change anything and you wouldn't want to, because it was good the way it was.

She liked field work because it wasn't the same all the time. After a time of fruit picking, you might do a tour elsewhere in the irrigation system ass-deep in mud making sure just the right water went where it was supposed to, and next you might be planting behind a narga-pulled plow, knowing that what you planted you would see grow and thrive and bear useful things for the community. Honest mistakes, even carelessness, were never punished; instead you felt terrible about it and everyone worked to reassure you and to teach you so that you did not make the same mistake twice.

And the work grew easier with time; she needed less to drink, felt hardier and more confident, and finished without aches and pains and tiredness much of the time as her muscles grew and her body conditioned itself. She grew no thinner, but her arms and legs began developing a hell of a set of muscles. It was not something she was conscious of, but it was noticeable in her neck and shoulders and when she flexed her arms.

Far from feeling self-conscious about her weight, she relished it as a reflection of power, the way a wrestler took pride in bulk, and no other girl had breasts so enormous; and because she could lose no weight the effect of muscle development in her neck and shoulders had the effect of pulling the breasts up and thrusting them out firmly so that there was little sag. She called them her "melons"—and she liked to flaunt them, never so much as during Endday, the one day of the week where they worked only half a day and threw a grand communal party and celebration that lasted well into the night. Then she would don her one fine patterned sarong and the traditional flower necklace and dance with the best of them. They took to calling her *Noma Ju,* which literally meant Big Tits, and she didn't mind a bit, taking it in the playful spirit that it was used.

She did, however, allow her roommates to do something of a makeover on her. There was a magic potion you could get from a friend or a relative of a friend who worked in the residence that would make your hair grow at a miraculous pace and they procured enough of the weakened formula to allow her to grow in a matter of weeks hair just below shoulder length, which set off her face and made her look much better. All the other girls had their ears pierced, so she did, too, even though it *hurt*, getting small rings inserted on which you could clip longer ones for special occasions like Endday Festival; and she started taking some care in her appearance outside of work and even in the way she walked and talked.

She found herself most comfortable around the women but the men seemed attracted to her and she *did* tease them a lot. Virtually all the Akhbreed peasant women were lean and muscular; her more padded form and largest attributes hanging out there seemed to turn some folks on. She found that she liked to be kissed and hugged and fondled but she didn't ever let it get too far. Although sex was rather casual among the peasant communes, a pregnancy meant an obligatory marriage and for some reason she just could not bring herself to take the risk.

And there were the dreams. Strange dreams, sometimes, of another person, another place, in some magical royal castle. A strange woman with a deep voice that was cold, eerie, aristocratic, and a fearsome nightmare figure in crimson robes and horns on his head. She felt that, somehow, these dreams were of the evil around the community, the evil from which they said she'd escaped, and so she did not talk about these dreams with anyone. Perhaps they were somehow shadows from her past, but she did not want to know any more. At least they were not common; she had experienced only four of them so far, and she could live with that.

Still, she was happy, *very* happy, and content, and she had no questions.

Up in the residence, however, where the peasant folk virtually never went and held in some awe, there were questions.

"This is a high desert," Duke Pasedo grumbled. "It has almost always been so and it stretches out for most of the continent. It rains for perhaps an hour every two or three years, and often less than that, and the land and the system, *our* system, is based upon it. And yet, in two months, just *two months,* gentlemen, it has rained heavily four times! Four times! Some of the crops are in danger, the irrigation system is a shambles in many places, and along the canyons there are now many landslides. I want to know how this can happen. What is causing it?"

The Director sighed and shrugged his shoulders. "Your Grace, these things happen. Some shift, somewhere, causes freak occurrences of all sorts of weather. You remember several years ago we had that freakish cold and actually a bit of snow over the night."

The Duke slammed his fist on the table. "That is one incident.

This is more of a long pattern. My son has watched these storms, since I feared they might be Sudogs or some other sorcery, but they appear to be just storms—but localized. Very localized, and with no apparent source of moisture. It rains only on *us!* It collects from nowhere, rains, then dissipates. That is not natural, gentlemen. Not natural at all. When you begin to get such magical storms, can the changewind be far behind, attracted to this very spot? Can you imagine what a changewind would do to this place, all our dreams? Yes, I see you are about to assure me that we are adequately protected, but the land is not! The river and canyons are not! The balance is delicate here."

"We are doing what we can to find the cause," the Director assured him. "Possibly a changewind deflection from some point. We will need to find it to see how or even if we can deal with it, though."

"I want the cause found. I want it stopped!" the Duke ordered.

Duke Pasedo was not the only one becoming aware of the phenomenon. When strong powers are exercised anywhere, those most sensitive to those powers grow aware of them, and with each passing incident the location and then the source grows more and more apparent.

Klittichorn, who liked to be known as the Horned Demon of the Snows although he was no demon and his horns were mere ornaments, was troubled. Several times now his concentration had been broken by a sense of activity somewhere far off. He liked it least because it was coming from a region where it should not be. The only one who had crossed through Mashtopol had been that courtesan girl, and he had forces looking for her and he knew at least where she was not.

Was it someone new, someone he'd missed in spite of his best efforts? Or had that son of a bitch Boolean drawn him off with a decoy?

No, that didn't make sense, either. If the courtesan was a decoy, then the real one would be well away from Mashtopol by now and in another direction. Hell, it had been over two months since the showdown with his trusted agent Asterial, Blue Witch of the Kudaan Wastes, and all it had done was have her trapped in a nether-hell with some nutty demon Boolean had cornered and coerced into service. That had been a major blow, since she was the only really trustworthy one with any real power he'd had there. Damn! With thousands of worlds it was pretty damned difficult to cover *everywhere* with quality people!

That silly Duke with the messiah complex might have nabbed the real one, but he sure as hell wouldn't hold on to her. He'd play Boolean off against him for the best advantage and fast. But there had been a split-off somewhere. The courtesan and that lunatic artist were missing their friend, the other one who'd fallen through. What if that one had lost her mind and perhaps had fallen into the hands of some of the crooked characters out there? Hell, she could be some kind of mindless slave or bound by all sorts of nasty spells somewhere in the Wastes with neither she nor whoever had her even aware of her nature.

Could she be the one? Could he have been a sucker, maybe still a sucker? That other one had been reported a tub of lard wed to a lesbian loony, hardly the sort, and yet . . . If the duplicate were ever physically transformed her effectiveness would cease, yet would putting on all that weight qualify?

He slapped his forehead. *Shit! I've been a double-dyed idiot! I could do battle with a great sorcerer or a greater soldier, but I keep getting taken in by that bastard of a con man! Outsmarting him was like trying to find the escape clause in a Satanic contract!*

But if the other was a decoy, then the magic worked by the first might be out of dreams or emotional periods, not conscious acts. If she was still in the Kudaan, that meant that Boolean didn't have her, either. He turned and shouted, "Adjutant!"

A man entered and bowed. "Sir?"

"I have reason to believe that Boolean's suckered us again and that the girl we've been chasing is a decoy. The one we want is the fat one, and I think she's under somebody's control and still in the Kadaan. Sooner or later somebody is going to notice the same things I have felt and find the source. I want her found first!"

The Adjutant looked thoughtful. "It won't be easy. Some of our patrols got massacred in there the last time, and if we take an army in they'll just go to ground and all we'll have is another Chief Sorcerer and perhaps a king as an enemy. To have any chance in that hole will require magic."

Klittichorn nodded. This fellow was a damned good man and he'd learned to rely heavily on his mind before going off half-cocked. "Yes, yes, I agree. And Sudogs aren't going to do it. We can't maintain them long enough there. We shall need Stormriders."

"But they themselves will cause some of the same disruptions as she would," the Adjutant pointed out. "And how are we to find her? A fat girl the same height as Her Highness isn't much to go on."

Klittichorn was thinking hard. "Their energy will be of a different sort. Still, you are right. Without a description all the spies on the ground and Stormriders in the air would be useless. And who knows what she looks like by now, within the limits? We'll just have to put people in there and wait for the next manifestation of storm-bringer power. With the riders present it should be quite easy to localize it. That could possibly take weeks, but if Boolean hasn't found her by now I think at least we start even. Better than even, since he has nothing like my forces at his command."

"As you will, sir. Should I call off the ones hunting the artist and the courtesan?"

"No. For one thing, we can't be sure of the decoy. If they are anywhere close to making a run for it and need a diversion, it's just like Boolean to arrange something like this to draw us off. Besides, if we miss this time the artist will give us another chance. They foolishly married one another back in Tubikosa and that invoked a spell. They are linked until the death of one of them, whether they know it or not, and it has certain other attributes that might prove useful just in case."

"As you wish, sir."

"And, Adjutant . . ."

"Sir?"

"We cannot afford to allow this to drag on. One or the other and quickly. We are reaching the point where limited and theoretical tests are of no further benefit. The conditions under which a full-scale operation will work are quite precise mathematically and do not occur every day or week or even month. We must show our strength to retain our allies and gain new converts, if not through the demonstration that we could actually win then through fear of our disfavor. I should not like any wild cards out there, as it were, complicating matters, no matter how remote the possibility."

The Adjutant bowed. "We will do all that is possible, sir; of that I assure you."

The sorcerer chuckled. "This is Akahlar, where *nothing* is impossible!"

Heat shimmered off the desert floor and made the air dance in strange new patterns, distorting distance and rippling the few shadows. The small caravan made its way slowly and deliberately across the floor, following no road but only the experience of its Navigator, who sat then on a horse walking slowly beside the lead wagon.

He was a big man; not merely tall, although he was certainly that, but broad and tough, a mountain man's physique. He had a broad-brimmed white hat, creased in the middle, and wore light, almost cream-colored buckskins that showed his perspiration and the grit of the trail but also helped reflect the heat.

His face was broad and weathered, his hair and full beard long and strawberry blond, making him a striking figure in any setting. His odd, steel gray eyes, protected somewhat from the glare by swatches of black dabbed on beneath them, scanned the horizon, almost as if they sensed something not quite right. He reached down and took out his binoculars and looked again, then put up his hand.

"Hold up!" he called. "Break but stand ready! We have a rider coming and I'd rather meet anybody out here on the flats where they got no place to hide."

Distances were deceiving in the desert, but this rider was clearly very close. The Navigator frowned, wondering why he or one of his crew hadn't seen the rider long before now. It was almost as if both horse and rider had materialized out of the desert shimmer. He didn't like that. It meant either a sorcerous enemy or an emissary from an old friend who was about as welcome news as the sorcerous enemy.

The rider approached to about a thousand feet of the caravan but then halted, standing there shimmering in the heat as if some bizarre apparition, waiting. The Navigator again looked through the binoculars, then sighed, and shouted, "It's all right. I know who it is, although I don't think I want to know what it's about. Full break and at ease. I'll be back in a few minutes." With that he spurred his horse onward to meet the newcomer.

The closer he got to the rider, the more ephemeral the vision. It was a man, or something like a man, astride a great black horse, but it was curiously flat, almost two-dimensional, and there were streaks or breaks in the vision that momentarily showed the desert beyond. Horse and rider almost merged into a black, streaking thing, but if you looked sharp you could see details, including the fact that the horse was standing not on, but slightly above, the desert floor.

The Navigator came very close to the apparition and stopped.

"Hello, Crim," said the dark rider, in a voice that was both ordinary and yet unnatural, with a slight echolike reverberation in it.

"I figured it was you," the Navigator responded. "You always liked to do things the dramatic way."

The dark rider laughed. "It is the only fun I get sometimes. I have an urgent problem that only you are in a position to help me solve."

"So what else is new?"

Again the laugh. "You are always one of the best I can turn to, Crim, in spite of your lack of any particular fear and respect for such as me. You have heard the rumors concerning the Storm Princess?"

Crim nodded. "Lots of 'em, and lots of activity as well. I can't say I approve much of the friends she has and the company she keeps."

"Nor do I, although from her point of view they are the only ones who would keep company with her so long as she persists in her prideful ambition. Klittichorn plays on it, and the military minds attracted to them know how to use all that power. I have spent years trying to convince the others to listen to me, but to no avail. My colleagues in the other capitals believe that I am attempting some sort of power play myself, or are too mad to care. The kings will unite against a common foe only when they personally feel threatened, and their minds are being expertly poisoned against me. I admit that I underestimated them, or, perhaps, overestimated myself. He is a great and cautious organizer and I am an opportunist. We were always that way. Now, perhaps, I finally pay for our differences, but it is not just me."

"You really think true empire is possible here?"

"Perhaps. Perhaps not. But it will not happen in spite of all their dreams, for Klittichorn is not interested in empire. He has an even grander design than theirs, and it could destroy all humanity everywhere. At the very best, it will eliminate civilization and most of the population of all the universes, not just those of Akahlar, in a form of devastation that would repel even him if he could see it. But he is blind to consequences, which is a common failing of his type. He is growing, Crim, but I can still stop him. Without the uniqueness of the Storm Princess both plans are doomed to failure. I found others in the Outplane. So did he, of course, but he killed them. I brought mine here, but they were ill-prepared for Akahlar or too easily recognized by Klittichorn's agents. They have me effectively boxed in, and I am running out of options. I believe I know where my most promising prospect is, but I dare not go to her myself or show any direct interest in her. This would be sensed."

Crim was intrigued. "Another Storm Princess? Huh! Think of that. And not far, I take it?"

"On your route. You recall the disaster that befell Jahoort's train?"

"Yeah. About three months back. He was a good man."

"Jahoort carried one of mine among his train, and another who precisely resembles the Princess. My doing—opportunistic again. It's worked fairly well, although I doubt if the young lady without the powers is exactly enamored of me or her role. I had arranged to separate them farther on, drawing off Klittichorn's people, but they were split in the disaster, or its aftermath. My people made the most thorough search of the whole region that has ever been made and could not find her. I believed she'd suffered some sort of injury to the head or fallen into one of the wild powers of this place. I would have known if she were dead. She has no real control of her powers and I have sensed her. It has already rained four times in the past eleven weeks on our august Royal Governor."

"The Duke? But why would he have her? I heard nothing about any survivors coming in and I've been through there twice since Jahoort's wipeout. If he didn't know who she was he'd have put her with me or one of the others who came through, and if he did he'd be trying to bargain her to either you or Klittichorn while keeping her buried. But he wouldn't hold on to her for this long. She's too hot to hold, even in this place."

"There is a third possibility that never occurred to me until now, lulled as I was by the same logic you just used. What if she was injured, perhaps in the head, and was found by the Duke's people? Or, possibly, what if she just kept her mouth shut and played poor little lone survivor? The Duke is a collector of injured animals and stray cats, as it were."

Crim whistled. "He'd give her one of their patented amnesia potions and she'd join the crowd. If she wasn't on staff or anything I might never have seen or heard of her. Those peasants won't hardly speak to an outsider. That means she'll have a new identity, maybe a new personality, and she won't remember anything of what she was. And they're almost never alone, particularly the women."

"The process is alchemical?"

"Yeah, I think so. They might use spells if they need to—they got a couple of pretty good magicians on the staff—but I'd guess it was alchemical. Their own concoction, though. And it's *permanent.* I never heard of a relapse."

"There is no such thing as a permanent potion if it leaves its taker alive and physically intact. I can deal with it, even from here, but first we will need her away from that commune."

"You don't know what you're asking! First I told you how it's nearly impossible to get one alone. One of 'em coughs and everybody in the group wipes their nose. And what if you could, and get out of the canyon district unnoticed—also no mean trick, by the way. You know he's got a small army there. You'd have a dull-eyed ignorant peasant girl fighting like hell and probably so mad and so scared that Klittichorn's men would only have to look for the permanent moving rainstorm and that would be me."

"You haven't heard the half of it. In order to make the decoy believable and the real one be overlooked, I took advantage of a situation she brought on herself and rendered her permanently quite fat. She is very short, and she almost certainly weighs at least a hundred halgs."

"Oh, great! Forget it! Klittichorn will just have to destroy civilization, that's all. It's impossible."

"I am an Akhbreed sorcerer, and not without power and resources. This is Akahlar. Nothing is impossible here."

"Then get yourself another sucker. This one values what he has."

"But you have unique qualifications of all those available, not the least of which is that you speak English like a native and that is her own old native tongue. I don't make that the primary qualification—the last time I did the bastard turned traitor on me and wound up cursed—but you are the only one I trust because I know of your distaste for Klittichorn."

Crim sighed. "I'll need a lot of help, and a lot of briefing as well. And I still need convincing. What are you offering to spring her?"

"Nothing. Not a thing. She is of no value to me merely 'sprung,' as it were. I need her *here.* The first one, anyone, who delivers her here, alive and physically intact, will gain the ultimate. One wish, and no funny business about the terms and conditions. Anything within the power of an Akhbreed sorcerer, Crim. *Anything.* But it's all or nothing."

Crim stared hard at the shadowlike horseman. "What's that sort of hovering there? A tree limb? You son of a bitch, you're riding in some nice park or forest all shaded and comfortable and I'm sitting out here in the middle of a desert hot enough to fry meat! You want her that bad, you ask the impossible, you give all the help and charms and information and everything else you have and you deliver three wishes."

"Two and it's done. One for you and one for Kira. Any more haggling and I'll make it a more open offer to others."

"All right, you bastard. But for that price you could just walk up to the Duke and get her."

"Perhaps, but he could not get her safely to me. And, of course, I cannot grant the only wishes that Pasedo would be interested in anyway, since even I cannot alter what a changewind has done. Nor could I trust him if he knew her value."

Crim sighed. "Very well, but this won't be easy. It'll take some time to figure out how to do it at all. I'll give you a preliminary list of what I think I'll need and soon. I'm only a few days from there now and we'll camp tonight at the river gorge. Take it up with Kira tonight at the gorge in the cool of the evening. If she still agrees, we'll make a good stab at it."

"This is the big one, Crim. Plenty for any whom you take into the plan, although of course the nature of the girl and my motives will be between us alone. Let the others wonder. But anyone who betrays us will find no refuge anywhere."

"Yeah. And we won't mention *my* reward, will we? Even the most trusted people can be tempted to knock me off and claim it themselves. No skin off your nose but plenty off mine."

"Agreed, for now. So long as you have and control the girl. If you lose her I reserve the right to broaden the offer. Now you are broiling and I have dallied long enough, so go, get a drink and make your time. All this riding fatigues me."

"Okay, you bastard. I'll see about your dirty work. At the gorge, tonight."

"At the gorge tonight," the strange dark rider echoed, then it turned and rode off.

Crim watched it go, away from him, out into the desert, until it was one with the rippling air. Only then did he turn and make his way back to the caravan, but he only idly gave the "ready to move out" sign with his hand. He was already beginning to formulate plans—not details, but a broad outline. Some of this would require subtlety, and that was more of a Kira specialty. Still, you couldn't dream of a greater reward, but by damn they were going to earn every bit of it! And if Boolean had to be squeezed and sweated a little bit in the process, all the better.

5

Of Slavery, Decoys, and Shadowcats

Comug, the chief slave administrator of the House of Hodamoc, did not like to disturb his Master unless it was absolutely necessary. For one thing, the General often took out his irritation on the slaves closest to him, although he regretted it later. When you've spent hours in pain or are bleeding from terrible wounds, a sincere apology isn't all that appreciated.

Still, this had to be done. He knocked on the door of the Master's study, then waited patiently.

"Yes? What is it?" Hodamoc snapped irritatedly.

"Comug, Master. A thousand apologies, but there is someone here who demands an audience with you."

The door had not opened. "Did you say *demands?* Who is this who demands anything of me?"

"A magician, Master. Third Rank by his garb. He says his name is Dorion and that he is an urgent messenger from Yobi. It was because of this last that I dared to disturb you."

For a moment there was no reply. Suddenly the door flew open, and the General, looking more puzzled than angry, stood there. Comug bowed slightly and just waited, being one of the few slaves who did not prostrate him or herself in the Master's presence. Since he dealt with the Master on a day-to-day basis it would be rather impractical.

"Yobi . . ." Hodamoc mused. "What the hell does that crazy old bag want of me?" He sighed. "Still, she's Second Rank. It wouldn't do to piss her off without first hearing her out. Very well, Comug. Alert the House Magician and Security. If they clear him I will see him, but you can never be too careful about his type."

"Master, he is as he says. Several of the slaves have seen him before in the bazaars and he is not completely unknown. He is a permanent resident and exile and does often do errands for Yobi.

Had I not already checked on this I would never have allowed him even this far."

The General nodded, subdued. After all, that *was* why Comug was around in the first place and held the position he did.

"All right, then—show him up."

Dorion was not the sort of fellow to inspire awe and terror. Of medium height, perhaps five nine or ten to Hodamoc's six three, he was stocky, a bit chubby, with a pleasant, cherubic face that he'd attempted unsuccessfully to harden by growing a far too thin and wispy beard and moustache. His long reddish brown hair was thin and stringy and had vanished on top to a fair degree, giving him a monklike appearance enhanced by the rumpled wool earth-brown robe he wore. His deep blue eyes had that glazed look so common to magicians, and while he moved with confidence it seemed as if he were seeing by some method other than the usual sight. He had one of those brassy magician's baritones, though, which in incantations and spells might well sound commanding and authoritative but which in normal conversation often sounded either insincere or shrill.

Dorion bowed slightly. "Your Excellency, I bring you greetings from Yobi of the Sarcin Caves. I am Dorion, formerly of Masalur, a humble magician surviving here by doing services for others."

"An errand boy, you mean," the General responded, unimpressed. "Very well—you asked for my time and while I cannot spare it at the moment I am willing to grant an audience, so have done with it and dispense with the flowery and meaningless rhetoric if you have not lost your capacity for speaking plainly."

Dorion gave a weak smile and shrugged. "Very well, then. Someone important to Yobi was waylaid first by some rebel force that tried to penetrate the river valley and then in its aftermath was taken by raiders from Shorm. They were brought here, auctioned to the high bidder, and enslaved. You were the high bidder, Excellency, and you have her. Yobi wants her back."

The General's eyebrows rose. "Indeed? You mean that pretty little whore?"

"Courtesan, Excellency. She is of some importance to Yobi, although I do not know the reason for it. *Very* important. Yobi understands your expense and is willing to be quite generous to regain her."

"The expense is irrelevant. She is a possession, part of my collection here. She was dear enough to buy in the first place; now you have added value to her. I collect, sir. I do not sell my collection."

Dorion cleared his throat a bit nervously. "Excellency, you know full well that while Yobi is of necessity banished to this place she nonetheless is a sorceress of great power and, in fact, some influence among the Second Rank. While she rarely gets involved in the affairs of the Kudaan, she can offer things of great value, and she is of the same sort of mind as Your Excellency regarding those things which she considers hers by right."

The General had to stifle a grin. It was the nicest and pleasantest threat he had ever received.

"And you, Sir Magician, know full well that the girl is bonded to me by blood and relics. I am not saying that you couldn't take her, but if she violated my will and left these grounds even involuntarily and could not get back she would simply die and leave you with nothing. Your Yobi might break that spell but only with full rituals, and she would never survive to get to those rituals. An attempt on me is also fruitless. I am protected from much by powers as great as your Yobi's, and even if you succeeded in a more conventional way I have no heirs. Upon my death my slaves will destroy all this, and then themselves, although even they do not know this. We have nothing further to talk about."

Again the magician did his nervous throat-clearing. "Uh, pardon, Excellency, but as a humble middleman I can but see two sides of equal will and determination. You are a soldier and great leader. A thousand pardons for bringing this up, but you exist outside your natural element here, in the Wastes, in relative comfort of exile I admit, but not as you would wish or should be. With Yobi it is different. She is no longer purely Akhbreed by the one power none can withstand. But neither is she retired. Are you truly content being retired here in the Wastes? If so, we can go no further."

The General sat back in his chair. "Just what do you have in mind?"

"As I am sure you are aware, Warog, the Imperial Akhbreed Sorcerer, is now so mad that he is beyond much of this world and, as is the eventual fate of all such powers, has become obsessed with the next world. It would take very little to push him completely over and remove him from the scene, but so wild and insane are his tempers now that only one of the Second Rank can even dare contact him. His acolytes are ruined as successors by this, so should he decide to seek First Rank status his position would become vacant. The number of Second Rank sorcerers capable of assuming the post and interested in it are quite limited. Should the successor be friendly to your own interests, it might fill in your one missing factor. Or, of course, it might well be someone inimical to your interests, in which case you will enjoy a permanent retirement."

The General stared at him. "Let me get this straight. You're saying that Yobi can push old Warog out of the picture and put a friendly young new fellow in the post who might be dissatisfied with the current political arrangement? Is that what you're saying? And all that trouble and work for a mere little whore?"

"I am but a messenger but I believe Your Excellency has at least a basic grasp of the message."

General Hodamoc sighed. "Well, first of all it brings up a sense of disbelief. I find it next to impossible to believe that Yobi or anyone else could pull it all off. But assuming against my better judgment and belief that this *could* be done, it brings up the question of just what makes this piece of fluff worth such work. You face me then with a problem, sir. If I give her to you, I must take on faith that all you say can and will be done. Not doubting that the old girl thinks she can do it, belief and accomplishment are two very different things. I know that well. It is why I'm stuck here. On the other hand, you have demonstrated that I own something of great value. If she is of great value to your mistress, then she is most certainly of great value to others. I believe I should see who else is offering something for her, then, perhaps of more certain value."

"That would be a mistake, Excellency," Dorion warned him in the same casual tone he'd used up to now. "One of your greatness should not make two grave mistakes in a lifetime. This is the business of sorcery, not practical men. Not merely Yobi but other high-ranking Akhbreed sorcerers are involved. Your protections come from Warog in better, earlier times, and they are formidable, but to have more than one of the Second Rank angered at you . . . Well, it would not be a clever thing for so brilliant a man to depend too heavily on those protections, particularly without Warog in his prime to back them up."

The General stood up straight. "You *dare* threaten me in my own house, in my own lands, in my own office?" he roared.

Sometimes the power of magicians stems not only from their supernatural abilities but also from their simple, nonmagical craft side. Having removed a small vial from a hidden pocket in his robe sleeve, Dorion deftly uncorked it without dropping that cork and even as he spoke to the General he turned the vial over and let its powdery contents fall to the floor of the office. The vial was then recorked and replaced in its hidden pocket, all in a matter of seconds, all in plain view, and all, thanks to manipulative skill alone, without the General seeing any of it.

"I do not threaten, Excellency, nor does Yobi. But this affair goes far beyond your own ambitions and interests, and involves the most powerful of people. I came here, unarmed and without rancor or malice or any evil intent, to convey to you an honest offer. My part is as an honest messenger only and that I have fulfilled. By your leave, Excellency, I will return and convey your sentiments honestly and truly to those who sent me. My part is now done."

General Hodamoc was having a hard time controlling his temper, but he felt he dealt from a position of power in this matter and the cooler part of his mind told him that it would not do to harm this insolent bastard. That would create a pretext for immediate retaliation by Yobi, and right now he needed time, both to find out just what was so important about this girl and to prepare defenses against whatever magic might ultimately be directed his way. He was of the Akhbreed blood royal, and even as an outcast and exile with a price on his head he had certain special rights and access by virtue of that blood.

"You tell your mistress I demand to know exactly why this girl is important and to whom, and then I might *discuss* the matter further," Hodamoc told the magician. "I make no promises, though. Now—get out of here! I am about to issue orders that if you are ever on my estate again you are to be killed on sight, and even your precious little whore will drive the knife into you if she sees you!"

The magician bowed, touched his forehead, then turned and walked out of the office at a brisk pace. The threat to his personal safety didn't bother him very much, but it was best to be out of this place as quickly as possible for—other—reasons. Hodamoc wasn't the only one who knew of the mystic bond that might be summoned by one of the blood royal, and how much time it would take, nor could Yobi afford to allow the General even enough time to start an inquiry on the girl. The General now believed himself in total control of the situation, and it was time to disillusion him by illustrating his one major mistake.

Back in his office, Hodamoc tried to think things through. Assuming that even a small amount of what the fellow said was true, this little bitch was of some major importance. Why? Perhaps she carried information in her empty little head even she did not know. A courier whose recorded dispatch could be extracted only by one knowing how. That would explain the foreign soldiers chasing her, but it didn't add up. Yobi would hardly need a courier to send and receive any sort of message. Those top sorcerers just sort of transported a part of themselves and talked securely and directly.

A sacrifice, perhaps? She was quite pretty, but hardly a virgin and not of much use in that regard. Perhaps the daughter of someone important, bound to the courtesan life as a runaway, whom Yobi had been asked to find. That made the most sense. Someone *very* important, since she'd be a pariah to the bulk of the population considering her current state.

He needed more information. He had a slave, Pocasa, who was a pretty good artist. A good, faithful drawing of this girl would be of great use, perhaps with a lock of that long hair for magical and alchemical analysis. Many of the troopers stationed at Duke Pasedo's were of his old guard, and they were handy go-betweens. Yes, that was the way to start.

"Comug! Get in here! I have some work for you!" he shouted at his loudest, which was very loud indeed. He expected an immediate response, and when nothing resulted he tried again, "Comug! Attend me! Anyone out there—attend me!"

He got up from his desk, suddenly aware of how still the air seemed in the office, and how deathly quiet everything had gotten. The office was well insulated from the rest of the estate but it wasn't a sealed room. There were always distant noises, shouts, muffled sounds and vibrations that one never paid any attention to until they were not there—and they were not there now.

Suddenly the entire floor of his office seemed to vibrate as if in an earthquake, and he made for the doors and tried to open them but they were sealed shut as if welded to the frame.

He turned and there was the sound of breaking wood as the very floor in front of his desk seemed to heave and push upward. Realizing instantly that the magician must have left something he missed, something that guided a more powerful magic, he made his way quickly around the edge of the office to a small cleared area and stepped within it, then made a few mystic signs. On the floor, barely noticeable unless one looked for it, was a true pentagram, created at great price by a master magician, and sealed with the ritual he performed.

The timbers gave way with a horrible crash and up, into the room, rose a strange and dreadful-looking figure. It was quite large, larger in all ways than the General by far, and it wore a broad black robe that seemed to conceal some great and gross inhuman body atop which sat a cowled head. Long, ancient fingers with sharp knifelike nails reached up to the cowl and threw it back, revealing the face of an impossibly old woman, a skull's mask covered with skin and punctuated with more wrinkles than there were stars, mostly covered with dull purple blotches and topped with only remnants of long, wispy snow-white hair. The long, broken beaklike nose sat below two blind eyes, yet the head and eyes fixed immediately on him and the toothless mouth twisted into a caricature of a wicked smile.

"Oh, I see you know you've been naughty and have fled to the corner," the creature croaked in a voice that was high and cackling. "And, oh, my! What a clever little pentagram! But, then, you always *were* ninety percent brilliant, weren't you Hoddy? It's the other ten percent that's made you a professional failure."

Hodamoc was not impressed. "Well, well. The great Yobi herself, who it is said has not left her cave in a century. This *is* an honor, even if it is a bit hard on the floor."

The sorceress thought that was uproariously funny, and cackled over it for several seconds. "Oh, my, always good for a laugh at that! Come, come—you expected something like this, didn't you? We are a lot alike, really. Both of us were big in our chosen fields, both of us made one big mistake, and both of us wound up in this asshole of a world. The only difference is that I do not make such mistakes twice. You seem to be bent on self-destruction."

"This display of theatrics is impressive but you know it will do you no good," he responded confidently. "The pentagram insulates me from your power and your presence, and even if you should kill me it wouldn't get what you want. And I am not afraid to die. I am a soldier."

"Oh, can the macho man bullshit, Hoddy! We're not amateurs, you and I, and I'm no third-rate shaman who thinks she can scare the big, bad general with a lot of demonic show and tell. The *last* thing I want is you dead, although I can't be absolutely sure that it won't result. How's your heart, Hoddy?"

She reached into the folds of her robe and brought out a small, grotesque wax figure and held it up to him.

"Look familiar, Hoddy? Oh, I know you brave soldier types only play with toy soldiers, but us girls, now, we get to play with dolls. Seems like a silly and impractical thing unless you're going to be a mommie, I admit, but dolls have their practical sides in a lot of areas."

He stared at the doll a little nervously. "I assume that is supposed to be me," he managed, trying to remain confident.

"Oh, it *is* you! I promise you that!" she responded with a cackle. "It has a bit of your hair and a bit of your nails and all that. No blood, but, then, I don't want you dead."

"That's impossible! All of my relics are destroyed or protected by spell and handled only by my bond slaves!"

"Except once. Bless you, dear, for being a total paranoid! You insist that every slave be relic bonded. That's smart, if you have a magician who can control an energy demon on a regular basis, but such ones are rare since those demons can ask a nasty price. But, you see, those demons can still be bargained with. They take your auric materials in with the relics. Not all is fused. Just leave out a hair here, a single small clipping there, and pretty soon you have enough to do some real mean stuff."

"Karella—the bond magician," he sighed. "But that's impossible! She is held by a Second Rank voluntary spell. She cannot betray her trust without destroying herself!"

"True, true. But she's only *Third* Rank, dear. She's not the one who betrays such as you. No, it is the demon who betrays, by not digesting one tiny little particle and instead depositing it very nicely my way where it can do the most good. I was dealing with that demon sprite before Karella's grandmother was born. I have *priority*." Yobi sighed. "So, let's get down to business. You give me the girl, and I forget all about this encounter."

He stared at her, defiant. "You can kill me with that thing, perhaps, even in here, but you cannot make me bend to your will!"

Yobi shrugged. "But, dear, I wasn't talking about *killing* you. Oh, no. Suppose I just pinch one of these cute little feet here . . ."

General Hodamoc screamed in pain and dropped to the floor, suddenly holding his right foot. Anxiously, grimacing, he pulled the boot off and revealed a crushed, bloody mass where the foot had been.

"You see, dear? It's not nice to be impolite to old ladies," the sorceress said sweetly. "Now, what's next? The other foot, perhaps. Then the right arm, then the left. Then we can start on creative anatomy. I wonder what would happen if I pinched right here in the groin where the two legs meet the body . . . ?"

In terrible pain, mad as hell, but ever the pragmatist, he gasped, "No, no! A good soldier always knows when his cause is lost! That's why I'm alive here instead of dead in Mashtopol. You spoke of a deal . . ."

"Deal's off, doll. I told you we were a lot alike. You know you wouldn't offer a nice deal like that again after somebody turned you down and then put you to all this trouble."

"I paid thirty-one fifty for her! At least I demand a refund!"

Yobi held up the doll and went into a mocking version of the auctioneer's chant. "How much am I offered for a foot? An arm? How about the pride of the male? Do I hear a thousand? Two?"

That got his temper going and she suddenly realized she'd overplayed the scene. "Bitch! Do what you will! If you bring her to me

I will order her to destroy herself! You cannot stop me, and I will follow in death no matter what torture you first mete out!"

Yobi thought fast. "Very well, General. I'll give you thirty-five hundred, a more than fair profit on the deal, and I'll also fix both your foot and the floor."

His hatred almost overcame him, but he saw a way to salvage his honor and bring things back to a more even keel and make the best of the situation.

"Not enough. I want the doll as well. And spells of protection so that my body and my home can never be so easily violated again."

She realized the opening and took it unhesitatingly. "Deal. But you forget all about this girl. Forget she was ever here, that you ever had her. Tell any guests who sampled her that she died or was killed and dismiss it. Betray the bargain and the spell that seals it will become undone. Time will curve, and we will be back here, as we are, and I will hold the doll. Be true to it, and it is done."

"All right. I will send for the girl."

"No need," said the sorceress. "I can handle that."

Charley was up top, on the surface and outside, just lounging in the sun and daydreaming about people and places far away, ignorant of all that was taking place. Suddenly she felt dizzy, and the whole outdoor scene seemed to blur, the heat of the sun to vanish, and in a moment she was inside a strange room beholding a strange and terrifying sight.

First she spotted Hodamoc and started to drop to the required genuflection position, but then she first felt, then turned and saw, Yobi just behind her, and even though the sight was terrifying the other automatic part of her slave programming took over. Someone was hurting the Master. Attack!

She rushed at the sorceress, but Yobi simply put up her palm and Charley felt as if she'd run into a brick wall and then fell to the ground, stunned. Still, she could not violate her standing commands and started to pick herself up, searching now for a weapon to use.

"No!" Hodamoc shouted. "Leave the creature alone and come to me!"

She immediately stopped, all standing instructions overridden, and turned and came to him. Or, rather, she tried to. When she reached a certain point on the floor very close to him she found herself unable to move another step.

"The slave bond can't move across the pentagram, dummy," Yobi noted, forgetting her spirit of reconciliation for a moment. "Have her bend down."

"Kneel and lean in as far as you can," Hodamoc instructed her, and she did so. He moved, painfully, and then reached out and touched the ring in her nose.

"Thy bond is transferred by my free will," he intoned. "That is Yobi. You will obey her as Mistress as you have obeyed me, and bond as she instructs. You are now her property, not mine, and all prior instructions and loyalties to me are canceled. Obey Yobi."

She felt dizzy once again, and then fell back a bit, but she also felt as if something of a weight had been transferred from her mind. She no longer regarded the man in the uniform as anyone special or unusual.

"Girl! Stand, turn, and face me!" Yobi instructed, and she did so with a sudden thought of *Here we go again!*

"Your former Master and I have some last-minute details to cover to seal the bargain. You will leave this place when I tell you, exit in the lower cave level, and at the boundary you will seek and find a magician in a brown robe. His name is Dorion and he will introduce himself as such and then state that he is from me. You will go with him and obey him and no other as Master until we can modify that spell of yours. Now—go!"

She found herself walking to and then out of the door to do as instructed, closing the door behind her.

Yobi turned back to Homadoc. "Now, I fulfill my end of the bargain. I keep my bargains, General. I expect you to keep yours. The monetary part will be on deposit in town within the hour." With that, she lifted the cowl back over her head and began a chant, gesturing as she did so.

It was suddenly as if everything had been placed in reverse. Yobi sank into the floor with an odd sound, and the floor itself came back seamlessly to its original state. Hodamoc found the pain in his foot suddenly gone and looked down to see it whole, although he still had to put his boot back on. He did so quickly, then got up, unsteadily, and made his way out of the pentagram and over to the desk. It was another couple of minutes before he could get complete hold of his senses, and then he looked down. On top of the desk was the small, crude doll that Yobi had been holding.

He wasted no time in finding a copper bowl and then some lamp oil. Placing the doll in the bowl, he poured the lamp oil upon it and then used a flint to ignite it. The blaze was something fierce but localized, and when it was done there was nothing left in the bowl but a puddle of melted wax and some bits and pieces of things, charred and burned beyond recognition. That hold on him, at least, was now gone.

But his pride had been wounded by the encounter, and he was very bitter. Nobody, *nobody*, did this to him! Particularly in his own home and in his own quarters! First he would arrange for his protections and be ready for any retaliation, although it would take a bit of time. No more ninety percent here. Then, one way or another, he was going to find out just what was so valuable about that little whore, and then he would use all the influence he had to make certain that any value she might have would accrue only to him.

Dorion waited for her just outside the boundaries of the main cave of Hodamoc. She came swiftly, and he couldn't help but get something of an erotic charge just watching her approach. Her every move was unconsciously erotic, and he had never seen someone so totally sexual before who was a real person and not some sort of demonic succubus a good magician knew to avoid. She was wearing a beaded outfit; the lower part hung on her hips and formed a multicolored beaded loin covering in front, and another elaborate set of beads shaped and highlighted but didn't really conceal her breasts. Otherwise she was naked, and might as well have been anyway for all the good the beads did.

She stopped just at the entrance to the cave, the first time in weeks she'd been even a few inches outside of Hodamoc's territory, and began looking for this magician.

Dorion stepped from the darkness of the cave and approached her. "I am Dorion acting for Yobi," he said, sounding a bit nervous. "Obey me as you would her."

"Yes, Master," she responded in a really soft, low, sexy voice.

For the first time Dorion realized that she would have to obey anything he commanded. Somebody like that was completely under his power . . . God, he was so turned on, he only wished he had the nerve to take advantage of it.

"Take my hand and come with me," he instructed. "We have a very long walk and we're going to have to take the back ways to avoid running into anyone we don't want to meet. I am told that you can understand but cannot speak Akhbreed. What tongues do you speak?"

"English, Spanish, and the Short Speech, Master," she responded.

"English, huh? Well, we have something in common. I've never been able to manage to speak English so anyone else can understand, but I can understand it pretty well. So you speak English to me and I will speak Akhbreed to you and together we might understand each other. All right?"

She felt almost a flood of relief. *Somebody who understood her!* "Yes, Master," she responded in English.

"You are from one of the Outplanes, I guess. Brought here by Boolean?" he asked as they began to walk in what looked to her to be total darkness.

"Yes, Master. Almost two years now, I guess, although I have no way to judge the time." She didn't like admitting that—there was no way of knowing if this guy was a nice fellow or if he was one of Klittichorn's boys. That *thing* in Hodamoc's office wasn't reassuring. That Yobi looked like a horrible version of the creature who had captured the others and almost gotten her as well after the flood. However, there were certain default conditions as it were built into the slave spell. All could be countermanded, of course, but they existed unless that was done. The first was total unthinking obedience whether you wanted to or not, of course. The second was an automatic subservience to anyone who could order you around. One did not speak unless spoken to and one answered just what was demanded—and absolutely truthfully. You couldn't lie, cheat, or steal something from a controller unless told to do so, and like a planet in its orbit you needed your controller as the planet needed its sun. There was no running away. It simply was not an option.

It was because of this that Yobi had been forced to act so quickly after Hodamoc had turned down the initial offer. She hadn't been able to afford even a questioning of the girl by her then Master, or it all would have come out.

It *was* quite a walk, and, again, she couldn't have retraced it if she tried, nor did she figure out how the magician knew the way himself, but eventually they emerged outside and relatively high up in the mountainous crags of the Wastes. From that point it was a narrow trail that wound around the top of a ridge until eventually it entered a cave originating in the floor of the rock itself and leading down a bit.

The place stank, kind of like the way Boday's lab had often smelled in the old days. Lots of odd odors and unpleasant fragrances, which identified it as a dwelling of either a magician or an alchemist. There were several small chambers and then a main one which looked, to put it bluntly, a mess.

A central pit was in the chamber, in which much was obviously cooked, and over which a kind of metal web was built on which could be sat large pots and bowls or from which you could hang kettles and tureens. There was a pot of something on, simmering, and from its look and smell Charley prayed to herself that it wasn't dinner.

Most of the rest of the cave was taken with shelves filled with all sorts of boxes, gourds, glass jars, you name it, as well as apparently embalmed bats and lizards and such and even a shrunken head and skull or two. There were also books—lots of books, all huge and old and moldy looking. The only area of the walls other than the entrance not so covered with bric-a-brac had an old and faded patterned rug hung on it right down to the ground.

"Not exactly comfortable looking, I know, but it's a lot better than most sorcerers' lairs," Dorion noted. "Just sit on the floor there. I'm sure Yobi won't keep us waiting long."

And she didn't. The rug suddenly flew up and the great sorceress entered the chamber, revealing an ancillary cave beyond that had to be her private quarters. Although Charley had glimpsed her back at Hodamoc's, it was not under the best of circumstances, and part of the sorceress had been stuck below the floor, as it were, out of immediate sight. She had not, for example, realized until now just how large the old one was, or how totally inhuman were her lower quarters, obscured as they were by a specially designed black robe. The face, though, was easy to remember. It kind of looked like the wicked witch from "Snow White," only without the redeeming qualities.

Yobi looked over at her with eyes that seemed glazed and blind, yet Charley knew she was getting a thorough examination on several levels.

"Shit!" the sorceress muttered. "All that trouble and all we got was a decoy. I thought you were better than that, son."

Dorion looked surprised. "A decoy?"

"Sure. Any fool can see that she's got Boolean's trickery written all over her aura. How the hell did you wind up looking like the Storm Princess wished she looked, child? You can speak English. I have been forced to learn the foul-sounding tongue."

"It is a long tale, Mistress, but it is as you say. The sorcerer Boolean did it by remote-control magic."

That struck Yobi as funny. "Remote-control magic! Wonderful. Well, speak, child. Tell us who you really are and how came you to this point. Take as much time as you wish—we are in no immediate hurry right now."

And, in general detail, Charley told them the whole story. Of how she'd been a friend and schoolmate to this rather odd girl in her own world and land, and how quite by accident and by not believing in this sort of magic she had wound up getting sucked down to Akahlar with Sam. She told how Boolean stepped in to save them from Klittichorn in the journey, in the process revealing himself as an active enemy of the horned sorcerer and making himself a target. How they'd been picked up and then betrayed by the mercenary Zenchur, but not before Boolean's magical device had caused her to appear to be an identical twin of Sam's.

And she talked of being sold to Boday, who gave her the beauty as well as the markings of the blue butterfly and changed her into a true courtesan, and how in rescuing her from Boday's clutches Sam had unthinkingly grabbed and made Boday drink a love potion that made the alchemical artist fall madly in love with Sam. And how Charley had volunteered to raise the money for the trip to Boolean by actually being a courtesan, and how Sam had grown fat and lazy and domestic under Boday. And, of course, how they'd finally made the money to get there not by selling herself but by creating and selling the patent to women's undergarments common back on their world.

How, then, they'd been attacked, and Sam's use of her power to summon storms to save them at the cost of a flash flood that had destroyed the train and killed many, with most of the survivors being captured, raped, and tortured by others of the gang led by Asterial, and how the demon prisoner of the Jewel of Omak had eventually saved them all. And, finally, how they had become separated and wound up where they did.

Both Yobi and Dorion listened intently, occasionally nodding but only rarely interjecting a question to clarify a point they didn't understand. When she was done, she knew that her life, and Sam's, were now squarely in the hands of this pair.

Yobi was silent for some time, thinking it all over, and then she sighed and said, "Well, now we know where we stand, anyway. I'm afraid I'm going to have to get this Boday as well, which might be easier or tougher depending on Jamonica's mood and whether or not she's really of use to him. He's a trader and he buys and sells everything, unlike Hodamoc, who's a damned *collector*. The gods save us all from *collectors!* He does not use relics, however, so it'll cost, damn it." She sighed again. "From what you tell me, you *should* have been the one and not your friend. You have the spirit and temperament for it. But, we must deal with what we have, not with what we want. In the meantime, I sense that much troubles you. I would like to know what, one at a time, please."

"Well, Mistress, I do not like being a slave."

Yobi cackled. "Why, we are *all* slaves, child! We only kid ourselves if we pretend otherwise. Why, Akahlar itself is a source of massive power and wealth and nearly limitless resources, yet ninety percent of its people are at subsistence level toiling for the few. The ones that are left over are subject to monarchies and governments in which they have no say even when some of those governments pretend that their citizens do have some say, and under a series of religions that oppress them even more. Wars and revolutions are always fought in the name of the dispossessed but always seem to really be about which side of a small elite shall be the oppressor. I envy you if you were born and raised in a different sort of place where this is not true. It must be strange indeed."

"Mistress, my land valued personal freedoms and liberties, although most of my world was as you say."

"Indeed? So your land was rich in a poor world, and so mere citizenship in it made you a member of the elite. Sounds like the Akhbreed here. Oh, there are poor Akhbreed, of course, but even the poorest in the hubs and colonies is better off than the average of all the thousands of races who inhabit the worlds they loot."

She wanted to protest that it wasn't really like that, but slaves weren't permitted debates with their controllers. But she remembered the visions of the migrant workers, the illegals from Mexico, who worked the fields in the Southwest, and the huge population of Mexico just out of sight of the tourist villas and fancy hotels. And how much say did anybody have in an election, anyway? Anybody could run, but only the ones with people and money and party support stood a chance. You got to pick between two people who were basically picked for you. And the seamy underworld neighborhood of Tubikosa where Boday had lived was not unlike that in any major city back home, nor, in fact, did pimps and prostitutes lack for business. Maybe it wasn't so great after all, but it was *comfortable.* And, for over a hundred years anyway, they didn't keep slaves.

"What would you have done, or thought you might have done, if you'd stayed ignorant of all this?" Yobi asked her, giving her some clearance for an answer.

"Graduated from high school and gone on to college," she responded. "Most women aren't chained to families and child-rearing there because of easy birth control. I was going for a degree in chemistry, with the hope of getting into the cosmetics industry."

"Indeed? Wonderful liberation, that. Learn all that so you can better your fellow woman by making her look prettier. Lots of money, no commitments, total pleasure-seeking off the job. Perhaps an occasional march or donation to ease the conscience now and again. So long as you can live well and have fun, what the hell. I've got mine and that's all that matters. If you've got the brains, and the talent, and the connections, and not many scruples, anyone can become parasitic royalty. I'm surprised you don't all die young of pleasure potions and venereal disease. Or don't they exist, either?"

"They do, Mistress. Drugs, alcohol, and many kinds of VD. One was around when I left that was always fatal. It was scaring a lot of people. I have worried about whether such things were here as well."

"Of *course* they are, you ninny! You don't have to worry about *those* kinds of diseases, though. What alchemy can't create here magic can eventually control, or, if such a disease is created in the changewind, as has happened, the Akhbreed move to—sterilize—it. You're immune to the hundred or so venereal diseases we have now, so don't worry about it. That's what makes courtesans worth so much. Of course, the general population isn't so lucky, but it keeps the populations under control and in check. But even the highest of the Akhbreed can become addicted to the pleasure potions. That's Jamonica's real trade, and why he'd pay so much for an alchemist slave. And that's Hodamoc's hope for eventually controlling Mashtopol. Addict so many of the pleasure-loving and decadent royalty and the bored movers and shakers that he will enslave them in a way just as effective as he enslaved you. Do not feel so bad. That ring tells the world that your situation was forced upon you and not self-inflicted, and there is no dishonor in that. I sense you have a question on it anyway. Go ahead."

"Then—Mistress? It is permanent? I can never be free?"

"Oh, no! It's a complicated ritual and a real pain in the ass but any Second Rank sorcerer and even some of the Third Rank can undo it if you have the Master's permission. Finding one that *will* undo it, however, not to mention a Master willing to let you go, is the trick. Pardon, my dear, but there is no percentage in it. Don't look so crestfallen. You haven't exactly done very well on your own up to now or you wouldn't be under such a spell. Your value was, is, and remains as a decoy. Klittichorn might suspect, but so long as he does not *know* he can't take you for granted, and that means he must try and hunt you. Your value is to lead them away from your friend—without falling into their clutches, which you both have very narrowly escaped doing up to now. However, before we can make use of you we must first locate and redirect your friend. Since this Boday had the audacity to trick your friend into that marriage spell, she is essential to the task. I fear your friend has fallen into the clutches of Duke Pasedo and is even now happily and ignorantly picking berries somewhere many leegs from here. That we will have to determine. But you have other problems and worries. Speak."

"Mistress, I am still trying to make peace with myself over what this world has made me."

"A decoy?"

"No, Mistress, a courtesan. One who sells her body. In my world it is considered the lowest thing a woman can be."

"And you are bothered by the fact that it sinks you low?"

"No, Mistress. You see, I—I spent over a year at it in Tubikosa, and I *liked* it. I fear that there is something wrong with me that I did not suspect. That I would rather be a whore than a warrior or a queen or have my own business."

Yobi shrugged. "Many queens and sorceresses have done pretty good jobs. Others have been lousy—just like the men. We are what our destinies make us. To be otherwise is to be miserable. Most people are miserable. If you liked it, then there's no shame in that. Spend little time thinking of what other people demand that you be and please yourself. Consider—would you rather be a slave and courtesan or would you rather have fantastic power and look like me and live forever with *this?*"

With that Yobi pulled away the draping cloak, and what was revealed made Charley sick to her stomach. The body was huge, bloated, and deformed, a pulsating and pulpy cream color like some sort of enormous monster insect larva or worm, and bits of slime and old skin hung to it or moved slightly with the pulsations.

Yobi replaced the cloak. "The Second Rank sorcerers are about as free as you can get in this or any other place," she told the still stricken-looking girl. "The things I can see, the kinds of things I can do, stagger even my imagination. I've lived six hundred years and I've seen and done most everything. Pretty soon the madness creeps in, and you begin to think and act like you're some sort of god. It happens to all of us sooner or later. And you begin to chafe at even the minuscule, meager limits still imposed on you. Your ego cannot accept them. First Rank or nothing! And eventually you dare, and you look in those places you dare not look and try those things you dare not try. The last barrier is the changewind, and you go against it. I was lucky. I managed to pull back with only this to remind me, and retaining—perhaps regaining is a better word—at least a hair of sanity. But, sooner or later, I know I will try again. It is inevitable. If one must live forever then one must gain and grow, or death is preferable. But—not yet, not yet."

Yobi sighed, then suddenly snapped out of it and bent down and looked at Charley's face closely. "How are your eyes, child?"

"Mistress, I was always nearsighted, and lately I have been so that my vision is quite poor. In the past weeks it had gotten progressively worse. I can no longer see anything except what is directly ahead, and without the sun or a strong light like your lanterns that I now face I can see almost nothing. I have been quite frightened of it."

The sorceress nodded. "You stood there, helpless, watching a knock-down-and-drag-out between a true demon prince and Asterial. There are—radiations—involved in most magic. That is why all magicians have very poor eyesight and Second Rankers are all blind in the conventional sense. It is unavoidable. But most in the magic arts have other means of sight that are not only as good, they're quite a bit better and more revealing. To be a decent magician, though, you must be born with the talent and also with an apitude for mathematics. It's quite precise or you don't survive long, which is why magicians are often powerful but rarely creative. You have no magic of your own to speak of and without that even a mathematical wizard would be helpless. Yet the dosage you received was probably quite intense. No, my dear, we must find some magical alternative for you. There is no way around it, but there are things that can be done."

Charley's heart sank and she was as depressed as she had ever felt at this. There was no way around it. She was being told that she would always be someone's slave, and, worse, even than that, a blind one.

"Boday is *crushed* by this!" the tall, tattooed woman grumbled. "First they make her a slave—a *slave!*—and set her to work in a happy-potions factory—me! A great artist! Hovering over what is no more than a soulless assembly line!"

Yeah, well, at least you're not blind as well, Charley thought dejectedly. Other than Sam, the only thing Boday ever thought of was Boday.

"And now they bring her here and duck both her and her finest creation into this moldy *slime pit,*" Boday went on, oblivious as always. Charley had hopes that Yobi or Dorion would command her to silence at least but when there were just the two of them there weren't any limits on that sort of thing.

Two gray-robed acolytes, a man and a woman never introduced

and so referred to only as Him and Her, entered and helped them out. Yobi, it appeared, had quite an operation here, and more people than had been immediately apparent. Some were students unable to apprentice to a Second Rank sorcerer in the hubs; others were exiles like Yobi and most of the others here.

Both women were now stood straight up and had water dumped on them in great quantities until the last vestiges of the goo was off. It had been worse for Charley than for Boday; for Charley they had prepared a sort of mud pack of the stuff and let it set and harden over much of her face.

Not that it had really mattered, except for the feel and the smell. Charley hadn't been at Yobi's two days before she woke up one morning on her mat and thought it was still completely dark. She had not seen a single thing, not even light and darkness, since.

It had been so gradual up to now that she had some suspicion that the sudden collapse of her eyesight was less natural than Yobi's doing, but she could not be sure and there was no way to ask and get a straight answer anyway. She resented it, but she could understand it. Yobi had wasted no time in having Him and Her begin training as a blind person. It was frustrating and boring and maddening, particularly since, with the slave spell, she couldn't take a break, couldn't give up, couldn't even complain as it went on and on, but it was now paying off. When you are ordered to walk you wind up walking with very cautious confidence after a while. Balance was more of a trick than she'd thought it would be, too, but she managed. You felt your way along the cave walls and you memorized where anything that might trip you up was, and you learned to use your other senses, and your feet as well.

Dorion entered the mud chamber and looked them over. He was still having a terrible mental problem over Charley, whom he was beginning to have wet dreams about, but there was just something inside of him that couldn't take that kind of advantage of anybody. If she was willing, that was one thing, but the master-slave relationship made that tough to figure out for real, and somehow actually having her would make him feel like a rapist.

"We've found your Sam," he told them. "Yobi's set to break her out of the alchemical traps she's fallen into and Boolean's set her up with somebody who's totally trustworthy, but we don't want to spring her completely until you're ready and underway. The trick is, we want them to chase you, but we don't want them to catch you. This is step one. Boday, your work is beautiful, but it's a beauty that is made to be seen. Frankly, the pair of you wouldn't last an hour in any hub with those tattoos, so off they come."

Using a thin razorlike instrument, Him and Her worked first on Boday, whose body below the neck was covered and thus was actually easier. Making sure not to cut the skin, they made a series of incredibly delicate incisions, and, thanks to the hours of soaking in the preparation, they then were able to peel off the tattoos from her body in segments. It was quite bizarre; they came off, layer upon layer, like decals, most fully intact, and while Boday was less than pleased with the whole thing she was somewhat mollified that they actually laid the designs on a paper form and managed to preserve most of them. The result, when done, was not that bad, since Boday had natural brown skin.

Charley was more of a problem, partly because the designs were so delicate and intricate with few solids and also because she was naturally light-skinned. Her exposed skin had turned a dark brown with all the sun and exposure, but the tattoos had blocked the rays from where they covered, and now she stood there, mercifully unable to see the result, with the designs somewhat etched in outline in light skin against the otherwise suntanned complexion.

With Dorion they always had a certain amount of freedom to speak, within limits and subject to cutoff, of course. Boday looked over Charley and said, "Boday likes it. It is a fascinating abstract."

"We'll have to fill it in with dyes, I'm afraid," Dorion noted. "We want uniformity. We'll also have to do something with the hair. It's been alchemically lengthened and stabilized, but I'm afraid knee-length hair is not only a sure giveaway, it's not practical in the circumstances. The object remains the same—reach Boolean in the shortest possible time, but by a route totally different than the one your friend will take. Perhaps curled a bit, dyed a lighter color, and tumbling a bit over the shoulders. Boday, we have a different but no less effective set of ideas for you. I know you won't like them but you'd like Klittichorn's Stormriders less."

Boday thought a moment. "Permission to ask a question, Master?"

"Go ahead."

"Boday cares not for herself, Master, but—how is her darling Susama and what new curses does she bear?"

Love potions conquer all, Charley thought with amazement.

"Heavier than she was, but a lot more muscle. That curse kept her weight up, which is good—she's nearly unrecognizable as a twin of the Storm Princess—but she's been doing heavy farm work. She could probably lift the both of you and possibly a horse. Her hair's shoulder-length, and thanks to a tough potion she's amnesiac. That's what Yobi will work on. She's been quite happy, though, in her ignorance. And, well, it won't be certain until we see her, but

Yobi's initial spells, now that we have her located, suggest—only suggest, mind you—that she might possibly be pregnant."

Both women gasped. "By whom, Master?" Boday asked at last, a bit shaken.

Dorion shrugged. "Who knows? We don't even know if it's true. But if it *is* and isn't just some byproduct of all those potions she was fed and the kind of life she'd been leading, it must be fairly well along, predating her current situation."

"Those filthy rapists," Charley muttered, then had a thought. "Or maybe it might be that friendly wagon train crewman she seduced out of curiosity. Poor Sam! It would be her luck to get knocked up the first time!" She suddenly caught herself, remembering that Boday didn't know about that one. Well, Boday didn't know English, either. "Please, Master, do not mention that one to Boday, though."

Dorion looked puzzled, but didn't pursue it. Boday, however, was now deep in thought.

"Pregnant . . . It could have happened to Boday as well just as easily, or those poor little girls. One wonders what the product of one of those—*creatures*—and Boday would have been? A great primitive artist, perhaps, or maybe an animist." She sighed. "No, with that mixture it would probably grow up to be a critic. Whatever, Boday will consider the child as her own. *Our* own."

"Yeah, well, it's just another complication now. We have to move, and fast. The word is old Horn Heart is getting set to pull something big. That's good in that it'll get him out of his citadel. but it's putting a lot of pressure on us. As soon as we get you two set up we have to *move*. We've been sitting on Hodamoc long enough anyway and it's been no end of trouble. We want to let him go, have him identify Charley as the Storm Princess's double, and draw them here. By that time you have to be long gone."

"Master, how can I do much of anything?" Charley asked him plainly. "I am *blind*. Totally so. And, out there, totally defenseless because of it. I was lucky once when I could see to shoot straight, but I didn't do really well with both eyes going. Now . . ."

"We are going to deal with that as well," the magician told her. "Of course it depends on whether or not you like animals—and whether any animals like you."

Walking into the small room was a strange and unnerving experience for Charley. Unable to see, unfamiliar with the layout, she was nonetheless overcome with sounds. Screeching sounds, scurrying sounds, barking, and mewing sounds. Had she not been commanded, and therefore compelled, to enter, nothing that could be offered would have gotten her there.

"Nothing here should harm you," Yobi assured her. "Pets, strays, mongrels—the animal part of the Kudaan underground. Castoffs, like ourselves. Sit for a while on the floor crosslegged so you form a lap and see what might like you."

She sat, but she didn't like all the implications of that one. A number of the animals approached her, but she tried to remain calm and not show fear. She remembered that animals could smell fear.

Suddenly something small and furry bounded into her lap and then tried to climb up her torso using sharp little claws. She cried out and recoiled and reached out—and knew that she was holding a cat.

Not a big cat, certainly, although it was no kitten. It struggled for a moment, since her blind grip wasn't exactly the best, but then she relaxed and so did it and she put it down in her lap and felt its form and started to pet it. The cat purred.

"It seems you have found a friend," Yobi noted. "That cat is a bit odd, very much like all of us here. It often seems to think it's a great tiger cat, taking on that which it cannot hope to vanquish, and other times it is a forlorn, mewing sort demanding attention. It's a bit scruffy and scraggly, but it is a tomcat through and through."

The cat seemed to snuggle up to her, purring loud enough to overcome the residual noises in the room. She found herself scratching its ears and stroking it and she liked it. She'd never had a pet before.

"A tomcat . . . Mistress, what color is it?"

"Gray with black stripelike spots, dirty white paws. Very ordinary."

Charley nodded. A typical alleycat, which kind of fit. Still, one thing bothered her. "Mistress—I like him, that is true, but I cannot see how this helps me. I have heard of seeing-eye dogs before, but not cats."

Yobi cackled. "Come. Bring your friend and attend me, and I shall work a little magic with you."

All had been set up ahead of time; the braziers were going, there was incense about, and Charley could feel heat from large candles. The big stuff.

"Bring your friend and yourself forward ten paces," Yobi instructed. "Then stop and wait, but do not let the cat out of your grasp."

The cat, fortunately, didn't seem to want to go anywhere except to scratch some primordial arboreal instinctive itch that made it want to climb up on her shoulders and perhaps her head.

"Many of us use creatures well suited to giving us information, culled from all the worlds of Akahlar," the sorceress told her. "However, they require special handling in most cases, or odd diets, or even controls of a sort you do not possess. For our purposes, the cat is fine."

She began a series of chants and Charley could hear a lot of sizzling sounds and smell odd odors wafting through the cave. Suddenly the sorceress broke into her heavily accented but quite understandable English.

"You shall have eyes once again, of a sort," Yobi told her. "There is also room in this equation for other attributes. Remain still. The cat will taste of you and it will hurt for a moment, but it is necessary. Do not move or drop it."

Suddenly the cat twisted a bit and she felt sharp fangs drive into her upper left arm. It hurt, and she knew instantly that it drew blood and she began to wonder just what was happening when the cat began to lick that blood from her arm and from the wound it had made.

"Mix, match, mate," said the sorceress. "The cat has become a familiar and shares your blood and a small part of your soul. Half in shadow, not in light, *link* ye two!"

Charley felt a sudden and uncomfortable hot flush, which took a few moments to fade. She began to see images; strange outlines and bizarre shapes and forms unlike anything she had ever seen or imagined, and, somehow, she was seeing them with her eyes. They were brilliant, dazzling, occasionally scary, as they briefly turned and twisted and for a moment here and there seemed to be not merely colored electrical lines but shapes both monstrous and, somehow, evil. They turned, they danced around her, reaching out, as if trying to touch her or even come inside her, and she was powerless to recoil or defend herself. Then, in a sudden flash that seemed to release all the brilliant and eerie colors at once, all was dark again, but only for a moment.

Then, slowly, incredibly, she began to see images in her mind, visions that were quite dim at first and faded in and out but which began to take on greater solidity, until at last they were quite clear, if very strange.

She saw the central cave of Yobi's complex, but not with her eyes, nor how her eyes would see it. The images were devoid of color, but infinite in their gray shadings, and they were also somewhat distorted, like the fish-eye lens of a camera, which showed an enormous field of view but showed things in perspective only in the center, and only a bit farther out. From there the image curved out like an inverted mirrored glass, elongating and distorting the images. Still, she could see Yobi now, and the smoky braziers, and all the rest, the candles momentarily smeared the view, and if you focused on them all else was dark. The focus was general rather than on anything specific, but if something moved, even the smoke or candle flames, or Yobi herself, the vision instantly locked that moving thing in at the center of vision. It took some getting used to.

Suddenly the image shifted, and she saw a giant human face and neck. *Her* face, but not as she had ever seen it before.

I'm seeing what the cat is seeing, the way the cat sees it! she realized suddenly.

"Yes, that is true," Yobi told her. "You and your cat friend are linking together in a number of ways. There is a price, for every so often he will need a drop of your blood to remain active and alive and you must give it. But that will keep him with you, inseparably if need be, no matter how far he may roam. The blood link will allow you to see through him whenever you wish, even if you and he are not touching, although always from his point of view, of course. It will take some getting used to. It's not as good as eyes, and you will still be blind, but you will now be able to see what you must."

The cat was now looking at Yobi's craggy face, as if also understanding the words.

"There is a side effect here that I did not negate, although it is a mixed blessing and curse," the sorceress continued. "While you hold the cat, your thoughts are open. Anyone fairly close to you, say as close as I am now, will be able to understand them as if they were spoken, regardless of language. You will thus be able to communicate with anyone anywhere in Akahlar, which is more than most can do, but you must be cautious. Your thoughts will be an open book to anyone looking at you or to anyone you are looking at or interacting with. You will have to learn to control your thoughts while you hold the familiar. I added that curse, for that is what it is, to enable you to communicate normally, and as a possible salvation should you be captured by the enemy. They will know immediately that you are the wrong one."

That was a strange and unnerving concept, but at least she didn't have to always hold the cat.

"Those—those shapes, Mistress . . . What were they?"

But Yobi didn't answer, and there was no other way to know.

Charley sighed. "Well, then. Well, we must have a name for you if we are to be so close, mustn't we? Half in shadow . . . That's not just a spell, it's me. All right, then, Sir Shadowcat, you and I will have to be very, very careful."

The cat purred.

6
Split Personalities

The Great Gorge was one of the most spectacular places in all the Kudaan, almost a fourteen-hundred-foot sheer drop to the rushing river below, unbridged and uncrossed. More than one animal had smelled that water and run to their doom, plunging over that sheer cliff so that by the time they reached what they craved from desert wanderings they no longer needed it.

To the west was the high desert itself; the river that ran far underground through stronger, tougher rock and only here, where the rock changed to the softer sedimentary variety, had its great tunnel been extended all the way to the surface, carrying away the collapsed material in the channel it dug over the eons, slowly enough so that it did not get dammed up but rapid enough to cause the impassable chasm.

The caravan stayed for the night just beyond the canyon, expertly limiting the animals so that while they could have food and what was left of the wagon they would not or could not wander off too far in the wrong direction.

She emerged from the Navigator's wagon and looked beyond the campfire to the starry darkness beyond. She wore only a thin, light robe tied at the waist, which was all that was required in the desert. It could get chilly here on occasion, but not tonight. Tonight she could almost sense that it would fall from broiling to merely hot; more comfortable but not exactly perfection.

Kira was perfection, or as close to it as a woman could aspire to. Without makeup, jewelry, or any aids, just as she was, she was almost a dream woman. The figure on her five-foot-two frame was perfection, perfectly balanced and shaped; her face an idealized, almost angelic one, the lips just right, the nose perfect, the emerald green eyes large and dark, the features giving just a hint of a playful, kittenish quality coming through the beauty. Her hair was thick, lush, with a natural body beyond the need of more than a regular washing, auburn with natural streaks of a dark blond, cascading down from her face, framing it perfectly, ending just below the shoulders. She moved with a natural catlike grace that was no studied affectation but simply a part of her, as totally feminine as Crim's big, muscular frame and swagger was so masculine. The word *sensuous* seemed invented for her.

The trail crew saw her, and nodded, but then went about their work. Kira was one of them in spite of her appearance, and while they appreciated her beauty she was nothing unusual to them.

She went over to the campfire and took a small amount of wine in a gourd cup and a couple of pieces of sweet bread and nibbled on them, not feeling very hungry. She was thinking, and waiting.

She felt, more than saw, him come. There was a charm they had, one that allowed Boolean to know where they were, and it seemed to have a sort of two-way effect. The feeling wasn't absolute; it had more than once played them false, and it was none too certain if it was Boolean or some other power from its tingle, but she was confident now. She put down her meager supper, got up, and walked out from the fire, out towards the gorge.

She felt someone suddenly beside her, although it was quite dark, and she found a rock and sat pertly on it. "So," she said, in a soft, musical voice that could charm a tyrant. "Now we shall talk."

"A pleasure to speak with you again, Kira," said that slightly hollow voice again, the voice of Boolean somehow both here and faraway. "I confess to preferring you to Crim even though I feel more at a loss around you."

She laughed. "I thought the great Akhbreed sorcerers were beyond all that."

"Some of them are, maybe most of them," he admitted. "Those who are have ceased to be human. Power can do that to you if you're not careful. Our kind of power." He paused. "You have considered the proposition?"

She nodded, even though it seemed a futile gesture in the darkness. "Crim prefers the more direct, fighting approach, which he is so good at," she noted. "But the mark of a great warrior is knowing when *not* to fight. As for myself, I could not even *lift* his sword, and the recoil from his guns would be as devastating to me as to whomever or whatever I hit. Crim is correct on one very big point, and that is no amount of force short of a total assault will get her out of there if she's in there under the conditions you surmise."

"Stealth, then."

"Caution, certainly. But the ideal method is extortion, if I had something to use, which I do not. We need the help of higher-ups in the Duke's entourage, that is definite. Access to them—the men, certainly—is no problem for me, but both cooperation and security cannot be secured by the basic methods. No, I will need something to trade, and with the entourage the magicians and alchemists are the most vulnerable. A sample of the potion used, I would think, would simplify matters a great deal."

"Immensely, even though analysis from this distance is going to be rough. It will keep me from falling into traps and making serious or irreversible mistakes."

"I thought as much. And we will need someone who can give us access to the girl. Finding her by hit or miss in *that* place might take forever."

There was a thoughtful sigh in the dark. "So we need something for each. A spell that any good magician might covet, particularly one of the sort that one who would spend his or her life there might value more than loyalty. The same in the chemistry department. The first one I can come up with fairly quickly, although I hate to give it away. It's a good one, and should be earned. Still, this is a prize for which the rules must bend. How about a spell that would regrow amputated limbs?"

"*Perfect!* They have much need of it and it will make them great in their little domain—and help a lot of unfortunates in the process."

"The one I have in mind is complicated as all hell and not very fast. It reads the genetic code and then slowly regrows what's missing over a fairly long period, but the results can still be spectacular. All right. But alchemy . . . That's tougher. They're apparently pretty damned good at that already, so the obvious probably isn't needed. I'll have to give that one some thought and perhaps some research." The sorcerer paused a moment, then said, "All right, so we use bribery. Now how the hell do we control the girl if she's been turned into a pea-brained grape stomper? With her build she'd probably be great at that."

"Surely if we can get to her there is some sort of simple hypnotic—"

"Yeah, yeah," Boolean muttered, still thinking. "But most of those are potions and I don't want to add anything that might complicate matters. I wish I had another equivalent of the Jewel of Omak. That was damned useful, but it also took me years. You don't trap demons every day. Your best bet, if possible, is to make some solution to that part of the bribe payment. They know what they're dealing with better than we do. I'll try some backup, but it'll be risky. Maybe theirs will be, too, but it'll be educated, not ignorant. The next step will be getting her out of there. She is not exactly unobtrusive."

"So you told Crim. No way to lift that?"

"It was demon imposed. I'd need her physically present to see what it did and how and they're tricky little bastards. Besides, it wouldn't matter even if I could. Once that thing's lifted she won't be any different. If she wants to be thin again she's still going to have to lose it. Any kind of spell that might restore her might also impair her. These things are all interrelated. Now if I'd had that weight put on by spell, or even the demon, it'd be a different story, but it's all hers. They don't check you much, do they?"

"On the way in it's pretty thorough," she told him. "They want to make certain that we harbor no surprises or are under no compulsions. Out is usually pretty casual, but even if there are questions I think we can deal with it. Once we are away, though, we shall have to restore her and I think we must break with the caravan. It would not do to draw attention to ourselves by not keeping to routine. It's going to be rough and overland."

"By now she can ride very well, and she fights when she has to. Don't sell her short because of her size or her looks. She's kind of weird, though, even when she's normal. Most girls dream of growing up and becoming princesses; she's got a shot at princess and she desperately wants to be a floor scrubber or grape stomper." Quickly, but in as much detail as he could—or knew—he described Sam and her past in Tubikosa, sparing no details. When he finished, he added, "Now I'll show you the last vision I had available of her from the Jewel of Omak."

There was a slight spark and Kira felt her forehead tingle, and suddenly in her mind there was a full, three-dimensional vision of Sam, animated, even speaking.

"I can understand her low aspirations," Kira commented dryly. "The others I see there with the painted bodies?"

"The tall, skinny one with the design riot is Boday. I told you about her. The other one is Charley."

Kira gave a low whistle. "And this Sam should or could look like *that?* I can see the resemblance, almost like sisters, but you cannot really see the potential of one in the other."

"I know. Part of that is attitude. Even when she looked like that she thought she didn't. You don't have to psychoanalyze or cure her of her hangups, just get her to me in one piece."

Kira gave a faint smile. "That will be a most interesting challenge."

* * *

Medac Pasedo did a low, lazy circle in the sky and then descended towards the caravan that had pulled in and made a basic camp near the supplies building just down from the Governor's Residence. The men would stay in the residence guest quarters tonight and sleep on real beds and eat decent food.

Crim watched the big man land on the run and then slow to a stop, get his land bearings, then walk over to the train. "Hello, Medac," he said, using no formalities. When the Duke's son had been changed by the winds he had forfeited all titles and claims automatically; legally he was lower than a commoner, although here in his father's domain he was certainly a privileged person, a high-born. To Crim he was neither the creature the Akhbreed considered him nor the near-deity that the people of the refuge regarded him, but merely an equal.

"Crim, it is good to see you," Medac said sincerely. "Did you have a hard trip?"

"Only the Kudaan, as usual," the Navigator replied. "If you all weren't here I'd skip this whole place, frankly. Ovens are for cooking, not for living. About the only good thing about Kudaan is that it dries up my sinuses and any cold I might have and keeps me from catching another for weeks. Even diseases know better than to live here."

Medac did not laugh, although he also was not offended. "I love this place," he said softly. "It has a beauty and an isolation that becomes a part of you. But, enough! We have gone through this many times before. What did you bring?"

"Some of the latest fashions of Court for your mother and her ladies, and some nice trinkets here and there for the rest. Morack coffee, which is the best as you well know, and the usual shopping list of chemicals and crap for your alchemical staff. I'll be glad to get rid of those. Two of those jugs break and mix togther in a bump and you wind up falling madly in love with a cactus and becoming a joyous pincushion when you embrace your love."

The winged man laughed at that one. "You are a little bit crazy, Crim."

Crim glowered in mock menace at him. "All us navigators are mad, sonny. Ain't ye heard? We gibber around campfires and howl at the moon and all that stuff. If you ain't crazy you wouldn't be doing this kind of thing, delivering all sorts of nice stuff to folks but never enjoying any of it yourself."

"You love it. You wouldn't do anything else and you know it."

Crim nodded solemnly. "Case for madness proved, sir. Only a

madman would love it and do nothing else." He cocked his eyebrows and dropped his joking tone. "Now, anything I should know before we get all this unloaded and I pay my respects and let these characters have some fun?"

"Nothing that would concern you. We have had a few visitors in and out, some unexpected. One who showed up just yesterday was Zamofir."

Crim suddenly tensed. "Zamofir . . . here. I'd like to have a real close private talk with that little bastard. He never just drops in. What's he want?"

"My father involves me in everything concerning the refuge, but nothing beyond it, which is how I want it," the winged man responded. "From what I hear, though, he's working as a ground man for a certain somebody from up north and his rainy girlfriend. They want something, I'm sure of that. There have been presences around—up there." He looked skyward. "I've felt them rather than seen them, and I think they're more powerful after dark, but they're there."

Crim was suddenly quite grim. "You make sure you steer clear of any of *them,* son. They don't care who or what you are. Interesting that Old Horny's still lurking around here, though. Guess he got frustrated when they used some of his patrols for vulture feed a while back, so they needed some heavy artillery."

"I have charms to keep us from meeting."

"Don't depend on no charms, boy," the navigator responded firmly. "They're okay so long as you aren't in the way or considered an obstacle, but no charm will keep them off you if you get between them and what they're after." He sighed. "All right, thanks. You happen to know where that moustachioed mouse is right now?"

"In the residence somewhere. He likes the mineral baths, you know. He usually takes a long one before dinner."

Crim gave a slight grin. "Thanks, son. I owe you one."

The Navigator went back and helped supervise the unloading, while lots of beefy members of the staff were ready with carts or to tote boxes to where they belonged. It took awhile, with a break for lunch, but Crim seemed quite businesslike. It wasn't until they were just about through that he turned to his trail boss and said, "I'm feeling a bit sore today, Zel. I think I'm in the mood to take one of those mineral baths." With that he walked off and up into the Governor's Residence.

If Zamofir had been any thinner or slighter of build he would have ceased to exist. He compensated to some degree with foppishly styled long curly hair and a waxed moustache that came out several inches on both sides and curled up into perfect rolls at the ends, and by dressing in a normally flashy manner. He had a long, thin face and a prominent Roman nose and would never be taken for handsome, but he certainly was unmistakable.

He called himself an "expediter," and that was what he was. He was never directly involved in anything, but if you wanted or needed something that was immoral, illegal, or fattening and paid him a fee he would make certain that Supplier A got what was required to Customer B. It might be drugs, human cargo, black magic, bribes—you name it. If you needed a criminal gang to attack a rival and put them out of business without any possible links to you, see Zamofir. If you needed someone assassinated, well, he knew a number of free-lance assassins. And if you needed slave girls, or beefy eunuchs, or your boss turned into a toad, well, he always knew somebody who knew how to do those things. And yet nothing was ever done directly by him, and his "consultant's fee" was a matter of public record. He was a businessman, a man who sold advice. You could never prove that some theoretical discussion of criminal activities was ever linked to the actual.

And now he sat there in Governor Pasedo's bubbling, soothing mineral bath, eyes closed, just relaxing and enjoying the experience and concerned at the moment only that the tremendous heat and humidity would wilt his moustache.

Suddenly something struck him, and he felt himself pushed violently underwater and held there by strong, powerful arms until he thought his lungs would burst. Then, mercifully, the pressure ceased and he broke for air, coughing and gasping. "Who *dares* do this to *me?*" he screamed shrilly between chokes.

"Hello, Zamofir," said Crim in a light tone. "Long time no see, but not long enough."

"Crim! How *dare* you . . . !"

Two strong arms came down again but did not push. "*Shut up, little man!*" the Navigator growled. "I'm going to say one name to you and then I better get a real convincing story from you or the next time I won't let up. The name is Gallo Jahoort."

"I—I don't know what you're talking ab—"

Suddenly he was dunked back under the water, and this time it was a very close thing. When he was released again, strong arms gripped him like a vise.

"Now you listen, you little motherfucker. You know damned well what happened to Jahoort because you were *there!* I *know* you were there. Public record, after all. You always do things on the record, don't you, shit licker? A whole train gets turned into mush and who just happens to be on that particular one? None other than Zamofir himself."

"I had nothing to do with that! It was a flash flood! You know that!"

"Yeah, and I suppose that Asterial behind a perch with a fucking hundred-round-a-minute automatic gun and a whole team of cut-throats working for her and trying to take over the train was just so much hot water too, huh? Why I ought'a—"

Zamofir felt the pressure and the anger and screamed "Wait! Hold it! All right, all right! Yes, I was on that train. I always travel that way, since I am always traveling in my business and I am no Navigator. I had no knowledge of Asterial or the raiders until they appeared, I swear it!"

"Uh-huh. And you just happened to survive that disaster that killed like three-quarters of the people and animals and you just happened to wind up in Asterial's camp with her friends and then you just sat there kind of nice and proper and watched them torture and rape and kill a lot of your fellow survivors because it was no skin off your big nose."

"Yes! I mean, no! They pulled me half-drowned from that place and took me with them. I'd done business with them before and they recognized me. What could I do but watch, Crim? Pick up a stick and beat them all to death? I could do nothing but survive and keep back, that's all! They were mad, Crim. The difference between me eating and sleeping and riding out with them and winding up myself on that torture pile was a word, a gesture."

Crim stared hard at him and cursed under his breath that time was running short. He was sort of enjoying this, and there wasn't anything even the mighty Zamofir could do about it. If the Navigator's Guild ever really even *thought* that Zamofir had deliberately aided that train and one of their own to doom there was no place in all Akahlar to hide and the dying would be horribly slow.

"They're all dead, Zamofir," the Navigator said menacingly. "Even Asterial, if not dead, sure as hell isn't anywhere where she can do harm to Akahlar anymore. One little courtesan girl and a dying old man shot to pieces did it. But, of course, they make a hundred of you in backbone alone. And, now, here you are, alive and ugly as ever. How'd you get out of there, Zamofir?"

"Asterial zapped the sniper and she had the girl under her control, but most everybody else was dead and with magic around I didn't want to be there no matter what happened. While Asterial was preoccupied I slipped out and around in back of the wagons, loosed a horse, and walked out of the light. Didn't get on and ride for ten minutes. Even then, I only had on a damned sheet and was riding bareback in the dark. I almost died before I reached friends." He paused a moment. "But—how did you know I was even there, let alone that I escaped?"

"Two survivors. The gutsy courtesan and the nutty painted alchemist. They made a report to a Navigator and it didn't take long before that report was everywhere—and with your name in it."

"*Those* two. Not the fat girl and the two kids, though?"

"Why do you want to know about them?"

Zamofir, still being held, tried to shrug. "Just curious. I didn't know if they made it or not."

"Yeah? And it's not because you're looking for them for a certain horned wizard and acting as the point man on the ground for a horde of demon sky riders?"

"I know nothing of that. Just curiosity—I swear!"

Zamofir was so convincing it wasn't hard to see how the little guy survived in his world of evil.

"You're violating your own rules, Zamofir. Never be directly involved. That's a good policy. It's kept you alive and free and untouched."

"What do they mean to you anyway?" the little man wailed.

"They were passengers and they're still Company and Guild responsibility until they're found, gotten safe if they can be, and settlement is made. Now, if I find out you're actively looking for them for somebody else, then I'm going to think that maybe they were what the ambush was all about. And if I think that, and you were on the train, and now you're actively involved in this, then I'll have no choice but to spread the word. There won't be anyplace to hide. Even the Duke depends on the Guild and the Company, and maybe now I'll bring up those missing passengers with His Grace even though I wasn't going to bother. But when I heard you were here, and then I see your interest, well . . ."

Zamofir's eyes grew wide as he realized he was between a rock and a hard place here. Clearly he had already tentatively broached the subject to the Duke, and gotten no positive response, but it wasn't something that could be undone. And if the Navigators got the idea he'd caused the death of one of them . . . hell, even the most corrupt and evil of them held to a code concerning *that*.

"I didn't know about Asterial," he said slowly and sincerely. "I didn't have anything to do with Jahoort's death. Yes, I'm looking for her now, but that's separate. The price being offered is . . . *irresistible,* Crim! You've bent as many laws and flaunted as much authority as anyone. I'll split it with you, Crim!"

The big man was conscious of the clock and knew he could not remain. Still he said, "No. Not this time, Zamofir. Not for me, not for you. I have only your word on Jahoort and this now looks real bad. And I don't care what the price is or why, if you have anything to do with finding this girl and turning her over to Klittichorn's bunch there isn't a Navigator in Akahlar who will believe you." He gave the little man a violent shove into the water, letting go this time, turned, and walked out of the baths.

Zamofir, bruised and shaken, waited until the big man was well gone before painfully climbing out of the bath himself. He lay there on the floor for a moment, breathing hard, looking up at the ceiling. Damn it, he *hadn't* had anything to do with the destruction of that train! But Crim was right—if Zamofir found the fat girl and turned her over to Asterial's ally, who would believe that? He would have to risk the horned one's wrath and resign. It would be a terrible thing, but better a chance of quick, angry death than sure and certain slow death later on. No reward was worth *that* certainty . . .

"Kira, my darling!"

Duke Alon Pasedo went to the door personally and kissed her hand, then drew her close and hugged her. "It is so *good* to see you so radiant!"

Kira smiled that man-killing smile. She *was* a stunner tonight, in a stunning sparkling burgundy slit dress and matching heels, golden jewelry and made up just right.

"You're just an old smoothie, Your Grace," she responded with a laughing tone. "You would swear we didn't meet like this every three months or so."

"Ah! It is because it is so seldom! You are the only one I have ever known who tempts me with lustful and unfaithful thoughts at the mere sight of you. Come—sit! We have a special meal in your honor tonight and we will sample our finest vintages and our best liqueurs."

"I doubt if Your Grace would still love me in the morning," she responded a bit playfully, then allowed her chair to be pulled out and then herself seated.

The Duke always outdid himself for her visits, and she thoroughly enjoyed them, too. She knew, too, that in his own way he was a man of great internal honor and would keep his lust platonic. Not so the other males in the overly large entourage that always dined with them. She was the object of every man's lust in that room and every woman's envy and she knew it and she loved every furtive glance and inattentive gaffe that situation caused. Even the

Duchess kept one of those cold bird's eyes of hers always on Kira, not at all pleased with the way her husband acted when the beauty was around.

So far none of these people's fantasies had been fulfilled. Not that she was averse to a bit of sex when she was in the mood and really wanted the man, or when it was to her advantage for other reasons, but until now that situation had not come up in the Duke's refuge. The only really good-looking man in the court was Medac, and that smacked a bit of kinkiness. The others were the average dirty old men.

Tonight, though, she didn't brush off Director Kano Layse's clumsy under-the-table passes at her leg, and she paid him far more attention than she ever did, to which he responded by getting very, very hot in his pants. Layse was, after all, the Director, and he was also what Akahlar called a physician, although that term here meant more "healer" or "medical magician" than anything else. He was, however, a better administrator than magician, which was why he was Director. Better to have a man who could run things and understand what the smarter, more talented, more powerful ones below him were doing and talking about than to have your best magician wasted on administration.

The evening went quite well, and there were songs and poems and lots of gossip, and she never once brought up Zamofir or the fat girl. She didn't know if Zamofir had really been involved in Jahoort's debacle or not, and she didn't really care. Crim's anger and suspicion were real, but the major purpose was to convincingly remove the competition's man on the ground. If Zamofir was here at all for that reason, then they were just in time, and time was what Crim's fearsome explosion had bought. The mere fact that Zamofir, officially a guest and holding talks with the Duke, had skipped the banquet was evidence enough that, at least for now, the ploy had worked.

One of these days, though, she was going to stick a stiletto between the little man's ribs and twist slowly, or Crim was going to snap that bobbing neck, and therein rid Akahlar of at least one source of contagion.

At the end of the festivities, when they were going for the door, she whispered to Layse, "Director, I should like to speak with you privately. Will you walk me to my room?"

"Delighted," the magician responded, certainly meaning it. They made their good nights to the Duke and the others and walked out and down the hall. It wasn't until they were in the quiet of the residence wing and in fact in front of her door that she said, "Director, I'm afraid a bit of a problem has arisen and you are the only one who might help. Would you mind coming in for a minute?"

The Director, who clearly had a totally different line of thought in mind that included that invitation, responded, "Of course."

She sat in the chair facing the mirror and he sat on the bed, the only other place to sit. She kicked off her shoes and began removing her makeup while watching him in the corner of the mirror.

"Director, I'm afraid His Grace is in a very awkward position, one that will cause him certain embarrassment and perhaps far more."

"Oh—what? Yes?"

"About three months ago, a certain young woman wandered into here who was under the protection of an Akhbreed sorcerer, and was mistaken for just another poor injured girl needing help. She could not tell about this because she did not know whom to trust."

The Director was now partly listening, even though it was hard to keep his eyes off her. "The fat girl with the two children."

"Yes. I am happy we do not have to play games," she added, while loosening her dress.

"That scoundrel Zamofir was also asking about them, that's all."

She sighed. "Then we *do* play games after all. I am not a patient woman—Kano. Unlike Zamofir and his employer, we *know* she is here. I was sent—ahead—to see if something could be done to keep disaster from befalling this nice place."

His voice was trembling, but he replied, "I will not betray my Duke even for a night with you." She stood up and the dress fell away. "*Oh gods!*" he almost sobbed.

She reached for a robe and donned it, although taking care not to conceal very much, and perched down next to him on the bed and gave him a seductive pout.

"My darling Kano, there is no betrayal here. There would be to Zamofir and his crew, but not to *me*. You see how it is. The sorcerer Boolean *knows*. If we can't settle this, then he'll have to contact and make public demands of and embarrass the Duke, and the Duke, to retain his honor, will have to deny it all, and then the full fury of an Akhbreed sorcerer will be brought on all within and this will all be destroyed. No more refuge. No more governor. Nothing but all the changewind victims who survived wandering the ruins. And even honor and reputation will also be crushed, for her mate is still alive and will lodge a formal inquiry with the Kingdom."

Sex wasn't off Kano Layse's mind, but it paled before the vision she was so softly and gently painting, a vision he could fully accept when he heard the name of the sorcerer involved.

"Good lord! W—what can be done'? You know His Grace can never admit to anyone what was done, even though it was an honest mistake made out of compassion and nothing else. No! If this were true surely she would have told us."

"Uh-uh. You remember that train that she was from? The one that got attacked and finally destroyed? They were after this girl. Just her. To kill her. You think she could just wander in here, ignorant of the Duke and the nature of this place, and *trust* anyone? Better to just leave and then contact the sorcerer."

He was sweating now, and he nodded, absently. "But—she got the strongest potion. We—we knew she was from the Outplane, so it was full treatment. Absolute obliteration and hypnotic compulsions to conform."

"Boolean says that there is no such thing as a potion that magic cannot undo."

"Yes, yes. In the strictest sense that's true, but this formulation is powerful because it goes to the heart of the affliction, as it were. The pain, the loneliness, the fragile ego and poor self-image . . . Our diagnosis was correct, damn it! She *wanted* to forget, wanted to become someone else, to be loved, to feel important, needed, for herself, and she didn't care if it was on the level of a base peasant. If she had, she would have developed differently. Many of our staff here had the same potion and all began as base peasants, but they could not find happiness at that level, so we allowed them to rise until they were at the level that met their basic inner needs. Not her. She loves the communalism, the tribal identity, the basic life with few demands and no responsibility. And the longer she's been there the more thoroughly she's become one of them."

"It is no longer her choice—it was *never* her choice, which is part of her problem I suspect—nor yours, nor mine, nor the Duke's. The freak rains that have been doing so much damage here will continue and increase in severity."

His head snapped up and he stared at her. "*She* is the cause of that?"

"The magnet that draws them, anyway. Klittichorn has Stormriders above, just waiting for it to happen again, and you have not had a nightmare as bad as the Stormriders running roughshod through this place to get at her. She cannot remain, and if you give her to Klittichorn then Boolean will destroy this place in his fury."

He was thinking now, all thoughts of an assignation gone. "But how do I know you are from this sorcerer?"

She got up, went over to an old, weathered leather saddle pouch, rummaged through it, and withdrew a small piece of paper. On it was a complex mathematical formula, written in the Akhbreed characters. She handed it to Layse without a word and he stared at it for more than a minute and his mouth dropped slightly.

"Do you know what this is?"

"I can't make sense of any of it," she admitted, "although it is in my hand. But I know what it is."

"But there is something missing! A variable not provided!"

"I have it. And you shall have it if we can work something out."

His hands trembled as he held the card. "This is the highest level of Akhbreed sorcery, far beyond anything lessers could manage. But—what would you have me do?"

"We need the girl, and we need a means of getting her safely and quietly out of here when we leave at dawn the day after tomorrow. A sample of the potion and whatever records you have on her would also help. Remove her and you remove all threat to the Duke or this place. She never was here after all."

He nodded. "I can pull her after work tomorrow to the clinic for a medical check. It's routine, although she's not really due as yet. We could keep her on a pretext, sedated perhaps. The most obvious way to have her voluntarily go would be a love potion, but that would have to be compounded—we do not keep any here—and I'm afraid of how it might mate with the present alchemy. It might cause even more dire personality changes, particularly in combination with that spell of legal mating she already has. Mild, transitory hypnotics might not give you enough time, since they wear off unevenly depending on the individual. Only a strong hypnotic, one requiring an antidote, is sure. She would be an automaton, requiring that you tell her everything to do, without thought. And if you lost the antidote, she would remain that way unless you returned here, since all of our preparations are proprietary."

"That will do," she told him. "I've had experience with that sort of potion before. But can her mind be restored?"

"It's only been three months. The potion does not actually erase—there is no known way to do that without damaging a lot more, actually turning an adult into a mental infant. What it does is block *access* to any past memories. The new personality is built by simply being in and around what you want them to be. Access is by exposure. She has been around only peasants of our sort, so she was able to retrieve and use all the words and phrases and such that they use and she hears. Then she adopts that culture, that belief system, that mode of speech, that way of life. The longer the period that this lasts, the more permanent it becomes and the brain, not accessing the old information, begins to stick it where it cannot be found, like memories of infanthood and fine details of our past. The more she wants what she has, the more she is comfortable that way, the more rapid and total the process of eliminating the past and its knowledge becomes. Eventually, it is irrelevant and irretrievable."

"How long does that take?"

He shrugged. "It varies. There's the age—the less to forget the faster—and various psychological and physiological factors. Those girls who came in with her, for example. They're happy here now, they're placed with loving families, and they are much better off. By now both are probably irretrievable. Your girl—I don't know. She's young, which works against her, but she's also from the Outplane, which makes it an unpredictable factor. You might well get all, or at least most, of the memories back to one degree or another, but the personality—that is a different matter. She had a very weak ego and self-image before; she has a very strong one now. I can only guarantee she will be different."

Kira nodded. "That's all right. I was asked to bring her in, not turn back any clocks." She leaned over and kissed him on the forehead. "You have been a *big, big* help. I won't forget it."

He stood up. "I'll need to have an alchemist in on this. We keep antidotes around but none of the strong potions, for safety's sake."

She stood, too, went back to the bag and pulled out another small card. "I think this will silence any alchemical questions. I trust you to be able to fake any convincing reasons that might also be needed."

He looked at it. "Some sort of chemical formula. Not my line. What is it?"

"A compound that can be made from common materials. It hardens and can be colored and then molded into flesh, and while there is no feeling I am told it will make the biggest scar look and feel like a tiny scratch—and it can be permanently bonded to skin, even breathe like skin."

He gave a low whistle. "Yes, that will be most—helpful. But there is one more condition to my doing this for you."

"Yes?"

"All of them upstairs saw us together, saw us leave. The porter saw us enter together. Please—could we just—pretend—that something happened here?"

She gave him her sweetest, sexiest smile. "It'll be our little secret," she whispered.

* * *

"That's *her?*" Kira asked as she peered into the low and primitive adobe clinic used by the field workers from a safe office. Layse nodded.

The young woman they were watching was the proof that both *short* and *large* could be used to describe the same person. She was certainly quite fat, and no area from the face to the hips, thighs, ass, stomach, and breasts had escaped excess. And yet she was certainly muscular—the arms took very little work to exhibit an amazing set of muscles, and the legs when they were tensed showed much the same.

Her face and skin were burned almost black by the long periods of hard work in the sun, and the skin also had an almost leatherlike toughness to it, as most of the peasants had. It also seemed that her lips had been sun-bleached to an unnatural pale, almost colorless point like her nails, but that might have been just the contrast. At least something in her ancestry had protected her from the most dangerous horrors of this climate, at least for now, but no one who had been out that long could remain totally unaffected.

She had long, straight dark hair down below her shoulders, which did in fact give her a more impish appearance and make her look more human. It was not well trimmed and curled up at the ends, but the sun had created an odd and shifting pattern of light streaks in it that might well be white.

"Nobody grows that much hair in three months," Kira noted.

"A potion. It's a common one and harmless, since if it doesn't work you can always cut it again. It's one of a number of innocent things we allow them to think they're stealing or lifting from us that does no harm and makes them happy. The rest is natural, a consequence of spending over a thousand hours in the sun. You can see it on the others, too."

She nodded. *What a life,* she thought sadly. Still, "She certainly seems bubbly and outgoing," she noted.

"Yes. She was rather quiet and somewhat withdrawn with us before, and I suspect with everyone she didn't know well, but without pressures and with a large tribal family she's been quite extroverted and extremely uninhibited. Physical differences aren't a minus here, you see, and there's no pressure on her. She's strong as a bull, too, which gives her complete self-confidence. My people have seen her hold up the end of a wagon while a wheel was fixed for quite some time without breathing hard, and at Endday she picked up a big, bruising fellow built like a stone tower and head and shoulders bigger than she."

"How'd you get her in here?"

"Slipped a small powder in the field drink today that gave her a nicely timed case of the runs. The treatment potion she'll be given as soon as the last of the other patients leaves is the hypnotic. It will cause some dizziness and she'll be told to lie down. Then I'll dismiss the staff."

She nodded. "We must get her out tomorrow. Zamofir is certain to be around somewhere, just more circumspect, and we have our heavenly host to consider as well."

Layse went over and opened a small case and removed two sealed containers, each with a label on it. "This gold one is the antidote," he told her. "The marks on it represent degrees of recovery. Half dose will represent the more classic hypnotic trance, where the subject is aware but suggestible. All of it should be swallowed for complete recovery, although she will go into a very deep sleep for a couple of hours while it flushes out the remnants. The light red potion is about forty percent of the dose of the amnesia potion that she received. Don't let anyone drink it and particularly not her. That kind of dose on top of the one she had would probably produce a childlike individual with no memories, no self to speak of. Basically an animal."

"Don't worry. We're not out to steal your formula or use or abuse it. We just want a means of getting her back without harming her."

"Where will you take her?" he asked, curious.

She smiled. "That is something it is better for you not to know." She looked back out through the peephole. "I think everybody else is gone. She's taken her medicine like a good girl and they're helping her over to a cot."

Layse nodded and was out the door. Timing was crucial here; there was no sense in having to convince the medic here that there wasn't anything untoward going on. He and Layse talked in animated terms for a while, then seemed very chummy, and finally the medic picked up a file on his desk and handed it to the Director, who went through it absently, then told the man to go, he'd take care of this.

The medic looked uncertain for a moment but didn't really want to argue for more work. It had been a long day, and he had staff privileges at the residence. He left, and Layse sat looking through the file intently, almost forgetting Kira. She waited patiently; no sense in showing up and then have the medic or somebody come back because they forgot something and see her.

Finally he sighed, put down the folder, and motioned for her to come in. She did so, then looked over at the young woman who was out cold on the cot, dead to the world. "Anything the matter?" Kira asked him. "I saw you studying the folder."

"Medical history. Environmental adjustments were the first priority so we didn't do much of one when she joined us, just the usuals to make sure she could stand the work and was as healthy as she seemed. There was supposed to be another one, a more thorough follow-up, a few weeks later but she seemed to be adjusting so well and the case load is huge, so it wasn't done. This was the first physical she had. She's gained eleven and a quarter halgs, which sounds high until you realize it's all muscle and some of it is fat into muscle conversion as well. If that's not allowed to go back to fat it won't be serious."

"Enough for me. I only weigh forty-three myself. Even Crim weighs only ninety-two. It's a good thing we won't have to *lift* her. Any medical problems we should know about other than that?"

"Only one, but it is really going to complicate your situation if you have a very long journey."

Her eyebrows rose. "Yes?"

"She's three months pregnant."

That was a stunner. "Oh, *great!*" Kira muttered. "Just what we needed. Does she know?"

"I doubt it. If she underwent any morning sickness she didn't report it, and who would notice any of the other minor symptoms out in the fields? It probably won't start to show until the end of the sixth month, and who's going to notice a bigger belly on *her* until it's well along? But it will weaken her, slow her down, there will be biochemical changes, that sort of thing."

"Yeah, but what you're telling me is that I've got six months or less to get her where she's going." She sighed. "Any idea whose? Somebody here, perhaps?"

"Possible, but doubtful. They don't usually take advantage of newcomers here, and it's normally a few weeks before there's any real social activity. From what you say it's unlikely she had any earlier male trysts on the move, so that leaves the rape."

Kira sighed and looked at her. "Poor kid. No way to get rid of it?"

He looked a bit shocked, but recovered. "Um, not without lots of work and recovery, no. Not *safely*, anyway, and the other, cruder methods at this stage risk infection, even possible death. If you take her tonight, either your sorcerer has to come up with something or she's going to have the kid."

The woman nodded. "Well, I'll let Boolean decide that one." She turned. "Think she's ready now?"

"Oh, yes. And the loose bowels was a one-time thing, really. Just a super laxative. However, she'll have no bladder control in this state, so remember that. Have her try going often."

Kira turned and walked over to the unconscious woman. She had come in directly from a day in the fields and she was filthy and smelled like shit. There was no way around that for now. "Misa, open your eyes, sit up, and sit on the side of the bed."

The eyes opened, but they were blank, as if still asleep, and she did exactly as instructed.

"Now listen to me," she said carefully. "You will hear only the sound of my voice and no other voice, so my voice is all that you will obey for now. Tomorrow, a man will come to you and say the words, 'I am Crim, obey me as well,' and you will hear him say that and then obey him as well as me and hear either his voice or my own but no one else's. Do you understand that? Answer."

"Yes," she replied dully, in a voice that was startlingly low.

"All right, now stand up. You will follow me, three paces behind me, and whatever I do you shall do until I tell you different. If I sit, you sit. If I walk, you follow. If I stop, you stop. Understand? Answer."

"Yes."

Kira checked to see that she had the antidote and the sample. "Does she have anything to wear except those filthy black panties she's got on?"

Layse shrugged. "Sorry, not here. Back in her room, yes, but there's no way to unobtrusively get to it now."

"All right, all right, I'll have to make do. Getting out of here is the only real priority right now, and putting some distance between us and the forces above. Can you put out all the lights?"

"Of course, but it will be pretty dark if I do."

"I am a creature of the darkness," she told him. "Still, there's enough residual light from other sources for her to see me. Do it."

He killed the lights, and she waited for Misa's eyes to grow accustomed to the dark.

"Misa, can you see me now? Answer."

"Yes."

"Then follow and obey."

Kano Layse suddenly had a thought. "Wait! What about the missing variable in the formula?"

"You have it now. It is on the same paper as the rest of the formula. If we leave this jurisdiction the variable will fade in and be like the rest of the ink. If we are betrayed, or caught while still in the district, the paper will burst into flame. That is fair enough."

Layse sat back down in the dark, disgusted. He had every intention of betraying them on this. He felt like a traitor to the Duke in this matter, but that formula—when he saw it, and knew what it was—was, well, irresistible. Tomorrow he'd go down to the labs and start tinkering. In a couple of weeks he'd come up with it, and his star would really shine and his position would be quite secure. But the price he paid still made him feel guilty. Creating Misa was the right and moral thing to do; he was still convinced of it. And while restoration was theoretically possible, he had never seen or done it, and no one he had known could do it, either. The gods knew what poor Misa would become now.

Getting out of there had been the easy part, although finding a shipping crate that would fit her without harming her was a real pain. The next morning, just at dawn, Crim had the caravan put together and everyone was ready to move. The cases of the Duke's private wines provided nice cover, and would bring a decent profit at some point.

Crim was not yet ready to feel safe, but as the mileage built up between him and the Duke he began to feel a little bit better.

They followed the river trail, as they always did, at neither a faster nor slower clip than anyone would expect, but with an eye to the canyon walls and particularly to side canyons and old slides which might hide ambushers. Thanks to agreements between the wilder denizens of this area and both the Duke and the Navigators, there was generally little risk so long as you were known and official and all that, but there was always the chance of newcomers and some of the folks in this country were just plain crazy.

By nightfall they were camped at one of the safety zones, a campground that was agreed to be neutral territory of sorts and thus safe. It was only a theoretical safety, of course, and they would have guards and spells and all sorts of things for insurance, but in all these trips they'd never been hit anywhere in this area. Anybody inclined to violate this place would also be too afraid of Yobi to actually do it. Only the crazy, and Klittichorn's bunch, might try it, and the latter only if they suspected something.

They were about thirty miles from the Duke's now, a fair distance in these parts but not really comfortable, not when the Duke's son flew with ease over great distances by day and there were Stormriders about at night. The latter were not strong without a storm from which to draw energy, but they could see well enough and if one could get a message off, they had a mistress who could whip up a storm of any fury desired. And even though the canyon now was broad, nobody on the caravan wanted to think about a real gully washer in the area.

Kira couldn't risk going out alone into this in search of who she wanted. Not even Crim would be really safe in this place, not alone, or particularly not with the girl.

They had checked on her from time to time. The crew knew better than to ask questions about such things; they all had hands in one shady thing or another now and then. Every once in a while Crim would climb on the wagon, crawl back to her, open the side of the crate, check her condition, have her eat and drink, and, using a bucket as an ersatz chamber pot, have her go if she could as well. They didn't catch that last need every time, and she was getting pretty gamy in there, but there was no way around it. To command someone to hold it invited forgetfulness, and you could cause a kidney to rupture or bowel blockage by doing so.

Now, Kira could only wait, although she decided to take the risk and attend to one matter. She brought her obedient woman to the river, and commanded that she remove all clothing left and discard it and then bathe completely. "Misa" was no work of art when she was done, but at least she didn't smell so bad.

Everyone was fast asleep except for Kira and one other guard, both of whom kept pistols on their hips and rifles at the ready nearby just in case, when someone came. It was the guard who first saw or heard or felt something, drawing on a near-sixth sense born of long trail experience. Kira had expected someone, but not old Yobi herself, who *never* left her cave. Yet, here she was, with two very inhuman attendants, slithering in, long ears twitching, pulling herself with the aid of two strong-looking canes.

Kira looked over at the rather stupefied guard. "It's all right, Garl. I know them and I've been expecting—someone."

Yobi came straight for her, and stopped when she saw "Misa" apparently asleep under a tree. The dark woman was hard to see in the shadows, but Yobi didn't use the same sight as normal people did.

"So," she rasped. "That is the source of all our machinations. My, but there is little that hasn't been done to that poor girl. I see the demon spell, with its inhuman mathematical insanity, and the marriage bond as well, thin as it is, trailing like a spider's web. And the potions, layered this way and that. The hypnotic is easy, then the memory one. Oh, my! That's a nasty one, that is. And under it all, what strange and unnatural *power* lurks! The threads that run wispily to the north are firm. Yes, yes, she is definitely the one, poor soul."

Yobi sighed and looked up at Kira. "Kid, this one's gonna be a real bitch to do."

Kira stared at her. "Do you think you can bring her back?"

"Not me. Mister Smartass Greenpants, maybe, with my help. You have the sample and the antidote?"

"Yes, in my bag. I'll get them."

"Bring that idiot sorcerer's calling stone, too. We're gonna have a long night here."

"You think it is wise to do it here? This close?"

"Of *course* it's not, you silly, blithering idiot, but if I can't recover from old Horny the Fart and his minions as long as I need I don't deserve to still be here!"

7
Stormrider

"The time has come to run swiftly and well," Yobi said to Dorion. "Just today that little shit Zamofir is due at Hodamoc's. Once the moustachioed twit hears the description of Charley and all that transpired, the full hue and cry will be out. They will even come to me to try and make a deal or somehow threaten me if they think they can. I'm pretty well invulnerable, I think, but they can cause a lot of trouble."

"We've worked on the disguises pretty well," the magician responded. "It's a delicate thing to figure out something that's effective but not *too* effective. That crazy one, Boday, is also pretty good with many kinds of weapons, including the whip and cross-bow. Charley, of course, is much more limited, but she'll make it."

The sorceress nodded. "Yes, they are a strange pair, this Charley and her Sam. Charley has already overcome things that would have beaten many a lesser person, but never have I seen such a determined and survival-oriented ego. She adapts incredibly. Already the blindness is simply accepted as an inconvenience and she is using her other senses more and doing much with confidence—including knowing her limits. She uses the cat's vision sparingly, when she needs it, instead of trying to make the animal substitute eyes. Yes, she is incredibly strong and yet the irony is that she believes herself to be incredibly weak. Somehow her ideal is to be a man with a better tailor and more clothing options." The old one sighed.

"Now, this other one—this Sam," Yobi continued, "she's a real mess. Charley does not understand that it is perfectly fine to enjoy being a courtesan so long as it was a valid choice on her part. Few men have the courage that she showed in tracking down Asterial and her whole gang in hostile country with only two pistols. This Sam, though—I'm beginning to wonder if the breakthrough will ever really come with her. She wants to run and hide. She wants to be docile. She'd be perfectly fine as a slave or some peasant. She wants to avoid all responsibility and all pressures. Even if I can pull her back from Pasedo's mental acids, I don't know if she'll *ever* have the will and temperament to take on the Storm Princess. That is another reason for keeping Charley alive, Dorion. The only act of bravery and will, the assumption of risk and danger, was when Sam rushed to save her friend. She draws strength and resolve from Charley. So it is not just as a decoy that our girl is important. I think she will be essential in the ultimate battle."

Dorion nodded. "I think I see what you mean. So how do we work this and who does what?"

"I, obviously, can go nowhere in the flesh, and I don't have an acolyte I'd trust on something like this. I've made arrangements to get them through with some various people who owe me in ways they dare not refuse my will, but they will need a native guide and helper, as it were, preferably one with some magical talents, odd and arcane as those talents might be, and a full Akhbreed citizen able to move freely throughout Akahlar."

Dorion stared at her a moment, then gulped. "You mean—me?"

"Oh, good! I'm happy you volunteer. Saves me the trouble of putting pressure on you."

"Hey, wait! I'm not—I mean, damn it, Yobi! You know the limits of my magic! That's why I wound up here in the first place! I'm in lousy shape; I'm a poor shot and even poorer with any other weapons. What the hell good would I be?"

"You're streetwise, as they call it in the cities. You think fast when you have to, sweet Dorion, and you're basically trustworthy and with a strong sense of honor that is almost nonexistent around here. That is worth more than muscle. I can command muscle, but never honor."

Dorion thought about it. "You mean—me? Alone, with those two, for all that distance?"

Yobi gave her cackling laugh. "Yes, indeed. I'm transferring complete control to you, but their Master will be Boolean himself. That means that even if someone should get to you, they would be useless and always driven to Boolean. Frankly, I'd remove their slavery if I thought it would be productive, but Boday needs discipline or she'll be more hindrance than help, and Charley needs the same external discipline because of her beauty and her blindness. And so long as they have those rings no one is going to abduct or make off with them, since they know their prize is both useless and dangerous. Nor do I want her wandering off lost somewhere, particularly out of fear. That's a very real possibility when she discovers, as she must, that she is not exactly blind."

Dorion, whose eyes were also little use because of the magical radiations of his apprenticeship but who was of sufficient power that he saw, as Yobi did, by other means, understood what the sorceress meant. This kind of blindness shifted the eyes rather than destroying them. As Charley would discover, there were many things she could now see that before she either could not see or could not see properly, nor could any sighted person. But seeing on a magical plane often meant one saw what one wished one could not see.

Dorion sighed. "All right. When?"

"Tonight. After dark. I have horses ready capable of taking you into Mashtopol itself in just a couple of days. From that point I have a list of contacts and methods along the route that you must memorize. You'll have sufficient supplies for the initial journey and sufficient money along the way for whatever you need. Since enslavement of an Akhbreed is technically illegal, although nobody really cares, I've had papers drawn up showing them to be indentured under a spell certified by a ranking sorcerer—the sort of thing everybody makes up to make this kind of thing legal and proper. Officially, you and your superiors performed a service of magic the price of which was indenture. That makes their enslavement a consequence of their own free choice, and thus legal. Gad, how I love bureaucracy! You can commit murder and pillage so long as the paperwork's right!"

He nodded soberly, thinking of the job. "All right, so what if we somehow manage, and I admit I'll be shocked if we do, to get them to Boolean? What do I do then? I mean, I'm not exactly a stranger to Boolean, and he wasn't too thrilled with me the last time I saw him."

"All is forgiven and forgotten if you deliver them," Yobi assured him. "After that, it's up to you. You can transfer their control to Boolean and get out with a whole skin from this mess—and with a nice reward to boot—or you can stick it out if you prefer and if you and Boolean can stand each other for that long. That's the other reason why it must be you, though. Others might be able to shepherd them to the boundaries of Masalur, but you are from there and you know the region better than any other that I have. If anyone can sneak them in right past Klittichorn's nose, you can."

"Yes," the magician sighed. "That is true enough. If I live that long."

* * *

Both women looked very different from the way they had looked in years. To eliminate the butterfly design outline, they had treated Charley with a potion that triggered the release of all melanin within each cell and added it if it wasn't there. The result was a uniform chocolate brown complexion that suited her quite well. The process could be alchemically reversed but was otherwise stable, permanent, and self-renewing. Her hair had been cut to shoulder length and given a great deal of curl, and it had also been colored a reddish blond that contrasted greatly with her skin tone. She was still sexy and gorgeous and all that, but she was no longer obviously a courtesan but rather an Akhbreed colonial who probably had her hair dyed.

The physical disguise was a deliberate and subtle choice. There were a lot of pretty girls in Akahlar, but the blind blonde would not be recognized without a very close inspection as one of the wanted women—but she would be remembered. The object was really to be recognized, but too late to do any good and not without a lot of work.

Because she was "indentured" to a magician, she wasn't a free agent and thus wasn't as well expected to live up to the local dress codes. This was a relief to her, really; it had been so long since she'd worn a lot of clothes that she wasn't all that sure she could abide a complete and cover-all type outfit, and she certainly had doubts that she could ever again stand to wear a pair of shoes.

The clothing thing didn't bother her—she always dreamed of having the body to dress lightly and sexily—but she remembered spending many fond hours shopping for shoes.

In point of fact, she knew that slaves were fairly common among the Akhbreed nobility and many others important enough and rich enough to afford to create them. It was somewhat ironic that the very colonial system made them inevitable. Since none but Akhbreed could enter the hub cities, all non-Akhbreed were excluded if you lived in a hub. But the level of obedience and service slavery provided to feed upper-class egos was simply too tempting to ignore, and the strictures of the society were such that if you didn't fall into the hands of the criminal element but were still outcast from tribe and clan, you could wind up commercial property. As erotic as Charley was, and blind to boot, there was only one assumption possible as to what sort of slave she was, and she would have to dress the part: Bare breasted, with the little beaded bottom she'd been wearing when taken from Hodamoc, and with a loose robe of semitransparent gauzelike material worn generally untied. To those were added dull bronze earrings, matching bracelets and anklets, and a thin necklace of braided chain.

Boday was still tall and lean, but she didn't look so exotic when shorn of her elaborate mass of tattoos. In fact, she really didn't look all that bad. She had nice curves, a tight ass, and surprisingly smooth skin, although without all the artistic pyrotechnics her breasts looked rather small for all their firmness.

The absence of the tattoos caused such a dramatic difference in her that they didn't feel they had to do much more. The only thing they worked on was her hair, although she hadn't forgiven them yet for not allowing her to dye it some nice rainbow colors. Instead it had become thick, wiry, and incredibly curly, and they had grown it out almost to a manelike stature. Through Shadowcat's eyes, Charley was able to see at least the basics and thought Boday resembled nothing so much as some *National Geographic* shot of some African warrior woman. With her Mediterranean-type features and all those tattoos and straight, short black hair she'd looked very different; it took this to see the real Boday—more black African than exotic Lebanese, for example.

Boday even admitted that this was how her own natural hair had looked. She had straightened it and lengthened it alchemically before.

But if she could no longer look so exotic, Boday was determined to dress that way and had designed and helped make most of her outfit. It was kind of a revealing leather bodice with silver rivetlike studs, long leather boots with fairly high heels, and a matching headband. Charley thought she looked like something escaped from an S & M porno movie, but, somehow, it suited Boday just fine. The whip, and the leather holster with its pistol, only completed the impression. Charley thought that when Boday started to sweat and move around a lot in that outfit it was going to become very uncomfortable, but the mad artist was not to be denied at least this much unless commanded to do so.

Dorion dressed in a mud-brown cotton outfit that matched his robes but was a more conventional shirt and trousers, along with a broad felt brown hat with a crease in the middle. He had his robes and his magic paraphernalia with him, but the regulation outfit wasn't practical for a long horse journey. Neither, of course, was either outfit the two women were wearing, but right now that couldn't be helped. The first object was to get them through the tightest squeeze, which was Mashtopol, with the place surely swarming with Klittichorn's agents. Once through the bottleneck, they might be able to change not only clothing styles but a lot else—perhaps might be forced to do so.

"I want to get a few things clear at the outset," he told them. "First of all, keep the abject slave stuff for the public, when strangers or any others are around. When it's just we three, you can dispense with the Master stuff and just talk to me pretty much as you would anyone else. Feel free to make comments and ask what you need. If I get sick of it I can always just order you to shut up, so don't abuse it."

He looked at them and at the horses and knew he really didn't want this shit but, somehow, he was stuck. Well, he'd been the one who'd started all this rolling—even though she wasn't even the real Storm Princess double, damn it!

"Now, Charley, I know you've been practicing but you're not going to be great as a free rider and you know it," he continued. "Your horse is old friends with the other two. It'll follow me, and that's where you'll be—just behind me. Boday, you're behind Charley and since you've got the weapons it's up to you to use your own judgment unless I countermand it specifically. Don't wait for an order if an attack or real threat appears, and make Charley's protection your first priority. Remember, I have some magical powers and they've gotten me this far alive and whole, so Charley's the one who needs your help. If I need it, I'll yell loud enough. Understood, both of you?"

Charley nodded, as did Boday. Charley was a bit fascinated by something that hadn't been so until now, but which was both inexplicable and intriguing. She found that, somehow, she could *see* Dorion—not with Shadowcat, but with her eyes. Not really him, but an odd, wriggling glowing shape that was mostly deep reds but occasionally showed or flashed other colors as well. This against the eternal gray nothingness was disconcerting; she could not see Boday or any of the landscape or the horses at all.

There were, however, a few other things in view. An odd yellowish glow from a point about eye level and off to the right—Dorion's saddlebag, maybe, with the magic stuff in it? And Shadowcat—Shadowcat was a small deep lavender fuzz. She sent her mind to the cat's, and saw, from a very low perspective, that Dorion was where the deep red was, and that there was certainly a horse where the yellow came from.

There was also a curious wispy light red string, almost like a single strand from a spider's web, that continually twisted and turned and seemed to go off into the distance. She realized suddenly that it came from Boday, but what it was and where it went was a mystery. Boday herself was in no way visible—but the wispy strand helped locate her.

She was still blind for all practical purposes, but she began to realize that the radiations that had taken her sight had perhaps given her another, stranger one. Was this, then, what the magicians and sorcerers saw with their own eyes, or did they see clearly what she saw as only bizarre and pulsating shapes and colors? It didn't matter, but it was at least something she didn't have before, and it would allow her to keep Dorion in sight no matter what the light. She could not use the magic, but she could see it, and somehow that gave her a lift.

They helped her on her horse and she settled in like the lifelong horsewoman she was. When they were down on the ranch many times when she was but a girl they had used their familiar horses and closed their eyes and tried all sorts of games and tricks that way. This wasn't so bad, as long as you didn't have to gallop for your life.

They had made a sort of sling for Shadowcat, which the cat had taken to right away. Clearly there was some magical thing now residing within or controlling the cat, for he was quite loyal and willing to submit to a number of indignities.

"I am surprised that Mistress Yobi did not come to see us off," Boday noted, taking advantage of the new freedom of speech.

Dorion chuckled. "Mistress Yobi is pretty damned busy right now, and part of it is making some arrangements for our future security—if we get that far. We've already delayed too long and it's going to be tight. One of Klittichorn's agents is right now a guest at Hodamoc's, and it won't take that little moustachioed son of a bitch too long to put two and two together."

Charley's head came up. "Moustachioed? Is that the word I understood in translation? Can this one you speak of be called Zamofir?"

Dorion looked surprised. "You know him?"

"The spineless swine of a mud demon!" Boday spat. "He was with our wagon train and then with the animals who tortured and defiled us! How much would Boday *love* to get his balls in her grasp and squeeze hard—if he has any balls."

"He's a freelance scum," Dorion told them. "Expensive, though, careful, effective, and, most important, he stays bought. The Horned One has offered him a bundle for you two and your friend, it's said, and he'll work like a demon to find us. If they've given him a bottomless money account, as they probably have, he can be a pretty nasty enemy, although, as I said, he's careful. He must have slipped up on that wagon train business, because he almost never gets close enough personally to get caught in anybody's hands." He sighed. "I'm not too worried about here to Mashtopol. I know this territory well and few will dare risk Yobi's wrath. But pray that your new look fools them in Mashtopol. It's so damned corrupt we can't count on anybody or anything."

Riding by night and sleeping by day made the journey much easier, since they didn't have to contend with the hot sun, but they could never have done it on their own unless they'd stuck to the road. Dorion, however, seemed to know every back trail and crack and crevice, and seemed to see as well in the dark as Boday did in daylight. Charley envied him that kind of second sight.

She liked Dorion, too. Oh, he was chubby and he got out of breath in a hurry when he had to do anything energetic, but, what the hell. So he wasn't Mister Wonderful with the body of a barbarian and the head of a Greek god. He seemed a pretty nice, level-headed guy, and it both impressed and somewhat puzzled Charley that, with them subject to his every whim, he had taken no advantage at all of that situation. She wasn't sure about Boday, but she sure as hell wouldn't have minded a therapeutic fuck or two in the wilderness. She began to wonder if the magician might not be as gay as Hodamoc.

Still, when you can't even see the sights and you're strung out in a line so conversation's pretty limited, it gets pretty damned boring pretty fast. Charley began to imagine herself, as she sometimes did, going back home at this point. It had been so long, and she'd gone through so much.

Hi, Mom! Hi, Dad! I'm back! I found a career I really like as a high-class hooker. I'm blind, and, oh, yes, I'm now black, and I'm a slave girl who dresses like a porno belly dancer, but other than that, everything's just fine. Oh, I almost forgot. You remember my best friend Sam? She got real fat and married another woman . . .

Their parents' sense of loss would still be there, of course, and maybe she and Sam had their faces on a million milk cartons, but there was no going back. Not now. The trouble was, it remained to be seen whether or not there was any real going forward, either.

This whole period, both the dull sameness of Hodamoc's place and the more active but still strange and isolated time at Yobi's, had left her for the first time with a lot of time for introspection, and she had come to some conclusions about herself while still wrestling with others. Part of it was this last stay with people who knew both alchemy and magic and who had taken away some of her mental props by separating what was really her from what had been imposed upon her. Many could be made into courtesans, for example, by the kind of alchemical magic Boday used to wield, but few truly enjoyed it. The distinction, in purely Akahlarian terms, was between what you *did* and what you *were.*

For example, she realized that she really loved men. Not in the sense of being heterosexual; it was a more encompassing, even generic sort of love. Oh, she liked those cute little asses and there were some that were simply *gorgeous,* but it wasn't just that. She liked them young, old, tall, short, fat, thin—you name it. She couldn't explain it, but she knew what her ideal was and she missed it. That wasn't alchemy; it was deep.

And she loved sex. Not just the screwing, although that was the hot fudge on the sundae, but all of it. She had liked it the first time, back home, but it had scared her as well, perhaps because she had liked it so much and it had dominated her fantasies and daydreams. Now she couldn't get enough of it, not anymore. It wasn't enough that she got off; she had to give as well as get in equal amounts. Now, having done it so much with so many, there were no inhibitions left, only a deep craving. Something that had always been there had been loosed by circumstance and now here it was.

She began to understand what Yobi had said to her. It didn't mean that she wasn't smart, or that she didn't want independence and control of her own life. She was proud of that rescue operation, and if she could somehow get this ring out of her nose she'd be overjoyed. She didn't want a husband; she wanted twenty years or more of one-night stands that would make her also wealthy and totally independent of others.

She wasn't gonna let this blindness hold her down, either. She missed her sight, sure, but it was only one sense and not the most important. She was already learning quickly how much she could do. A lot of it was just plain common sense, like putting your thumb inside a cup where you want the fill line to be and pouring until it reached that point; others were trial and error, or just doing things a bit slower and more cautious than before.

She liked Shadowcat, and appreciated what he could do for her, but she was sparing in using him. Dorion, after all, understood English, which left Boday out rather than her, and she'd much rather talk to Dorion than Boday anyway, so she didn't want that telepathic thing unless she needed it. And when the cat was let free to roam, she discovered quickly how you didn't really want to see what he was doing. The first mouse and insect kills kind of cured the romance right out of her. But it was convenient to be able to look over a campsite and memorize it, or to check on things when she had to. But she was determined from the start not to use him as a crutch.

Blind, she could saddle and unsaddle a horse and ride with confidence. She could prepare her own food and drink to a fair degree on the trail, and she could attend to her own personal needs. She managed her own sleeping bag from unpacking and setting it out to repacking her gear. She would rather have her sight back, but she wasn't about to give up living because it was lost or wallow in self-pity waiting for it to somehow miraculously return. It would be nice to have it, but it was something she could live without.

Perhaps this Boolean could restore it, although they said that most all magicians and sorcerers lost real sight so if they could get it back they would. Dorion was a bit vague on it, admitting that his eyes were shot and yet he could see with remarkable clarity better than he had with them. He was not blind, but his methods were those of sorcery denied to her.

The strange things she *could* see puzzled her. Why was Boday nonexistent save for that odd and fragile red strand, and the horses and the landscape a seamless deep gray, but Dorion this strange, fuzzy red blur and Shadowcat that lavender blob?

"Your eyesight, like mine, has been shifted, not canceled," Dorion told her. "It is very hard to explain to a lay person, but you can read a lot into the shapes, colors, and types of patterns you see. You are seeing perfectly well, but in dimensions beyond the capability of normal eyes to ever see. It is like being in a haunted house and being able to see the ghosts but not the house they haunt. Still, if you could see fully into those other dimensions you would probably go mad. Only that which is in this world but gives off radiations into the others is visible, and that's for the best. Some things of the magical world are best not seen, but you might see them. Be prepared for it, but control yourself as well. It is better to see those who would do you harm from that realm than to be at their unseen mercy."

On the third day they rejoined the main road very near the border of Mashtopol, but Dorion decided to camp yet again in the Kudaan before going through. "Best we move still by night, at least for a while," he told them, "and be fully awake and alert going through there."

"Boday does not understand what risks there might be," the artist noted. "Surely this pig Zamofir is behind us, and after all this time those still alerted for us must be mere hired hands and ruffians, not the sort who will keep a steady watch or be difficult to fool."

"Yeah, perhaps," Dorion responded, "but it's best to take no chances. Zamofir has birds and other means of communication that are far faster than we, and he has access to a magical network with near-instant communications. We have to assume that they're expecting us. From tomorrow until we're clear of this place we're going to have to depend on all aspects of the disguise, including our cover."

"You mean the slave business," Charley said, nodding.

"Yes. You will have to be total slaves and act the part at all times, even when it seems as if no one is around. Charley, you're going to have to be the slave girl Yssa, the total and uninhibited sex slave who's also subservient and docile to my will—and mute unless I say otherwise or unless we need to be alerted to a danger, since you can't speak the language. And you, Boday, will be Koba, and you will have to be different. Do not use your name at all except to answer 'Koba' if asked what it is. If you must speak in the third person, then use humble and self-deprecating terms like 'this unworthy one' and 'this humble slave.' I know that will kill your ego but it's essential. You are our defender, a warrior slave. If anybody asks too personal or specific questions just tell them it's not permitted for you to answer or that your past life has been wiped out. In all cases you are *my* slaves and there will be no references to others."

"Boday has spent her life seeking recognition," the artist noted. "This will not be easy for her."

"You don't have to be inconspicuous, but you must eat, sleep, think, act the part at all times," he told them firmly. "Only if we are discovered and unmasked are you on your own, using your own discretion. And I will have to treat you as my slaves, too, acting my own part. I'll apologize later. I never liked this slave business, and I'm uncomfortable with it."

"Use us as you must," Charley told him, "and don't worry or feel guilty. We have already been through so much, and what you ask me to be is a role I very much enjoy playing."

The Kudaan exit station was unusually crowded, with a number of tough-looking men about, mostly armed, and to no apparent purpose, but both the officials and the men spent most of their time looking at Charley and not very much looking at the documents or anything else. She gave them a good show, lounging sexily on the saddle and doing offhanded obscene things in a playful way. They would remember her, all right, but not a one of them seemed to entertain the slightest thought that she was anything more than she appeared to be. In fact, you didn't have to read minds to know pretty much all the thoughts those guys had.

She couldn't see them, of course, but she didn't have to. The comments and the sounds and the panting and the many attempts to bribe Dorion for a little while with her said it all.

Shamelessly, she loved every minute of it. In a way, this was a different kind of power and no less real for all that.

And beyond the gate was what looked like a great yellow wall rising from ground level as far up as the eye could see. It looked amazingly solid, and imposing.

"Each null zone has a shield like that," Dorion told her. "It is a great shield of an Akhbreed sorcerer, and it prevents any but Akhbreed from going through it to the land beyond. In that way all non-Akhbreed, all changelings, all the ones who don't fit the definitions, are prevented from ever moving from world to world. It's not absolute because you can't ever be smart enough to write a spell that covers everything, but along with the entry gates it keeps things so manageable it may as well be impenetrable to all others."

Maybe not as impenetrable as they think, Charley reflected, remembering that when she'd first entered this world there had been a centauress hiding out in a cave within a hub itself. But, as Dorion had said, nothing couldn't be beaten, but that centauress *was* hiding out and would have been killed instantly if discovered.

For them the boundary was paper thin; they passed through it with no sensation at all and went into the null zone itself, and that was something else again for her. She could not see the ever-present thick white mist, but she found she could see the massive spurts of energy that had previously looked like occasional sparks here and there. It was a forest, a fairyland of color and light and constantly shifting patterns, and there seemed to be a kind of yellowish rain connecting it to the unseen clouds above.

As they entered and passed through it, they interacted with it, causing the area around them to become intensely more active and to constantly change colors as well. This was the beauty and wonder of the magic sight. Outlined against the darkness of her conventional blindness, it was breathtaking.

There was no magic to see beyond, in the hub itself, but far off in the distance, she couldn't guess how far, there seemed to rise a single pencil-thin beacon of brilliant gold, like a searchlight beacon breaking the night.

"That comes from the city," Dorion explained. "It emanates from the royal Akhbreed sorcerer himself. We're going to avoid that and try and stick to the borderland, although we can't avoid some civilization. All roads really lead to and from the capitals, and the crossroads are intended for local use only and we'll have a very crooked path to follow because of it."

Dorion worried about Boday, no matter what the commands, but he wondered about Charley. He was the first to admit that he never really understood women, not even if they were six hundred years old and built like a cross between a crone and a slug. Charley was bright, resourceful, adaptable, everything—and yet he got the very strong impression that if she were free of him, of the ring, and of all obligations she'd become a full-time professional whore, a seller of her flesh. She wasn't just acting back there; he had the distinct impression she would have been delighted had he taken any of those men up on their offers. Yobi had said as much and had seemed to find nothing wrong with it. You never argued with Yobi, but it sure as hell seemed wrong to him somehow.

Both Charley and Boday were relieved to reach the Mashtopol entry station. Finally, at last, the Kudaan was behind them, with its merciless heat, its strange denizens, and its bizarre risks. It had taken so long to get through it that it was only by great luck and a hairsbreadth that they'd not wound up spending the rest of their lives there.

The duty officer at the entry station found both women fascinating, but he was also far more officious and more steadfast in his duties.

"Indentures, huh? Permanent?"

"Yes, sir," the magician responded. "Neither originally to me, though. I was in the service of a great sorcerer who saved the tall one's people from a demonic attack and got her because the old boy outgrew his need for servants. The other, well, you see her. I had to pay a high price in spells and services to talk her owner out of her, as you might guess, but you can see why any price was good enough."

The duty officer looked at Charley and nodded. "Yes, I can see why you would want her, but not why anybody'd sell her."

"She's blind. That made her inconvenient to her old owner, but there's no problem with what *I* wanted."

The officer *tsk-tsked.* "Too bad. So pretty. What about the cat? We have to check on all animals, you know."

"I have it on the documents here. The cat is mine and used with some of my magic, but it's just a cat. The girl took a real liking to him, though, and he to her, so they stay pretty well together when I don't need one or the other."

The duty officer sighed. "All right, sir. All in order. Big festival in the city the end of the week, you know. Lots of folks in town, so you might have trouble finding rooms if you haven't already booked them. Also, this time of year, there's a lot of the bad element creeping in to take advantage as well. Been some girls disappearing here and there, and some murders. You watch your pair there, sir."

"I will," he promised. "But in Koba's case they better watch out for *her*."

The officer stamped the documents, and Charley wondered just how easily those things were forged and just how few were real that came through these stations, anyway.

"All in order, sir," said the duty officer, handing back the papers to Dorion. "You're cleared for as long as you wish to stay, exiting either here or at the Northwest Gate. Have a pleasant stay."

Dorion thanked him and remounted, and they were off into Mashtopol. Charley, in fact, felt suddenly very relaxed. When they had gone about a mile inside the hub city, Dorion stopped and drew them close and gave Charley permission to speak this once, since she seemed dying to anyway.

"Master, there is no danger here to us," Charley noted. "Could we not take a room with a *bath* and perhaps purchase more useful clothing? I should like to feel and smell the life of a city after all that time in the Kudaan."

"Sorry, no, it's not that easy. We have problems," he told them. "I just didn't think of it, but if Zamofir talked to Hodamoc he knows you both came in together and that you were both auctioned and enslaved. I don't think the word's gotten here yet, or that officer would have taken us on some pretext, but it's sure to draw the wolves in a day or so. There's not much open country but we're going to have to stick to the side roads if we can stay out of any real civilized areas. They'll have all the gates covered, and the odds are good they'll have the nulls covered somehow as well. With everybody drawn to this city festival we might make it across okay, but we might just face a fight in exiting. I'm afraid your bath and city feel will just have to wait."

For two days they traveled through the outer periphery of the Mashtopol hub without much incident. There were some curious farmers and some negotiations for overnight camping rights, but clearly they were keeping well off the main drags. There was also a lot of curiosity and some very high-moral-tone commentary about the two women; the conservative farmers and small-town types weren't at all anxious to have *those* kinds of women around, and they were forced to buy what they needed and move on fast—which suited them just fine.

Shadowcat was delighted with the region, where the rodents were very tiny and apparently pretty stupid and the bugs were big and crunchy. She let him roam and have some fun, knowing he would not stray far and that somehow his link with her would call him back if they needed to pick up and move. She was even getting used to the occasional tiny prick he might make to get just a small bead of her blood to lap up and renew that link. He was good to take it unobtrusively and take only the minimum required, and while it stung for a second it healed over in a matter of minutes, almost as if when he lapped up the blood drop he somehow also undid the hole.

And maybe he did. This was magic now, in a land where the difference between black and white magic was strictly in the motivation of the magician. If the magic of Akahlar had any coloration, it was gray.

But the land was not rife with magic, even though the locals thought it was, for she could see magic if nothing else and, aside from the magic in or attached to her companions, there wasn't much here.

It was a pleasant land, though, for all that. It smelled of flowers and new-mown hay and the sun was comfortably warm rather than broiling hot, and when on the second day they ran into a brief shower it took an order by Dorion to get either woman to take shelter. It had been a long time since they had seen rain or felt it fall on them, and it was *wonderful*.

Here was the magic that all could see and few ever did. The sound and smell of a gentle rain on field and forest were true magic and life and full of promise and wonder.

By the third day out, even Dorion was beginning to think he was being overly paranoid. No secret agents were about, no attacks had been made, and there was no sign of any real pursuit. It was only because he was beginning to relax that Boday, in particular, got worried. When things went *too* well in Akahlar, you'd better watch out, something was lurking there ready to bite you.

"We will have to exit by night through the fence," he told them. "I don't want any record of us exiting at any exit station along here. There will be patrols, but it won't be any big deal I don't think. Once in the null, though, we'll have to be patient and pick and choose with care. If I do a Navigator's trick and force a world on my own at this point, it'll be noticed by everybody and they'll have a perfect trail. We're going to have to sit and wait out there and hope something decent comes up that I either know or can handle and cross at that point. If we can cross a colonial wedge undetected and cross from there into Quodac, there is no way they can find us except by luck. If Klittichorn had enough agents and wealth to cover all the possibilities he'd be in charge already, and Quodac's officials aren't nearly as corrupt as Mashtopol's. Quodac means a breather, and then we can plug in to some of Yobi's muscle."

They approached the border with little trouble, but Dorion didn't want to cross at any point close to civilization. He suggested that, after dark, they move a considerable distance from the gate along the border until the land would no longer support the horses without having to turn inland or force them into the null zone.

It was an eerie sight for Charley, who could see all along her left side the enormous power and energy of the null while all elsewhere was dark nothingness to her. They rode for about thirty minutes, and then Dorion called a halt.

"Construction equipment here," he explained. "They appear to be building a fence completely around this region. Wonder why?"

He got down from his horse and walked over to it and examined it.

"Huh. Copper wire. Looks like enough on that one reel to run from here back to the exit station. Insulated fence stakes, odd post fasteners . . . It's as if they're going to run something through the wire and they don't want it grounded. Very odd. Oh—you two can speak freely now. Pretend time is done."

Boday jumped down and looked at the stuff all laid out there. "Clearly it is more than a mere fence," she noted. "Boday has seen small areas for security that are electrified with materials such as this. They would kill anyone who touched them. Could that be what they are doing? Although it begs the question of who they would be doing this against."

Dorion nodded. "Yeah, that's a real question, all right. A lot of the hubs have fencing, but it's mostly to keep animals from wandering in. It's easier and cheaper to barrier the small section of overlap with the colonial worlds than entirely ring a hub. Besides, where would they get the kind of power a fence like this would require? They can barely power the central district of the capital with what they have."

He thought a moment, then mused, "But if there was a very low-level charge, a trickle, of any sort of energy, even a bit of the null bled into it if somebody figured out how, then it would be enough to close a circuit. It wouldn't keep anybody in or out, but you'd know when your border was breached, and roughly where. Yes, I'll bet that's it. Probably just a test section now, but nobody goes to all this trouble to prove a theory. I wonder who or what they're suddenly afraid of."

"Does it matter?" Charley asked him impatiently. "Let's get someplace where we can cross out of this place and begin to relax and maybe have time enough to sleep in a real bed and—take a *bath* . . ." She added the last less wistfully than reverently. She knew how she had to look and she knew how her hair felt and she certainly knew how everybody smelled. These Akahlar people didn't seem to take too many baths, but that was an area too gross for her to compromise, and gross was the word for all of them by now.

Dorion thought it over. "Well, here's as good a place as any, although who knows how long we're going to have to wait out there until a world we can live with comes up? If we go any farther north we'll hit the exit station area, and if we go south we're going to probably wind up cutting holes in their nice, shiny new fence that isn't even ready yet. *That* would sure tell them where we exited and give them something of a lead. All right—here it is. Boday—mount up and stay behind Charley as usual. We're going across!"

They went in; Dorion in the lead, Charley almost slipped once as the horse tried for a decent balancing act, but she hung on and felt the horse suddenly level out and speed up as they went out onto the null.

She liked the null because she could see it, and, more to her surprise, she seemed to also see the sky, although it looked kind of weird, like some trick photography or something, the swirling clouds outlined in dim and unnatural colors and hues and crackling with a dark, demonic energy.

Shadowcat, in his harness and perch, gave a sudden yowl that would wake the dead, and Dorion whirled and yelled, "*Stop! Turn around and head back for the bank! It's a trap!*"

Charley didn't react at first; the demon clouds seemed suddenly to take on a shape, and then out of those clouds, or perhaps of the clouds, a giant and horrible vision formed.

The gaunt was outlined in hellfire; a great pterodactyl with hollow, burning eyes and a mouth that seemed filled with flame. The rider was even more terrifying, outlined boldly in whites and crimsons, a gigantic figure who rode the flying beast as comfortably as they did horses. The Stormrider was easily ten or twelve feet tall and proportioned to match, and there was a semblance of armor in the magical energy outline, and of a helmet with visor up inside which burned deep crimson flame out of which two dark, demonic eyes peered.

She didn't need any more encouragement. She couldn't see the hub itself but the very lack of vision was enough of a visual cue. She kicked the horse and let it take her back.

The great gaunt screamed at them, its cry echoing off the land and piercing their very souls as it did so. Charley could only hang on for dear life and pray that she could make it back before that thing could single her out and its talons take her.

Clearly, though it was a creature of sorcery, this was no invisible monster to anyone, cursed with the magical sight or not. Boday tried to keep pace with Charley and keep her on the right track, but she turned, watching the great Stormrider on his gaunt pivot, turn, and start to dive in towards them; and she reached for a gun, turned in the saddle, and, certain she couldn't miss something that big even at this distance and under these conditions, fired.

The bullet found its mark but it had no effect, cutting right through the fearsome apparition as if it did not represent anything real.

An incredibly deep, resonant male voice filled the air with mocking laughter.

Furious but frustrated, Boday watched Charley's horse make it to the edge of the hub once again and scramble up that short but irregular ledge. The horse slipped, and Charley suddenly found herself thrown, falling into the mist and hitting the soft, mossy ground of it hard. She managed to get up quickly, adrenaline pumping and masking any pain or injury, but she was shocked, confused. Turning, she watched as the great horror swooped down on her, perhaps only seconds away.

Suddenly she felt herself being picked up and held against a horse, then bounced as the horse made it up the side of the hub to the ground above. She felt something touch her, sting her thigh, and there was a rush of air and a foul stench, and then suddenly she was dropped onto the dirt of the hub.

Boday was breathing hard. "Hurry! Do not delay! We shall find your horse later, but, for now, come up with me and get away from the edge!"

But Charley just lay there, hurting, unable to move. She looked down at her thigh and saw it shining a burning crimson, the same as what had been inside that creature's armor. Her leg was suddenly numb, paralyzed, without feeling or the ability to move except for the burning.

She could only sit there and look out and watch the horrible thing finish its circle and come in close again. There was nothing she could do, no place she could run, and she just watched it come closer, ever closer—until it was virtually at the hub border.

Suddenly the rider pulled up, and the gaunt and rider remained suspended in the air just a few feet away from the border, the great flying creature's wings going gently up and down in an apparent attempt to keep it there.

Charley abruptly realized that for some reason the thing couldn't come in. Perhaps the same power that kept out the colonials and the nasties prevented even this form from crossing into one of their sacred hubs.

The two deep, burning eyes fixed upon her.

"The power of the storms in a null is great," said the Stormrider in that low, resonant bass. "Because of the mixing of the air masses and the constant shift in access to the colonial worlds it is always turbulent. Even now forces obedient to me have cut off access and soon will be closing in on you from all sides but this. You cannot win. You cannot escape. Rise and come to me!"

Charley felt will in her burning leg, but it wasn't her will. It tried to stand, tried to force her into motion, but it was simply not enough.

Suddenly Boday was there, pulling her back from the edge, pulling her back behind cover.

"I have fifty men who have no morals or scruples at all and whose reward is great when they bring you to me," the Stormrider chided them. "They also do not care for the lives of your companions. You cannot cross except through me, and your pitiful weapons mean nothing to a prince of the clouds."

Dorion came up beside them, crouching low. "Damn it, he might be right," the magician muttered.

"What *is* that thing?" Charley asked, scared.

"Stormrider on a gaunt. Creatures of the Inner Hells, beyond Akahlar where no humans may exist. They can cross, though, into our existence if there is sufficient energy and if they are called by a sorcerer, and they very much want to cross into here."

"It's that horny bastard again, isn't it? *He* brought that thing in!"

"Yeah. He's got something going with them. It's all tied in with the same plot somehow, if we knew what it was. Never mind the history lesson now, though. I don't think he's bluffing about those men, either. Damn! I should have thought of this! Their powers are lessened in daylight."

"Enough to get across through it?" she asked.

He paused. "No. Not that lessened. Damn! I wish I could *think!*"

"You are a magician, oh mighty Master," Boday said sarcastically. "Can you not divert it so that we might cross?"

"I'm not *that* good a magician! Besides, the cure might be worse than the disease."

Charley felt something furry brush against her and looked down to see the shining lavender fuzz that was Shadowcat. The cat went to her burning leg, climbed on it, and seemed to rest there. She felt a sudden tingle and watched as the cat began to take on some of the crimson coloration of the magical wound. It was incredible, but, somehow, Shadowcat was absorbing the spell, restoring her leg!

She began to think furiously. "Look, didn't you say that the fence they were building was mostly copper? To conduct some magic energy?"

Dorion stared at her. "Yes, but what of it?"

"How was the fence wire stored?"

"On a big reel. That's the only way they can handle it." He was beginning to get interested.

"Hollow core?"

"Yeah, but it must weigh like lead."

"How far are we from it?"

He looked out. "About a hand. Why? What are you thinking of?"

A hand was around 125 feet or so. "Something impossible, probably. If you could turn that copper wire coil and mount it somehow on a spindle so it'd turn, and if you could pry off the end from inside and fix it to something iron here, in the hub . . ."

Dorion's eyes lit up. "I think I *see!* Yes, it's worth a try!" He turned and explained it as quickly as possible to Boday. "Stay here," he ordered. "Boday and I will go see."

There were several reels of the stuff at the work site, and the two of them could barely move the smallest one on its side, but they managed. Boday looked around at the rest of the work site and the tools and equipment there, found a number of things, and began to improvise.

"Ha! Not a mere *winch,* a sculpture that shall enter into legend!" she muttered, and began to assemble a very strange-looking device from bits and pieces of boards and equipment she found lying about.

The activity took time, and did not go unnoticed by the Stormrider.

"What is this? A fence of magic, perhaps? Effective, to a degree, but hardly a good defense against bullets and knives and swords I should think," he noted.

"Silence, pig!" Boday shouted back at him. "Boday is creating and she *detests* critics enough later on; she cannot *abide* them looking over her shoulder as she creates!"

The Stormrider seemed somewhat taken aback. "She is truly mad," he muttered, almost to himself. "But this avails you nothing."

Dorion suspected that he might be right, but it took less than fifteen minutes for Boday to come up with what might just be a workable winch—if they could keep the damned roll on the spool or even lift it on there in the first place. However, after failing for a few minutes to convince Boday that decorative carvings and shaping of the edges into artistic forms was a luxury they couldn't afford and finally commanding her as a slave to obey, they managed with great difficulty to get the reel up onto the spindle, which sagged just a bit but seemed to hold.

Boday fed out several yards of the wire while Dorion reached in with a knife and finally found an end piece; then, with a knife and with Boday steadying the reel, he got enough out to be manageable.

The artist looked at the inner end. "You will have to hold that down and firm. When this reel turns, it will want to pull that end back up into the reel."

He nodded. "I'm going to loop it around this iron fencepost and then jam it into the works of the bonding device here. It must weigh a thousand halg. If the wire is tied and the post wedged firmly enough it should hold. Can you shoot such a stiff wire, though?"

"Boday would prefer a cannon, but she will manage. See, she has already taken off at least two hands of wire, and that is about as far as the crossbow will reach with any accuracy. Still, we shall have to bring him in a bit."

He nodded. "I'll get Charley and the horses. Either this works or we're going to be in deep trouble. I think I can hear riders in the distance now."

Shadowcat had somehow completely absorbed the evil from her leg. She had some feeling again, and managed, somewhat wobblily, to stand. She reached down and picked up the cat, who seemed all in with the effort.

"Don't you worry, Shadowcat. You just earned whatever you want from me," she told him.

Dorion came, startled to see her standing. "It's done—I think. Boday may be crazy but in her own way she's a real genius." He paused for a moment. "So are you," he added softly.

She handed him the cat. "Here. I don't know if that bastard can understand English but the last thing we want is for him to read my mind right now. Bring me around until I can see him and he me, and pray that Boday gets the idea. Be ready in a flash, because that might be all we have. Even if this works, who knows what'll happen?"

He sighed. "Yeah. Nobody's ever even hurt a Stormrider before in all this time."

"Yeah. I'm counting on him knowing and believing that, too."

With the magician's help, she stepped out from behind the rock-and-bush cover and saw the edge of the null and the great, fearsome, hovering shape that waited.

Boday had the crossbow rigged, but she was still too far away to be effective. "Over here! Towards the sound of Boday's voice!"

Charley shifted, and, keeping just a few yards in from the edge, she managed to cautiously move towards the fence line where Boday waited.

After what seemed like an eternity, she felt and heard Boday behind her. "Good enough, but you will have to bring him in," the artist whispered.

"I have to admit I am curious," said the Stormrider. "Just what has all this been about? Do you think you can somehow sting *me* with that crossbow and some puny wire? Sticks and stones can't break *my* bones for I am a creature of sorcery!" he mocked. "And that half-baked magician of yours is no match for me no matter what magic he intends shooting up that wire."

"Yeah, well, if you want it, come and get it," Charley said in English, and walked slowly towards the edge of the null.

"Ah! The bait for my trap! Come, come, then, my pretty one! Come to me and try your worst. Here, mad one, I will make it easy for you!"

With that, the Stormrider slowly moved down and in, until he was perhaps twenty feet, no more, from the hub's edge. Thunder rumbled ominously and Charley could see the energy from the null storm transferred not to rain or mist but to the Stormrider, energizing him, making him more and more solid.

Suddenly Boday bolted past Charley and went right to the edge. "Very well, sir! Try *this* stick!" she screamed at him, aimed, and fired the crossbow.

Boday didn't allow for the wire that was suddenly shooting out and she felt a sudden sharp pain in her back that knocked her over and sent her tumbling down into the null itself, screaming curses. In the same time that it took Boday to fall, the arrow struck low into the Stormrider's gaunt.

The laughter stopped abruptly, and there was a sudden, piercing scream from the gaunt. Instantly, creature and rider were turned into a giant ball of flame like a miniature orange sun, and what happened next was so fast that Charley could not follow it. It seemed as if the sun raced towards her, and she fell on her face and felt a burning sensation and then there was nothing but a terrible crackling sound and a monstrous roar of thunder so close it rattled her eardrums and knocked her senseless.

Dorion was out in seconds with the horses. He didn't wait for Charley to recover, but picked her up and somehow got her on the horse, where she sat, stunned and confused, only half-aware. He led the horses and their lone rider down into the null, stopping just inside.

Boday was still cursing, and he helped her up. "Are you hurt?"

"Boday's ears are stuffed with cotton!" she screamed, although it was no longer necessary to do so. "She is bruised and sore and perhaps hurt, but not as much as that flying son of a bitch!" Unsteadily, she mounted the same horse as Charley and held on to her. Dorion led the procession, with Charley's horse carrying only a dazed and very tired Shadowcat out into the null mists.

The riders were now very close, and some could be seen in the distance. There was no time to waste and Dorion knew it. No matter what, they had to ride like blazes across the null and hope that something decent came up before the riders caught them.

8

A Chase Down Memory Lane

Yobi held the potion up, studying it. "Interesting stuff," she muttered in her raspy voice. "There's some real creative people there."

Kira gasped, horrified, as the old witch suddenly drank a small portion of the memory-erasing potion. "No! Wait!"

A toothless grin spread over Yobi's face. "Smooth . . ." she whispered. "Good stuff. Oh, don't worry, my dear. I just want to see what it does and where it goes. I'm in perfect control of it. It's a foreign substance by my spell and will."

They waited for what seemed interminable minutes in the darkness.

"Fast," said the witch. "They must have put it in her morning breakfast juice or something. It'd knock you over before you knew what hit you, and then it goes for the jugular, as it were. Forces the victim to cooperate with it, it does. Fascinating. It sort of gets to know you. Then it finds your lowest common denominator, as it were, and allows those feelings and impulses to remain while it blocks all nonessential memory, anything keyed to 'self.' It appears to actually displace, even replace, certain chemicals or enzymes in the brain itself. It has a very long life and it doesn't get thrown out as a foreign invader, but eventually it does wear out, but not before the new pattern is reinforced and there's been some rewiring, as it were. It establishes Misa as the mind, the identity, then it wires in a whole new set of connections so that only those things relating to 'Misa' as 'self' are referenced. By the time it's learned 'Misa' and worn away, there's no connection with the old self. Needed memories—language and the like, common sense about not sticking your hand in the fire, all that—are duplicated as new 'Misa' information and then the old references are replaced by the potion. When it wears away, there's no more connection to the old. Fascinating."

Kira nodded. She didn't follow all the mechanics of it but she got the general idea. "In other words, whatever they tell her she is when she wakes up is what the potion takes as true. It then takes whatever the new personality needs from the old and cuts off the rest. It almost sounds *alive.*"

"No, no, merely a wonder of modern chemistry, my dear. Dangerous, too. You could make an army of devoted, soulless killers with the same stuff. I hope Old Hornass hasn't got hold of this." She sighed. "Well, it's gonna be rough. The tricky part is that the only thing that's holding any of her to her old self is the potion. We can get rid of the potion easy enough but then we'll just be stuck with Misa. If we leave it we just get Misa because it's blocking. The worst part is, we can't wait. There's been damage done now, and every day that passes does more. I hope the mighty Akhbreed sorcerer who bills himself as nearly a god can figure a way around this 'cause I sure can't. The only reason we got any crack at it at all at this stage is that marriage spell, which only a magician's court can fully dissolve and provides a connection of sorts with the past, and the link to the Storm Princess. But even they wouldn't matter if she'd been there another couple of months. Better call out the gods on this one!"

"I'm afraid I'll have to do," came a pleasant man's voice, sounding slightly hollow with a trace of echo. It came from even further into the darkness, and from no clear fixed source.

" 'Bout time you showed up, Smartass," Yobi commented.

"I was here. Your analysis was just so interesting I didn't want to interrupt. Kira, give her half the antidote and let's bring her up to a trance state. I can't deal with a zombie and, frankly, that mental blankness only makes that potion's work easier."

Kira got it, poured to the measure in a small cup, then went over to the apparently sleeping fat girl. "Open your eyes, take this cup, and drink all of its contents," she instructed.

"Misa's" eyes opened, she took it, and drank obediently. While they waited for it to circulate through the system, Boolean discussed the problem.

"It appears that we have to take what's left in there and replace that potion with something equally good that doesn't block. If we can, then she may be missing parts of her old self, some permanently and others temporarily—the brain's pretty good at finding alternate routes if given half a chance and some time—but she'll be basically back. You have the formula?"

"I think so," Yobi told him. "Here—catch!" Blue-white sparks flew from her head into the darkness, yet did not illuminate anything around them.

Boolean whistled. "Wow! No human mind ever worked out something that complicated on its own, I'd bet on it. This was developed somewhere in the upper Outplanes, out where they have very big computers for our nasty-minded people to use. It could take *months* to break this sucker down and understand what's doing what! We're going to have to try some desperation patches, slow and easy, trial and error, and see what we can get. The only way we're going to break through is for her to do it herself. Maybe try and convince *Misa* that *she* needs this information. Well, let's see what we can do. Kira, open her up to us."

Kira knelt down. "Misa, listen to me. Just after I say your name again, you will hear two other voices. Hear both voices, answer, and obey them as you would Crim or me."

"Yes, ma'am," came the slightly slurred response.

"Misa—now."

"Hello, Misa," said Boolean gently.

"Hello, sir," she responded, not sounding as blank as before she had the antidote.

Boolean allowed Yobi to repeat the process, then asked, "Who are you, Misa? Tell us about yourself?"

"Ain't much t'tell," she responded. "We be peasant girl. We helps t'plant things 'n help 'em grow so's they gives t'fruit and stuff, and then we helps pick'n pack 'em so's folks can eat and drink and wear good stuff. It be hard work but when we sees the seeds b'come the trees and give th' fruit we feels real good like magic, almost."

"Do you ever think you'd want to do anything else?" he asked her. "Maybe be on the staff or even somebody important in the Duke's office?"

"Nay, we be happy. For som'thin' else y'gots to get th' schoolin' 'n learn all that readin' and writin' shit. And we's borned t'do what th' gods made us t'do. Ain't no bad thing to grow stuff. We wasn't meant t'be but what we is, an' ain't no shame in bein' no peasant. We's *proud* of that. If we don' do it then som'body got to or there ain't nothin' to eat."

"What about your personal life, outside of work?" Yobi asked her. "What about boyfriends? Would you like to get married, have children? Tell us the truth, now."

"Oh, we got lots'a frien's. Th' boys they always tryin' t'fuck us, 'n we guess sometimes we'll let 'em, 'cause y'got t'have kids if y'can, y'know. Truth is, though, we don' get hot 'n juicy with th' boys.

Dunno why, but we ain't th' only girl what feels like that. Ain't no big deal, nohow, though. We take th' boy 'cause we gotta 'n the girls 'cause we wanna and it's all right."

"There's not enough access to her old self for that to be a factor," Yobi noted clinically. "It's got to be the marriage thing that's holding her."

Boolean thought a moment, then asked, "Wouldn't you like to have riches, all that you needed? Fine, pretty clothes and a fancy place to live and servants of your own and the finest foods and wines? Maybe use some of it to help others?"

The fat woman thought that one over. Hypnotized, totally honest, she was giving very plain responses without consideration for her audience.

"No. sir," she responded. "We guess them things might be nice f'r them that needs 'em, and we likes th' pretty things, but we thinks a lot of 'em is not so good as horse shit. They don't really do nothin', ain't good f'r nothin' 'cept givin' the lords 'n ladies ways t'show off to each other. Anybody cares more 'bout how they look than how they act ain't worth shit nohow, 'n all the pretty shit won't make a pig a lord, sir. We's just as soon work a good day 'n be friends with them what does, too, 'n get what we really needs in pay. Ya owns stuff ya got to worry 'bout it 'n keep it 'n try'n be better'n the rest and we don't wants that shit. Horse shit's an honest thing. Ya give it to the ground 'n it gives itself to th' plants and th' plants gives ya food. Ya eats the food and ya gives the shit back. And if y'don't want nothin' but friends 'n food 'n work, ya don't wants nothin' nobody else got. An' any friend who's friends 'cause of what ya got or what ya work at or how ya look ain't no real friend nohow."

"My God!" Boolean exclaimed. "She's been turned into a saint!"

"We're getting some threads," Yobi noted. "Want to go for more?"

There was silence for a moment, and then Boolean asked, in perfect, clear, American-sounding English, "But you're married to a woman, aren't you, Sam? And what about Charley?"

She did not react, and instead looked very confused.

"Looks like the English is cut off, Boolean," Yobi noted. "She's still understanding good Akhbreed, but clearly her mind-set is such that she doesn't believe it's her place to speak or think except in that peasant garbage. She has gone too far."

"She *can't*," he responded firmly. "There's not enough time left and I need her. They're planning something big, Yobi, and within the year. Something horrible. I haven't quite gotten exactly what—

not the full-scale thing at this point—but something so terrible it scares the hell out of even their own who have hints of it. They've just about stopped their small testing, and that means preparations for something more ambitious. I've *got* to have her!"

"Then you've got to be drastic," the witch responded. "You have to give her something that will force a break through that block."

"I know, I know. I was just hoping we could undo without doing more to her than has already been done." He sighed. "All right, then. Kira, I want you to put the little amulet of mine you carry with you around her neck. That will establish a direct link here. Maybe I can jolt her out of this."

Kira, fascinated by all this, did as she was instructed. The small, green gem was an ordinary-looking stone set in a rather drab setting and fixed to a thin brass chain. It wasn't intended to look like very much, but those who had it, or similar stones, throughout Akahlar were those who had either done Boolean a service in the past or were known to be trustworthy or mercenary enough to call upon if needed.

"Ah! Now I see you, little Misa Susama Sam," Boolean whispered. "Now I can truly deal directly . . ."

She felt a series of soft blows inside her head, and because of the potion she could do nothing and could not resist.

You are married already, Misa! said a voice.

"No!"

Yes! Look at your hand. See that mark there, the witchmark? See the thread flowing from it, out and away into the night? You must believe what I tell you. You must believe all that I tell you. You are married, and your mate is worried and wants to find you. You know it is true! Now, who is your mate? What does your mate look like? What is that name?

Flashes . . . Intermittent, fleeting visions of a strange, tall, thin woman with short black hair and a painted body . . . The potion fought to suppress these visions, but the belief command together with the reinforcement of Boolean's will was more than it could stand. This was now a part of Misa, required information. A process began.

"Boday," she whispered, sounding amazed. "We's married to a girl named Boday . . ."

Who is married to Boday? Picture the marriage. Where was it? Who was there? Who is Boday? Why does she love you ? You must answer me. You must find the answers to these questions in your mind! The questions and commands came fast, thick, furious, compelling.

"Susama Boday . . . is Sam. . . ." Scene of her rushing Boday in some oddly half-familiar setting, like a laboratory only not, and when she was knocked down feeding the painted woman something, something . . .

"Artist . . . Alchemist . . . We is married to an alchemical artist . . . Boday . . . Love potion . . ." It was like a brick wall that first crumbled in only a spot or two, revealing only a tiny part of the view, but the more view it revealed the more it began to crumble.

"He's a pretty powerful bastard at that," Yobi noted approvingly.

How? Why? All pressure, all commands, no let up.

"Save . . . Save—Shar-lay . . ." Visions of a pretty girl with artwork around her eyes and on her beautiful body like an azure blue butterfly . . . "Friend . . . *Best* friend . . . Name was . . . Shari. Yes, but also . . . Char-lee. Charley."

Remember. You must remember. Charley, Boday, Sam . . . Fill it in. Break it down. Remember . . . remember . . . remember!

Things began to fill in quickly now, as her new personality was now told to want, even require, that information. There was too much, far too much. She couldn't sort out the details, or make sense of it all. It was also being filtered through the Misa personality as the controlling one, and evaluations were being made involuntarily as the information was accessed or copied to where it could be accessed. This Sam was parasitic, unhappy with herself, unsure of anything. But *she* was Sam, but she didn't like Sam very much, either . . .

"Quickly!" Boolean snapped. "The rest of the antidote! All of it and now!"

Kira poured it, praying she wouldn't spill any of it, and said, "Misa—take this and drink it all, to the last drop!"

It was an automatic gesture, and Kira held her breath when it looked as though the girl was going to spill it, but she obeyed, almost absently.

Suddenly her eyes opened wide and she stared out not at them but at something beyond that only she could see. The cup, empty, fell to the ground. "Oh! Oh! *Oh!*" she said, and then collapsed in a dead faint forward and lay there silently on the ground.

"I'm not sure what we'll get when she wakes up except a woman with a headache," Boolean told them, "but that's as good as I can do by remote control, as it were. It's crazy, though. The most whacked-out part of her was the only way in that I found. If she'd liked boys, if she hadn't gone along with Boday in getting that thing formalized, it might not have been possible. If we had to actually break that stuff down and find an antidote there would have been nothing left at all to grab and hold on to. I owe you one, Yobi, for your analysis, your insight, and for keeping the Hellhounds off. I already owed you for the other two. If Boday had died out there, then the spell would have broken and that would have been that."

"You bet you do," said the witch. "And one of these days when the time is right I'll collect. For now, screwing that madman is enough of an excuse."

"I dare not risk remaining any longer," the sorcerer told them. "Already, even with Yobi's excellent blocking, they know I am roaming the ether and they're trying to track me."

"If you're so all-fired powerful why don't you just will yourself here?" the witch wanted to know.

"Because it would invite a power down that canyon that even I am powerless against and would finish us all," the sorcerer responded. "Why the hell do you think I'm stuck here? In my own hub, I have power to draw on and acolytes to marshal. Outside of it, I'm just another Akhbreed sorcerer no stronger or weaker than the others. Our side's losing, Yobi. It's weak and fragmented while Klittichorn grows stronger and bolder. This girl isn't a pawn, she's a last, desperate chance."

"Go, then," Yobi responded. "I'll get them at least on their way."

You could sense almost immediately that Boolean had gone, even those without any magical powers of their own like Kira.

The pretty woman looked at the witch. "What did he mean by that, old one? What are they planning in the cold north? What is it that even ones such as yourself and Boolean fear it? And how does she fit? The Storm Princess has great and unique powers, but hardly of a world-shattering sort—or have I been missing something?"

Yobi cackled. "That's what's so slick about them, my dear. Klittichorn is marrying the sorcerer's power to that of such anointed ones as the Storm Princess, each complementing and aiding the other. You know that the changewinds have been blowing more frequently and a bit more violently of late in certain parts of Akahlar?"

"Yes, but what of it? We have always had to live with them and in fear of them."

"The whole of a world is greater even than a changewind which affects only a small part of it," the witch explained. "Even the changewind is subject to the forces that make up a world, its greater patterns of wind and sun, gravity and centrifugal and magnetic forces. No matter how great a change the winds may wreak on an area, it is relatively small and the rest remains and partly recovers the damage. All the factors that affect weather and climate affect the changewind too, you know. It even enters Akahlar through a combination of transitory weaknesses at that given point. Klittichorn, it is said, has found that combination. He can summon the wind, but he cannot control it. The Storm Princess, however, can influence its local factors, its course, and even to a degree its intensity and duration here. They don't even like each other, but they need each other. Together, they have the potential to be a god of wrath."

Kira nodded. "I can see it as a horrible weapon, but not what good it would do. They still cannot determine what changes the wind will make, nor make good use of it except as a weapon of terror. In the face of it, the armies and sorcerers of the Akhbreed kingdoms could destroy Klittichorn and kill the Princess no matter where they were if they tried to use the weapon as blackmail, and that is all it is good for."

"Perhaps," the witch responded. "But I hardly think that the opposition is stupid, my dear. The Princess's end is politics. Klittichorn sees the politics as a means to a darker end we cannot yet fathom, but will know well to our horror if he manages to pull it off."

Something exploded inside her head. She didn't understand it and it frightened her, but she was helpless to resist it or to cast it out.

At first it was beautiful, like staring into infinite facets of the finest diamond, all colors shimmering this way and that, the triangular shapes turning and twisting, but soon it was all around her, enveloping her, trapping her suspended there in the midst of chaos.

Suddenly, near her, there was a tiny black dot, also suspended, and the dot grew into a long black line and the line suddenly turned and revealed the shape of a man. No—not a man, but the shadow or outline of a man, all dark and featureless and somehow as thin as paper.

She cried out and thousands of triangular facets seemed to echo her cry and make it something terrible.

"You are right to be afraid," said the figure, "but not of me. I did not make you or have a hand in the destiny you must follow, but I can help save you from it if you'll let me."

"Go 'way! I want nothin' t'do with you!" she shouted, and the twirling facets echoed and mocked her.

"You don't really fear me," said the shadow man. "I'm so thin that if I turn I'm not even here at all. I can't harm you, and I have no wish to do so. You didn't choose to be what you are, but you are what you are and you cannot change that. From the moment you were born you were set on a path that gives you no choice but to follow it or die, and only at the end can you gain your own freedom."

"What—what do you want of me?"

"Look into the center of the gem and see the source of your destiny," he told her.

She looked, and as she did images formed: clear images, as real as if they were there, although something told her that they were not. They could not see her, but they were real . . .

A tall, gaunt figure in robes of sparkling crimson, who either had two cowlike horns growing out of his head or was wearing some crazy kind of crown or cap with them. He was an old man, and there was hatred and bitterness in the lines of his face, in the glare of his cold eyes, in the way his small mouth twisted naturally into ugliness atop a lantern jaw.

"Behold the one who calls himself Klittichorn, the Horned Demon of the Snows," said the shadow man, "although he is no demon but a man, a sorcerer of tremendous power and learning but without wisdom. A man from another world and another culture whose intellect was so great that he became almost godlike in Akahlar. He schemes to destroy all Akahlar, all its people, its cultures, all its worlds, and all the other worlds as well. He does not mean to destroy them particularly, but he is beyond caring if he does—and he will. Everyone you know, everyone you have ever known or might ever know, will be destroyed by this one man."

She was appalled. Maybe it was magic, but, looking at him, she couldn't help but believe what she was being told was true.

The view shifted. No longer was there a crimson-robed sorcerer, but instead a young woman, perhaps no more than twenty, a bit chubby but not at all unattractive, with long black hair and in beautiful jewel-encrusted furs, wearing a tiara surely made of pure gold encrusted with every great gemstone ever known. The girl was very different from anyone seen so far in Akahlar, but, somehow, she was also very, very familiar.

"She is known only as the Storm Princess," the shadow man told her. "Klittichorn found her among common stock in one of the colonial worlds. Much like you, she wanted neither power nor position, but she had it thrust upon her because she was born different from other girls and because something happened to her that changed it all. She was a witch and the daughter of a witch although she'd never asked to be born that way. Her people farmed the land in a place where the mountains kept the rains away and where no natural rivers flowed, and they did so because of her mother. She was born with a gift; a magical gift, perhaps a reward for some intelligence we might call supernatural because we cannot understand it or know it, to an ancestor who did some service or made some bond. A gift passed down from mother to daughter—one child, no more, with the gift, and always a female. A power beyond those of the Akhbreed sorcerers. For she could call the storms, call the rains, and they would obey her. She alone could summon the waters of life and tell them where to drop their most basic gift of liquid life, and in what amounts.

"And the child wanted for nothing that was truly important," he continued, "because she and her mother gave the people of the valley the waters of life, and they in turn returned a part of that bounty to them."

And she saw the place in the center of the facets; saw the beautiful, lush valley and the small peasant village and farms that dotted it, and she understood just how rich and beautiful it was.

"And then the Akhbreed soldiers came," the shadow man went on, "and they marveled at how they had missed so rich a place. The people had no army and no lords to protect them, yet they resisted as best they could, and even when easily subjugated they refused to recognize the soldiers' king as their lord and to give much of their bounty to him and his armies. And when the witch, her mother, called down lightning and struck down many of the army and turned their camp into a quagmire so that the people of the valley could set upon them and kill them, those valley people rejoiced. It was a short-lived celebration.

"For the king had more soldiers alone than a hundred times the population of the valley, and more came, this time with sorcerers and mighty magic as well, and they showed no mercy. They were more than mere lightning or the creatures of the storms could count, and they slew without mercy. The girl saw her own mother slain before her eyes, and found herself captive to a sorcerer of terrible power. He understood that she, too, knew the secret of the storms, and he coveted that knowledge and took her. But, of course, there was no secret and there was no knowledge She was what she was. And the valley became dry and barren, as lifeless as stone, and she was the last of her people, and she hated them for it. Hated them all."

Tears came unbidden to her eyes as she saw what the valley had become and the stains of blood still there after several years because there had been nothing more to wash them away.

"By the time the sorcerer understood the girl's ignorance of her powers," the mysterious one told her, "and knew that such powers were somehow forbidden those who had all the others, Klittichorn had heard of her. So powerful was his magic that he was able to spirit her away from the very palace grounds of the king and his sorcerer. He used her hatred, and fed it. He showed her the Akhbreed empire, with its subjugation of the races, its feudalism and slavery, its cruelty and oppression. In his northern palace, in the land of eternal snows, he crowned her the Storm Princess, and convinced her that, together, they could end this cruelty, revenge her mother and her land and people, and liberate all of the oppressed. Many who were terrified of him, more terrified of him than of remaining under the Akhbreed kings, rallied to her. They have now not one army but many armies, trained, hidden among the vast colonial worlds, waiting for the call to liberation."

She understood what he was saying, understood and believed it all, but she did not understand her place in it. "She is good!" she shouted at the shadow man. "Her dreams are noble and proper!"

"They are," he agreed, "but life is not that simple. She and all her armies cannot overthrow the Akhbreed sorcerers in their hub citadels or hope to match the great armies of the rulers. She needs the power of true sorcery behind her, and that Klittichorn brings. He has convinced her that he shares her dream, but he does not. For if the power of the Akhbreed sorcerers is somehow halted, and if the Akhbreed themselves are destroyed, there will be no controls. Instead of all hating the Akhbreed, the thousands of races will begin to suspect and hate and then war with one another. And out of this chaos will come the only remaining, untouchable source of great power, which will be Klittichorn. This he believes, but he, too, is wrong. To destroy the Akhbreed and their sorcerers he must loose the terrible changewinds themselves, the only things against which no Akhbreed sorcerer has power. He will loose them by the score and the Storm Princess will guide them."

"Is that—possible?"

"Klittichorn thinks so. *She* thinks so. He has somehow managed to summon many small changewinds to the places he commands, although how this is done is a mystery, and she has managed to shape and turn them. But those were small, and one at a time. To control great ones, all at once, and all over Akahlar—that is something reason says cannot be done. Reason and experience also tell that such an event, done all at once, would create such an instability that the worlds themselves would collapse upon each other, that the changewinds would roam unchecked and over vast areas, and none would be safe. Such weight alone might draw all of creation down to the Seat of Probability and to oblivion. All that has ever existed, all that exists, and all that can or will exist will be no longer."

"But—surely she knows this, or senses it!"

"She is a farm girl the same age as you; a peasant girl, really, with an inherited power she can wield but not comprehend. Seven years ago she was ignorant that anyone or anything outside her valley and people even existed. Since then she has been a victim or a dupe. How can she know, or even comprehend? Certainly she has seen the winds and knows the risk, but such is her thirst for revenge and so skillfully has her hatred been fed that she would prefer oblivion to inaction, which are the only choices she has. Those who follow her blind themselves to the risk for they see no other choice but eternal subjugation. They would rather risk the end of time and space and all within than accept the permanence of their condition. Understand well that Klittichorn is prepared for either event. He believes that should the end come in such a manner he will be left, alone, to re-create the universe, the one lone supreme being. Lord of Akahlar or the one true god. He feels he has nothing to lose."

She was appalled. "Can he—might he really become *god?*" That man, that ugly man with the ugly soul that showed?

"Perhaps. He is one of the strongest sorcerers ever known. Together, however, the rest, even a relatively small number, might defeat him. But if they are removed, if the changewind crumbles the Mandan castles themselves and sucks the very air from the shelters, then who is to say what he might become? Either way, the Storm Princess's dreams are hollow and stand on no foundation. She will replace a bad system with pure evil, or with oblivion for all. Not just death—the nonexistence of the universes!"

It was a terrible vision. It was worse than terrible, for it gave no hope. It was a choice of lesser evils over greater ones and there was no way out.

"But why me? What has this to do with me?"

"Search those memories that are slowly returning to you. Search within yourself as you gaze upon the face of the Storm Princess. You recognize her. You certainly recognize her. Remember back, remember before you gained your weight, remember the face and form in the mirror. *Remember!*"

A face, a form, reflected darkly in some wall of glass in some far-off place. A strange vision, with storms all around outside, yet a great deserted village totally enclosed . . .

A face and form reflected in a window. *Her* face. *Her* form.

"My god! She looks a lot like me . . ."

"No," responded the shadow man. "She *is* you. The Storm Princess is you."

"But how can that be?"

"There are many worlds encompassing Akahlar. Each is its own complete and unique world. The people of those worlds differ, usually, in some major or minor degree from Akhbreed purity, but a few do not. The same is true in the vast Outplane of millions of universes all stretching out from here. Almost anything possible has happened in one or more of them. Given that, it is not surprising that not just one but many women were born in those universes who, by chance, are genetically identical with the Storm Princess even if they have nothing in common with her, not even genetically identical parents. It happened. One of the ones so born was you."

"But I had no power over storms!" *How did she know that? She couldn't remember . . .*

"No. But Klittichorn worried about this, about such doubles being discovered by his enemies and brought here. The gift, or curse, of the power is keyed to a particular person—the Storm Princess. But it is a power, not an intelligence. It cannot tell the difference between you and so it endows you both with that power. Once the way was opened from Akahlar to you the power knew you and of you and it became yours as well."

"If there are many girls, then let me be! Use one of them!"

The shadow man sighed. "There are—were—not many. There were some. Klittichorn, using the Storm Princess herself as the object, was able to seek them out ahead of his enemies and kill them. They died, never knowing why or how. Only a very few were saved, such as yourself, and brought here by other powers. They were nothing like you—except physically, of course. Oh, they preferred the same things generally and they tended to like and dislike certain things and do things in certain ways the same, as twins might, but they were products of different parents, different worlds, different cultures. Like you, they were subjected to the rigors and strange magic and powers of Akahlar. Most succumbed."

She was shocked. "They're all *dead?*"

"No. Some are. Others have been changed by the changewinds or by demonic sorcery. Others have been rendered useless by falling into powerful and evil clutches. You are the one most likely to make it as of now. You are the only one we know the location of, and condition of. We did not choose you, and, frankly, had we been able to choose we would have selected someone different.

We have no choice, just as you have no choice. Klittichorn is hunting you. He has more difficulties here, in Akahlar, than he did in the Outplanes because he cannot locate you by sorcery. The presence of more than one of you destroys the effectiveness of all such spells. He must do it the hard way, as must we. If you fail to reach the safety of Castle Masalur in the hub of that name then you will die, and others around you will die. It may also be that hope to thwart Klittichorn will die. If you succeed in reaching Masalur, and if you then are able to aid in the defeat of Klittichorn—something not assured by your merely reaching the castle or even fighting—then, you will be free. There is no other choice. There is no other way."

It was a sobering, flat-out statement. No choice, no other way.

"What do you want me to do?" she asked, resigned.

"First decide who you are and what you want to be."

It was an odd comment. "What do you mean?"

"Who *are* you?"

Who indeed? The question was in its own way more unsettling than what had preceded it. She wanted to be Misa, but she couldn't be Misa. Misa could not do this, could not stand against such powers, and would only bring down horror on her people.

There was—another. Sam. Vague memories, disjointed thoughts, many grave gaps. She remembered the Sam of Akahlar, although still with some gaps here and there, but there had been yet another Sam before that and that one was hazy, strange, impossible to focus.

Who did she want to be? That was easier. Both Sams had been unhappy. They had reacted, never acted. Everything they had done they had done either to try to conform to others' expectations, others' standards, never her own. They had made fun of her low voice, her liking for sports and competition, her grades, everything . . . That first Sam had rebelled, but in the wrong ways. Constant diets, to keep super-thin. But forget pretty clothes and cosmetics and all that. Wear boys' clothes, take on a boyish manner, talk tough and dirty, play roughhouse.

But her body turned female anyway and when the boys shot up she stayed very short. To be with the boys now took something else.

Sudden scene in the mind: she and a boy named Johnny out back of a bowling alley after dark. They were both sixteen and had grown up pretty much together. He was big, though, and she was short and slight. He made some passes. Scared but curious, she responded. From the way he acted it wasn't his first time, but she knew what to do only from the romances and the soap operas. She liked the feelings, the hugging and the kissing, but she didn't want to go all the way. That was too much. He had a different idea. He dropped his pants and revealed his—his thing. *It was big and stiff and* enormous *and not at all like she'd thought they were, although she didn't really know what she had thought. And he wanted to put it in her* mouth, *to* suck *on it, for god's sake! It was ugly and, and, he* peed *out of it! She had been revolted. She thought she was going to throw up. This wasn't like it was supposed to be at all! She'd run away from him, away from all of them . . .*

She could not put together the world or frame or life around that experience, not even at the moment remember what a bowling alley was, but she could remember that, and she could still feel the revulsion. If *that* was what guys wanted and what girls were supposed to do then she wanted none of it.

Scene: she and another girl, frightened, alone in a remote cabin someplace. She was scared to death. She clung to the girl friend—to Charley—the only real friend she had in the world at that time. And Charley had responded to her need and they had made love and it had been wonderful, for a time. She knew that from Charley's point of view it had been an act of compassion, not love, but it hadn't seemed wrong.

Scene: Boday, who loved her because she was the first one the artist had seen after inadvertently taking a love potion. Boday's sexual tastes were bizarre and her appetite insatiable, but it was also secure. No worry, about what her Sam looked like or sounded like. The love and the strength were absolute, unquestioning. Sam had grown very fat and lazy under such love and security, but she still was insecure inside. Because Boday's love was chemical, she could not bring herself to think of it as genuine and so give some of it back. Because Boday was a woman, it was, somehow, still wrong. She was no damned freak!

Scene: on a big wagon train in Akahlar. She had compelled by the magic of a hypnotic charm, out of jealousy, guilt, and curiosity, one of the trail hands to make love to her and he had done his best. And she had felt little but disappointment. Nothing he had done was nearly as good as what she had gotten from Boday, and the end for him came all too soon and was nothing much to her.

Scene: Tied down on the rocky ground as three ugly, brutish, foul-smelling men had at her, over and over, as she closed her eyes and tried not to feel the foulness . . .

But Misa had been accepted. Misa had to conform to no standard in the refuge. The men had made passes but that was okay and the girls had been earthy as well. No one had made fun of her low voice or her fat or her lack of knowledge or anything. So long as you worked hard and did your share it didn't matter at all, and there hadn't been any guilt or shame or pressure, and she had enjoyed being female and all that meant. Nobody had judged, and nobody had cared except one equal to another.

And the fucking Storm Princess was fat, too! Maybe not as fat as she was, but really a chubbette. Charley was a lie, a "duplicate" made not to reality but to an ideal and kept there by sorcery and alchemy. She could never be Charley. Left to her own devices the best she'd look like was that Storm Princess! More, why in hell did Sam ever *want* to be Charley? To be seen only as a body, a sex object, a fly trap for men?

Her reflection came up to her in a huge facet and she stared at it. Okay, so she was fat. But she was still kind'a cute, damn it, and she didn't really *feel* uncomfortable this way. *Comfortable,* that was the word. She was comfortable and she didn't give a damn what anybody else thought. Sam had never liked herself but Misa had liked herself just fine.

By god, she was gonna *keep* liking herself just fine!

The facets whirled, became less reflections than a maelstrom, and she felt herself falling, falling . . .

And suddenly she was aware that she was on her back on something hard and moving, and that it was incredibly hot.

She sat up in the wagon and opened her eyes. It was odd; her mind had never seemed clearer, her senses never more acute than now. That included the basics; she was damned thirsty, and starving to death.

She crawled out of whatever she was in—a box of some kind!—and looked forward. She was in a wagon being pulled by a narga team; in back she could hear the sounds of one or maybe two horses, possibly tied to the wagon and walking with it.

The driver was a big man in Navigator's buckskins with a broad-trimmed felt cowboy-style hat on his head, and beyond the landscape was unmistakably still the Kudaan but back out in the harsh desert land far from the river.

She felt distrust of Navigators. One—when and who?—had supposedly been her friend and had tried to betray her. The memories were kind of fuzzy, hard to hold on to and make sense out of, so she didn't try. Maybe it would come back to her, maybe it wouldn't. But for right now she was crawling out of a box in a wagon in the middle of nowhere, stark naked and with a big guy the only human in sight.

He heard her but didn't turn around. "If you're awake and feeling all right, there's drinkable water in the cask with the water sign on it and warm ale in the one with the mug on it. There's also hard rolls and dried trail meats in the box just to the right of them with the diamond on it."

She jumped, then caught herself. Uh-uh. No more of this "poor little old me" bullshit. She was naked, thirsty, and hungry and this guy could have done anything to her by now but hadn't, so relax. The beer sounded great but not when it was hot enough to take a bath in. The water wasn't much better but at least it didn't surprise, and the food wasn't exactly great but it did fill. Only when she was done did she climb forward to see what this new man was like and what the situation was. She was still naked but it didn't matter to her. Let the guy have his jollies if he was that way.

He *was* a big man, well over six feet and with the look of one who is trim and lean but still had muscles to spare. His face and hands showed weathering and evidenced hard work and that said a lot about him as well. He was about as solid and all-around masculine a man as she'd ever seen in real life.

"I'm Crim," he said in a friendly tone. "And who are you today?"

"I—I'm Misa," she responded. "But I'm also Susama and Sam and some long name I can't really remember right now." Her tone and inflection was strictly peasant and bottom class, but her grammar and general vocabulary and structure was more standard, sort of like a peasant girl who'd spent a fair amount of time as the servant of somebody high up. It was kind of folksy, but nobody would ever mistake her for an aristocrat. The accent was strictly Mashtopol sticks—down home, *way* down, on the farm. "I'm sort'a all mixed up inside my head."

He nodded. "That's understandable. Hopefully it'll sort itself out over time. In the meantime, do you know who I am and where we're heading, sooner or later?"

"I guess you're somebody hired by the shadow man to bring me to him," she responded, then frowned. "Seems to me somebody else dressed like you was supposed to do that a long time ago but he double-crossed me."

Crim nodded. "I heard about that. Well, like most of the independent Navigators I have my problems and my hangups beyond the normal kind, but that kind of thing isn't one of them. For one thing, I'm being paid only on delivery and the pay is so high nobody can outbid it and be trusted. Boolean may be as crazy as the rest of 'em but he always keeps his word. For another, it's not just the pay. There's no way I'd ever work for the other guy, and he's the only one who really wants you other than Boolean."

"Boolean." She repeated the name. "Yes. I remember that name now. Is he the shadow man?"

"I have no idea, not having seen any shadow men. He's usually either a voice or a vision, though, so maybe that's as good as any. Hell, even his name's a joke. In the tongue he uses when he thinks, it's not a name at all but a number system. Algebra, I think. Invented by an Outplaner named Boole a long time ago. I think he took it as a sort of private joke."

She stared at him. "You know the Outplanes? And the languages?"

"Well, some. It just happens to be some knowledge I—acquired along the way, as it were. You're from the Outplanes, too, originally, I'm told."

She hesitated. "I—I know that I am, but I don't have no real clear memories of it. Just bits and pieces here and there, some making no sense at all."

He turned to her and said something that sounded like an ugly string of monotones. She stared at him and shook her head.

"You understood none of it?"

"Didn't sound like nothing at all."

"That was English," he told her. "I was told it was your native tongue. We'll try and work on it and maybe it'll come back to you over time. It's a handy language to know when dealing with Boolean. That's *his* language. One of them, anyway."

She sighed and shook her head. "There's just so much—missing. I remember all sorts of scenes, but they don't make no sense and don't go together. Kind'a like memories from when you was real small. Some basic shit, maybe, but no details."

"What *do* you remember clearly?" he asked her, probing a bit.

"Well, all of bein' Misa, that's for sure. All but that last night when I had the runs and went to the clinic. Ain't much after that, 'cept I can, well, remember a real pretty woman, maybe the prettiest I'd ever seen, and she was takin' me someplace. That's about it. Or did I dream her?"

"She's real," said Crim. "That's Kira. You'll meet her before too long with a clear head. But is that it? Just Misa?"

"No, no. But the more you go back from there the fuzzier it all gets. I lived a while in Tubikosa. A long time. Not in the straitlaced world of most of 'em, but in the entertainment district where them hypocrites snuck down to blow off steam and do all that shit they preached against. My lover's an artistic alchemist. Creates beautiful girls for the courtesan trade. I remember all that, too, only it's a little bit fuzzier. No dates or real order, just the whole thing sort'a running together in my head. Old friend of mine was a courtesan. Me and Boday we sort'a lived off her and doin' stuff for the other folks down there. She didn't mind none and that was the funny part—my friend, I mean. She's smart and she was gonna be the big wheel, the queen of big business and all that, and she found out she loved bein' a whore. Most of the girls either hated it or had no choice or were under drugs and all, but she really liked it. Crazy."

Crim shrugged. "Maybe. Maybe everybody's so busy trying to be what everybody else tells them they should be that they never have time to be themselves. No offense, but it's the people who enslave and victimize those girls that are the real criminals. It'd be a pretty victimless crime if only the ones who wanted to do it did it and got to keep the profits. Nobody ever held a sword to somebody's throat and said, 'Go fuck a prostitute or I'll kill you.' They buy what they want and need but for some reason, like pleasing all the others, never can get in normal life. It's not my thing, but I can't condemn somebody who does it for herself and because she wants it. Problem is, you mostly can't keep the crooks out of it—and, of course, when you get past your prime you haven't got much of an old-age job."

"Maybe. I guess maybe I been so busy tellin' myself that I don't much care what nobody else thinks about me that I kind'a forgot not to do the same thing to other folks."

"Do you remember even further back? Before Tubikosa?"

"Not clear, anyway. I didn't have much fun or much of a life back then, I don't think. It's like I said—a scene here, a scene there, and some funny memories of things that ain't in Akahlar or not the way I somehow think they should be. I ain't tryin' too hard to remember, truth to tell. I don't think I'd want to go back there, somehow. I know where we're goin', sort of, and I know why I gotta go and what I gotta do—sort of. I know I got to go if I can and I got to do it—if I can. And I want to find my lover and my friend. Any sign of 'em?"

"Oh, yes. They would have wound up where you did except they thought you were captured by the rebel troops. They got captured by a witch gang who took your friend for you and hauled them off to their camp. With no word about you, Boolean wanted them to lead the enemy away from the Kudaan, so they set off ahead. If both they and we make it, then we'll meet them in Masalur. Not much hope of meeting up ahead of time, and I don't think we want to. The enemy suspects the trick now and they're off hunting both them and us. If we link up it'll be all the easier for them."

She nodded. "I guess so. I just, well, don't want to screw it up at this point, not when I finally got myself a little put together. The Misa in me wants what Sam had but doesn't want to be Sam, if that makes any real sense. Sam was such an asshole. She didn't know what she had or what she wanted and let everybody else do her thinking for her. Hell, she even lied to herself. I'm done with that. You got to make the most of what you are and not waste it all tryin' to be or dreamin' of bein' what you're not and can't never be. For the first time in my life I'm damn happy to be what I am and I don't give a flying fart what nobody else thinks. I can't free myself from this job, and if I can't do it then this is all the time there is, but while it is I'm gonna make the most of it. I liberated my mind and now I'm gonna liberate the rest of me as much as I can."

She suddenly got up a little and looked out and around the wagon and to the back. "Are we it? Nobody else?"

Crim nodded. "Just us. My train had to keep going on its scheduled route in order to keep anybody from noticing and pointing a finger right at us. They're all around, even here. They're looking, and many of the lookers aren't human in any way. Just be sure you don't make it rain. *She* has more experience with that than you do and she's got a sorcerer right next to her to use that energy and send things through."

"Don't worry about that," she assured him. "But what about the pretty woman? Are we gonna meet up with her separate?"

He cleared his throat. "Uh, well, not exactly. Aw, hell, I'd better explain the whole thing to you. In about four hours you're going to know it all anyway."

She stared at him. "Huh?" From the looks of the sun that would be about sundown. "What is she? Some kind of vampire or something?"

Crim chuckled. "No, although you're not the first to suggest or suspect that, and there are many, I think, who believe it. It began a while back now. She came here accidentally from one of the Outplanes, like you did."

"Oh, yeah?" She was getting very curious about this now.

"I didn't start out to be a Navigator. When I was very young, I worked as an apprentice to a shady trader named Yangling. I had some natural magical talent—that's where the navigating comes in—and Yangling had high hopes for me as a tool, more or less. Then Kira quite literally fell into his hands—at least she was found, unconscious, near his place and taken to him by those who found her. As soon as I saw her there I think I fell in love with her, even before she recovered. I was assigned to find out from her all that was possible, since Yangling had made me study an Outplane language which was her native and only one. I spoke it poorly, awkwardly, and probably made only a very little sense, but she seemed appreciative that I could speak to her at all and that she could be somewhat understood. This was particularly important because the language here was an illegal one. A number of the younger and newer Akhbreed sorcerers had taken to using it as a sort of standard for some reason. It was thought that some knowledge of it might prove useful."

She nodded. "All right, I'm following this so far. Sounds kind'a romantic."

"It was, in a way. We got to know each other quite well. She improved my English immeasurably, but she never could get the hang of Akhbreed. It's that sort of tongue. She was a wonderful person, but tragic, too. She had not many months before been in an accident that was not even her fault. It had broken her neck and spine. She had some jerky movement, nothing useful, in her arms and fingers but not much else, and no real feeling below that. That beautiful body was useless and unfeeling and she was basically no more than a talking head."

"What little memories I have seem to show her pretty lively."

He nodded. "Anyway, Yangling was furious. He called in a bunch of top black magicians he had on his payroll and they went to work on her. Didn't do any good, though. Nothing short of a changewind or some terrible magic would have her mobile. Well, Yangling was more interested in the fact that she could read intercepted communications from top sorcerers with ease and then I could translate them to him. They thought of changing her into an animal, using a curse of some sort, but there are few animals that can read and speak in human tongues and nothing was certain there. The changewind option, if chance provided it, might alter her mind or her sanity. Yangling had a garden filled with erotic statues, and with her face and body there was talk of turning her into stone, her soul imprisoned, and animating her head only when her services were required. I couldn't have stood that, and I told her enough that she seemed to just want to die. I had to do something."

"You got your own magician?"

"Sort of. The blackest of the black, really. A grotesque figure who wandered the mountains there filled with hatred. No one dared seek him out, or could conceive of wanting to, but I did.

I offered to trade information—many of the complex and totally incomprehensible Akhbreed spells we had been intercepting. To my surprise, he agreed, although he said I would have to raise my own demon and do my own bargaining. At that point I was ready for anything."

She was shocked. "You sold your soul to a demon for her?"

"No, no. That's for fairy stories. Demons might like to eat you, for they hate all humans, but they couldn't care less about souls. I did the ritual, scared to death, and I raised the demon in the pentagram just right. It was a horror, worse than any nightmare imaginable. There were only two ways to make him do anything he didn't want to do, and one involved human sacrifices—this one of children. That was sure, but I could never do it. The other was risky and involved a way of threatening a demon with being trapped in the netherhells, regions of nothingness between the Outplanes. That's possible, but when a demon is doing something under duress, particularly for a human, he's not honorable. This one basically gave me one choice or it said it would rather spend eternity in the netherhells—and you believed it. I took the choice, and while he was mean he wasn't very bright. They often aren't. It's worked out."

"Yes? And the choice?"

"I wanted not just her body restored, I wanted a way for her to get out, to escape becoming the inevitable courtesan or slave. We became—fused, in a way. All that Kira was, is, is inside me, inside not just my head but all of me, yet it isn't a part of me. I have her memories but they're somebody else's memories, not mine. I'm still the same as I ever was, and maybe a little more. In some ways it's been quite—useful. My command of English is absolute, and my knowledge of Outplane science and devices is improved. More important, I understand the feminine outlook, which is both a more similar and more different view of the world than I'd ever thought. I also know what attracts them and what turns them on, what they want in a man. That's been—useful. Not just in the way you think, but in various dealings as well."

"But—I saw her!"

He nodded. "It's my turn from sunup to sundown. That's the way the curse works. Then it's her turn. For me, it's just going to sleep, and she takes over, physically and mentally. Like me, she has all my memories, and so she knows what went on during the day—she will know about you and this conversation as I know about last night—but she will not be me. She likes men, by the way. Sorry. Apparently more now than before, and for the same reasons I gave about women. She's formally registered as a citizen of Holibah, the kingdom we were in, which took some bribes and connections. This business seemed perfect, since any kind of permanent relationship with anyone is kind of out of the question for either of us, and because she's sleeping all day and I sleep all night there is a presence here who needs no sleep at all, which is quite handy, particularly out here. In most ways she got the better of it. She gets to be wined and dined and romance men in the dark, and I get to do all the shit work during the day. I pay a bit by not having a night life and she pays by lonely nights standing guard at four in the morning, but we are best at our appointed times. Still, the joke is really on the demon. It was going to keep us lovers forever apart, unable to kiss or embrace, but we are closer than if we could."

She whistled. "And I thought *I* was havin' identity problems!"

"No, no!" he laughed. "There's no conflict. I'm not Kira and she's not Crim. Just remembering what the other said and did isn't the same as being them. Still, as I have her English, she's got my native command of Akhbreed and my knowledge of its people and its territory. And, there's an odd by-product. We age only when we are 'alive,' as it were. Each of us is aging at half the rate."

He paused. "It's hard to explain, but when you talked I couldn't help thinking that in a way that's what you've got to come to grips with yourself. Sam doesn't pop out at sunset, but she's still a part of you that you have to deal with. You're not the Misa we saw last night. You're totally different. You're Sam with a Misa outlook and maybe that's not so bad."

She considered it. "Well, we'll see. I got to see this change, though, before I'll believe it."

"You'll see it. Or, rather, you'll be around many times when it happens. It's *very* quick. But we, all three of us, luck willing, will be with each other for quite some time. Months, probably. It's a long way to Masalur."

"You're a Navigator. How come we just can't go straight there?"

"Because the Earth is round. All of them are."

"What? I don't see . . ."

"Akahlar intersects with thousands of worlds, but the only common points are the hubs, the points of greatest force and power. The rest are compressed around the hubs and only intersect at certain random intervals. But when they *do* touch, they are worlds touching round worlds—so that actual point of overlap is very narrow. Kudaan is a world, not a desert. This is the Kudaan Wastes, a large desert on the planet, but not all of the planet is this way by any means. If we go outside that narrow overlapping strip then we'll simply wander the face of Kudaan and never intersect a hub. The only way to go is along the strips and through the hubs. We're being a little roundabout in our routing, but we're still going to head for the border of Mashtopol and we have to go into and through that hub to go farther. There are no short cuts, for anybody. At least there I have a number of contacts. We'll get you new identity papers—as Misa, I think, a colonial peasant of Kudaan whose services are bound to me by your liege lord as a favor because I'm short some experienced animal tenders. That won't be citizenship or anything—you'll be little more than a bound slave I can't sell but that's about the only restriction—but it'll explain your appearance, ways, speech, and the like."

"That's okay. I don't mind."

"We'll probably play a bit with your appearance, too, just to make it even harder for them. Maybe dye your hair and a few other simple things. The real colonial women of the Kudaan, as opposed to the refuge people, have certain cultural things about them and we want to be right just in case. They're considered primitive and terminally crazy from the sun and because they generally like to live in that sort of place. I wouldn't worry about the dialect—your class dialect is okay and there are probably dozens or hundreds around just the dry continent."

She nodded. "Okay, but I want to keep myself up as well. I don't want these muscles to go, 'cause once they're gone I got an awful feelin' they'll never come back. I'm gonna lift weights and put myself through a pretty damned hard routine and stick to it. And I want some training from you, too."

His eyebrows rose. "Training?"

"You're a pretty big guy. I seen the swords back there, and the rifles and pistols. I want to learn how to use a sword. I want to learn how to shoot and hit what I aim at. I want to know about and practice with just about every kind of weapon and defense thing there is. If it's gonna be months, then we have time for some of it. We ain't gonna be movin' all the time."

Crim liked the idea. "If you're really serious, I can run you through swords and other heavy weapons every morning before we start out. Give you as much as I can. Don't expect to be a master—you haven't the height or agility for it—but maybe I can have you hold your own. We'll do some horsemanship, too, and everything else time permits. Kira—she can teach you as well. Pistol shooting is a close-range thing and she's good at it. She can also fence, which is something I never had the control for, and she knows a number of ways for somebody relatively small and weak like she is to throw a heavy attacker across the camp. It'll be frustrating for a while and it'll take practice, but if you really want to learn it's a very good thing. If anything happens to me or Kira, or if there's any kind of a fight, you'll be much more valuable."

She nodded. "I was just thinkin' 'bout what you said about these worlds only touchin' at narrow strips and us havin' to go through the hubs at the gates. I mean, the enemy's gotta know that, too, right?"

He nodded. "And that's why we have to turn you into someone else as quickly as we can."

9
On Dangerous Ground

They had a pretty good head start but it was a very long distance across the null to the colonial boundary, far more than you could expect a horse already well traveled to make with maximum effort.

Still, Dorion, Boday, and Charley did not have quite the pressure of an armed mob after them. Some had been close enough to the border to see the Stormrider destroyed or whatever they did to him and it had a major effect. There had been no immediate pursuit, and when the rest of the gang had gathered and been told how the Stormrider had been defeated and possibly killed, something considered impossible up to then by anyone, there was a lot of debate and hesitation about going after them. Anyone who could take on a Stormrider and win had powerful magic, and what were guns and swords to that sort of power?

Still, nothing builds courage like greed, and a few of them were still game for the chase no matter what. Perhaps they didn't believe the large number of witnesses, or perhaps they had little to live for unless they got a very big score, but finally a half dozen men broke ranks and galloped off into the null.

By this time, however, the fugitives had built up a lead of more than two miles, and Dorion, thinking as fast as he could, had angled them well off the straight-line path to the colonial boundary. He knew well that at some point the horses were going to need a rest, and if they were out of sight then the null became a fairly large place indeed to hide in, one also shrouded in dense electrical fog and covered by incessant heavy clouds and occasional rain, and in which darkness was a great ally.

Charley rode like she had always ridden this way, with confidence in spite of limited vision. In fact, her vision was far worse here than it was back in the hub, since the magic of the null spread out all around her and obscured somewhat Dorion's own form. It was fortunate that his aura or whatever it was was a different and contrasting color, and that it seemed to float over the mists. For a while, though, it was nearly too bright, as Dorion took them for a long stretch at right angles to the boundaries and thus created the mist ahead of her as far as anyone could see, sighted or not.

Finally, after an interminable number of zigs and zags and a lot of all-out riding, the magician slowed and shouted for them to stop.

"We'll stop here and rest the horses," he told them. "Boday, stay on guard in case those bastards somehow spotted us, or start this way. I think we can relax for a little, though. Feels like it's going to rain through here any minute, which will discourage them and cool off the horses, and we won't be easy to spot in here until daylight."

Charley slid wearily off her horse. "I said I wanted a bath, not a storm," she noted tiredly. "Still, I prefer anything to those men or that *thing*. It went so fast I can't be sure what happened to it, though."

Dorion shook his head in wonder. "How in the world did you get the idea of *grounding* it?"

She shrugged. "Well, you said they were gonna power the fence with some kind of magic energy, so when Boday said her bolt just went right through it I figured the thing had to be made of some kind of magic energy. Magic energy, I figured, had to work kind'a like regular energy—electricity and all—because of the fence."

"You were most certainly right," he responded, still not really believing it. "I wonder why no one else has ever thought of it, though?"

"Maybe 'cause nobody else happened to have a mile-long roll of copper wire handy when they met one," she suggested. "It's not exactly something you keep around for the right occasions. We were damned lucky there to have it."

He nodded, mostly to himself. "Lucky—or something else. Maybe that's why Yobi was fairly confident we'd make it."

"Huh?"

"Destiny. It is a difficult concept to explain to anyone not versed in the magic arts and probability theory as well, but I'll try and boil it down. Everything, not just life but mountains and flowers and air and fire and water, is or contains energy. It—you, me, Boday—is a collection of mathematical equations that make us what we are and who we are. From the moment we're born, perhaps even conceived, this energy construct interacts with everything and everyone around it."

"I can't figure if you're talking astrology or genetics," she responded honestly.

"Neither. Both, sort of. But we each have a thread, a destiny, that we follow. It is layered, from primal to inconsequential. Some people just seem to be naturally lucky; others seem to always have a little black demonic cloud over them causing them untold and undeserved misery. It is not dependent on intelligence or courage or anything else, or its lack. That's why so many rotten people get all the breaks and so many good ones still suffer. Your destiny pattern is randomly assigned by so many factors that one can only influence a few of them. Magic is really an attempt to alter or change some of those patterns. The more powerful the magician, the more factors for more people or places or things he or she can influence."

She thought about it and didn't much like it. "You sound like we're actors going through somebody's script, only we don't know and can't really read the script."

"Well, it's not quite that bad," he told her, "but that is one way of looking at destiny. You *can* change some things, of course, and the fact that your destiny is so complex that no one can ever completely figure it out gives things a certain amount of spice, but basically the script idea is valid. Magicians can read a few lines and directions of the script; sorcerers can read whole pages or scenes. But no one can grasp it all. The First Equation, which set all else in motion and created the universes and all they contain or will contain, created the complexities of everything's destiny. If you believe that was the product of an intelligence, then that is your religion. If you believe that it was random, then you're not religious. Religion has little really to do with magic for all its trappings. Even the gods and devils and spirits are creations, like us, of that destiny and not lords of it. Only the changewind, being of the same sort as the First Equation, can actually alter those equations. It's the random factor that keeps everything from becoming scripted, so to speak."

She was fascinated, but felt a bit uncomfortable at the idea nonetheless. "And you're saying that it was our destiny to beat that thing and its destiny to die or dissolve or whatever? That it wasn't chance or even somebody's design but destiny we just happened to show up where the wire was and I figured out how to use it?"

"Not quite. What Yobi felt, what the others might be learning now, is that it is your destiny to survive. You are a survivor, and probably your friend, too. That's what attracted Boolean to your friend in the first place. In fact, it makes sense. If she's created genetically the same as the Storm Princess, then the two probably share much of the primal parts of destiny as well, and the Storm Princess is a true survivor. It means that you will always have the means of a way out. It doesn't necessarily mean that you have the will to take it, but it is there. Consider that flood that destroyed your wagon train as an example. Most died, yet all three of you survived. The rest, for the most part, were killed later—but not you three. You survived. You fell into the wrong hands but somehow eventually fell into just the right ones. They do their worst against you, and you are still going. You see? That is what Yobi could see. That is why the copper wire was there, and that was why you had the knowledge to put it together."

"Damn!" she sighed. "And here I was feeling real good about how clever and smart I was to come up with that."

His tone softened. "But you *were!* I—I can't tell you how—impressed—I am. To have been so cool and calm and analytical under such pressure, to have put it all together—it was *brilliant.* You are a very remarkable young woman."

He said that sincerely, and she liked the sound of it a lot better than that destiny crap. She was brilliant, he said, and brave, he said, and she was also every heterosexual guy's wet dream to boot. What more could you want? For a minute it might turn your head and take your mind off the fact that you're starting to get rained on in the middle of literally nowhere, you have guys with guns looking all over for you, you're effectively blind, and you're a hell of a long way from anyplace safe.

"Hey! Magician!" Boday called, and the other two tensed, wondering if she heard something. "Boday caught your half of that discussion. Her destiny is unknowable so Boday does not think about it. If one is ignorant of it, then what good is it? But if you magicians can see even a bit of it, then why are we cowering here in this shower afraid of a bunch of brigands? Why did we all wind up in such a spot to begin with? Where are your powers? Why is it that you cannot whip a spell up that would curse our enemies and protect us all?"

It was a fair question, but not one Dorion liked talking about. He cleared his throat nervously.

"Well, uh, it's true I know the stuff and it's also true I have a fair amount of power, but my powers are a bit—odd—and restrictive," he replied uncomfortably.

"So? If those hordes of men show up now Boday can take only a very few with her. She would need your magic or all is lost."

He sighed. "I'd use it if I had to," he said carefully, "but not unless I do."

"Your power is not great?"

"Oh, it's great—potentially," he admitted. "It's just, well, *unpredictable.*" He sighed. "All right, then, I guess I may as well tell you. It's control. Some say concentration. Some have said I've got some kind of brain damage or something that makes it happen. Others, well, they have been less kind. That's why I was out there in the Wastes with Yobi and a few others. I was scared to get back into civilized company where I might do more harm."

Charley, too, was interested now. "Harm?" She paused a moment, sensing his embarrassment. "It's all right. We should know, and we won't tell."

He thought a moment, trying to figure out the best way to explain. "I was born the child of magicians and a grandchild of a great sorcerer," he told them. "The power in me is strong. And I know how to use it. Really, I do. That's what is so tough about it. The ability to tap magic is inbred; you are either born with it or you're not. But it's not enough. You also have to be able to use what great power and energy you can draw, and that means you have to have a tremendous mathematical mind. There are set spells, simple things, that anyone with the power can learn to do, even me. And if you have the memory and years of study, you can memorize even huge spells and make them work. I know a couple but I was never that good at rote memory. I get bored too easily. An acolyte is one with the power who can work the simple spells. Third Rank knows enough of the big ones to demonstrate it and get his or her ticket. Those are the craft ranks. Second Rank, like the Akhbreed sorcerers, are mathematical genuises who can size up a situation they've never been in before and create complex spells in their head and impose them, improvising as they go. Me, I knew enough to reach Third Rank, but just barely, but I can't help *improvising* and it just doesn't work right."

Boday shrugged and Charley looked blank.

"Look," he tried, talking to Boday, "you're an artist, I understand. If somebody learns enough to copy great paintings and sculptures perfectly, they have perfected their craft but are they artists?"

"Of course not!" she huffed. "Art is not something one *learns,* it is something one *feels.*"

"Okay, so I'm a barely talented craftsman but I have the urge of an artist. I keep improvising in spite of myself, even with the simple stuff. I had to take a hypnotic drug to pass the Third Rank tests. Only I don't have the mathematical ability to build equations into infinity on the fly. Even if I work 'em out, or have time to, somehow they don't stay that way when I use them."

"You mean your spells don't work?" Charley prompted.

"No, no! I've got great power, but no control. The mathematics is wrong, or fuzzy, or incomplete. The spells work, all right—they do incredible things. But they don't do what I designed them to do or want them to do. Sometimes they only half work. A spell to take us all to a desert island might take us to a desert instead. A spell to make us invisible or invulnerable might well make everyone *but* us invisible or invulnerable. No matter what I try or how careful I am, it goes wrong. I work a spell and gold is transmuted to lead. I once accidentally turned a handsome young fellow into a toad. Stock spell, but not the one I was trying to do. Rather than try to undo it I decided on the usual remedy, got a pretty girl to kiss him. She turned into a toad, too. I am a danger and a menace. I've been exiled by many governments for their and my own good. Don't you see, I don't *dare* use any magic if I can help it. Particularly when it involves Mashtopol. I only hope Boolean will understand my service without killing me first."

Charley's head shot up. "Boolean? You *know* him?"

"All too well," Dorion admitted sadly. "How do you think I got to know English? Several of the newer Akhbreed sorcerers are English speakers. For a long while, before my time, it was something called German but they're pretty well gone now. Boolean speaks English and German and a lot of other languages, too, and not all by spell, either, but he *thinks* in English and he's most comfortable using it, so everybody around him has to learn it."

"There's a world of Akahlar, then, that speaks English?" Charley asked him. "That's why he does?"

"Uh-uh. There's thousands of tongues, and probably a few close to English or one of the others, but none that really speak it. Boolean and many of the others, they aren't originally from Akahlar. They're Outplaners, like you. Some of the best are Outplaners. They were born with the power but either never knew it or were too far away from the Seat to really use or draw on it or something, but they were whizzes at mathematics and real geniuses. They get here and put it together in a flash and do in a few years what it takes ones like Yobi hundreds of years to attain. Boolean says that it's because Outplaners don't have to unlearn a lot of the crap and mysticism that we're brought up with. That they have a different perspective. Maybe. How could I know?"

Charley's mind flashed back. Long ago, so long ago now, in the maelstrom that brought both her and Sam to this place, Boolean had saved them from Klittichorn, had stalled the horned sorcerer to get them past and out of his clutches. She hadn't understood Akhbreed at all at the time, not having Sam's mysterious link to this world, but she realized now for the first time that she'd understood that exchange between the sorcerers. They had spoken in English!

Boolean—from the Outplane, maybe from her own world or one very much like it. And maybe this Klittichorn, too? Jeez! To be dropped here, suddenly, and find that somehow you could learn to have godlike powers . . . No wonder they all went nuts!

Dorion was obviously uncomfortable discussing his own magical past and abilities and she decided not to press it. Still, it gave him a more human dimension. He was a pretty nice guy, and smart, and he sure had guts. His guilty secret, his embarrassment, was actually kind of sweet.

Dorion sighed. "I think we've gotten wet enough," he told them. "Let's mount up and make our way carefully over to the colonial border. If those guys didn't spot us by now then they're not going to."

Boday nodded. "Still, if Boday was in their saddle, she would have men riding up and down the border area hoping to spot us, and if she couldn't prevent us she could at least signal the others to get into the same world that we did."

"Right, and so we're still going to have to be careful," the magician agreed. "You can only take this destiny business so far. Maybe Charley will somehow get through, maybe destiny will take you in sight of the goal only to thwart you—we can't know. But even if it's your destiny to reach Masalur, it might not be mine. I'm not taking any chances."

They rode along in relative silence for more than an hour. Dorion had to bring them in a bit; they had wandered so far north that they risked the true null point, where they might well fall into the void or into a netherhell. Only a strip of each world was touching Akahlar, and all those worlds were round. There was a point where the curvature of each earth rolled off and another rolled up and on, and in that region many things were possible, none of them desirable.

Dorion thought of this, but his thoughts were most of all on Charley. She was unlike any woman he had ever known, even for an Outplaner. She was beautiful, sexually uninhibited, almost every male kid's private fantasy. Only they were just sex objects, not real people, and the beautiful and sexually uninhibited women he'd known were generally ignorant, dumb, broken in spirit, or had a screw loose somewhere. Charley, though, really was brilliant, imaginative, and as strong-willed and independent-minded as a queen or sorceress might be. Slave ring or not, nobody, particularly no man, would ever be her real master, that was for sure.

Hell, he knew as much about electrical properties as she did, maybe more, and he also knew far more about the nature of Stormriders. He had seen and known about the same materials that she had suggested using, but it would never have occurred to him to use them, or that they were of any use except as a barricade for a last stand. He, and probably Boday, would have stood and fought and died back there, or at best been captured and held by an enemy too powerful to defy. Not Charley.

She didn't need any magic, or regular sight. Her own abilities were far stronger than that. If she understood that, if she ever saw herself the way she was instead of just a pretty girl with common sense, there was nothing she could not do or have. The fact that she did not realize that her mind was far more exceptional than her body was the only thing holding her back.

Damn it, he was falling in love with her and he didn't know what to do about it. Hell, he didn't even have any real experience with women. It wasn't for lack of desire, it was just, well, he'd never exactly been handsome or athletic or had the kind of personality that attracted women. Now, here he was—and, as usual, he was a comrade, not a lover. He hadn't had much attraction before, he knew, but now that she also knew his terrible secret about his magic he felt he had no chance at all.

They were all surprised to find the colonial border essentially peaceful and undefended, not knowing that only six of the small horde of gunmen had gone off in pursuit of them. Still, crossing in this far from the entry station was not without its risks. Roads were deliberately engineered so that they led only to entry stations; people in general were not allowed to live close to a border or have access to it in order to make it more difficult for anyone coming in the back way, and there was much use of natural as well as artificial boundaries to make anyone coming in far from the gates very miserable.

Dorion was nervous. Knowing all this, he didn't want to take the first reasonable world that came along, but he was also conscious that the longer they remained there, poised at the boundary but still within the null, the more likely that someone would come along. *They* might hide, but not the horses, and without the horses their chance of crossing a strange colonial world undetected was much slimmer.

Charley had always been fascinated by the ways the border changed—very abruptly, as if it was a colored slide of some place that just faded out as another faded in—but this scene was no longer possible to enjoy. She could see only the energy part of the null's mists and the fuzzy colored shapes of Dorion and Shadowcat and that wasn't much. She got down off the horse and from her pack located the box with a preservation spell on it in which there was ground meat for Shadowcat. The cat ate like a pig, and even though it wasn't that old she was already running low.

The cat ate with his usual gusto, then crawled into her lap for a pet, oblivious to the wet conditions. Well, she was wet herself. The cat climbed up so its head was looking over her right shoulder, body limply down and held, and purred like an outboard motor as she scratched and petted him.

Charley was conscious of the curse of holding and stroking the cat by now. It was nice to be able to project yourself to anyone, regardless of their language, but having your forward, surface thoughts broadcast whether you were trying to communicate or not was unnerving. It was impossible to lie under such circumstances, and at least once already Boday had become offended by a stray thought of Charley's. The trouble, really, was boredom, which had allowed such stray thoughts to creep in, and she found that the technique she'd developed from those nights as a courtesan and refined further during her interminably boring stay at Hodamoc's helped a lot in both regards. She had two personalities inside her head, and by just relaxing she could push her real self well into the background, almost on standby, and allow the simple courtesan Shari to assume forward control. Shari didn't think very much, and she was quite content to just sit there blankly petting Shadowcat and awaiting some order or instruction.

Dorion watched the slowly changing procession of worlds and tried to stave off boredom once one came up that was obviously unacceptable. High granite walls had greeted their approach. The next two, at roughly twenty-minute intervals, were both seascapes; vast stretches of salt water without land or dock in sight. Even land didn't mean much, really. The average world was three-fifths or more covered with water; it wouldn't do to step out into a fairly nice-looking place only to discover you were on an island. That was a favorite of this particular region as well—islands big and small.

In a way, it was a tempting fantasy. Marooned, the only man on a tropical island with two women, one of whom was Charley, and both with the enslaving rings bound to him. He knew it was ego-centric and self-centered and didn't take the women's interests into account, but, hell, it was *his* fantasy . . .

In the end, it wouldn't even matter to the scheme of things or the shaking of events. It was the other one, this Sam, who mattered. It was such a tempting thing, he and Charley, romping naked in the surf of some tropic isle . . .

He was so lost in his own dreams that he almost failed to notice the sudden change in the colonial tableau. It was speeding up, taking on almost a blurry appearance. After a minute or so he suddenly realized what was happening and jumped to his feet.

"Mount up fast!" he shouted. "A Navigator's working on the border! That means that whatever comes up will probably have people and some kind of civilization, so we're not likely to get stuck in some monster-infested swamp or another Kudaan!"

Charley suddenly snapped back to control, jumped up, and with a little trouble found Shadowcat's socklike carrier and slipped him in, then mounted up. She was getting very good at this now, she thought to herself with satisfaction.

The view that suddenly came up and locked in looked quite pleasant but it wasn't a hundred percent encouraging, either. A wide landscape illuminated by bright moonlight lay before them, covered with thick grasses going down to a white sandy beach and a beautiful bay beyond with some dark areas showing a light or two that might have been islands. The beach wound around the bay, and on both sides there were low rocky mountains that on the right came to a major promontory and on the left seemed to stretch out into the darkness, a few small lights showing that it went for a considerable distance. That meant shoreline, and the possibility that if this was an island it was a damned big one—and it was possibly a main land mass. Hot, humid air struck them.

"It appears to be the start of an ocean," Boday noted. "Are you certain that this is the one we can use? We will have to cross that, you know."

He nodded. "We'll have to cross some ocean anyway to get where we're going, so it might as well be where can see a lot of land. Move in now! We don't know how long whoever it is will be able to hold this position!"

They went forward, and suddenly the air seemed very thick and heavy and there was the smell of salt spray in every breath and the sound of small but steadily advancing waves striking the shore. Somewhere ahead Charley could hear the clanging of bells, possibly markers out in the bay itself or even beyond. She just kept her eyes on the crimson blur that was Dorion.

Now there was the feel of the horse in sand—fairly hard-packed, wet sand at that, and she could both feel and hear that they were within the reach of the waves themselves.

This was one of those times when she was really hit by her lack of sight. They were out of the null now, and all was just that deep gray with those few fuzzy colored smudges she'd come to recognize as Dorion and other magical things.

They rode for quite some time at the water's edge, although at a slow pace to keep the horses from collapsing. She wondered why, and finally shouted the question out to him.

"I can see the high tide mark, and the tide's coming in," he yelled back. "It's vaguely possible that somebody might stumble on our tracks entering this world, but even now the waves are totally wiping out our new tracks and our direction. If we can find some place, like a shallow stream cut, to go inland with the same effect we'll do so and make camp. We can do with some rest and I think we can risk a campfire for some decent food. I think we want to explore our situation in daylight."

He eventually found what he sought, and they made their way away from the sea, although not terribly far, the horses making their way in the shallows of a rock-strewn stream, until he found a place with reasonable cover. The ground was fairly hard, but the stream water was fresh and drinkable, and the small fire would not be visible from the beach area and wasn't likely to be observed from the bordering junglelike forest.

Charley barely touched her food; Shadowcat wandered out after they had finished to explore the area, and she found herself basically wet and grimy and all-around miserable but, most of all, she needed sleep. The bedroll wasn't the most comfortable place on such hard ground, but it didn't matter. She was soon fast asleep.

The next morning she awoke feeling a bit guilty. She'd slept solidly and well, not being able to share in the duties of being a camp guard which kept the other two from enjoying a long and uninterrupted sleep. It wasn't so much that the blindness limited her activities, since she was learning to deal with that and barely thought about it now, but the fact that it limited her usefulness in such a situation to the others. She checked for Shadowcat and found him curled up sound asleep at the bottom of the bedroll and a little miffed that she had the temerity to wake up and move and spoil his comfortable bed.

Boday saw her rise and came over to her. "Boday has been exploring the area a bit, and has found a large pool just inside the bush which the stream has dug deep," she told Charley. "It would be breast-high on you, and it is a bit colder than one might like, but Boday thinks you might want to use it as she did."

Charley did—and *how* Charley did. Boday was right—the pool was fairly chilly relative to the air, but the water seemed clean and smelled okay and there was enough of it. She might have liked some soap, and particularly some shampoo, but even as basic as it was it was *wonderful*. Somehow it made her feel human again, even though she wondered if her hair would ever dry in this humidity. Not only that, but she could wash out her really smelly, filthy clothes, although again the drying would take time. For a while, all she'd have was the never-before-used cape, which was kind of sexy without anything under if a potential modesty-preserver. Any saddle sores that might develop in the interim had developed long ago; she was pretty toughened now to riding bare-assed in the saddle.

Dorion could not wake up without his thick, super-strong coffee that could be smelled a ways off, so Charley had to wait until he and Boday had drunk their fill of the filthy stuff before she could get the pot cooled, cleaned, and boil some water for her tea. Then it was time for discussions on what came next.

"We must go east," Dorion told them. "That's the only way to Quodac and that in turn is the way we must go. It's going to mean a boat, from the looks of it, and that means finding civilization. The main road from the entry gate's got to be no more than thirty or forty leegs tops from here, probably closer. The odds are good that if we can find it it'll take us to a coastal city or town."

"Well, aren't we gonna be a little conspicuous?" Charley asked him. "Even if they aren't on the lookout for us, which they might well be, three strangers showing up not even knowing what the world is called are gonna raise a few eyebrows. At least somebody'll check and see that we didn't come through that gate. And you said some Navigator called up this place, so they're likely to be there waiting for a boat, too. They got to have heard about all the commotion over us back there, and they'll put two and two together."

"I know." Dorion nodded. "Still, I can't wave my arms and materialize a boat for us with a knowledgeable pilot aboard. I can *try*, but I'd probably wind up with a sea monster working for Klittichorn. I don't think it's going to be as bad as you say, though, and there's always the age-old method of bribery." He sighed. "Well, let's saddle up and see if we can find this town or port or whatever it turns out to be. We can't know how to solve our problems until we find out what the problems are." He thought a moment. "There were some lights last night father on up the coast where we're heading. Not enough for a town, but maybe some private dwellings, maybe even native. Just stay loose and relaxed and we'll see if we can find somebody to give us the information."

That somebody was a good two hours' ride away up the beach. It was a strange-looking shack made out of native woods with the design looking like everything had been compromised. Certainly the oddball lumps, deliberately sagging roofs, and very small additions sprouting out from it made it look very strange indeed.

Stranger still was the creature who peeked out curiously from a trapdoor in the top of the thing as they approached and watched them come up to the place and stop.

It was totally hairless, a very pale green in color, with a leathery skin and wide, somewhat webbed feet that ended in very mean-looking claws. Its arms were rather short and ended in hands with three gnarled fingers and an opposing thumb that terminated in a sharp, spikelike nail. Although a tailless humanoid, its face was more reptilian than Akhbreed human, its nose just two indented nostrils above a wide, flat mouth, its eyes bulging from its head and covered with thick, rubbery lids that barely moved. It wore some sort of necklace but no clothing, and yet its sex was impossible to determine just from looking at it. It did not, however, seem afraid of them, merely curious.

"Uh-oh," Dorion said in a low tone. "Looks like this world has a very different set of natives. Maybe *too* different. I'm not sure that mouth could form Akhbreed words or sounds if it knew it. Still, no harm in trying."

"If it does not try and eat us," Boday responded nervously, putting a hand on her pistol but not drawing it lest it provoke an attack.

"Good day," Dorion attempted, a bit nervous himself. "Do you understand my tongue?"

The creature stood there a moment without responding, then let loose with a string of sounds that were a cross between a hiss and an impossible collection of all consonants.

Charley couldn't see the creature and so picked up Shadowcat who deigned finally to look at the native. Even with Shadowcat's strange vision, the native was something of a shock, as alien a creature to humans as Charley had seen in Akahlar, even stranger than Ladai, the Ba'ahdonese centaur. Suddenly, though, she realized that she could communicate—if one way. She stroked Shadowcat.

"*Please,*" she thought, directing it at the native, "*I know you can read my thoughts with this spell although I cannot read yours. We are strangers in your land and we are lost. We seek the main road and perhaps a place to get passage west. Is there any way you can help us? We do not know your language, but while you can understand me we have no way of understanding you by speech, I fear. Can you help us?"*

The thing looked very surprised. It was amazing how much very human emotion came through that reptilian form, although you never really knew if the reactions meant the same thing. At least it seemed to understand and thought a moment. Then it turned, went back into its house, and returned a moment later with a strange barbed spear, although it didn't seem menacing with it.

The creature leaned over, smoothed some sand, and began to use the spear point to draw a crude design.

"A map! It is making a crude map for us!" Boday exclaimed. "How—primitive—the style."

Dorion got down to study the design, finally having to turn the other way when he realized he was looking at it upside down. Yes, there *they* were, and there was the coast, and there was a road or trail or something leading inland a bit farther on. It appeared that this was some sort of peninsula, and that the town was on the opposite side and a bit before the point.

"I think I've got it!" he told them. "If we can find the trail. Charley, thank him or her for the help and let's be off. I can't tell from the sun how much time we might have left, and I'd rather be in a town used to Akhbreed travelers than in the middle of a strange jungle by nightfall."

She did so, and they started off, leaving the native standing there and watching them go.

"At least the language barrier keeps us from being asked embarrassing questions," Boday noted.

"True, but not from *thinking* them," Dorion responded worriedly. "I hope after this world we'll be able to keep in areas closer to Akhbreed types, though. Keep a sharp watch, too. Remember, we're Akhbreed and we aren't exactly the most popular folks in the colonies to the colonials no matter what our personal opinions are. It was probably being legitimate and nice, but you can't tell when one of them will direct you right off a cliff."

While the trail wasn't easy to find and wasn't really designed for people on horses, they *were* able to spot it by going slow and having Boday check out every likely access, and they were able to use it single-file, although Charley had some tough time avoiding low-hanging branches and the like that she could not see ahead of her and which were low enough to unhorse anyone not ready. Finally, after falling off and getting bruised, Dorion took her horse as a lead while she climbed onto Boday's mount, riding behind her doubled up in the saddle. It wasn't very comfortable and made her aware of her limitations more than she liked, but she preferred that to breaking her neck or even getting permanent rips in her face and body.

The trail was a bit over eight miles long and slow going, but at last they reached the downward slope and the jungle gave way rather suddenly to thick grasslands and a picturesque view of a second and smaller bay below. The town was easy to spot and not much; one main street, some warehouses, a two-block-long row of facing buildings, none over two stories tall, and, most important, a dock.

"Remain here and relax," Dorion told them. "I can't see any sign of a train down there and the place looks more Akhbreed than what we saw on the other side, but you never can tell about anything. If I go in alone at first I can get the lay of the land without rousing too much suspicion. A magician can always travel between the worlds on his own, and without you two I won't stand out so much." He looked around. "I'd go back up close to the woods and off the trail and just wait. From the looks of the sun we've got about three hours to sunset. A half hour down, one or two in town, and then maybe three-quarters of an hour to an hour back up here. You are commanded to hide, wait, and make no contact with anyone until I return. Avoid contact unless it's forced, defend yourself in that case if you have to, but avoid being seen. Understand?"

Boday nodded. "Yes, we understand. But it will be very inconvenient if something happens and you do not return."

He thought about that. "Well, I don't think it'll be that serious, but if I don't return by sunrise you are to consider me dead and are to make it on your own to Boolean by whatever means you wish. Your one overriding command is to reach Boolean. In that case you, Boday, will be the warrior slave Koba and you, Charley, will be the courtesan slave Yssa, as before, and no torture, no spell, will prevail to get your true identity. And while you will do anything you must to reach Boolean as fast and as safely as possible, you will not reveal the name of your Master, only that you must go to him. Understand?"

They both nodded. "Take care of yourself," Charley told him sincerely. "Don't make us go off on our own again."

He grinned. "I don't intend to." And, with that, he was off and going down the trail towards the town.

"Come," Boday said firmly. "We must get off the trail and hide ourselves." There was no hesitancy or thought of disobedience in any way. Although they were quite casual with Dorion, they were bound to carry out his commands.

They found a spot about a hundred yards off the trail that had a means of getting into what Dorion called the woods—more like a jungle, really. The horses could be brought to cover, however, and still have something to graze upon, and they would be able to monitor the trail without being seen.

"Boday is uncomfortable with this situation," she growled, sitting as guard just behind a few trees and with a clear view of the immediate trail. "She is an artist, not a slave and a warrior, although there are many she would love to kill right now. Still, she perseveres for the sake of her beloved Susama."

It being still daylight, Shadowcat had no interest in being anything but a lump, and Charley disturbed him and then sat petting him, making a sort of conversation possible so long as she watched herself. The distance to the trail was much too long to carry her thoughts.

"You really miss Sam, don't you?"

Boday seemed surprised and also surprisingly soft. "Yes. Boday loves her. Do you think that anything else would have brought her forth from her comfortable studio, her art, and keep her going through all this?"

"But—it's due to a potion. One of your own potions. You know that."

Boday shrugged. "What difference? One feels what one feels. Boday dreams about her, thinks about her all the time. It is real. It is now a part of Boday, the most important part. All those husbands, and all those lovers—male, female, and other—over the years, and Boday never really loved any of them, nor felt any love really from them, either. It made her heart cold, her art surface and cynical. Now Boday both loves and suffers. One day she will create art that none will deny is great and glorious and immortal—if she lives. The potion was perhaps part of Boday's destiny." She paused a moment, reflecting. "You, however. You have never loved. You have lusted, as Dorion lusts for you, but never loved."

Charley was startled. "Dorion lusts after me? But he could take me anytime he wanted to! I'd have to obey! Hell, he could have *both* of us if he wanted to, and you know it."

Boday gave a slight smile. "Yes, but he is from a cloistered youth, and he has never learned how to approach women properly, nor read them, as most do when they are just teens. What he did learn during that time was a strong sense of honor and propriety which is keeping him dull and miserable. His status as a magician is the only thing that gives him any sense of self-worth, and he feels flawed in that. Far worse when he has to admit it, worse yet when he must admit it to women."

Charley was stunned by this. "How did you figure all this out?"

"You are too young, my precious flower. You may have had hundreds of men, but they were just a commodity to you, all the same after a while. You mistake your expertise in sex for expertise in people, but they are not the same. Most men see women more as objects than equals; do not make the same mistake in reverse or you become like what you hate in them. Boday is close to twice your age, and, she suspects, has lived four times your lifetime. Boday knows these things."

Charley made no reply, but the words hit home and were very uncharacteristic of Boday. Perhaps she, or maybe all of them, had missed something in the woman, seeing only the flake. And, of course, that's just what Boday was accusing *her* of doing. Seeing only the surface and never looking beneath. Her two-level personality she had mostly taken for granted as, like Boday's love for Sam, it was alchemically induced. At least, she'd been telling herself that all along. But was she kidding herself, really? It wasn't magic, it was drugs of some kind, permanent or not. Wasn't that really the difference between magic and alchemy? Magic created and destroyed; alchemy only enhanced or depressed what was already there.

Now Boday was saying that most, maybe all people acted on several levels, the public one being perhaps the best perceived to others but the least important in terms of really understanding the person underneath.

"You are learning, my sweet," Boday commented, and Charley suddenly realized that while she held Shadowcat her inner musings were basically public knowledge.

Boday looked out and frowned. "It is growing dark now and there is no sign of him. Boday begins to be nervous. Each of these paths so far has led to a bottleneck that has spelled trouble."

Charley began to share the nervousness. "What happens if he doesn't come back by dawn?"

Boday sighed. "We have our orders and we must obey them. First we go back across the border. Then we use some of the valuables in the saddlebags and we buy incongruous clothing and create for ourselves still other appearances, and then we bribe our way across or hire aid or we make it alone. If Boday can get some alchemist's supplies she can change us yet again. We can do only that because we can do nothing else. Our free will is limited to improvising how we carry out our commands."

Charley knew that Boday was right, although she didn't relish it. There was still a long way to go and a lot that could go wrong.

Later on in the night someone did come up the trail on horseback, and Charley peered out and looked in the general direction of the sounds approaching from below. Boday was instantly at her side.

"It's Dorion," Charley said with some relief.

Boday didn't know English but she could understand that much. "How do you know? There are clouds tonight and the moon is either hidden or not yet up. Boday sees little."

The dark, however, was the same as bright daylight to Charley. She groped for the Akhbreed words. "Shari see Dorion *melagas,*" she tried, fumbling for the word for "aura" and settling for the one for "soul." She had stared at little else for quite some time now.

Boday was still worried. "I hope he is still in control of himself," she muttered. "Still, what could we do if he isn't? If he commanded us to surrender to the enemy we would be forced to do so."

And that summed up their dilemma and their frustrations all at once. They were subject to Dorion, and dependent on his own wit and independence.

Dorion stopped at the top of the trail at the edge of the woods. "Come out! Bring the horses and packs!" he called. "I think we might actually have gotten a break this time!"

Charley gave a mental summons to Shadowcat, and they got the horses and saddled them, packing up with a mixture of apprehension and relief. Charley worried when they made their way slowly out into the open because the cat had not yet shown up, but suddenly there was a flying fuzzball of lavender jumping up on the saddle, barely holding on with all claws. She helped him up and then stuck him in his makeshift riding sling.

"Don't cut it so close the next time," Charley warned the cat. "Remember, you need me as much as I need you."

The cat reacted with typical indifference.

Dorion was patient but seemed excited. "The town's an Akhbreed colonial town, although it's got a fair number of natives working there," he told them. "The thing is, I ran into an Imperial courier down there who's somebody I used to know. Somebody I was a kid with way back when. He's the one who brought this world up, by the way—carrying dispatches to Covanti. This is one of the fastest places to cross over, it seems, which is why it came up."

Boday wasn't so certain that this was a good thing. "How much does this person know?" she asked him. "About what happened back there, that is? Or about us? And how trustworthy might he or she be?"

"He," Dorion told them. "His name is Halagar. When we were kids we all looked up to him. He was a natural leader type. The kind you admired and hated all at the same time. You know—he was stronger than you, better-looking than you, always smarter than you. That kind. He's gotten older, just like me, but he hasn't changed all that much. As for what he knows—well, I've never known him to betray a confidence or an old friend. He might if he had direct orders, big pay, and believed in it, but I don't think that's the case here."

Boday still wasn't so sure, even as they made their way slowly and carefully down the trail to town. "If he is so Mister Wonderful how is it that he is a mere courier?"

"Oh, couriers are highly paid and highly skilled," the magician assured her. "And you're on your own and pretty independent of bosses and the like. They might have to be anywhere. He says he's taking it easy for now after some experiences that were a lot more harrowing. He talks about being in the military but whose and where I don't know. I think he might have been a mercenary, and ex-mercenaries don't like to advertise that. Some folks think a mercenary can always be bought."

Boday was clearly thinking along those lines as well, but there was nothing to do but follow Dorion's lead.

"There's a ship due in here tomorrow," Dorion continued. "It's a freighter but it'll carry passengers as well. A few days' sail and we'll cross the null into Covanti. When we do that we'll be buried enough that it'll be a lot easier to move, and we can rely on some of Yobi's people to take the load off."

"Sounds good," Charley responded, sharing some of Boday's doubts but not voicing them. "Maybe too good to be true."

Dorion had apparently been talking over old times with this Halagar in the bar of the small inn there and carefully getting what information he could about the town and the situation before figuring out a way to introduce and explain the two of them. His cover story here was pretty close to the truth: that he had been conned by an Akhbreed sorcerer into taking two female slaves consigned from one sorcerer to another.

"He knows that there's a whole mob on the lookout for three women wanted by Klittichorn," Dorion told them, "but the general word is that one's short and fat, one's got a painted body, and the third resembles the Storm Princess but has the butterfly tattoos.

Neither of you now matches any of those descriptions, really, and if you just keep your slave personas from this point on I don't think anybody's going to associate you two with them."

"That Stormrider did," Charley noted. "And those guys chasing us . . ."

"Not the same. The Stormrider no more 'sees' in the conventional sense than you do—or I do, for that matter. The patterns he saw are invisible to those without full magic sight, and I don't think he had much of a chance to have reported them to anyone. None of those men ever got close enough to get a good look; they were being summoned by the Stormrider by magical means. Now, that doesn't mean I want to stay around here any longer than we have to. The sooner we've crossed into Covanti and even beyond the more obscure all trails will be and the less likelihood of even a smart guy figuring out what's what there'll be. If Halagar is what he says and still basically honest, he can be a real help as far as Covanti hub itself."

"And if he is not?" Boday pressed. "If he turns out to be an enemy?"

They were coming right into the town now, and Dorion looked around, then sighed. "Then we will dispose of him as discreetly as possible. Any old friend who would betray me deserves no more respect from me than he gives."

Boday smiled. That, at least, was unambiguous, but left her with a great deal of latitude.

"There won't be many people in the inn," Dorion told them. "I think we're the only ones other than Halagar with a room there, which is a good thing since I don't think they can have more than four rooms total. They don't use this world much; mostly it's used by people like Halagar who want speed over all else, and for shipping emergency and highly perishable stuff. Ah! Here we are! Let's get the horses stabled and then we'll get some real food—not great but a lot better than what we've been eating—and sleep in real beds."

Until now Charley hardly remembered that she was wearing just the cloak, but now she suddenly felt self-conscious, not only about that but about how rotten her hair and her overall appearance might be—and she had no way to improve on it. Boday sensed her sudden feeling.

"We can not do much about the clothing—the old outfit never was much and is a mass of shrunken wrinkles right now—but we can at least comb the hair and get it looking somewhat presentable . . . so. Both of us would prefer a true bath and a wider choice of wardrobe and perhaps some slight makeup, but we do what we must with what we have. There! Not as lovely as you could look by half, but more than good enough."

It was no longer enough to simply follow Dorion's crimson aura; now there were steps and obstacles about which she could know nothing, and it was up to Boday to take her hand and guide her as well as she could.

Charley had never particularly liked Boday, but she was beginning to see why Sam had stuck by her. Boday was more and more showing her other, more hidden side, at least to Charley, and, most of all, she was totally trustworthy in a world where everybody seemed against Charley, Sam, and all that was good and holy. There was certainly no getting around the fact that Boday felt no guilt for turning young girls into mindless courtesans and whose only objection to slavery was which end she was on, but that wasn't all her fault, either. This world had bred Boday, and Akahlar bred harder, harsher people with ideas and standards formed in a quite different world than Charley's home. And even back home, there were people brought up to believe with all their heart that suicide for god was the best thing you could do so long as you took enemies with you and lots of equally weird stuff. Didn't the same guy who wrote "All men are created equal" own slaves? You couldn't blame them so much as you could blame the system that created them.

If nothing else, Charley was beginning to learn perspective.

The inn *was* small; a bar and back kitchen area opened onto a relatively tiny room with just five round tables. There was no electricity or other modem conveniences; even by Boday's standards this place was pretty primitive. In back and opposite the bar was a steep wooden staircase and rail leading upstairs. If the top floor wasn't any bigger than the bottom, then the four rooms up there were pretty small and the bathroom had to be in the back of the place.

Boday described it softly to Charley, who sighed and said, "Well, there goes the dream of a nice bath."

The inn was run by a couple of middle-aged Akhbreed types, the man of medium height but with bushy red hair and moustache and a great belly that no tunic could disguise. The woman, presumably his wife, was a bit shorter but of equal girth, wearing the traditional baggy dress and sandals and with short graying hair. They appeared to be in their fifties and they looked well suited to this sort of job in this middle-of-nowhere location.

The man greeted Dorion. "Well, I see you are back with your charges, magician," he said in a gravel voice that suited him. "You'll need two rooms, you know. No way to put three of you in one of ours."

"That's fine," Dorion responded. "I think the best thing to do would be to get settled in as best we can. Do you have any facilities for bathing? I think after so long on the trail that's a top priority."

The innkeeper scratched his chin. "Well, sir, we got one tub and heating the water's no problem. You understand, though, there'll be a charge."

"Just add it to the bill. If you can get started on that now, I'd also like to find some more suitable clothing for this pair. The elements have pretty well wrecked what they came with."

"We usually just go over to Quodac for that," the innkeeper responded. "No use in keeping much stock here, being so close to the border and all. Benzlau, he runs the dock and warehouse, keeps a stock of things, though, in case there's need. Might not be much of a fit, or much at all in women's clothes, but I'll get down there when we're through here and see if he can get a wub to open up the company supply store there. Closed now, of course."

"Wub?"

"The lizard folk. That's what we all calls 'em. They ain't too bright but they does a lot of heavy labor with no complaints around here. Most folks use 'em for most everything, but I don't allow 'em in here. For one thing, they get really nutty in the head when they get some booze in 'em, if you know what I mean, and they'll steal that sort of stuff. Best to keep 'em out of places like this."

The good old Akhbreed colonial mentality strikes again, Charley thought sourly. For people who weren't that bright that one back on the beach sure got the message fast and had no problems with a map. The fact was, they probably had more interaction with the "wub" than this guy did who lived and worked here simply because he treated them as the animals he saw them as being, while they'd treated the one as an equal human being. She couldn't help but wonder what most of this world, inhabited by only its natives, might be like. There might possibly be "wub" cities and "wub" kings and all the rest. The government probably knew, but to these people who lived here it was not only irrelevant, it was unimaginable.

"Thank you, that will be fine," Dorion assured him. "Have you seen my friend?"

"The courier? Yes, sir, he went out a little while back to check on the shipping and just take a walk down by the water, he said. He'll be back at any time."

As Dorion predicted, things began to work out, at least for a little while, in their favor. Dorion decided to try for the clothing problem first, while the bath situation was percolating, so to speak, and one of the wubs came after a while with a bunch of keys on a ring and led them to a door in the side of a big warehouse and then into the structure. At the rear was a separate room containing clothing, shoes, hats, boots, you name it. Most were in men's and boy's sizes and clearly were designed as replacements for clothing of the Akhbreed who lived and worked here and perhaps who lived and worked on the ship or ships. The women's clothing was mostly the sack-like dresses and, as slaves, they weren't allowed to don "respectable" clothes, something that distressed neither of them.

Nothing really fit Charley, but they found that large men's cotton T-shirts came down almost to her knees and they provided some protection and improvement over the bare nothing she really had. Boday found a couple of pairs of boys' black work pants that were okay at the waist although the legs weren't long enough. She decided the effect was all right, and went with them plus the same kind of shirt situation as Charley. Since Boday was so tall, the shirts were large and baggy but didn't come down nearly as far as they did on Charley, which made things work out.

"We will win no fashion awards, but it is acceptable," Boday pronounced.

The baths were crude but compared to the lack of them for so long Charley was not about to complain. With water a bit cooler than she liked it but with a big bar of soap she managed pretty well on her own, impressing the innkeeper's wife with her ability to manage without sight very well indeed. She didn't really want to get out, but considering that it was also Boday's turn she reluctantly did, now recapturing what it was like to actually have towels to dry off with once more. There was no doubt about it; no matter what else she was, Charley wasn't the wilderness-trail type. If there wasn't a good hotel every night, decent food, and the other creature comforts, she really wouldn't be happy.

As expected, there wasn't any indoor plumbing, but the inn's lone toilet was inside and reminded Charley somewhat of the port-a-johns back home. It had a regular seat and seemed to be made of metal, and it had a tank of something that kept it from smelling up the place and which took the crap to a holding area. She had the uneasy feeling that the contents of that tank wound up fertilizing the local gardens from which the inn and others got their fresh fruit and vegetables, but she didn't want to think on that very much.

Finding the cotton shirt acceptable and after then spending some time walking about and memorizing the general layout of the place she had it down pretty pat. She knew that many people might have a terrible time with this sort of thing, but somehow she just had this unsuspected talent. Give her an hour and she knew a place at least well enough to navigate if need be. Of course, with chairs moving, things changing as other people went in and out, and the like, you had to be cautious, but if need be she felt that she could leave her room, make her way down the stairs, find the john in back, do her business, and return to bed without help.

Dorion was right on the food. It wasn't all that great, but after what they'd been eating it seemed like fancy cuisine. Charley decided that her inclination to vegetarianism served her well here; the fruits and vegetables and even some nuts were quite good and fresh, leaving Dorion to grumble and Boday to sigh when eating the cooked parts. Charley did try a piece of the pie, but it was gummy and far too sweet and she didn't eat much of it.

They were just about done when Halagar entered the inn. Boday immediately saw what Dorion had meant in his description of his friend: Halagar was tall, broad-shouldered, muscular, and extremely handsome. He carried himself with the confidence of a professional soldier and officer at that, and what age and experience had added to his face and hands had only added to the effect. He was clean-shaven, with thick, black hair perfectly cut, and dark complected but not deeply so. His rich, baritone voice was just what you expected, and it had a melodic, almost hypnotic quality about it. This was the sort of man heads turned to see whenever he entered a room, and who was automatically the center of attention. Boday thought him perhaps the most attractive man she had ever seen, and immediately made a note never to turn her back on him for a moment. He might be all right, but people like this were always dangerous.

"Well, Dorion! Returned, I see, and with your two lovely charges!" Halagar's twinkling blue eyes fell on Charley and he paused for a moment. "And you vastly understated the little one's beauty," he added in a low, appreciative tone.

Charley felt suddenly very strange. She couldn't see what he looked like or get the effect Boday got by looking at the man, and yet she *felt* him, *felt* his gaze and sensed his instant attraction, and his voice just seemed to reverberate through her. There was something indefinably magnetic about him that instantly drew her attention and to some extent turned her on. He'd spoken perhaps twenty words in the minute or two since he'd entered the room and yet already that other side of her was in control, the irrational and emotional one, and she was thinking of nothing but him. She'd been horny as hell for a couple of weeks and something in this guy just tapped that and drew it out.

Halagar walked over, took a chair, and leaned back. "The wine here isn't fit for salad dressing," he muttered. "Innkeeper! A tankard of dark draft, if you please!"

"Yes, sir! Coming up, sir!"

As the tankard was delivered, Halagar sighed again. "What a pity that such beauty can not gaze upon itself, even in a mirror," he said, sounding totally sincere. "Her very manner is—magical."

Charley felt a tingle go through her. It was only the hold the slave ring had on her that kept her from responding or seducing him right on the spot.

"She is not magical," Dorion assured the man. "No powers at all. Some alchemical enhancements from when she served her trade, but that's all."

"Incredible."

She could feel him staring at her even though she could not see.

Dorion cleared his throat. "Both of you go up to the room now," he ordered. "Wait for me there."

There was no argument even though Charley in particular wanted very much to stay. They got up, said, "Yes, Master," and made their way upstairs. Once there, however, Boday exploded.

"Just when Boday thinks you might be learning something you turn back into the silly, immature sexpot again! You know nothing of this man and he is potentially as dangerous to us as the devil monster we slew!"

Charley sighed. Without Shadowcat around she could only be lectured to, not respond herself, but she did not feel apologetic. *I'm what you made me, Boday,* she thought angrily. *It's what I am. It's who I am. It's also the one thing I can be good at here.*

Dorion entered not long after. "I saw how you reacted to him," the magician said to Charley. "And I sure saw how he reacted to you. He asked me—well, whether or not you could be with him tonight."

"You refused, of course," Boday responded sharply.

"No. I have to think of the objective. I can't let my own feelings or anyone else's get in the way. Free, safe passage all the way to Covanti, and connections once we're there. He knows he can't have you forever—he's well aware of the fact that you belong to a high Akhbreed sorcerer and nobody crosses them. He doesn't know which and won't. If you hadn't been so damned hot there, I might have said no, but if you want him and it helps us then I can't see how I can't go through with it."

Charley didn't hesitate. "It would please me very much. Is he as good-looking as he sounds?"

"Yes," Dorion sighed. "Damn his soul. Go to him, if it's of your own mind and will to do so. He's two doors down. But don't let him pump you for information. Be dumb and ignorant. Short Speech only. You understand?"

"Yes, I understand." She turned and went to the door. "Do not worry, either of you. This will be strictly—physical."

She walked out, knowing that Boday would probably have to be ordered into silence but not caring. She felt down the hall—one door, two . . . Here it was. She made to knock, and suddenly there was a strange, eerie, inhuman voice in her mind, saying the one phrase she firmly believed that only she and Sam knew in all of Akahlar.

"Charley be gone," said the inhuman voice in perfect English as she knocked. And, in that instant, Charley ceased to exist as an active or accessible personality in her mind, leaving only Shari, the girl of pleasure, who knew nothing but service and wished to know no more.

From the darkest part of the hallway, two unhuman eyes watched as the door opened and Halagar bid her enter. For a moment the light caught the eyes, causing them to reflect it back and making them shine, but it was not noticed, and soon the door closed again leaving the watcher in the darkness it preferred. Satisfied, it crept silently to the top of the stairs, then went down to the inn. It went over to the open window, judged distance, then leaped up to it, then went out into the small port town.

Shadowcat had a lot to learn about this place.

10
Some Self-Reevaluation

It had taken some adjustment to get used to the idea of Crim and Kira, but the actual changeover was a letdown. Oh, Crim would make camp before sunset and then slip out of his buckskins and into a robe, but even if you watched real close it wasn't any spectacular thing. One moment Crim was there, the next it was Kira in a robe now very oversized. The same thing happened in reverse at sunrise.

It was also difficult to accept that this was no transformation; they really were two entirely different people, and had they been able to walk side by side you would have thought them a near-perfect couple but hardly each other. Crim had literally given half his life to Kira, and that's the way it was. They shared some sort of existence, but they described it as dreaming; each "awoke" at his or her appointed time with vivid yet dreamlike memories of what the other had experienced. But the innermost thoughts and feelings of each were separate and closed to the other; they had information, but were not merged.

The hardest thing for Sam to get used to was that they never slept in the usual sense of the word. Even so, it made Sam sleep a little better just knowing that Kira would not. Still, there was a feeling of guilt in going to sleep on her out on the trail. This was a very lonely existence for her. In the towns and cities, Crim was often frustrated that he could do the heavy work but not partake of the night life, and Kira, so pale even here, longed for the feel of the sun now and then and more of the day-to-day activity and friendships that would not come with this kind of life. Each had clearly paid a price for the bargain, but it was also clear that neither regretted the price and thought it was well worth it.

There had been many rumblings in the sky, particularly at night, as they traveled circuitously around the Kudaan Wastes to the main road once more very close in to Tubikosa. Sam had managed a measure of clothing using one of Crim's undershirts, and it was casual enough to get them through the checkpoints, but as soon as they actually entered the hub Crim had arranged for them to be put up at a roadhouse while he used his contacts to get what was needed.

For all the bureaucracy, so long as you met the basic physical requirements for being called Akhbreed you could get hub documentation. The small black passportlike folder said she was Misa, an indentured field servant of Count Bourgay, Prefect of Allon Kudaan, which was within the rough boundaries of Duke Pasedo but far from the canyon regions and far to the north and east of the refuge. Allon was an oasis built around a solitary but fruitful well where water from streams far underground made its way to the surface and provided an arid but workable farm environment. The Count was actually a warlord of unquestioned criminality and highly questionable nobility whose alliance with Pasedo had allowed him some measure of respectability and kept the law off his back, but he was not a popular man in the region and was rarely seen and little known, which suited their purposes just fine.

For cover purposes, the story was that Bourgay, who was on Crim's regular route, had "loaned" Misa to the navigator while he broke with the train to do some business in the northwest. This wasn't an altogether unusual arrangement when Navigators were off on their own, since it was assumed that the trains must keep their schedules and to take a paid—highly paid—member of the train crew would be ridiculous. In effect she was a slave, expected to do the cooking and washing and tend the horses and nargas and even drive the wagon if Crim wanted to sleep. The peculiar nature of Crim and Kira was not public outside his regular areas, since such a thing would have disqualified Crim as an Akhbreed and prevented access to the hub and produced an instant loss of citizenship at the very least. By now, Crim and Kira were pretty adept at keeping their duality a secret. Sam's certification as an Akhbreed was necessary for hub entry at all, and unless you were Akhbreed you couldn't go from world to world at all, leaving the colonials isolated and separated and thus helping maintain the system.

Sam not only acted the part, she enjoyed it. She was a quick and eager learner, and had no trouble learning how to cook over an open fire, what things would keep—and how—and what would not, how the animals were cared for, hitched, and unhitched, and even elementary carpentry and mending of the wagon area. Her strength surprised and delighted her, and she was eager to keep it up. The broadsword that Kira could hardly move seemed rather light and easy to manage when Sam picked it up, and she worked out a regimen using heavy iron pieces used in the wheels and other things picked up along the way to keep those muscles. By rarely riding in the wagon but mostly walking or running beside it her leg strength and endurance not only maintained itself but actually increased, providing she had some oil on her inside thighs to keep them from rubbing themselves raw.

The practice sessions with Crim each morning and with Kira each night didn't turn her into an expert swordswoman or marksman or a great archer, knife-thrower, or martial arts expert, but they helped. She had the feeling that if she worked on any one exclusively over many months she could become pretty damned good at it, but for now all she wanted was a working general knowledge for defense. As Crim was fond of pointing out, the vast majority of people who used such weapons and techniques weren't very good at them, either—but they were far better than those who knew nothing.

The most frustrating part, at least from Kira's point of view, was Sam's continuing inability to relearn English. She had much from that period, including a habit of using archaic English measures like pounds and feet and miles even in Akhbreed, yet she had no clear-cut, specific memories of her old home world, only major, usually traumatic, scenes from there. After a while, Kira got the idea that Sam was actually fighting it; that the old memories and old life might be there, at least most of them, but that Sam unconsciously or otherwise didn't want them to come back, didn't want to even think of that place.

Although there was lots of paperwork and connections with Crim's underground friends, they stayed well clear of the Mashtopol hub's capital city and even camped outside of the small towns. This didn't prevent either one from going into those places when and where necessary, but it was thought best to leave Sam in a less obvious, less exposed position just in case. This was partly because Mashtopol was the most dangerous point, theoretically, until they reached Masalur, since if the enemy suspected that she still lived and was hunting her, as seemed obvious from Zamofir's comments back at the refuge, then here was where there would be a plethora of spies, mercenaries, and opportunists mobilized to look for anyone new or suspicious. Also, while Mashtopol looked to Sam to be physically a carbon copy of Tubikosa, its government was far more corrupt.

In Tubikosa, only "bad" women would go about without the long, baggy dress and bandanna on their heads, and only "wicked" men would be seen not fully and formally dressed at all times. There *were* some like that in Mashtopol, particularly in the small towns, but the majority of people were far more casual, with women casually wearing colorful print skirts hanging on their hips and comfortable tops, and men in more casual pants and shirts, usually of dark, somber colors, and wearing vests of various colors over their shirts. Hats, however, seemed to be out of fashion for either sex inside the hub. Social norms still hadn't progressed here to the point of seeing women wearing pants, but it certainly was a lot more casual than back "home" and some of those skirts were hanging pretty low and some of those tops were pretty damned tight. It also beat those stretch outfits that always felt like they were cutting her and grabbing her in all the wrong places.

The Kudaanese fashion, though, which Sam was expected to wear for consistency, was for light solid colors in the skirt and a halter-type top, sometimes set off with a matching blanketlike cotton garment that had a hole in the center for sticking your head through, but there was also a small pocket on just one side that contained a pull-out integrated hood with tie strings. Wearing it that way you had your head pretty well covered and the rest became something of a cape. The light colors, design, and all-cotton nature reflected simple attempts at dealing with the horrible sun of the Kudaan region. Sam's hairy legs and underarms were also reflective of a colonial origin; most hub women shaved them.

The last touch wasn't so much fun but made the most dramatic change in her. Kira had mixed a nearly alchemical mixture of foul-smelling chemicals and had thoroughly and repeatedly treated Sam's now long black hair with it. It had taken most of the color right out of the hair over repeated rinsings, giving Sam what she thought of as "dingy gray" hair. Kira called it silver and tried to be nicer about it. Still, Sam's sun-darkened complexion and weathered look combined with the long and full "silver" hair to provide a striking change in appearance. Only Sam didn't like it, but she preferred it to meeting Klittichorn face-to-face.

She had just the right image, which was why the fake origin was picked, but there was still a real risk. Agents of Klittichorn might not know her appearance very well, all things considered, but Crim had had that run-in with Zamofir who had told him pretty much everything, and somebody was certain to be suspicious of the fact that the Navigator had now suddenly left his train and was heading in a general westerly direction in the company of a Kudaanese woman.

Sam came back up from the woods near where they camped to see Kira checking supplies. "Something up?" Sam asked her.

Kira nodded. "The hub's filling with all sorts of strange and not-so-strange faces," she told her. "There's also a rough sketch of your face making the rounds, unofficially. It's not very accurate or very good but it won't stop them from looking hard at every—heavy—young woman they come across. You look different but it's a no-questions-asked reward and many won't bother to ask questions. A number of short, fat women have been reported disappearing, and the police and militia here are as corrupt as the rest. We have what we need and we've been here long enough. Once we get into the colonies on the other side they'll have a hard time finding us. There are just too many possibilities, even if they know our direction. It's only in the hubs that we have to really worry. Get a good night's sleep. How are you feeling?"

"Pretty good," Sam told her, " 'cept it seems like I got to pee every twenty minutes. Maybe that's the price of girls havin' muscles. I dunno. Why do you ask?"

"Because this is still a big place and it's our turf, as it were. We have as many people bought here as they do and we know the land better. That's why we haven't run into ugly scenes so far. But those who hunt us know that as well, and they also know that the one place we have to show up is at the exits. There are only eight possibilities there and you can bet that there's a ton of people looking over the most likely exit points and enough looking even at the out-of-the-way ones."

"Can't you just avoid the guard posts?"

"Not without ditching the wagon as well and cutting our way through fencing. Then we'd have to take random choice on whichever colonial 'petal' was up and we'd be reported there sooner or later by any officials or Guild trains we might meet. And, going west and north, we're going to be out of our normal and familiar grounds ourselves, and that means we have to watch it. Some of these places are pretty dangerous."

Sam looked at her. "You got any bright ideas?"

Kira shook her head. "No, and I've been thinking of little else. Maybe Crim will come up with something in the morning."

"The problem," said Crim, "is the wagon and supplies. Two of us on horseback wouldn't have much trouble sneaking out of here, although we'd have to take pot luck on which petal happened to be up. When you start getting into unfamiliar territory, though, it's best to stick close to the main roads and have the bare essentials with you, and for this type of journey I don't want to ditch the wagon and head for the hills until we have to. The worst thing this rebellion business has done is to bury honor. There are lots of possible friends and allies out there but we can take none of them for granted. That means going legitimate whenever we can. And that means going right through one of these checkpoints."

She stared at the map. "What about doing a go-'round?" she mused aloud. "I mean, you go through *there,* alone, with the wagon, and I go through on the side, here, by cuttin' through the fence and meet up with you out in the misty zone. I know there's bound to be a border checkpoint wherever we're goin', but there's a pretty long distance between the hub and the colony."

He shook his head. "No, it's not that easy. First of all, they stamp your identity papers when you go through. Yours wouldn't have the exit stamp."

"Then maybe I go all the way myself. You know, like paralleling you, keepin' you in sight but off a bit. I sneak in the other side when you bring up the right world and meet on the other side of the border."

He frowned. "I don't like it. First of all, that's over forty leegs to cross, and you'd have to be pretty far off me to avoid being seen. Maybe a lot of magicians could make a horse invisible but I never got that far in the course. Second, things seem to have a way of happening to you. If we get separated at this point and you wind up in some other, nastier world all alone, I might never find you, and while I wouldn't help the other side on a bet I'm doing this for profit, remember."

She was undaunted. "The big thing is just to be close enough to you to be sure I can get over to you but without them guys seein' me on either side. How close could I get in that mist without gettin' caught up in the wrong world?"

"Fairly close. You can see where the connection is made because the mist doesn't sparkle and it's darker. Why?"

"Well, why can't I try it on foot? I got myself built up pretty good."

He sighed. "That's not across the street, you know. I know you've been running a few leegs a day and walking more, but it'll take you some time to make it that far. Too risky."

"Not near as risky as goin' through a hole where there's bound to be a bunch of tough guys waitin' for me who'll take no chances, maybe with the guards lookin' the other way and you with a bullet in your head. Uh-uh. I been in that crap before. It ain't so bad. Just gimme a canteen of water and some candy for energy and I'll make it. You said it yourself—once we get clear over there we'll be harder to catch, and once we cross out of this turkey of a kingdom it'll be even harder."

He still wasn't convinced. "That's the region where two alien air masses meet, remember. There are always clouds and sometimes storms. If they get any idea at all that you're there, the Stormriders will be on you."

She thought about it. "What are these Stormriders?"

"Creatures. Some say they used to be warrior magicians who went too deep into the black side of their arts and became inhuman. Others think they're renegade demons. Whatever, they're Klittichorn's protective guard and they're fiercely loyal to him."

"Can they be killed?"

He shrugged. "Nobody knows. Unlike the Sudogs, which are minor spirits requiring the storm's energy to feed them and the clouds to give them shape, they're independent and only draw additional energy from the storms. They can exist by day but are far more powerful by night. I've seen one, once—there aren't many of them, but you don't want to meet them."

She fumbled and brought up the white cotton hood. "Well, with this on and short as I am I ought'a be pretty hard to see in daylight, and if they got less power then it's when we should cross. I'll take a pistol and a spear. The spear's light enough to carry easy and I'm gettin' pretty good with one. And don't worry so much. Up to now I been a pretty naive kid lettin' other folks and events push me around. Now it's my turn. How in hell am I gonna take on that Storm Princess or anybody else with power if I can't even manage this?"

It was a good point. "Okay, then, we'll adjust to camp just before the border tonight. That'll give us a chance to see what we're up against. If it looks in any way bad, then you'll be off just before dawn. I can't give you but a few hours' head start, though, or *I* won't get across in daylight at the speed I can go with this rig, and I can't stall much in bringing up Briche, which is the land we're going to use. You must be there when I get there. Understand?"

She nodded. "I understand. What's this Briche like?"

"Not too bad. Heavily forested, a number of small towns and one or two big trading centers, but pretty peaceful. The natives are formidable-looking, I'm told, with hair all over. They're supposed to look something like giant apes only with a more human build. Civilized, though, and pretty peaceful, really. I was warned not to eat with them, though. Among other things, they make soups and pastes out of hordes of insects and flavor them with tree leaves and grasses."

"Yuck."

"There's also a lot of fog and rain in there, but seldom a thunderstorm. As soon as you enter start heading for the road and come into it as close as you dare. it's pretty easy to get lost fast in a forest, particularly when you can't see the sun and you don't know all the rules in force there."

She nodded. "Let's do it, then. And I'll put in extra hours today gettin' myself up for this."

The edge of any of the worlds of Akahlar was always an eerie sight no matter how many times you saw it. The land just ended, and below and stretching out far into the distance was a flat plainlike region covered with a thick white mist that rose perhaps three or four feet from the ground, and within which were little flashes like hidden Christmas lights turning randomly on and off under the white shroud. In the distance, on the other side, you could see another land rising up out of it, but every few minutes that land would change. Where there were mountains there were suddenly valleys, and where there were farms there might now be the shore of a vast sea. It was almost never sunshine on a border, either; clouds always boiled and churned as two alien and incompatible air masses met but, somehow, did not quite mix.

From time to time there'd be a crossover of insects or birds or other such things, even rarely some plant spores, but nothing actually lived for long in the transition zone. There was nothing really to feed or nurture life, and nothing at all would grow there.

A small wirecutter was the only thing needed to breach the long fence that surrounded the hub. It wasn't really there to keep people in or out; those who were not of the Akhbreed were prevented from entering by the spells of the chief Akhbreed sorcerer. Crim and Kira could enter and leave the hubs only because they were truly two different people who were both Akhbreed. The spell might exclude a curse or changewind-induced departure from the norm, but when Crim entered he was just Crim to it.

The fence was basically there to bar wild animals who might wander across from getting in, and as a political statement. Colonial races who could not enter a hub could never attack, let alone overthrow, a seat of power.

Kira was as dubious about all this as Crim had been, but just a casual visit to the border station convinced the both of them that this was the only way. Mashtopol was corrupt as hell: the guards had a picture of the Storm Princess herself hung in their entry station, and around and nearby were a number of shifty types apparently idling in the area for no particular reason.

So it was that Sam, when it was just turning light enough to really see but before dawn broke, had received a kiss and hug for luck from Kira and slipped through the opening in the fence and down onto the mist-covered floor. It felt as wet and spongy as she remembered it, but it was firm enough. The far horizon was still dark, although you could occasionally see isolated lights here and there when one or another world would come up. Looking back from perhaps half a mile, Sam could see the lights of the entry station for the hub, and even farther out that glow always kept her oriented.

As the sun rose she conserved her pace and repressed the urge to sprint or hurry along. Forty leegs was about twenty miles, give or take.

Once she felt she was out of sight of any but someone looking directly at her through field glasses, she stopped and removed all her clothes and put them in the small backpack Kira had fashioned for her. Better not to have to deal with a skirt and top until you had to.

Crim had worried about her ability to cross in the needed time, but she was having no trouble and feeling very proud of herself for that. The big problem, which they'd also discussed, was the lack of a far reference point in the ever-shifting landscapes beyond. That meant, as soon as it was fully as lit as the cloud-shrouded nether-region ever got, picking an area on the fixed hub and checking back every once in a while to keep herself in line with it. She picked an odd-shaped bluff just beyond the entry station that was shaped kind of like the face of a fat guy doing a big pout. It was fairly easy for a while, but the farther across she got the harder it was to make out that feature or distinguish it from the other bluffs and crags of Mashtopol's end. She began to get a little worried and disoriented as now the far "shore" appeared closer, and she slowed to an easy walk.

Ahead of her now was the shore of a vast ocean, filling the horizon and making orientation even more difficult. There was no entry station in sight, either, which didn't mean much. If you were coming along here you'd better have a boat waiting or you'd be stuck anyway.

She took a drink and decided to walk diagonally to her right and wait for something better to use. She was walking for some time when the scene flipped, showing some barren, yellowed hills leading down to an ugly-looking lake. The air coming from it reached her, smelling foul, sort of rotten-egg type, and both hot and humid. She could hardly wait for *that* one to be out of the way.

Suddenly she heard noises of animals and equipment and shouts of people and stopped dead. For a moment she couldn't see them, but then, suddenly, they were there, coming almost right at her! One of the wagon trains, damn it! She was too far over, maybe right between the two stations!

There wasn't a whole hell of a lot of time, but she dashed back the way she came at top speed and the sprint, after all the rest, finally got her winded and feeling a bit dizzy. She collapsed to her knees, breathing hard, and tried to let the mist cover her, peeking up just enough to see how close they'd come to her.

It was pretty damned close. The outriders on this side almost trampled her, and she could see the wagons clearly and the people in them. This was one of the passenger types like she'd started out with, and it contained a fair number of families and tough-looking men and women dressed in various garb. One man sat on a wagon seat holding a furry creature that seemed all eyes and teeth. The thing seemed to sense her presence and its cold eyes looked where she was, then as the wagon got closest it tried to leap from the man's grasp and come after her. Instinctively, she grabbed the spear and crouched down.

My god, it's all mouth! she thought nervously.

But the man held on, and the pet or watchdoglike thing or whatever it was finally gave up.

Then the train stopped. The Navigator, she knew, was going to pull his magic trick, not tremendous as the sorcerer's went but one hell of a trick nonetheless. She turned and watched it, always fascinated.

The scene changed. First slowly, then more quickly, worlds flashed by, mountains rose and fell, seas stretched out and receded, trees grew and then shrunk, summer turned to snow and then to torrential rains. Suddenly it slowed again, settling on a peaceful-looking meadowland with lots of flowers and gum trees and plenty of green. It looked like a pretty nice place, and off in the distance the sky was even blue.

There was a series of shouts echoing up and down the train and then, slowly, it began to move once again, off the mist and onto a nicely maintained road, and within ten or fifteen minutes tops the whole train was out of transition and into the new world.

Almost immediately after the traditionally buckskin-clad Navigator made his final checks and rode in himself, the world was lost, but this time not to just another scene. Like a deck of playing cards bent partway at a cut point to expose a single card and then let go, the rest of the worlds held there now began to snap back as the vast worlds piled upon worlds of Akahlar sought equilibrium once again. Scenes, whole worlds, flashed by, dark, light, cold, hot, wet, dry—all the combinations, going by too fast for the eye to gain more than a general impression of the place before it was gone. She had never seen this end result of a Navigator's magic before and was fascinated by it.

Suddenly, all around her, was the sound of thunder very close, and lightning split the heavens again and again. She whirled and looked up to see ominous black clouds and a tremendous display of energy, and then *something else* before sheets of pouring rain hit her. *There were things up there!* Things with great, leathery wings and heads on long necks that looked like chisel-points, with glowing coals for eyes, atop which were strange, wraithlike giants in saddles riding them as if they were horses. The riders were transparent, outlined by pulsating borders of energy that seemed to form both body and some semblance of armor.

Stormriders! Made visible by the Navigator's work and all the turbulence it set up and now drawing on that tremendous energy.

The rain was still driving, but the lightning was no longer striking the ground but rather seeking out those great black things with their ethereal riders, who grew brighter and more horrible as they absorbed each bolt.

She dropped down below the mist, the rain so hard it was almost stinging her, afraid to look up, afraid that one of those *things* up there would instead look down and spot her with those cold, empty outlined eyes. Above, there came the noise of horrible screeching that pierced even the noise of the storm as the ghastly black mounts screamed their defiance of storm and all else in creation.

And the strange thing was, she didn't *have* to see. In her mind, throughout her body, she felt the storm and its deadly occupants in ways she could never explain, almost as if she and the storms were one and the riders were tearing at her. Somehow, she and the storm were one, and she felt almost violated that they were draining the energy from her even as she lay there, frightened. She wanted to lash out at them, order them to stop, or, at least, to divert some of that energy to herself, but she dared not. If they knew, if they so much as *sensed,* that she was there or anywhere about then the talons of the leathery-winged creatures would be upon her in an instant.

It seemed to rain for an eternity, although it probably wasn't more than a few minutes, but even after it tapered off suddenly, then stopped, she lay there, in what was now a couple of inches of water, listening for more of those screeches and afraid to stick her head up.

There was a slight but steady current to the water, and it began to recede quickly, going off towards the nearby land. Soon there was little left, save that the ground was kind of squishy, like a sponge, and oozed water wherever it was pressed.

After a while, she knew she *had* to risk looking, and fumbled in her now thoroughly soaked pack for the white hood that might give her a little extra camouflage. It was soaked through, but so was she, and she wrapped it around her head and then, very cautiously, peeked up.

She could still see them, but they were not close and seemed to be going away from her. She decided not to move, though, or do anything, so long as any of them were in sight, and the clouds, going back to their usual swirling gray, now seemed more menacing, as her mind feared a great black shape with an electrified neon warrior atop it hovering just above, waiting . . .

The "petals" of the worlds had stabilized once again, and she looked back in hopes of seeing a lone and familiar wagon. She could see nothing, hear nothing, but the world that now was locked in, at least for its time, contained an entry station not that far in and with a number of uniformed men and horses there.

It was impossible to see the sun through the cloud cover, but she had the impression that it was getting quite late in the afternoon. At least, as far as she could see inside the revealed world, the amount of light was more consistent with afternoon than any other time, and she began to worry. *Was I too late? Did he have to go without me?*

She rejected that almost immediately. If Crim had dialed in whatever that world was called there would have been the same kind of thing she'd just gone through almost surely. So where was he? Stopped at the border? In some kind of trouble? What?

She didn't want to spend a night out here, alone, particularly with those *things* around. Almost nobody crossed at night. Not even a Navigator could see all the landmarks and keep dead on at night, and it was generally only done when it was some kind of military or medical emergency or in the case of urgent diplomatic dispatches which would be aided and guided by sorcery. Night crossing wasn't a real option anyway. Kira couldn't navigate—it was a talent you had to be born with, or so they all said. You could only learn to control and develop it, not bestow it on someone else. Besides, while Kira was real smart in a lot of ways she'd been a female jock. Something called the Biathlon, she'd said. Crazy kind of thing that had to do with cross-country snow skiing and rifle shooting. That was why she was such a good shot, but the deserts of the Kudaan were a hell of a place for a snow skier to wind up!

But it *was* beginning to get darker, though, and not from any impending storm—she could tell that now—but because of the lateness of the day. Her hair and everything she had was still soaked through, and there was a chill wind blowing from whatever world was up right now.

She was still trying to figure out what to do when she heard the sounds of others approaching from the hub. *Crim!* Or—was it? Not one wagon there, but two! She moved off a bit so she wouldn't be right in line once again, but she wanted to stick close enough, risk or no risk, to make sure just who was in what.

The lead one *was* Crim! She felt some relief at that, but what the hell was the second, trailing wagon? Two tough, weathered men in front, on the seat, and probably two more in the wagon since four horses were trailing behind them. This didn't look good, and it was unlike Crim to take this long to get across. Hell, what if it was sundown before he could clear the entry point? What if it was sundown *while* he was at the entry point?

She shadowed them at a distance, taking a wide semicircular route around them. Wherever Crim was going, that's where she was going, and to hell with those other guys. If he was being shadowed by suspicious characters, maybe with too many guns, figuring on just what they were pulling and hoping to catch her when she caught up with the Navigator, then that was a problem, but not an insurmountable one. She was sick and tired of being hunted like an animal and kicked around by the fates and something within her had hardened her. If she was mortal then they were mortal, too. She'd rather take her chances with Crim and Kira, even if it meant taking these men on, than wander around another unknown land until she bumped into another Duke Pasedo or worse.

After you saw the Stormriders, four guys with guns didn't seem half as frightening as they might have.

Crim had gotten a bit ahead of her, but now he stopped, very close to the border region, as the trailing wagon crept up to him and then passed him, allowing her to draw roughly even but maybe a few hundred yards down. It was risky being this close, but this was a new circumstance. She was going in with Crim, no matter what Crim did.

The Navigator looked nervous, maybe even tense. There were two more guys looking out of the back of the wagon and they had guns of some kind, that was for sure. So why had they decided to pass him?

Suddenly she realized the reason. He was the Navigator—none of them were. He had to be behind to bring up the world and stabilize it for them to cross. It would also hold only a couple of minutes after he let it go at best, so she had to be really ready now. It was maybe a quarter of a mile to the border. She didn't feel much like more exercise, but she was prepared to *float* over if she had to. She took off the backpack and let it fall. The hell with that waterlogged dead weight. She had other clothes in the wagon. Besides, some cruel god or fate seemed to like her naked for some reason. At least this time she was armed.

The worlds began to flip, faster and faster, and, after a couple of minutes, they stopped on just what he had described—a great forest, in the first throes of dusk, with another good road leading up to an entry station carved out of the forest that already had some lights on.

She started to go in, for some reason held herself, as she watched the men in the wagon proceed in and then up onto the road itself. Something, perhaps in Crim's manner or perhaps a sixth sense she hadn't suspected and which hadn't been very useful until now, warned her.

Suddenly the forests vanished and several worlds flipped past before slowly coming to a stop again. *He'd gotten rid of them! He'd dumped them in that world and then let them go!*

"Misa! If you're out there *run like hell now!*" Crim called at the top of his lungs, and she ran as if the Stormriders were right on her tail.

Crim slowly edged forward as she took off. He was buying her all the time he could, but it was still an ordeal for her after the rest of the day and no picnic at all. She was going on sheer determination, every muscle aching, not even seeing what kind of world had come up.

Suddenly there were trees and leaves batting her face and she grabbed some limb and brought herself to a stop, then dropped on the ground, gasping for breath. It was several minutes before she could get hold of herself, and when she did she knew that Crim had crossed the border. There was lightning and the start of a storm out there in the void.

She took stock of her surroundings. It was getting pretty damned dingy, but they *were* going west, after all. This sure wasn't the world Crim had planned on, though, and she wondered if he had any more idea about this place than she did or had just picked it as the first decent-looking one that came up before he lost control of the "deck." Probably the latter, but the odds were he'd spotted a road or something, so her best bet was to head back over towards that road—if the land allowed her.

The humidity was tremendous, and the vegetation was incredibly thick and seemed to reach almost into the mist itself. She worked herself around as best she could, using the spear as a probe and walking stick. It was getting *very* dark *very* fast, and she wanted that road. If it was dark and nobody crossed late, then the odds were it was a pretty safe area so long as she avoided any entry station.

It wasn't easy. Several times she almost slipped off the slick floor into the mist, and while she had no fear of the transition zone as such she had no desire to lose Crim now that she'd kept up with him. Or maybe Kira by now. She hoped that after all there hadn't been some kind of awkward embarrassment ahead.

Finally she made it to a cleared area that was most certainly the main road. It was more than a little muddy, although none of the rain that she could see had escaped from the transition zone, but she wasn't going to be on it, anyway, but rather walking along it.

About ten feet inside there was a strong and very high fence with a kind of barbed wire on top, and she realized that when she'd dropped the pack she'd also dropped the wire cutters. Smart. If she *had* tried to press in, she wouldn't have been able to get through. The road was open, though, and the gate there was a simple wooden slab on a hinge.

Just beyond was the entry station, a pretty small affair by its look, with just room for a couple of people. There was a small cottage made of bamboo or the like nearby with a thatched straw roof, kind of looking like a fairytale house, and a couple of horses grazing in a nearby clearing.

Crim's wagon wasn't there—he had to have cleared the place and gone farther up, maybe to wait for her. By now it was sure to be Kira, and Sam didn't want Kira out in a strange place alone right now. Kira was skilled, but this wasn't her kind of element, and against a gang or perhaps animals of who knew what variety she was just one woman alone.

The lights for the entry station and outside the hut weren't electric but plain old torches, but they gave off a good amount of light and definitely lit up the entire gate area. Suddenly a dog started barking over the hut and Sam didn't like that at all. It was definitely a dog, and maybe a big one. She tightened the grip on her spear.

Funny, she thought. *Like a half hour ago I was ready to kill four human beings, but I'm not sure I can kill a dog.*

A woman came out of the hut and said something sharply to the unseen dog, who quieted down but only a little. She went on over to the guard shack and called in. A man came out, then reached back in and turned off his inside light. Sam couldn't tell too much about them from this distance, but they both looked kind of average. Thin, though. They looked like the kind who could eat a chocolate cake apiece and still lose weight. They were also kind of romantic, as if they hadn't been married long—if they were married now. He said something, she laughed, said something back, they kissed, and then walked hand in hand back to the hut. Sam thought it was kind of sweet.

But that damned dog better be on a chain or something.

She suddenly sensed an odd building of energy, and almost immediately after there was a crack of thunder and it started to rain. It wasn't the kind of very hard, driving rain like out in the mist, but it was a steady rain with pretty good volume, the kind that soaked everything through and turned the mud to worse. She risked at least a bit of a bond with the storm, trying to sense if it were normal and natural or if some ghostly airborne riders were within it, trying to use it. There was nothing but the storm, though, and she relaxed. If it was a normal thing, then it could be used. She doubted the dog liked it any more than anybody else, and it was noisy enough to mask most sounds.

She went to the fence, then to the gate, and squeezed through. The horses made irritated sounds, not at her particularly but at being left out in this crap, and she walked back into the shadows sinking in mud to her ankles now.

Within a few hundred yards of the entry station it turned pitch dark; so dark it was impossible to see a thing, only feel the rain and mud. She slipped a couple of times, but it meant little, since the rain was giving her a rinse. She was, however, beginning to long for very short hair again, and mulling over the virtues of shaving her head. Hell, considering how she looked now what difference would it make? Boday would still love her, and Charley would still be her friend, and Boolean would still need her. Still, she had the uneasy feeling that maybe looking like some freaked-out Hunchback of Notre Dame might not be something *she* could live with.

Odd to be thinking of Boday and Charley at a time like this, but she really missed them. They were the only two people she really cared about in this godforsaken place, the only two who cared anything about her. Oddly, and particularly these past few days, she missed Boday more than Charley.

Charley had changed so much Sam wasn't sure she knew or understood her old friend anymore. Jeez—she didn't have any more to do with working as a hooker than Sam had with getting fat, but Charley *liked* it.

Boday—Boday was security. Hell, it was more than that. She'd lived with the crazy artist for a real long time now, and she knew her better than she knew anybody. Oh, not that you could *understand* Boday—that was probably impossible—but you got to know her real well. She admired Boday's egocentric confidence, her real genius at almost any art form she wanted to tackle, her inner strength and toughness in a world that was far more of a man's world than anything Sam had known before.

That was something. It was starting to come back after all. She was starting to remember "home," or at least the Earth she'd come from. There were lots of gaps, mostly personal ones, but she remembered the music and TV and cars and all that. She could remember Boston, and Albuquerque a little, but she couldn't remember any faces. Not even her Mom and Dad. No faces.

It bothered her, but only that. She hadn't ever been happy there, and God knew where she'd have wound up if she hadn't gotten pulled here. If only they would just leave her alone here. If only she had some time and some peace to find out about herself once and for all . . .

Where the hell was Kira with the wagon? She couldn't have kept going far in this weather. She *knew* Sam would be along, and it wasn't out of friendship that the strange two-in-one couple was helping her, but for profit. She was *sure* that Crim or whichever had made it to this particular world, and equally sure that customs or whatever had been cleared because there was no sign of the wagon or any problems back there.

Clearly something had gone wrong *after* clearing the gate, and that something was almost certainly not related to the entry gate itself—that couple hadn't looked like they'd had anything unusual happen back there.

So now there was just the rain and mud and darkness of a strange world, and she began to feel miserable and alone.

I'm sick of this! she thought sourly. *Sick of running and hiding and being chased and abused, sick of having everybody crap on me in this world and having everything go wrong to boot! Damn it,*

I've been nothing but somebody's ping-pong ball since we got here! This has just gotta end! There's just gotta be an end to all this!

The storm rumbled, and there was now thunder and lightning. She had been conditioned to fear such storms, first by the dreams, then by the reality of being hunted by ones who used them, but suddenly she began to think things out. She was a clone or something of the Storm Princess, or the Storm Princess was a clone of her. Who cared? And the Storm Princess was being conned or was going along with this Klittichorn clown who wanted to kill her, right? But why did this big-shot sorcerer who had enough power to find her back home and chase her here need the damned Storm Princess at all? It wasn't just a big plot, it was something that Boolean guy had said long ago.

Klittichorn didn't have any power over the storms! That's why he needed this Storm Princess! Sure, he used those ugly creatures of storms, but *they* were dangerous when they were around, maybe, not *him.* And she'd actually *called* a storm once, here, to save them. It hadn't turned out so right, but it saved their personal asses anyway. But it hadn't worked out so right not because of Klittichorn or those monsters. Why was he trying to kill her, anyway?

Because for some reason he was scared of her. She was a wild card he had to kill because he couldn't control her and her power was dangerous to him! That wasn't putting down the real threat from killers and sky creatures and changeling witches and all that, but she was running into them *anyway.* And—why were they all chasing her?

'Cause he's just as scared of me as I am of him!

She stopped dead in the middle of the muddy road, closed her eyes, and took a number of deep breaths. There, in the dark, in the rain, she let her mind go, let it rise up to the clouds and turbulence above.

And she felt *power.*

She was one with the storm, and the storm was hers. She was where she stood but she was also everywhere touched by this great tropical storm. The winds were hers to command, to bend branches or whip through the treetops; the lightning was a plaything, a toy, a weapon if she wanted it to be.

She was aware, suddenly, of a *presence* in the storm, a thing not of it that hid within it and took from the storm's center a bit of its power to give it form. It used clouds to form a skull face, a demon face, and electrical energy to feed it and give it strength and solidity. She did not know what it was, but she knew immediately, somehow, that it was looking for her. Looking, but not seeing, because the rest of the storm was hers and she would not permit it to see.

The Sudog felt resistance, felt its will being blocked, but the force against it was too strong. It looked anxiously in all directions for the source, but the source didn't seem to have a center, a locus. The storm itself was somehow alive in the same way as the Sudog was alive, and the storm was much larger and greater than it could ever be.

Winds whipped around it, creating an upper-air twirling, a tornado within the clouds, and with it came the force and power of a vacuum, tugging and pulling at the Sudog as it strove fruitlessly to break free. Sucking it up, tearing it apart . . . It gave a mournful, anguished moaning scream as it came apart, on a level few could hear, and then it was gone, leaving the storm to her alone once more.

My God! she thought, feeling both exultation and disgust at herself. *Boolean should have told me! All this time I been* runnin' *from storms, cowering in lonely rooms, scrunched up in dark corners. All this time I've been afraid of the thunder, and it was my greatest ally, my one true friend!*

She felt the soaking rain on her body and found its touch no longer terrible but instead a friend, a lover's caress.

She shifted her mental focus again to the storm, using it now, directing it. Lightning within the storm could be used as well, could illuminate the very road ahead, if only briefly . . . *There!* Off to the side and not too far ahead, partly hidden by the tall trees! Horses!

Just whose horses she couldn't be sure, but so long as she had the storm, and she knew now that she could have it if she needed it, it wasn't as important. She started walking again, this time using the illuminations as a guide in the rain and mud and darkness.

Yes! There! It *was* Crim's wagon and the familiar team, still all hitched up as if waiting for the rain to pass. The wagon wheels were sunk deep in mud, and even she was now struggling in the mud of the road, sinking down well past her ankles and going on only because of her hard-won great strength. Clearly, though, that wagon was going to have lots of trouble unless things dried out.

She approached the rear of the wagon cautiously, unable to figure out why she had been forced to walk so long a distance. Satisfied as well as she could be that there was no one lurking under it or in the nearby trees, she stood there and shouted, "Kira! It's me! Is there anything wrong?"

There was no answer, and so she climbed up and started to look inside.

Something lashed out from the dark interior of the wagon, catching her on the head and knocking her back, stunned, into the rain and mud. Confused, she made her way painfully to her feet, slipping a couple of times before she made it, and looked up.

A dark figure stood there just beyond the tailgate, a figure that wasn't of anyone she had ever seen. The occasional lightning illuminated it slightly, showing a mean, scarred face with deep-set, wild eyes and a frizzled gray beard, and he had a pistol in his hand like he knew how to use it. He reached down and came up with something—they looked like chains or maybe manacles.

"Ye just stay right there, Fat One," he shouted menacingly at her. "Ye ain't worth nothin' dead, but I'm a dead enough shot even in the dark at this distance to hit one of them fat drumsticks of your'n with a high-powered slug that'll keep you there. No funny moves, now. I'm comin' out in this crap but there ain't no way ye can move or take me without me gettin' ye bad, and if it's my life or your'n I'll drill a hole right through ye."

His accent was strange and low-class but she had no trouble understanding his words. Her head throbbed, but this was no time to worry about a headache.

"What have you done with Kira, you pig?" she shouted back at him.

He laughed as he reached down, let down the back board, then sat on it, all the time his eyes and pistol never wavering from her. He was definitely a pro, all right, for all the rest he might be.

"Yer pretty friend's inside, all trussed up like a stuffed goose. She tried to give me some trouble when I popped up and ordered her to pull over, so's I had to whack her one good. She won't pull her changeling trick again, neither. I seen the big guy turn, but it won't do her no good if she tries it. Got a wire noose on her pretty neck. She turns now and that little neck gets big, well, she's gone and hung herself is all. Now ye turn 'round, back to me, hands behind ye, so's I can stick these things on ye. No tricks, now. I know 'em all and by the gods you'll feel a bullet rip through ye like ye never dreamed."

Think! Concentrate! Got to get him farther away from the wagon! Move back a little. Make him come to you!

"Gad it's awful in this miserable hole," he grumbled, easing himself down into the mud. A sudden gust of wind whipped the rain right into him, and he was momentarily off-balance. Not enough to jump him, but when he recovered she was several steps back.

"Oh, no ye don't! Ye don't move a muscle 'cept I tell ye," he said menacingly. "Ye been warned. Do anything but what I say just *'xactly* as I say it and I'll plug ye through and do it myself while ye writhes in pain in the mud! Now—*turn around, hands behind your back! Now!*"

It wasn't far enough, but it had to be. She reached out to the storm, surprised at her lack of fear. Fear was irrelevant now. She was too damned angry to be afraid.

"Go fuck yourself, Deadeye!" she shot back defiantly. "Don't you know who I am, *what* I am, to be so valuable to them?"

He hesitated, not expecting such defiance and, frankly, pretty curious about the answer to those questions.

"Ye look like a fat peasant pig t'me," he growled.

She felt a sudden, total coldness within her, a cold and calculating dangerous part of her she had never known or suspected was there.

"You know the Storm Princess? That she knows how to bend even storms like this one to her will?"

He frowned, now thoroughly soaked himself. "Yeah? What of her?"

"Well, *so do I,*" she responded.

The lightning bolt was strong and powerful; it came in an instant from the great clouds above and struck him dead on and went on through him to ground. The displaced air caused a loud thunderclap and went off with such force she was momentarily thrown backwards, landing again in the muck, but there was no shot. The moment it struck him it so heated the powder in the bullet that the gun had gone off, but she wasn't aware of anything except an ass full of mud.

It took her a moment to collect herself and get up again, and when she did she looked at where the man had been. He was man no longer, but instead a charred and gruesome-looking corpse, still smoldering, the manacles and pistol still sizzling as the rain struck them where they lay.

She felt momentarily grossed out at the sight, but ran quickly to the wagon and hauled herself in. "Kira!"

She looked around, fumbled with the lantern, found the flint and, removing the glass, struck it at the wick until it lit. Replacing the glass, she waited for the flame to stabilize and then looked around.

Kira was bundled up really good. Since the man had seen the change but hadn't realized it was involuntary, he didn't want Crim suddenly popping in, breaking bonds, and coming after him. He'd tied her hands and feet with wire, then stuffed her into a sleeping bag and tied that off as well. He'd also stuffed rags in her mouth to gag her. Finally, he'd rigged the wire noose he'd spoken of and nailed it to the wagon floorboard.

She was awake now, but she didn't look any too good, and there was a nasty welt on her forehead and a small cut that had bled a little before drying. Kira's beauty was going to be tempered, at least for a few days.

Sam pulled the rags from Kira's mouth and she started to cough and gag.

"Stay still!" Sam told her, "I've gotta find something that'll cut you out of that thing. I sure as hell can't undo that stuff. Never seen nobody who could do that with wire."

She went and got the trail shears. "This'll probably screw these things up, but I think I can get through that stuff with 'em." She knelt down and first tried to cut where the noose was fixed to the floor but that seemed to strangle Kira and she stopped, first cutting the bonds around the sleeping bag and then getting it off her as gently as she could. She got the tight bonds off Kira's legs, but the woman was face up, arms beneath, and that noose just had to go first.

Sam looked at the hammer but it had a back kind of like a pick instead of a pry groove. Another invention to file away for future profit. She sighed. "Turn your head a little to the side and hold on," she warned Kira. "I'm gonna have to get in there around the neck and cut. There's no other way."

It was tricky, nervous work, but she was careful, and with her powerful arms she managed to apply enough pressure to eventually snap the cord, although Kira was also going to have a bruise around her neck and particularly on one side for a while as well.

Kira sat up, coughing and gasping, and Sam quickly freed her hands and then got her some water. Kira felt her throat and gagged a few times, but seemed at last to recover enough to try talking.

"Sloppy on Crim's part," she managed. "But I wouldn't have thought of it, either. They—suspected—somehow, or—at least—this one did."

"Take it easy," Sam cautioned her. "No rush now."

"He—you—got him? How?"

"Tell you later."

"He crawled—into the wagon—must've—during the long wait. Just lay there—quietly—in the back. Probably got in when Crim took a crap. The border guard either—didn't look—or didn't care." She kept stroking her neck, but she had to talk. "Caught me—by surprise. Tried to—take him—but he had—something. Long weight on a chain, I think. Got me good." She suddenly stared at Sam. "You, too?"

Sam was so muddy and cruddy in general she hardly realized it, but when she touched her forehead it hurt like hell. "Ow!" Suddenly she felt a stinging in her left thigh and looked down. There was a gash there, and blood not fully clotted. "The son of a bitch still shot me!"

"Sit down! I'm all right, now—honest. Better than you," Kira told her firmly. "Let's get that cleaned out and some salve put in there. Then I'm going to put a tub and the cistern on the wagon sides. If it's going to rain like this, the least we can get out of it is drinking water and a bath."

The pain was starting to rise up with a vengeance, but Sam managed a satisfied smile. "Don't step on the mess outside," she warned. "And don't worry about the rain. It'll rain just as long as you want . . ."

Klittichorn, the Horned Demon of the Snows, fumed, and those around him quaked in awe and fear.

"Who are these girls who survive every torment?" he thundered. "One burns our agents with fire and strangles the Sudog in its cloudy lair, and the other—the *other*—manages to destroy a Prince of the Inner Hells, a *Stormrider!* They avoid our armies, exile the Blue Witch to the netherhells, and we seem powerless to lay hands on them! Well, this will have to stop! They cannot both be magic, yet they do things even I had not dreamed to do! No, my lords and ladies, this must not be permitted to continue!"

Suddenly his fury seemed to vanish, replaced with cold calculation. "We can never hope to snare them both and we have lost them as well. Let the mercenaries keep trying, but otherwise pull back. We have failed at stopping them so far, so let them through. Ease their way. But marshal local allied forces off Masalur hub. I want them ready to act when we are ready."

"I see, My Lord Klittichorn," said one of the generals. "Let them grow confident and then grab them where we know they must go."

The sorcerer whirled. "No, idiot! I care little now if they reach the place or not. Too much time and energy and expense has already gone to that goal without result. It would be convenient to know their location, of course, and even more convenient if they both made it to Boolean within a few weeks' time, but it will not matter in the end. Without him they are not relevant."

They all looked shocked. "You mean, after all this, you intend to let them reach Boolean?"

"Let us just say I no longer care to prevent it. But double our spells upon Masalur, concentrate our magic, poll and deploy our demons and allies so that the bastard remains where he is. Lose him and we might as well be lost. No, my friends, let us not combat fate any longer. The mathematics of destiny appears to protect them. Let it. But whether they meet or not, we shall cheat destiny and alter their heads by the one means that neither destiny nor Boolean can fight. We must have one final test. We must know if our calculations are correct, our dreams realizable."

"My Lord, you don't mean—"

"And why not? We must know if it works. What better target is offered, that rids us of the only enemy that might defeat us? If they get together in time all the better—we shall eliminate all threats at once. But no matter, the time will be set and fixed and the one most dangerous will most certainly be there."

"But the girl—she might . . ."

"Might what? Without Boolean she is helpless, without training, without direction. A wild talent, no more, soon without anyone who knows how to use her properly. Remove the canny Boolean and they will fall victim to the fates they have so narrowly cheated up to now. No Storm Princess, but merely a girl who can play tricks with the weather."

"But, My Lord—a *hub!* We are the strongest single force it is true, but to attack a single hub and eliminate a single powerful sorcerer is to confirm all he says! The other kings and sorcerers will band against us! It is tipping our hand too soon!"

"Ridiculous! They are mad fools. One they will put down to the same chance as they put down all the others through history, not only because it is most logical but because they *want* to believe it is mere chance! A few might suspect, but out of fear they will tip our way. The rest will cry a few tears and make sacrifices to their gods in thanks that it did not happen to them. Come, my friends, this is not boldness but caution! If we cannot murder Masalur and Boolean with it, what chance do we have of ever accomplishing our wider, grander dreams?"

He turned on them, eyes blazing, "Now the changewind shall come to Mashtopol! And soon, my friends, upon that disaster and with that blood to feed us, the Akhbreed empire will cease to exist!"

PART III

WAR OF THE MAELSTROM

For Randall Garrett, another old friend of my youth and a writer's writer, gone too soon.

PROLOGUE
Seizing Destiny's Threads

She was a short young woman, in no more than her early twenties but far older in the eyes, where it revealed damage to the spirit. She was not conscious of what her eyes showed, although it drew the attention of all others. She was dressed in a full-length blue satin robe without belt to conceal the chubbiness that only she thought was important.

She stood on the balcony of the castle looking not at the vast forests and high mountains beyond, but rather at the sky, where clouds seemed to swirl and dance in unnatural combinations for her amusement, as indeed they did. They had always done her bidding, first with her mother's help, and then, after the Akhbreed bastards had slain her mother, fully in command herself of the weather and storms that most others, even powerful wizards, found impossible to control.

Her mastery over these clouds and this weather and the strangeness with which the sky moved terrified most who could see it, even those who lived in the region and were now used to her experiments, pranks, and moods, but, to her, at least, something was very wrong.

The clouds suddenly stopped their wild movements and began to sort themselves out into more normal patterns as the natural conditions were allowed to reassert their influence upon the patterns. She uttered a mild curse of frustration under her breath, turned, and stalked back inside her rooms, but she did not remain there. Instead, she went to the door, where guards with beaked faces and hands resembling birdlike travesties of her hands stood guard in crimson uniforms, pikes at the ready.

She went down the winding stairs as rapidly as her robe, slippers, and dignity would allow and then stalked down a hallway that was the only unguarded one in the entire castle. It had no need to be;

he who lived and worked on this level was one to be protected from rather than the other way around, and only she of any of them would dare even enter this one level without first asking permission.

Klittichorn, Horned Demon of the Snows, master sorcerer of the Akhbreed, was in his study working as he usually did on his magic box. No one else there understood what the box was or what it did; it was one of those great magical things that only the Akhbreed sorcerers had or understood, although it looked somewhat like a mechanical device, with a lot of little buttons all clumped together, on each of which was a different magical symbol none but the Akhbreed could decipher, but which Klittichorn used with rapidity to create his spells and do whatever else it was that sorcerers of his rank did.

The magic was in the square, barely the thickness of a hand, on which strange symbols like those on the buttons but grouped almost as if they were, well, words—occasionally with small pictures of unknowable things—would appear in bright blue against a metallic gray background.

A tiny little alarm sounded and a small red light went on just above the buttons, and Klittichorn cursed and sighed, and for perhaps the millionth time since he himself had arrived unexpectedly on this strange world of Akahlar, he wished at least he'd had an extra battery charger. It had taken him a good two years after setting up here just to rig a way to adapt the localized and unstable current used in the Akhbreed castles for basic electricity so that it would recharge the damned thing.

The woman burst into the room at just that moment—always the worst moment, he grumbled to himself, when he was in the foulest mood. She alone could get away with it and know he would check his considerable wrath, although he had fried people with a glance or turned them into stone for less effrontery than this. It wasn't out of any love or respect for the woman, or any relationship, either. She wasn't all that bright, really, which was to his advantage, but he needed her as he needed his magic box and all his other tools of power, and she knew it.

"You might try knocking," he said acidly.

"This is serious," responded the Storm Princess sourly, in a surprisingly deep, almost mannish voice. "It has happened again. First the dizziness, then the sudden weakening of power and control. It was intermittent, but stronger than any of the last times. I have not felt such a lack of control since control passed to me upon the murder of my mother. Something is very, very wrong, wizard. Dangerously wrong at this stage."

He tried not to betray the fact that he was as concerned about this as she was by maintaining a calm and clinical tone. "Yes, I have been increasingly concerned about these lapses of yours and I have been trying to analyze what is causing them."

"It's that girl! The one you have failed after all this time to locate, let alone kill. She invades my sleep and creeps in corners of my mind."

"Your twin, in fact," he responded, nodding. "I agree that she is at the root of this, but not in the way you think. She has the same power as you, but it is untrained, armed only by emotion, and would be no match for you. No, it's something else. A new factor has been added to the equation, and, yes, you are right, our inability to nail her hide to the wall is the root of our problem. Somehow she, or fate, or, more likely Boolean, has come up with something we failed to anticipate, some new equation that is challenging the neat and ordered set we were dealing with. Do not be too hard on me, my dear. I have killed you in a hundred worlds a hundred times; it was inevitable that I'd miss at least one of you. The problem was that there were too many of you in various worlds of the outplane; our very attempt at insurance drew attention to what we were doing and allowed Boolean to finally figure it out. Forget recriminations. We must now deal with what conditions we have."

"And just what *are* those conditions?" she demanded to know. "Am I losing my powers or what? And, if so, what comes of all our planning, all our schemes, all the blood and hopes of our vast but fragmented army and the oppressed people all this would liberate?"

He sighed. "You aren't losing your powers, but they are being diluted, almost as if yet another version of you was—" He snapped his fingers. "No! Blast me for a fool! It's so obvious that it never once occurred to me! In spite of my precautions the worst happened anyway! *Blast!*"

He was clearly angry as hell with himself, and even she grew a bit nervous when he was this way. He didn't like to show that he still had a human side left to anyone. Under normal circumstances she might have left him for a while to cool down, but this was a unique circumstance. It was her powers that were in question here, and her powers were all she had.

She would never have believed that she had a near total immunity from his true rages; at least, she would never have believed why she did. He needed her very much, simply because he needed someone he could talk to, rant and rave to, just *interact* with, who wasn't so terrified of him that they were clearly play-acting. The fact that she was neither smart enough nor sophisticated enough to understand much of what he discussed was actually a plus. Ignorance was often the safest confidant.

"You know what is causing this?" she prompted him, trying to divert him from his anger.

"Yes, yes! It's obvious now! And Boolean probably had nothing at all to do with it. I have kept you too sheltered, my dear. Had I considered this threat I could have dealt with it, but no more. That girl out there—Boolean's Storm Bitch— she's gone and gotten herself pregnant!"

The Storm Princess looked surprised. "That is all it takes to cause *this*? that she be *pregnant*? Why did I not hear of this before? Out there, on her own, it was almost inevitable sooner or later."

He sighed. "I—I thought not. When I sucked them down to Akahlar I had them in the Maelstrom you created for me. I was about to shove them into the storm when Boolean appeared. He took me completely by surprise—I had no idea until that moment that he even suspected what was going on, nor certainly that he would have the skill, let alone the guts, to tempt the changewind. I had to draw my attention away from the girls in order to block him. He actually *challenged* me in there, knowing that if either of us so much as touched the walls of the Maelstrom we would be consumed by the changewind. It took more skill and concentration to just remain there than even I thought possible. I refused, but realized that so long as he was there and the danger so real I had no chance to make a stab at the girls, who were being drawn down and past me. I could have removed them, but to take my concentration off Boolean would have given him the opening to destroy me. Still, with Boolean in the act, I knew that there was at least a slim chance that our quarry might elude us in Akahlar, where they could not be so easily located. The flow of air from the storm is always an upward spiral, as you know. I risked a small spell, down, below all of us, figuring that Boolean would not notice such a minor thing directed elsewhere than at him or the girls—and he did not. The spell caught in the spiral and came up, lost in the overwhelming blast of power coming from the storm's walls."

"Just—what did you do?" she asked him, not quite following all this.

"They looked so similar I couldn't tell which girl was which," he replied. "Two terrified teenage girls pouring out every emotion possible—it was confusing. As the resemblance struck me, though, I knew it would also strike Boolean. I know how he thinks—now.

I knew what he would do, and I knew that one had to be in so many ways your duplicate. He would inevitably make one look just like the other to carry on the confusion, but it would be merely physical. I knew that at their age and stage they would not be certain of their own minds and feelings, and so I made them choose and harden the extremes which conflicted within their natures. A yin and a yang, as it were, so that they could be differentiated. Our target would become a lover of women and gain no pleasures from a man; the other, the false one, would tilt to the other extreme. A simple system, and, yet, one Boolean could do nothing about without negating the duplication as well, and one that would make our quarry stand out in our society and, not incidentally, would prevent the natural experimentation that might have resulted in a pregnancy."

"With all that I have undergone I am yet a virgin, although I do not know why I was not violated in those early days. I have *chosen* celibacy, which she certainly has not."

"You weren't violated because it was your power that interested everyone, and there was a great deal of fear that virginity was a part of it. Needless, as it turns out. You are celibate by choice because your nature makes you incapable of desiring a man and you hide, as she did, from your attraction to other women by denial. Yet your mother was like that, and hers before her. It is a part of it."

"How could my mother have been thus?" she demanded angrily. "She had *me* and her mother had *her,* and we were not products of virgin births!"

"They carefully picked the fathers in elaborate rites, and then stood for it in order to bear their heirs," he responded. "The gift, or curse, of the Storm Princess included this always, because one of such powers must be apart from society, both above and different from its rules and conventions, so as to never compromise that position of power. In the absence of a Storm Prince, who does not exist, it was the way to distance the paranormal from the normal, and as a part of the gift itself it is an essential part of a Storm Princess's makeup. But she had not yet fully realized or accepted her different nature and was still experimental. I thought by freezing it I would preclude a child."

She frowned. "Well, consider it now, because it is done. Boolean must be laughing at you now. You can not deceive the master deceiver."

"Boolean!" he spat. "He has a damnably charmed destiny! Head to head Boolean is easy to deceive. His brilliance may be equal to mine, but he lacks both talent and imagination. He is the brilliant thief, the master trickster, bright enough to comprehend what the greatest minds come up with, and steal it and make it his own, but incapable of coming up with it himself. Why, right now I have him convinced that four Akhbreed sorcerers await his exit from Masalur; four who together could crush him or keep him for me to finish. That is what imprisons him there—that belief. It was easy enough to fake convincingly. We sorcerers have certain procedures for checking for dangers. It was enough to show him that danger clearly lurked in sufficient force by all the signs. Would that I truly *had* four such allies!

"Still," he added, "it is a trick more in his style than my own, which is mostly why it worked. He has preyed upon me for a decade because of my naiveté in such things, but I am capable of learning a lesson well."

"And yet she is pregnant anyway, and possibly by Boolean's own machinations."

"Nonsense!" He spat. "The failure was mine, so easy to see in retrospect. I, who have sent thousands to Hell, somehow never considered rape. And by our own agents, too! Those bestial idiots with Asterial's band were dumb enough to probably gang rape the lot of them. Blast! And probably the only time she was or ever will be penetrated by a man happens to be the time she is most fertile! Destiny fights my attempts at meddling with it!"

She shook her head in puzzlement. "Still, how can this matter? It only incapacitates her and makes her more vulnerable. Another one who can control the storms I can understand, but a *baby?* An unborn one at that!"

He sighed and looked at her as if she were a small and not overly bright child. "You are the only daughter of an only daughter who herself was an only daughter, and so on, as far back as your line goes. That is the only way to pass along the powers of the Storm Princesses, and that is why it is such an exclusive club. The power connects the child to the mother. That power is not within you; it is, rather, drawn to you. You are a magnet, a lightning rod, for it. The power is finite, and connects you to her and her to you as well in a nebulous way. That is why you dream sometimes of her and she must of you. But now there is a child and it grows within her and is *physically* connected to her. You are magnets, all three, but together those two are a larger magnet and therefore a stronger one. Whenever she draws power in, the power draws also to the unborn child. You get less. The older the child grows, the more power she will draw as well as the mother, and you will be the loser. Do you understand?"

The Storm Princess felt like she wanted to sit down, and fast. "You—you mean that the mother and child together will draw so much power to them that eventually I will get none?"

"Well, not none—you will always attract that part that is closer to you and far from them since you will be a stronger *relative* magnet—but it is true that you are being slightly weakened now, on an intermittent basis, and it will get worse. It is also true that the two of them together, even one as a babe in arms guided by her mother, would be able to totally drain you if you were within the same sector. This is very dangerous, and may just be what Boolean is counting on. Time, which has always been on our side up to now, has become our enemy and Boolean's friend. We can wait no longer." He strode over to a massive and mystical red tapestry-covered wall and pulled a bell rope.

"Then the solution is obvious," she said, steeling herself. "No matter what, I, too, must arrange to conceive a child."

He sighed. "My dear, there can be only one heir to the powers in all Akahlar. If we fail to eliminate her before the child is born, there will be no other. The moment she conceived, your own capacity for conception ceased. No, we must act pragmatically now with what is possible."

The Executive General of the Armies entered in response to the bell pull, his toadlike face and bulging eyes seeming strangely incongruous atop the resplendent blue, gold-braided uniform and shiny boots. He stood there and bowed slightly to both of them.

"General, we have two problems and we must now advance our timetable to meet them," Klittichorn told him. "We must have the duplicate. It's the fat one we want, and there is no reward too high to pay for her—dead. I no longer need to see her. The one who kills her need only bring me evidence of the deed and he can name his own price."

A snakelike tongue ran around the upper lip of the toad-faced general. "Very well. Do you still want the decoy? I ask although it appears they both lead extraordinarily charmed lives."

"No, don't capture the pretty whore, but put people on her and keep them with her. She and that crazy artist both. They are the magnets that may draw our quarry out from wherever she is. Just do not allow them to get all the way to Masalur hub and Boolean. Take them alive if possible at that point but not before, and hold them for me. Something in the back of my mind keeps telling me that they are the key to locating the duplicate but I can't put my finger on just how yet, so keep them ready. I want to know where they are and be able to put my hands on them if it comes to me."

The general bowed. "Very well."

"That's not all," the sorcerer added. "We have a growing danger to all our plans the longer we wait. The duplicate might still continue to elude us, since we haven't been able to find her in almost two years and we now have far less time and Boolean might be well served to just hide her. How long would it take to get the word to all the armies in the field to assemble?"

"All of them? For the full assault? Months. There are many hundreds of worlds that would have to be notified, given orders, and there's assembly time, and, of course, it must be done without alerting the Akhbreed," the officer replied.

Klittichorn did a little figuring in his head. "Let's see. . . . Assuming it was those apes with Asterial, it would be—hmm—six months, give or take." He thought a moment. "You have eight weeks, General. Exactly fifty-six days and not one more. No excuses. Those who are not ready at that time we will do without. We will attack in full force starting at precisely twelve noon, our time here, progressively around all of Akahlar. You must not give me any excuses or objections, General. I tell you that if we do not attack then we may *never* be able to attack. There is a new and potentially fatal element in our game and only this timing will block it."

The general clearly didn't like it, but he made no objections to the basics. "Still, though, I am uneasy and so will our allies be at the lack of a truly valid test. It is one thing to create dust-devil changewinds in the deserts and high country here and there, but an Akhbreed Loci is a totally different matter. They will not rally, sir, in sufficient force to do the job, unless it can be proven that a hub, an Akhbreed hub, guarded by a great Akhbreed sorcerer and supported by thousands of lesser ones, can be as easily taken out. I mean no disrespect to you, Ma'am, or to you, sir, nor do I reflect my own confidence in saying that. It is a practical matter."

"The masses are sheep, General! You do not need any mystic powers to hear them *baaing*, nor to know that there are precious few wolves. We are all either predators or prey, General. You have only to pull the right levers to get the sheep marching to the slaughterhouse, one by one. If you cannot do that, then you are a sorry wolf indeed and perhaps not the man to lead this great crusade."

The General was not intimidated. "Then give me that lever. Give me something so startling that there can be no resistance. I can move them, but distance and the need for secrecy ties my hands. Give me something that will not betray us but which will none the less be so loud I will not have to raise my voice to reach the farthest colony of Akahlar."

The sorcerer nodded. "Very well. I have been itching to do this ever since we managed to contain Boolean inside Masalur. I was going to do it anyway, but you and others pressed me not to out of fear it might tip our hand. I think we can do it so that it will not. I think we *must* do it, both for the reasons you name and to eliminate the only effective threat we have. Without Boolean, the threat is lessened greatly. Without the girl, it is effectively eliminated."

"Then you intend to move against Masalur as a demonstration." the general said more than asked.

"I do. It will be an excellent test no matter what, and we might just eliminate Boolean in the process, although I fear he leads a life as charmed as that girl we have been chasing." He paused a moment, then said in disgust, "*Augh!* He has bested me for so long he has gotten me trained to his mind-set. Damn him!"

He got control of himself, then added, calmly, "We already have forces in the region. They can seal it off, block immediate word of the tragedy, and control that word when the navigators dare approach."

The general nodded. "And when do you plan this demonstration to occur?"

"It must be early enough to serve as such, *and* build confidence. I assume that you will be assembling the General Staff for the final preparations. That will take a few weeks. All right. Four weeks. Four weeks from today, at precisely two in the morning Masalur time. That will mean most of them will be asleep and there will be little time to flee or act on a major alarm. That date and time and the object are classified from this point. General Staff only, not even aides. We need enough people to know that we are the ones who did it and to be able to get that word back. Not enough to leak to Boolean or be intercepted by spies. You understand?"

"Perfectly, sir. The timing will also be right in that it will spur our forces onward to assemble on the ready and will also be rather short even if the Akhbreed suspect. We will know if they do by whether or not an assault is made upon us here."

Klittichorn chuckled. "Yes, and even if they do they will find us gone, and there will be too little time to take proper countermeasures. Very well, General, it is decided. In twenty-eight days Masalur will cease to exist. And perhaps Boolean and his fat bitch as well."

The Storm Princess stared at the sorcerer. "Then I should get in some last-minute practice with you, I should think. I am relieved that the waiting is over and that we will finally act. The General can take care of the military matters here. You and I, Lord Klittichorn, should leave for the Command Center as quickly as possible."

The horned one nodded. "I agree. It is all or nothing. The die is here irrevocably cast. Now we will seize the threads of Destiny and play them to their ends, and, no matter what comes of this, or what decision is ultimately reached, all the worlds of Akahlar and perhaps all the worlds of Probability will be transformed forever."

1
The Mirrors of Truth

It had not been a good trip, and it hadn't gotten any better. Now, at least, they were with a qualified Navigator's train heading in the right direction, although that didn't give Sam a lot of comfort. The last time she'd been in such a train, it hadn't helped at all. In fact, she was one of the few survivors.

Maybe the only one by this point. She had thought long and hard about that and all it did was make her own personal depression worse. The kids at least had some kind of peace back at Pasedo's with their minds mercifully cleansed of the ugly memories of rape and murder. Charley and Boday—who knew if they still lived, or where, or under what conditions? Even Boolean might not know, or might not care to know. She was the only one that was ever really important to him.

She only thought she used to have nightmares; now she awoke, sometimes with a scream, drenched with sweat and shaking like a leaf. Her attempt to overcome the demonic fat she carried was out the window as well; she no longer had much energy, and she often felt a bit sick or strange, and she really no longer felt like doing much of anything other than eating and sleeping.

The worst part was that she was having trouble remembering things clearly. She knew she had come from another world and had spent most of her life in that other place before being drawn here as a pawn in these sorcerers' games, but she couldn't really remember it, sort it out, or make sense of it. She had no clear vision of her old, pre-Akahlar self, nor any real memories of her family, although she must have had one.

Rather, it seemed, somehow, that she'd always been this way, had sprung as she was, as if one of Boday's fantastic creations, cast out into an angry world she didn't understand as the plaything for others, the quarry in some fantastic supernatural chase. And now she moved towards Boolean, whether she wanted to or not, in a seemingly endless journey divided between those who wanted to kill her and those who didn't care about her, both companion and prisoner to the strangest split personality she could imagine.

By day, her companion was Crim; a big, brawny, powerful man wise in the ways of Akahlar, a mercenary who, at least, was on her side. By night the big man vanished, replaced with the beautiful but no less tough Kira, a mysterious woman also from another world and place but now very much at home here. Once they had been two, but now, cursed, they shared an existence, the man by day, the woman by night, each otherwise a passive observer in the other's mind, an unimaginable marriage. It was hard enough to get to know or understand another person; Crim and Kira remained ciphers, friends or not.

"We're going to have to cut out of the train," Crim commented to her as he sat on the wagon seat staring into nothingness. "We're coming in to Covanti hub, and the heat will really be on there. I'll want to scout it out before we risk passage through the city-state."

She nodded absently, not really caring any more.

"Perhaps," Crim mused, "we can make use of the layover. Kira's quite concerned about your mental state and moodiness, and I think she's right. If you don't care if you make it or not, then you won't make it. Monanuck, the Pilot for this leg, tells me of a reliable physician in Brudok, a town near the border. I think we'll stop in there."

Physicians here were different than what the word conjured up in her mind from some past, little-remembered life. They were sorcerers, usually Third Rank, but with particular skills in the healing spells and generally teamed with a top alchemist for those ills and injuries requiring potions.

"I want no more drugs," she told him flatly. "They have been the cause of much of my misery, I think. Drugs and potions that bend and erase the mind and play nasty tricks on it."

"Not that kind of physician," he responded. "But I think you ought to try her. There's little to lose, and you might find out what's wrong."

Actually, Crim knew most of what was wrong with her even though she did not, but he had no quick fix for the problem nor any confidence she could deal with much of it if she heard it from him.

"Why not?" she sighed.

It was Kira, however, who took her to the physician's office in the small but prosperous-looking colonial border town. There was no telling who might be about looking for her in this sort of place, and night was far safer, even for two women on their own, than day.

The physician was a woman in her mid-thirties, with a bit of prematurely graying hair she hadn't bothered to color out but had cut very short. She wore a satiny yellow robe, no makeup, and her only jewelry was some fancy, overlarge rings and some sort of charm necklace with various tiny things attached to them. That wasn't unusual for a sorceress—those were various magical things or symbols used for invoking powers, Sam knew.

It was immediately clear why Crim and Kira were keen on this particular one; she asked no probing questions about why they were there or where they were going or anything like that. In fact, she asked very few questions at all except for her age and the usual vital statistics. Then she probed, by laying on of hands, various parts of Sam's body, particularly her fat stomach, and then placed both hands on Sam's head, one on each side, shut her eyes and seemed to go into a light trance. Sam found she didn't really mind the exam: the sorceress was kind of attractive and the feelies evoked pleasant memories.

Finally the physician broke her trance and sat down in a chair opposite Sam. She seemed to be thinking for a minute or two, then she said, "Well, you are not suffering from any physical diseases other than a minor and easily treatable infection that could lead to boils—and you may have a cold coming on. However, there are some severe complications here that will take more than I can give, I'm afraid. You have a number of complicated spells acting on you, some of which are acting against others and causing some of your problems, and a couple of minor ones old enough that they are integrated into your very being. That was what took so long to detect. You further have some serious neurological problems stemming from an ingestion within the past year of a powerful potion that is unfamiliar to me. I could treat any one of them, but the combination is far too complex."

Sam sighed. "Tell me something I don't know. So there's really nothing you can do."

"Not me," the physician agreed, "but I think there is someone who can. In Covanti hub itself, however, is, I believe, someone who can help you a great deal."

Kira cleared her throat. "Uh, it is not easy for her to go through the hub, and it must be done quickly and without delay. I had hoped to have her stay over here for a day while I went over and checked things out, but for her to go into the hub to actually see a specialist is, uh, *indelicate*. I am afraid I can not explain further, except to say that there are people there who would do her harm."

The sorceress sighed. "I see. Well, there is no way around it. If you do not get this straightened out, I'm very much afraid that it will consume and destroy you. It has already gone on far too long. The one I would send you to does not live in the city proper but in the hills along the eastern border. If you must pass through anyway, it seems far more dangerous to me, as a physician, not to make the stop than to make it."

Kira nodded. "I see. Well, give me the details and I will see what can be done. Sam, go get dressed and I will be out in a minute."

Sam was under no illusions that she wasn't being shoved into the next room so the two could talk, and she very much wanted to hear the conversation, but short of making a scene there wasn't any way they were going to say what they wanted to say with her there. She sighed, got down from the table, and went off to dress, figuring she could worm it out of Kira somehow later.

As soon as Sam was out of the room, the physician whispered to Kira, "She doesn't know she is pregnant? Even though she is clearly more than six months along?"

"She doesn't," Kira responded. "There has been no good way to tell her without depressing her even further. You see, the odds are quite good that it was the result of a rape. As for her ignorance, she is so used to thinking of herself as fat and ungainly that the additional burden, while it saps her strength, isn't the sort she would notice, as opposed to either of us."

"Well, she's going to find out in another eight to ten weeks," the physician noted. "I think this specialist will be the right way to solve that and many of her other problems. I have known great successes from Etanalon, although there is danger. In such a mixture of spells and experience, she alone can be the ultimate physician to herself. Even Etanalon can only give her the means to cure herself as much as she might be cured. She should not have gone this long without a Second Rank specialist treating her. Her depression, her nightmares, her moodiness, her lack of control, which is only exacerbated by the pregnancy, saps her soul. Without the will to cure herself, she will go mad with the treatment or die without it."

Kira considered that. "She is stronger than she thinks she is. Deep down, she has shown great courage and resourcefulness when she had to. I think it's still there. Tell me where this Etanalon is, and I will do what I can."

It was a quick and relatively easy passage into Covanti hub, much to Kira's relief. There were only two sleepy soldiers on guard, no particular hangers-on except a couple of dogs sound asleep on the border station porch, and the document checks were perfunctory at best. It was, in fact, so easy that Kira began to worry that some kind of a trap lay ahead. Either that, or they had successfully shaken their pursuers at this point and they were now regrouping beyond this point, where they knew that Sam would have to pass. She didn't like the idea of having such a solid and waiting line ahead, but at the moment she preferred it to complications here.

Even so, they took no chances, travelling the outer loop road around to the east. It was well after midnight when they reached the small village nestled in a valley surrounded by low, rolling hills, and if anyone was about at that hour they certainly kept to themselves.

Covanti was wine country, both the hub and some of its colonies. The vast bulk of Covanti wine came from colonial vineyards, but the really good stuff, the select stuff, came from small privately held vineyards within the hub itself. The sense of it being a peaceful and highly civilized region continued along the roads, which were generally well lit with oil lamps on high poles. The village had electricity, a rarity outside of the big cities, and looked less like a remote town on a mystical world than some tiny and quiet European village, right down to the red slate roofs and white stucco buildings.

Etanalon lived above the village, in a small house overlooking the town and the valley. The road up was steep and not as well lit, and it took them almost an hour to get up there. Still, Kira didn't want to wait for daylight. She preferred to be up there before anyone saw them, and to remain up there until darkness again could shield a proper exit. Covanti had been easy to get into, but it might be hell to get out of.

Sam had been all right up to this point, but, now, looking at the ghostly small house with only the hint of a glow inside, she began to grow nervous. Nothing really good had ever come of her experiences with sorcerers. She didn't trust the ones she knew, let alone ones like this about which she knew nothing.

What was a Second Rank sorcerer doing living in a gingerbread-style house up here, anyway? They were all crazy as loons from their power and experiments—particularly the ones that went wrong—and all they seemed to ever be interested in was increasing their own power and knowledge no matter who else got hurt.

Looking at the house in the dim light and thinking that way, a thought came unbidden into her mind from that part that was mostly cut off. Hansel and Gretel. This didn't look like the kind of place where you'd want to help the old witch light her oven, that was for sure.

Even Kira seemed a bit nervous. "It certainly doesn't look like a sorcerer's den," she noted, then sighed. "Well, here goes."

She raised her hand to knock on the gnarled wooden door, but before she could do so it opened with a strong creaking sound and a dark figure stood just inside.

"You are Etanalon?" Kira asked, wondering somehow if this wasn't a sophisticated trap, with them now irrevocably committed. A Second Rank sorceress out of the political way would be just the kind to be a friend to Klittichorn.

"Oh, do come in, both of you," responded a pleasant, high, elderly woman's voice. "I have some tea on the stove."

They entered, primarily because there was no graceful way to back out, and found themselves in a cozy living room, with over-stuffed chairs and a couch with flowery upholstery, a big, loud grandfather's clock that ticked away, and rugs of exotic and colorful designs on the walls in the Covanti fashion.

Etanalon reentered from the rear of the house bearing a tray with a teapot and three teacups. She looked a lot like everybody's grandmother should look—seventies, perhaps, but in fine health, with thick gray hair and a cherubic face, round spectacles perched on her nose. She was wearing a long, baggy, print dress and looked nothing at all like any Second Rank anything. About the only odd thing about her was the glasses, which were consistent in fashion but looked to Sam as if they were entirely black and opaque.

She put the tea down on an antique coffee table, poured, then got herself a cup and settled back in a padded rocking chair.

There was a sense of unreality, sitting there in dim light in this Victorian setting with an old granny, sipping tea at two in the morning.

"We are . . ." Kira began, but Etanalon stopped her.

"I know who you are. I have been expecting you. When Amala contacted me and described you, I knew just who you must be."

She saw Kira start at this, and raised a hand. "Oh, rest easy," the sorceress said reassuringly. 'If I were going to betray you there would be nothing *you* could do to stop me."

"Then—you are on our side?" Kira asked her.

"I take no sides, dear, in such mundane conflicts. I withdrew from that a couple of centuries ago. Such mundane political maneuvering and bully boy contests are so *boring* after awhile, and they never settle anything except which new bully is going to be king of the hill. Since then I've been engaged in pure research, to expand knowledge, and I help out people now and again without regard to who or what they are if they come my way."

Even Sam was shaken a bit from her lethargy by the attitude. "They say that if this one goes bad it will destroy all life everywhere. That doesn't bother you?"

"Oh, pish and tosh! It is far more difficult to destroy all life than these petty materialistic bully boys think it is. Even if it did, the Seat of Probability would eventually reform it anyway. And if it doesn't, then it changes little in the basics, does it? A study of what really is gives one *perspective* after a while."

She finished her tea, then sat back and looked at Sam through those dark glasses. "Ah, well, I see the problem, or, rather, problems," she commented. "It brings up an interesting question, though. Do you want to live, child? If you don't then there's nothing more I can do."

Sam thought about that. "Yes—and no," she responded carefully. "I want to live, yes, but not like now. Not alone and wandering around with everybody after me and no end to it. There has to be an end to it."

"There is an end to everything," Etanalon told her. "Some of it is Destiny, predetermined by Probability, but some of it is our own choices, right and wrong. Your problem seems to be that you don't really know what end you desire. You think you were happiest when you had no choices at all and let destiny sweep you along, but that's not happiness. Mental oblivion isn't happiness. Drifting isn't happiness. It is turning oneself into a vegetable. Most vegetables are ignorant and happy as long as it rains enough and gives sunshine enough for them. But the end of a vegetable is stew, and even then it doesn't really care. So far you have been content to be a vegetable and let all the choices be in other's hands, lamenting those choices you were uncomfortable with and either blaming or accepting fate. And see where it has brought you—to this state. Most people are like that, which is why they end up carrots or stew themselves. Excitement, energy, comes only to those with the courage to kick destiny in the rear end, take its thread, and shake it. They might end badly, or well, but at least they will have *lived*."

"What kind of choices could *I* have made?" Sam asked her.

Etanalon stood up. "What's done is done. What matters is where you go from here. If you really want to live, to grow, to make a mark, then you must undergo a trial that will not only give you those choices but compel them. It requires no strength of body but it does demand character and the courage to face a single enemy on the level of your soul, that enemy being yourself. You will either emerge strong and alive, or you will fall into the pit of your vegetative half and will consume yourself. This is your first choice. Take the treatment, as it were, or walk away, out of here, as you are. That pit will consume you if you do, but more slowly, and you will be absolved of any responsibility because you will be incapable of action."

Sam grew uneasy. "What kind of trial?"

Etanalon shrugged. "I can not say because it is never the same for any two people. There may be other methods, but this is mine. Even I have no idea what you will face since all that you will face is inside you right now. What do you say? Take a chance—or walk away?"

"You want me to decide on this *now?*"

The old sorceress smiled. "Why not now? You can debate it endlessly and never resolve it. You have been moving more by night than by day of late, as I can see, so you should not be any worse off now than later. Call this your first test. Your first real decision as a newly independent person. Choose!"

"I—I—" Sam was caught completely off guard by that. Choose some kind of unknown sorcery *now,* without even thinking it through? This wasn't fair! This wasn't the kind of choice she craved!

"In life," said Etanalon, "you don't get to pick what choices are there, only from those that present themselves or ones you make yourself. You very rarely have time to think about the ones that count until after you have made them."

Suddenly Sam realized why the sorceress was putting on the pressure. This was just what she'd been talking about. The choice at least was clear—a risky cure or walk out the door. Yeah—walk out the door to what? More of the same? Hell, they were probably gonna blow her head off before this was through anyway.

"All right—I'll take your test," she told the sorceress.

"Ah, good! Then something still burns inside you after all. Come and follow me. No, Kira, you remain here. Have some more tea. You can not be a part of this one."

Sam expected them to go down into some great magician's den, with bubbling pots and eyes of newts and all that stuff, but instead Etanalon led her into a small but cozy bedroom that matched the living room in decor. About the only unusual thing in it was a large, thin object against a wall covered by a black drape.

"Remove your clothing, any jewelry, anything else you might have on," the sorceress instructed. "Just lay it here on the bed. This little journey must be taken with nothing but yourself."

Sam did so, then stood there, wondering. Etanalon went over to the thing masked in black cloth and carefully removed the cloth, revealing an antique full-length floor to ceiling mirror. It was quite beautiful, and for a moment Sam couldn't see why it was covered. Then she looked again. The reflection was—odd. Brighter than it should be, but, more, it reflected back only herself and Etanalon, not anything else in the room, against a shiny mirror finish.

"Step up to it and look at yourself in the mirror," Etanalon told her, while getting out of the reflection and back into the doorway. "Everything will be more or less automatic from that point. Go on—there is nothing there that can hurt you externally. The only wounds that you can suffer will be self-inficted, and that's always up to you, isn't it? Go on—look in. That's it. Just look into your own eyes."

"The last time I did something like this I had a demon possess me," Sam commented dryly, but she did as instructed.

There was a moment of contact—eye contact with her own reflection, and a sudden but very brief sense of disorientation, and suddenly she was no longer standing in the bedroom of the sorceress but instead within the mirror itself. She looked back but could see nothing but another mirrored wall. She turned again and looked ahead at her best reflection, such as it was.

Now what? she wondered. *Do I just stand here staring at myself or what?*

"What do you want to see?" her reflection asked her in that deep, gravelly voice she'd been saddled with since childhood, a voice that had grown only deeper with age.

She jumped, startled, and the reflection didn't.

"Who are you?" she asked it.

"You," the reflection replied. "I dwell here but I have no existence, no reality, until someone is reflected within me. Then I become the mirror image—left-handed to your right, and so on. But only the image is reflected, inside and out, not the baggage you bring with you. Not the spells or potions or any external things. Still, I am you. I have your mind, your memories, all of it, for as long as you are reflected in me. I am a separate entity, but I can exist, can live, only as another."

"Well, you didn't get much of a bargain this time," Sam responded.

"Oh, I don't know. When you have no body, no memories of your own, it is good to be alive. I would be quite happy to step out, to live your life, if I could. What do you see in your reflection that is so wrong?"

Sam chuckled dryly. "Well, for one thing, I'm *fat*."

"Yes. So? Why is being fat so terrible and thin so good?"

"Well, people look at you different, treat you different, when you're fat. They make fun of you. Kind'a like you're cripple or something, only it's your fault."

The mirror considered that. "Then why are you fat?"

"You know, if you got all of me in you. It's a curse."

"Did the demon make you fat?"

Sam thought about that. She'd blamed that demon since the start, but it really *wasn't*. "No, I did it to me. Kind'a fast, too. Boday encouraged it. She drank that love potion so I'm always attractive to her, but she didn't want nobody else to feel that way, I guess."

"Oh, so now Boday did it. *Which* of you drank that love potion?"

"*She* did, of course!"

"Uh-huh. So, after that, she was no longer a free agent in these matters, but you were. You ate out of boredom, perhaps, or perhaps it was just because you felt secure and didn't have to put on for other people. You have a family tendency towards overweight on both sides. Your father was heavy, and your mother was once very heavy, wasn't she?"

Memories, forgotten until now, reaching around the blocking points in her mind, flooded into her. Her father—big, strong, built like a wrestler. Her mother—heavy, not obese but definitely well rounded during her early memories. Herself at nine or ten, chubby, being teased by the other girls, coming home crying, hating herself. In her teens struggling to take off the weight, fighting to keep it off . . . She thought she was still fat then, but how she'd love to be that weight now.

Back in Boston, that girl—Angela what's her name. Pigging out and nearly skeleton thin. One time walking into the lavatory after lunch and seeing Angie deliberately forcing herself to puke up the lunch she'd eaten so it wouldn't go down and make her fat . . . .

And then, after the breakup, how hard it had been to keep from eating and how her mother struggled with near starvation and every fad diet in creation to get down, so she would be "presentable" to get hired. Mom always on that, "You're too fat" kick and "Thick thighs" comments. Mom went nuts keeping it off, but not Sam. Sam got to a certain point and could, it seems, go no further.

"Then why did you stay fat?" the reflection asked her.

"*That* was the demon. It cursed me not to lose weight until I got to Boolean."

"That curse ended when the demon was removed from Akahlar," the mirror told her. "And yet that spell remains. It remains because you didn't really want it vanquished. Tell the truth, now. You can not lie to me, because I am you, so tell yourself the truth. Don't you really like not worrying about it?"

The truth, huh? Well, the truth was that the reflection was right. She *was* generally eating right, without denying herself some pleasures. She was no glutton, no compulsive overeater, not in the past few months, anyway. Oh, she might like to be a little lighter than this, but she was sick of trying to be thin for other people or watching some girl eat two ice cream bars and stay thin as a rail while she gained walking past a bakery and smelling. Even thin, she never was gonna be no glamour queen. And, well, yeah, on her own, she liked big tits, she didn't feel all that awkward, and she thought she was kind'a cute.

"Yeah. I'd like to take off some pounds, but it ain't worth that kind of fight," she admitted, knowing that billions of women would groan and gnash their teeth at that comment.

"So being fat is no big deal to you," the mirror concluded. "That means, then, that you're only unhappy with it because of the way other people treat you. Perhaps that would be true back home or under other circumstances, but what about here and now? You envied Charley her slimness because she didn't have to work at it. But, here and now, knowing how people never seem to look inside a person or past their skin, have you noticed that people here treat you as an adult, a social equal, where Charley is always assumed to be an airhead and a bimbo? And that is so transitory. We grow older. What demand is there for a fifty-year-old courtesan? Was she not always the smart one, always getting the best grades? Give her that curvaceous body and sweet face and look what she not only becomes but *enjoys being*. She would be more formidable in your body than in hers."

Again, she had to admit that the reflection spoke the truth. She had envied Charley's looks because it was an idealization of her own self, but that's what it was—an idealization. Without magic and alchemy it could never have been truly attained. And it had both limited and imprisoned her friend.

Hell, Charley's body really was designed for only one thing: attracting men. And that it did really well. As for herself, well, that wasn't what she wanted at all, although that, too, bothered her.

"Accepting bein' fat is one thing," she told the reflection. "but I'm a fat dyke. Always an outsider in any society. It's against God and nature and it bothers me, but it's there."

"Indeed? If there is a God or gods, perhaps it or they have lapses. There are far worse afflictions to bear. Birth defects, retardation, cerebral palsy, whatever. And if it is mental, it is certainly preferable to becoming a catatonic or a homicidal maniac, a beaten wife or a child abuser. It harms no one, forces no one else into it, and allows the person to become a productive member of society at peace with themself. Your tendency was reinforced by Klittichorn while still on your way here, as a way of insuring that if you survived him you would remain childless and thus give the elementals who empower the Storm Princess and her double an additional one with whom to divide their powers and thus weaken his own."

She was startled at that news. "You mean—it wasn't just me?"

"No. There is a point early in childhood where the unisexual bonds are strongest, when girls prefer playing only with girls and boys only with boys. Even in the teens these boy and girl groupings exist, with your closest friends and emotional bonds being with the same sex while your sexual urges draw you to the opposite one. There is a point where the barrier is crossed, where it is possible to be as close to a member of the opposite sex as to your own and where physical gratification between the opposites is strong as well. That insures children and a next generation. For some—not a lot but a very large number in real terms—that barrier is never crossed. For some it is physical—a minor birth defect, one might say, with the chemicals of the mind not dropping wholly into the right places. For others it is mental. For many it is only a combination of the two. You always thought you should like boys, and wished you did, and you even resigned yourself to marrying one day, but it wasn't what you felt, it was what society and family and other people expected of you. It was worse than being fat in a society that prized thinness; it was something society considered so repulsive they campaigned against it."

More memories of the past. Of Daddy, idealized, heroic, wise, tough, strong, yet loving her always and spending all that time with her. It was Mom—cold, always clear that she was an intrusion; an unplanned, long-term inconvenience, slapping her around for the tiniest fault, taking all her frustrations out on her kid. Yelling, screaming, fighting all the time with Daddy, too. She remembered the pain, the hurt in Daddy's face after one of those bouts. And yet, when Mom finally got her degree and decided to split, she'd fought like hell for custody, and when they'd awarded joint custody Mom took that job twenty-five-hundred miles from Boston just to spite him. And joined that Bible-thumping evangelical, Hell and Damnation church to boot. Trying to fix her up with all those dumb guys in suits who were weenies when compared to Daddy or even to normal humanity. Not that the guys at school were much better. All that pawing and strutting and shit they did that was so, well, juvenile. The only thing in their minds was to stick that thing of theirs up every girl's dress. She needed love, *not*—that. . . .

"You can't really fight it any more, you know," the reflection commented. "You could have, once, even up to the point where Boday took that potion. You might still have lost the fight, but you might not have. It is hard to say. But the tendency was there, and the spell forced a choice, and considering your background and how you felt there really was no option. It was there inside you, but you chose to fight it. Klittichorn ended the battle: his spell compelled that you win the fight or stop it. You could never totally win, and conditions were always against any other way, anyway. Deep down, you have been so satisfied with that choice that the spell is hardly detectable; you have made it a part of yourself. The only thing you have never done, never faced, is acceptance of it. That is what tears at your mind. Not that you are this way and will be so, but that you still feel unnatural, an outcast, somehow wrong or deformed. You keep treating it like some kind of disease that will pass or waiting for a cure to be discovered. It hampers your actions, limits your freedom. It is killing you."

"What the hell can I do? It don't seem *right,* somehow, that's all."

"Forget that. What's right is what's right for *you,* not everybody else. It's not what could be, it's what *is.* You didn't pick it, and it's not your fault, and you can't change it now. You really don't want to at this point. It's not a crime, it's part of what you are. Who really cares? Society? Yeah, they'd rather see you miserable or trapped forever in a loveless, sexless marriage and getting so miserable you finally become a drunk or an addict or kill yourself. That would make them happy. If it wasn't your choice to be this way, then you're as natural as they are. You just scare 'em 'cause some of them are afraid maybe it's in them, too. That same society that doesn't blink an eye when young girls are sellin' themselves on street corners, or thinks it's too bad but not scary that other girls are rotting their minds with drugs and booze, or who can accept the idea of teenage girls havin' babies and rotting on welfare—yeah, they're the ones who say you're a greater evil than the others. They can forgive the others, right? But not you. You're not hurting nobody, not even yourself. Makes you think, don't it?"

"So what's your grand solution?" Sam asked the mirror.

"I can only work with what's in you that's reflected in me. I'm the other side of what you are, remember. I say you got a right to be as unconventional and abnormal according to their lights and set your own standards rather than live with somebody else's. I can tell that's what you really want, too. I say don't pretend for nobody, and if they don't like it, to hell with them. You got Boday. She's still alive and out there someplace and your destiny is to see her again. The spell of union still exists and I can see it. So what's your problem?"

Sam sighed. "Boday," she replied. "The attraction on her part is chemical, not real. What if it wears off? What if a spell frees her, or something else, and she suddenly finds me repulsive? *Then* what do I do?"

"It probably won't happen, but what if it did? You know you aren't the only one like yourself. If you're comfortable with yourself and out in the open and honest to everybody else, you'll make out. Go out there with a feeling that you're gonna *live* your life with the cards destiny deals you, not curl up and die in a self-pitying cloud that you and things aren't what you want them to be. Consider that society's happiness does real harm to you, but your own happiness really doesn't hurt them at all. It's an easy choice. Be strong, be decisive, live on challenges, don't run from them or worry about what might be."

It was good advice, advice that was, she realized, really what, deep down, she had wanted to say to herself but never could. "It'd be easier if I had Charley's brains, though," she commented. "God knows she ain't usin' 'em."

"So who said you were dumb? Some junior high guidance counselor waving his I.Q. tests around in so stupid a manner? Coming straight out and saying you were dumb, so you believed it, just like you swallowed the rest, and you stopped trying. Your grades were fairly good until that time when he told you you were below average. And who was he to tell you that? You picked up the tools and skills of carpentry just watching your Dad. You know, in every case where you haven't just given up and surrendered, you've out-thought and out-maneuvered just about everybody. You escaped from Klittichorn back on your own world. You escaped from traitors on this one, and you have survived quite well here. It is only when you quit, when you listen to *them* rather than just go out and do what you want that you fail. Forget about *them.* A lot of great minds flunked out of school but not out of life. Ever wonder what that guidance counselor's I.Q. was? Or how much of it he used? Who cares whether you're smarter than some and dumber than others? That's another thing. What do those numbers mean? There are always people smarter than somebody else, and lots dumber, too. You're probably a lot smarter than some smart people in some areas as it is. So, forget it. If you can't learn something you figure out a different way to do it and you go on. How many brains could have survived what you've already survived? You got big problems to solve ahead. Get rid of the old ones. You can't afford 'em."

She stared at the reflection, as if sensing for the first time that this was a true dialogue and that this creature that looked like her was anything but.

"Just who and what *are* you?" she asked the reflection suspiciously.

"You might say a spirit. A kind of life that exists outside the kind you know or understand. All things which are not energy are created by energy. That trapped energy breeds us; the matter contains us, or natural laws shape us in energy itself. My kind is called by many names by many people of many cultures. Some call us elementals, some ghosts or spirits, *manitou* and *turgerbeist.* I was born within the casting and polishing of the mirror, and am sustained by its perfection. Because I reflect you, I become you, for a time, as I said."

"But you aren't reflecting my thoughts, not even deep down! I never thought this heavy or thought any of this through."

"Because you reason, so can I. I know all that you know, and all that you are, but it is secondhand. I did not live it or experience it. I can, therefore, be objective about it. First we deal with what is and is unlikely to be changed, for good or ill, right or wrong. You are a Storm Princess, a magnet for the elementals born of storms and a mistress of them. Those are powerful ones who have no feeling for matter; they are bursts of pure emotion who must live their lives in the briefness of the storm rather than within the lifetime of a tree or a rock—or a mirror. They obey neither sorcerer nor demon, although they might cooperate if they feel like it—or turn on them and devour them. Those of magic fear them, as do even the other elementals. But, long ago, there was a compact of some kind. Some great one performed a service which even they can not now know or understand, but a debt, an obligation, was created. Girl children of that one line, descended from that first who created the debt, they will obey and never betray. They are the Storm Princesses."

"But I'm not born of that line."

"Perhaps not, although who's to say? They recognize you as a legitimate heir to that debt and that is all that matters. They can not tell you and the one born in Akahlar apart. As you already know, they will come if they are summoned, and they will obey you, at least as you are in Akahlar or connected to it in some way, by interacting with those forces that flow from it."

Sam sighed. "So how the hell do you get to tell me the way I should act and think?"

"As I say, first we take what is. You are a Storm Princess and you can't change that. You are fat, and unless you intend to be constantly at war with your body for the rest of your life you are going to stay fat. And, you find men sexually unattractive and not even all that interesting on the whole. You have been fighting that up to now and you can fight that for the rest of your life and pretend it is not so and be unhappy because of it *or* you can just accept it as something no different than a tendency to be overweight or being short the rest of your life and get on with living. Your problem is that you have not thought it through. You think of these things as wrong rather than as simply different. Do you remember your life as Misa on the farms of Duke Pasedo?"

She nodded. "Yes. That, too. In many ways it was a happy time."

"Yet almost all of the peasants and workers there were different. Victims of the changewinds, or of other spells and curses that made them abnormal, unnatural. The Duke's own son has hollow bones and wings instead of arms and flies as a bird might fly. Did you find all those who were there who were not totally 'human' to be repulsive? To be unfit company? To be denied your friendship and help? Should they be treated as animals, as less than humans?"

"Of course not!" she retorted immediately. "They were some of the nicest people I found here. A lot more human where it counted than most of the Akhbreed."

"But many were ugly, deformed. Surely they bore the mark of sin and the wrath of God and were punished by God, condemned to look like that and live like that."

"No, no! They were all victims. Just victims of circumstances beyond their control!"

"Do you believe, then, that the Akhbreed are the inheritors, the truly superior race who has a right to forever rule hundreds upon hundreds of other races on other worlds who do not match their own physical standards or accept their culture?"

"Of course not! The system here is obscene. Kind'a like the worst parts of all the racism and sexism and shit back home."

"And do you remember your vision of the changewind?" the elemental pressed, reading her memories. "Of a young boy caught out in the great storm and changed by it into an inhuman, demonic creature?"

She *did* remember. "Yes! And when the soldiers found him afterwards he pleaded with them that he was the same boy on the inside still, but they murdered him! It was—awful!"

"Then we should accept them as they are? Treat them according to how they act and contribute, whether they are good or evil people, without regard to their looks or what they eat or what language they speak or what culture they follow? Or should we consider the different our inferiors and treat them as such, and perhaps kill all the maimed and deformed and the crippled among even the Akhbreed who do not attain the Akhbreed standard of physical perfection and behave exactly as all Akhbreed are expected to behave?"

"That's stupid! Where are you goin' with all this?"

The reflection looked her straight in the eye. "How major are your problems compared to theirs? How can you condemn them while eating your heart out that you yourself don't quite meet their standards? You are no different than those people at Pasedo's, than the colonial races, than the cursed and deformed and handicapped, except that your differences are so minor you can even exist in Akhbreed society. How can you at one and the same time condemn the Akhbreed for their ways and yet be upset because you can not fully meet the Akhbreed standards yourself? You would not be upset if you were caught in the Winds, if you suddenly had a tail or grew wings. Or even if you caught a terrible infection and lost your hearing or an arm or a leg. You admired those people for overcoming their differences, which were in most cases very severe."

For the first time, really, she *did* see the mirror's point, and see, too, how very silly her own feelings must look to such a one.

The reflection, however, wasn't true. "Now think of yourself in their position. They could be horrified at what they had become and give up, become vegetables, die by inches in a morass of pity. They might have been so forlorn that they committed suicide. Many do. Those who you saw were the survivors. The ones who decided to accept what was and *live.* That self-loathing, that lack of ego and self-worth that consumed many of the ones who did not survive, is what also is consuming you. And for what? That, through no fault of your own, you aren't what other people think of as normal, attractive, perfect."

Damn it, the thing was a hundred percent right. She knew it now, understood it, and also understood what kind of a hypocrite she had been. She would have saved that boy. She would liberate the colonies. She wouldn't care a bit if she shared more meals and living quarters with the folks at Pasedo's.

And yet, without that potion, she might well have shrank from some of them, or been worried or revolted by them, and that knowledge made her feel ashamed. The potion had done more than wipe away memory; it had wiped away hangups as well. Because she did not remember then, those people were the only ones she knew.

They were normal.

They were a far better lot of human beings than almost any of the so-called "normal" humans she'd run into. Those bastards back at the cliff—they were "normal" humans. Zamofir was "normal." Probably even Klittichorn was "normal."

"Just understanding and realizing that makes you wiser than almost all of the Akhbreed of Akahlar," said the elemental. "And most of those of your home world, too. One who matches all of society's rules and perhaps is even a genius can still be insane or even evil. But the only true measure of superiority is one's wisdom."

Sam sighed. "What do I have to do?"

The reflection smiled. "Look inside yourself and then look at your reflection and decide that it will do just fine. Be ashamed of nothing not of your own doing, and cast off all the worries over things that have no meaning and no relevance and which can not be changed."

"I—I want to very much, but I'm unsure that I can! I grew up set in one way, and even though I hated it, it was still a part of me. That's what I've been trying to get rid of by my memory lapses. I understand that now. But I'm back. I'm Samantha Buell again. It's not that easy to do it all at once, like this, now, and know that it'll stay."

"If that freedom is what you truly want," said the reflection, "then I can give it to you. I can not force it. I can not do it for you. But if you truly wish it, if you let me in, if you do not fight or fear or doubt, then, now, at this point, at perhaps *only* this point, I can heal you."

Choices. . . . Crossroads. . . . This way or that. This is what Etanalon meant. This is the moment of decision. Not to be transformed into some artificial beauty as Charley was, nor to become anything other than what I am. Rather, to accept what I am and go on from there. To be content to be just me. . . .

It wasn't an easy choice for all that, for it meant surrendering forever the fantasy of changing, of giving up even the desire for the magic wand that would make her perfect. Instead a Sam with no illusions, and content with that. One who would never please the public, but might well please herself. It was a tough thing to choose. Nobody outside of fairy tales ever really lived happily ever after, but it was damned tough to give up the dream of it.

The reflection seemed to shimmer, and parts of it began to fade, and Sam was suddenly afraid that she had made a choice by not making it.

"Wait!" she called. "I—I'm ready."

The reflection solidified once more, this time becoming very much her reflection, her perfect mirror image. She stared into her big brown eyes and the image seemed to come closer, floating to her rather than walking, until they were nose to nose.

Then the image and her own body merged, and inside the mind, throughout her whole body, there was almost an explosion, a tingling, an excitement. Barriers within her mind fell like dominoes, one after the other, until she remembered her whole past, her whole self, right up to this point, but with a kind of clinical clarity she had never known before.

Yeah, she'd been dumb, all right. Dumb all the way through. All the time it was *them* she listened to; all the time it was herself she'd been fighting. The barriers continued to fall. *What a mess I made for myself—back home and here,* she thought sourly. *Well, I'm not going to give a shit about* them *and* their *standards and* their *rules and demands anymore. It's time to stop being afraid of living. Okay, I'm not like* them. *I'm different, in a lot of ways, and they aren't really so bad at all.*

It was as if she was suddenly reborn, grown-up and wise. She liked herself now, and she found her old self pretty damned pitiful and repulsive. She liked the image of herself as a survivor, as somebody with power who might be able to do important things. No more dishonesty, not with herself, not with other people. Anybody who didn't take her as she was, wasn't worth knowing anyway. Let other people be embarrassed for her differences. She wasn't gonna be, not ever again. Who the hell wanted to be "normal" anyway? That was just another word for "dull."

So now what? She was sick and tired of being led around by the nose, of running and hiding and being scared of shadows and the future. She had power here—great power. Maybe it was time she used it. Maybe it was time to test it out and see if the journey was really worth the trip.

She turned, and suddenly realized that she was no longer within the mirror but back in Etanalon's bedroom, just standing there. She turned back and looked into the mirror once again—and there was no reflection there at all.

Etanalon came back into the room and covered the mirror once more. Sam went to the bed and got dressed once more, then sighed, turned, and looked at the sorceress. "I think I can handle it now," she said simply.

"Indeed?" Etanalon replied, sounding a bit skeptical. "Then you believe that there is nothing that can crush you, nothing that can stop you, even unto death. You're now ready for any new challenge. Is that it?"

"I think so. I'm gonna try and avoid that death part as long as I can, though. I ain't sayin' I'm not gonna fall flat on my face, but at least it'll be my decision, up front. I'm through running. From myself, from others. I didn't pick gettin' dropped here or what I have to do, but it's right that I do it. That I face her down and screw her ass into a thunderstorm. Not 'cause Boolean wants it, but because it's the right thing to do."

The sorceress nodded. "That's nice, dear. Come back in and I'll hand you your first crisis of your reborn self."

Sam was suddenly wary. "Something happen while I was—in there?"

"Oh, no. Nothing's changed. In fact, the entire process took only a few minutes, no matter how long it seemed to you. It's something that already was, but which has been kept from you. Both a severe complication to your plans and, well, a potential advantage as well. But you should be sitting down for it."

Kira was curled up on the couch but looked up and then sat up. "That was fast."

"I'm a lot better, Kira. Inside, anyway. I still feel like I'm carrying a ton." Sam settled down in one of the padded chairs.

"Not a ton, dear," Etanalon said softly, "just a baby."

Sam stiffened in shock. "*What!*"

"You're pregnant," Kira responded, affirming the news. "Six months along."

"Holy shit! You *knew* about this? And you didn't tell me?"

Kira shrugged. "In your mental state it was tough to know whether or not the news wouldn't push you off the edge. But, as the physician said last night, you weren't too far from finding out with a vengeance."

Sam sank back down. "Jeez! Pregnant! I come out of there ready to march into battle against the forces of evil and now maybe I can waddle a little. I know I ain't had a period since lord knows when, but I figured it was the potions or the shock or the weight or something. Jeez! One of them bastards back with the Blue Fairy in Kudaan, probably." She paused a moment, thinking, all the memories now clear in her mind. "Or maybe not. God, I hope not!"

"The rape was the only sexual experience with a man?" Etanalon asked.

She thought a moment. "No, it wasn't. A day or two earlier, really. I realized I had this—power—with that demon amulet, and there was Charley screwin' half the train, and I just *had* to know. I just picked a strong, nice guy and kind'a bewitched him into seducing me. It was no kick at all. I didn't even get off." She thought a moment. "But he did. Jeez, I *hope* it's his! He was a pretty nice guy for all that and I think he was killed in the attack. Huh! I guess we'll never really know, unless he or she grows up to be an ax murderer or something."

"She," Etanalon told her. "Storm Princesses have only girls, and generally only one child. She, too, will be a Storm Princess, at least as long as she remains on Akahlar. More importantly, it will preclude the native Princess from a child, since such things are determined by the elementals. More and more they will take you for her, dividing their support less and less between you."

Sam was still pretty shaken by the news, but she was thinking clearly now. "Wait a minute. Are you telling me that because *I'm* havin' the kid she can't? And that once the kid is born she'll lose her powers?"

"That is the way we believe it works, yes," the sorceress replied.

Kira, too, was fascinated by this. "Then we might already have won. The only way they can retain their power and keep to their plan is if they kill her and her unborn child. There are a number of very pleasant, tranquil places deep in the colonies where someone could hide for a year or more. We need only take Misa there and wait until the child is born. Then the Storm Princess's power dies and with it Klittichorn's dream of controlling the changewinds."

"Sam," she responded. "Misa was just another place to hide. Susama in Akhbreed, Sam for short in any tongue. I like the picture you're painting, but it's all wrong."

"Huh? What do you mean? Etanalon just said—"

"—What Klittichorn already knows," Sam finished.

"We don't know for certain that he knows," Kira retorted. "We don't even know that he's not chasing Charley all over the map."

"Maybe he is, but I doubt it. For one thing, I tune in every once in a while to the Storm Princess. I got to figure she somehow tunes in on me. And I don't sell old Horny short. They got a pretty good idea of me by now, I think. We had to fight off the hired guns back off Quodac, remember, and I think maybe that slimy bastard Zamofir has got to know more than he's putting out. He saw me on the train, maybe even arranged the attack because I was there. He was them at the rock camp, too—the only survivor from their side. Figure he saw it all, heard everything. Then, later, he shows up at Pasedo's and narrowly misses me."

Kira sighed. "Yes, and Pasedo's people knew you were pregnant at that point. Crim should have drowned that little creep. All right—so Klittichorn knows. What good does that do him if he can't find you?"

Sam sighed. "Well, suppose I was him. Six months. . . . So I got three months to go, give or take, right? He'll figure from the rape Zenchur would have reported to him, which is good enough. Now, he's spent *years* building his armies and making his plans. Years finding and shaping and building up this Storm Princess until she'll do exactly what he wants her to. He's got Boolean bottled up, everything shaping up nice whether I'm around or not, and then he finds out he made one tiny mistake. He kept her a virgin instead of getting her knocked up when he had the chance."

"It would have been difficult unless the soldiers who took her from her homeland had ravished her, and no doubt they had strict orders on that," Etanalon noted. "This is a lengthy plan of Klittichorn's, carried out with much patience. He arranged everything so that she would be his willing accomplice, from the massacre of her people and mother onwards. Do not doubt it. He manipulated the threads of her destiny to create what he had. A child would have interfered with that."

"Yeah, and I guess he kept her on a tight enough leash so she couldn't fool around on her own," Sam noted.

"Most certainly. She would have been most public, you see, and always guarded. But remember, too, that she is in all senses except her background *you*—another version of you. On that level, she might have been no more likely to 'fool around,' as you put it, than you would—at least not with men. Of course, she would not admit it, even to herself, and she would expect an arranged marriage at some point, but she would run from such feelings in horror, as you tried to do. It was a factor that Klittichorn overlooked. Or, perhaps, one he simply took for granted and reinforced in you. It simply never occurred to him that there were other ways than romance to cause pregnancy. In his own way, he's rather conservative and old-fashioned in his outlook. It never seems to have occurred to him that, in spite of all, Storm Princesses are still born. At any rate, it is done."

"Yes," Kira put in, "but now what can *we* do? All it's done is to start the clock ticking on the end of the world."

"I don't see how, even with all his tricks, he can get her to go along with him on this," Sam commented. "I mean, no matter what, I don't think I could trust that horny bastard."

"Hatred and revenge fuel her," Etanalon told them. "She is convinced that only as the liberator of the colonial races and the destroyer of Akhbreed power and rule can she both avenge and give meaning to the deaths of her mother and her people, as well as give meaning to her own life."

Sam nodded. "Frankly, I wouldn't mind being the liberator myself, but not at the cost of having old Horny around to pick up the pieces. The system here is bad, but I can imagine worse." She turned to Kira. "Don't you see? If I was old Horny, faced with all this work and all this power goin' down the tubes, I'd move it up. I'd go with what I had and take a chance, ready or not. He's gonna do it, Kira. He's gonna do it before my baby's born. I don't want my baby growin' up in *his* world, or even in the wreckage a defeat would leave behind. We don't have much time, Kira. You got to contact Boolean. You got to tell him that the whole deal's off. Tell him either we hit them now, or it's going down and soon. We need to get together whatever forces we can and move on them before they move on us. No more bullshit. No more sneaking around. We hit them first, quick and dirty, or it's all over."

2
Political Pictures

Such was the luxurious and glamorous reputation of the Imperial High Court of Covanti that Covantians had a saying that it was better to be the one who emptied the King's toilets than to be a merchant prince. And, after a few days there, even Charley and Boday had some reason to believe it.

Halagar, the old friend and one-time schoolmate of Dorion who was now an Imperial Courier for the Court, had brought them straight in to the palace without incident, and in record time. It was far easier when one was travelling with clear Imperial protection; there might have been all sorts of thugs, thieves, and murderers waiting to claim Klittichorn's reward for them, but none of them dared act against people under the protection of one from the Court. Rewards were only of value if one lived to spend them, and Halagar's large, jewel-encrusted ring gave him some kind of psychic contact with the Akhbreed sorcerers who maintained and guarded this land.

Of course, that protection extended only to the land and colonies of Covanti; once outside of that domain, they were also beyond the reach of any sort of Covantian imperial protection, supernatural or otherwise. And there were still five worlds, four of which were under other kingdoms, before they reached Masalur and Boolean.

As far as Charley was concerned, she didn't care if she *ever* reached Boolean now. She had been giving a lot of thought to that, although, to be sure, the decisions about her future were not hers to make.

She had come to Akahlar not by anyone's grand design but simply because she had been with Sam when the two great wizards had come for their Storm Princess clone; one to kill, the other to save. Like the innocent passenger in a car crash, she'd had nothing at all to do with the accident but she nonetheless suffered all the consequences.

Then Boolean had taken advantage of her presence and her superficial resemblance to Sam to make of her a decoy; to make her appear as Sam would have if everything had gone exactly right, if the idealized potential in Sam's genes had been a hundred percent realized. She was beautiful, sexy, perfectly proportioned, and, after falling into Boday's alchemical hands, virtually engineered to be a courtesan, a high-class whore, whose sole function was to give pleasure to men and to find high pleasure in that as well.

And although she had had "I'm gonna conquer the world" Superwoman ambitions in her old life, and now sometimes felt guilty remembering them, the fact was, she liked the job and the situation. The only problem she really had with it, and it was a big one, was that she was designed to stand out in any crowd, the better to attract the attention of those forces seeking Sam who would see the resemblance and take her for her friend. She was the decoy, dependent on her own wits and the powers and authority of others to save herself without benefit of Sam's powers or anything else. That was why she was here, on the road, in the middle of a strange world, on her way to Boolean. Until she, or Sam, reached that safety neither could hope for any long-term peace.

Or so she'd thought. Now, in the Imperial Court, she was beginning to wonder. For the first time since she'd worked the high-class geisha route back in Mashtopol, she felt safe and comfortable.

More, the odds of her really getting any further were slimmer even than the odds she would have gotten this far. Set upon by the gang in the Kudaan Wastes, she'd managed to escape and to rescue Sam and Boday and the others, but at the cost of her eyesight. Witnessing the supernatural battle between Asterial, Blue Witch of the Kudaan Wastes and Klittichorn ally, and the demon from Sam's amulet had caused some kind of radiation effect. All sorcerers who dealt in or with such powers had suffered the same fate and had alternate ways of seeing, but they knew magic or had powers she did not. Even Dorion didn't see with his eyes, although nobody could really tell that just from meeting him.

Not that she was totally blind. Rather, her eyes could see things of magic; the supernatural had its own colors and auras that were revealed to her when she was in proximity to them, but there was a lot less magic in the world than even most of the inhabitants thought. She had been able to see the terrible Stormrider in the Quodac void, a sight she might have chosen to avoid, but most of the time the world was a dull and meaningless gray null. It was an irony, really; most people in Akahlar, from the lowest to the highest, feared magic and the supernatural because they were things they could neither see nor understand. Magic, however, could not sneak up on her, but she was totally defenseless and at the mercy of the normal world.

More, having fallen into captivity in the Kudaan and sold into slavery, the small gold ring in her nose bound her with strong magic as a slave who could not escape her master and who was compelled to obey that master. Right now that role was delegated to Dorion, a rather sweet and shy sorcerer's apprentice who couldn't make himself take advantage of the situation, but, thanks to Yobi, the powerful witch and his own mentor, Charley really "belonged" to Boolean.

Her only convenience was Shadowcat, a medium-sized tomcat somehow bound to her as she was to Boolean. Through a tiny sharing of blood, she and the cat were somehow linked, and if she willed it and concentrated, she could see, in the strange fish-eyed and monochromatic way a cat saw, and from that small and low vantage point, just what the animal could see. This was handy only to a degree. Shadowcat might have been something supernatural, but deep down he was a cat, and cats didn't go where you wanted them to, nor necessarily look at what you wanted to see.

The other advantage Shadowcat gave her was a two-edged sword. She had been unable to master the complex polytonal language of the Akhbreed; it was doubtful that anyone not born to it or who had not absorbed it in some magical way as Sam had done, could ever master it. After all this time she understood it well enough to get by, although following a fast-talking multiparty conversation was sometimes impossible, but that was about the limit. She could understand Boday, for example, but not speak to her, except in the servile Short Speech of the courtesan whose few hundred words were designed strictly for the job of woman of pleasure. Many magicians, including Dorion, could handle English, having learned it by spell, since for some reason English, or a form of it, was a major language of the high Akhbreed sorcerers, but without Dorion or Boolean around she was cut off there, too. On her own she was effectively both blind and voiceless.

The Shadowcat binding spell also gave her a way out of that; when she held the cat others in her immediate vicinity could read her thoughts. The problem was, everybody could read *all* her thoughts, so she didn't use that much unless it was an emergency.

Still, for the only thing she could really do, and the thing she like doing the most, she didn't need to see or speak. She had concentrated not on dwelling on her problems but on coping with her situation, and, with a lot of patience and thought she was as self-sufficient as she needed to be or could be. She could memorize the basics of almost any room of normal size in a half hour; she could find the bathroom or chamber pot or whatever was available for the need and tend to herself. She could dress herself as much as one of her class and station dressed, fix her jewelry and her hair, apply perfume and even some limited cosmetics. There were tricks you just worked out for doing that. Even pouring a drink—the finger unobtrusively just below the rim of cup or glass telling her when it was full. That sort of thing. She'd arranged what little supplies she'd picked up so that she could find them and use them in the same ways every time.

In the Covanti court, they had placed her with the royal concubines, in a sort of loose harem that was pretty good and had a lot. There were real hot showers, and slaves to do your hair and nails and the like, a pick of perfumes, cosmetics, and assistance for her in putting them on, along with good-tasting things to eat and fine wines of the region and coffees and teas served regularly. Each concubine slept on satin sheets and pillows atop feather beds and had little to do until summoned but play around with the luxury. There wasn't much of a level of conversation that she felt left out of; while the Short Speech was reserved for when they were outside, just about all the women had been born and raised to this position and purpose. They were all illiterate, and appallingly ignorant of the world or much of anything outside the immediate Covanti royal grounds. They mostly did superficial comparisons of the men of the Court, and how they were in bed, and did and redid their own and each other's hair, makeup, and the like, did exercises and tried out dances. They were all pros, just like she was, only they had a kind of status and a gilded cage and they neither knew of nor wanted much else. This was the highest level to which they could aspire.

Charley found herself quickly slipping into their vacuous lifestyle without any problems. If they had no depth, they were at least all friendly and sympathetic, their competition between themselves limited mostly to boasting about their own sexual prowess or trying to top one another in style. It was more like a girls' luxurious summer camp back when she was, say, thirteen or fourteen. That lonely, friendless feeling she'd had since losing track of Sam in the gorge back in the Kudaan Wastes was filled, to a degree.

Too, she had not realized just how much pressure she had been living under until it was removed. Here, with the Royal Courtesans, protected, cared for, she felt reasonably safe, and slept long and well without nightmares. Particularly considering her handicaps of language and sight, this was also the highest level to which *she* could reasonably aspire. Even in twenty years or more, when beauty was fading and demand for older women was lessened, the royal honor was kept, and all needs would be attended to for life. No worries, no insecurities, no real responsibilities—it was a seductive thing, empty as it might be, particularly when you considered how she was, what she'd already been through, and what was waiting out there should she leave.

And if it got too boring, there were the wines of Covanti and an endless supply of mild drugs that would take you for as long as you wanted into a state where everything was pleasant and wonderful and the silliest little things were endlessly amusing.

She indulged herself in all the pleasures because she knew it *would* end, probably sooner than later. She was property, and not of Covanti's royal family as the others were, and she was being taken to her master.

And then there was Halagar. She had seen him only through Shadowcat, but she had known him far more intimately than that. He was a big, strong, muscular man with an equally strong and handsome face, with a bodybuilder's frame and muscle control, and so worldly wise and experienced that he had taught *her* some new things in the bedroom. He was rough, yet tender, too, somehow, and he seemed to be as smitten with her as she was with him. On his part it was a strictly physical attraction, but that was the only kind she really knew and it fired up her ego and self-image to think that out of all the choices available to him he had chosen her.

It *had* to be physical; somehow, for some reason, every time she was alone with him Sharlene Sharkin just ceased to exist, leaving only Shari, her perfect courtesan alter ego, who had no memories beyond being a courtesan, thought only in the Short Speech, and existed only to serve and please. There was a spell that would do that, of course; Sam had created it so she could have some fun back on that wagon train without betraying anything by accident. But that spell's words were English and known only to Sam and herself. Even on her own and without the spell, she could slip into Shari as easily as slipping into a dress, but she had always been there, as a sort of rider, able to regain control if needed. It was her "professional" persona. But this was different.

She wondered, sometimes, if perhaps that spell were breaking down. That maybe it was her subconscious doing it; that, deep down, she really just wanted to be Shari and to hell with anything else. In Akahlar, Shari was all that she needed, required, or could actually be. The rest, Charley, was excess baggage. She knew, at least, that if she ever did wind up permanently in a harem like this, she would quickly become all Shari and remain that way. And, truth to tell, she wondered if that wouldn't be all for the best for her own sake. She would always prefer to be in total control of her own life, but, if that could not be, and if there was no hope of ever returning home and she had to live her life here, as she was, wasn't it better to forget what wasn't relevant and just enjoy, like the girls here?

Sure, she was the brave, blind courtesan who'd outwitted and caused the destruction of a feared demon Stormrider by merely remembering a bit of high school physics, but there were only so many times you could get away with that, and she knew how lucky she'd been. One of these times, she'd lose. If not the next time, then the next, or the next. And, although one of her fantasies from the old days back home had been as the fierce and feared Amazonian warrior, it was different when you really faced those kind of things. On the whole, in real life, she knew that if she had to choose between being a warrior or a lover, she'd much rather be a lover.

Boday remained as personal slave to Dorion, although the plump, sandy-haired apprentice sorcerer would much rather have had Charley around. At least Boday was also subject to his commands, although, truth to tell, Dorion just wasn't all that comfortable in the role of master. And Boday was just a bit too weird a personality even for him.

Boday, tall and thin, now had a dark, chocolate brown complexion just like Charley, and for the same reason. Boday's body, tattooed from neck to feet, made her instantly recognizable anywhere and hardly somebody you could sneak through civilized areas. The sorceress Yobi had, therefore, dyed them both with an incredibly natural-looking skin dye to cover the designs. In Boday's case, it hadn't helped much. Neither did the fact that she assumed the name of Koba (and Charley was Yssa) so their names would not only not be obvious flags but also would match their new apparent nationalities. Neither dye nor a mere alias could hide Boday herself.

"Your humble slave is desolate!" she wailed to him in private. "When will we leave this velvet prison and resume our journey?"

Dorion knew well why Boday wanted to go. Early on, she'd accidentally swallowed a powerful love potion of her own design and the first person she'd seen after waking up had been Sam. It was incredibly strong—it had to be, since Boday often made references to one or another of her seven previous husbands—and its composition was known only to Boday, so only she could mix an antidote for it. And, naturally, under the potion, the last thing she wanted was an antidote or anyone else to slip it to her. She had even registered Sam and herself as a "married" couple in the Kingdom of Tubikosa, where it was allowed with disdain for the convenience of the authorities as a strictly legalistic means of straightening out inheritances, powers of attorney, and other such complexities that would otherwise tie the State up in knots. She certainly considered herself totally and monogamously married to Sam; how Sam felt about it Dorion didn't know, never having met that member of the trio, although Charley had indicated that Sam was the sort who liked it just fine.

Dorion, as a magician, could understand Boday, but ones like Sam made him well, *uncomfortable,* somehow. Boday was not a woman attracted to women, even now; she was just compelled by potion to be madly in love with one of them. But somebody who, without benefit of spell or potion, was still attracted only to members of the same sex was, well, creepy to him. He had known only a few in his short life, mostly men, and didn't know whether he was more disturbed that they were that way or that the ways to change that were available by spell and potion were rarely ever used.

"We're waiting for a report on what's ahead," Dorion told Boday for the umptyumpth time. "From here on in there's no choice of routes, and things are going to get tight and more dangerous than before, and before was dangerous enough for me."

"Koba knows you just like sitting here eating and drinking fine food and wines and ogling all the half-naked slave girls, some of whom might believe your tales of mighty sorcery and battles, but you are on a mission, commanded by our true master to bring us to him. How long do you believe that he will like us being kept here?"

Dorion sighed. She was dead right, of course, but the encounter with the Stormrider had unnerved him. Truth to tell, although his brown robe marked him as Third Rank, he really wasn't much of a wizard. His spells rarely turned out right or did what they were supposed to do, and he did as little as possible in that area. He also wasn't in the best physical shape and most weapons scared him; he would hardly have been his own choice for doing this job, and suspected that he'd been given it because, if he died in the attempt, it would be no great loss.

About the only reason he really was thinking of pressing on wasn't any fear of Boolean or Yobi, but mostly Charley. Halagar had been more an acquaintance than friend in their youth. In point of fact, time had dimmed the old feelings he'd had for the man, but now they were brought back full.

Halagar, in fact, was the kind of guy that boys like Dorion had hated. Handsome, sexy, debonair, the best athlete, the master of all he attempted, the dream of every local girl. Hell, even though he'd tested near the bottom of the "magically talented" group, he'd gone off to his apprenticeship mostly to get away from Halagar.

Halagar, on the other hand, had joined the army, risen rapidly in rank, gained position, then quit and become a mercenary and gotten pretty rich at doing that. Now, here he was, Imperial Courier to the King, and, worst of all, Charley had clearly fallen for him like a ton of bricks just like all the other girls always did. Hell, every time she was around Halagar she just seemed to melt away, leaving only a servile, mooning airhead. He liked Charley for her looks, sure, and he was as guilty as any man of looking at the pretty ones first, but it wasn't just the looks or even the moves, no matter how alluring they were. But he also was enormously attracted to the Charley who, blind and helpless, when faced with the monstrous, demonic Stormrider, had calmly figured out its weakness and directed its destruction. It was the strength and brains and nerve beneath the beauty that was, in fact, the most important to him.

Sure, she was a slave and compelled to obey him. He could have forbade her making out with Halagar and in fact commanded her to make love to him, but he didn't want it that way. He was a sorcerer, at least of sorts. He knew how easy it was for spells and potions to substitute for what was real. To compel it was no different to him than going down to the low-life district and buying it. His mind and heart just had no craving for or even use for gratification like that. Magicians above all others prized most that which was genuine and real.

It was the thing that puzzled him most about women, particularly strong and decisive women. They all said that they hated and detested men who treated them like sex objects rather than people and judged women by looks alone, Charley included—and said so often. Then they'd make real good friends with the kind of man who saw them the way they said they wanted to be seen and treated them accordingly—but they'd then walk off to bed with the guy who was best-looking and treated all women like sex objects and leave the guy who treated them first and foremost as people, the way they said they wanted all men to treat them, and who didn't look like a god but just ordinary. And then when you asked them why they were saying one thing to a guy and then teaching him the other, they turned and snapped and said, "You treat sex like it was a reward or something." Well, it sure wasn't punishment and it was sure a pleasure, and a guy who didn't get much sex himself sure couldn't figure why a woman would want to go to bed with a guy who acted all "wrong" and leave a guy alone and without sex who was their kind of guy.

In the absence of love, sex was either a commodity or a reward, at least to any guy he'd known. If there was any other thing that it was, it was unfathomable to the male mind.

Women and men sure didn't think alike, that was for sure. To him, Charley was basically sending the message that he was a sucker for not treating her as his sex slave and to hell with all that respect crap.

The trouble was, while he got the message, he just couldn't bring himself to be that way. Halagar, too, had gotten the message long ago, and he sure was never shown any reason to change his views, either.

Still, Halagar had been vital; Dorion had to admit that, even to himself. Were it not for the courier, his contacts, his quick sword arm and sure shot, and his rank in Covanti, they might not have made it this far. And now he was using the same power to get the information they needed to complete the journey that, like it or not, they had to complete.

He sighed and got up from the comfortable divan on which he'd been sitting. "All right—I'll see just what's up. I know how anxious you are to go on, but the gods know we needed this rest."

So far he'd been pressing Halagar for news; now he sought out others, the bureaucrats of the Court through which all such information had to flow, to see if maybe he was being played for a sucker in other ways. It took a little sweet-talking and a bit of bravado and bluster, but he finally wormed out the situation.

First was the interesting news that the dogs had been called off of Charley. That alone was amazing, wonderful news to him. Apparently it had happened many days earlier, and was now common knowledge among the underworld of Covanti, who had shifted their search to "a fat and probably very pregnant girl" exclusively. This took enormous pressure off; surely Halagar had known of this as soon as the word had been put out. Why hadn't he told them?

Of course, the answer was obvious. Now that there was no longer any manhunt, or, rather, womanhunt, for Charley, there seemed no particular reason for them to hurry on to Boolean. They had become, very suddenly, no longer really relevant to events. That meant that Halagar could enjoy all of Charley's favors until he tired of them without actually affecting the course of history or even events, and without getting a big-shot sorcerer mad at him.

Of course, Dorion's reaction at the news was just the opposite. His charge was to get the women to Boolean; now this seemed less an impossible task than a relatively straightforward affair. Not even Boday was at serious risk; it was she had the love potion, not Sam. It wasn't all that certain that holding Boday hostage would cause Sam to do anything dangerous or foolish—if, indeed, she even heard of it. Indeed, now that Klittichorn knew that Charley wasn't the one, the smart thing to do would be to facilitate their journey and do so in a manner that they would feel no reason to continue to be secretive themselves. That Sam was still trying to reach Boolean was a foregone conclusion; Charley and Boday. then, became valuable travelling the same road as bait.

To have revealed this to Dorion, or even Boday, would have meant their immediate departure.

Not that things were risk free. Covanti had mobilized some of its reserve forces and moved most of the regular troops from the colonies back towards the null zones. Rebellious forces composed, incredibly, of mostly colonial races had begun actual attacks on Akhbreed outposts and had also begun to marshall forces near the inner borders with the hub. The level of coordination was amazing; hundreds of colonial worlds, separated irrevocably by their lack of hub access to get communications or coordination between their various worlds *still* were moving as if under a unified command. Such actions were not merely dangerous, they were unprecedented.

They were also inexplicable. No matter how many forces they marshalled at the null's edge, the armies of the Akhbreed could always defend the nulls with superior weaponry and in-place defenses, and even if the colonials gained a bit and managed to cross worlds—what then? They'd be cut off from their own supply and support, unable to blend into the new world, and would only present an easier target for Akhbreed forces to mop up. Without control of the hub, what they were doing defied all sense. And they could never control the hub so long as the Akhbreed sorcerers guarded it so well and so effectively. It was the hub, its circular shape so perfect for military defense and supported by the vast powers of the great sorcerers, the heart of the Akhbreed kingdoms and of the race's control of all the worlds of Akahlar. Without the hub, they could be deadly, costly, even inconvenient, but they couldn't really win anything except their own death and the harshest repression for their worlds and peoples afterwards. They knew this. Why other than mass insanity would they now organize and march?

Dorion frowned. "Then is it safe, or even possible, to get through the colonies at all?"

The bureaucrat nodded. "Oh, certainly. Their worlds need the trade from the other worlds just as much as always. It is their interdependence that gives us power over all of them. They might stop or overhaul a train, but except for Mandan cloaks and blankets and weapons, they take nothing and let the trains continue. Most, travelling with sorcerers and under strong military guard, get through not touched at all. I wouldn't want to go through that kind of colonial territory on my own, but in some of the bigger trains it's still as safe as always."

Dorion thought it over. "Yeah, until the troops and sorcerers leave at the border and we cross from Covanti territory into Tishbaal."

"Oh, this is happening all over, not just in Covanti," the clerk assured him, sounding rather blasé about the situation. "In fact, it's worse in Tishbaal and they're thick as flies in colonial Masalur. But they seem impossibly well disciplined, and, while cocky and confident, they still seem to be letting most everybody and everything through. The High Sorcerers of all the kingdoms are in almost daily conferences over what it all means, as are the general staffs of the armies, but, so far, there's been no consensus. Your friend Halagar has been arguing with the King, advocating that we go almost to a seize mode and close the borders and shut down the trade. Right now, though, the economists agree that such an action would harm us far more than the colonials. I would be careful, though, my friend, if I were you. You are associated with Boolean and many of the monarchs and sorcerers believe that he might somehow be behind this."

"That's insane!" Dorion retorted. "He's been trying to stop this! He saw it coming years ago and has been trying to warn and unify everybody, and nobody would listen to him!"

The clerk sighed. "Yes, well, that's the problem, or so the rumors I hear go. He's had a hateful rivalry with Klittichorn of Marpek for decades, and he's been trying to gain allies to defrock or destroy—or whatever it is you wizards do to one another—his rival ever since. Klittichorn has always treated Boolean with contempt but has never tried to get sorcerous and political action against him. Also, Boolean has been outspoken for years in his contempt for the Akhbreed way and consistently a defender of colonials, as if they were capable of governing themselves. Comparing the two's actions and words over the years, there are a lot of people who don't like Boolean very much and who think he might be mad enough or frustrated enough to have somehow orchestrated this just to force them to act against Klittichorn."

"But it's the other way around!"

The clerk shrugged. "Perhaps. Consider, though—the champion of colonial rights is saying that he is defending the system he abhors, while a defender of Akhbreed rule stands accused of being a mastermind that the colonials will die for. Which would you believe? Remember, too, that you are a sorcerer yourself and you work for Boolean. If you were a neutral party with only a stand-off knowledge of the pair, you might feel differently. Klittichorn's domain is cold, poor, and remote, and he has done many favors for his brethren in the other kingdoms and never asked much in return. Boolean is in the middle of the richest and most powerful kingdoms on Akahlar and he's not been known for doing favors for anyone nor being particularly nice or even civil. You see where this leads?"

"Yes," Dorion muttered angrily. "To Klittichorn's victory and the destruction of Akahlar."

Still, it presented him with several immediate problems and many decisions to make. Until now, he'd never really understood how Klittichorn could be so brazenly successful and Boolean so ignored. Now it was at least clearer—the Horned One had laid his groundwork well, being the wonderful fellow, the man with great power and knowledge who would always help, always share, and demand nothing but cordiality in return. Boolean, he knew, had a less than wonderful and outgoing personality and tended to lecture those who, whether they were or not, considered themselves his equals, and he had little or no patience with stupidity, nor had he ever been quiet about his contempt for the system. Now Klittichorn's glad-handing was paying off. He was moving his forces openly, making low-level attacks and high-level threats against the kingdoms in the most brazen manner, and because they liked Klittichorn and considered him a good-fellow-well-met who said all the right things, and they had a personality problem with Boolean, who always spoke his mind, it was the latter who was getting the blame and taking the heat!

If this was really becoming official policy in Covanti, then if they stayed, they'd *stay*. Grotag, the chief sorcerer of Covanti, was known as a pretty genial fellow, but strong. Dorion knew he'd not be a match for the power in one of Grotag's hairs. He'd take no chances; he'd turn Dorion and maybe Boday into a pair of pet monkeys and give a re-enslaved and newly bewitched Charley to Halagar as his pet.

Damn it, it was time to use what powers and abilities he had and get the hell out of here!

He was heading back to tell Boday to make arrangements for their immediate departure when he ran into Halagar.

"Hold, old friend! Where are you going in such a hurry and with such a wretched expression?" the courier asked.

"We've been here long enough," Dorion answered carefully, "and if we're here much longer I'm afraid we'll be interned for the duration."

Halagar shrugged but did not deny the possibility. Instead, he argued, "Would that be so bad? This is not exactly the worst place in Akahlar nor a bad place for withstanding a siege, either."

"That is true," the magician admitted, "but I'm afraid that such safety would be very short-lived. I have been talking with various officials here and they have told me the, uh, political situation, as it were. They are fools to be taken in by a popularity act; the objective situation is upside down from their view. They are too safe, too fat, too confident that the way things are are the way things will always be and that no one can change that."

To Dorion's amazement, Halagar didn't seem offended by the remark nor defensive about it either. Instead he replied. "Yes, I agree. The massive coordinated movement of raw colonial troops who have theoretically never been schooled in the military arts shows much cunning and long work. One would have to be incredibly clever to have organized that sort of thing, and someone clever enough to do that and brazen enough to do that is not stupid enough to make the old mistakes. You only come out in the open to this degree if you've found a massive chink in the enemy armor. Still, what is the percentage in moving? What can any of us do about it?"

That was a stumper. "Not much, perhaps," the magician admitted, "but if a great war is upon us and if the power of the Akhbreed is so threatened that even the hubs are not safe, I think at least I would rather be with one of power who will fight to the last. Perhaps there is nothing we can do. Perhaps there is nothing Boolean can do. But, so long as there is a chance of anything I prefer action to complacency. I know Boolean, although he and I are not exactly on close terms right now. It is true he would not lift a finger to defend the system unless it was threatened with replacement by a system far worse—or even direr consequences. Imagine a wizard who could control the changewinds, Halagar."

The big man *had* considered it. "I am most troubled by that, and it is clearly the object," he admitted. "However, it might not be as clear-cut as you think. Do you really believe that Grotag and the King and all the high advisors are that dense? Or that the other kingdoms and Akhbreed sorcerers can't figure out the plot? They are scared—make no mistake about it. They are still unconvinced that it could occur on a global scale, though. Many see it as a basically localized fight between old rivals. Klittichorn with *his* Storm Princess versus Boolean with his, if he can ever find her or she him. One on one. The greatest colonial rebel massing is against Masalur and the approaches to it; that is clear. Klittichorn's ambassadors have been going around assuring everyone that it's a local fight, and that he is considering a preemptive attack with all his powers on Boolean before Boolean can attack the rest of them. The sorcerers and kings are mostly willing to sit it out, perhaps rooting a bit for Klittichorn, seeing who wins. Then if the winner moves against any of the others the rest will take him on. Because of his views, they consider a Boolean victory more of a threat to them than a Klittichorn one."

"I don't know how the horned one is going to do it, but I am convinced that this will be no localized quarrel. If Klittichorn can sit off safely with his Storm Princess in his remote northern citadel and still somehow draw and guide the changewind through Masalur, then he already has the means to hit anyone, anywhere, that he wishes. Boolean may wish he could do that, but if he could, he would."

"There is currently a wait-and-see attitude among the sorcerers," Halagar told him, "but once they see how things are developing they will most certainly mass on the victor to force him to share his new powers or be taken on."

Dorion considered that. "But if they take him on, they will have to mass together to fight him. What a tempting target for a changewind to blow through!"

"Huh! I hadn't thought of that! I'm a fighting man, not a sorcerer. I take your word for it, though. You have convinced me, Dorion, although we would never convince the others. They are, as you say, too sure of themselves. As for me, I would rather die fighting than sitting here with the winds blowing." He thought for a moment. "The odds of getting a train towards Masalur are slim right now. Few are willing to risk ambush by the colonials, particularly with Mandan cloaks in such short supply and the colonials practically holding some roads hostage. Armed escorts would only be good to the Tishbaal Null. We could make better time going overland ourselves, avoiding the main roads and routes."

Dorion's head looked up at the courier in surprise, " 'We'?"

"Why not? With my gun and sword arm and your sorcery we ought to be able to stand up to any minor colonial backwater irregulars we might be unlucky enough to come across. And I can have the maps and learn the roads and routes straight to Masalur, particularly if you can navigate at the nulls. With any luck at all we might reach your Boolean in, oh, three weeks."

"The King is not going to like your change of loyalties," Dorion noted, not at all enthused by the prospect of having Halagar along, nor all that happy that he might well be called upon to show how hollow his own boasts to the big man were about just what magical powers he might have. He wondered, too, if Halagar was *that* infatuated with Charley or if he was instead leading them into some sort of double-cross. "Nor am I that comfortable with someone who would shift loyalties so casually," he added bluntly.

Halagar shrugged. "I am a mercenary, an employee. I have been such almost all of my life. I give my utmost loyalty while I am in anyone's employ, but this will not be the first time I've quit a job. I am sick of arguing myself hoarse for a solid and unified defense of the hub with fat generals who have never fired upon anyone who could fire back. When I must commit to dull and stupid minds, then it is time I sought a different employ."

"Boolean or Masalur would certainly welcome your services, but I have nothing with which to buy your loyalty and arms."

Halagar looked at the magician, a strange, crooked smile on his face. "You have command of Yssa," he noted. "Delegate that command to me."

Dorion was shocked but not really surprised. "How can I do that? She and the other belong not to me but to Boolean personally. And she has an overriding compulsion to seek Boolean with or without me. I can not give what is not mine."

"That is understood. The commission is to get the three of you to the sorcerer Boolean, and that I will do and in the most direct manner. My fee is that she will be mine absolutely during that period only. Once there I must negotiate a new commission with Boolean. Once there, she is of no more value either as decoy or lure. I have sufficient money spread around and reserves hidden for when I truly need them. I have no wish for political power; I have seen what it does to men like me. I am certain that your Boolean will find my fee quite reasonable and affordable, and I will give my all for it."

Dorion was amazed. "She attracts you that much? You who have all the women swooning over your every move? Are you certain that you are not under an enchantment?"

"Sometimes I think so," Halagar replied. "And it is true that I can lie with most any woman I choose, although a few have eluded me. I have lost count of the number of women, free and slave, noble and common, that I have lain with, but she is, somehow, different. I have never married, not out of lack of suitable candidates, but rather because my life and chosen occupation would make it unfair to any woman and subject her to either far too much danger and strange places or force me to give up the life I love and settle down. Any such woman would also be a sword my enemies could use at my throat if all else failed. Courtesans of her caliber were always the best, but they always belonged to someone else and were heaven for merely a night, and not a one can hold a candle to her. She is blind, yes, but it hardly slows her, and she can see magic, which I cannot, and that gives me an advantage I did not have before."

"How did you know that'?"

Halagar shrugged. "She remarked on the color of some charms I have carried for some protection that first night back in Quodac. I knew then that she could see the magic, although she did not understand what it was."

"Oh," Dorion responded, interested that Halagar had still never seen or experienced, nor even suspected, the real Charley.

"She would be always loyal, totally obedient, would be uncomplaining no matter what the conditions or situation, yet she would serve me in all ways and ease my loneliness. She is the best of her class that I have ever seen and the first within reach. She is a pretty jewel who can neither be purchased with money nor taken by force, and, with her, I need not compromise my lifestyle nor situation."

Dorion nodded. "I see. And this period would be a sort of—trial run, as it were." He only wished Charley could have heard the way Halagar was describing her. He envisioned a time when a lustful Halagar would bring another woman to his tent and order Charley to serve them both. Still, the deal wouldn't be made unless Boolean okayed it, and Boolean knew just who and what she really was. In the meantime, perhaps three weeks or so as Halagar's "property" might reveal his true nature to her. Either way, this seemed the only reasonable chance of reaching Boolean under current conditions. He just hoped he wouldn't go mad watching the two and listening to them from the next bed.

"What occurs once we reach Boolean is your affair," he told Halagar. "I will accept your bargain as much as I can in the meantime, though, provided we leave as quickly as possible."

"It is late now, and there are preparations to make," Halagar noted. "Still, if you all can be ready, we could leave just beyond first light tomorrow. I will have everything ready by then, and will have cleared things here as delicately as possible. Is that soon enough?"

"I would as soon leave tonight," the magician told him, "but it will have to do."

Boday was no longer the first destination. He turned and decided that he'd better inform Charley.

She emerged from the harem, where men were not permitted, into the anteroom where he waited for her, looking puzzled but expectant. She no longer looked merely gorgeous; after some time and a make-over by the Imperial courtesans, she looked spectacular. Dressed in the light, gauze-like finery of the harem, with long, painted nails perfectly manicured and toenails to match, her hair streaked with blond, her lashes long and luxurious, she was the epitome of male fantasy. By the gods! How he wanted her, and how he hated himself for this!

"We leave tomorrow, just past dawn," he told her in English. "Be prepared."

"I am prepared," she replied. "I don't exactly have much to pack. They don't have riding outfits for people like me, but I'm sure I can find something that'll do."

"Halagar is coming with us."

That news excited her. "Really? I hoped against hope he would!"

"He is leaving the service of Covanti and coming over to us. His fee for taking us all to Boolean is you."

"Huh? How can that be?"

"He wants me to delegate my authority over you to him for the journey, which will still take several weeks. Once there, he expects Boolean to give you to him permanently in exchange for his service in the defense of Masalur."

She was intrigued by that, but not as delighted as he'd expected her to be. "I know this ring in my nose is kind of a turn-on, but I'd kind'a hoped that once we got to the old boy he'd at least neutralize it or something."

"You object to this arrangement?"

She thought it over, "No, not for a few weeks, I guess. But, you know, something funny happens to me every time he's around. I go bye-bye and Shari takes over. I love Shari when I can turn her on and off, but bein' her all the time isn't my idea of a future. I don't like the idea of being out there in the middle of nowhere without my brain in my head, either."

"Well, I don't like what happens, either, and I can't explain it, but I don't see we have any choice." Quickly, he filled her in on the whole situation.

"I get the picture," she told him. "I also get a real feeling that you don't like this arrangement much."

"I don't," he admitted, "but he's just the sort of person we need to have a chance of making it."

"Well," she sighed, "it's got to be. I don't have much choice these days anyway. At least it's kind'a flattering for me to find a guy with that much experience wanting me so much."

"Uh—Charley, he doesn't want to *marry* you, he wants to *own* you. Or, rather, he wants to own Shari. I, uh, well, he doesn't think you're the perfect woman; he thinks you're the perfect slave."

"Yeah, I figured it was something like that. And, as Shari, I *am*. I guess I should feel lucky. Very few people are ever perfect as anything. Still, it's not exactly been a burning ambition of mine to even discover that I'm the perfect slave. It's sort of like dreaming you're gonna be a great genius or something and discovering that you are really the world's greatest toilet cleaner. Still, it's in other people's hands now, really. If Boolean goes along with me, then I'll sure give Halagar his chance and see if he wants me anyway, but if Mister Green decides I'm no longer of any use then I guess I'll spend eternity washing his socks and loving it."

"You've gotten so cynical and too fatalistic," he responded, a bit angry at her. "That's not like you. You're sounding more like the local women here."

"Yeah, well, show me where I've had a crack at anything else. Seriously, though—you worked with Boolean. How do you think he'll take me?"

"It is hard to say," Dorion replied honestly. "Under normal conditions you would be free, liberated as much as he could, and treated extremely well, but these are not normal conditions. What's right and wrong under normal circumstances seems out the door now. Too much is at stake for ones like him to think much about an individual's rights."

She nodded. "Yeah, sort'a like Bogart in *Casablanca*. That's what I figured."

"All we can do is get there and see. Now, listen to me and obey my commands. Until I say otherwise—and, I emphasize, until *I* say otherwise—you will regard Halagar as your lord and address him as Master or however he commands. You will obey his every command as you would mine, as if your commands were from me or from Boolean—with a few exceptions. You will not obey any command that would betray us or our mission but will instead immediately report it to me. You will obey no command that would harm yourself or Boday or me, or cause us to come to harm, and you will report as soon as possible to me if any such command is given you by Halagar. Further, if anything happens to me, or we are separated, then you will be a free agent commanded still to reach Boolean as quickly as possible thereafter by any means you can find. And you will neither reveal nor repeat these conditions and exceptions to Halagar and you will deny to him that any such exceptions exist. Those are my commands. Obey them exactly."

She heard herself responding, "I hear and obey, Master."

At that moment, she felt a sudden, strange disorientation. Dorion, somehow, seemed to be less overpowering to her, more like Boday or anybody else she knew. He seemed, maybe for the first time, just kind of, well, *ordinary.* Her Master, whose voice must be obeyed, was elsewhere, and as of yet she had no commands from him. It was a weird sensation.

"I have to go," he told her. "Boday still has to be told and we have to get packed and ready. That's if Covanti lets us leave. If not, all bets are off."

She could hear the regret in his voice, and thought of saying or doing something, but she wasn't sure what to say or do. While she was still a bit confused, he left her standing there, alone, in the harem anteroom.

Neither Dorion nor Boday got much sleep that night, not only from the nervousness at going on, but also because of Dorion's fear that Halagar was either pulling a fast one or that the powers that be in the Court would stop them as soon as Halagar made ready to leave with them. Boday, who had no real liking for Halagar at all, saying she'd seen a thousand like him in her time, slept uneasily within reach of a whip and a short sword, ready for any sort of late-night intrusion. However, when light began to creep into the windows, and they began to hear the first stirrings of life in the castle area, nothing had happened.

Boday had agreed with Dorion that Halagar, if he were being straight with them, was an asset they couldn't afford to turn down, but she swore to Dorion that before she would let Charley be permanently given to the mercenary, she would kill either Halagar or Charley.

It was difficult to tell if Halagar had gotten much sleep, either, but he seemed to be true to his word. Two household grooms came for Dorion and Boday and their things, most of which were replacements picked up in Covanti, and took them down to the courtyard, where Halagar was waiting. He was dressed now in a plain black riding outfit with leather jacket and broad-brimmed black hat (none of which were adorned with any symbol or insignia), matching boots, and a thick, black sword and pistol belt.

Charley was with him, dressed in calf-length high-heeled black leather boots from which thin black leather straps came, interlaced up the leg and thigh and forming a cross-hatch pattern that led to a pair of black satin leather panties. Above the waist she wore an overlapping gold-braided neckpiece, matching gold bracelets and earrings, and a light, satiny black cape tied at the neck, but not much else.

Boday leaned over and whispered in Dorion's ear, "You see? Boday said she knew his type."

Dorion shrugged. It seemed an odd comment for Boday, who was rather fond of revealing leather outfits herself and, indeed, had one only slightly more modest on herself. "Seems like kind of an exposed riding outfit for so long a journey, but we're still in the warm latitudes. Still, it's in character with him and not as bad, I guess, as what she was forced to wear before." He frowned. "I see three horses, but one's a pack horse. Where's he expect *her* to ride?"

The answer was the kind of leather saddle placed on Halagar's big, black stallion. It had smaller, independent, leather stirrups attached forward, and the saddle was a bit longer than the norm. A saddle built for two. Either Covanti had two riders common enough so that such saddles were made routinely or Halagar had had this fantasy of his for a long time.

Charley was clearly in her Shari mode as well, servile and submissive and empty-headed. She always was around Halagar, something Boday and Dorion had both noticed and which had confused and disturbed Charley for a while as well. None knew the cause but while Dorion didn't like not having Charley's quick mind and courage on hand, he certainly didn't want Halagar to see that part of her, either, nor anyone else. Shadowcat in her lap broadcast her thoughts; as Shari, those thoughts betrayed nothing.

Still, Halagar's dominance and use of Charley disturbed the magician on a less practical and more emotional level. The idea of seeing her moon over Halagar and kiss him and maybe even make out with him on the trail raised emotional wounds in Dorion that he hadn't even suspected were there.

Still, he consoled himself as best he could and hoped he could stand it, knowing that just as Charley was now a tool of Halagar's, so Halagar would be a tool of Dorion so long as it served his purpose to get them to Boolean. Once inside Boolean's circle of power, Halagar was going to find his dreams a bit harder to hold on to.

It wasn't that Halagar was an evil man, it was just that he'd been, by benefit of being handsome and strong and the best at everything physical all his life, a spoiled and pampered center of attraction. Egotistical, self-centered, Halagar just wasn't the type to ever consider others as anything but tools or employers. Even now, he didn't really understand why he was lonely, or why he was so fixated on Charley even at this level—and he probably never would.

"We want a minimum of sixty leegs a day." Halagar told them, "and more if we can get it. The packhorse is strong and will keep up the pace. With so much of the colonial country infested by rebels, I intend to keep off the main roads if possible and travel mostly by day. Dorion, if you can manage solid Navigation, I intend to pick worlds where there is little report of rebel massings and plentiful water and reasonable terrain. There are a few in each track we must follow. Still, we can't count on anything, and there have been reports of minor changewinds in the least active colonial worlds. I've got Mandan cloaks for us on the packhorse, so don't let us lose him, but that could also make us a target. They've been gathering Mandan in great quantity on their raids and I can guess why. If you could do the impossible and actually predict a changewind and have troops ready at its periphery, you'd want to carpet your people in Mandan gold."

And that, of course, was the crux of the whole battle to come. Klittichorn and the Storm Princess together could somehow summon a changewind to any spot they chose; the Princess could then do what even the greatest and most powerful sorcerer, demon, or magical creature could not—she could direct even that great storm, at least to a degree. Not what it could do, of course—that was beyond anyone to predict or determine—but it didn't really matter to Klittichorn what it did. It changed, it transformed, it replaced for all time (or until the next changewind) what it touched, and if you could send such a storm roaring into the hubs of the Akhbreed, even their greatest sorcerers and spells could not stop it or even slow it down. And if you had a rebel army, well armed, well trained, and united in its hatred of the Akhbreed, following that storm quickly in, before even those who could get shelter had come back up, you would have an enemy army in your midst that perhaps even sorcery could do nothing against.

Halagar checked out everything, then put Charley up on the saddle and climbed on behind her. At the last moment a small, fast shape darted out from the shadows and leaped on to the big saddle where Charley and Halagar sat. Halagar was startled, and reached around her to pick up the creature and throw it off.

"No!" Dorion shouted. "They need each other. Remember that! The cat is a familiar and essential to her well-being."

The mercenary hesitated, then sighed. "All right," he growled, "but I'll not have a cat in my way here."

"Cats will do what they want to do—particularly this cat," the magician told him. "He will stay out of your way generally, and he will hold on as he must. But they go together, the girl and the cat. It is both or neither."

Shadowcat spent some time figuring out a comfortable place, irritated that his carrier sling was not fixed, but finally found a position that would do right against Charley and settled in, oblivious to argument.

"All right," Halagar growled at last. "But he better stay out of my way and hang on or he will be cat meat no matter what you say."

Dorion and Boday mounted their own steeds, and Dorion looked around at the luxury and comfort they were leaving and gave one last sigh, and then they were off, heading back into dangers worse than any yet faced. The only solace, and it was cold comfort to him, was that within a few more short weeks they would either be with Boolean—or in Hell.

3
Practice Session

Etanalon was startled to find Crim relaxing on her living room couch when she awoke, even though her magical sense told her that this was no enemy. No one, and nothing, could pass her threshold without being invited, and she'd never seen this fellow before. Most disturbing was that she got the same feeling from the stranger as from the pretty woman who was there the night before.

"Don't be alarmed," he said reassuringly. "I am Crim, Kira's—other half, you might say."

Etanalon frowned. "A curse? A very strong one, by the looks of it."

Crim nodded. "Kira resides within me as a passive passenger by day, and I inside her by night. It was a bargain to save her life, and, while inconvenient at times, it has not been a terrible thing. I believe, knowing what we do now, that we would still have made the choice."

Etanalon looked thoughtful. "Fascinating. A strong, handsome man of the world and a beautiful young slip of a thing. . . . Yet, listening to you and feeling your energies, I can see how intertwined the patterns are. I can also understand why Boolean chose you for this task. You have grown much alike, one to the other."

Crim's eyebrows rose. "Really? Nobody ever said *that* before."

"Not in the mere physical or sexual sense, but where it counts. In your manner of speech, choice of words, radiation of strength. I see not two auras there but more a greater whole. You have her memories, her innermost thoughts, and she yours?"

He nodded. "Yes. That was the hardest part at first. There was almost a descent into madness until such things could be sorted out and dealt with."

"Many would not have had the strength to do so. Almost all who know you both believe you to be separate people, I suspect. Perhaps you still think that way yourself—but you are not. In spite of what you say, the auras tell me that she does not ride with you now, nor you with her last night. I would have known. There were two of you once, quite different, but you escaped madness not by acceptance but by becoming as one. When you are a man, big and strong in the daylight and with the body's natural masculinity, you interact with the world as totally male; when you are a beautiful woman by night, you interact with the world as totally female, but you carry the same mind, aura, and inner strength in both incarnations. You have made a fascinating, almost unique, adjustment. Every male has some feminine aspect to one degree or another or they would be mere brutes, and every female has some male aspect to one degree or another or they would lack the hardness to survive on their own. Only in you, it is equal and without a dominant side."

Crim thought about that. "Maybe. I hadn't really thought about it that way. I certainly never felt attracted to other men, nor Kira to other women, though."

"Each aspect dominates with the body you wear," the sorceress noted. "That is how you avoid madness and enjoy what you have no control over becoming, but each of you draws what is needed from the other aspect. Strange, is it not, that you, who are truly two opposites in one, have no sense of confusion, while the girl, who is herself a single individual. does. Indeed, many would feel threatened or uncomfortable by you if they knew, yet I get the impression you actually enjoy the duality and would feel its loss greatly. Yet even you are uneasy with the nature of our outplaner Storm Princess."

He nodded. "It *does* make me uncomfortable, but I can't really explain why."

"Her situation is not as uncommon as we tend to think it is. It is only that it is out in the open with her that is uncommon. Sex is such a complex thing, such a part of us, both physical and mental, and yet, next to eating and sleeping, it is the most overpowering thing about us. The wonder is not that it goes awry now and then, but that it does not in so many more of us. Still, the combination, physical and mental, biology and environment, is complex and filled with countless variables. Hence, we get the pedophile and the nymphomaniac, the sexual murderer or sadomasochist and we get the impotent and frigid. The variations are endless. One wonders what the so-called 'normal' folk who would condemn her do in their own beds, or in the brothels and entertainment districts. Take any crowd of men and women and you will have a vast horde of sexually abnormal folk there, far more than her relatively minor situation. No one really cares, so long as it is swept under the covers and out of sight, any more than anyone really cares about your own true nature unless it is brought forcefully to their attention. Would a man attracted to Kira lie comfortably with her if he knew that in the morning she would be a tall, strapping, muscular and masculine Navigator? Would the women who swoon over you react the same if they knew that at sunset you would become more beautiful and feminine than they? I think not."

He shrugged. "It is true that I feel more comfortable the fewer who know my situation, and we have encountered far stranger aberrations in bed than we would have dreamed of otherwise. But we are a special case. Barring the unlikely meeting and compatibility of our opposite number, who might be female by day and male by night and both parts attracted to the other, we are best living somewhat separated lives *She,* though, is not cursed."

"Of course she is! Not by magic spell, perhaps, but by being different in a way that society strongly disapproves. Still, so long as she hid it, from society, even from herself, she could function—except that she was neither happy nor comfortable hiding. Like Kira inside Crim or Crim inside Kira, it was creating great stress and unhappiness and had the potential to drive her mad—a potential almost realized in her initial situation with this potion-created mate of hers, and after, where she has always taken the easy way out to flee her own inner demons. She has been victimized repeatedly here by an inner drive to forget who and what she was, to cease her own growth as a person. Many people can afford that luxury, although it is difficult to see how it is a positive thing. She can not. She has a destiny from which she can not run, and if she tries then it will destroy her."

Crim nodded. "So you decided that she had to like what she was and feel confident and comfortable with it, no matter what the social cost."

"In the end, it was she that did it. I simple removed the fear inside her, the social inhibitions that stood in the way of her accomplishing what she must. She now is happy with herself and absolutely uncaring about what others think about it. With that comfort comes confidence. Her ego, which the inhibitions kept fragmented and weak, strengthens constantly now. She will probably grow less pleasant and a lot harder to take, I fear, but this is the sort of person needed to stand up to the challenges ahead."

It was late afternoon when Sam finally woke, after the best sleep she could remember having in a very long time. Her old memories, her complete self, was back, but she didn't think about that past too much because it wasn't all that pleasant. In fact, it was almost an alien past, really; she could hardly believe how fucked up in the head she'd been all her life.

A fragment of a Golden Oldie song from that past rumbled through her mind, though, and she found herself humming it.

You can't please everyone, so you gotta please yourself.

Not, however, that she was particularly thrilled with the situation as it now stood. Now that she finally felt comfortably at peace with herself, she wanted to go out and pick up her life and *do* things and *see* things and enjoy that life, but her changed attitude towards herself hadn't changed the situation at all.

She was still a fugitive, still lined up for a battle she didn't really know much about or what was expected of her or how to fight it, and she was still pregnant to boot and none of that had changed.

Oddly, it was the pregnancy that dominated her thoughts. She preferred to think that she got knocked up that first time, when it was her own will and choice, and that this was no rapist's child, but it didn't really matter. The kid was still a kid no matter what the father had been.

The crazy thing was, in spite of it all, she *liked* the idea that she was going to have a baby. She wanted that child more than she had ever wanted anything in her whole life, but it stuck her between a rock and a hard place. If she didn't go into this fully, if she didn't face down this Storm Princess and beat her at her own game, then the child had very little future and she even less of one. She wasn't scared for herself, but what if it came down to victory or the child? That slimy, horned bastard always knew the weak points in anybody's armor, and it was a real concern.

But everybody had weak points. Even this guy Klittichorn must have them, or he wouldn't have had to take so long and be so sneaky to get to this point. Maybe the trick wasn't to dwell on the weak points but just try and cover them as much as you could and instead concentrate on your strengths. Or maybe use the weakness—the child inside gave her incentive to win, a motivation to dominate those forces that threatened her. Frankly, she wanted to take on her opposite number right now, one on one, and get it over with, but that wasn't the way things worked.

Damn it, I need a gynecologist, not a green-robed sorcerer, she though sourly. Etanalon was different—she was kind of a shrink, and she certainly was at least as effective as any of the shrinks back home. She just didn't make any bones about working voodoo and doing it with mirrors, that was all. This was different.

She sighed, pulled on the old dress, and wandered into the main house. Baths were few and far between here, but at least breakfast was still breakfast.

"I wish you would join with us," she heard Crim saying, presumably to Etanalon. She walked into the living room and saw the two of them sitting there, talking.

"At the moment—no," the sorceress responded. "I have retired from all that. Someone else must save the world once in a while. I'm tired and pretty well disgusted with the affairs of kings and back-room magicians. Grotag had a meeting just the other day to press for a united front against Boolean, who he is convinced is the really dangerous one. Many of the others who are still sane enough to care agree with him." She broke off the line of conversation and turned to Sam. "Well, hello! How are you feeling?"

"All right, I guess," Sam replied. "Not as ready to take on the world as yesterday, and maybe a little over-tired, I dunno. At least now I know that the reason I been feelin' so weak and washed out lately is the kid. Any chance of getting something to eat? I'll fix it if you tell me where all the stuff is."

Etanalon chuckled. "No need. Sit there in the chair and just think of what you're most in the mood to eat."

Sam sat, and it wasn't hard to come up with a vision of breakfast, even if it was late in the afternoon. Lots of hot cakes, melted butter, real sausages, maybe with some fruit and powdered sugar, with a pitcher of orange juice, fresh squeezed. It had been a long, long time since she'd had a real breakfast like that.

Suddenly, in front of her, was a stand-alone tray with dishes containing just exactly what she'd dreamed of. It was a startling appearance, and she jumped, almost spoiling it by knocking it over. "Hey!" she shouted in surprise.

"Relax," Etanalon told her. "There are several advantages to being a sorceress. No shopping, cooking, cleaning, dusting—unless you want to. Go ahead—it's real. *You* bite *it*, it doesn't bite you."

Sam stared at it for a moment, though. In all the time she'd been in Akahlar, she'd seen demonic spells and mystic potions and strange and magical creatures, but she had never until this moment truly seen flat-out magic. The smell of the food and her hunger drove out any further hesitation, though, and she tore into it. Still, as real as it seemed and as good as it was, it just seemed, well, impossible. You didn't get something for nothing, *that* she'd learned.

Etanalon seemed to read her thoughts. "Sorry—I forgot. You

haven't had much experience face to face with Second Rank personnel, have you? If you want the complete technique and its complexities I can give it to you, although it will do you no good. Only those with the power can do it, and only those with a great amount of power and control can do it that effortlessly. No, it is not materialized out of nowhere—I simply took the image from your mind, extrapolated the ingredients, and then did a simple matter-energy-matter transformation on it. So long as we have molecules of *anything, even air,* to work with it's not that hard."

"You sure don't have to worry where your next meal is coming from," Sam agree between bites. "Uh—you get hold of Boolean?"

Crim nodded "I made the call early this morning using the witchstone. He agrees with you that it is far too dangerous for you to attempt the last leg to him at this point. The lands between here and there are filled with colonial rebels, and they have figured out that Charley isn't you, which is good for her but means you're the sole object of everybody's attention now."

"Yeah—thanks a lot," she responded glumly, "Uh—does that mean they got Charley? I mean, we've heard so little. . . ."

"No, right now they're safe, and even in Covanti," Crim told her. "But they have already crossed the null and are heading towards Tishbaal. A pity—had we known we might have linked up again to form a company of sorts."

She sighed. "Yeah, I could really have used them now, just for shoulders to cry on. All right, so what's his idea for us?"

"We know that Klittichorn is planning something, but we aren't sure what," Crim said. "Spies in the lower ranks of Maripek, which is Klittichorn's domain in the frozen north, report that he and the Storm Princess left there a day ago. No one is quite certain where to, although there are rumors of some sort of fortress or redoubt Klittichorn has used in the past when he wants absolute secrecy."

"You're tellin' me that we don't know where they are?"

He nodded. "That's about the size of it. We don't even know if they're heading for this fortress, even if we knew where it was. They could be headed here, or anywhere."

"Yeah, but how far could they have gotten in just a day?"

"A lot farther than you seem to think," Etanalon put in. "Do not forget that he is a master sorcerer. Within certain complicated limits we can move very far very fast if we have to."

"Oh, yeah? Then how come I been goin' through Hell to get even this close to Boolean? And why hasn't Boolean just used this power to get to me?"

"Klittichorn has convinced many of the sorcerers of the Second

Rank that Boolean is the threat," the sorceress reminded her. "Boolean can't move without some of his colleagues knowing where and when. If he were to leave now it would simply cement in the minds of many Akhbreed sorcerers that he is deserting his position and is indeed behind what is happening. He can take Klittichorn, or so he believes, but not several sorcerers of that rank working in concert against him. I believe he is fairly itching to break free, and has been for some time, but he dares not until forced to do so, and that means waiting for Klittichorn to either make a move or make a mistake."

Sam discovered that this was indeed a magical breakfast. So long as she was still hungry, the moment she cleaned the plate it was renewed. She enjoyed it without guilt, knowing this might be the last decent meal for a while. "So—we're back to square one, like all the shit we were put through never happened. I can't get to him and he can't get to me and we don't know where the enemy is. So where does that leave me?"

"Not here," Crim responded. "That's a small town down their and the odds are pretty good that within a short period of time our entry into Covanti hub and village curiosity are going to come together and reach the ears of folks we don't want to know about us. Right now we're going to pick a comfortable colony east of here which doesn't border on Tishbaal and lie low. When Klittichorn tries something it will take energy—lots of energy. Boolean is monitoring all over and he hopes to be able to trace it when it comes. *Then* we can move on them."

"Uh-huh. Hurry up and wait as usual. Seems to me, though, that we got in here real easy. If this local sorcerer is against us and if they now know Charley's not me, it might be a lot harder gettin' out."

"Searching everyone who comes into and out of a hub is difficult," Etanalon noted. "Concentrating just on those leaving is far easier and more efficient. From this point the hubs are in hands friendly to your enemies and the colonies are heavily infiltrated. I agree, though, that caution outweighs everything else and that you must leave and quickly. I can not really use much sorcery on you since that would disturb the aura of the Storm Princess that is the key to all this. There are a lot of people who fit your general description, so perhaps subtlety, doing just a few minor things, might be far more effective than an elaborate disguise."

The racial restrictions of the hub system and the nature of Covanti's economy made for some unusual and exceptional sights for an Akhbreed hub region. Periodically, when the grapes in the small private vineyards were ready for harvesting, a fair number of agricultural workers were needed. In the colonies, where most of Covanti's wine and all its export was grown, this was no problem, but only those of an Akhbreed race could enter the hub. Grape harvesting was not unskilled labor—especially when specialty grapes and the royal vineyards were involved. And few of the Akhbreed race had ever bothered to learn anything so menial as grape picking!

Out of this need had grown the tradition of the clan call, in which leaders of family clans would call upon the women members of that clan to come aid the harvest in the name of clan unity. Such a gathering of the females of the Abrasis clan was even now in its final stages at one of the clan estates near the border, and it was there that Etanalon sent them, after suitable preparation. The harvest and subsequent stompings and the like involved hundreds of women, many from different colonial worlds who knew each other not at all, although all were at least very distant cousins.

Small spells that did not involve any sort of molecular transformation would not have any real effect on Sam, and they were rather simple for one such as Etanalon. It was a rural tradition in Covanti that a woman's hair might be trimmed but not cut. Hence, a small spell that caused her hair to grow right down to her ass overnight was in order. Sam had always preferred very short hair because it was almost effortless to care for, but she accepted this both out of need and because she knew it could always be cut later. The hair was also darkened to inky black, but with some white steaks that were a particular characteristic of the Abrasis clan. Not everybody had them, of course, but it was more common than not. More irritating to her, at least at the start, were the very long teardrop-shaped silver earrings that were fixed permanently to her earlobes. The only time she'd ever really worn earrings was after Charley had convinced her to get her ears pierced at the mall, but they had been little fake gold and pearl things and she'd eventually taken them off. These things weighed a ton and weren't removable.

But it was another Covantian custom, and she accepted the discomfort as part of the disguise. She *did* have to admit to herself that the very long hair and the long earrings did in fact suit her fat face and form pretty well.

Finally, some very bewitched eyeglasses that really changed her general appearance more than she expected them to. When she wore them, they were clear transparent glass, of no real effect except as a nuisance. But, if they were removed and someone else looked into them, they would present a convincingly distorted and blurry picture as if she had serious eye problems. It was one of those neat little touches a major sorceress could give you.

Covanti hub was both peaceful and pretty, but it was carefully guarded. A check of the border showed regular patrols by civil guardsmen and a fairly thorough scrutiny by militia at the border posts of anyone leaving. Clearly somebody had put two and two together and concluded that perhaps she was indeed within the hub.

Sam had spent most of the civilized part of her life since being dragged to Akahlar in Tubikosa, a rather strict and somewhat fundamentalist place with covered women and lots of hang-ups, and even though she'd lived all her time there in the inevitable capital city entertainment district, she had a strong idea of just what the typical Akhbreed were like and she'd been none too thrilled by them. They had their lapses, usually for their own convenience, but they were basically straight, uptight, and kind of like those pictures you saw of the most backward parts of the Middle East back home. Since then she'd come more or less through the back door from place to place, mostly hiding out, or sneaking through.

Covanti, however, was a much looser place. It was almost too bad that it was ruled by such dumb guys at the top, since otherwise it was almost the opposite of what she thought of as proper Akhbreed society. It was more class-bound, sure, but she had never identified with anybody other than the lower classes here anyway and so that didn't really bother her. The big city folk dressed more comfortably and with a lot more variety than the suits and baggy dresses of Tubikosa, and, while nominally all Akhbreed followed the same general religion, there was nary a veil in sight and a lot of skin. Upper-class women were still somewhat cloistered and withdrawn, but middle-class women were at ease in colorful saris and light sleeveless tops and short skirts, and even the men wore loose-fitting colorful shirts and slacks most places.

The peasants were even looser, more so than even some of the colonials she'd seen. The climate was warm and wet, at least in the hub, except in the few high mountain areas to the north and west, and it was kind of startling to see peasant women, often with huge jars or boxes on their heads, walking topless down the road wearing only a colorful, light-colored sarong or short skirt, apparently all of cotton. The peasant males weren't above being bare-chested, either, although their normal dress was a kind of white or tan baggy shirt and matching pants, usually with sandals, and wide-brimmed white or tan leather hats.

"In many places it's hard to tell the classes apart," Crim commented, noting her surprise. "In the subtropical and tropical regions things are clearer. Somebody with royal blood wouldn't be caught dead even in this heat and humidity without being fully and formally overdressed to the point of heat stroke, which is why you never see them much in the day. The middle classes show off their relative wealth—or hide their lack of it—with fashion. The peasants—well, you see how they dress. It's not only tradition, it's the law, really. The gradations of class are actually a lot more complicated than that, but you can actually get thrown in jail for dressing inappropriately to your class."

"I'll stick with the peasants," she told him. "No complications or hang-ups and they just let it all hang out and to hell with it."

He nodded. "Now, the vineyards of the Abrasis clan are loose, and the women brought in from the colonies to handle it are all officially peasants here no matter what position they might occupy back home. It's not quite as loose as it looks, either. There's an effective if unobtrusive security guard for them and the women don't go anyplace alone, only in small or large groups. The women don't have much more in the way of political or civil rights here than anywhere else in Akhbreed society, either, outside the family. The only real exceptions are those with magical powers and those with political connections, who have a kind of *de facto* position and respect. Needless to say, the plantation owners and colonial managers don't send their own wives and sisters and daughters to these obligatory things—they send the peasant-class women in, usually the daughters and such of the field supervisors, overseers, and the like. Lots of peasants hire on cheap to the colonial corporations because, while they're the lowest here in the hub, and the lowest Akhbreed in the colony, they always have a whole native race to feel and be superior to out there. It's an ego thing. You'll find most of these women ignorant, totally unschooled, lacking much imagination, and about the most bigoted group you ever met. Take it easy in there. The object is to blend in, not draw attention."

She nodded. "I'll try. How long do I have to stick it out in there, anyway? I know as much about wine—other than it comes from grapes and if you drink enough you can get tipsy—as I know about, well . . . *babies.*"

Crim grinned. "You won't have to know much. You're starting to show and that means they'll make you a cook or something like that. Women are coming and going all the time there during this period so it's unlikely anybody will think your showing up is anything unusual. For most of them it's an excuse to get out and away and many of them spend more time in the villages, maybe buying stuff or just seeing the sights, than actually working. You just walk in, keep your story and your accent straight, and do a little acting so you won't pick fights and draw attention to yourself. I'm going check the lay of the land and security on the eastern borders. I'll stick myself in as a Navigator going into the colonies as a dead head interested in escorting any who want to go home and thereby picking up some spare change. I've got about fourteen different Guild cards, so don't panic if I come in with a different name and a slightly different look."

"I still ain't too sure about this," she said worriedly.

"We're gonna hav'ta pick up a small bunch of girls to make it a group, and unless we ditch 'em fast Kira's gonna be kind'a obvious, but if we do they'll be after our heads."

"Don't worry about Kira," he soothed her. "For one thing, these are colonials, not hidebound hub-huggers. I've had a little experience here. Just make friends, not waves—understand?"

She nodded. "I'll do what I can."

Infiltrating the harvest gathering proved to be very little of a problem. Sam looked right, talked more or less right, and the security men weren't about to even ask whether or not every woman in the group she joined had been there from the start. The idea of a woman actually sneaking into one of these peasant camps just would never enter their head.

Sam had always thought of wine as something that came from more or less cold regions, and, back home, she would at least have not found lush wine grapes in a tropical setting. This was not home, though; this was Akahlar, and the rules were quite different here, as were the animals and vegetation, even if much of it looked the same.

The festival looked less like hard work and more like the Campfire girls, although the Campfires never dressed like this. The ancestral castle was off on its own grounds so far away from them it was simply a distant and tree-shrouded speck; the women were put up in open-sided buildings with thatched roofs, about twenty women to a unit, or block, sleeping on straw mats. There were communal cooking areas between each unit; generally fire pits and crude stone ovens that looked like giant backyard barbecue pits. The makings came out in wagons daily from the estates, were prepared, then distributed on a regular basis to the women unit by unit. To eat, you lined up, grabbed a hubcap-sized wooden plate, got what you wanted, then went over on the grass and had a picnic. The food was of surprisingly good quality—these *were* of the clan, after all, peasant branch or not—and drink was, naturally, local wine.

It seemed to Sam almost like an all-girl's picnic and camp-out. Nobody seemed to be working very hard, most seemed to be enjoying it, and almost all of them were young, the majority in their mid or upper teens and the oldest perhaps in their mid to upper twenties. They came from every kind of colonial world Covanti controlled—Sam counted maybe sixty variations of telltale earrings before she stopped counting.

And, although married women were rarely sent to these things and she met none in her first day there or after, there were a fair number of pregnant girls around, many looking no more than fourteen or fifteen. Kids having kids. Peasants couldn't afford the magic charms and alchemical potions that were the only forms of birth control in Akahlar, and abortion was quite literally a mortal sin to the religion—you did it and got caught, you died by public dismemberment. That was what drove many young colonial peasant girls to run away to the hub cities, where, of course, they wound up feeding the appetites of the patrons of the entertainment districts.

Of course, it depended on the locals and the clan, and the local priests as well, how such a bald indiscretion was taken. The pregnant girls here were sent here mostly to get them out of sight for a while, or until the family back home could figure out what to do next. Legally, none were allowed to have their kids in the hub, though; that would make them hub citizens, not colonials, and the government would then have some responsibility for their support and upbringing. Some would think just that way, sneak off to the city, have the kid and have it taken away and given to the church, then delivered to the pimps and lords of the entertainment district if they refused to be neutered and made wards of the church—usually janitors, housemaids, and the like, de-sexed and then cloistered for life—although few if any of the colonial girls who ran off to the city either knew or believed this. The rest would go home, but Sam wasn't sure what kind of reception they'd get at that point. She decided she'd try to find out, although she was pretty sure it wouldn't be a great life or a happy one.

This system not only oppressed and controlled the nonhuman and not-quite-human colonial populations, it was also quite effective in making even a large number of its own miserable for life.

Few of the pregnant girls with whom Sam was naturally quartered and placed seemed to think about that, though, or the alternatives awaiting them. Some of it was just the usual teenage "It'll work out" or "It won't happen to me," and some was just trying not to think about the future so long as they could be here.

She picked up her assigned goods, which weren't much—a couple of light brown panties, her personal cup and plate, and her small toiletries kit of comb, brush, and the like that she'd brought with her—and found her assigned sleeping space. Not much, but at least there was a bit of breeze and not many bugs out here.

"Hi! Welcome to the Disease Pits," she heard a pleasant teenage female voice say in a very provincial but understandable accent. Sam turned and saw a pretty young girl of perhaps sixteen or seventeen, maybe five-five or six, her waist-length hair held in a great ponytail and slung over her left shoulder so it hung down the front. She was very well along in her pregnancy, her natural thinness just making her distended belly all the more prominent, and she was wearing just a yellow panty almost like a bikini bottom. The brief dress was practical; there was no way she was going to get a sarong around her that would stay on. The fact that almost all the women around were wearing the sarongs but Sam had been issued panties indicated that dressing by class was taken here even to the lowest common denominator. "My name's Quisu," she added.

Sam kind of stared at her distended belly for a moment. It was the first time she'd ever seen a girl this far along—not in a maternity dress—this close up, and the sight was unnerving. Unlike Sam, who was fat anyway, this girl really looked like a normal teenager who somehow had swallowed an entire undigested watermelon. Quisu held herself oddly, didn't look either well balanced or comfortable, and waddled when she walked.

Is that the way I'm gonna get in another month or two? Sam couldn't help thinking. Aloud she said, "I'm Sahma, of Mahtri. Uh—how far along are you?"

"A few days over eight months. Less than a month to go." She sighed. "They're gonna throw me out'ta here this week, looks like."

"Oh yeah? Then what?"

Quisu shrugged. "I ain't decided yet. Guess I got to real soon now, though. I been thinkin' of sneakin' out in the city but I don't know nobody or nothin'. I ain't never been in no city before. Hell, this is the biggest group of Akhbreed I ever been around at one time. I don't even know how far it is or how to get there. You *believe* that?"

Sam nodded. "You're better off not knowin'. You get out on the road here, some guy'll come up and promise you all sorts of stuff and take you there. I saw some of the vultures and I know the type. I been in cities. Girl like you, they'd let you have the kid then slip you some stuff so you wouldn't remember nothin' 'bout yourself, your past, even what you looked like, and you'd be just nice and cooperative. You'd just be another street whore on some guy's string."

"Aw, we all heard all that shit. Maybe it's true for some, maybe not, but it beats goin' home for a lot of girls."

They walked out to the grass and sat, Sam curious and wanting to make a few friends right off the bat. "Is it that bad?" she asked Quisu. "Goin' back, I mean?"

"*Uh!* I hate this part of it. You can't even get comfortable sittin' or standin' and you got to pee every ten minutes. Uh—I dunno what it's like in—where'd you say you was from?"

"Mahtri."

"Yeah, Mahtri. But you take like Dolimaku, where I come from. The natives look like big lizards, even hiss when they talk. Ain't that many Akhbreed there, and the ones what are, are real strict. If I go back, they let me have the kid, then I get strung up, get enough lashes on my back to make permanent scars, then they carve my face up so's I won't never tempt no more boys. Like the boys ain't never at fault! Shit, I bet Coban maybe got a lickin' and grounded for a couple weeks or somethin', if that. His dad's the chief overseer. Kind'a big shot. Big deal! But that Coban's so damn cute, with the tightest little ass and the deepest big brown eyes you ever seen, and he was so smooth, I—I guess I fell for him like everybody did, only I was dumb enough to think he was gonna marry me."

Sam was appalled at the first part. "You mean they'd actually carve your face up?" No *wonder* the girls lit out for the cities, dangers and dismal futures and all.

Quisu nodded. "Yeah. Only thing is, though, the kid would be accepted like a regular member of the family. Have a chance, a future, you know what I mean? And I could see it, hold it, even care for it, watch it grow up, you know? Even if I couldn't never tell it I was its Momma. Things any different where you come from?"

Sam felt a little sick, but didn't want to press on for now with the subject.

"Well, I ain't gonna be exactly welcomed with open arms," she responded, being careful, "but I'm in a little different way than you. Train I was travelling with, comin' back from visitin' relatives in the city, got hit by bandits. I got raped."

"Wow! And I thought *I* was through somethin'! Now Putie—you'll meet her, she's a nice kid—she got raped, too, but it was by the Company Supervisor's brother. He claimed she seduced him and was only claimin' rape 'cause she got knocked up and, well, you know which one they believed. She's from Gashom. She says they shave your head there, then rub some gunk on it so it never grows out, stick a brand on your forehead, and then you become the property of the Company, which in this case includes the guy who raped her. Ain't much, but the guy gets the kid, and in her case that means the kid's raised with the upper class, so it's something. Her friend Meda's also from Gashom, but she's from a town and got knocked up same as me. She'll get the same shave and brand, but her kid'll go to some orphanage someplace and she'll wind up property of the town—kind'a like what they say you get in the city, only without the forgettin' juice."

"I guess you're all sort'a thinkin' 'bout goin' back or not," Sam responded, "and maybe comparin' notes."

"You try not to think about it," Quisu said softly, then patted her bulge. "But sometimes you just can't get away from it. Meantime, we're kind'a the bad examples here. Not that you're treated bad. There's some that're holier than the gods or real smug and superior, but most of 'em'll talk to you, sometimes ask you what it's like, that kind of thing, even be real sympathetic or extra kind. We don't do no work here 'less we want to, and those of us this far along don't want to much. It's kind'a borin', but it's the way things are. Sometimes you get to hatin' the kid, sometimes you get to hatin' yourself sometimes, you just lie there and cry a lot, but mostly you just relax and try not to think much. There's always some girls assigned to watch us, like them over there tryin' to pretend they ain't, just to make sure we don't try'n kill ourselves or somethin', but nobody stops you if you just slip away and off the grounds."

"Are there many girls who try and kill themselves?" Sam asked, wishing she could do something, anything, for these girls.

"Sometimes. One tried it while I was here. Real sloppy job, though. Many got a lot worse to go back to than me or the others I told you about. I mean, what's a little balding or scarring compared to havin' your tongue cut out, your eyes put out, and your eardrums shattered, like they do in Fowkwin?"

There wasn't much to say in answer to that. And this festival would be winding down in a few weeks; they'd all be forced to choose at that point.

Damn it! Boday used to take kids like these and make them into mindless sex bombs, while others on the street sold the less desirable ones into slavery or worse. The lucky ones would wind up permanent, free, peasant labor at a Pasedo-type place. And she'd sat there and accepted it!

The fact was, she'd just ignored all the bad parts and hadn't looked very hard or thought about it at all. It didn't make her feel very good right now.

If she had her way, and the power, she'd create some land somewhere on one of these colonial worlds as a refuge where all these kind of girls could go and have their kids and have a kind of life without being slaves or property or worse! A Pasedo kind of place without a Duke or hierarchy at all. But she didn't have that power, and so long as the Akhbreed maintained their rigid cultural attitudes and tight colonial grip there never would be such a place, not really. And she was supposed to save these damned Akhbreed from such destruction! Hell, this was just one small part of one branch of one clan! How many girls like this *were* there? Maybe, just maybe, she was coming around to the real Storm Princess's point of view. She'd been around Klittichorn a long time—she *couldn't* be *that* dumb.

Could it be that the Storm Princess knew just what she was doing, but could not imagine even dominance by a godlike Klittichorn any worse than what was now here?

Her old problem was coming back now, in spades. The problem that had overshadowed all her other problems, all her personal problems, and the one no magic mirrors could resolve for her. It was the one she'd been running from, consciously or not, since it had been first put to her, and she was no happier with it now than before. Sure, Klittichorn was a damned murderer and something of a power-mad maniac, but what in hell was Boolean? Etanalon had said that Boolean disliked the Akhbreed way and was outspoken in that dislike, and that was, more than anything else, why nobody else liked him or would help him or even believe him. But he'd done nothing to change the system and was still working against the odds to preserve it. Nor was Etanalon a really good source on this—she, with her power, could never comprehend the horrible choices these girls faced, and the most she might do with the system was fine-tune it, remove some of its more gross features, but leaving everything else intact. Etanalon, at heart, was a believer. Why else was she still on the fence?

Damn it, she didn't have enough information! Never had. She needed to meet Boolean, talk to him, take his measure, not as some distant and mysterious ghostlike figure but man to woman. How the hell could she muster the confidence and will to beat back the Storm Princess unless she was sure she was doing the right thing?

She felt a sudden, sharp, uncomfortable twinge in her belly, and must have registered surprise or discomfort on her face.

Quisu chuckled. "I think you just got kicked."

But the kick had made Sam abruptly aware that the hot sun was no longer beating down and she looked up and saw swiftly moving clouds gathering, and she forced herself to relax. *That* was the way to draw a lot of attention fast, and that was in nobody's interest right now.

"Wanna meet some of the others?" Quisu asked her.

"Yeah, sure. Why not?" Sam responded, needing to move or do *something* right now.

"That line of trees over there is the river," the girl told her, pointing. "That's the bathtub around here. It's shady and a little cooler there, so it's kind of a hangout for those of us with nothin' much else to do. I used to be there a lot this time of day, but you get to feelin' so awkward and dumb-looking and so damned tired quick."

Sam got up slowly, then helped Quisu to her feet. It wasn't all that far, but it really was hard on Quisu, and Sam let her take it slow and easy and knew that, fat or not, this was her in not too much longer a time. If, of course, she lived that long.

There were a dozen or so visibly pregnant girls there under the trees, and it was a sort of instant comaraderie that made things a lot easier for Sam. Quisu's friend Putie was something of a shock; she was so tiny she looked maybe twelve or thirteen, no more than four-foot-ten and if she weighed eighty pounds. even with her extra baggage, she'd be at fighting weight. Putie was, in fact, simply very small and slight, but she was among the older girls in the Disease Pit at seventeen. Quisu was sixteen. and Putie's fellow Gashomian Meda, a chubby girl with very large tits, was fifteen. All were well along, although in Putie's case it was hard to tell since she was so very tiny and the child was certainly at least normal size and the distention was gross. Sam couldn't help but wonder if Putie was too small and weak to survive the birth.

Sam let them do most of the talking, if only to avoid having to come up with details of a world she'd never actually been to, or making references to people and places she shouldn't know about. They talked freely, and, as Crim had warned, it was kind of tough not to object to some of it. as when Meda referred to the native population of Gashom as Slimeys, but Sam restrained herself, realizing that, no matter how wrong it was, these girls right now desperately needed somebody, some category, lower than they were, and they took the first and only cultural target of opportunity available.

Okay, terrible things portended for them; they were headed for the very bottom of the Akhbreed ladder—but they would still be higher than the natives. It wasn't much, but if it's all you got, you go for it.

Sam had always kind of wondered how, back home, in Civil War times, all those thousands of church-going southern people, most of whom had never and would never own plantations or any slaves, would be willing to march out and fight and die for slavery. Maybe this was the answer. If you were some dirt-poor Appalachian farmer plowing rocks and in hock up to your ears and had kids you couldn't feed and very little else except what you might get sharecropping for the rich, you were pretty damned low. But so long as there were slaves, there was somebody lower. Like these girls, lowest of the low, who would still be so appalled at a colonial native uprising that they'd fight and die rather than let the natives take over.

Well, she was learning a lot about people and about herself, Sam thought. The trouble was, the lessons didn't seem to lead to any clear conclusion.

The ignorance of the girls was appalling, too. As much as they were being screwed by the system, they still believed in it and could conceive of no other. They thought the sun moved around the Earth and that the stars were holes through which a little of the Kingdom of the Gods shone through. They had seen so little electrical that they considered it in the same realm as magic, and the concept of flush toilets or cities larger than small towns was just not in them. None could conceive of snow or really being cold.

None of them had ever seen any real magic, yet they believed that the spirits were everywhere—in the trees and wind and water and even the rocks—and they prayed to them or asked them for favors.

Most amazing was their total acceptance of their class. They could no more conceive of being anything but peasant class or lower, than they could conceive of suddenly turning into a dog or a lion. The very idea of *aspiring* to move up in class or position or that it was possible or done in other places was so totally alien to them that there was no use in trying to explain it. This was why even the stories of what happened to girls like them in the towns and cities held little terror, but it was also why only a small percentage of these young unwed mothers really did run away. They had a near total fatalistic outlook that sustained them and kept them from madness, but which would lead most of them to mutilation and dishonor back home simply because that was the way things were.

That was frustrating. They couldn't help their ignorance, but the idea of accepting even this was really too much for Sam, yet she didn't try and argue them into any kind of alternative action.

The fact was, they *had* no alternatives she could recommend. Oh, they had choices, all right—mutilation and permanent dishonor back home, becoming a whore or a slave or a eunuch in the city, or maybe death. And no matter what they were feeling inside, they accepted that. The completeness of Akhbreed political, religious, and cultural control was amazing and something she had never really fully faced before. And by so tightly controlling themselves they were able to control so many other worlds and people and cultures.

And the future was always on their minds.

"Men," Meda said in the same tone you'd use for vermin. "They always got to be the bosses, push everybody around. We bear 'em and raise 'em and they grow up to be strutting assholes just tryin' to overpower and outdo each other, and the ones that can't come back and beat up on the women. It ain't fair. There oughta be someplace where the women are the bosses. Yeah. I know, it's sacrilege, but who says it is? Priests, right? Men. I ain't felt too religious lately."

"Well, I dunno," Quisu responded. "I still like men. I guess I'll always like 'em no matter what. There's lots of good ones—my dad, for one, and my brothers ain't all that bad, 'though I'd never say that to their faces. It'd be nice if we had some equal say in things—I mean, they trust us enough to eat our cookin' but not to do business or sit in on councils. There's good and bad men just like there's good and bad women. It don't make no difference. We just run into the wrong sort once too often, that's all. I ain't even really blamin' the boy that knocked me up. I mean, I was crazy for him and I wouldn't listen to nobody. I never even thought about *this*." She patted her belly. "Never entered my head, and probably not his, neither. I ain't sure if I could do it over I could stop myself from havin' him inside me again."

"Yeah, but most girls got crushes on somebody, only they don't go all the way," Putie noted. "Most stick it out 'til they get married. *I* stuck it out, but it didn't do me no good. He was a damned spoiled brat who never thought 'bout nothin' 'cept what he felt like and he was half again as tall as I was and three times my weight, and his girlfriend just broke up with him and got engaged to somebody else. He couldn't take it out on her so he took it out on the first girl he saw, the bastard. And when I went and told about it they all acted like it was my fault or somethin', like I came on to him. That's the way *he* told it and they all just believed it even though they knew what a louse he was. Uh—I just about made up my mind I ain't goin' back, you know."

The others turned and said, "Huh?" almost in unison.

"I don't care 'bout me," Putie told them, "but he ain't gonna have this baby. No way. I don't care what happens to me or where the baby winds up, but he ain't gettin' it. Shit—what if it's a girl? Imagine *him* with a girl kid! Uh-uh."

Sam could sympathize. "Where will you go?" she asked the tiny woman. "Into the city?"

"Uh-uh. I ain't never been in no city but what I hear 'bout it I don't like. I'll cross the null and take the first colony that comes up that I can sneak into."

"Putie," Quisu said softly, "if you have that kid without a midwife and maybe a healer around, you'll probably die."

Putie shrugged. "Maybe that's for the best. But it'll drive 'em all nuts in any case 'cause they'll never *know.* None of 'em'll ever be sure. Maybe I'll luck out and get some colonials that'll help me."

"Yeah, that'll be the day," Meda responded in disgust. "They'll probably eat your baby and then chain you as a pet. 'Com'on! Everybody rape the Akhbreed girl!' Uh-uh. Not for me."

It went on and on like this until Sam could take it no longer. Finally she and the others wandered back to the camp, where hordes of young women were now gathering for the meal or helping prepare and dish it out. Sam ate well, but didn't rejoin in the constant conversation testing out all the alternatives these girls were playing with. She was so damned depressed she wanted to have a good cry, but there wasn't even a good place to do that.

Lying there later on her mat, she tried to sleep, tried to put all thoughts out of her mind, to at least not face the darkness that the thatched roof covered long enough for sleep. Blank your mind, relax. . . .

She was wearing a full-length fine satin dress with gold belt and jewelry, and she was walking down a set of stone stairs to a great chamber. It was a very strange place, sort of like a great hollow dome, only it had concentric stone steps going down in row after row to a round and flat stage at the bottom, kind of like some great ancient theater.

On the floor of the chamber were several designs painted on the floor. The designs were all identical—perfect pentagrams—but were arranged in a kind of mathematical symmetry and each was a different color, the pentagonal centers all pointing inward. And, at the center of the chamber's floor, there stood a strange, violet-colored, pulsating, round globe, transparent enough so that you could see the other side through its outer skin, and the globe was moving, slowly but surely, west to east. On it were evenly spaced dots of bright orange light.

There were others in the chamber as well. She glanced over and saw Klittichorn, in full crimson robes and horns, sitting on one of the stone rows and working with some kind of strange object.

Suddenly Sam recognized that object with a shock. A computer! The son of a bitch had a portable computer! How the hell did he get it or know how to use it?

The others were also in robes, although of dull greens and browns and blues. There were both men and women there, and while none looked like very strange creatures, all seemed to have something odd or amiss about them, something not quite right. One had tremendously pointed ears and a giant cyclopslike eye that seemed segmented into at least three parts: another appeared to have a broad tail sticking out from under her robe, and the last one she could see might well have had batlike wings. Yet all were dressed as sorcerers, and all seemed to be busily checking out something or another in various parts of the chamber.

Three of these oddities, plus Klittichorn and her. Five, Five pentagrams on the floor, each color coded to the robes of the others except for the golden one that was obviously hers.

The Storm Princess turned and approached Klittichorn. "Well, wizard, has your demon box given you what you sought?"

The sorcerer didn't answer right away, but finished up on the keyboard, then watched as the small screen filled with incomprehensible numbers. He nodded to himself, smiled slightly, and looked up at her. "Indeed yes, my Princess. It would be nice to test it out, though, before going straight against Boolean. We know it works, but accuracy and control are crucial."

The Storm Princess nodded. "Very well. Whenever you're ready. This place is unpleasant, almost haunted. I would soon do what it was built to do and do so quickly."

"Patience, patience," Klittichorn responded. "You won't believe what went into its construction, let alone its powering. What brings you here now?"

"I had another brief weakening. I felt it, this afternoon, even though I was doing nothing. It disturbs me."

"Yes. If we only knew where she was. . . . A good test, I would think. Go, rest, practice your control. We will need it soon enough."

The Storm Princess turned and walked back up the chamber,

lifting her dress slightly so as to keep from tripping and falling back into that pit.

Sam had not had one of these cross-over episodes in a very long time, and never one as clear as this. The longer it went on, the more vivid it became, almost as if she and the Storm Princess were truly one, and it was Sam and not her duplicate who was now walking in that chamber. They were so mentally close, so attuned, Sam couldn't help wondering. . . .

"*Wait!*" Sam called out to the Storm Princess.

The Princess stopped suddenly, then turned and looked around, but saw no one. Clearly, though, she had heard!

The old Sam wouldn't have dared this, and maybe the new one would have been more cautious, but the day spent with the poor girls had disturbed her deeply, causing her to dare the risk.

"*This is your sister, whom you seek to destroy,*" Sam told her.

"*Get out of my mind bitch!*"

The thought was so sharp, so violent, and so filled with rage that for a moment Sam was taken aback, but she knew she had to press onward. She had to know.

"*I am not your enemy! Not necessarily, anyway! This system sickens me! I don't want to defend it! But all you and Horny there have done is tried to kill me, and I know that you know he's a slimeball! Give me your reasoning! Tell me your plans! Show me why I should not fight you!*"

The Storm Princess whirled. "Klittichorn! The bitch is *here!* In my mind! Get her out! *Get her out!*" The unnaturally low voice she shared with Sam echoed across the chamber and everybody else froze.

Klittichorn looked up at her, then stood up and stared straight at the Storm Princess. The distance was fairly great, yet it seemed as if he were looking not only at the woman but through her. A tiny, thin beam of white light seemed to shoot from him to the Storm Princess, ricochet off the woman, and land somewhere on the pulsing violet globe.

One of the yellow lights on the globe changed to white.

"She—she's in Covanti!" one of the others shouted. "In the damned *hub!* Low hills . . . near the border. . . ."

"Got her!" Klittichorn shouted. "Princess, get back down here at once! Places, everybody! Full power up! We got her!"

Suddenly contact was broken—completely, absolutely, leaving Sam there wide awake in the darkness. It was still—Jesus! So fucking still you could cut it with a knife!

What have I done? she wondered to herself.

She got up, and managed to carefully step over and around sleeping girls and get to the edge of the enclosure. There was a fire still burning in the fire pit, although it was slowly dying, and she went over to it and tried to think. Five places, five pentagrams—but only one Storm Princess. That spinning violent globe—Akahlar? The shining yellow lights—hubs? *Think! Think!* How much time? Had to be. Had to be hubs. The white one had been near the middle, where the hot places were, and this was sure one of them. Covanti, then.

Five places but only one Storm Princess. That was important, somehow. What the hell did the globe do? The five of them stand there, they concentrate on someplace, the pentagrams point, and where they all come together is the target. That had to be it. Made no sense but what did around here? Four of them . . . sorcerers. Akhbreed sorcerers, probably, the others like Yobi, misshapen, changed, by their own misfired powers, but powers they still had.

What would they send? Some great demon Stormriders, perhaps, or great magic spells, or what? No time to run, no place to run to. Ten minutes alone in the dark on that road, right around here, and she'd be in the hands of slavers and it would be bye–bye Sammie anyway.

Wait a minute. . . . Wait a minute. . . . Stormriders, big spells—they wouldn't need *her* for that. The Storm Princess could do only one thing, and it was the one thing none of them could do. Could that gizmo maybe *broadcast* that power? Send it here like it was some kind of radio or something? But what good would it do to send even a hurricane here? Her powers were at least the equal of the Storm Princess's, and she now knew how to draw the power from the storms, shape them, direct them, and she'd be closer to the storm than the Princess, closer to the elementals, whatever they were, who guided and fueled it and obeyed the Storm Princess, They would know that.

Changewind!

The term itself explained everything and yet was the greatest terror she knew. That big gadget—some way to focus magic power. Could those four sorcerers do what no sorcerer dared to do and actually cause or call or create the conditions for a changewind? Poke a hole someplace?

Call it, yeah, but they were powerless to control it or do anything with it. The Akhbreed sorcerers feared changewinds as much as anybody, since they were just as much helpless victims of the storm as the average person. But they were far away, inside that domed chamber, far from the changewind they would call, safe from its effects.

Could the Storm Princess even command a changewind?

The temperature seemed to be dropping, the very air thinning. Deep within the darkness there were terrible rumblings that caused the ground to vibrate. Sam stood up, turned, and looked around into the darkness. The conditions and the vibrations were already waking up most of the women, but they were sleepy and confused.

Let's see. . . . You could save yourself from a changewind by covering yourself completely with Mandan gold, the only stuff that could shield you. But there was no Mandan here—not in hubs. They carried it on the trails and in the colonies and in Crim's wagon, but not here, in a place like this. It would take a lot, anyway.

She had never faced a changewind in person, although she'd seen one in a vision, through other eyes. These fancy places were supposed to have crypts, big underground chambers lined with Mandan, for everybody to run into! That's how it had been. But even if the manor house had one, it wouldn't be big enough for everybody here, and the house was like three-quarters of a mile away. Forget it. They'd panic here and most wouldn't make it anyway.

Think. . . . Think. . . . Damn it, something in what you just thought. Think, Sam!

If they sent a storm she was of equal power at least to the Storm Princess, and closer.

Was the changewind, for all its fearsome results, actually just another big storm? It *had* to be! Otherwise none of Klittichorn's shit would work!

There! Tremendous sound and lightning just off to the east, between here and the border. Tremendous explosions, and women screaming all around her.

Far off, the sound of a siren kind of like a volunteer fire department came to her ears, and to the others, and immediately the large number of women began screaming in panic, "Changewind! Changewind! Make for the house!"

Sam moved away from the panicking mob, away from the enclosures, towards the storm. Was she enough? Was she up to this yet? Was she forgetting something, maybe?

She realized, suddenly, that she'd picked up a long stick from the cooking area without even thinking about it. She made to throw it away as the sounds of panic receded behind her, then stopped as she was about to throw. A pointer. Something to focus on, like *they* had.

She pressed the stick in the dirt and with all her might began to trace a circle, unsure in the darkness whether or not it was even taking real shape in the ground. Then a line here, then there, then again, and again, and again. If there *was* a pentagon in the middle of the star, she was within it, and it was pointed towards the terrible lightning and thunder and explosive sounds that now seemed so close.

She heard some people behind her and turned. "Who's there?" she called. Even now, the wind was starting to pick up, to blow things about, but that was not the changewind, only the effects from its leading edge. It was coming, but it was not here yet.

"It's Quisu and Putie!" she heard Quisu's voice call "Come! Get under some shelter! It *might* help! There's no way we gonna make it up there in time!"

"Stay back!" Sam shouted to them. "Don't go into the shelter! Get everybody still there out in the open but behind me! You understand? Out in the open and *behind me!* Sit on the ground! This wind's gonna be real fierce real fast!"

"You crazy!" Putie shouted. "Nobody faces down a changewind!"

"Maybe I am," Sam called back. "We'll know in about two minutes! Now—do what I say!"

Tremendous gusts now hit her, and the leading edge of rain that would become quickly intense. She heard somebody yell as they were knocked down, and she heard the sounds of things blowing this way and that, things that were normally too heavy to blow anywhere. Within another minute she could hear the sound of thatched roofs coming apart, and the cracking sounds of some of the enclosures starting to give way. There were screams as well, but she couldn't pay attention to anything now except that coming storm, invisible in the darkness.

Strangely, she felt remarkably calm, as if something inside her was relieved that a climax had actually come, that action was required without nagging questions of right and wrong.

She reached out into that thundering that seemed marching straight for her, not denying it, not hiding from it, almost welcoming it. She felt the strength, the energy, flow into her and she suddenly stiffened, a look of pure amazement on her face in the lightning's glow, as her whole body felt not the sudden, pounding rain and wind but rather the most intense, sustained orgasmic feeling she had ever known. The power flowing to her was enormous, beyond belief, but all she could think was, *Come on, you stupid bitch of a princess! Let's see how you take on this fat, pregnant, peasant dyke who hates your god-damned guts!*

4
The Victorious Trap

The storm was small by weather standards, but what it could do was something no ordinary storm, regardless of size or power, could do, and that was why it was so feared.

And yet, as she concentrated on it, as she felt its power and grabbed for it, she understood that, for all its strange nature, it was still a storm. She reached out in ways she could not explain to anyone and saw it as an entity, raw yet conforming to the rules of storms so long as it was within Akahlar's domain. It had some dominion over matter and energy, of what it touched and what it might do, yet upper steering currents still held it in some tight fashion; landforms, even those it could transform, nonetheless bounced and jostled it, turned it, and reshaped it even as it reshaped them.

All storms had a distinctive shape and obeyed their own internal rules of consistency, and lost their power once those internal rules were altered. With an ordinary storm that was not impossible to do, but with this one the internal rules were hard to find in all the confusing masses of hissing, snapping energy. Fed as it was by a tiny particle of the monoblock whose instability had created all that was, it was the most alive and active thing in all nature, spitting off particles of matter and energy, mating with what it found and changing it in ways that seemed at first totally random but which she came to realize were in some way mathematical. The random bursts of particles and waves from its tiny but super-powered center were only half the equation; the process was only completed when they interacted with what was already there, binding the random fury to their laws and creating a fearful symmetry in what was created.

There was no way to grab that center and guide or direct it; it was unfathomable, a brilliant, sputtering, incomprehensible mass.

The trick was to control the storm by its edges, to shape it, pick up the myriad whiplike appendages of energy that flew from it, and hold them in the mind like reins on a herd of wild horses.

And something, *someone* else, was busily locating and getting hold of those whiplike energy reins. Sam could sense the other, feel it, watch just what was being done. She didn't understand it; she didn't *have* to understand it; the practical demonstration was enough.

The other's power stemmed from intense but measured hatred; Sam used rage, which was rawer and less controlled but in its own way just as strong. She began to reach out to the energy reins that the other had so considerately already grabbed and stabilized and began a mental tug of war for their control.

For a while, it seemed an even match, the storm oscillating first this way and then that, but having something of its own way as the struggle for its steering energies was in dispute, but there was a grave difference between Sam and the Storm Princess, one that had nothing to do with children in wombs or experience or even proximity.

If Sam did not stop the storm, it would quickly swallow her and all the others helpless in the open behind her; the Storm Princess was safe far to the north in her dome, under no threat no matter which way the storm or struggle went. In the test of wills, experience versus self-preservation, self-preservation had the emotional intensity to give Sam a slight edge.

One by one, she pried the tendrils of the changewind from the grip of the Storm Princess and gathered them to herself. The first few did not come easy, and there was much back-and-forth tugging and twisting. The Storm Princess tried strategy, letting her enemy have several very suddenly while making a grab for others to hold tightly, but it was a tactic that worked only once. Slowly but inexorably, with a building sense of power and satisfaction, Sam gained complete control. Klittichorn had miscalculated; even with all his studies and planning, he had too much fear and respect for the changewind, too much faith in its ability to dominate. Now he would know.

You do not send a storm to do in a Storm Princess.

Sam felt the other's control weaken and then fade away, and she quickly gathered up the balance of the whiplike energy leads and gained complete control of the changewind. She had it, absolutely, and she was exultant. *She'd done it!* She'd beaten the Storm Princess and Klittichorn and now was mistress of the one thing in Akahlar everybody feared!

The godlike feelings were punctured by sudden confusion. Okay, she had it—now what the hell did she *do* with it?

Clearly so long as it remained relatively in place it was drawing strength—intensifying if anything—and that was the last thing she wanted. She had to get rid of it, send it on a course that might cause terrible effects but which would dissipate it as well, send it, weakened, up into the outplane. To kill a storm you spent its fury.

It was close enough to the null that she tried to send it there, but while it shifted a few miles it could go no further. Powerful energies and upper air currents forced it back upon itself, refusing to let the storm approach the null. The conditions the null exerted against storms from the worlds was what kept Akahlar functioning; there was no way out there.

The hub, then. It had to be the hub. There were mountains someplace, mountains that could dissipate a storm, but she didn't know where they were or how to find them. All her concentration had to be on holding that storm; there wasn't much of a chance to check a road map even if she had one.

The circle around the star. Hubs weren't perfect circles but they were close; she was on the eastern border, so west, or north and west, were her only alternatives. She searched for upper air currents high above the storm, found them, and began to tie the upper tendrils of the storm's steering energies to them. She began to tie them—one, five, ten—and still the storm remained, so she frantically began to tie all that she had in messy clusters, until she reached the critical number where she felt a sudden wrenching, felt the storm begin to move, lumbering, but away. She realized that now was the riskiest part, for the only way to send it was to let it go, and she didn't understand enough of the complexities of storm movement and the influence of other things on it to be certain it would not double back on her. Still, there was no other way.

She released the reins and suddenly felt as if a great weight had been lifted from her and was speeding now away.

She was suddenly standing ankle-deep in mud with wind and torrential rain cascading over her body, the darkness so absolute she could see nothing at all. She felt a sudden rush of self-satisfaction, and in the midst of the more ordinary storm still raging around her, she laughed and raised her arms to the heavens.

Oddly, she felt neither tired nor drained; in fact, she felt really alive, energized, as if somehow the energy she had absorbed from the storm's periphery had somehow supercharged her. Not only did she feel so incredibly alive, but her mind seemed to be working with the crystal clarity only absolute self-confidence brought. She knew she could not celebrate for long; they had failed to kill her with all their power and gadgetry and magic, but they knew just where she was now. The changewind would wreak havoc in the local area and that and the aftermath of the more conventional storms that spun off the great wind would make it as difficult for her pursuers as for her, but it wouldn't take long for them to compensate for that. Not even the mighty changewind could touch her; she knew that, now. But a bullet, or a sword, would have little trouble making that fact irrelevant.

She also remembered what the Akhbreed did after a changewind, how they mercilessly came down with their armies and massacred the changed victims. She could do nothing to stop that, not now, but it would mean the Covanti army would be moving this way as soon as it was clear and there was light. The fact that she had saved the Abrasis estate meant little except that this region would be an ideal staging ground for the soldiers going into the changewind-ravaged areas. And with them would come men contacted by Klittichorn, charged to find her at any cost.

The wind, the rain, were dying down rapidly now, as the great storm sped swiftly away on its new track. Sam was able to hear herself once more, and immediately turned into the darkness. "Anybody!" she shouted. "Shout out! Is everybody okay?"

There were a number of cries in response, some quite close to her, and soon there were a few dozen voices yelling back.

"All right! Listen to my voice and come to me!" Sam shouted. "Everybody who can hear me shut up and come to me!" She kept repeating that over and over, and, slowly, they came. With the skies still totally overcast, the fires and torches all drenched into uselessness, and all lighting, even in the distance towards the manor, out, they were still effectively blind, but Sam's solution began to gather them.

"Sahma! Is that you?" she heard Putie's voice call out.

"Yeah! Over here! Everybody over here so we can find ourselves and figure our what to do next."

Others were now shouting off in the distance, but they didn't seem close enough to hail. One by one, though, the drenched and mud-caked survivors made it to Sam.

The Disease Pit, as the enclosure for the pregnant girls was nicknamed, was the last in a line and a bit off to itself, and it was no surprise that almost everyone who came to her was from there. The ones left were the ones like Putie and Quisu who *couldn't* run in panic and knew they'd never make the manor house and so had simply remained to meet their fates.

The rain had become nothing more than a fine mist in the air now, and the wind was down to a gentle breeze. Sam took time to grab her Covantian super-long hair and try and squeeze out what felt like a ton of water. It was like putting a wet mop in a wringer. Maybe very long hair really did make her look better, but she wondered if appearances were worth the price.

Nine of the fifteen girls sleeping in the Disease Pit, including Sam, were there. A few from the other enclosures also showed up, but Sam told them to go see if they could find others and gather them to themselves. The ones who weren't pregnant had a lot better mobility and were in general in a lot better shape.

Not that anybody who'd undergone the storm's approach was in *that* good a shape. All were soaked, mud-covered, and scared. Sam noted that the pregnant contingent seemed, oddly, to be holding up better than some of the others, judging from the yells and screams and hysterics coming to them in the dark. She wondered just how many of them, if only for a fleeting instant, had hoped that the fearsome storm *would* come their way, overwhelm them, and end their problems.

"Ain't nobody gonna ride down here and get us together?" Meda asked nobody in particular. "They just can't let us rot here in the mud in the dark."

"They can and they will," Sam assured her. "I've seen this kind of thing before, only in daylight. They'll wait in their shelters until they are dead certain the storm's gone, then slowly come out. First thing then they'll ring this place with what security they can until the army gets here, and then they'll wait for dawn. They're scared, too. They know a lot of us got caught out here but they don't know how close the storm got or what it might have done or not done. They won't take any chances until they can see properly. Anybody checked the shelters?"

"I was near one when it collapsed," somebody said. "Made an awful racket and just missed me. With that wind I bet there's not a one standing, or, if there is, not a one anybody but a fool would get under."

Sam nodded to herself. "That's what I figured. Can't see a thing in this pitch dark, and I ain't so sure I even know which direction's what, so there's no use in moving right now. Best thing we can do is kind'a huddle down here and wait for light. It's gonna be a pretty miserable night, but until we know what's what, there's nothin' we can do."

That fact made Sam even less happy than the others. She wondered if Kira had been out there, maybe camped on the way here from whatever she was checking out. What if Crim was now cut off? If the storm cut the roads between here and the capital they'd be blocking them off and nobody would be allowed through for days. More than enough time for Klittichorn's henchmen to come here and ferret her out. Worse, it was equally possible that Kira had been caught dead center in the storm. If that was the case, nobody would be coming for her.

"I wonder what they gonna do with us?" Putie wondered aloud. "If everything's wrecked and all, there ain't no way we can just go back to normal here no matter what." She sighed. "I gettin' tempted to just start walkin' towards the null at first light."

Sam chuckled dryly. "Yeah? And just how far do you think you can walk, Putie? Or most of you? Even if you got some food and water, it's maybe ten leegs to the border and another thirty or forty leegs across." That was, at best, something like twenty-five miles, a fair day on a slow horse. "Besides, they'll be heavily patrolling all the way. There was lots of folks living in the path of that Changewind and they ain't dead, but they ain't folks no more, neither. We got to play it by hunch, that's all."

"Who you all kiddin'?" Meda said derisively. "We ain't got no say in it at all. We gonna sit here 'cause there ain't noplace else to go, and then when day comes we gonna do just what they tell us t'do, like good Akhbreed girls. It just the way things *are,* that all. Only time I disobeyed and did somethin' on my own, 'gainst the rules, I got myself knocked up. The gods made the rules and every time we go 'gainst 'em we get screwed."

That started up something of a debate that, while on a basic level, was actually over the proper role of women in this society and also the class system. Sam listened to them, slightly bemused by it. Not that any of them sounded like revolutionaries; every one of them would have been overjoyed to just go home and pick up where they left off, get married if anybody would have them, and keep house and have lots more babies. But that wasn't a choice they had, and so there was a natural human tendency to try and cheat fate. Finally Sam decided to take charge.

"Hold it! Hold it! Look, I don't know how long it is 'til dawn and I don't know what the hell will happen then, but it's startin' to get a little bit better here and there's a fair amount of grass. Each of you take a hand of the one closest to you, and let's get over where it's more comfortable and try and settle down. We're not doin' ourselves or our babies no good by sitting up all night in rotten muck."

They did get together, and she led them to an area she could feel was fairly thick grass. It wasn't dry, but it wasn't muddy, either, nor did it have a lot of debris, and in the swiftly rebuilding heat and near-suffocating humidity, it was an island in the midst of chaos.

"Everybody just sit or lie down and try and get a little sleep," she told them. "I know that probably isn't possible but give it a try. It's been a hell of a night."

A single firm voice and a little confidence was really what they needed, and she was a bit surprised although pleased at how her authority, even though a newcomer and stranger to them, was accepted. For a while there was quiet, and then somebody whispered to somebody and finally there was something of a set of whispered conversations. Sam didn't try to hear them nor care what they were saying; she moved a bit away, staked out a plush plot of grass, and sat, staring out at the darkness.

Contrary to all that Meda said, there was at least one woman in the group who wasn't about to wait around for the men to decide anything. The darkness was frustrating; there was a little light now as the clouds broke and some stars shone through, but there wasn't any sort of moon around Akahlar, at least not the sort that would illuminate the landscape well enough to see.

At least now she knew she could do it—turn and twist the changewind. The most feared thing in this whole crazy world was the one thing that did not threaten her at all. She already knew that she could summon more common storms and use their power as a weapon; she had killed with that power. There might be more things one could do than that, but she hadn't been able to test it all. It didn't matter. What she did know was enough. No matter what happened from this point on, she would no longer be defenseless, nor hesitate to use that power when necessary.

The reaction of the Storm Princess infuriated her still. She couldn't comprehend it, not really. If this Princess was her twin, then she at least had the same amount of brains. She had to know it was Klittichorn who killed her mother and that he was using her. Maybe she was bewitched, under some kind of spell—but it didn't seem like it when she was inside the Princess's skull.

Revenge, they'd said. She was fueled entirely by a fanatical desire to revenge herself and her people against the Akhbreed kings and their sorcerers. Did she, could she, hate so much that she didn't even *care* that she was being used? That the only thing that mattered to her was the destruction of the Akhbreed empire? My God!

Did she see her relationship with Klittichorn as a sort of deal with the devil? Had she willingly sold her soul to evil so long as it carried out her hateful wishes?

No matter what, Sam knew, from now on the Storm Princess had to be treated as an insane enemy. There could be no more attempts at reaching a compromise or understanding with her. Perhaps that was why Boolean stood so firmly against them in spite of his own alleged lack of enthusiasm for the system.

Or was Boolean just a sort of reverse Storm Princess, hating Klittichorn so much that he'd preserve the power and the system and oppress billions forever—pay any price just to get his own revenge?

Shit—she wished she knew the answer to that one.

If she knew what direction was what, if she had any real landmarks, she would have set out that night to get some distance between her and her inevitable pursuers. It certainly wouldn't do to just start walking and perhaps walk right into Covanti, or worse, into whatever the changewind had wrought. They wouldn't have as easy a time cleaning up *this* mess as they had the previous one she'd seen in her vision. The area was much wider, the warning had been too short, and the region too densely populated. Well, whatever they were now, they also had the night to prepare, to evacuate, or to make ready to defend themselves. It might take an Akhbreed sorcerer as well as an army to control that region, and that was one type of person she didn't want to meet here right now.

She was also more physically limited than before, when she'd built up all those muscles and done all that running and lifting. She would walk if she had to, but if there was a way to ride somehow she preferred it. As for Crim—well, she'd make it possible to follow if she could, but no matter what, Crim was gonna have to find her.

Someone approached her in the dark, and she turned and strained to see who it was. Putie, from the smallness of the figure.

"I thought I told you to try and get some sleep," Sam admonished her.

"Couldn't. Ain't had much sleep nohow, so out here and on grass it ain't possible. That's true for most of us. We sorta been—well, talkin'."

"I noticed."

" 'Bout you."

Sam frowned. "What's this all about? You speakin' for the group?"

"Sorta. See, most of us, we was right behind you, no more than two hands back." A hand was roughly six feet. "In the storm, I mean. Everybody else was runnin' 'round in panic and scared shitless, but you was real calm, you told us to sit down, then you walked to the storm. We could see you clear—first in the lightnin', then even more when you started glowin'."

Sam was startled. "I *glowed?*"

"Uh-huh. Swamp fire we call it back home. Green light that just come from the sky and set you glowin'. Real spooky. But there you was, just standin' there, facin' the storm, and gruntin' and groanin' and sometimes wavin' your hands in the air and the like, like you was pushin' that changewind away from us."

That was uncomfortable. "Putie, you know nobody, not even the greatest sorcerers and high priests, can do anything with a changewind."

"Yeah, maybe. That's what we all was told. But, back home, the Slimeys, they got this crazy goddess they call the Queen of Thunder. They make these crazy carvin's of her and they worship her. They say she's an Akhbreed goddess who can control the changewinds and got sent someplace 'cause the others were jealous of her. That she's plotted revenge for thousands of years and will one day come back and strike down the sorcerers and their gods with the changewind, and that all the lesser races who come to her side and fight for her will be raised up over the Akhbreed. They spend a lot of time findin' shrines to her and destroyin' them. But Quisu says that the lizards in Dolimaku have almost the same thing, only it ain't just Akhbreed but the rule of men she's gonna get rid of. That she rules a goddess court of women only and she bears a daughter as a virgin. Another girl said she's in her world, too, only a peasant goddess, who brings the rain to breathe life into the soil."

"Well, that's not exactly true," Sam responded, trying to limit her reply and having an uneasy feeling where this was going. "There is somebody who has power over storms, and she did come from peasant stock, but she has only that one power. Otherwise she's as human as anybody else—and forget that goddess and virgin crap. There's a bad sorcerer who's got her and he's using her and these cults to build an army so he can knock off the Akhbreed sorcerers and take over."

"Yeah, well, I thought you'd say somethin' like that. But you ain't really one of us. Like you was talkin' just now—low but some big words, too, like you was tryin' to hide yourself. We noticed. And the way you take charge—give orders. More like a guy would, or somebody from high up, anyways. You wasn't scared of that changewind. Ain't nobody not scared of the changewind, but you wasn't. And now you tell me all this 'bout this storm goddess and this evil sorcerer. Ain't none of us ever heard anything like that. Who *are* you, Sahma? And what?"

Sam sighed. "It's kind'a hard to explain to you who I am, but I'm human, you got to believe that. No goddess, no princess, no Akhbreed sorcerer or magician. My name is Susama Boday, and I come from Tubikosa." No use in trying to explain the concept of outplanes and worlds beyond Akahlar to Putie; she barely understood the other worlds adjoining her own.

"You're *married*, then?" It was the almost universal Akhbreed custom that you had but one name and that you took your mate's surname when you married.

"Sort of. Yes. I know about the evil parts of the cities, Putie, because that's where I came from and lived. Boday is an artist and alchemist who took pretty young refugee girls on the run like you and makes them into beautiful, living works of art—so they can work for a master and he can sell their bodies to the higher classes. Not just women but men and even kids are turned into playthings for those with strange appetites who can afford them. Those who can not be made attractive for that flesh trade are turned to slaves to do all the dirty work and cleanup. That's where the ones from the colonies wind up when they run to the cities."

"But you weren't no slave."

"No," Sam admitted. "It's made me feel guilty for a while now, that I didn't feel guilty then. Oh, I *might* have wound up a slave, but in a complicated set of things Boday swallowed a strong love potion and I was there and so the potion fixed on me. That is why I say I am sort of married. It gave me someone to protect me and my friend who became a high-class whore, so I went along. I—well, I found out things about myself, that I had some strange needs, too, and it kind of worked. What I didn't know was this storm and evil sorcerer business. Another sorcerer who wants to stop the bad one found that I was another, maybe the only other, who was born with that power. Even I didn't know it at the time. He forced me to try and come to him, since the evil one has him kind'a pinned down. That's how me, Boday, and my friend Shari got on a Navigator's train, and the enemy hit it, killed most, captured me, and that's when I was raped. Not once. Over and over, by lots of filthy creatures who called themselves men, while I was tied to a rock."

She was suddenly aware that she had more of an audience than just Putie, and sighed again. What the hell? They'd seen her in action. If she couldn't win them over they could buy favor, maybe even out of their misery, by turning her in the next day.

"So did they kill your husband and friend? And how'd you wind up *here,* of all places?"

"No, my mate and my friend are still alive, or at least were the last time I got word. It was my friend and a badly wounded man from the train, the father of two captive girls, who rescued us. But more bad guys chased us, we got separated, and that was the last I saw of them. I worked on a plantation for a while as a picker and they gave me a potion to forget all, but the sorcerer who needs me didn't forget and sent a mercenary to get me out and get me to sorcerers who restored my memory. The rest up to here is a long story, but we got to here and found that Covanti decided to throw in with the bad sorcerer 'cause they're scared of him, and they figure if they can turn me over they'll buy out of whatever he's plannin'. I got in okay but gettin' out is the trick, so we came up with this idea when we heard of the gathering here. Tomorrow or the next day my mercenary, who's a Navigator, would show up and volunteer to take some girls home who might be on his route. I'd go along, and just be one of the girls. No papers, no mess. That's how it was *supposed* to work. Now, if he wasn't devoured in the changewind, he'll be cut off for days, maybe weeks, and I can't wait around for him. They know I'm here. Not just in Covanti, *here.* They'll be comin' for me. They tried with the storm but we were even there. Now they'll come with men and guns."

The audience was spellbound, not so much by her real predicament as by the romance of it all.

Quisu's voice came from the darkness. "You mean you made it this far, against all those forces? And you're gonna try and keep ahead of them, even now?"

"Sure. I'm not defenseless, no matter how I look, and I've got a lot of experience now. I'm not gonna get taken in or screwed again."

"But—one woman, pregnant, alone, *out there*. . . ."

"You had your brains washed with your faces! Meda was right in one sense—the system's set up by men for men. But that's the system, not any edict from the gods! Maybe we're not as tall or as strong as the men, but people didn't get to living in houses and growing food and having all the things they have and do 'cause they were bigger or stronger. The *narga* is both bigger and stronger than any man, but who works for who? Do horses ride *us?* So long as we're just as smart as men—and we are—we can do what they do. If I was a man I'd still be in the same fix as I am now and chased by the same folks."

That silenced them for a moment, and then Putie said softly, "Take us with you when you go. If brains are all that matters, the more brains the better."

"I wish I could. Lord! Do I wish I could! But you're all further along than me, and my fat hides some of mine. I mean, they might not notice one woman, but a cartload of pregnant women are gonna be kind'a hard to miss. And what happens when you're due? And I ain't even headin' for the sorcerer any more. They'll be lookin' for me that way most of all. I'd love to take you all, but I don't even know where I'm goin' myself, or if I'll get there. You see how it is. Now, go on back and get some rest. And, remember, my life depends on you not giving me away tomorrow. These vultures are going to attack much of Akahlar soon, I know it. Perhaps I can do nothing, but so long as I live I might be able to fight them. No one else could."

They didn't respond, but slowly drifted away, back to their grassy plots, visions of romance and adventure still in their heads.

Putie, however, did not go back, but waited for the rest to get out of earshot, then lowered her voice.

"This Boday's not your husband, right?" she said more then asked. "It's a girl, isn't it?"

Sam was startled again. "What makes you think that?"

"The way you talked. I ain't had no learnin' but I ain't dumb. Boday is female case, and the only time you didn't say the name you used a word ain't nobody uses for their husband. That, the bit 'bout the love potion, and how you found out you was kind'a strange, too, all fit with the goddess stories. And there you was married, but the kid's a rape child. It all fits."

"You *are* pretty smart." Sam responded. "But I told you to forget the goddess bit. It's more like a curse on the family line than any kind of big magic. Does it bother you that I'm married to a woman?"

"It might bother some, but not me. I uh, well. that is . . . I love you, Sahma."

Sam wasn't shocked, merely exasperated. "Putie, you've only known me for most of a day! And I bet you had crushes on lots of boys."

"A couple, when I was a kid," she admitted, "but not like this. When we met by the river, I couldn't keep my eyes off you, and when you helped me up you was so *strong* and I felt my whole body shiver. When the changewinds come I came to be with you, and then you saved us all and stopped the changewind and you wasn't scared or nothin'. I ain't never felt such love, Sahma. but I didn't know what to do 'bout it. Then when it was clear 'bout Boday and all, I couldn't keep quiet no more."

"Putie, you're still just a kid and this is just a crush like the others, maybe made worse by the scare we all got tonight and the fact that sometimes this bein' pregnant plays hell with your emotions."

Putie took Sam's hand and put it on her swollen belly. "Nobody with a tummy like this is still a kid," she responded. "And we all got them rushes when all you do is bawl for no reason, or all of a sudden want to do everything at once or stuff. Sometimes I just feel so small and helpless and lost and I need somebody bad. You can't tell me you don't feel that way sometimes, too, and you're gonna feel it a lot worse, and when you don't want it the further along you get. You need somebody along who knows what you're feelin' and can help. And who's gonna deliver *your* kid? You? I helped bring a baby brother and sister into the world. It ain't that hard, but it ain't somethin' to do alone."

Sam had the uneasy feeling that some wisdom was coming out of this desperation crush, and she didn't like the message.

"All right," Sam replied. "Depending on what the morning brings and what we find, and depending on the opportunities, I'll try and take you and others who might want to take the chance with me, at least until we can find some better places for you. It still might not be possible, but, if it is, I will. That's the best I can do."

"Maybe *we'll* figure it out," Putie responded, sounding very happy. "Outsmartin' men one way or the other has been women's way since the beginnin'."

Finally, with Putie beside her, she managed to doze, but it was a light and troubled sleep filled with terrible images from her past. Stretched out on that rock, with the eerie glow of the fires against the cliffs, as those filthy men came at her again and again. . . . It was a recurring nightmare that she had never been able to banish. But, this time, there was an overlapping, distant image, of a place of near darkness with just a small light within, casting a demonic, horned shadow on the walls.

"There is no way to get from the city over to the district; they've got everything sealed off," a man's ghostly and distant voice was saying, like out of a bad transistor radio "The army will cross in there. Why not get them to do it?"

"No!" replied the horned one sharply. "That would involve the law and procedures and we can not chance that Grotag might do

a full examination of her and determine the truth of the situation. He is a fool but a cautious one."

"Well, we have a few men on the eastern border and they're going to move towards the Abrasis lands at first light, but they'll have to sneak in. The incoming border is sealed. I have at least two dozen good men over in Dhoman, but it will take them at least a day to get to the border and cross the null."

"No. Even if let in, their options will be limited, for by that time the army will have a division in there. Have them camp in the null and ride picket along the vulnerable crossings of the border. There is no civil authority or army in the null. No witnesses. We know that she is with child and probably disguised as an Abrasis."

"Yeah, but that's a pretty vague description. Are you telling me to simply murder any pregnant women who try and cross the null?"

"I leave the details to you." responded Klittichorn. "We will never have this specific an opportunity again, though. If she slips through, you and your men will wish you had been more imaginative and more ruthless."

Sam sat up suddenly, sweating.

First light showed a disaster of a magnitude even Sam had not imagined. There wasn't a single structure standing anywhere in the encampment area, and many of the shelters were unrecognizable as anything other than kindling wood.

There were bodies, too. Not many, but some who apparently were crushed in the shelters or struck by flying debris and a few who might have been trampled in the mad, panicky stampede. There was also a wide variety of injured, some with pretty bad-looking wounds or breaks.

Most startling was the view to the north of the encampment site. Where the day before had been rolling hills and countless vineyards, now stood a vast and eerie plain of purple grasses and bright orange mud, and here and there steam seemed to rush from the ground and spout plumes of water high in the air from time to time.

And scattered around, thicker the further in you looked, were groves of tall trees much like great pines. but with huge red and yellow ball-like fruit or flowers clinging to them.

Of people there was no sign, but they would have lived beyond the vineyards, beyond the road that now was cut and gone, and out of immediate sight. Sam was grateful for that; she had no desire to see what they might have become, what new race might have been formed here. If they still had their wits about them, though, they'd be off for the null *en masse* about now, before the army got here in strength. The law called for the systematic murder of every Akhbreed transformed in a changewind, and it was ruthlessly applied.

Estate and clan personnel, with the healthy girls organized into details, managed to get their own area straightened up, the wounded onto wagons for the trip up to the manor house where healers were even now converging, and to collect and remove the dead for return and burial. The rest of the girls combed the rubble for personal effects.

Sam hadn't lost much, although she did locate the twisted and smashed pair of enchanted glasses. They hadn't even survived long enough to be used as a disguise.

They bathed in the river in groups. The river had also been changed, going underground now at the new area, but it flowed north, so the water coming past the estate was from unchanged sources and thus was judged safe. They also got fed, cold and not elaborate but it was the best they could do. And got a fresh set of clothes—which in the case of the pregnant girls wasn't much—although they were very short of combs and brushes, each of which seemed to go through countless hands.

By mid-day contingents of troops, mostly from the colonies, were coming in to cordon off this side of the "infected" region and work out plans for going in and "disinfecting" it as soon as sufficient forces arrived. At least they paid little attention to the estate and the encampment, except, of course, to ogle the girls as all soldiers did.

Also by mid-day, civil authority had moved in and attempted to impose some order on things. Rumors swept the gathering that they would all now be sent home as quickly as possible and that plans were being made to do just that. Sam hoped to get a ride to Mahtri, since that was certainly where Crim would look first, but she wasn't particular. If the first batch was for someplace far away that she'd never heard of in her life, she fully intended to go there. They set up tables on the grass with clerks behind them to take names and destinations.

Sam grew nervous when they ordered all the unwed pregnant women to one side; the vividness of the dream she had had was still very strong and the sense of ruthless menace stayed with her. She wondered if she could somehow sneak off in this mass, maybe steal a horse. She wondered, too, if some of the other girls, Putie in particular, would let her do it. *Damn!* It was always the worst case!

Still, Sam wondered just how many would actually come along

when the adventure—and risks—were so immediate. Putie, certainly—the small girl hadn't left her side and kept trying to show real affection. That was tough because Sam really had the need for some of what Putie offered right now but couldn't bring herself to encourage the kid.

But before she could do much of anything, one of the clerks emerged from the crowded area of tables and records and came over to them.

"Is this everyone?" he asked them, sounding official. He was carrying a clipboard and pen but not the sheaves of documents that the clerks at the tables had.

"All right, listen up, and shut up," he said brusquely. "You've been real lucky up to now. First the changewind abruptly changes course at the last moment and moves away from you. Now I got some more luck for at least some of you. We're trying to move everybody out as quickly as possible and send them home, but we haven't got Navigators or Pilots on the other end set up for everybody yet, and it's gonna be unpleasant here for a while, but you know what's waiting for you when you go home. You're all whores who have dishonored your families and the Abrasis clan. Don't give me any lip! You know what you are. Now, a clansman arrived here yesterday, mostly in the hopes of working out something about a few of you. We were going to take more time and interview you, but under the current emergency he can't stay and doesn't want to."

They listened silently, some seething at his terms for them. But they said nothing, not knowing just where this was leading.

"I won't mince words. Now, there's a colony called Nayub. Probably you never heard of it. It's not the world's most wonderful place, but it has among other things an Abrasis-run company that was started up a couple of years ago as an experiment with a small group of convict laborers. It's now starting to pay, and the laborers are being offered full commutation if they settle there and keep working at it. And, yes, none have seen a woman in at least two years. There's little of any civilization near their camp and it's off the beaten track. We'd like to get a true colony going and make the place permanent. We're offering to send you there instead of home. Any questions?"

"Uh, sir—you mean send us to these *criminals?*" one girl asked, a bit taken aback. "Guys who haven't seen a woman in *years?*"

"They are no longer criminals. They have been paroled under condition of exile. As for the other—well, I'd think that girls like you would have a ball as the only women for twenty love-starved men. Eventually it'll be a full-fledged colonial outpost, with lots of regular people, but that's going to be a slow build, and they'll be professionals with their own families, so it won't be rugged forever."

"You mean he wants twenty of us to go with him out there?" another asked.

"He does, but due to the emergency he's limited to his own wagon and existing supplies. Everything else was commandeered. We had planned on doing this methodically, over time, but the Emergency authorities have ordered all non-residents out as quickly as possible. That means no round trips, and by the time he might get through to hire other wagons, you will all be gone home. At the moment we can take only five. We'll take the names and homes of the rest who might want to go, but there are no promises."

No one said a thing, but they all could do at least that much arithmetic. *Each of us with four husbands. . . .* It wasn't the turn-on it seemed. Even if all four turned out to be decent sorts, which wasn't all that likely, you'd have to be wife to all four. Not just conjugally, but cooking, cleaning, keeping house, and all the other drudgery multiplied by four. The clerk knew they understood that, but, like the clan lord and the man with the wagon, was counting on it still being a more attractive alternative than going home.

"Uh—what kind of crimes did they do?" someone asked.

"What's the difference? You go home, you become a slave. You go this way, you gain some legitimacy. But, remember, they all volunteered for this colony and permanent exile afterwards rather than take their sentences, so they probably were hanging crimes. It's up to you, though. We legally can't order any of you to do this, but you have to decide and now. He's being forced to leave today, and we have your routing papers to send you home over there if you don't want to go. Lord Abrasis has cleared and approved this, and will clear all legal hurdles."

The vision still clear in her head, Sam tried to weigh the alternatives while wishing desperately that she had more time.

The trouble was, this colony was most certainly not anywhere near the intersection point between the colonies and the hub. As Crim had reminded her, those weren't little slivers of land, those were whole *worlds* of which only a narrow strip a few degrees wide overlapped. How would Crim ever find her, or she escape, from such a wilderness?

She thought furiously. Maybe, though, there was another line to take here. This guy taking them in would expect no trouble from five pregnant girls who volunteered. The guy would have the same low opinion of them that the clerk did, and would consider them helpless nobodies. If they couldn't overpower him and take the wagon over once inside this Nayub, she could fry him with lightning. It seemed an ideal solution. A wagon, nargas, supplies, and probably only one road to retrace. And it would get her out of here *today.*

"I'll go," she said loudly.

The clerk nodded. "Step over here. Who else?"

"Me, too!" Putie yelled. The clerk almost hesitated when he saw her tiny size; she noticed it immediately and added, "I'm a lay midwife as well."

The clerk's hesitation disappeared and he sighed. "All right, over with the fat one. Three more."

"I shall go," announced a rather sexy-looking young woman of perhaps sixteen or seventeen, pretty and nicely built, she managed to look ready for a man and a bed even at maybe six months or more pregnant. "I have known men with three wives. Far more interesting to have four husbands."

"You'll be very popular, I'm sure," the clerk noted, not being sarcastic, and gestured.

"All right. I will, too," said Quisu, stepping out and over with the rest.

"One more," the clerk announced, looking at the group. Sam, Quisu, and Putie all stared at Meda, who seemed to be trying to avoid their gaze. Sam couldn't help wondering if she was either all talk and no guts or if she just hadn't caught on to the plan.

"I will," a short, stocky, buck-toothed girl of fifteen or sixteen said in a soft, shy voice, and stepped over with them.

"All right, that's it, then, for now," the clerk announced. "Everyone else get in the proper lines for your homelands and register to be taken out. When you get to the front, if you're interested, give the clerk your name, village, and family and, if things work out, we might notify you. You five, follow me."

Sam dropped back a bit and whispered, "Just go along with everything until we're completely out of here." The others nodded sagely.

They were put on a wagon and taken up to the great manor house itself, then off and down a small set of outdoor marble steps to a basement area. The other girls were almost awed by the size and splendor of the place, which was more than they had ever seen. Then they were taken into what looked to be a kind of waiting room with some comfortable chairs and told to sit. "We want you to be off within the hour," the clerk told them, "so we'll get through the formalities one at a time as quickly as possible."

Sam felt suddenly uneasy about this, almost expecting to see some of Klittichorn's men come out and grab her as she sat more or less trapped. Why this delay if they were in a hurry? They had no particular belongings or wardrobe or the like; just load up and go.

The clerk emerged, pointed to Putie, and said, "You. Come with me." The small girl looked nervous but went inside and the door was shut. The five minute wait or so seemed interminable, and when the door opened again it wasn't Putie but the clerk, who pointed to the sexy girl. Another five minutes, and Sam began chewing her nails. What was going on here, anyway?

Again the door opened and the clerk pointed to her. "Now you," he said, and she got up and went inside.

There were no gunmen or uniformed officers there, but the place was the sort that filled her with instant apprehension. Suddenly she wondered if history hadn't repeated and, in spite of her confidence and cautions, she hadn't walked into another trap like she had at Pasedo's. The place was clearly a magician's office, probably the chief clan sorcerer, and he was there, a rather young fellow with a goatee wearing a loose light blue robe.

Shit! It is *another Pasedo deal!* she thought, panicking, her eyes darting around to look for the exits. The sorcerer saw her reaction and simply waved his hand at her and suddenly she felt all her fears and anxieties drain away and a sense of peace and well-being came over her.

"Don't be nervous, child, this will only take a moment," the sorcerer said in the kind of voice your family doctor used just before he gave you a shot. "Just sit in the chair here a moment and give me your hand. Yes, that's nice. Left hand, please."

There were burners going and the smell of something unpleasant cooking. He reached around, picked up a small object, tossed it a few times in his hand and then blew on it. She saw it was a thin gold band, like a wedding band, only it had four tiny different colored gems set in it. He took the ring and slipped it snugly on to her ring finger.

Instantly she felt strange, different. She had all her memories, she knew who and what she was and where she was, but something inside her head had changed. She realized that the ring contained a spell or a combination of spells that acted on the wearer, and that if she removed the ring the spells would not longer be active.

The trouble was, she had no desire to remove the ring, not ever. She felt good, happy, even content, and excited as well about the future. She remembered everything about the changewind and the

Storm Princess and Klittichorn and the rest, but somehow they were no longer important to her, no longer even relevant. She knew it was the spell doing that, but it didn't make any difference. For the first time she realized what Boday must have felt like when she'd taken that strong love potion. The fact that she knew better, knew that there were other important priorities, knew that she was the victim of a spell, didn't matter in the least. Even that was irrelevant.

Her whole view of herself and society had been turned upside down in an instant as well, and it, too, didn't bother her. She was a helpless, pregnant girl, out on her own, and she couldn't make it on her own. She wanted her baby and a home and solidity. She wanted somebody to take care of her and support her and she wanted to take her place in that household and have lots of babies and be an uncomplaining wife and mother. She was excited by the prospect, anxious to begin. Her world was instantly redefined as her husbands and children and home to be; all else was irrelevant.

Even sexually, the world was turned upside down for her, although right side up from most points of view. A few moments before she would have thought the idea of a husband, a man, silly, and as for the idea of desiring and needing a man—ridiculous. Now, strangely, the idea of having not one but many husbands excited her all the more, even turned her on a little.

The sorcerer helped her out of the chair. "Now go join the others out the back door there and wait in the wagon."

She got up and went out the door as directed and found a tall, burly, bearded man there next to a covered wagon. He helped her up the back steps, and she appreciated it, and found Putie and the other one already sitting there. Putie looked up at her and smiled. "It's all changed, hasn't it?" she asked in a voice that seemed softer, dreamier, and gentler than before.

"Yes," Sam replied, her own low voice sounding softer and sexier in her ears. "Isn't it *wonderful?*"

Boolean, Lord High Sorcerer of Masalur, was royally pissed. "What do you mean, you *lost* her?"

Crim's voice came distantly out of the glowing green crystal. "I lost her, that's all. All hell broke loose in Covanti all of a sudden. As near as I can figure out, somehow, Klittichorn found out where she was. Not generally—*exactly* where she was. I don't know how or why, but that's the word I'm getting. That changewind that roared through was their attempt to nail her."

"It didn't. I had definite energy readings afterwards showing she was still very much alive and still whole. Then, very abruptly, the readings stopped. Cold. Like she no longer existed. It wasn't the changewind, so what the hell happened?"

"I couldn't guess," Crim responded. "It wasn't Klittichorn's men. They're all over here now moving heaven and earth to block her exit and nail her. If somebody'd gotten her, the news would spread around here like wildfire."

Boolean thought for a moment. "I'm still getting some readings indicating that the fetus is whole, a new proto-Storm Princess. But they're weak and vague and don't allow me any sort of location except that she's still somewhere in the hundreds and hundreds of possible worlds of Covanti. That means she's been neither killed nor transformed, which is something, but something upset her matrix, her mathematical perfection that made her a Storm Princess. She's not now. I can only guess she's under some sort of spell that's changed something about her that the matrix deems essential. Timing is everything now, Crim. You should not have left her."

"What could I do? They got drawings of a fattened-up Storm Princess at all the exit stations now, and the border's pretty well monitored here. It seemed the easiest way to slip her past, and it was—until that damned changewind. Now we got a state of emergency here, martial law in the immediate Abrasis area, and a hundred of Klittichorn's guns on both sides of the border, not to mention colonial forces out looking for her. The only good thing about this is that they can't find her, either."

"Well, the radiations from the fetus are enough to convince me that it's no big deal of a spell, nothing that I can't reverse in an instant," Boolean told the Navigator, "but first we have to find her. Are you in a position to move?"

"Depends," Crim replied. "I can get around the changewind mess okay, but they're using the Abrasis estates as the eastern staging ground for their operations into the new region. I'm going to try and get in there from the south if I can and see if I can get any information at all about her, but it's such a mess that they may not let me."

Boolean sighed. "Well, do what you can. If you can get in and find out where they sent her and what's happened to her, well and good, but don't waste time if you can't."

"Well, I can't exactly scour the colonies for her when I don't have the slightest idea which one. We don't have years, you know, and lots of the Covanti colonies have their main settlements, even Akhbreed settlements, far from the intersection points."

"If you can't get anything definite and fast, then don't try," the sorcerer told him. "There is another way. The other group, the one with Charley and Boday, is still headed here. They have suddenly become very important again."

"But that other girl is no longer a decoy; they're wise to her. And she certainly has no powers."

"I wasn't thinking about Charley. That crazy artist with the love potion had a legal registry of marriage performed between her and Sam back in Tubikosa. I noticed that they used a connectivity spell for the seal when we treated Sam after pulling her out of Pasedo's. A typical bureaucratic simplicity, but short of death or a change-wind, it'll stick, so there's a tenuous thread of magic energy linking the two. I believe that if I had Boday, I could use that thread to find Sam. That group left Covanti starting for here only yesterday, so if you can't find anything on Sam, or get into the Abrasis estates, then don't bother. I have no way of tracking them now, but I know they went via Ledom, so you ought to be able to pick up their trail from that point. As soon as you reach them, notify me, and I will get them into here."

"Don't they have a magician with them? Why can't you reach them through him?"

Boolean gave a dry chuckle. "Dorion? He means well, but he's a total incompetent and a klutz to boot. That's why we sent him with them. He was more than expendable. In any case, they were the decoys. No particular need to have contact with them. Frankly, I didn't think they'd get this far, let alone still be loose or even alive. That's irony for you. Now they're the only hope we have of finding Sam. The clock is running, son. Sam's disappearance and the sudden full restoration of the Storm Princess's powers will not escape Klittichorn, but he'll also get the vibrations off the child. He'll figure it the same way. He'll send Hell itself after Boday if he has to, and the worst part of it is, that they've been told the heat's off and they're no longer being chased."

He snapped his fingers. "Wait a minute! There *might* be a way to warn them after all, although I'm not sure what good it'll do. I'll give it a try, anyway. In the meantime, you make sure you reach Boday before they get her."

Crim sighed. "Damn it, they're riding right into the thickest concentration of rebel forces in all Akahlar, and they got one hell of a lead."

"You don't try, you *do* it," Boolean responded. "Otherwise Hell itself will be preferable to what will happen next."

5
The Darkling Plan

The first two weeks out on the trail had been surprisingly easy, or so they all felt.

The colonial world that Halagar had picked for their exit from Covanti had proven comfortable, if a bit rugged. The intersection point, which wasn't something anyone could change, was a region of high, rocky desert, strange and eerie landforms, and little to support a population. The road, of course, was well maintained with a complex series of junctions that apparently took you to anyplace worth being in that world, but Halagar wanted to stay away from the main roads and they certainly had no need of junctions.

The country seemed even more desolate than the Kudaan Wastes had felt, although that might be hindsight now that they knew some of the Kudaan's secrets and secret places. Still, this was a world that seemed to have no secret places, or towns, or thieves' hideouts, or even anything flying about far above. Even the silence was deafening.

They had crossed at an unmarked border point, well up and out of sight of the official road and known only to officials of Covanti. None of them were really certain why such an alternate way in was there, except that it might provide a less public entry or exit without going through prying eyes or fooling with officious bureaucrats. And there were more than their share at the "official" crossing; the main road was a rather stiff toll road, to cover the cost of water and grain waysides at the various junctions.

Halagar kept them well away from that road, on rocky ground without so much as a trail, navigating, it seemed, from old experience. Each night, after they would make a cold camp, he would go off with the horses, leaving the rest of them there, alone, and very nervous. He took the animals to the road under cover of darkness and found the waysides where travelers were not camped, and there was able to feed and water them.

When he first did that, Dorion in particular was nervous, although Halagar did not take Charley, and it provided a chance to have something of a normal conversation.

"Well, Charley, what do you think so far?" Dorion asked, hoping she was already a bit sick of being treated like one of Halagar's possessions. His hopes were quickly dashed.

"It's not bad," she responded cheerfully. "I wish I could see, but from your comments I gather I'm almost better off keeping this place in my imagination. I kind'a hoped, though, that he'd take me with him tonight. It must be a lonely and dull job out there in the dark with just horses."

Dorion translated, rather glumly, for Boday.

"Boday just hopes he comes back at all," the artist grumbled. "There is something about that man that gives her unease. She has seen his type too many times in the back rooms and dark alleys of Tubikosa's entertainment district. No man, or woman for that matter, remains so handsome and so competent after all that experience without it costing something in the soul."

"Well, he didn't sell it, anyway," Dorion commented. "That's something I could pick up, and even Charley might be able to see. He has a few magic charms and amulets for various minor protections, but nothing else. They aren't much, but he chose them well. No, he's always been like that. A charmed life, everything going his way. That's why I accepted his offer to take us the rest of the way."

"Bah! Sooner or later all that unnatural luck will be used up, and he will be collecting the unpaid balance of disasters," Boday responded.

Dorion chuckled. "If there was justice in the world none of us would be here now—or need to be," he pointed out dolefully.

"I think he's just *wonderful,*" Charley said, sighing. "If I could only see, I'd go with him on my own in a minute. I might anyway."

"As his personal slave?" Dorion was shocked.

She shrugged. "What the hell is better for somebody like me? This world always seems to be trying to eat anybody with ambitions alive. Let's say we get to Boolean, he restores my sight and takes away the slave ring, then he and Sam go off and beat the bad guys and have a real happy ending to all this business. Then what? I can barely speak the language, I can't read or write it, and probably never will, I have no magical powers or knowledge or abilities, and only one sure way of making money. The only independent women seem to be ones with magic powers or who are educated in something that's useful here. I'm stuck back in the Middle Ages, and that means you find a strong and powerful guy to hitch on to."

When Boday got the gist of it—Dorion had some problems with the term "Middle Ages" since it meant nothing to him—she spat and responded, "You have more potential than you realize! That breast halter you created back in Tubikosa should tell you that! Such ideas mean money, and a woman with money in Akahlar is in many ways as powerful as a man with money. Men may have the power, but most men are for sale if you just find the right price."

Charley chuckled. "The bra, you mean. I didn't exactly invent that, but, yeah, you're right. I probably could come up with a lot of good ideas for the women of Akahlar, since nobody else seems to be bothering, but it would mean going back, building a stake, settling down, and, somehow, that's not what I find appealing. It's pretty much what I set out to do a million years ago back home, I guess, but it hasn't got the same appeal here. No movies, no TV, no pink Mercedes and Dior gowns and all the ways you show off your wealth or really enjoy it, and I couldn't even really run the thing. I'd need somebody just to write a letter or make a sale or sign a contract or just write the instructions for whatever I came up with. And for what? So I could live in a place that got the cool breeze and maybe had inside plumbing and a couple of erratic electric lamps and where—no matter how much money I had or how many princes I could buy—I'd still be looked on as a low-class common whore. Uh-uh. If I'm gonna be in a place like this, it may as well be with a classy Conan out seein' and conquering the world."

Dorion tried to translate, but when he got to "movies" and "TV" he became exasperated. "You must stop using those alien terms," he told her. "Where is Shadowcat? At least with Shadowcat you can project your thoughts and save me this mental torture!"

Charley frowned. Where *was* Shadowcat? She relaxed and sent her mind out to find him, expecting to tune into some night tableau she'd rather not see with the big tomcat stalking or devouring some cute little desert creature, but she was receiving nothing. Where *was* he? Why couldn't she summon him or see with his eyes?

She'd taken him for granted up to now, hadn't really thought much about him, but this was worrisome. "I can't seem to make contact with him," she told Dorion.

"Huh? That means he's out of range. I hope he has enough sense not to get lost in this territory. He's a familiar—he can't survive indefinitely without you."

That worried her. "I never knew there was a range, or that he could survive without me at all."

"Oh, the contact spell of that sort is basically line of sight. He could still find you, though—the two of you are psychically linked—if he could catch up with you before his psychic energy was depleted. If he could find someone of the same blood type who was willing, he could probably survive for a week on his own, maybe longer, but it wouldn't be the same as if it were you, and he'd draw less and less each time until he couldn't get enough to keep going. I'm afraid I don't remember much about that course beyond that, but I do know he'd have trouble finding anybody with any blood type in this forsaken place. Don't worry—he'll be back at the last minute tomorrow morning as usual."

"Yeah, maybe," she responded, still worried.

He decided to redirect the conversation back to its roots to take her mind off the cat. "I'm still amazed that you'd consider going with him, even if I admitted your points. I don't know if you noticed it, but be has a rather odd effect on you. You stop being yourself and just become that vacant eyed, empty-headed courtesan."

"Yeah, I know. I can remember all that when I'm me, but I can't remember me when I'm her, if that makes any sense. It's actually easier that way. It bothered me at first, but now I find it, well, sort'a convenient. There's not much conversation in this kind of riding, even if I could get into it, and I'm not equipped for sightseeing, so I'd just be sitting there getting bounced around and brooding and feelin' sorry for myself and maybe going nuts. Maybe that's what triggers Shari around him; I dunno. But Shari, now, she isn't a real person, sort of, at all. She's got no ego of any kind; she exists only in reaction to somebody else. Except in the courtesan role, where she's still on a kind of automatic: she doesn't brood, she doesn't wonder, she doesn't really think at all—she just exists. She doesn't even have any sense of time or place. I tell you I'm scared to death—I been scared to death most of the time since I got here. Not thinking for all the boring times just makes things more peaceful, that's all."

"But if you were with him all the time you'd be like *that* all the time," he pointed out. "To me, you might as well be dead."

She shrugged. "Maybe. He's not the type to be around all the time, though. Maybe you're right, though. I'm just not the type to kill myself—the old way I was raised still has hold of me, I guess. Maybe just becoming Shari is a way out that gets around that. There's a way that only Sam and me know that forces me to become Shari and just Shari. There's been lots of times when I was tempted to use it, to solve all my problems, and nobody could ever know how to get me back."

He was shocked. "Don't do that! In the name of all the gods, don't even *think* of doing that! I don't think I ever saw anyone so smart and capable as you, who had such a low opinion of themself. Besides, what about your friend Sam? What about all this impending conflict we're trying to avoid?"

"I no longer care about Storm Princesses and changewinds and the like. It's not my fight, Dorion. It's *never* been my fight. For a while I was a decoy, and all that did was almost get me carried away by a monster and scared to show my face in public. Now, well, I heard it being talked about back in Covanti hub. They know I'm not Sam, so that's it. My one remaining bit of usefulness to your cause and boss is over already. I can't lift a sword, I can't see to shoot anybody, and it would take a second and a half for a wizard to turn me into a toad or something. It's like atomic bombs back home. I was against them, and scared that one or two old guys could destroy the world in a flash, but there wasn't anything I could *do* about it. And I don't think protests and petitions would do as much here as they did back there, which was nothing."

"And Sam?"

She sighed. "Don't translate this for Boday—since I don't need shit fits right now by anybody, least of all her—but if I hadn't been around Boday all the time I wouldn't think of Sam at all any more, and I don't think of her much anyway. We were teenagers together, yeah, a million years ago, but my life got shorted out because I went beyond the call of duty to help her and got sucked here with her, and since that time we've gone such different ways that I don't think we have anything except the old times in common any more. It's like somebody in the neighborhood when you were growing up-they're not a part of your life any more. She got me into this, and since that time I been ying-yanged around and here I am and I'm stuck. Stuck in this world, stuck in this class, stuck blind and mostly dumb to most everybody. Yeah, I hope she gives some meaning to all this by getting to Boolean, becoming the Storm Princess, being a combination of Mommie and Joan of Arc, becoming rich and famous and powerful and a legend in her own time, but it's nothing to me. To me, she's as remote as Boolean and less interesting, who's done nothing but mess up my life, and I have to take the cards I was dealt and live my own life. I just don't give a damn about Sam."

Dorion *didn't* translate, but he opened his mouth to reply and then closed it again. There wasn't really anything to say. In her own way, she was absolutely right—this was no longer her fight and there seemed nothing at all she could do from this point, and she had little cause to love Sam or bother with all these matters of high importance. Struck by her beauty, personality, and intelligence, he'd put her on a kind of pedestal, never really considering just how much a helpless victim she was in all this, how totally out of control of her life she had been since being caught in the maelstrom with Sam. It was a shock to realize that she was not here out of choice, nor because she was any more part of it, nor did she really even have a stake in meeting Boolean, in having curses lifted or anything else. She was here only because that slave ring ordered her to be; she had no choice. She'd had no real choices since coming here, and not much chance of future freedom, either. In Akahlar, her intelligence wasn't a blessing but a curse, since she understood her situation full well and had no real hope or stake in much of anything. No wonder she envied being Shari! She couldn't even marry and have children—Boday's long-ago alchemy had seen to that.

"This is Akahlar," he reminded her, trying to sound like he believed what he was going to say. "*Anything's* possible here, you know. You're not like the peasants or low-class riffraff of the entertainment districts and courts. You have powerful friends, with real power. There is a way out for you. There is always a way out. Not everybody has the connections or the patience or the will to find it, but it's always there. Don't give up until the last possibility is explored. Never give up."

"Yeah, a way out. Find one of those changewinds and walk into it. Come out some kind of monster or hybrid or something. I don't know those powerful friends you're talking about. Boolean's no friend. He's cowered for years from his enemies and subjected us to this, and he's so busy with his plots he doesn't give a damn about the discards. If I could be released from this compulsion to go to him, and not have to, that's all I would want as a gift. I'd like my sight back, yes, but neither you nor he nor any other magician has normal sight yourselves, so I figure if you can't heal yourselves you're not likely to be able to do it for anybody else, either. Oh, I know, your magic lets you see not only normally but all over, but I don't have that magic and you can't give it to me. With that in mind, the *last* thing I want is to see Boolean."

"But he'd lift all the spells, all the compulsions!"

She chuckled. "Dorion, I didn't look like this when I grew up or when I got here. I was frumpy, buck-toothed, and I was in the process of growing thunder thighs. Boolean made me look like this, and I believe you that he's a man of his word, so he'll remove the spell when I get to him and I'll go back the way I looked before. Dorion—this *body's* all I got in Akahlar. The only payoff this trip'll have for me is to take away the last and only thing that I want or can use. I won't even be desirable. I'll be a nothing. And that's even worse than what I am now."

They were asleep when Halagar returned and bedded down himself, but in the morning Shadowcat was there, with no real indication as to where he'd gone, nor could Charley get much indication. She fell asleep as Charley but awoke as Shari and stayed that way through the day and, it turned out, the night to come and several after, since after the first night Halagar did indeed take her with him when he went off to feed and water the animals, confident now that they weren't being trapped or trailed.

Indeed, to the null that separated the entire kingdom of Covanti from the hub and satellite worlds of Tishbaal, they were inseparable, and, at least for now, Dorion felt a little better about it.

Even so, he spent most of this time trying to figure out a way through her arguments and her brooding pessimism. As long as she had it, she'd have this modified death wish, which would become a self-fulfilling threat if it went on.

Damn it, *He* would take Charley in a moment, even if she changed outwardly into a rather ordinary-looking young woman. That wasn't what had attracted him so much to her; he'd seen enough Sharis—made gorgeous by sorcery or alchemy and reduced then to mere sex objects. In fact, he almost preferred her to be less attractive. That didn't mean less sexy, but it sure meant a little more security.

Halagar sure wouldn't be interested in her any more, not then. But, damn it, he was no classical male god himself. He had a sort of cherubic look but was by no means handsome, and carried a bit of fat himself. Women had never exactly fallen groveling at his feet and never would. Oh, he could buy a potion or cast one of the standard spells, but what the hell did that mean? Lust fulfilled. But if he didn't love her for her body, then her body without her will wasn't at all attractive.

Guys who looked less than great, or were anything but Mister Masculine, and didn't have the benefit of family-arranged marriages, still did attract women, of course, but by other routes. By being rich, or powerful, or famous, or supertalented, or superheroic. He had no money, and Boday had pointed out that Charley had the ability to make it if she wanted to—and Charley had shot that down.

He was a magician, yes, but one who hoped that nobody found out how lousy a magician he really was. Oh, he could use The Sight and all the other basic tricks, but you were either born with that or you weren't and he was. But he wasn't just Third Rank, he was third rate, and he knew he'd never get much beyond that. Give him a book of formulae and spells and good instructions and he could work all the classical things, do amazing stuff—amazing, that is, to somebody who neither had the power nor knew what it really was capable of. A competent Third Rank magician could create spells in his head, invent some new ones, maybe, and certainly do all the classical stuff without needing reference books and instructions for all but the most incredibly complex work. Without his books, like now, his magic was pretty damned poor and erratic, and usually unpredictably awful.

He'd been little more than a janitor for Boolean, but just a little experimentation, a little fooling around, and he'd caused a lot of disaster and wound up getting kicked out on his face. He remembered Boolean's rage, his yelling about some sorcerer's apprentice, and someone or something called a Mickey Mouse. You didn't need the references to understand the meaning. Exiled to the Kudaan, "where nobody will notice your disasters and mistakes," building fires for Yobi's cauldron, and straightening up the laboratory, because at least he knew the contents and uses of the various jars.

No, he'd never be powerful, not in that sense.

Famous? He hardly had a hope of becoming infamous, let alone famous. And as for talent—well, maybe he had one, but he hadn't found it yet. And while he wasn't a coward, or he'd never have gotten this far on this journey, he wasn't much of a fighter and he'd rather hide than battle if it could be arranged, and nobody gave medals for skulking.

Although he had more freedom of action, in his own way he was just as much a loser at life as Charley, he thought. Worse, really, since her fall had come from attempting to do good above and beyond the call of friendship, and hadn't really been her fault, while he'd had all the opportunities and blown every single one.

He had tried to promise her that there was a way out, that there was always a way out, but she hadn't believed him, and why should she, coming as it did from somebody who hadn't found a way out himself.

* * *

There was little evidence of rebels anywhere in this desolate place, or anyone else, for that matter, but that changed when they reached the null that formed the border between Covanti and its colonial worlds and the outer colonial worlds of Tishbaal. There would be no hiding from Covantian forces here; at least two divisions of its army were deployed in specially prepared defensive lines just inside the null; the men, horses, and equipment, their tents with small pennants flying, sticking eerily out of the fog-enshrouded region.

It certainly made sense to defend the kingdom from its side of the null; an attempt to guard the borders of hundreds of Covanti colonial worlds that might come up and interact with the null at any moment would have required a population many times that of the entire number of Akhbreed in all Akahlar. The question was, would they let travelers through at all, and, if so, did they have some orders about them in particular that would make this a short journey.

Halagar surveyed the scene grimly, then lifted Charley down, and turned to the others. "I'm going to go down there and see what's what," he told them. "The odds are that I know some or most of the officers setting up here, and I might get both a pass and some information on why the army would be establishing such a frontier at this point. I hate to betray our otherwise successful exit—it makes all the discomfort of the route meaningless, damn it!—but unless they have warrants for us, I'm sure I can talk our way through to Tishbaal. I'm more concerned with what I'm talking us into, considering this size of fortification."

He rode off, down into the null, while they got down and tried to make themselves as comfortable as possible. At least Charley was returned in mind for the first time in a week.

"Looks like a war," she commented.

Dorion was surprised. "You can see it?"

"I can see the null, and I can see where there isn't any null, kind of like a shadow play against the brilliance. It's all in silhouette, but it's not hard to see what's out there."

"Halagar is more concerned with what is beyond, and Boday agrees," the artist commented worriedly. "Tubikosa has a small army that is mainly used to guard the crown jewels, the palace, march through the streets on parade days, and handle emergencies, but this is more uniforms than Boday has ever seen before in one spot. If they are also covering the other borders, then they must have half the men of Covanti under arms."

"I doubt if they have anything like this at the other borders,"

Dorion replied. "Maybe they should, though, if there's a threat this big. If I was a rebel with some way to get colonial fighters from one place to another, I'd do a big show of force in one area and then attack from the rear while the whole army's over here."

"Good point," Charley agreed. "As Boday said, most of the armies of these kingdoms are toy soldiers—big on uniforms and brass but most of 'em never really had to fight anything big. They're used to marching into some colony and putting down some strike or local uprising by some poor natives without the weapons or organization to do much against them. They're not used to thinking in terms of armies against armies, both sides with weapons and generals and all the rest, and trained to fight, and they're sure not used to defending hubs. They depend on their sorcerers to keep the non-Akhbreeds out." She chuckled. "You know, while this all makes sense on paper, I guess, I kind'a wonder what the hell all those guys could do if Klittichorn just sent a bunch of the Stormriders in here. They wouldn't even kill many of these guys. Just a bunch of 'em making passes and zapping a few tents and horses and big-mouthed sergeants, and the rest would run like hell for back here, leaving their equipment behind 'em."

Dorion sighed. "This is ridiculous! We, a two-bit magician, an alchemical artist, and a courtesan who came from another world, are all able to sit here and figure out all the intricacies of what these professional military men are doing wrong and how to whip them easily. If the likes of *us* can see it, why can't *they*?"

"Cockiness," Charley sighed. "That and arrogance. They been the bosses so long, taught from their mother's breast that they're the superior race, the lords of creation, that they just can't get it into their heads that maybe the only thing they're really superior at, is a few good sorcerers and the keys to the gun locker. How many colonial worlds intersect this null? Hundreds? Thousands? I dunno. But if ten thousand of those not-quite-right humans from those colonies showed up here, each with a gun, they'd grind these guys to pulp. These guys, though, just can't imagine such a thing happening."

"And why should they?" Dorion asked her. "Even if the colonials somehow got together in the nulls and even if they hit and destroy this army out there, they still can't enter the hub. Grotag and his unknown number of acolytes and assistants have the spells sealing off entry to the hub from all non-Akhbreed locked up tight. So long as they sit in the hub, there's no way the rebels can enter."

"Yeah, as long as they sit in the hub," Charley echoed. "So the Storm Princess brings a changewind right into downtown Covanti, the one thing they're powerless against. Maybe it gets them; at least it scatters them and keeps 'em from thinking much about defensive spells. By the time they got regrouped you'd have thousands of organized troops inside the hub against an army still running. Besides, this isn't the hub—it's the colonies. Jeez, I still remember from my high school history classes what a siege is. If they take the colonies and then put up a wall like this around the hub in all directions, the hub'll be cut off. It'll take a while, but no more raw materials, no more fresh fruit and vegetables. . . . They'll be eatin' their grapes before they crush 'em. The demon forces like the Stormriders will protect the rebels, and there won't be much of an army in there for a breakout."

"Then the sorcerers would have to spearhead the breakout," Dorion pointed out.

"Uh-huh. And that means they got to leave the hub, right? So they break out of any side and the other three sides get invaded. Neat. They'd slaughter every Akhbreed they found and leave the sorcerers with nothing to come back to. I bet some of these sorcerers would make deals with them when that happened. Besides, who says the rebels don't have some sorcerers, too? Isn't that what Covanti thinks Boolean's up to? And isn't Klittichorn a full-fledged equal?"

Dorion thought about that. "Um. . . . Maybe I've got the same disease that those troops do. I can't see a hole in it, but you make this whole system sound so vulnerable. I can't believe that it's that easy to break through, or somebody would have done it by now."

"They didn't have Akhbreed sorcerers on the rebel side before," Charley noted. "And they didn't have those sorcerers running messages and even troops between colonial worlds or coordinating things, and they *never* had anybody who could use the changewind as a weapon before. No, it's gonna be a bloody, rotten mess now, and so many are gonna die it makes you want to puke just thinking about it. Still, if it wasn't for one thing, I'd just as soon see this rotten system fall."

"What? Klittichorn?"

"Us. If the colonial races are all organized then the Akhbreed's outnumbered from a hundred to a thousand to one, and not a one of those other races has any reason to do anything but hate Akhbreed. If they win, bein' an Akhbreed is gonna be the worst thing you can be. And we're Akhbreed."

That brought him up a bit short. "Um, yeah. I hadn't thought of that."

They might have continued their conversation but there was the sound of a rider coming, and as soon as Halagar reached them and dismounted, Dorion could sense Charley vanishing before a wall of blank blandness. It was amazing how it happened every time.

"There's no problem moving through," he reported to them, "but there might be big problems on the other side. The word is that somehow large numbers of infantrylike units and mounted units appear to be able to move out from the worlds of colonial Tishbaal as they come up, and they are doing so. It's irregular, but no one can tell if the main bodies are moving in towards Tishbaal hub, or if they are fortifying in the null, or in some assembly world. The odds are pretty good we'll have to make our way through some kind of colonial force to make it into the kingdom, and probably an enormous force surrounding the hub."

"But we've got to get in and out of the hub to go west," Dorion pointed out. "And if Tishbaal is that bad, imagine what Masalur will be. And just *what* we might have to get through as well."

They had long ago dropped any pretense of assumed names for the women and Boday was able to speak freely under Dorion's very loose leash.

"Boday is ready," she proclaimed. "If it comes to a battle, she will do her part!"

Dorion looked over at her, then back up at Halagar. "Uh-huh. So the three of us are going to take on a nurbreed army. The odds at best may be only a few hundred to one. The pair of you are mad!"

"There will be gaps and weak points," Halagar responded confidently. "There always are in the best of formations, and the border there is quite long, and the guards might be good fighters but they have no experience. Come, my friends! It's not as bad as all that. We shall have to forego our pack animal, however, and that's too bad. Come—let us eat a little something and transfer what we can to our own mounts and get some rest. I want to cross entirely in the darkness, when most are asleep and guards are bored."

"And jumpy and likely to shoot first and ask questions afterwards," Dorion added grumpily.

Halagar shrugged. "There is grave risk from here on in, but you knew that going into this. I would certainly prefer being shot to being captured by these sort of people, though. There is still time to call this off, if you do not want to make the journey."

Dorion sighed. "No, that's not really an option for us. All right."

"Well, then, is there anything in your magic that might be of help? A spell to disguise us to look like whatever *they* look like, for example, or to charm us against bullet and sword?"

"I don't think you can depend on magic," Dorion finessed as carefully as he could. "For one thing, those that you ask require much preparation and paraphernalia, long incantations, that sort of thing. Not to mention that I'd have to know what we were supposed to look and act like. No, the odds are I'll be far too busy dealing with any precautionary magicks on their side to also handle us. You'd need a true sorcerer to do it all."

"Fair enough. I did not really expect much help from that quarter," Halagar responded, in a tone that made Dorion unsure whether he'd been insulted or not. "Very well," the mercenary continued, "we improvise."

The Klutiin guarding the extreme western sector were spread thinly and certainly not expecting anything. They were tall, thin creatures, particularly ugly to Akhbreed eyes, with mottled yellow and olive skin resembling that of an exotic snake, a pair of deep-set black eyes, and a thin and very long proboscis that shot straight out from their faces and then angled down. They had forbidden, semi-automatic rifles slung over their backs, but seemed more comfortable and at the ready with their tribal spears, which they held in their hands.

The stretch of border was as mist-covered as the rest of the null, perhaps a bit deeper as the border range was nearby, but it wasn't difficult for Klutiin sentries to see and hear horses coming towards them. They were a good thirty yards apart at this point, walking back and forth, more a warning line than a barrier, with a company encampment back near the true and "real" colonial border of Tishbaal, whose worlds changed slowly but with eerie regularity behind them. Clearly they weren't there in strength or with intent to build and attack Covanti; they were, rather, a psychological deterrent, visible through the telescopes and binoculars of the Covantian Akhbreed soldiers far across the eternal mists of the null, and intended to be. A deterrent, and if need be, a holding action in case Akhbreed troops from Tishbaal's neighbor should come to the aid of their sister kingdom to the northwest.

When they heard the eerie stillness of the null broken by hoofbeats, the sentries were startled, and rather than raise an immediate alarm or go for their rifles, they went out of habit to their warrior stances with the spears.

"Riders!" one called out in the harsh guttural language of the Klutiin, but perhaps not loud enough. Almost instantly he heard a cracking sound and was gasping for air, pulled back and down by a leather whip expertly entangling itself around his neck, and he vanished beneath the mists.

The sentries on either side turned, unsure whether or not their comrade had been downed or simply had slipped on the spongy, soft, wet null surface. A moment later a figure wearing the sickly yellow tribal robes climbed unsteadily to its feet, shifted the rifle on its shoulder, and again assumed the readiness stance with its spear.

The one closest to the other frowned, as if sensing something wrong, but not being certain just how to cope with it. There was a sudden pull on his own neck from the back and he went down, a cry muffled by a knife swiftly and professionally cutting his throat.

Now, suddenly, the horses were visible, heading for the spot right between the recently fallen pair. The sentries further on now gave the cry of alarm and began to hurry towards the spot where the horses would cross, but Halagar on the one side and Boday on the other swung their newly acquired rifles on them and cut them down with short bursts.

Dorion, riding Halagar's horse with its special saddle with Charley in front of him, slowed just long enough for Boday and Halagar to quickly mount the two riderless ones he led, and then they kicked the horses' sides into the fastest possible speed and headed for the true border as shouts and shots and flying spears showed up all over the place.

There was no way to choose or determine which colonial world they would enter, although they'd delayed their attack until a border came up that seemed relatively unfortified and smooth enough for the horses to make a clean run inside. It was a strange-looking fairylandlike forest of the deepest greens imaginable, with lush vegetation but with some clear openings, and, most important, only one border fence, set in from the null.

Halagar and Boday stopped after they reached solid ground, turned, and began shooting at the disorganized but very angry soldiers now rushing towards them from all directions. Dorion pulled up at the fence, saw that it was mostly just barbed wire like it had looked through the binoculars, and began hacking away at it with a sharp sword. He cut three of the four main strands away; the bottom one was just too low for him to reach and not also fall off or cause Charley to fall off. He urged his horse through the breach and it cleared it.

Boday turned, saw the opening, then broke off and headed towards it as well, leaving Halagar to lay down some fire. When she made a small jump through, he turned in the saddle and followed.

The null was out of sight in a moment, but the trio rushed on for a bit until they felt safe to slow down and await the others. Dorion in particular didn't want to lose Boday and Halagar in this stuff, and he certainly didn't want to have to yell to find them. There was no doubt in his mind that a heavily armed and very nasty patrol would be sent after them on the double.

Boday, still wearing the tribal robe, caught up to him and stopped, then pulled off the robe, and threw it away. "Smells horrible," she commented. "Like it lined the sty of a hundred sweating pigs."

Halagar joined them in another minute, a broad grin on his face. "Now, that worked rather well, didn't it?" he said with evident satisfaction. "Rank amateurs, even for colonials."

"Almost too easy." Dorion agreed, "although I did sweat a little right in there. Anybody hurt?"

"I've got a scratch where a bullet winged me, but it's nothing more than that," Halagar replied. "You?"

Boday was scratching all over. "Boday fully believes that the soldier was not the only one inhabiting that robe!"

That gave them a bit of a laugh, although it wasn't funny to Boday, and Halagar jumped down and examined the horses. "No shots—I doubt if they've trained much with those rifles, if at all. Not a single one put their weapon on automatic fire, which would have done us in but good at the fence. Still, we came through that one pretty well."

"Yeah, and, just think, we have three more of those to go," Dorion said grumpily. "If we were lucky this time, how many times can we afford to do that?"

"Not many," Halagar agreed. "But we'll have to take each one as it comes and solve it somehow. Best by stealth, I think, and trickery, rather than directly as here. We also have to get from here to there. If that was all the force they really are putting on the kingdom borders, then their main force must be elsewhere. It is inevitable that we will run into it sooner or later. I certainly wish I knew just what they were up to, though." He thought a moment. "Perhaps not so much holding off Covanti or threatening it as perhaps securing a vital area for other activities, like bringing in more troops by whatever method they've found for doing it. We shall have to watch our backs." He looked around. "Dorion—have you ever seen or heard of this colonial world before?"

"Beats me," the magician responded. "There's far too many to ever keep track of."

"I don't like being in these woodlands not knowing what might lurk here," the mercenary noted. "Let's find a reasonably open area and camp here for now. In the day, we'll head east towards the main road and follow it as much as possible without risking ourselves unnecessarily. I dislike moving by day, but in a strange world with an enemy about it is better to risk being seen, rather than not see what is lurking for you. From now on, though, everyone keep a watchful eye and ear at the ready. We want no surprises."

"You're going to camp *here?*" Dorion said nervously. "They'll be all over here in a matter of minutes!"

Halagar chuckled. "I think not. They can't know any more about most of these worlds than we do, and they can't spare many, if any, troops to go off into this darkness looking for us. Oh, they'll send a patrol or something that we can hear two leegs off, and they'll clomp around for a bit and make like they are doing a major job, but it'll be half-hearted and I doubt if those unlucky souls will really even want to find us. No, they'll just send a message forward that some folks stormed the line and trust to those further on to take care of us."

"Yeah, that helps a lot," the magician responded glumly.

It was amazing how quiet, almost dead, the place felt and sounded. But for the wind in the trees and an occasional sound of some insect or tree-dwelling animal flitting about, disturbed by their passage, there didn't seem to be anyone home at all. When they reached a shallow creek, the horses stopped to drink and didn't fall over, so they decided to make camp there. They set a rotating watch, of course, but if anyone was out looking for them, they missed by a country mile.

It was the quiet that got to them, both in the night and through the first few hours of the next day. This was not the kind of region where no one would want to live or work; the climate was at least subtropical, the vegetation lush but apparently not dangerous, and there seemed to be no predators lurking about anywhere. Still, there were no signs of paths or trails or large animal droppings anywhere about; nothing to indicate that this was a place that had ever seen any sort of man.

Dorion tried to use the daylight to good advantage, hauling out and paging through his *Pocket Grimoire* for any stock spells he was capable of throwing that might help them out. The invisibility spell held promise, but it was very limited and, being a basic public domain-type spell, was so easily countered that it would probably just trap them. It was strictly a one-person deal anyway, and transitory.

Let's see. . . . Love spells and charms, aphrodisiacs. . . . No, even if they might be useful, he couldn't see being fawned over by a love-starved Klutiian or something. The curses, too, seemed both too specific and too complex to be useful in a live or die situation, although they were fully half the book. Well . . . maybe. Here was blindness, deafness, striking someone dumb, that sort of thing. Fine if he had something organic of the subject's or was face to face with him, but otherwise next to impossible.

The hypnotic spells were a better choice, although they were simple and few and easily broken or stalled by someone with great will power. Those sentries back there, however, might have been easy marks—if he had the nerve to pop up near such ones and invoke the spell first. He didn't know what was best, if anything, but he was determined to keep looking.

They found the road without much trouble and followed it along the side, always keeping nearby cover in mind, and cautiously scouting every bend and every hill before venturing forth.

There was, however, no apparent traffic and no threats from either direction. At Halagar's insistence they kept playing it supercautious, which slowed their progress to a crawl, but they soon began to feel alone in a strangely desolate world.

Four days in, they came to a town center. Clearly established as a main support link on the road, it looked to have supported perhaps a thousand people in various forms of activity, but now the nearby fields stood untended and the streets seemed as deserted as the forest.

Halagar waited until nightfall and then went in on his own, looking over the whole of the town and taking his own sweet time about it as the others waited. He finally returned, shaking his head in confusion.

"No one! Nothing!" he reported. "It is strange. Almost as if everyone along here was ordered evacuated. Everything's been put away or carted away that was of any use or value, and the thing has been just abandoned. From the looks of the dung, feed barns, and the like, I'd say it's been this way for perhaps two weeks. There are some ugly signs, though. The government house had suffered a major fire—it's in ruins. A number of the Akhbreed houses and shops had been clearly ransacked—not closed in an orderly manner like the rest—and there were old, dried bloodstains in great numbers. I think it's safe to go in there now, though, and even sleep in those unused beds and perhaps work up something hot out of what we've got. There's nobody left now. Besides, I'd like to examine the town closer in daylight."

They'd brought along mostly practical food, so there wasn't much chance of a real cooked meal, but it was nice to be able to brew coffee and tea at least. The real beds were comfortable, too, but both Dorion and Boday felt as if they were somehow going to sleep in a gigantic grave; as if the place were somehow haunted, tinged with evil.

The next day, Halagar discovered that their feelings were somewhat justified, although nothing supernatural needed to be involved. He brought them around to a place near the old government house and pointed. "Buildings weren't the only things they burned," he noted.

Someone had dug large pits behind the government house and filled them, then poured something flammable on the piles, and lit them. But bones didn't burn all that cleanly or well.

Halagar sifted through the charred and blackened remains with a stick and uncovered some blackened skulls. "This one had his head crushed in," he noted clinically, "but some of the others appear unmarked. That doesn't mean much, but there are a *lot* of remains here and they look almost all Akhbreed in both pits."

"What must have happened here'?" Boday asked, appalled.

"Not an invasion, certainly," the mercenary replied. "They would have just sacked the town and left the remains to rot. This was orderly, organized. Only Akhbreed places were burned or ransacked; only Akhbreed were thrown into the pit. Whatever the natives look like here, they're certainly smaller and different than Akhbreed, and there's none of their remains here. I would wager that if we looked hard we'd find true graves for them. I think the inhabitants of this town—the native inhabitants—awoke one day, or perhaps performed by a signal what they had rehearsed for a long time, and systematically slew every Akhbreed in the town without regard to who or what. Then their places were ransacked, their bodies dumped here and disposed of, and they then very calmly packed up all that they wanted or needed and every man, woman? and child went off."

"They would not dare do that!" Boday protested. "They would know that they would be hunted down to the last survivor and tortured to death, and the whole province would be under military occupation."

Halagar nodded. "That's the drill, yes, and it's worked for thousands of years. The Akhbreed colonials here surely thought that way, which was why it was so easy. But, who is going to look at this and vow revenge and hunt them down, Boday? By whose authority? By whose power'?"

"Why, the Tishbaal, of course!"

He shook his head sadly. "I doubt it. They're probably withdrawn to the hub boundaries and fortified just like Covanti's. They're not coming in here now, not when they can't be reinforced from the hub. I think you're still thinking too provincially as well. Don't just look at this pit and this town—think about *all* the towns and colonial outposts and farms and factories and whatever on this world. All of them. The odds are there are a half billion or more natives on this world and maybe two, three million Akhbreed tops, spread out all over the place, all secure that their sorcerers and soldiers will protect them—taking it for granted. I should say that there *were* two or three million Akhbreed. Ten to one the survivors number in the thousands or less. They sealed the world off and then they rose up and claimed it for their own. I wonder how many worlds like this one there are where this has happened, and nobody knows? And not just Tishbaal, either."

"But—they must be mad!" she maintained. "Perhaps things are bottled up now, but they can not crack the hubs, and sooner or later the Akhbreed sorcerers will come with or without the troops and make this entire race wish it had never been born!"

Dorion, also a product of Akhbreed culture, was as stunned by this as Boday was, but he understood what Halagar was thinking. "You're right," he agreed. "They wouldn't dare this knowing what must eventually come—if the hubs are in fact impregnable. Clearly the natives here think they're not. I wonder what convinced them? This isn't something you do on faith alone."

"Perhaps we'll find out—further along the road," the mercenary responded, and they packed up and prepared to ride.

It was close to sundown when they reached it, just over a hill. Sitting on their horses atop the crest of the hill, they looked across a vast valley that was unlike anything they had ever seen.

The ground was yellow and purple, and strewn with tall, spindly plants growing from it up into the heavens with tendrils waving about—and not from any wind. The great, green weeds with thorny plates like bones thrashed like some alien squid half-hidden in burrows in the ground. Although planted, some were so close together that tentacles would occasionally touch and there would be a furious battle, ending only when the contacted tentacles of one were pulled out of their trunks by the other. The remains of dead ones littered the landscape as well, where two of the things had been too close for both to tolerate survival.

"Changewind," Dorion breathed.

Halagar nodded. "And note its symmetry. The storm touched down up there—you can actually see the start of it—then progressed in an unnaturally straight course along the center of the valley, stopping just at the edge of the fields up there. I've seen a thousand changewind regions, and never one as regular as this. Here's the answer to our puzzle—and an unnerving one at that. A demonstration of a blessing from the gods. Can't you see the effect this would have if it were announced in advance, through the high priests or whatever of the natives here? On such-and-such a date and such-and-such a time we will produce a changewind just in this valley as a sign of our godlike powers. Word would get around fast—and if the Akhbreed were curious as well, or heard the rumors, or wondered where some of the natives were going and followed, what difference would it make? This would be a sign from the gods writ too large to miss. The uprising must have followed almost immediately. That's why there are still plants out there fighting for their space. There hasn't been enough time to gain balance as yet."

"Could Klittichorn actually have done this?" Dorion wondered aloud. "By the gods! If he can do that on cue and to such precision then what chance has *anybody* got?"

Halagar shrugged. "Who knows how they do it? I suspect it's not as bad as all that, that they need the precise coordinates and limits at the very least. Otherwise they would have to be physically present—both a top sorcerer like Klittichorn and the almost irreplaceable Storm Princess—at each attempt. Too much risk there to them, and too much attention drawn. I doubt if this was done too many times—yet. It was practice at an ideal place of their choosing and with careful preparation that also was an effective demonstration of their power to the locals and perhaps visiting dignitaries and potential allies as well. But, think now how easy it would be to get the coordinates to the central government district of a hub, for example. They're fixed, unmoving amidst the constant world shifting around them."

"Yes, but then why have they not just taken out the hubs one by one?" Boday asked him. "There must be more to it than that."

"Maybe. Maybe not. You start taking out the hubs one by one, and you get two or three in a row all this precise, and you can't keep it quiet or quiet the suspicions of the remaining sorcerers. They'd get out of the hubs and fast, I'd think, and then they'd go hunting for Klittichorn as a group and that would be the end of this scheme. No, to get them, or at least most of them, you are going to have to attack all over Akahlar simultaneously, or as close to that as possible—before they can know what's happened to the others. The power is awesome here, but Klittichorn's had to tread on eggs none the less. He and his storm witch are still vulnerable and they'll only get one shot at this. That's what this is about. They're doing selective demonstrations to get sufficient rebel colonial forces to move to the hubs, so there will be an invasion and occupation force when the changewinds hit. There will still be a hell of a fight. But this is genius. An all or nothing gamble for all Akahlar!"

"You sound like you admire the guy," Boday noted sourly.

"A professional soldier's admiration for a great strategic general, that's all," the mercenary assured her. "I'm just beginning to wonder how we can ever hope to get through the forces inevitably massed around Tishbaal hub."

Dorion looked back at the hostile, ugly valley with its monstrous plants. "Even more immediate, I'm beginning to wonder how the hell we get across this valley."

"We don't. Not with what we've got. But you can see where it begins and ends. I'd say we make an early camp here now and get some rest. Tomorrow we'll have to blaze our own trail around. It shouldn't be too hard—the people and animals of that village would have had to do the same. At least we know now why they have such a flimsy force at their rear and why the town would want to put themselves between the hub border and this valley rather than exposed behind it. At least I doubt if we'll have to worry tonight about guarding front and rear."

Boday looked back at the scarred valley and then at the peaceful and empty road. "Boday feels as if she is a horseshoe," she muttered, "with the smith's hammer behind and the anvil ahead."

6

The Armies of the Winds

Charley awoke suddenly from a sound sleep and sat up, puzzled. It was still quite dark, and she was very tired, yet something had forced her awake even as the others, including the light-sleeping Halagar, slumbered on.

That was odd, too, she thought suddenly. There is Halagar right there and yet I'm me, I'm all here.

"*Many men coming. You must wake and warn others,*" came a strange and eerie English-speaking voice in her head that seemed composed more of hisses and growls than human speech.

"What? Who?" she said softly aloud, startled.

"*Hurry! Not much time!*" the voice warned urgently. Suddenly she saw a vision in her head through catlike eyes; an eerie, glowing scene without color or much depth, of creatures that were not quite human, riding animals that were not quite anything, either.

She frowned, puzzled. "Shadowcat? Is that you? You can *speak?*"

"*I hoped to keep that secret, but hurry now! Wake guard, tell him, then wake others!*"

She got up and looked around in the darkness. Dorion was supposedly on guard duty but she saw him slumped against a tree, dozing. She crept up to him and bent down near him "Dorion!" she hissed. "Wake up!"

He stirred, then jumped in reflexive panic and almost knocked her down. "Who? Wha—?"

"Shadowcat's out there and sees a small army moving this way, not far off," she told him. "You must wake the others!"

"Charley, I—*army?*" He was instantly on his feet if not quite fully awake. "Halagar! Boday! Trouble!"

Halagar was up and awake in a flash, Boday a bit more slowly and grumpily.

Halagar grabbed his rifle and quickly went over to Dorion. The automatic rifles they'd stolen from the sentries were very handy, but they hadn't a whole lot of ammunition for them.

"She can see through the cat," Dorion told him, nodding to Charley. "She says the cat's seeing a lot of armed men coming."

Halagar frowned and looked at Charley as if wondering how such a simple creature could even understand or convey such thoughts, but he was a professional. Such questions were for later, not when danger lurked close at hand. "Pack up what you can and quickly!" he hissed. "Dorion—get the horses. The three of you retreat into the woods a safe distance so the horses won't betray you. I'll come for you."

"Yes? And what will *you* be doing?" Boday asked him.

"I want to see who and what they are, if they are there at all and not one of Dorion's wet dreams. Hurry! And don't worry—I won't be seen. Which way are they coming from?"

"No way to tell, I think," the magician replied. "It's just visions from a cat."

They gathered up what they could and did as instructed. Dorion wasn't sure how far in they should go and wanted to continue a good ways, but Charley was adamant. "Just far enough! We want to be able to find him and him us again! Besides, I want to tune into Shadowcat again."

They stopped perhaps a hundred yards within the woods and Charley sat on the grass, cross-legged, and concentrated while Boday and Dorion held the horses nervously.

"Yes, I see them!" Charley told the others. "Shadowcat's up in a tree or something, looking down at them. Big, ugly sorts. Hideous in some ways. No hair, it all looks like bone. Sort of diamond-shaped bony heads out of which eyes peer kind of like, well, maybe a turtle or something. Just slits for noses, and the mouth looks more like a short beak. Bony plates down their backs, too. Mean-looking mothers. Riding what look like baby dinosaurs or something, with the same kind of bony plates and heads."

"They sound too big to be of *this* world," Dorion noted.

"Well, they got like machine guns or something. All of 'em," Charley reported. "Jeez! It's like a small army!" To Shadowcat she shot the thought, "*Why didn't you ever tell me you could communicate?*"

"*Quiet!*" came the eerie-sounding reply in her head. "*I have enough problems just keeping balance. People do too much talk, say nothing.*"

"Listen!" Boday hissed. "You can hear them even this far back!"

The horses stirred a bit, getting an unnerving scent and strange sounds in the darkness.

They were past in a few minutes, the sounds slowly vanishing in the night, and things were suddenly quiet once more.

There was a stirring in the dark forest to their left and guns came up, but Halagar said, "Hold it! Know what you shoot before you fire!" and stepped out.

"What were they?" Dorion asked him.

"Galoshans," he replied. "About fifty of them, all heavily armed with weapons of a kind I've never seen before, although I can imagine what they can do. They're a particularly unpleasant group and I'm not surprised to see them in this. They live mostly on a mixture of beast's blood and milk, and their skins or whatever are hard as rock. You've got to practically hit them dead on with a bullet in the face to stop them. They're tribal nomads from a world that could stand a lot of improvement. I was once part of a detachment who had to hunt some renegades down. The idea of them with mere rifles, let alone any kind of repeating weapon, is chilling."

"They were heading towards the Tishbaal hub," Dorion noted. "So they're between us and where we want to be."

"Well, there'll be that and worse," Halagar assured them. "Make what camp you can here, just in case they have a rear guard or are only the first wave." He stalked over to Charley and pulled her up roughly by her arm and off to one side, away from the others. He pulled her to him and slapped her face so hard that her head snapped back and the resulting pain that came a few moments later brought tears to her eyes.

"You listen to me," he hissed. "You are *mine!* If you need to warn anybody again, you wake *me* up and tell *me,* understand? You're *mine!* The next time you forget that or fail to please me, I'll break your damned arms! And you tell neither of them about this, understand? You just tell them you worship me and want to be mine always. And if anybody should ask if I beat you, tell 'em you love it." Then he grabbed her by her hair and almost dragged her back to the camp.

She was shocked by his reaction, and confused. He'd given no orders before that she had to obey on this, and she would have found it next to impossible to tell him in Short Speech what was coming and how she knew it. This was a side of Halagar she'd not seen before and one that frightened her. She began to wonder for the first time just what things would be like if Dorion and Boday weren't around to keep him in check.

"How did the girl know?" he asked Dorion, seemingly calmed down. "How did she tell you with the air she has for brains?"

Dorion sighed, wondering how much to tell, and deciding to tell as little as he could get away with. "Like most of her type she comes from someplace else and she has her own language. I understand the tongue, but few others do. When there's danger she reverts to it, knowing only the Short Speech."

"*Hmph!* I thought the potions took all that from them."

Clearly Dorion hadn't heard the altercation in the woods and it was too dark to see any effects. "What's got the bug up your ass?" he wanted to know. "If she couldn't do it, she couldn't have warned us, and we'd have been spotted by their forward scouts. The girl and the cat saved us!"

Halagar did not respond, but stalked off to prepare his own bedding once more.

Charley felt scared and confused. What the hell was going on now? It had been going about as well as she could have hoped, and then *this.* She needed to put this out of her mind, be Shari again, but Shari, who was almost automatic, wouldn't come. Her face still stung, and when she touched it, it hurt a bit.

"*Shadowcat? I need somebody to talk to. Are you there?*"

"*Go sleep, stupid girl!*" came the response. "*You wanted him, you have him and he have you. You want furry friend to talk to you, next time pick dog.*"

She didn't get much if any sleep that night, but in the morning Shadowcat returned and took his accustomed berth in the saddle blanket having refused to say another word to her. She did not revert to Shari at any time then or during the next few days, but she acted as if she had to Halagar, who seemed both rougher and more callous towards her than before. She wondered if this was just his ego at not awakening until a rather noisy force was almost upon them when he'd convinced all of them, even himself, that he was nearly infallible in these situations—or whether that was simply the catalyst for the real Halagar to appear.

Still, as they neared the null border and had to stop and make camp well off any roads or paths, she found herself left alone with Boday as Halagar decided to scout what lay ahead and wanted Dorion's magical eye and experience with him. Boday came over to her and bent down and examined Charley's face.

"Boday thought so," the artist muttered. "The dark skin dye hides the bruising but the eye shows it still. So Halagar beats you, does he? Boday noted the resemblance to her late and unlamented second husband."

Shadowcat crawled out of his perch, stretched, and as if on cue crawled into Charley's lap. Although she wasn't too certain about the cat, if it really *was* a cat, at this stage, Charley had reasoned that at least the thing was on their side. If not, why warn them at all at the cost of betraying just what intelligence lay behind those feline eyes? She began to stroke the cat, and, thanks to Yobi's spell, her thoughts became audible to Boday.

"I do not mind the beating. In fact, I enjoy it," she said to the artist although those weren't the words she meant to send. That damned slave spell!

"Ah! He commanded you to say that, didn't he? And that you're a masochist, and you love him, and would die for him, and all that crap. Yes?"

"Yes," she responded, at least thankful for Boday's worldliness.

"Ah! My little butterfly, how you are still having your education, even if you do not see all the truths or understand the values, or learn all the lessons! Back in the long ago you were a courtesan, a cultured creature pampered and kept with only the best sent to you and you thought that was what it was all about. The romance of the erotic, yes? But there you were protected from the average by Boday and her procurers. The girls on the street, they must take what comes, and those who are out there are not simply poorer but far stranger. The men who love to beat up women, the mutilators, the fetishists—the men who are sick in the head. Anyone who will pay. That is where you would have wound up eventually, as courtesans are prized for being young and even the most pampered grow old too fast. That is why the memory potions or happy drugs are so necessary. In so many ways, after all this, you are still a child, relishing no responsibility, seeing the world not as the cesspool it really is, but as a playground."

"I've had a choice?" Charley retorted.

Boday shrugged. "Life deals mean cards many times—most times. The point was not what you were forced to become or do, the point is that you enjoyed it, relished it. embraced it. Boday should not have made you so beautiful. Boday should have made you walk the streets. Then your brain would have been plotting and planning escapes and working against your lot. You have been a fighter, but only when you had to be, and only so long as the danger was imminent. Then you quit and retreat into this oh, so comfortable shell."

"What can I do? I'm blind and I'm weak and I must obey him. You know how the spell works."

"Indeed. But your blindness isn't just in your eyes, it's in your heart and soul. Do you believe for one minute you would have been given as some kind of payment to Halagar if you had raised even the smallest objection to Dorion? We survived this far without him, and if we survive, it will not be because of him. But, no. You *wanted* dear, sweet Halagar, Mister Muscles with the perfect cologne and the granite prick. When you begin to think of yourself as an object, a thing, a pretty flower and nothing more, then you start judging everyone else by that as well. Very well, you have his outside—but you must take his dark inside with the rest. He is an evil, twisted man. His kind, who choose killing as a career, usually are, and Boday has seen many in her life."

"But he's on our side!"

"So? He is an evil man who is on our side. There are probably countless good men, holy men, on their side. Whose side someone is on only matters when someone is attacking you, but no matter how dangerous the situation, you are rarely under attack. The rest of the time you must co-exist with swine. Not that all men are swine, but the ones who are attracted to girls like you—or women like me—tend to be. That is why Boday found her darling Susama such a joy and a relief."

Charlie was suddenly struck with a revelation. "You could reverse that potion, couldn't you? A top alchemist could always figure an antidote."

"No, it is a good one, but love potions are very simple, really. To counter it you need only take an overriding potion that redirects the fixation to something neutral and harmless. More commonly, and with fewer side effects, one just finds a good magician and uses magic to overpower and neutralize the potion. That is what some of my friends and associates did back in Mashtopol a few weeks after I took it, when they recognized the symptoms."

"You mean—you *haven't* been under a love potion all this time?"

Boday laughed. "Darling, Boday has had nine husbands, and the only one who was any good died of heart failure after a night of passion. The rest were rich or intelligent or sometimes handsome but they were rich, intelligent, or handsome scum. Boday murdered three of them herself, although if the facts were fully known and she was not such an expert at alchemy, she would still have been freed. Those weeks with the potion, she realized that she did not, never had, needed a husband—she needed a wife. Boday had to live a long time and fight the world before she learned why she was so miserable and what she really needed, and the difference between love and lust."

"And you gave all that up—voluntarily? For *this?*"

"Well, not for this, my little darling, but she gave it up, yes. To tell you the truth, Boday was at a creative dead end and no longer expanding inside as an artist. It was all too easy. No offense, my little creation, but Boday was trapped in the comfortable but sterile world of the purely commercial artist and in serious danger of becoming a hack. It all had become so—*boring.* This—the challenge, the adventure, the dangers, the horrors—this has energized her. If she survives she will become the greatest artist of her age! If not, well, she will have died for love and for her art. But you, little butterfly—you will have lived and died for nothing. Not love, not art, not for a cause, or friendship, or even ambition. Royalty and sorcerers are born to their destinies; the rest of us must carve out our own with courage and will, or we will not matter at all. You have given up your ego and your dreams, and, frankly, the only difference of late between Shari and Charley is that Charley has a better vocabulary. I—"

Boday suddenly jumped up, her rifle swinging around to cover in one motion, but it was only Halagar and Dorion returning. Shadowcat looked up, climbed off Charley's lap, and went back to the bedroll.

Dorion was breathing so hard that it sounded as if he was going to drop dead any second; Halagar had barely a whisker out of place. "We've got it!" said the mercenary triumphantly.

"Got what?" Boday responded.

"This," he replied, bringing a small pendant and chain from his shirt pocket. The stone hanging from it was undistinguished and ugly; it looked like a pebble picked up from the side of the road.

"You stole a rock?"

"Uh-uh. Better. Had to kill for this one, but it was worth it. I got the idea when those Galoshans trooped by the other night. There were two Akhbreed with them, riding those big lumbering beasts of theirs like natives, dressed in black uniforms with unfamiliar insignia. Of *course* there were Akhbreed involved on the other side, from Klittichorn and the Storm Bitch to the men who worked the hubs for them! I had to wonder—after seeing the remnants of that massacre, how could they tell *their* Akhbreed from the rest of us? Most of those colonials can't even tell us apart. That's why I wanted Dorion along. I was certain it had to be some kind of spell or charm."

Dorion was still breathing hard and sweating like mad, but with a few interruptions for coughing spells, he managed to join in.

"Yeah, that's it. A real simple thing and they all wear them, colonials and Akhbreed traitors and mercenaries alike. I know it doesn't look like much, but it doesn't have to. It's a generic spell but fairly complicated, so they can be mass-produced but not easily neutralized. Anybody wearing one instantly knows friend from foe."

Boday frowned. "So how does this help us?"

"Don't you see?" Halagar responded. "It's just a stone on a chain. Almost anything will do. We got two—courtesy of a couple of very careless guards who will be careless no longer. We got rid of the bodies—I doubt if they will be easily discovered. But with these on, Dorion and I can ride right through that line and encampment and be recognized as friends. I'm a known mercenary, so even if somebody recognizes me, it's not hard to believe I'm working for them now, and they've got dozens of Third Rankers down there, so Dorion won't even be noticed."

"Mostly magicians who ran into trouble along the way and blame the big-shot sorcerers," Dorion added. "I'd bet on it. There's lots nursing grudges. And if any of them should happen to know me, unlikely as that is, they'll also know that I'm the *last* guy to be working for Boolean these days, and the first with a grudge."

Boday thought about it. "It seems a bit too easy, but even if it works there is still a problem. Where does that leave Shari and Boday? We have no such charms."

"Thanks to those rings in your noses it's not as much of a problem as you might think," Dorion told her. "They didn't kill all the Akhbreed colonials after all. The ones they captured—men, women, children—they hauled in to the magicians they had where available and fitted them with slave rings. There are hundreds, maybe more, Akhbreed colonials down there, all slaves, all doing whatever their former subjects and now their masters want. I'm not sure you're gonna like what you see down there—I sure didn't—but just keep very quiet and very obedient and prepare for some rough talk and treatment for a little while, and you'll fit right in."

Boday didn't like the sound of that. "How many are there down there, anyway?"

"It's indescribable," the magician replied. "You'll have to see it for yourself, and hold your stomach." He paused for a moment. "But first I'm afraid the two of you will need a little preparation. Uh, this may seem odd, but I'm afraid both of you will have to take off everything you're wearing and, ah, maybe roll in the dirt a bit."

This was one time when Charley felt her blindness particularly frustrating, but Shadowcat was peering out as curious as she was and giving her at least a cat's eye view, which was enough.

It was like a cross between a giant city and a massive armed camp. Coming down the last hill to the null, people—or sort of people—and animals and tents and even temporary buildings seemed to stretch along the border as far as the eye could see in either direction. While it extended a ways into the null, the bulk of the encampment, the people, and supplies seemed to remain on the world they had just crossed: one of several, it appeared, that were being used as staging areas. "Probably any world where they had a successful revolt," Halagar guessed. "They probably have sufficient navigation to bring in forces at will from several worlds—totally protected reserves that can be almost instantly brought to bear. It's brilliant."

Less brilliant was the organization down below, which was close to nonexistent. Most of these races had never seen each other before and appeared as strange or exotic or monstrous to one another as they did to the Akhbreed themselves. They spoke a dozen languages and a hundred dialects, and the only thing they really had in common was that they and their ancestors had been kept under the rule of a single race and subject to the tyranny of an absentee king and his own requirements for thousands upon thousands of years.

Nor had they slaughtered all the Akhbreed in their regions. That would have been too easy and not very satisfying. As with most former subjects suddenly liberated after so long under a cruel system, they found less wrong with the system itself than with their own people's place within it. Those Akhbreed who had been taken alive and unhurt, who had surrendered, who had not gone down fighting or committed suicide, were brought here, packed in wagons like pigs, and in an almost assembly-line fashion were fitted with slave rings by busy magicians working in crowded tents. Stripped of all they had, broken and naked, these people were then given over to the rebels to do whatever bidding was demanded of them.

Filthy, beaten, driven to exhaustion, suffering every degradation, they hauled stuff, waited on their former workers, shoveled dung, dug field latrines, all the worst stuff, while others suffered the depths of public degradation and humiliation for the amusement of the crowds. They looked empty-eyed, the walking dead.

The bulk of the natives were of three groups—the Galoshans, of course, and the Mahabuti, whose world Charley and the others had just crossed, revealed for the first time as short, squat little people with wrinkled hides of the dullest grey, with broad bearlike clawed feet and hands that matched and short, barren, ratlike tails. Here, too, were the bulk of the Klutiin, in the wrong political jurisdiction but not seeming to mind a bit. Clearly it was not Covanti that was threatened, at least not yet.

Although they had all tensed when they crossed the first line of pickets, and hadn't relaxed much when they reached the beginnings of the camp itself, few paid them much attention. Clearly the stones were working, although neither Halagar nor Dorion believed that they alone would solve all their problems. Such a generic sort of badge was necessary because of the sheer numbers involved, but the masterminds of this rebellion were far from stupid. The more generic you made something, the easier it was to steal or copy. It served as a uniform, but there must always be a wariness for spies.

Somehow, in the bedlam, Halagar heard gruff, guttural Akhbreed being spoken and headed for the source. It was one of the crested Galoshans barking orders to a number of Akhbreed slaves. It looked up more in curiosity than in fear as it saw Akhbreed approaching fully clothed and on horseback. Halagar halted just in front of him and saluted.

"Your pardon, sir!" he shouted above the din of the mob. "Captain Halagar of the mercenary militia. Where's the command center?"

"Why?" the creature shot back with a roar, making it very clear that he didn't like Akhbreed as allies at all.

"I have orders to report to the commanding officer," the mercenary responded smoothly, ignoring the tone. "Orders directly from Colonel Koletsu of the General Staff."

"Field command is out *there,*" responded the Galoshan, pointing towards the null. "But you'll need passes to get out of here."

"Well, who do I see to get them?"

"Commanding officer. But, yes, you wouldn't *have* a commanding officer. All right." He turned and pointed up the border. "See that big red tent about a leeg north? That's combat support. Somebody there can help you." And he turned and went back to making the lives of several Akhbreed men and women miserable.

It was their eyes; the eyes of the Akhbreed that were otherwise so vacant, that haunted them. Those eyes came alive, if only for a few seconds, as the quartet passed them, as if searching for help, for allies, for some sign of kinship or hope. They all regretted that they dared give none, nor did they have much to give.

Going through that mob was difficult not just for the sights but because of its overall atmosphere. It stank of strange and unpleasant scents; it was a cacophony of noise, with everybody seeming to speak at the top of their lungs all at once and constantly in a tremendous number of strange dialects, and it was also dicey, since all four were Akhbreed and these people were united only in their intense hatred of the ruling race. Dorion was fairly safe because they depended on the renegade magicians and because they still feared the magic, but even Halagar had to watch it, since, ally stone or not, rank or not, it would take very little provocation by this kind of mob to bring him down.

In fact, both Charley and Boday had felt stupid and ridiculous after being ordered to roll in the dirt and some man-made mud until they were satisfactory to the two men; Boday had bitched loudly, and both had wound up feeling ratty and gross. Now, both women wondered if they were ratty or gross enough for this crowd.

For a measure of protection, Boday was riding double behind Dorion and Charley in her usual spot in front of Halagar. The third horse, riderless, was being led, with the bedrolls and other supplies. As they went through the crowd, though, creatures of the various races would come up to them, some shouting epithets or spitting on the ground or towards them. Some struck, and Halagar had to caution them it ignore it.

Less was directed at Dorion, for they still feared magic, but his cherubic face and stocky demeanor simply was not the sort to inspire awe and fear no matter how grim he looked or how much he glowered at them, and some were bold enough to come forward and attempt to grab Boday, perhaps pull her off the horse.

Dorion wasn't the world's best magician, but he wasn't *completely* powerless; a mild shock was enough to discourage.

That had the effect of turning the various natives' attention to Halagar and particularly Charley, who, it had to be admitted, looked pretty good even with dirt and mud. She looked somewhat like the idealized Akhbreed woman, and for colonial races raised as inferiors on their looks and held up to Akhbreed standards of what was beautiful or handsome, the pair in front drew much attention. Halagar quickened the pace, but more than one native got a hand or claw or something on her with intent of dragging her off, and a bit of Halagar's leather uniform was torn as if it were paper. He simply had to bear it and do his best; not the greatest of skilled mercenaries nor any great rebel rank, real or not, could have defended against a mob.

Now, for the first time since seeing the system of Akahlar. Charley began to have doubts about the wisdom of rebellion. This was the future they were seeing here; a future of confusion and brutality, in which revenge rather than just freedom was the primary motivator. Take away the Akhbreed authority, and these people would quickly be fighting among themselves for what was left. Revolutions, particularly when they had a self-evident just cause, had always seemed romantic affairs, the morality all black or white, the rights and wrongs perfectly defined. For the first time she began to wonder if things really were as simple as all that.

The combat support tent was guarded with better, more experienced troops; obviously the hard core of the mostly disorganized irregular army building here. These, too, were the tough, diamond-crested Galoshans, but they had a different bearing that was all military. Again, Halagar gave his spiel, which, to Charley's ears anyway, sounded a bit too pat and convincing. She began to wonder how he knew all the right names.

"Captain Halagar of the mercenary militia, on direct orders from Colonel Koletsu of the General Staff. I must get permission to pass into the null."

The Galoshan stared at him. "Why? What orders do you bear?"

Halagar sighed, aware of the innate hostility and also of the vast potential mob behind. "With all due respect, soldier, I can't reveal that to you, any more than you would to me. If I could just see the commanding officer, though, I'm sure we could work this out."

The sentry thought a moment. "All right. Just you, though, Captain. The others remain here, along with your weapons and horses."

Halagar nodded, dismounted, and the others did likewise "Just stay here and say nothing," he whispered to them. "I know it's a nervous situation but consider that the alternative is trying to fight or sneak through all this. At least you're safer inside this picket line."

There was no arguing with that, so they sat, Boday and Charley sitting together and keeping very quiet and very still. Dorion tried to look unconcerned, but he wasn't at all thrilled, either. At any moment, the slightest hint of anything suspicious would make things instantly unpleasant.

The nearest sentry came over to him and gestured at the two women. "They his, magician, or yours?"

"Personal slaves. They were slaves even under the old order, so this isn't much different for them." The conversation was making him uncomfortable. Too much chance of a slip of the tongue here.

But the guard just nodded. "That explains it, then, I thought I noticed a different look about them. They say they're going to be pulling the women out of these camps soon. Going to start a breeding program. Some of the animal husbandry experts are opening up a whole new business in slaves. Akhbreed, mainly, but some of the other races who won't join us will wish they had, too. That bother you, you being born Akhbreed and all?"

It did, more than this sentry could know, but that wasn't the required answer.

"The system's been just as bad to some of us as to most of you," he responded. "You don't know what some of those big-shot sorcerers are like close up. I do. I've been a refugee in the wilds for many years, seeing little of my own kind, living and dealing mostly with halflings and changelings and the like. The system's done such horrible wrongs that it's only to be expected that setting it right will cause suffering as well. I had a mild brush with a changewind anyway, so I'm not wholly acceptable to them any more, either."

The sentry nodded sagely. "Most all the magicians working on our side have some problems like that, either from magic backfiring, curses by higher-ups, or occasional changewind problems. Nobody ever knew how many like that there were until this."

And, with that, he slowly wandered away. Dorion allowed himself a nervous sigh, and Boday caught his eye and seemed to understand.

It took Halagar almost an hour, but when he came back it was with an escort of soldiers. "Come, Dorion! The General was most understanding, and we're getting a security escort to the border. All I had to do was mention Masalur and all barriers dropped. You two—take the third horse, double up, and ride between us!"

Boday was immediately on her feet and lifted Charley into the saddle and then climbed on behind. They both were thin enough that a common saddle wasn't all that cramped. It wasn't until they were on their way that either could wonder just how easily Halagar seemed to have managed all this. Was he working both sides or not? Or was this some kind of trap for all of them?

The guard parted the ways of the crowd down to the null border itself, and then took them in, past the equally professional picket line. Out here was no colonial rabble; the soldiers of the rebel forces holding the colonial side of the null looked tough, efficient, and businesslike. The commanding general, a rough-looking creature with mottled rust-red skin and a serpentine face, who was of no race either Halagar or Dorion had seen before, was crisp and businesslike. This man was a pro, trained and prepared for this point in time.

He pointed a long, clawed finger out into the null. "That's the enemy, about twenty leegs beyond. From my front line here, it's a no-man's-land until their frontier line. They're established quite well—their commander seems to know what he's doing—but when we're able to move they will be vulnerable with little or no cover."

Halagar was the professional military man all the way. "You really think you can take them? Your troops here look excellent, but there are not enough of them, and the bunch back in Mahabuti, if you'll forgive me, would be cut to pieces by any good defender, and not inclined to obey your orders."

"Well, we're doing what training we can with them, but you're right. They're strictly a rearguard force, or cannon fodder, depending on the situation. I have sufficient forces, though, both in reserve in other colonial worlds and more coming all the time. I'll need more time than I have to whip that rabble into shape, but I have enough time to get sufficient forces for the real fighting together." He paused a moment. "So you're on a special mission from Colonel Koletsu. How is the Colonel?"

Halagar was unfazed. "I'm afraid I've never met him, sir. My instructions come by courier. I've never actually seen any of the people I work for."

That was the right answer. "Well, neither have I, although I saw this Klittichorn once and he impressed me as one nasty character. I confess I'm uneasy about building his power so much, but if you're going to have to deal with the power of sorcery you're going to have to deal with the devil, and if that power's on my side I can't quibble about it not being perfect. I assume that you're going to pass into the hub as refugees? If so, don't get shot by a nervous sentry over there."

"We'll be as careful as we can. I'm hoping to pass us off as double agents. Get a convincing story and pledge allegiance to the king and like that. Enough to get me through, anyway."

"Like you did here," the general muttered. "But I don't care who or what you are, Captain. If you're truly with us, then you'll wind up rewarded and living in the only remaining center of Akhbreed freedom in Klittichorn's immediate domain. If not, then you'll join those wretches you saw back there, if you survive. Pretty soon the last obstacle to us will be removed and then it will be time to strike. I've grown old waiting for this; I'm not about to fail."

"Well, I'm counting on us all being evident Akhbreed to tilt any doubt on their side in my favor," he told the general. "Am I going to have to go through all this on the other side as well, though?"

"Not much. There's just enough force against the west border to secure it so we can bring up our own forces as need be, nothing like this. But when you get near Masalur hub, it will make this look like an unpopulated desert. If all goes well with you, though, then you ought to reach there just in time for the fun."

Halagar didn't know exactly what that meant, but he responded,

"Well, that's when and why I'm supposed to be there. Those of us with combat experience need to evaluate what's what."

The general nodded. "Yes, indeed, we do need that. We will win, but the casualties are going to be a hundred times greater than they need to be because we're using, of necessity, all green troops. Very well, Captain. I'll give the orders for you to pass."

And, like that, they were through the line and out into the middle of the no-man's-land of the null.

When they got far enough out that the others felt free to speak, Boday said. "You were very chummy with those slime, and very free with the right names. One might wonder with that general just whose side you're really on."

Halagar chuckled. "I'm a mercenary, and I'm on the side of those who pay me, which in this case is Dorion. As for the names, I picked Koletsu because it's a fairly generic name. I have no idea if a Colonel Koletsu exists anywhere, let alone in the rebel general staff, but I took the gamble that those people wouldn't, either. A military command is a vast bureaucracy; nobody knows all the players, particularly those on the operational level. I wish, though, that I knew what the general meant by getting there just when the fun begins. My best guess is that they are going to move for practice on your friend Boolean, and quickly, to test out their system."

Dorion looked ahead at the slowly appearing hub border on the horizon. "He was right about us getting shot coming in, though. Shoot first and ask later, I'd say, particularly if these guys are as nervous as the ones back at Covanti."

"Well, I picked up some yellow cloth for a pennant when I was back in combat support," Halagar told him, the yellow pennant being Akahlar's symbol of truce. "I'd say we hold it and come in openly, slowly, and wait for the challenge. If we talked our way through back *there,* we should be able to talk our way through here, surely."

None of them talked much about what they had seen back at the border, but it was on all their minds. For Charley, it had always been a cut-and-dried situation: the Akhbreed should give the colonials and natives their independence and deal with them as equals and everybody would live happily ever after. Happily ever aftering, though, wasn't the result. Oh, you could argue that the Akhbreed had brought this on themselves by maintaining such a system for so long, but did anything excuse what she'd seen back there'? Did mere oppression warrant genocide? Or would she think it did, if *she* had been one of the oppressed? And what were those people going to do once they had totally destroyed the Akhbreed culture and its knowledge and skills? They knew the basics of getting raw materials, but did any of them know how to build the buildings and repair the machines or engineer even a sanitary system? Who would keep them from fighting each other in constant wars? Were they in fact anticipating something that was going to wind up reverting thousands of civilizations back to the Stone Age?

It was much too heavy for her; there shouldn't be situations where all the solutions were bad. All this war and hatred and savagery was so unnecessary and so tragic for all of them. Things had been so much simpler back home—or had they only seemed that way?

Well, the bottom line was that she couldn't do a damned thing about it, and that fact, instead of frustrating her, made her a little happier. God, she'd never want *that* kind of responsibility. . . .

"Did you *really* have a brush with a changewind?" Boday asked Dorion.

"No, I was making that up as I went along. All my life my best asset has been my voice. One on one, anyway, I've always been able to talk my way out of just about anything. It explains why there were so many magicians there doing their bidding and yet getting along in that crowd of hate, though. Changelings and those somehow deformed by delving into forbidden magic way beyond them—that's who those guys are. Now their differences, their deformities, become an asset and not a curse. Hounded out of the hubs, made to feel like monsters—the kind of folks like we saw back in the Kudaan. Now they got a chance to get even with all those fine Akhbreed types who looked down on them before. You know, until now I never could figure why somebody like Boolean, who never missed a chance to knock the whole Akhbreed system, would risk his neck to defend it. This is the first time I think I can understand. It's all hatred and revenge. This whole revolt is all hatred and revenge, from Klittichorn and the Storm Princess on down to those people back there. That's what their whole new society is gonna be built on—hatred and revenge. Makes a society built on callousness and indifference seem downright nice by comparison."

It took several hours of slow, cautious travel to reach the outer defense line of Tishbaal hub, and when they did, in spite of their pennant and their precautions, they still got shot at.

"Hold your fire, damn it!" Halagar shouted. "We're Akhbreed and we're not with *them!* Let us talk to your officers!"

There was no immediate reply and he grew impatient. "Damn

it, look at us! If you have anything to fear from the likes of us, then all the guns in the world won't save you!"

Suddenly an entire squad of uniformed soldiers rose from the mist, guns pointed directly at them. "All right, sir," said a nervous sergeant. "You just keep those hands free—all of you—then dismount and follow us."

In a stroke of luck, the intelligence officer of the forward defenses knew Halagar. Not personally, but they had met in the performance of the mercenary's old duties as a Covantian courier. After that, there was no question that they would be admitted, although first they had to be thoroughly debriefed on what they'd seen back where they'd come from, and how the hell they'd gotten through.

Without identifying the two women and letting the officer's mind assume the obvious about them. Halagar gave the basic story flat out.

"Perhaps we should hire you on," the intelligence officer, whose name was Torgand, remarked. "We've tried infiltrating people over there regularly and none of them ever get back to report."

"The Akhbreed they have working for them keep well back of the border and in their own camp," the mercenary told him, "as would I in their place. I'm not certain any Akhbreed will be safe once the fight begins."

"Yeah, well, we're still trying to figure out how that can be. Our shield is strong; they can take out our forward element, of course, but even our picket line is within range of hub artillery. And even if they send that rabble in wave after wave, they're not going to break the psychic shield that prevents any non-Akhbreed from entering the hub. They've got a bunch of magicians, maybe even a few real sorcerers on their side, but all of them together couldn't break the kind of shields the hubs have."

"I thought so, too, until I saw that changewind valley. Those shields, like all magic, are as nothing to the changewind, and I am convinced that their bosses can drop one wherever they want it. Right in the center of the capitol if need be. No sorcerers, no shield. Or even a changewind that simply sweeps from inland to the border, breaking it in a wide swath. An avenue in. I'm not certain what they plan, but I am certain that they are confident of success."

"Nobody has ever been able to influence a changewind, you know that," Torgand responded. "That valley might seem impressive but I've seen the winds do things just as regular and just as odd. They follow their own rules but they do follow rules. And even if there was somebody who could do it, they'd have to do it one at a time, and it wouldn't take much to find out who and from where and all the other sorcerers would track them down and destroy them out of sheer self-defense. No, it just doesn't fit the way the universe works."

Dorion was having none of this. "Then why are you holed up here in fortifications, shooting at yellow pennants, and scared out of your skulls? Those poor people we saw being abused are *citizens,* damn it! They have *rights.* And the right of any citizen is protection and defense from his King and all the power at the command of the Crown."

"He's got a point," Halagar noted. "Why wasn't this nipped in the bud in the usual manner, with massive force, even big-league sorcery? That's what the damned army's for—keeping order and law in the colonies. Instead you withdraw everybody to the hub and let it spread."

"I know, I know," Torgand agreed. "You think it hasn't gotten to us, either? Complacency, mostly, I think. The Chief Sorceress here has been cracked in the head for more years than I can remember. Senile, batty, and mean as hell. She no longer emerges from her quarters at all, and nobody can tell her anything she doesn't want to hear. She ignores even the King's commands, and she's powerful enough to zap even some of the strong adepts who'd normally take care of this. You know how nuts she is? She keeps calling His Majesty King Yurumba, and Yurumba died over two hundred years ago! She insists that this isn't happening and seems to really believe that she was on a tour of the colonies only weeks ago. She's completely lost, senile, and mad, and nobody dares cross her since she's never allowed any of the adepts to live who came close to approaching her power or threatening her position. She's the only one we have who can keep the shield up, and since that's the case we had very little choice. We can't go against them without sorcery to back us up, not on this scale, and not with those damned illegal automatic weapons that are better than anything *we* have. All we can do is pull back and rely on her to at least keep up the shield."

Dorion nodded knowingly. "I thought as much when I saw this. They're all too old or too lazy or too incompetent at this stage to really do the job. I wonder how many centuries we've been running on sheer reputation? How long we've kept the colonies in line with fear of sorcerous power that in many cases just isn't there and hasn't been for some time? The best Second Rankers don't want to be Chief Sorcerers—they want to experiment or specialize or pursue their art to the bitter end. They retire and separate themselves from politics, or they get into territory too dangerous even for them, and they wind up malformed creatures—or they wind up summoning the changewind and vanish into the Seat of Probability. That leaves mostly mediocrities as our defenders. Damn! That's what the enemy saw. He wined and dined and socialized with them and he saw what frauds our whole way of life, our whole world, was built upon."

"That's water under the bridge," the mercenary pointed out. "I am far more concerned with the rebel general's comment on the forthcoming 'fun' at Masalur. You have any information?"

Torgand shook his head. "None. We've been pretty much pinned down here for weeks. Right now, you know as much or more than we do about all this."

Boday caught Dorion's eye and he went over to her and bent down and she whispered, "Ask him if he has any knowledge of a short, fat girl about the age of our own coming through here."

Dorion nodded and went back to the soldiers. "Any sign of a girl, maybe twenty or so, pretty fat with a deep, almost mannish voice, who might look like the overweight sister of the pretty one there?"

Torgand shook his head negatively once again. "Sorry, no. At least, if she did it was before we were set up here. You might check with Immigration and Permits to see if she cleared before that, but since we've been here only a few refugees have made it across and none of them sound like somebody like that—and I've had to interview them all. Why? Somebody else trying to get through here that got separated from your party?"

"You might say that," Dorion responded carefully.

"Well, think about what you went through to get here. If she didn't make it by now, my guess is she either can't or she's dead or she's some colonial's slave over there. You were damned lucky. It'd take a full-blown sorcerer to get as far as you have at this stage."

They had spent several days in Tishbaal hub, like the other hubs a relatively compact city-state, but, unlike the others, one that had been under siege for some time. At one time it must have been a bustling metropolis, an exciting place to be. As they had progressed north and west, the kingdoms had seemed to be looser and far more liberalized than the more conservative Mashtopol. Here the women had some fashions, the dress and moral codes seemed loose, relaxed, sort of the way Charley remembered things back home.

Now, though, it was looking like a fading shadow of its former self, its factories and distribution centers closed both for lack of raw materials and for lack of ability to deliver anywhere. Shops were running out of many things to sell; electricity was rationed due to the lack of coal and other fuels that kept the plants going. Nearly half the city was unemployed and mad as hell about it and about the government's seeming impotence to deal with it.

And it was incredibly crowded and dirty, with far too many people living in quarters barely large enough for two or three people and many more sleeping in parks or tent cities. The refugees and the panicked, come to the hub for protection, and further straining its resources.

About the only thing that had kept the lid on was that the layout of the hubs included managed truck farms that produced an adequate supply of food for the population. Still, meat was rationed and there was a lot of hoarding. People who were used to thinking of themselves as the height of creation and masters of all, were now forced into decisions between their pride and the government handouts of food and other supplies that kept them going on a basic level. Although a fair number of colonial populations had remained loyal (or so at least was the word from a few brave folk who made it across the null from the other, less defended, border points), no colony was truly safe for Akhbreed or the great wagon trains the Akhbreed had depended upon for so long. Loyal colonists simply could not enter the hub to deliver things themselves, for to drop that prohibition would have invited the rebel forces in as well.

Leaving the hub, they entered what was supposed to be a friendly colony named Qatarung, their identity stones and Halagar's glib tongue giving them few problems in getting by the paper-thin rebel line on the Masalur side. The rebel force was there merely to enforce the siege; it was clearly not ever intended as an attack force, although if Tishbaal in its desperation overran them, their commander was confident that reinforcements sufficient to crush such an attempt were easy to bring up. Halagar did not disbelieve him.

Qatarung was vast fields of sugar cane and palms and other tropical agriculture. The large, apelike natives seemed mostly ambivalent to all that was going on around them, more than truly loyal. It was easy to get the impression that they would love to join the revolt if they could believe even for a moment that it had a chance of long-term success. In spite of their brutish appearance, they weren't at all stupid or even naive; if the hub could be broken that was the end of it and they would be overjoyed, but they were as convinced as Torgand had been that the hub could not be broken and overrun, and, if it could not, eventually there would be vengeance of the most horrible sort, no matter how batty the chief sorceress was or how dismal the conditions were in the hub itself.

In the meantime, they were exactly what the rebel sentry on the other side hated—the ones who, by taking no side, had profited the most. Tens of thousands of Akhbreed colonial families had moved into the hub for safety or, after the troops had closed the hub because it simply could accept no more had moved well away from the intersection points, in many cases thousands of miles away, where there were neither natives in any number or rebel troops on the march.

The Qatarung, in fact, were for the first time running their own place, pretty independently of the Akhbreed and under their own tribal rules, and they seemed to be coping just fine. If the hub held, their loyalty would be remembered and their relative racial position vastly enhanced; if it did not, they would cheer the victorious rebels. Dorion and the others suspected that most of the colonies were really like this, with only a few totally committed to the rebel cause. Still, those few would outnumber the Akhbreed by a fair amount, and the level of weapons they had made up to some extent for their lack of real training.

Not all Qatarung were playing both sides, though. The rebellion still had a good deal of emotional appeal, particularly to the young, and there were signs of looted plantation houses and even uglier events here and there.

They were three days in when they were set upon by a gang. It was on the quiet road going between endless tall stalks of sugar cane, in the middle of the day, with the sun shining brightly. Shadowcat was napping, and while he heard something rustling it was far too late to give a warning by the time any of them, including him, realized it was danger.

They emerged from the cane with shouts, panicking the horses, and surrounding the quartet of Akhbreed in a flash. Their weapons were two single-shot stock rifles, a shotgun, and three enormous machetés; a half-dozen young Qatarung males showing solidarity with the rebels and contempt for their clever elders.

Through Shadowcat's eyes Charley saw them—round-faced, barrel-chested, with muscles on their muscles and thighs bigger than watermelons, nearly covered with brown hair, kind of like a cross between Bigfoot and Alley Oop.

"What do you want?" Halagar demanded to know in his best

command voice, which really was impressive. "Why do you greet us this way?"

"Get off your horses, Akhbreed—all of you!" growled back one of the thickest, if not the tallest, of the natives and clearly the leader of the pack. "Your days of arrogance are past. Qatarung is *ours* now." He turned to his gang. "Five seconds or you shoot both the men. And shoot the magician if he so much as raises his hands. Shoot him in the head."

7
A Little Practical Treason

"You misjudge us," Halagar told the gang. "We're not with the kingdom; you can surely see that just by looking at us. I'm a mercenary in the employ of Lord Klittichorn's general staff, charged to go to Masalur in advance of, well, what will happen there, to evaluate it for them."

"Shut up and dismount!" the leader barked. "We're not as cut off as you think. We know who you are. You match the description perfectly. We want the woman. The rest of you might live, if we feel like it; the woman's our only concern."

Halagar put his hand on Charley's head and jerked it around a bit. "Her? She was wanted once, but no more. Didn't you get the word on that?"

"Not her," the Qatarung gang leader responded. "*Her*" He pointed to Boday, whose mouth dropped in sheer surprise "No more questions! Get down! Now! I'll count to five! One—"

Halagar judged their position and the position of his own party, then nodded. "Everybody do as he says," he said calmly, eyeing the leader, who held the shotgun.

The four dismounted, Halagar helping Charley down. *Clearly not professionals,* he decided at once. *Otherwise they would have realized that we were better targets and easier to cover up there than down here, on the same level as the horses.* There was no time to alert or prompt the others; they would just have to follow or get the hell out of the way.

"All of you up here where we can see you!" commanded the leader.

"Yes, right away, sir," responded Halagar, taking out the pocketknife he carried in his pocket and then sticking and slapping his horse.

The horse whinnied in shock and pain and reared up; the other two backed up, startled, and at least Boday got the idea, grabbed her whip, then slapped her own horse hard on the rump and leaped into the fray.

Halagar went right for the leader, grabbing him and spinning him around, so that the shotgun discharged into the rifle-toting gang member nearest him. Dorion, knocked back when the horses unexpectedly bolted, recovered quickly and rushed the other man with the rifle. The gunman was twice his size and four times his muscles, but Dorion was able to discharge his shock spell, which also had the effect of firing the rifle harmlessly.

A fourth was bringing his macheté down on the magician when there was a sudden *crack!* and it was plucked from his hands with a whip that left a bleeding wound. Dorion was startled for a moment as the big knife fell narrowly missing his head, but he rolled, picked it up, and plunged it into the nearest abdomen.

It was still an unfair fight; the two remaining ones with the machetés, plus the leader and the rifleman recovering quickly from Dorion's shock were more than enough in muscle and bulk to take the others on, but by this time Halagar had the leader in a viselike hold, one arm twisted back and his head pulled back with the knife at this throat.

"Everybody freeze or I'll cut his damned throat here and now!" Halagar bellowed, and it caused enough of a pause for the others, except the two writhing on the ground from wounds, to see what the situation was with their leader. It was too much for two of them; they dropped their weapons and fled into the cane. That made the score one leader with a knife at his throat, one rifleman with an empty gun, and two badly wounded on the road. The rifleman muttered a curse in his own language, threw down his rifle, and made for the cane himself. They let him go.

"Your friends aren't very loyal or supportive," Halagar taunted the leader, who struggled but not only couldn't free himself, he didn't seem to believe it was possible for a mere Akhbreed to hold somebody as big and strong as he in any kind of grip at all.

"They will fry in the netherhells for this!" the leader grumbled. "I will chase them for eternity!"

"Never mind the regrets. Who put you up to this? And what's so special about that woman?"

"Courier from the Masalur border," the Qatarung responded, giving up his struggle. "They bring us news and link the cells together. They gave us the descriptions of those three and at first said to let them pass if they came by. About a week ago we had that changed. They didn't care about the magician or the little one, but the tall, skinny one was to be taken at all cost and whoever brought her to any active border post would be rewarded beyond their dreams. That's what it said."

"Why?"

"How the hells should I know? First they said find a thin, pretty girl and a fat one. Then they said never mind the thin, pretty girl, just kill the fat one if you see her and bring something of her for a reward to prove you did it. Then they say they want the tall, skinny one, but *alive.* We just try and keep the orders straight and follow them. Fellow saw you all and recognized you a couple days back. He contacted us last night and we came after you, that's all."

"Are there more of you ahead?"

"I dunno. Maybe. Probably. Most of our side's gone to Masalur, together with some of the tribal chiefs, to see the demonstration."

"What demonstration?"

"I don't know! They don't tell people like me stuff like that! Just that anyone who wants proof of rebel victory should be at the border of Masalur hub by the evening of the Feast of Glicco. That's eleven days from now. It was supposed to be last week, but they had to postpone it for some reason so they say then for sure. Most have already left, 'cause you need big-shot magicians to get into Masalur and most of them on our side'll be going to the hub border as well."

"Thank you, my friend. You have been most helpful, in your own crude way," responded Halagar, and very cleanly and neatly slit the Qatarung's throat and left him gurgling and writhing in the road, choking to death on his own blood, next to the other two, one of whom had stopped all movement.

Halagar ignored them. "Damn! The gods know how far the horses have bolted, but at least they bolted our way. Dorion, pick up the guns. Boday, search those pouches on their loincloths for ammunition. We may need these." He looked up at the sun. "We will also need all the light we can get."

Boday came up with about twenty rifle bullets and six hand-loaded shotgun shells. It wasn't much, but it was better than being almost totally defenseless.

Halagar held one rifle in his left hand and took Charley's hand with his right and began walking down the road.

For Charley, the attack and the brutal defense had been a mixture of sounds and long-term fear, but she'd simply fallen back and hoped that it would all miss her and it had. She still wasn't very sure of Halagar, but at least today he'd earned his pay.

"Surely they must have mistaken us," Boday insisted as they

walked. "It is insane. Why would they want Boday? Perhaps, within tall, short, fat, thin, man, woman, we all look alike to them."

"Uh-uh," Dorion responded. "They knew who we were. Magician, pretty little one, tall skinny one—and even that reference to the fat one. And their news was recent, too, because they knew the hunt for Charley had been called off, and were apparently ahead of the gang back at the borders or they'd have taken us. That means the word is going back from Masalur's border where the bigwigs are. No, they weren't very good at being a rebel band, but they knew a jackpot when they saw it and went after it, and apparently you're it. The question now is why? As near as I can figure, you just came along for the ride through all this. Something you know? No, that can't be it. You've been with us since the Kudaan, so anything you know we should know, too."

"Boday came along because her darling Susama needed her and needed to be protected," the artist pointed out. "And to find new inspiration."

"Beats hell out of me," Halagar agreed. "I can't figure it, and I sure didn't figure it. It means we're going to have to find some kind of disguise for you at the next and last border crossings, though, and stay out of real visibility."

But as they walked it kept going through Dorion's brain, again and again. Why Boday? Why particularly Boday? The only thing she'd done that in any way linked her to this was that she'd made that rather bizarre marriage to the missing Sam, and. . . .

He snapped his fingers. "Yeah! That's *it!* It *must* be it!" He turned to Boday. "I knew you were married to this Sam, Susama, or whoever, but I figured it was kind of a love match. I never really connected. . . . That marriage spell you got—that's a real civil Tubikosan marriage spell? To her? They actually let you do that?"

Boday nodded. "Indeed yes. It is considered immoral, true, but it is not illegal. In fact, it is actually mandatory if one is going to do it, since they wish their—ha!—deviants known and registered and classified instead of hidden, so we can be kept in our own place and not sully the temples or be mistaken for polite society."

"It just never hit me before," the magician told her. "Look, so this Sam, or Susama, is still missing, and she's another incarnation of this Storm Princess—without whom Klittichorn can't control the changewind, right?"

They were all three all ears now. "Right," Halagar responded.

"So now they're gonna do their big demonstration, which might be screwed up if another Storm Princess pops up—and *maybe* they're gonna do the whole rebellion not long after that. Maybe she's no threat. Sorry, Boday, but maybe she's a slave or under a tight spell or something like that and is safely out of the way. She's not dead—now that I look I can see the thin marriage spell thread still running from you off and away in back of us. But they don't know and they're nervous. It's like a random, loaded gun pointed at them, the only thing that can queer their deal. Nobody, not the greatest sorcerer in all Akahlar, can find her on his own. Nobody thought of this before, just like we didn't, but somebody now has. The only way is to have you and then follow that magic thread all the way to her. A good enough Second Rank sorcerer could do it. Hell, Boday—that makes you the second most wanted fugitive in all Akahlar."

That sobered them all up fast, and made all but Halagar feel rather stupid that it had been there all the time and had occurred to none of them. To Halagar, this whole business of the marriage thread with another woman was news. It was also unsettling to him, evoking the same emotional sensation as, say, vomit. The fact that, to him, this whole thing suddenly turned on a legalized perversion somehow changed things, although he wasn't quite sure how yet. There were certainly humorous elements to it, but, somehow, after seeing all that he had seen, it didn't seem very funny. He had begun to attempt to think this all through almost from the start, in a mental battle of honor versus pragmatism, and he still wasn't quite certain he'd resolved it. He had never feared death in battle, but it was beginning to feel more and more like death in the service of a lost cause and lost ideal. He had never had any causes beyond his own self-interests not any ideals beyond his sense of personal honor.

He had never yet betrayed a commission undertaken, but he *had* failed a few times because the commission had proved impossible. Even if these others hadn't yet made the connection, he knew full well what was going to happen in only eleven days. It was obvious. As obvious as that marriage spell should have been to the likes of Dorion, who could not only be told of it but actually *see* it. If they actually found the horses today and they were all right, and if they made good time with no more major problems and delays, they might make the border of the Masalur hub in about eleven days. The odds of that were very slim indeed. The odds of bluffing their way through that horde of soldiers, of who knew how many races as well as major tribal leaders on the fence and probably bigwigs from Klittichorn's headquarters as well, were nearly nil. He began to wonder if there was perhaps a single logical course to take.

Boday, however, had a less troubled reaction. *Boday, the key to history! The entire future of the Akhbreed and all Akahlar revolved around Boday and her fate!* How simply *marvelous!*

It had taken the whole of the day to eventually find the horses, thankfully not stripped of supplies, although they lost a few things in the scramble. The stuck horse seemed no worse for wear, the wound superficial and healing well, and Halagar was much relieved at that.

Charley, too, was relieved to find a very happy Shadowcat, out of his perch now where he'd ridden on the runaway horse, but absolutely overjoyed to see her. The only thing he commented to her, in spite of all her prodding, was "*About time!*" but the purring seemed to be genuine and indicated a bit more softness inside than he wanted to admit.

There were some nervous moments and narrow escapes on the remaining three and a half days to the null and the border with Masalur, but by being quick and cautious they managed to have no further cause to fight.

The most surprising thing about the Tishbaal-Masalur border was that there were practically no colonial troops there at all. Oh, there were signs that at one time not long before there had been massive movements of men and supplies through the region, with a long camp, but they were gone now—inevitably into Masalur. So confident were the rebels at this point that they had only a few roving patrols going up and down the border on the Tishbaal side, and those were easily avoided. The Masalur side, however, looked like trouble.

They stood in the mists of the null and surveyed the scene with binoculars. Finally Dorion sighed and put them down. "No doubt about it," he told them. "There's some kind of shield prior to the boundary. It's not strong like the ones the Chief Sorcerers do for the hubs, but it's stronger than *I* can handle. From what I can see of it, it's not specific to any particular race or kind, just a real barrier to everything. Any second ranker could knock it over in a moment, but there don't seem to be any second rank sorcerers around—at least not on our side."

"So you mean we're stopped?" Halagar asked him, actually feeling a little relief at the news. "We can't get in?"

"Not exactly. There's a single point where the two halves join that looks designed as a passage, but that's the only place. It means everybody and everything has to go through just that one point. There'll be no sneaking in to this one, and the only way you can maintain something like that is with a top magician actually present to control it. If we go in at all, we go in there—and that means right up to a very good magician at the least, into the colonial world *he* wants us to go into, and that's that. We have to assume they have the wanted posters on us there, too. I don't see how we can do it."

Halagar thought a moment. "Well, they're looking for two female slaves of a certain description travelling with a magician. They don't know about me and they don't really want Shari. With my stone, the two of us are as likely to get through here as we were at the other places. If we tried it, say, several hours apart, and if you somehow could manage to not look like a magician, then they might not even connect us. It's either that or you two wait here and we'll try and make time and reach Boolean somehow and then come back for you."

"No. We should still travel the last road together," Boday responded. "Them are too many chances for one as valuable as Boday to be lost skulking about in these regions for days or weeks. Boday is both artist and alchemist, and she has her small kit taken from Covanti. With a few hours, she might be able to make sufficient changes not to be recognized during that brief crossing. In fact, perhaps she should go first, since it is the greater risk."

"No," Halagar replied firmly. "If you go in first and are still recognized, and we don't know what sort of powers we're dealing with there, then there is no way we can help you or hope to get close. If we get through—and you can probably get close enough to watch it all through binoculars, Dorion—then we can take up a position over there and cover you just in case you have problems. And if we don't get through, for some reason, you'll know that there was no way for you to get through in time to avoid capture, which is all that's left."

"Sounds reasonable," Dorion agreed. "All right—let's try it."

They found a position where Dorion was still reasonably out of view from the entry station but could observe fairly clearly not only the station but perhaps a quarter of a mile into whatever colony was coming up as well. It wasn't until they were set and Halagar and Charley were on their way and pretty much beyond recall that Dorion was suddenly struck by the idea that they might not be admitted into the same colony! Well, he knew Masalur very well, and the barrier was a good distance inside the null. If need be, he'd just see which one Halagar went into, go where he was directed, then slip down and back out inside the barrier and call that one back.

It was likely, though, to be the same one. This bunch liked crowds.

Halagar approached the entry station slowly but confidently. He held Charley tightly and whispered, "I know Dorion or that cat creature or both have probably put checks on my authority, but listen to my orders. You will say not a word, and do nothing, no matter what happens, and if that won't remain a valid command then I will take my knife and slit your tongue and break your legs. And if that cat creature so much as moves from his comfortable pouch I will destroy him. Now, put your hands behind your back."

She obeyed, wondering what the hell he was talking about, and was surprised to feel leather straps tying them securely behind her. Jeez! She was blind, stark naked, and a slave. What the hell did he think she could do?

Shadowcat remained still, not because he feared the big man, but because of the big man's will and position and what he might do to Charley if anything was pulled. Besides, it was better to find out what the hell the bastard was planning first.

The soldiers guarding the gate were Hedum; he'd seen them before in his travels, and they no less impressed him now than they had when he'd first seen them as a young soldier of fortune. Over seven feet tall, with long, spindly-looking arms and legs, a glistening coal-black skin, totally hairless, and all the more intimidating for it. Still, they looked basically human, until you got to the head, which looked like a coal-black sunflower, only the petals were not petals but thick, tubular tentaclelike shapes that were in constant motion. Some terminated in eyes, some in hearing or other sensory organs, and two were mouths. Of all the races of Masalur they were the strangest and also the meanest and most incomprehensible to Akhbreed. Just the sight of them with automatic rifles and a criss-crossed set of ammunition belts across their chest was intimidating.

The Hedum also quite literally talked through their nostrils; the effect was eerie, unsettling, and about the most inhuman around. Two flanked the theoretical opening in the shield, and the one on his left stepped forward.

"Who are you and why do you come here?" it asked, in that mixture of honking and wheezing that was the only way they could manage the Akhbreed speech.

"I am Halagar, a mercenary. I answered a call for men with past military experience and was told that if I got to the Masalur hub border in the next week or so I would find a great deal of work.

"She's an Akhbreed slave girl. Not mine, although responding to my commands at the moment."

Eyestalks leveled themselves on her. "She does not look as though she is responding well to your commands," it noted. "Still, wait here. I will summon the magician of the gateway."

The Hedum turned, faced the barrier, and placed both enormous hands on it, one on either side of the theoretical opening. There was a chilling, ringing sound and an almost immediate response from inside a tent in back of the gate. Presently a middle-aged man in black robes appeared—an adept! High power indeed. Klittichorn couldn't have too many adepts on his side or he'd not have waited this long nor been this cautious. Adepts were essentially Second Rank themselves, although not as powerful as full sorcerers—yet. Basically they had the power, but not yet all the skills and experience. Still, they were formidable.

The adept stood there, looked at both of them, frowned, then said, "Dismount and walk through. We'll bring your horse through after you."

Halagar slid down, then picked Charley off and virtually carried her through. He was not blind to the fact that several more Hedum within the barrier shield were pointing guns right at him.

The adept went up to Charley, seemed to examine her top to bottom, then put his finger on the tiny slave ring in her nose and stepped back. "She's bound to Boolean." he noted. "Not *by* Boolean, but definitely *to* him."

Halagar nodded. "I know. I know of no one capable of removing the spell."

"I could, but it would be a lot of trouble and time. However, the fact that she is not bound by him makes for an easier remedy. Has she ever been in his presence?"

"As far as I know, no."

"Then it's easy. Now tell me why I should bother."

Halagar hesitated only a moment. "My name is Halagar, a mercenary most late of Covantian service. I was hired by a two-bit magician named Dorion who's working for Boolean to bring her and another woman to him. The other woman is Boday, wife of Susama. Interested?"

"Very. But if you betray them, why should I believe you won't betray us?"

"No percentage," Halagar told him. "I know what you're going to do and that will make the whole mission moot anyway, since there's no way I can practically do it from this geographic point and I know it, and since in less than a full week the spell would dissolve of its own accord, wouldn't it? I keep my commissions, but not when they are obviously beyond my ability to perform."

The adept smiled. "Now I am very interested. Where is this Boday?"

"Not so fast. First, I want that slavery spell transferred to me. Second, I want an officer's rank in your forces, and protection and safe reward at the end, if I serve loyally and honorably and survive."

The adept shrugged. "Sounds fair enough. Very well, as a demonstration." He walked over to Charley, who was now livid and suddenly felt no loyalty or attachment to Halagar at all and a very strong urge to warn Dorion. The adept knelt down and made a few passes with his hand, however, and she suddenly stiffened and went into a deep trance.

"Fascinating," he said aloud to himself. "She's got a regular bundle of stuff in there. Even demon spells. She's got a familiar, too! Where is it?"

"In the saddle roll," Halagar replied, but even as he turned to look at the horse he saw the shape of the cat leap from the bedroll and run like hell through the startled soldiers and out of sight. Attempts by the Hedum to catch him proved more comical than effective, and he was soon well away into the countryside.

"Forget it, then," the adept told him. "Just make sure it gets no more of her blood. That's the way to kill them. If it shows up, don't kill it—that'll only cause problems. Trap it and let it starve. They're devoted but generally not very bright. All right." He turned back to Charley. "Girl, what is your native language?"

"English," she responded dully.

"All right," he responded in clear but heavily accented English, "now listen to me. I am telling you a secret and you will believe it. Now I tell you that Halagar is Boolean. Boolean and Halagar are the same. He chooses to use the name Halagar for now and so should you, but only you and he and I know that he is really Boolean, your lord and master. You know it, you believe it to be true, and nothing, no one, no evidence, no thing, shall convince you otherwise. He is your lord, your master, and your god and you belong to him and must always obey him. You are his to do with as he wills. When I snap my fingers you will not remember that this has happened but you will suddenly know and realize this as if it were divine revelation and you will believe and act accordingly. Also, your cat familiar is an evil creature, a demon who wants to harm your master. If he tries to contact you, you will shut him out and never seek him out, and you will never let him feed upon you. If it tries to contact you, you will not understand what it is saying nor obey, but you will tell your master. Now. . . three, two, one. . . ." He snapped his fingers, then got up and turned to Halagar.

"It won't hold if she actually meets the real Boolean," he told the mercenary, "but in a few more days that won't be a problem. In fact, upon Boolean's demise the spell will be permanently affixed, replacing the original, until your own demise. Now, what about this Boday?"

"If we're seen to be safely leaving, in no more than a few hours she will try and walk right in here with Dorion." he told the adept. "And she has the same slave spell Shari has, so she'll be easy to lead away and very cooperative."

"I see. Now about how powerful is this Dorion?"

Halagar smiled. "I seriously doubt if Master Dorion can successfully palm a card or make a coin vanish. He used to work for Boolean but the old boy exiled him to Yobi in the Kudaan, apparently for incompetence. This was supposed to be how he'd get back in."

The adept suddenly reached up and Halagar felt a tug on his hair. "Hey! What—?"

The adept took out a pouch and put a lock of the mercenary's hair inside, then put away his small clippers. "Just a bit of insurance that you will have no second thoughts and will stay on our side," he said lightly. "With this, I can curse you anywhere in Akahlar."

For Charley, sitting there, things became momentarily confused and then suddenly there was no confusion at all. When things had been going wrong the Master had suddenly revealed himself and his power to her and all was suddenly clear. Now she understood that Halagar was Boolean in disguise and thus her true master. It came as a complete shock, like a bolt from the blue, that revealed his power, but now everything was in place. She did not understand what he was doing or why, but it was not her place to do so. Such powerful beings were more than human; she could no more comprehend them or truly question them than a pet could comprehend or question the actions of their owner. In fact, that's just how she felt—like a pet dog, there to serve and obey, unquestioning, dependent, too low to comprehend.

Halagar was none too pleased about an adept having a part of him but it was a small price to pay to resolve his future. He came over to her, untied her hands, and saw in her face and demeanor the great change wrought within her. "This will be our secret," he told her, "to be revealed to no one. From now on you are Shari, slave girl of Halagar. That's your only identity and your only loyalty. Now, come—give me your hand. We must ride. We must not be late for their big show."

"Yes, Master," she responded, and that was all there was to it.

Dorion had been watching from the null, and while he had some bad feelings when they were held up by the adept, seeing them mount up and ride off made him feel relieved. Maybe they were going to make it after all!

Boday had used her kit to paint elaborate and colorful designs on her face and upper torso. She certainly looked— different—like some primitive savage, and maybe it would do. Dorion played with a simple by-the-book illusory spell that would make his robe appear to be some uniform, but when he saw the adept he knew that his simple and stock tricks would be of no avail. The hell with it; he would wing it as he was.

They mounted up and headed for the gate. The Hedum challenged them as it had challenged the first two, but the adept came out from his tent quickly and bade them come inside. The magician was just beginning to feel confidence returning when the adept said, "Well, brother-in-magic, I thank you for bringing us that which we have long sought."

Dorion frowned. "I do not understand, brother."

"Sure you do. You are Dorion and this is Boday, mate of the one we have sought for so long. Don't look so shocked or come up with any denials—your comrade betrayed you. And don't try anything unless you wish to test your own powers against mine."

Dorion hesitated, but he had too much respect for what it took to get that black robe, and too much understanding of how little power he himself possessed to do it. "No, brother, it's your game."

The adept smiled. "Let me make a bit of adjustment in our rather colorful slave here so that she believes me to be her true master, and then we can depart."

"Depart—for where?"

The adept smiled. "Why, we are going where you wanted to go. To Masalur hub! There we'll watch the final demonstration of My Lord Klittichorn's power and then meet up with some more of my brethren, and then together we will reunite this woman with her lover—an all too brief and sad reunion, I fear. And with those two steps we will erase forever the last hope of the old order in this world."

Out in the woods, Shadowcat had no luck in contacting Charley; she had shut him out entirely, even to the visual link, and now, with just she and Halagar on a single horse, it was clear that he could not hope to keep up with them. It was time to think it out.

The imp was a minor demon charged and bound to Yobi, who had no true existence in this dimensional level without inhabiting a body. Yobi had placed him inside the cat when Charley had selected it, and since then the imp had maintained himself through her blood energy while maintaining the cat body in the usual way.

Trapped in the body, which he needed to have corporeal existence on this plane, he needed her blood to survive, to replace the type of energy that was part and parcel of the very atmosphere and makeup of the netherhell to which the imp was native. By preying upon locals he might sustain himself for some weeks, but the link was to Charley and the energy level would be down at the very time he needed it the most. Worse, the locals here would probably not be Akhbreed and their blood, let alone blood type, was probably unsuited to his needs. Without Charley, he would die.

He cursed himself for not simply tearing Halagar's throat out one night as he'd been sorely tempted to do. Instead, he'd kept her in the courtesan mind-set, having learned of the spell from her own brain, so that she could not betray the full facts about herself to the man the imp had never liked or trusted. He could not destroy the cat body deliberately; that was against his nature and the rules here. He could provoke a killing, which would free him, but that would only take him back either to the netherhell or perhaps to Yobi's laboratory in the Kudaan, very far from here. It was a last-chance option, but it might well be too late if they killed Boolean.

Looking out from the bushes, he saw the Hedum bring up a sleek coach with six fast horses. To his surprise he saw the Hedum driver get down and Boday climb up and take the reins. Bewitched, certainly, and under the control of the evil ones. Two Hedum put large chests and blankets and bedrolls on top of the carriage in the luggage rack and secured them, then jumped back down, and Dorion emerged from the tent with the black-clad adept and both got into the coach. Dorion looked unhappy but not bewitched, which might or might not be some advantage. Shadowcat wondered what blood type both the magician and Boday were.

He eyed the luggage rack and judged where the coach had to pass and the probable speed of it when it did, then looked around for a convenient and climbable tree. It might be for nothing, he knew, but it seemed the obvious thing to do.

The rebel forces around Masalur were so confident that they even had bleachers erected for the big shots.

It was a far thicker but better organized crowd than the one back at Tishbaal; only the best rebel troops were here, all well-trained and eager to see some real action. They, and their support troops remained relatively apart from the others, who seemed to be of all races, shapes, and sizes. Here, too, were large numbers of robed magicians and sorcerers of all ranks, although Third Rank types dominated with a smattering of black-clad adepts, and there were very few with the colorful robes of the Second Rank. The fact that there were any at all was impressive to the observers. The one thing they all had in common was that they were on the outs with their own establishment, either having been changed or malformed or having committed some political or ethical violations that had at best estranged them from their own kind and at worst embittered them towards it.

Here, too, surprisingly, were a fair number of distinguished-looking and not so distinguished-looking Akhbreed; men, and some women, of obvious wealth or power in key areas with their own axes to grind, hoping to carve out wider niches in the wreckage the new order would leave, and very useful to ones like Klittichorn. Men like Duke Alon Pasedo, whose family was barred by Akhbreed law and spells from coming this distance, but who had many grudges against his kingdom and many friends among those who sought to inherit this world. There were a lot of Pasedos about, although they were dressing plainly and keeping a low profile. There was no use in giving any of the colonial troops who would have to fight in this, any idea that they might also be serving the interests of some Akhbreed types.

Most of the Akhbreed on hand, however, had gotten the slave treatment. Much of the stands, the temporary buildings, field kitchens, and pit toilets had been built by them, and vast numbers continued to do the manual labor and dirty work of maintaining the whole place. They weren't really needed to the extent they were being used, but the rebel command staff guessed rightly that the sight of them in such low situations and so debased would keep morale among the native troops high.

The Hedum acted as the traffic cops, keeping the various factions separate and out of each other's way. They were polite but very firm and imposed a sense of order and strength on the vast assemblage.

One look at such a mighty, organized, and confident force and Halagar knew he had made the right choice. Any Chief Sorcerer who would remain bunkered inside his hub and allow this so close to him was another who was more smoke than fire, a sure sign of the system's rotten core.

Somehow, this Klittichorn had stumbled onto the great power that the Storm Princess possessed. He probably wasn't the first, but he was the first to realize the weakness in the center of the system after so many thousands of years; to realize that he might get away with using that power simply because his colleagues in sorcery could not believe that they were not impregnable. To have godlike power means nothing in the end if you have not the wisdom for it.

The Hedum traffic director pointed him towards a small three-sided tent pavilion. Sitting there were three officers, a senior and two juniors. One had pea-green skin and bug eyes and looked more like a giant lizard than a variation of humanity; another was bald, squat, with an incredibly wide face and hairless skull from which protruded two bony horns like great but misplaced carnivorous teeth. The third was a tiny, gnomelike creature with huge upturned pointed ears, a rather stupid expression, eyes like dinner plates, and who looked like he had been born old. None were races he recognized, and the quality of their uniforms—and the sameness of them in this vast jigsaw army—indicated that they were probably from Klittichorn's own staff.

"Yes, name?" the gnome asked him.

"Halagar, sir. A mercenary officer by trade but a volunteer to this cause. I have proved it by capturing the fugitive Boday and turning her over to the adept at the Masalur border."

"Indeed. Well, welcome, then, sir. We have no billeting for such as you—unexpected, that is—but you are welcome to set up anywhere over there near the tree line where you can find space. There's a cold field kitchen there and pit toilets just in the woods. I would suggest, to avoid problems, that you remain in that area. You'll get as good a view as anyone from that camp." He looked over at Charley. "And this, I take it, is a prize of battle?"

"My personal slave," he responded.

"Well, the rules here are that all slaves are put in the pens and assigned work and cared for *en masse*, so to speak. It avoids, ah, nasty situations."

"I understand, but for practical reasons she should stay with me. She is blind."

"Indeed? Then why keep her, then? What good is she?"

The horned giant looked at Charley and then over at the gnome. "Stupid question," he rumbled.

"I, uh—oh, I see. Yes, *ahem!* Well, she'll have to be with you at all times, even when taking a leak, and because she's blind I suggest you see one of the smiths and get a collar and chain for her so you can stake her and not have to constantly be watching out for her. Just see one of them along here—they'll do it."

He nodded. "Thank you, sirs. I believe this is going to be a most interesting new time for me as well as Akahlar."

The green-skinned one looked over at him and said, in a surprisingly pleasant and mellow upper-class accent, "Tell me, as a soldier of fortune and professional, what do you think of the operation so far?"

Halagar shrugged. "To be frank, sir, it shows the other side as stupid, dry-rotted, and impotent. If I were this sorcerer over there, I'd have waited until everything was in place over here, then sent my entire army in with everything they had backed by all the sorcerers and sorcery at my command. As cramped and exposed and backed up as you are here, your automatic weapons would shoot as many of your own people as them, and you would be broken and destroyed. The fact that he has not done this shows that he must lose, and he's supposed to be one of the smarter ones."

"You are not alone in that line of thinking," the gnome told him. "Many of us recommended a low-key and covert build-up even with the organizational problems that would cause for that very reason. However, we tried build-ups of this kind in a dozen areas where we could bring a concentration of forces, and the reactions were always the same. If they will not help one another, our sorcery is at least the equal of their sorcery out in the open like this. You do them an injustice when you think them stupid, however. Think of the cost in lives and materiel to put down something like this. Their militia is designed to hold and maintain the colonies, not fight a frontal war. Far easier to endure, and allow our own weaknesses to consume us."

"The only weakness we have," the horned giant picked up, "is that the basic compactness and circular shape of the hubs makes them ideal defensive positions both from a military and magic point of view, and we have a less than cohesive force. They can reinforce from the center as needed, either power or men or both. They know it, and that's why they sit, waiting us out, believing we'll not be able to keep our forces together for a long siege—and it might even be the correct strategy under the old rules. This is a collection of independent races not used to dealing as equals with anyone other than themselves. Different, squabbling, with little in common except the thirst for freedom. But you remove that center out there, before your own forces begin to fall apart, and you have them. Tomorrow, at three in the morning, we will remove that center and attack from three sides. Tomorrow night, we will turn that center from enemies into automatic allies."

"Uh, do you have a Mandan cloak?" the green one asked him.

"No. We lost most of our supplies early on. Would there be a problem from this point? I know changewinds never cross nulls."

"That's true, but it means you should wait a day before going in yourself and seeing the aftermath, just in case there are spin-offs. With a storm of this concentration the weakness down to the Seat of Probability remains unstable, and in spite of buying, begging, borrowing, or stealing every Mandan gold cloak we could lay our hands on for several years we haven't nearly enough. Well, just watch from here and wait. When it's all secure, we'll see if we can spare some for people like you. Thank you—that's all."

Halagar set up the bedroll in an area that had a fair number of Akhbreed, including some of his own kind who he recognized and who recognized him. Some were men like himself, who saw this side as the winner and thus the more profitable to be on; others were pirates, bandit chiefs, and other very tough customers, some of whom he'd gone after as a lawman.

To Charley, the collar and chain was the ultimate in degradation. The metal used was light and thin, but the collar was welded around her neck and the chain, maybe six or seven feet of it, was welded to it. Very quickly she had been reduced to being paraded around, filthy and naked, on a leash, like a trained dog, and Halagar wasn't above having her basically do tricks as well. In fact, he bragged and showed off so much that eventually he yielded to the social pressure and new comradeship and actually loaned her out to them. She had always liked anonymous, uncomplicated sex up to now, but these men were filthy, brutish, and a little sadistic, and she had no choice but to go through her entire vast sexual playbook with them on the grass for hours, unable to put her mind on automatic because of their nature, feeling at the end bruised, battered, and utterly defiled, and she was commanded to act like she enjoyed it and beg for more.

And some of them were only nominally Akhbreed, and many had very bizarre turn-ons, and those caused her both shock and disgust like she'd never known.

And they were in no mood to turn in. They were all killing time until three o'clock when the major battle would begin, and that seemed like forever. When it finally ended, about an hour before Zero Hour, she was so battered and so exhausted that she just lay there, unable and unwilling to move, but she couldn't stop thinking, even in a state of shock, trying to hold on to her sanity. Boday had been right; she'd still been a child, naive and stupid about this kind of life, romantic in a world that was truly a cesspool. She was property and treated worse than his horse, and it would continue to be this way, over and over, because that was all she was good for, the only use she was to the master. And it would go on like this, day after day, week after week, year after year.

She couldn't stand it, she knew that, but she also had to obey, had to do it, without choice, without thinking, with no hope of rescue. She thought of those hollow, dead expressions on the slaves back in Tishbaal and knew that she would be as shriven and without hope inside as that in very short order. The time had come, now, here, tonight. She knew she had to do it before she was commanded to speak only Short Speech or to never use English. "Charley, be gone!" she said aloud, firmly, and slowly her expression changed to one of dull acceptance, her manner relaxed, as one who thought only in the most limited ways and matched her situation.

The slave spell was not gone, but Charley was, and little Shari actually managed to drift into an exhausted sleep.

Masalur was an almost fairy-tale land; its central castle and government offices, with their many spires and minarets shimmering in their Mandan gold sheathing, were known far and wide as the most exotic and distinctive such buildings in all Akahlar.

Beyond the government center with its architectural beauty and landscaped gardens and parks was a ring road, and just beyond on all sides was the commercial heart of Masalur, with its shops and bazaars and business centers for everything from commodities to insurance. One actually had to go about three miles from the center to hit the first all-housing areas, and these were densely packed, multistory apartment buildings containing hundreds of small flats. The final ring was the region of wealthy merchants who outdid each other with lavish homes and grounds. Only beyond that, perhaps an eleven-mile-circular city, did the land become rolling hills and farms sufficient to feed the city population, more than two million in normal times, perhaps double that now with the refugees inside.

Although it was in the early hours of the morning, after even the last of the clubs and night spots had shut down, there was no mistaking that a major storm was rolling in. Clouds seemed to rush in and thicken around the government center itself, the storm center appearing to form almost directly atop the royal castle. Those with the magic sight might have seen a glow in the clouds and wondered, and also seen the outer edges of the storm appear to take on the looks of strange beasts whose eyes and mouths were illuminated whenever lightning discharged inside the storm. The better magicians and Chief Sorcerer's staff would have recognized them as Sudogs, more here than could be remembered to be in any one area before. The Sudogs were weak and minor imps attracted from the netherhells by the conditions of great storms, but they were generally harmless and could not sustain themselves in Akahlar without the cloud "bodies" which would dissipate with the storm itself.

It would have taken an expert in both demonology and military tactics to recognize that the Sudogs were not merely using the storm for a brief reality but were moving around purposely, cautiously, almost as if directing the storm's shape and makeup. This they could not really do, but a sorcerer with contacts in the netherhells could use them to "see" from their unique vantage point, and if that sorcerer had power over storms, this information would allow very precise targeting.

For the first few minutes, those who were awake below ignored the storm as just another inconvenience; subtropical regions were used to being rained on at all hours. Now, though, the storm seemed to exude a strange sensation to those with the magical talent, as if those below it were descending in a fast elevator, and men and women in various places suddenly woke up, grabbed their robes, and headed for the alarms.

Changewind! A changewind coming, in the hub itself!

Hub cities were far too dense to allow for full shelter and warning, but the alarms rang anyway all over the place, and sleeping people were roused and headed for what shelters there were if they believed that they were in any real danger. The government centers, of course, were sheathed in Mandan, the only substance that would deflect a changewind. The royals, the permanent staff, the nearby senior bureaucrats, and the military command began quickly shutting the windows, pulling the shutters, fixing the seals to keep even the breath of changewind out, then going down to the below-ground shelters where the winds, if the shields held, could not penetrate at all. A surface covered by Mandan gold was also safe below it: that was why, even out in the open, a pit or trench and a cloak of Mandan on top might well save you.

Particles no larger than small stones broke free from the great mass known as the Seat of Probability on a dimensional center far "below" Akahlar, which was only the closest-in point where carbon-based life could exist and did. The small particles immediately shot out, breaking down, colliding again and again, gaining speed and momentum, breaking free of their parent block, and shooting up through the Lower Hells, punching through one after the other, their explosive reactions widening more and more and attaining a circular, cyclonic shape, remaining in the Lower Hells only until they found a weak spot to continue through their outward, upward journey towards the dimensions and realms of men.

Klittichorn and his associates, through the "eyes" of the Sudogs who were too dull to realize their own danger, were providing that weak point, and the Storm Princess in full possession of her powers was holding and shaping the resulting storm center, waiting for the changewind to break through.

Since the changewind was supposedly random, and Mandan gold scarce, not even the richest of kingdoms nor the greatest of sorcerers ever lined the below-ground shelters. Mandan would protect you from a changewind bearing down upon you, but the odds of one breaking into Akahlar under your very feet were so small as to not be worth calculating.

From their aerial vantage points, the Sudogs watched in fascination as the very ground of the government circle and into the business circle seemed to glow with a dull, white magical fluorescence, then grow stronger and stronger, more and more brilliant, until suddenly there was a tremendous rush and a great, swirling, tornadolike maelstrom broke free and reached for the storm clouds above.

Buildings, grounds, trees, streets, and all upon them seemed to shiver and melt at the touch of the white cyclone; the Mandan gold sheathing on the government buildings turned dark but held, yet began to crumple inwards into a heap as the supporting structures under them were melted away by the power from below; blackened gold foil that protected now only itself.

The maelstrom and the gathering storm mated in a dance of power, obliterating the Sudogs and all else and widening the regular storm into a monster of wind, rain, and local tornados which, while not changewinds, were nonetheless black angels of death in the dark.

The mass now covered almost the eleven-mile radius of the city proper, with the white whirling maelstrom at its heart the center of its own meteorological solar system. Its energy partly expended on what it was touching, it could not remain still, and instead began to move with the storm itself. The core maelstrom widened, becoming less powerful only in degree, touching and changing all that it contacted, and moving now, out of the center, with the great storm.

Normally its passage would be swift; fifteen or twenty minutes and the white maelstrom within would find its weak point and travel upwards once more leaving the lesser but still devastating storm to blow itself out in the null, but this was not the pattern here.

The storm took a turn and began a slow, steady march around the city, dragging the changewind at its core with it, as if somehow orbiting the center of its birth and unwilling or unable to break free. In less than an hour it had made an unprecedented, impossible three-hundred-and-sixty-degree circuit in a widening spiral, obliterating, then reforming all out into the farm belt itself. Masalur was not merely to be devastated or decimated, it was to cease to exist.

Across the null border between the colonies and the hub, from three sides, whole divisions of rebel troops began to move briskly across; thousands of men on foot following lines of calvary that seemed to stretch from horizon to horizon, bearing down on the armies of Masalur, who were now caught between the oncoming force and the changewind at their backs.

Even with the strongest telescopes, it was nearly impossible to see just what was going on at the hub border, but, unaided and without even magical sight, the entire horizon seemed to be glowing and the enormous booming claps of thunder rolled across the null and mixed with the distant sounds of artillery opening up.

Halagar stood on the ridge and watched from afar. He'd given up on the telescope, but just the fact that he could hear so much rumbling from so far away and see the whole horizon apparently ablaze awed him and his companions. They watched, too, open-mouthed, as great, demonic stormriders came out of the null clouds and right into the command areas of the rebels with reports and information, and carried instructions from the general staff back with a speed that nothing else in Akahlar could match and that no defender could slow or even affect.

Less than a half a mile from Halagar, Dorion stood atop the coach that had brought them here only an hour before, open-mouthed and with heart sinking. With his magic sight he could see and psychically *feel* the power out there, the finger of white barely glimpsed now and again as the spiral widened outwards. There was nothing else to see, of course, and no way to know just what it was like over there; Boday, exhausted from driving much of the past few days and through some of each night, had watched for a few minutes, then curled up and went soundly to sleep on the driver's seat.

But, somehow, even with nothing really to see, he couldn't stop watching.

He had actually been treated with the utmost respect since being captured. The adept, whose name was Coleel, proved a rather pleasant, even interesting fellow, with enough power and skills to be totally confident of himself; second rank in all respects save having successfully stood the examination by a committee of full Akhbreed sorcerers—something that, shortly, might be a bit difficult to assemble anyway.

His fall had been dramatic, although not for the usual reasons. As an apprentice to a sorcerer far to the east, he'd been posted as a magician in residence in a colonial capital, where, because he was already so powerful—a natural, as it were—he'd spent some of his copious spare time studying the natives and their culture instead of working all the time on his skills, and he had regaled Dorion with tales of these people, the Grofon, on their trip to this point. To hear him tell it, they were a particularly beautiful people, inside and out, almost angelic, and very similar to Akhbreed in appearance, but they were hermaphroditic—their whole world had developed unisexually—and had some "trivial" and "beautiful" differences like multicolored hair and bushy tails. A city boy and true believer, he'd expected to be posted to some primeval, primitive world with monstrous creatures more animal than Akhbreed, and instead he'd found a beautiful folk with a gentle culture. He'd become quite close to them.

Then there came a ritualistic period in a local tribe's life, a period of just four weeks that came only once every twenty years, which fascinated him, but which had the inconvenience to come during the peak harvest time. The Imperial Governor, a royal relative on his first assignment, had blown his stack at having all the natives cease work for so long a period during so critical a time, and he ordered them back to work. When they ignored him, he ordered troops in, only to find that in the one matter of religion, they would rather die than work. Infuriated, the governor had declared a civil insurrection although none really existed and ordered mass executions in public—children as well as adults, randomly. Coleel was ordered to protect the troops; when he refused, the governor threatened to bring him up before an Imperial Court of Sorcery for violating his oaths. The governor had too many spells of protection from the Chief Sorcerer for Coleel to do anything to him, so the magician had done the most pragmatic thing available and shot the man in the head. He had then fled and lived with the natives in a far region of Grofon, for sixteen years a fugitive, until word of the rebellion had reached him and Klittichorn's cause and protection was offered.

Dorion thought it was too bad the guy was screwed, and wished he'd known him under more pleasant circumstances. Now an act of compassion and self-sacrifice was being turned into complicity in the greatest butchery in the history of Akahlar.

It seemed it wasn't nearly as hard for Klittichorn to get good recruits with high magical skills as it would have seemed.

Dorion had no idea what they were going to do with him, but, although no spells had been cast on him and no guns were leveled at him, he had no more choice in that than did Boday. He looked back across the great null, and wondered what hell was going on over there. If Boolean still lived, he surely had been transformed into something far different than a sorcerer, and that was as good as being dead.

8
The Fugitives

Halagar finally decided that he had to get at least a little sleep or he'd be shot to hell when anything interesting happened.

For a while, he and his new comrades had watched and received relayed battle reports and wished they were in it somehow, but after a while came the realization that this wasn't his fight, not this time, nor would there be much to see before perhaps a day or so later. Better to be at your best than to waste yourself on this, and then look lousy just when you wanted to impress somebody.

He went over to where Charley had passed out a few hours before and frowned as he thought he saw some smaller shape, like an animal, dart from her still form and off into the darkness. *If I didn't know it was impossible, I'd swear it was her damned cat,* he thought to himself.

He went over and looked at her, and it *did* seem that she had a wound on her right breast, but that might well have been from the earlier night's play. Probably was, considering the location and considering it sure wasn't bleeding. *Over tired,* he told himself, lying down on his sleeping bag and stretching out.

The boys had been a little rough with the girl, but, hell, that was all she was good for, and she'd survive. Besides, she'd paid off already. Letting them have their fun with her had turned a bunch of mercenaries and misfits into a kind of comradely unit with them all feeling kindly towards him. She was unique; the only one of her kind in captivity, maybe the only one anywhere if they did to other hubs what they were doing to Masalur. Hell, she'd be real useful in keeping a unit happy out in the bush and a real inducement to ride with him.

He shut his eyes and relaxed and tried to get to sleep. With Boolean dead and the rest lining up for the slaughter, and with him and his pet and his new comrades and position, things were about as good as they could be.

Suddenly his eyes opened wide in sudden shock and pain; he tried to yell out, tried to scream, but nothing came. With tremendous force of will he reached up and grabbed onto whatever *thing* was tearing into his throat and came down on a small, furry body. In desperation, unable to breathe, hardly able to think, he grabbed the animal's torso and squeezed with all his might, trying to crush it, pull it away.

It was a death grip, and he knew it, even as he pulled the creature off him, its gaping mouth taking much of his throat with it and threw it with all the force of his command down to the ground. He sat up, trying to talk, pointing at two glowing eyes in the dark, then sank back for the final time in death. The last thing he heard before darkness fell upon him was an eerie, gruesome voice inside his brain.

"Bad man! Evil man! Die! Die!"

At the moment Halagar died, Charley woke up and sat up. She was feeling sore and bruised and very frightened but she was suddenly very wide awake. She was also not Charley, but Shari, making any conclusions or decisions nearly impossible.

Shadowcat was hurt, badly hurt; Halagar's will to live and his dying strength had been unexpected and particularly brutal. Most of the familiar's ribs had been crushed in the death embrace and he could barely move. He was bleeding inside, and he knew he didn't have a whole lot of time left. He reached out to Charley's brain and found only Shari there. It confused him, but he knew the trigger and sent it.

"Charley return," he managed, glad that it required only mental contact.

Slowly, and with some horror, Charley felt herself once again, and she didn't like it a bit. *"Oh, god! It didn't work! I can't send myself away!"* But there was something odd, something different. Halagar—that bastard! Somehow she'd been tricked into believing he was Boolean. What in hell was happening to her now?

"Charley," came a familiar voice that both startled and frightened her.

She looked around and finally spotted a magical aura of lavender fuzz about ten feet from her, although it didn't look right, somehow. It was constantly changing shape, and the whole center seemed the deepest black.

"Shadowcat?"

"Quiet! You want to bring the others? You know what they will

be like. You can do nothing for me. Halagar is dead beside you, but he has had his revenge. Do not weep for me; only the cat dies. I return home free and clear. You must get away. They will think you did it and what you have suffered will be nothing in comparison to what they will do to you. Go directly back, away from the null. This is cover and no one left."

"But—I can't leave you! And what can I do back there? I'm blind!"

"Trust your instincts. Survive. Use what you have. You must believe me, and in yourself. I do not know how long it will take, but if you survive then help will come, and if you survive then there is still hope. I can say no more. Now, leave me. I die now, and I prefer to die alone."

"No!" Then, *"How will I know the help when it comes?"*

"You will know. Farewell, Charley Sharkin. And, next time, pick the dog."

The blackness inside the lavender fuzz grew and engulfed the color until there was nothing left. No—not quite. A tiny ball of twinkling crimson, a jewel or starlike thing no bigger than her thumbnail, burst forth from the blackness and came towards her, then touched her for an instant, and then was gone.

She got up and almost immediately stepped on and almost tripped over her chain leash. She grabbed it, followed it, and found where it was pegged with a tent stake in the ground. With both hands she pulled the stake out and then gathered up and coiled the chain over her shoulder. There was a lot of noise around so she wasn't worried about that, and if those foul creatures were around she couldn't tell. Made no difference now; she had to act as if it were still dark and everything unseen. What she *could* see was the null, and that meant she knew the direction to go. She got up and walked away from it, and within no more than eight or nine steps she walked into a bush. She worked around it, met another bush, then a tree, and, using one hand to feel ahead of her, she continued on back.

She didn't know how far she was going, or even if she was making any progress, but using the sounds of the throng on the border as a guide she thought she was going well away from them. She wanted to hurry, but every time she did she tripped and fell. Several times the chain slipped, and she had to pull it back and wrap it, often tugging to free it. After that, it was very slow and cautious, using her hand and a lead foot. She suddenly stopped and thought a moment, then uncoiled some of the chain and began waving it back and forth in front of her. It wasn't a white cane, but it did help.

Suddenly she felt herself step into mud, then she slipped and fell into it and down a short embankment and into cool running water. She lay still for a moment, afraid that the chain had hung on something, afraid that this was a broad river, but after a while she got confidence and pulled on the chain and it came. Getting to her knees, she cupped her hands and put them in the water, not knowing or caring if it was fit to drink or not. She tried it, it tasted okay, and she drank.

Feeling a little better, she got to her feet and wondered what to do next. Was this a little wadeable creek or a broad river with slippery rocks and deep spots? If she tried to cross and slipped, then the chain would most certainly be the death of her.

But—back there, it probably was light by now. They probably had discovered Halagar's body and that she was missing and they might even now be looking for her, figuring she couldn't have gotten far. If they found her, then the horror would begin again, only worse, and eventually they'd drag her to one of the big-shot sorcerers there and. . . .

No. She was going to die, almost certainly, probably by stepping where she shouldn't or victimized by insects or wild animals or maybe by accident or drowning, and certainly eventually by starvation, but she would die free. For the first time since she'd fallen into Boday's clutches, she was really free, with nobody to rescue and nobody to obey. Compared to that, somehow, none of the rest mattered. Being on her own, being free, even if for a short time with death the only reward, suddenly seemed the only thing that was important any more.

She walked into the creek, carefully, and found it shallow, no more than hip deep at the center, the bottom a mixture of mud and tiny rocks or pebbles. When she realized that it was getting shallower again, she stepped back a bit and knelt down, so that the water came up to her neck, and she splashed it on her face and even immersed and wrung out her hair. Somehow feeling much better, she got back up and continued to the bank—where, of course, she found more soft mud. Somehow it didn't matter. It was *new* mud.

She knew, though, that she was spent. The hair weighed a ton as wet as it was, and she'd had a horrible night and very little sleep. On the other side, she decided to follow the stream for a bit, checking, until she found an area that seemed to be an irregular row of bushes almost as tall as she was. Wishing she knew how much, if any, cover they really provided, she sank down in the grass or weeds or whatever, stretched out, and more passed out than went to sleep.

It was six in the morning; the sun was not yet up, but false dawn gave a gray and colorless beginning to the day, and allowed the whole scene to be visible.

Dorion was dead tired, but he still resisted sleep. Just from hearing various people talk as they passed nearby, and checking occasionally with anybody who looked like they might know something, he had a fair picture of what was going on.

Before the changewind had exited, it had covered perhaps a third of the hub, including the entire capital and center and touching probably eighty percent of the swollen population. The land was now a swampy region with thick, bizarre vegetation, and most of it was under a thin layer of water; a shallow sea dotted with countless hundreds of tiny "islands" of thick growth that rose no more than a few feet above the swamp. The water area, too, was covered with vegetation, although, as usual, it was of types and kinds that hadn't been seen before.

Mandan hadn't saved the city center, and it hadn't saved those in the public shelters, few as they were, or the private ones of the wealthy further out, either. True, unlike the center they had received only the changewinds the shelters were designed to protect against, but the changeover in topography had opened up the regions around them, and the swamp water had come flooding in through the air intakes and flooded those shelters. It probably would never be known how many drowned that way.

The first rebel units into the transformed region were using loudspeakers urging the inhabitants of this new land to come forth, assuring them that they would be well treated and welcomed and would not be harmed in any way, let alone killed. That because Akhbreed role was dead not only in the hub but in all of Masalur, they would be helped to rebuild, to grow, as a new race among the many—equal now, but no longer superior or masters of all. First reports told of the appearance of "very large women" with deep green skin, long, purple hair, with four arms and four breasts, one set atop the other, and long, thin, prehensile tails coming forth. So far, no males had been seen, and all of the "women," at least to the eyes of the colonial forces, looked to them to be exactly alike in appearance.

The new Masalurians, Dorion thought. And possibly Boolean

among them, although nobody really knew what happened to anyone who was sitting on a changewind when it broke through. He and the others might now be just part of the energy of the storm rising through the outplanes.

Although the rebel forces were jubilant that it had all worked as they'd planned and dreamed it would, there were some sour notes and long faces among the celebrants. The Masalurian troops, who'd not been touched by the changewinds, had fought with exceptional skill and ferocity and, with nothing to gain or lose but revenge, near suicidally. The rebel forces, who had never actually fought before and had neither the training nor the discipline of the defenders nor the defenders' knowledge of the land from the hub to the transformed region—divided as well by racial loyalties, conflicting generalship, and language barriers—had been cut to pieces. Losses among the victors were not merely high, they were astronomical, and the remnants of the broken Masalurian army were still fighting guerrilla actions in the hills and might take weeks or even months to completely dislodge. The top generals here and the members of the General Staff were conferring in secret in the command center now.

When word inevitably got out about Masalur to the Chief Sorcerers of the other hubs, there would be much consternation and concern, but they would still not accept the truth—not enough of them, anyway. Although a changewind had never broken through in a hub center in recorded history, it was not impossible. The whims of chance, really. The odds of it happening again—billions to one, old boy. Why, no one can or would dare summon a changewind—you'd have to be right on the spot to even try and you know that would be the end of you. As for controlling and directing it—impossible! Why, in thousands of years of study and experience nobody had ever. . . .

Well, so it would go. Klittichorn got this one for free. But if it happened a second time, and in the same manner, reality would shove aside dogmatism. They'd know that indeed somebody *could* do it, and then they would remember Boolean's words and warnings. They'd be watching, they'd track down the horned one, and they'd burn him to the netherhells no matter what the cost, just for insurance.

Next time, Klittichorn couldn't stop until he got them all. Never mind Boolean's worried questions about the effects of so many changewinds all roaring through at the same time; did Klittichorn in fact have enough rebel armies for it? And after the inevitable word of the massive losses and gross slaughter suffered here, would he still find enough eager volunteers?

Dorion looked over and saw Coleel walking quickly towards him. *Never mind the philosophical questions,* he thought apprehensively. *The question now is whether I'll be around to find out and, if so, just what condition I'll be in.*

"You're still awake, I see," the adept said, sounding not very cheery. "Good. Saves me time. Come with me. There's something I want you to see and comment on."

Dorion got down, feeling a bit dizzy and light-headed from the lack of sleep but still too worried to do anything else. "Yes?' "

"Follow me. It's some walk up this way, but I think you might be able to answer some troubling questions."

They began to walk, and Dorion asked, "You're not going to tell me any more?"

"Wait until we get there. You can see it, about a leeg up and towards the trees, with all those people around."

Dorion shrugged, puzzled but intrigued, and continued walking. "Well, can you tell me if it's true about the new Masalurian being a green woman with four arms and four breasts?"

"Yes, it's true. And it seems that they're all like that and all really do look alike. They have some sorcerers going in now to examine them more closely—I was supposed to go with them but this took precedence. Right now the preliminary word is that they're some sort of plant-animal hybrid, unisexual, possibly capable of photosynthesis but bearing and nursing live young. Of course, we don't know that for sure, and we're guessing about the latter, and will until we see some live young in who knows when? I mean, those people don't even know themselves yet. The breasts indicate live, nursing young, of course, which poses the question of why a photosynthesizing species needs mammaries, and that tail—the end of it resembles, well, a male sexual organ. They're like nothing anyone's ever seen before. They're in shock, of course, and most will need our psychic help to adjust, but it should be fascinating to see how they develop as a species. It's never been done before with civilized people—they've always gone in and wiped them out. Only among primitive colonials who weren't found earlier, and even then the number was small. This could be a species that begins in the *millions.* Ah—here we are."

Coleel parted the crowd and Dorion followed, then stopped short when he saw the scene, being kept clear by Hedum sentries.

It was Halagar, all right, his eyes wide, his expression one of stark terror, frozen there now until the elements ate it away, his throat a bloody mess. Dorion felt a mixture of revulsion and satisfaction at the sight. The bastard had gotten what he deserved, and quickly, too. Maybe there *was* such a thing as justice in the universe after all.

"The girl?" he asked. "Where's the girl?"

"We don't know. Gone, that's all."

"Charley wouldn't—couldn't—do *that.* Not like that. And she was under your spell. . . ."

"That spell was broken the moment he died, so right now she's free meat, with a slave ring and no master. She'd become the property of the first person who touches that ring, and that might have been what happened, although nobody else nearby seems to be missing or unaccounted for according to the group here. But, no, she didn't do it. *That* did."

Dorion looked where the adept pointed and saw the still form of Shadowcat, eyes also glazed in death, caked blood on the side of its mouth and in a pool beneath its head in the dirt.

"Well, I'll be damned," Dorion sighed. "I didn't know a cat's mouth could open that wide. Remind me never to have one if I need a familiar. But how did it get here?"

"The only way short of very powerful magic is embarrassing, I'm afraid," Coleel commented, "and will do my standing no good at all. It had to come with us, maybe even feeding off you or Boday. It wouldn't have dared touch me, but have you noticed any small wounds or punctures on yourself or Boday?"

Dorion frowned, lifted up his robe, and there was a large, bruised area on his thigh and tiny puncture wounds. "I'll be damned! It's been itching like crazy, but I just figured it was a bruise."

The adept nodded. "That's how it kept going, although it wouldn't have had full strength. It must have made psychic contact with the girl, came here, waited, somehow fed on her and gotten strong again even though my spell would have her reject it so she must have been asleep, then waited for its chance." He sighed. "There's a lot of loyalty and a lot of guts there in that little form. I disagree with you, Dorion. I think a cat like that is *exactly* what I'd want for a familiar."

Dorion walked around the site, wishing he wasn't so tired so he could think more clearly. Suppose, just suppose, Coleel was wrong about Charley. Suppose the cat had used her for strength, and by killing Halagar, had broken Coleel's spell. If Shadowcat did his job, and made certain Charley had all her wits about her, she wouldn't just wander into the crowd. These other tough mercenaries would have been sleeping on both sides and she'd have walked into one of them, who would have grabbed her. She certainly wouldn't have walked towards the null, even though she could see it, because it would have meant going through more masses of sleeping bodies and guards. No, she'd go back into the woods and try and get as far away as possible. That *had* to be it. Otherwise she wouldn't have gotten far enough to be lost in this mob.

It wasn't certain, but it was the only possibility with an out for him or her. But if she did go back there, then she didn't stand a chance of survival. Not blind.

He went back over to Coleel. "Well, there's nothing more to be done here. Can I ask what's going to be done with me now?"

"Just hang around. Go to sleep—it looks like you need it. We have the Boday matter to handle yet as well as mopping up here. When they can spare the people and time, a board of magicians will be convened on you in accordance with our oaths, and you'll have a chance to justify your continuing existence. If you fail, you will be stripped of your powers, cleansed of your spells and geases, fitted with a ring, and thrown in the slave pens."

That was a chilling end to all this. "Considering that, you've been pretty generous with my freedom."

Coleel shrugged. "What can you do? Forgive me, but I can tell your relative magic strength and abilities, and they are not threatening. You haven't the proper spell and charm to be authorized past the borders of this camp, so all know you are a potential enemy. If you tried anything foolish, you would simply lose your right to the board hearing, and it would save everyone time and trouble." He looked out at the null. "Besides, what would be the point? You no longer have a master or cause to serve. Now, forgive me, I must get this mess certified and cleaned up and tend to my regular duties. You can find your own way back, I trust." And, with that, he walked off back down to the tent city.

The crowd was dispersing now; there wasn't much left to see, and the gory sights being hauled back in wagons from across the null provided more prurient interest to those who loved to gawk at such things. Dorion walked slowly away, trying to think about what to do.

If only there was some way for him to slip away. He wished he had the nerve even if there was such a way, but he was between a rock and a hard place as it was. They'd give him his board, but they couldn't trust him or what he said and, frankly, he wasn't powerful enough to warrant their attention. With power, even solid Third Rank power, they might purge his mind and "turn" him to their cause because they needed more magicians than they had, but he was nothing, almost a fraud.

He watched as four Akhbreed slaves, looking exhausted and drawn, walked through the crowd towards Halagar's remains, there to get rid of the body and clean it up. Everybody just, well, ignored them, and why not? They could only obey, after all, and there were tons of them doing the shitwork around. . . .

Almost a fraud. . . .

He walked down towards the small tents where the prisoners from Masalur were being fitted with slave rings. He stayed there a bit, talking "shop" with the overworked magicians, who knew he was not one of them in all respects but who just didn't give a damn, and, after a while, he wandered away again. The rings had been there by the carton load; sensitized, but "raw," waiting for the binding spell and the insertion. It was no big trick to palm one, which he now fingered loosely.

In here, the tents were so packed it was difficult to walk between them. He went over to where the VIP horses were informally stabled, ducked between two tents just before the stable area, then kicked off his boots, leggings, robe, undershirt—everything. He looked at the ring and let the simplest of slave spells flow into it, the kind they were doing out of necessity. He wished he could totally fake it, or make the owner tag his own, but that would be seen through very quickly. He therefore sensitized it to Charley and, taking a deep breath, invoked the final spell that caused the ring to pass relatively painlessly through the bridge of his nose without breaking skin and lodge, hanging, inside.

Waiting until it was as clear as it could be, he slipped around the back of the tent and into the rear of the stable area. The water troughs there had splashed all around, causing a nice mess of red mud, and there was other dirt around as well, although he decided to pass on the most obvious scent. Now, filthy, ringed with a spell that wouldn't read false, and looking lousy from his lack of sleep in any case, he got up and simply walked out into the mass and back up towards the tree line.

There were loads of people around, Akhbreed and colonial alike, but none gave him more than curious glances and then ignored him. A couple of brown-robed magicians walked near and he felt their automatic probe for anything unusual, but he read true to them and it probably didn't even register in their minds that they'd done it.

Normally his nerves would have given him away, but since the first activated items in the sensitizing spell for the rings was a compulsion to present yourself to your master, he had no choice. He *had* to find Charley, and that quieted all other fears and replaced them with wariness.

He passed quite close to where Halagar's body had lain, and close, too, to many of the people who'd been there when he was, but, as usual, they had seen the brown robe more than him, and he looked quite different now. Before they had seen a magician; now they saw a slave moving with purpose and obviously carrying out a command. Not even the Hedum guards gave him a second glance. He headed for a likely spot—the field latrines just in the woods—but as soon as he was close to there he veered off to the right and doubled back behind the death scene.

There were no obvious signs immediately behind, and he paused a moment. *Think, Dorion, tired as you are! You're blind and you have to get away and be sure you do. You can't see, and you don't have the null reference after this point, so how can you be sure?*

Hearing. That assemblage out there made a constant, terrible racket that he'd gotten used to through the night. So you walk away from the noise. Well, that gave him a place to start.

After several hours, he was beginning to panic, fearing that he'd made a dreadful mistake. The area, even assuming walking generally away from the noise, included a wide triangle, and there was almost a certainty that she wouldn't have managed anything close to a straight line. Might there be something up there that would stop her? A wall or steep drop, perhaps? Go directly away and see—it was the only thing he could think of that he hadn't already tried.

About a third of a mile in the woods, he hit the creek, meandering peacefully through the forest. At first it was only welcome water, far too small and too shallow to be the kind of barrier he sought, but as he went down to it to drink, he lost his footing in the soft earth, and slid down into it. Now a bit bruised and mud-caked, he sat them in the water suddenly feeling like a fool and hoping it was only exhaustion. Sure—he could see this thing and know it wasn't much, but she couldn't! To her this might be nothing, or it might be a great, wide river or sea. He drank, then picked a direction, and started walking.

Now, for a change, the fates were with him. Less than a hundred yards from his starting point he found a part of the bank given way and signs that someone had done pretty much what he'd done. It was so broken he thought she'd fallen down and then clambered back up, and he did likewise and searched the area but could not find her. He returned to the break and looked across the stream and now could see what might be signs of somebody getting out the other side. That was discouraging, since it meant the creek hadn't stopped her after all, and he might have an even wider area to search. Driven by his self-imposed compulsion and against the protests of his body, he waded across to the other side and climbed up on the other bank, telling himself that no matter how wrecked he was, he was still in better shape than those poor wretches back at the border.

Still, he knew that even to complete his compulsion he'd have to get *some* rest. He was feeling dizzy, had a hell of a headache, and was seeing things all blurry. He began searching along the creek bank for some kind of decent cover he could use to lie down just for a little bit, to get himself back into some kind of shape.

And suddenly he saw her, lying there like some dirty, limp rag doll, unmoving behind the bushes. He ran to her, fearing that she might be dead, and knelt down beside her. He took her, shook her gently, and said, "Mistress! Mistress! Are you all right? Wake up and speak to me!"

She stirred, mumbled something, then suddenly her eyes were open and she was aware first that she was in someone's grip and began to scream and push away, but then she *saw* him. Not Dorion, of course, but that magic aura whose distinctive shape she'd shared most of a long journey with.

"Dorion?"

He felt like crying. "Mistress, you live! You are all right!"

She frowned, unable to see the shape he was in, reached out, and began to run her hand over his body. "Dorion—why are you—oh my! Sorry!—naked? And what's this mistress crap?"

He lay down beside her and tried to relax, then told her the whole story. She had slept so hard that, while still exhausted, she felt wide awake and clear-headed, although her head was killing her when she moved. She listened, fascinated.

"Let me get this straight. To get out of there without getting noticed, you made yourself *my* slave? Jeez! All the time I been here, I been somebody *else's* property. Will it wear off?"

"No, Mistress. It can only be removed by *two* magicians of some skill, Third Rank, or a Second Rank sorcerer with some time and a lot of work. It's not supposed to be easy to undo."

"Even if I gave you freedom?"

"No, Mistress, that would be worse. Then I'd be a slave with no master, and the first free person who touched me would be my new master."

"Well, I wouldn't, if I could. I don't want you away from me from now on, and this'll keep you close. You made your bed and you're stuck with me, but cut that Mistress crap. It sounds wrong when it's addressed to me. Just Charley is fine."

That pleased him. "As you wish—Charley."

She suddenly came over and gave him the hug of his life, clinging to him, breaking out into tears. "I need you, Dorion. I need your eyes, your strength, and, most of all, I need your company."

"Whatever you want, I'll try to do, Charley," he told her sincerely, "spell or no spell."

"Just hold me," she sobbed. "Just hold me close until I can believe you're really real."

He did so, and felt better and more important than he ever had in his whole life. It wasn't until much later, lying there, her head in his lap and him stroking her hair, that he suddenly was struck by a wrongness. Not from Coleel or that bunch, but something wasn't quite right. Looking down at her still angelic face, as dirty and scratched up as it was, he suddenly realized that he'd been looking at it all the time.

Like Coleel, he'd assumed that the slave spell had neutralized when Halagar had died, making Charley temporarily free but only until someone, anyone, else touched her ring. Anyone but him, of course, since a slave could not be a master of his own mistress. But there wasn't just the sensitizing spell in her ring; it was complete. It was still Yobi's original—he knew her handiwork well enough. But that spell bound her not to Dorion—that was only temporary and had been neutralized by his own actions—but to Boolean. If Boolean had died, or been swept away, or had even been transformed into some four-armed, four-breasted plant girl, the spell would have been negated the same as Coleel's had been when Halagar died. The spell, however, was intact. Although Charley didn't seem to realize it, she, too, was still a slave.

His own excited start bumped her head a bit and frightened her for a moment. "What's the matter? You hear something?"

"No, no, Charley—your ring! Yobi's spell's still on! Don't you see what that *means?*"

She sighed. "You mean—I'm still a slave after all?"

"Yes, but it means a lot more than that. Charley—it means Boolean's still alive! Still alive and still unchanged." He gave a low chuckle. "It means either that he was as smart as I thought he was, or that, for all that, the bastards missed him!"

She frowned. "That explains it, then. Just lying here, feeling a little safe for the first time in a long time, I suddenly had this thing in the back of my head whispering that I should go to Masalur hub and find somebody. But—if you're right, Boolean couldn't be *there,* not *now*. Jesus, Dorion! I'm gonna wind up with a full-scale compulsion to find Boolean, and I no longer have his address!"

"Then you must use your head to fight it. You know he can't be in Masalur, so going there does not fulfill the command. You can not find him, not with things as they are. Your duty, then, is to simply remain free and alive and out of anyone else's hands until he can find you—or until some clue presents itself."

She thought that one over. "I—I guess you're right. I guess that's why I *can* fight it, why it's not overriding everything. Why I didn't really know until you told me. But that means it could be a real long time. Out in the woods, naked, savages, really. Sort of caveman and cavegirl, only without the cave or the skins. And fugitives, too. We can never be seen or mix with others. Around here, Akhbreed's gone from being the highest to the lowest of the low."

"I know. But it's a big world, a whole planet, and it's real warm here all the time, and it's thick forest around here. We'll be hard to spot or catch. If we can only find a source of food and water, we could make out okay." The fact was, Dorion didn't feel hesitant about it at all. Except for the food problem, which would have to be solved and soon, this came about as close to his private fantasies as he could ever come.

She frowned, still thinking, although this wasn't one of *her* fantasies. "Dorion? How can you be my property if I'm still a slave to Boolean? Property can't own property."

"That's what fooled me for a while. Because I wasn't bound to you—that would be beyond the spell—but because I bound myself that way, freely and of my own will. It's the only way possible."

"And you gave the magician's life up and came after me to live like this—for me." She said it like she couldn't get over it.

"Yes, Charley," he replied, not adding that it was certainly the best of his possible alternatives.

It was well past noon when two high rebel officers and a sorcerer of the Second Rank sought out Coleel, who was beginning to think that the mop-up work from the night would be never-ending.

The Second Rank sorcerer was one of only two on site during the whole battle; the rest had participated, somehow, remotely in a way only Klittichorn knew. The rebels had a large number of acolytes, magicians, and adepts, but very few of the Second Rank. Their powers and egos did not in the main make them terribly cooperative with one another nor willing to be under one of their own.

This one was a mean old fart with a face that looked like he'd died about three centuries past and refused to recognize the fact, but he had a fairly strong walk. His name was Rutanibir, and he was short-tempered, mean, and pissed off at the universe in general. What his motives were for working with Klittichorn wasn't known, but he was a key man in the field.

"You have this homosexual woman?" Rutanibir asked him in a shaky voice.

"Yes, Master. I—"

"Silence! Why wasn't I notified immediately of this? Take me to her at once!"

Silence was one thing he didn't want to concede. "Master, this *was* reported, but so close to the start of the battle that word did not apparently get to you. She's under my control as a slave, though, and she was commanded not to move. Come. I will take you to her."

They walked briskly along, the throng parting rapidly and averting its gaze from the wizened old man in the silvery robes. Because of the fear he generated, it took only a few minutes to find the coach and go up to it.

"Boday!" Coleel cried out. "Come! Attend me!"

There was no reply, and he frowned, suddenly nervous. He jumped up on top and saw that she wasn't in the seat or foot well, nor under the tarps. He climbed down, looked inside, under, and all around. She simply wasn't there anywhere.

"Incompetent idiot!" Rutanibir snapped. "No wonder you never made Second Rank! Whoever gave you those black robes should be drummed from the Order! You *knew* she was important, even vital! Yet you let her sit here, unattended, all night, with all hell breaking loose, and didn't even *think* about her! Didn't think at all. . . ."

"Master, I—" Coleel suddenly stopped and stood straight up, a tremendous look of confusion on his face. "Why in the name of the Seven Sacred Words *did* I do that? You are correct, Master—it makes no sense at all. And that magician—Dorion. I gave him free run of the place! And parked right here, not two leegs from the rest of his party. And I spent five days in the coach and never even *sensed* the presence of an unwanted familiar. I admit to abject incompetence, Master, and throw myself at your mercy."

Oddly, his talk calmed rather than enraged the old sorcerer, who waved off the comments with a casual hand gesture. "That son of a bitch," he muttered under his breath, more to himself than to any of the others. "Sixty-one-percent casualties and we still missed the old bastard. It *has* to be. All that—and he wasn't even home!

He's been standing *here,* next to all of us, playing games with us and laughing at us all this time!"

The two military men turned and stared at him, and it was finally Coleel who asked, "Pardon, Master, but do you mean I was bested by superior power? Who? Who would have such power and such audacity?"

"Boolean, of course, you idiot!" the sorcerer snapped. "Son of a bitch!" He turned to one of the generals. "You said you had a man back in Covanti who thought he'd tracked the girl. At the time it didn't seem worth pursuing, but if Boolean's *here* then we still have a chance."

"Yes, sir. Fellow's name is Zamofir, one of our best agents. He thinks that she got caught up in a move to give brides to a bunch of ex-convicts developing a valuable business in one of the Covantian colonies. He's got a band of men with him, loyal to our money if not to us, and he's willing to go. He's in Covanti still."

"Good, good. It's no mean feat even for one of Boolean's skills to follow such a slender and nebulous thing as a marriage thread over three kingdoms and into colonies. It'll take time. Lots of time. I can reach some of my people planted in Grotag's office in a matter of hours. All I need is my kit and someplace quiet. Your Zamofir and his band can be riding to her before Boolean is even clear of Masalur." He put one wizened hand into a fist and gently struck his other palm with it. "Yes, indeed. So he's outsmarted us, has he? Escaped and all that. Well, precious little good it will do him if your man's right. And he'd *better* be right, General. He'd better be right. . . ."

He was a small, thin man with long, thinning black hair just starting to turn gray; the most outstanding feature of his sharply angled face was its long moustache, which he usually, as now, kept waxed and perfectly shaped so that it stuck out from both sides of his face and curled up nicely. He would never be considered handsome, but he could be charming if he wished; still, no matter how he dressed or where he was, he always looked dapper and out of place beyond the casinos and social gatherings of the business set.

Now he was dressed in casual riding clothes; a simple cotton shirt and tough denim pants with boots, all of which looked new and had some unnecessary fancy stitching. He took out a long, thin cigar from his pocket but did not light it; it was just a pacifier at this point. You didn't want to smoke, not in *here.*

Several large, burly men dressed in the sort of clothes one knew instantly were not bought special but were the ones in which they lived and worked, entered the cave as well, all illuminated by magical hanging lanterns that had plenty of light but no heat or flame to speak of.

Zamofir, their leader and employer, pointed to a carton. "There. Use the crowbar behind that box and get the lid off that one."

One man got the crowbar and another assisted, and the lid broke open revealing a box full of large metallic guns packed in straw. One of the men reached down and picked one up and looked at it quizzically. "Looks like a rifle of some kind, but it's too fat to steady," he noted. "And where do you put in the bullet?"

"Idiot!" Zamofir snapped. "Let me have that. This, gentlemen, is what is known as an automatic rapid-firing gun, known where it came from as a submachine gun. These, and the cartons of ammunition around, were gotten with great skill by Lord Klittichorn using his powers to extend to the outplane. They use these big, fat clips, like this. You turn it over, press here, insert the clip so until it clicks in place, then throw the safety here and it's ready to fire. To reload, you just press here, the clip drops out, and you shove another in. Clear so far?"

They all nodded, crowding around. "But how do you hit anything with it?" one asked. "I mean, it doesn't even have any decent sights and it's too square."

Zamofir sighed. "Follow me, gentlemen. I do not want to demonstrate in here."

They went outside with the loaded gun, and Zamofir picked a small, thin tree about thirty yards away. "Watch the tree. Each one of these clips holds a hundred carefully packed rounds. You just point the gun in the general direction, then pull the trigger. Even *you* can do that." And, with that, he demonstrated, and the rattling filled the air and smoke poured from the top of the machine gun, although nobody noticed.

They were all watching as the tree was sliced almost in two and much of the surrounding area was also pockmarked.

"The shells are ejected automatically. Don't bother with them—we have a sufficient number of clips here. Each man will take one of these and as many clips as is practical for him to carry. We'll practice on the way, although little is really needed once you learn how to keep the gun reasonably steady. Now, there are twenty-one men and four women there at the camp, but it's unlikely that more than half the men will be there at any given time. Their big product is a key mineral found in certain kinds of ocean fish in that world, so they're out in shifts for days on end on small boats trawling, while the rest work the refining process back at the village. Twenty of us, with *these* should be more than enough."

"How far is it?" somebody asked.

"We are riding hard and light, but the village is out of the way and far outside the intersection point. Once we turn off the main road, it is unlikely that there will be any people at all between us and the village, so we'll be on our own but unimpeded. If we *do* meet anyone, kill them and go on. With consideration for the horses, it might well be seven or eight days to the village, depending on conditions. Once we get there, there is to be no quarter. Men, women, children, livestock—if it moves, it dies. *Particularly* all the women. If they surrender, we take their surrender, and then execute them. All are to die and all buildings and structures burned, and any boats, even so much as a rowboat, also burned. We want the place devastated, so that even if someone should escape, they would have no place to go and nowhere to turn."

"Aw, can't we even have some fun before—" somebody else started, but he cut them off.

"Listen! We're working for a big-shot sorcerer who can reward us all handsomely or punish us beyond our wildest nightmares. If we fail, then killing ourselves before he gets the word of our failure will be the only way out. Likewise, we're in a race against another, equally powerful sorcerer. The only good thing is that he doesn't know exactly where our girl is and I do. He's got to do things the hard way, and that takes time. If we're not out of there, and I mean *well* out of there, before he finds the spot, then we'll get it from the other side. For almost the last two days' ride there's only a single road, in some places too narrow for two horses to run abreast, for most of the length, shut off on either side by a wall of dense and nearly impenetrable jungle. If we don't get in, do our job, and get out past that trap, we'll be caught in it. Understand?"

They nodded soberly, and clearly a few were having second thoughts about this. Zamofir was quick to sense this and counter it.

"There's only one reason for any of us doing this—the price. We go in, do it, get away with it, and get back safely, there *is* no price too high. Name your own ticket. Your own little kingdom with all the wine and honey and slave girls you want—and I mean for each of you. This is the first job I've ever had where the prize was worth any risk, and I've worked for these people a long time. They pay off for success. Nobody, however, fails them twice. Now—get your weapons, ammo, and gear and saddle up. We ride *now,* and go as far as we can, then get as short a sleep as we can stand, and ride some more."

"What about the border?" one of the men asked. "Between the soldiers and the rebels it'll be hell getting through."

"Not *this* one. The rebels are on our side, dummy—they won't block us. They have their orders. But there's no army, no pressures, on this side. We've drawn them all to the south and west. The most we'll have to deal with are a few officials and the usual border guards, and under these conditions we can dispense with the niceties and just blow them to hell."

That didn't prove necessary. The border personnel weren't at all concerned with anyone going *out;* they were much too harried with the refugees and nervous ones from the colonies wanting *in,* and were more than glad to wave twenty Akhbreed through who wanted to go the other way.

Even Zamofir was impressed with the huge numbers of people along the road, even the main road across the colony he and his men wanted. The crowds slowed his progress considerably, and in some cases stopped them dead for some time. They were in no mood for that sort of thing, but the fact was that, in this case, they were twenty against an endless stream, and many of these colonial types, even with their families, were tough and hard-looking people with plenty of fight in them as well. You could machine-gun a whole mob, but they'd just keep coming, and then there'd be a ton of folks after them and blocking the only exit. Even with all that firepower and the clock ticking, Zamofir's group simply had to wait and cope.

The eastbound road was only slightly better, and it took them almost a week to finally make it to the final cutoff over to the sea. It was less a road than a tunnel through the jungle, dark, narrow, and forbidding, and they had better than two days on it to the settlement. At least, here, there weren't any crowds or refugees; indeed, there seemed to be no people, no habitation, at all.

There was the sudden crack of a rifle shot, and one of the men fell backwards out of his saddle and onto the ground, where those behind trampled him. A second shot came and another man fell, and now they suddenly all pulled up and dismounted fast. The dense, forbidding jungle was the only cover available aside from the horses, and none of the men really wanted to go into the jungle. It might be just what the shooter or shooters wanted them to do.

"Where did it come from?"

"I dunno! Over to the left, I thought, but the echoes made it hard to tell for sure!"

"Is it many people or just one guy?"

"One guy, I think. There were only two reports, both sounding the same and just about the time it would take to shoot and reload. We're like fish in a barrel on this damned road!"

Zamofir hunched behind the horses and cursed. "Well, if you hear anything, you open up with the machine guns," he told them. Spray the whole damned area if you have to."

"Who the hell's shootin' at us, anyways?" one of the gunmen asked him. "And why would anybody do it? They don't know who we are or what we're fixin' to do."

"It's that damn' sorcerer, that's who!"

"Don't be an ass," Zamofir told him. "Sorcerers have better ways to deal with us than shooting high-powered rifles. Maybe somebody who's working for the other side and is paid to delay us. But how'd he beat us here? Shit! More delays. . . ."

"Yeah," the man nearest him grumbled, "and we got at least another day and night in this trap of a road."

"Well, he *can't* dog us all the way," the little man maintained. "There are no other roads, and even the natives here can't fly. I say we can get pinned down here and picked off one by one or we can ride like hell and leave him in our dust. When we're well clear, we'll drop one man and he'll give our pursuer the same treatment."

"Yeah? Ever think that maybe his horse is *ahead* of us? That he's already gone, and maybe even now is mounted up and riding maybe an hour on and settin' up the next ambush? That's what *I'd* do."

"Fuck it!" Zamofir snapped. "I'd rather be shot than face either Boolean or Klittichorn. I say we spray all around, three-hundred-and-sixty degrees, then we mount up, and ride as fast as we can. Either we outdistance him if he's behind or, if we're fired on again, we *keep riding* no matter what. If he had more than a rifle he'd have wiped us out by now. Our only chance is to get ahead of him, and if we overrun his horse so much the better. What say you?"

"Beats hidin' out here," somebody muttered, and flicked off the safety on his machine gun.

After two days of being rained on, bitten by insects, and weakened by lack of food, the primitive life had lost its romantic appeal, even to Dorion. For Charley, it was about as bad as she could imagine, short of another round with those bastards back at the camp, but something that had to be endured.

"Dorion, we will have to take chances while we're still strong enough to move," she told him. "We need food to survive."

He nodded. "If we have to, we'll head back up towards the

camp. It should be breaking down now as troops leave and as the rest move into the unchanged areas of the hub. And, if I remember rightly, there used to be a small town a few leegs in from the border, as usual. It's probably not much now, but they had orchards and stuff. If it wasn't picked clean to feed all those troops, there might be *something.*"

"Let's go there, then. We haven't much choice."

It took them two hours to reach the road, and then they had to parallel it within the forest. There was a lot of traffic there, mostly wagons and such, almost all going away from the hub in steady streams. The conquerors were leaving the scene of victory now, taking what remained with them. For a victorious army who'd just done the impossible, they looked pretty damned grim.

Much of the town had been destroyed; cannibalized for the wood and other materials to build the structures at the border, but some of it remained. A small group of colonial natives remained; small, hairy humanoids with short, thick snouts and shiny yellow eyes the size of egg yolks, but it was hard to say whether they were the remnants of those who had lived there or if they were part of the force. Dorion did not remember seeing any of them at the campsite.

A couple of hours reconnaissance convinced Dorion that they probably weren't part of the attack force or anybody official. Apparently they were scavengers; opportunists there at battle's end who made forays into the campsite and came back with whatever wasn't nailed down that they could get away with. There were only a dozen or so, but they were tolerated because they were the "host" race and this was, after all, their world and their region now, Too many to take on, particularly when one good yell or scream would bring some of the passing "allied" forces to their aid. And, as expected, the orchards and such nearby had been picked clean.

There was, however, a mounting pile of discards out back, including a lot of soldiers' kits—cold rations and the like. They were either quite choosy or quite wasteful, and Dorion was too hungry and in too much need to quibble. When it grew late, and the inhabitants of the town ruins bedded down and the procession halted or at least slowed to a trickle, Dorion led Charley across the road and to the back. They were not particular, and Dorion didn't give Charley the exact details and she didn't want to know. It was enough that the food was edible, that it filled, and that it wouldn't harm them. The fact that it was somebody's half-eaten garbage showed just how low they'd fallen so fast.

"If we can get enough for a little journey, we'll head south again and off towards the west," he told her. "There's a bunch of groves and orchards down there, maybe two- or three-days' walk, that I'm sure the locals would have protected. They were parts of old plantations here, as I remember. I'll rig up some kind of shelter in the bush nearby there, and every night I'll go down and pick what we need so that they won't notice. We might be able to survive almost indefinitely."

She sighed. "Indefinitely. Like animals. And how long would it be before we crack, Dorion? How long before we talk each other out and stop? How long before survival becomes the *only* reason for living? Maybe it's different with you, but you can see. The sheer boredom would kill my mind in weeks once we got set up and got a pattern established. I'd flip out, be nothing more than a naked chimp in the wild. We're not living any better than that now. No, I'd rather die than that."

He shrugged. "What other choice is there?"

"Dorion, we have to get out of Masalur. We have to go where they don't control things yet. Not back, though. Not where *they're* going. You lived here in the glory days. There must be decent colonial worlds that aren't a part of the rebellion. Ones with gentle people we might find some help from. You told me yesterday that Coleel hid out from his king and sorcerer and all for like fifteen years. We got to do that, too. You can still navigate, can't you?"

"Yeah, sure, but. . . . What if I pick wrong? The only places that might be likely, and that's just by reasoning it out, are ones to the east. That was the side that they didn't attack from, probably because they didn't have enough allies there. Or we could guess at one right here—if they had to import folks from Covanti to fight, then there's got to be a lot of colonies who didn't want to join up."

"Yeah, but you'd have to call it up from the null. I kind'a think that would draw attention. No, that east is best."

He stared at her. "But that means going right through the camp, across the whole null, and through part of occupied Masalur hub!"

"Yeah," she agreed, "but it would scratch *that* itch in my head. It's gotta be a mess over there, and I can fend for myself in the null. Sam once did something like that. I say try it. If we're caught, we're caught. If not, we at least got a chance at some kind of *life.*"

"All right," he sighed. "Then we'd better eat good and cross in the dark tomorrow. And pray to whatever god you have that all the Stormriders are gone and that there are no magicians in range. Otherwise you'll go back to being a pet, and I'll be at hard labor until I drop."

9
Boolean

There were still a *lot* of people at the border, but a fair number seemed to be male Akhbreed slaves doing massive cleanup and even more massive burials. Apparently, with their furious working, the rebel magicians had created literally thousands of Akhbreed slaves out of both the survivors of the defending army and the locals who lived in the nearest unaffected hub areas. The slave spells were generic, and thus easy to do. They had to obey *any* order by just about anybody who was not Akhbreed, subject to the hierarchy of rebel rank.

Clearly some order and better treatment was already initiated. Large numbers sprawled, asleep, on the grass where not many days before armies had waited, while others seemed to be feeding on the leftovers of the invaders.

They appeared to be mostly males, and although some were very young, they all seemed at least past puberty. What women there were looked old, at least past menopause. Where the younger women and all the children were, Dorion couldn't guess, but he remembered the sentry's comments about breeding programs. The Akhbreed had never done much enslaving of the colonials, primarily because there were far too many of them and far too few Akhbreed, and that required subtler means. But if you could pick out just one race, known on sight by every intelligent being in Akahlar, you might well enslave it and breed it to serve. And all in the name of "justice."

Charley shivered. "This place, this life, isn't fun any more. Thank god at least I can't have kids. Boday's potions killed off my eggs or something."

"Sorcery can always undo alchemy if anybody takes a real interest," he responded. "Remember, the way you look was only streamlined by Boday; it was a product of sorcery at the start. Unravel that spell and the alchemy ceases to exist, like it never was. Don't feel too sure of yourself. You still want to go through with this?"

She nodded. "It's just something I feel I have to do. Or, at least, try."

"I can not disobey your wishes," he noted literally, but without any real enthusiasm.

Getting across the almost half a mile of open area before the null wouldn't be easy; still, Dorion reasoned that the center along the main road was probably the really dense and active area and would remain so; further down, well down, there might be nobody at all.

Indeed, they'd gone no more than a mile in the woods just off the border region when they were out of sight of apparently everybody. Oh, there were some tiny little dots very far off, too far for him to even make out what they were, but he wasn't as concerned with that. Taking her hand, and a deep breath, he walked her out into the open and down towards the null. He didn't rush or run; that might have attracted some attention from folks to whom *they* were just little dots, but his forced walk was brisk and steady and, to her credit, she kept pace with his reduced steps.

Even so, it was about as tense a few minutes' walk as he'd had yet, and he felt tremendous relief when they reached the edge of the null itself. There appeared to be no super alarms, no complex spells or shields, along the border; why bother? The only place you could go was the hub, and that was by now crawling with rebel troops and magicians and would probably be next to impossible. It was something he preferred not to think about until he got there.

Charley felt odd in the null mists; it gave her a sort of limited vision that was quite welcome, and it felt a bit cooler and cleaner, somehow, than the forest they had left. More, her presence in it had a certain *rightness* to it she couldn't explain, not to Dorion, not even to herself. Like, well, that she *belonged* here, doing this. That it was the proper thing to do.

They were too weary and too apprehensive to hurry the crossing, though, taking it nice and leisurely. It was a good twenty miles across, and, while they'd slept, eaten, and drank, they had nothing with them.

They were well out in the null, more than two hours out at least, with the fading "shore" of the colonies behind them looking far off and, now that they were within the hub, shifting and changing every few minutes. They finally decided to rest a bit. She was very tired, but had been waiting for him to call a break. It was only when she realized that he wouldn't call one, carrying out her command, that she called one herself. This mistress stuff was complicated.

"Have you been thinking about where we might go, assuming we make it through?" she asked him.

He nodded, although it was meaningless to her. "There are a couple of possibilities over on that side. Warm, good cover, and natives who didn't have as much of a grudge as many did. Boolean did a lot for Masalur—that's why they had to import troops from Covanti to supplement. He couldn't break the system, of course, but he introduced a large measure of self-government and administration in many of the worlds that had more advanced types, and even allowed colonial ownership on a limited basis of many of the commercial enterprises there. Most colonists hate their Chief Sorcerer; Boolean's probably the first to be more disliked by his fellow Akhbreed than by their subjects. Not that there weren't a few who spurned everything—you saw that type here. The Hedum, for one. But not many, out of hundreds."

"I'm surprised the kingdom let him do any of it."

"They didn't want to, but his power was *enormous* and they wanted to tap that. They let him try it in a couple of places just so they could prove to him how wrong he was, and, in the year or two after he allowed the natives to set up their own shops and keep a lot of their own profits, even from the quotas they furnished to the Akhbreed, productivity increased and unrest went down. When they all worked for the big companies or the government they worked the minimum; when they began working for themselves, on their own land, they worked like demons. They still fought extending it, but he was making headway. Now . . . well, I guess every colonist owns his own, huh? And all quotas abolished."

She nodded. "He sounds like an interesting man."

"Well, interesting has several connotations. He's as nutty as they come, only in his own unique ways, and sometimes he's not at all easy to take, but. . . ." He stiffened and she sensed it.

"What's the matter?"

"Head down and quiet! Somebody or something's coming this way and I can't tell who or what it is."

They hunched down so that the mists covered them and almost held their breaths. Charley could hear now what Dorion had heard, but it sounded odd, like muffled footsteps rather than the steady beat of horses or other beasts. Just a couple of people, very close, although she was certain there had been no one near only minutes before.

The footsteps stopped, and a man's voice, very near them, said, in English, "Well, it's about time! A few more hours and we would have been forced to give you up. I was beginning to doubt Yobi's competency, or yours."

Dorion knew that voice; even in English it was hard to forget it. He poked his head up and saw a man standing there wearing the buckskin outfit of a Navigator and for a moment it threw him. Then he saw the face and said, "Holy shit!"

"And the same to you, Dorion. Get up, Charley. You've been itching to meet me for quite some time so you might as well do so. You can't run from me."

She felt herself rise and turn towards him even though she hadn't really willed herself to move, sort of like a slave spell interacting, and then she saw the speaker with her magic sight, all deep crimson, but not like Dorion's rust-red aura; this was intense, and a churning, throbbing mass. All but a little blob of emerald green that seemed to be perched on his shoulder or someplace like that, and move a little on its own. That part confused and bothered her.

"Come on, you two. Why, Dorion! That's the filthiest I think I've ever seen you, and out of uniform, too. Come on, you two. Boday is waiting for us and we have wasted too much time now. Also, I don't want to run into old Rutanibir, who's lurking all over here of late trying to find me. He's the same old incompetent asshole he always was, but I can't afford any more delays."

Charley found herself following the man and yet terribly confused. Dorion sensed her total befuddlement and said, "Charley—we don't have to go any farther into the hub. That's Boolean. We found him—or he found us."

Boolean! Here! Alive! And with Boday! It seemed too good to be true, coming out of the blue as it was. And yet, after this, *this* was the great Boolean, the wizard of wizards, sorcerer of sorcerers? He sounded so, well, *ordinary,* more like her old high school English teacher. She wondered just what he looked like. Then an unsettling thought hit her, and she whispered to Dorion, "Are you sure? Remember how the adept fooled Boday and me."

Dorion shrugged. "Fairly sure. Might as well accept him, anyway, since if it isn't him, then there's nothing we can do about it."

"You're going to have to tell me how you wound up a slave with a ring in your nose without first being defrocked, Dorion," Boolean said as they walked. "You know the rules of the Guild. You defrocked yourself when it happened. Can't have anyone with the power enslaved." He paused. "Save it for now, though. We have a long journey and a lot of time for stories once we're under way."

Dorion hadn't thought of that angle to slavery. No wonder nobody had spotted him as a magician back at the camp. He wasn't one any more. It was a small loss, but it stung his ego greatly. Still, he wasn't going to admit *that* to Boolean, particularly within earshot of Charley. "H—How'd you find us? And why not sooner if you could?"

Boolean chuckled dryly. "Same old impertinent little twerp, aren't you? Well, you know it was kind of a crowded mess over there, and it was no mean feat keeping myself out of sight and undetected as I watched their little show. I knew where you were and I figured I could just pick you up when I was done. I knew you were there because my spells at the kingdom's borders told me so, and I had one of my associates unobtrusively there to sort of invisibly suggest to Coleel a few courses of action. But Charley vanished in that mess, and then you vanished after her while I was over surveying the damage, and I barely got Boday out of there before Rutanibir was called in. So, with all hell breaking loose and our appearance urgently needed elsewhere, I had to cool my heels and pray that Yobi's spell—which mandated that if anything went wrong Charley was to come to the capital and find me—would lead you into the null. Glad I got you, too, Dorion, but, frankly, you weren't on my priorities list. Once Charley got into the null, though, she was in my element, so to speak. I knew immediately and got here as fast as I could."

"Damn it, she'd just been raped! You expect complete recovery and cold logic from somebody who'd just been through *that?*"

Boolean sighed. "Well, no, but I'm not omniscient, Dorion. I really thought that fellow was far too possessive to allow it. All right, score one for your side. I apologize to the lady, but things were getting critical fast."

Dorion's anger was mollified somewhat by the unexpected concession, but he was still confused about the details. "But—how could you know? That she was in the null, that is?"

"The spell, you poor excuse for a magician! She's keyed to me! That ring makes her mine, right? I sensed it as soon as she entered. I've been looking for it for a couple of days now. Oh—I'm sorry, my dear. Feel free to speak your mind and say what you please. Sorry for the lack of nice introductions, but time is wasting. I'm James Traynor Lang, Ph.D., although here I call myself Boolean. It's one of their silly customs that sorcerers have to have ridiculous trade names."

"I—I hardly know what to say. *What* name did you say?"

"James Traynor Lang, winner of the Nobel Prize in physics and formerly a full professor at the Massachusetts Institute of Technology. You've heard of it?"

"Of the college, yeah. Of you—I'm sorry."

"Well, I'm not surprised. I don't think I won the prize in your world, just in mine. Our worlds are close by, but they're not identical."

"*Your* world! Then you're not from here?"

He laughed. "My dear, almost *none* of the Second Rank sorcerers who amount to much are born and raised here. You've got to be a genius to be a native and a power. No, we're mostly mathematicians, a few physicists, even one engineer, god help me! Different worlds, of course, but all from the upper outplanes. For a while, most all of 'em here had German accents, but in my time English has been the language where much of the big work in math has gone on and it's displaced German as the dominant tongue of the Second Rank—thank heavens. In English we just appropriate whatever local words are handy and invent new ones if needed. In German you have to run together old words to make new ones and it gets unwieldy as hell in this environment. We still have a smattering of old Germans, plus a couple of Italians, a Dane or two, a couple of Russians and even one Japanese—he's the engineer. Ah—there's Boday!"

So that's why English was so popular among the sorcerers! she thought excitedly. Suddenly she didn't feel so alien and alone any more.

"*Charley!*" Boday screamed—her only English word, really—and ran to her, picking her up off the ground and hugging her. "Boday is so happy to see you! That you are all right! We were afraid we would have to desert you here in this desolate place!"

"All right! Calm down!" Boolean shouted. "I wish I could give you time to sleep and feed you filet mignon and get you bathed and rested and all that, but, first of all, my old quarters have been kind of blown to heaven in little particles or changed into tree-lined swamps. Second, in spite of my getting to Boday first, they know where our missing Sam is. She's in a Covantian colony and the only lucky part is that she's stuck in the middle of nowhere in a place that's damned hard to get to, and I had somebody there to slow the bastards down. But time is wasting and it's a long trip, and we still have to beat them or she's dead and probably this was all for nothing. Crim can't keep a whole horde down forever—he's got the same problems with geography they do."

"They've got Second Rank sorcerers," Dorion pointed out. "How come they can't get there by the quicker routes that only sorcerers use well ahead of us?"

"Because they don't know where she is. Without Boday, they're at the mercy of a mercenary bastard free-lancer named Zamofir who's been dogging her the whole way. He found her the same way Crim did, but Crim can't break that damned spell she's under so there was no use in him rushing to her first. He was better used guarding the door. Zamofir's going for the big payoff, biggest of his career. He tells them where and they don't need him any more. Of course, if he fails, he'll be enslaved to the demons in the neth-erhells for a few thousand years of torture, but he's going double or nothing for the big payoff and he knows it."

"Zamofir," Charley repeated. "The little man with the moustache? The bastard who joined up with the raiders on the train?"

"That's him. He's very good at what he does, which is anything at all that pays handsomely. No morals, no scruples, nothing. This is a rare time when he's doing his own dirty work instead of hiring it done, but since he took responsibility he also takes the blame or the reward. Now—Charley, you can ride with Dorion, since you make such an interesting couple. Dorion, lash her down and hold her tight. We're going to have to make real speed here. Boday, you take the point in front since you're my confirmation that we're going correctly, and we'll take the rear. Don't worry about guidance. I'll be handling things."

Dorion took Charley over and guided her foot into a stirrup. She started to help herself up, when she realized it was a pretty low and fairly shaky saddle and froze. Then slowly, she felt *under* the saddle.

"Dorion—there's no horse under this saddle!" she whispered through clenched teeth.

"Yeah, I know. You get used to these things with real sorcerers. You think we could make it by *riding?*"

He hoisted her up, secured her as best he could, then climbed on in back of her. "Hold on," he warned her. "I have a sinking feeling that we're going to go very fast and maybe very high."

"All right," they all heard Boolean's voice as if he were right next to them, "let's get going here. Hang on and don't fall off. We've got close to a thousand miles—two thousand leegs in the local parlance—and with breaks for stretches, food, and drink, and one sleep, it's going to take us two or three days to get there. It's going to be *very* close as it is."

And, with that, the saddles rose straight up in the air, lined up in his predetermined pattern, and paused there for just a moment. Boday was muttering very nervously and Dorion wasn't too thrilled himself. Charley could only imagine the sight, but she could see just how far down the null was.

Boolean sighed and looked back at Masalur hub spread out before him. "It used to be one hell of a town," he muttered. and suddenly the saddles were off like a streak, back across the null, across an unfamiliar colonial boundary, high above the trees and roads, heading back to Tishbaal, back to Covanti, and, eventually, to Sam.

Dorion held her tightly, but Charley had the distinct feeling that he was holding on to her just as much for his own sake as for hers. As for her, her head was still spinning from this rapid and dramatic turn of events; she hadn't had time to collect her thoughts and emotions or even catch her breath.

"Dorion—how is it possible? Are these some kind of saddlelike vehicles or something?" she asked him.

"No, just saddles. They look like ones off army horses."

"Then how—?"

"It's fun to be a sorcerer, Miss Sharkin," Boolean's voice said to her. "Don't worry—you'll get used to it. Besides, it beats broomsticks, even if it is the same general principle."

Charley had met some magicians, and Yobi, of course, but she had not until now experienced the real power that these high ones possessed. Even after all this time in Akahlar, and with all the demons and charms and spells, somebody who could do this, apparently with a wave of his hand, was as shocking and inconceivable to her now as it would have been on the streets of Albuquerque.

And yet, in many ways, it was power from a man who seemed both very friendly and ordinary and yet so callous of lessers, too. He'd lived and done his work in Masalur for many years; he had to know its people, really like both those people and the place itself. All that had been destroyed; whether or not he'd had the power to stop it was not the issue. What *was* the point was that he didn't seem very broken up about the fact that everything and everybody who meant anything to him in Akahlar had just been totally destroyed, and all he could do was make light conversation and comment that it used to be a hell of a town.

Dorion had warned her that Boolean wasn't quite right in the head, but she couldn't help being disturbed by the man's reputation on the one hand as a social critic and reformer and the most vociferous battler of Klittichorn with somebody who could be like that, and she said so to Dorion, not caring if the sorcerer could hear her or not. He *had* given her permission to speak her mind.

"He's always been nearly impossible to figure out, like the other

Second Rank sorcerers," the magician responded. "But he's always hidden a part of himself from even his closest associates. I think he feels it, though. More than he'd admit."

"No, not more than I'd admit," Boolean responded to them. It was eerie how, even with the wind rushing by and them whooshing along at a good clip it sounded like he was right next to them. "This was the most agonizing time I had since I learned how to do miracles. When I first wound up here, I apprenticed in this region and they were all good to me. I was fascinated by the place and by the possibilities. I had a lot of close friends there, and there were a lot of good people rolled over in that mess."

"Well, you knew it was coming," she responded. "You weren't just not at home when it came by accident. Why didn't you warn them to get out?"

"To where? If I started any major evacuation or gave them much warning at all, it would tip Klittichorn that I was on to him. He'd have come in with everything he had right then and there and it would have been far worse even than now. They're in shock, but they're not dead, and a fair number have kept their wits about them. I went back in and sought some of them out—after. Not that easy to do, by the way. They really are absolutely physiologically identical. Fortunately, I knew where to go and what names to call. There will be a ton of mental breakdowns and some suicides and perhaps other problems we can't imagine, but there are enough folks there with level heads and strong personalities to pull it together with hard work. It's better than the alternative."

"Alternative! You sneak out and leave them to be turned into—whatever it is they are. What we heard about them makes them total nonsense."

"Green French porn queens who have been double exposed is about the best I can give it," the sorcerer replied, chuckling a bit at the description. "Yes, I agree, a species that is apparently born animal and becomes plant doesn't make sense, and I have no notion as to what the extra set of arms, let alone breasts, are good for, but we aren't exactly well designed, either. We only make sense because we're the norm to our own selves against which we measure everybody and everything else. We could be designed far more efficiently, I'll tell you. But it's only form, and it's not a bad one considering that many of the results of changewinds I've seen have looked like refugees from a bad Japanese horror movie. I expected far worse. I *did* get as many members of my own staff out as possible, since I didn't want them to lose their power, but some volunteered to stay, both because it was their home and because somebody had to maintain that shield while I was gone for a sufficient time to convince old Rutanibir and his flock that I was still home. The rest I couldn't help. They would have been chewed to pieces in a panic evacuation, and, frankly, the majority are far better off as a new race than as millions of slaves of the new administration."

She hadn't thought of that. "You said it was better than the alternative. You mean total slavery?"

"Oh, no. Klittichorn's been getting very good at using the maelstrom effect of the practice changewinds his princess has been calling up all over the place. In between the outplanes, dead center in the storm, it's a calm, almost a sort of vacuum cleaner effect. She's been quite good at putting it where he wanted it and he's been very neatly scooping up what he needed and dropping it down to him here. The effect is hard to explain, but you have at least experienced it. It's what he used to pick *you* up. You remember dropping through the maelstrom to Akahlar. It's a natural phenomenon of the wind, which has picked up and dropped a ton of stuff on Akahlar and the colonies and the lower outplanes over the millennia, including probably the first Akhbreeds. There's some evidence that nothing is actually native to Akahlar; this is, as I once told you, the ass end of the universe. Among the things he's picked up, other than people, are heavy weapons and ammunition and, among other things, a few thermonuclear devices."

She was shocked. "You mean atom bombs?"

"They're primitive. They are hydrogen at least. And it didn't take him long to figure out how to bypass the fail-safe mechanisms and replace them with his own, either. He didn't wind up down here with just the shirt on his back, you know. Among the things that came with him because they were caught in the same vortex was his portable computer and much of his current notes and fancy mathematical programs. That's what's made him a top dog so quickly. Once he grasped the basic mathematics of magic here, he was able to build and solve enormous equations with the thing, far beyond the abilities of even the greatest mathematical minds here. Once he had a little experience, he could work out how to do just about anything and knock over any big-shot sorcerer who stood in his way. And, of course, he *is* a genius, one of the rare true ones. Another Einstein, da Vinci, or Fermi at least."

"Smarter even than you?" she asked him, wondering about his reaction.

"Oh, my, yes. Certainly. Although I am one of the few minds capable of not only understanding but using and perhaps refining his work. I, for example, never dreamed it was possible to enter the Maelstrom through the weak point after it had passed, but once I saw that he could, well, I figured out the way. That relative intellectual position, alas, is why all of this came to be. In a way, it's all my fault, although I have days when I wonder if that is entirely true. Certainly some basic defects in my character helped shape this crisis. You see, I'm a very good wizard, my dear. I'm just not a very good man."

And slowly, as the miles passed far beneath them, Charley learned what lay behind all this mess, and it was sadder still for being so, well, petty.

Lang had been a professor at Princeton at the time; a boy genius—he'd had his Ph.D. and his voter's card at about the same time, and had already accomplished a lot by the time he first met the man who was to become his enemy.

Lang's interests lay in the far edge of theoretical physics; the kind of pure intellectual activity in which men still sat in small offices and thought deep thoughts and imagined the unimaginable and then built mathematical and computer models to illustrate various principles that, in fact, probably had no practical application ever, and in which only the mathematics would ever indicate whether or not they were right, or had wasted their whole lives on a falsehood.

He became particularly attracted to a relatively new field called Chaos Science, which sought to really explain the unexplainable. How could a random explosion of dense matter from the monoblock that created the universe form into such a useful and beautiful pattern, with its own very comfortable natural laws and limitations? Why did the freezing of water vapor form such complex and beautiful crystalline structures, and why were no two apparently exactly alike? Order, often highly complex order, almost always resulted from the most random events. There had to be a law, or a set of laws, that explained it, at least to a degree.

Doctor Lang became a leading theoretician of the relatively new science, and, as such, those also interested in it wanted to study under him. Among them, and the best of them, was a young Cambodian refugee born Kieu Lompong, who adopted the Americanized first name of Roy, a combination he joked he'd gotten by playing with numerological tables. He was young, intense, brilliant, but with no social life and no outside interests and, most of all, Boolean noted, no sense of humor at all.

Little wonder. As a child, he'd already been to hell, having seen his parents slowly hacked to death in front of him while black-clad revolutionary soldiers held him and made him watch, then put into virtual slavery in the rice paddies where he had to pretend to be a peasant and disguise his genius at all costs, for the new rulers killed the whole intellectual class.

He had finally escaped, and his genius had been recognized in the refugee camp, and he was made one of the exceptions to be brought to the United States under foster care of distant relatives who now lived there. His now unshackled brilliance produced an even greater rise in academic achievement than had Lang's; he was, under Lang, a Ph.D. candidate at the age of seventeen.

Under Lang's tutelage, and with access to the big university computers, Roy Lompong, in just a few short months, was able to come out with something that apparently had been percolating in his head for years; a unifying mathematical principle, a single equation, in its own area as significant as Einstein's in his, that unified and revolutionized the whole chaos science community. The thing was, he was in such a pure intellectual area that he didn't realize what kind of a breakthrough he'd made. To him, it was just a tool to use in studying specific phenomena. It was a whole new mathematics that made work in the field really amount to something in much the same way as Newton had invented calculus just so he could do the mathematical proofs of the theories he was interested in. Instantly obvious to Lang, it nonetheless would never have occurred to him. And yet, only the Princeton team knew it.

"He was so wrapped up in his projects on the creation of the universe, already with the best minds in the field, and he simply never got around to publishing it. He'd stopped reading the literature anyway; it was all beneath him, in the same way that Hemingway wouldn't bother to ever read Doctor Seuss. But I was his advisor and the head of his doctoral committee. And it *was* published, under my name, with Roy and three others credited with assists, just a few months after he got his degree and accepted a chair at Cal Tech. I doubt if he was even aware of the furor the article caused—his head was always in the clouds. In fact, I think it wasn't until three years later, when I got the Nobel for it, that it really hit him what I'd done."

Charley gasped. "You *stole* his idea? And took full credit for it?"

"Yep. And the money and the worldwide acclaim and all the rest. I mean, they looked at me with my reputation, and they looked at this twenty-one-year old who was my 'protegé,' and drew the obvious but wrong conclusions. It wasn't the first time it was done. In fact, it's done all the time—it's just rare to win the Nobel for it, and particularly in so short a time. I did, and he flew into a rage about it. It was his life's work to date and it was all his, and I'd taken it from him. More importantly, I'd hit him right in his Asian sense of honor. The fact that it was done fairly often didn't mean that he knew that. That the young discoverers often get professorships and posts elsewhere as rewards by their tutors who take the credit. It's not science, it's a crooked way of getting ahead in money, power, and prestige in the university environment. And he had no forum. Oh, the news was interested in his accusations about me, for about three days. But when the newsmen discovered they couldn't even comprehend the basics of what I'd stolen, it was old news fast. And the scientific and academic community, well, they were more comfortable with good old establishment me than with young firebrand Lompong, whom they'd hardly heard of. What he was doing just wasn't done—not cricket, old boy. You'll get your turn later. You see where it got him."

"Yeah. Nowhere. So Klittichorn's from the same world as you, huh? You must have a pretty nasty home world from what you say about those soldiers and his parents and all that. I never even heard of the country you said he was from."

"It's irrelevant. Your world's history and ours diverge quite sharply because of various key assassinations and a major nasty war we lost that yours didn't fight, but yours had its share of misery as well. All of them do. At any rate, I went from obscurity in an obscure field to department head at a quarter of a million bucks a year at M.I.T., and I was on top of the world. He was a bad boy, bitter at his colleagues as much as at me, bitter about everything. He became unglued and started thinking about some practical applications for his theories. He went up to Livermore Labs, which is a think tank run by the university for the government; it's where they sit around and invent new bigger and better terror weapons. They have a hell of a budget, though—as close to bottomless as you can get—and among the most sophisticated computers the world ever dreamed of. I'm not sure what led him to it, but he got real interested in crazy phenomena. The wolf boy in Germany, people disappearing in full view of onlookers, spontaneous human combustion, rains of frogs—all sorts of weird stuff. A fellow named Charles Fort used to write books on it. Unexplained appearances and disappearances and odd-ball phenomena of every sort."

"Flying saucers and stuff."

"That, too, but there's a lot weirder and more substantiated stuff as well. Somehow, in trying to explain it, he hit upon the theory of the changewind and its key maelstrom. I don't think he was prepared for the changewind effect, but the multidimensional effect, the worlds over worlds, tied in with other areas of new physics. He wanted the primal cause, the mechanism, for random events, both major and minor, to tie it in with overall chaos theory. He needed Livermore's computers to finish the work, and somehow he managed to convince some politicians that it had weapons potential. Maybe he *had* a weapon in mind from the start—I don't know. But it boiled down to a practical experiment many years ago out on the Nevada test ranges, where they blew up the atom bombs. Some kind of device, maybe part Tesla and part Lompong, that would create a weak spot in the dimensional walls. He got more than he bargained for. He drew a changewind, and he was dead center in it, and he dropped all the way down to here. They say the whole plateau just vanished with everything on it, leaving only virgin-colored sheetrock."

"Tesla?"

"Nikola Tesla, one of the types like Einstein, so much a genius we have units of measure in science named for him. He was obsessed with controlling the weather and, back before the turn of the century, and in full view of everybody, he did. But his device was banned, its principles still classified to this day, even to people like me, and experiments in that are even banned today in the Geneva Convention. The connection of weather and magnetic forces and fields should not be lost on you."

"Well, I think I'm sort of following it," she told him, fascinated but not real sure. "It's still magic to me, though."

"Magic has rules, Charley. That's why you need the charms and amulets sometimes or the magic words to focus the spell or anything else. Before the miracle can take place, the priest must incant and say *'Hocus Pocus!'* That's all a magic spell is, either in the legends and racial memories and religious rites that are all that's left in our world, and the spells here that do almost anything—if you can figure them out. Roy had a leg up. He recognized the spells here as being a variant form of his own mathematics. Unlike the ones here, he had his computer and much of his notes and a thorough grounding in conventional science and physics in particular. It's probable that the Akhbreed were mathematical geniuses with a high order civilization while ours was still in caves or maybe worse off. Over the years here, they lost much of their ancient knowledge, becoming fat and static, unmoving, comfortable with their spells and their empires. Most science vanished, leaving only the sorcery, as happened many times, apparently, with many civilizations. The main thing here was—the magic still worked, if you had sufficient mathematical aptitude to use it. The better your aptitude, the higher you rose in the magical priesthood. That's the difference between Dorion, here, and me. I can solve equations thousands of lines long in my head. He couldn't add two and two without pen and paper."

Dorion bristled. "Come on! I'm not *that* bad!"

"Uh-huh. Well, it's higher math, I admit, but you can't keep a ten variable equation in your head, so your spells have to be looked up and done step by step out of a cookbook. Your highest achievement was a unique formula that gave everybody electric shocks."

"Okay, you two! Enough!" Charley responded. "Those electric shocks came in handy on this trip, sir, which is more than you did. I mean, if you knew all this and could sneak out, and you can fly and all that, then why did we have to suffer like we did all this time, and go through the hell we went through?"

Boolean sighed. "It's hard to explain. It was only a few months ago that, quite by accident, I discovered I was being conned. That the substantial and hostile Second Rank presences I felt all around the border were being faked. Roy came up with some kind of projection device. I can't begin to imagine what or how, but he did. It only betrayed itself as a convincing false signal when he had to do that close-in demonstration of how he could guide and project a changewind over in Qatarung. It caused him to lose contact for a while with his illusion, caused all sorts of flickering in and out of it. Until then, I was convinced that I would have to face several of my colleagues and maybe Roy himself if I stepped out of there, and they sent that message loud and clear. Even when I *did* find out, it didn't do me much good. Between my duties here to an increasingly nervous king and country, as it were, and my attempts to find out just who was working for Klittichorn and what they were planning, I didn't have much time to spare. I was also trying to track down just where his projector was. In the back of my mind, I figured that if you all got in any real trouble I could break off and either get you out or send some of my adepts to do it. Then, when Sam just sort of vanished off the map, as it were, we went frantic. I'm afraid your side just got lower priority."

"Thanks a lot," she said dryly.

"Well, without Sam this isn't going to mean anything. With her, then you have a certain importance as well."

"Me!"

"Wait a while. We'll get to it. I think, in fact, that if we can beat them to Sam this might well all work out for the best. Enough for now. Suffice it to say that you aren't *crucial* to the scheme, but you are none the less important."

He would say no more on it, and she finally didn't press, but it started her mind wondering like crazy and coming up with the most outrageous, and unappetizing, possibilities.

Eating with a Second Rank sorcerer was an experience as well. He just picked a clear, remote, uninhabited spot and set them down, and, almost with a wave of his arms and a few mumbled phrases of sheer nonsense, materialized a full table complete with hot dishes, silverware, and the right wines, all uninterrupted by company, weather, or even ants and flies. It was pretty bizarre, but they were the best meals any of them had enjoyed since Covanti hub. Nothing to wash or clear away, either—another few waves and incantations and it was gone.

Boolean could say what he wanted about physics and math and chaos theories; this was sheer fairytale magic.

It was at the first meal stop, too, that she discovered that the green fuzz had not only a life of its own, but a voice that was so deep and raspy it sounded like a small child speaking by continuously belching. Dorion described the creature, whose name was Cromil, as a small pea-green monkey with jackass ears and a nose that resembled an eggplant. A longtime companion of and familiar to Boolean and his remote "eyes," in much the same way as Shadowcat, he was not nearly the quiet type that the cat had been, although he disliked speaking around strangers more than he had to.

"You just *love* to show off, don't you, you big ham," Cromil croaked as Boolean did the meal with extra flourishes.

Boolean chuckled. "That's why I keep Cromil around. He keeps me in my proper place because he doesn't care what happens to him."

"You need me more than I need you," the creature reminded him. "Without me, who would act as intermediary with the netherhells? Who'd make the best deals with all those imps and demons you love to use?"

Now, at the one rest and sleep stop Boolean had decided upon for all their sakes, Charley and Dorion were both at last able to get themselves clean of days of grime and garbage. The sorcerer had merely picked, not materialized, the waterfall and pools, but he'd made certain that the water was both warm and pure, and he even provided her with scented soap. It seemed to Dorion that she was *never* going to get out of the water, and that she was going to compulsively scrub her skin completely off. He was out and dried off long before she first considered coming out, and that meant he had to play lifeguard for her.

It was Boday, as usual, who gave him an answer. "Boday felt the same way after those foul beasts had her on the rocks back in the Kudaan," she whispered in his ear. "We all did, but Charley, she did not experience what we went through. Now she has. She is trying to wash them out of her. All of them out of all of her. She will not succeed, any more than Boday has even after all this time, but, let her try. Sooner or later she will realize that, once you have been violated like that, you can never wash it all away."

It explained much, but left Dorion with the same confusion over the sexes he'd always had. Charley'd been a whore, damn it. One, two guys some days, for a year, and after that she'd screwed almost anything with a male voice and it hadn't been anything *but* fun, and most of the countless guys she'd had were strangers, too, about which she'd known little or nothing. Hell, she even did sexy come-ons to the townies and border guards. And yet, somehow, that gang-bang orgy with her at the center back at the camp had been different, had really changed her. It was one thing for a violent-type guy to stalk and pounce on a woman, any woman, and force himself on her. That he could understand. But, damn it, if you're going to glory in being a sex object and advertise the fact, how'd this one really differ except that they were rougher, cruder, and smellier. It wasn't even the bruises and soreness she still had—it was something inside, like Boday said. There was something new—fear, maybe, although she still had guts enough to cross that camp and go into the null and a personality decisive enough to shape her own destiny if she could. Maybe it wasn't fear. Maybe it was doubt. Self-doubt.

Maybe it was just that the one night back there at camp she had to face what she really had become—and what she'd been all along—and she didn't like it. He wondered.

He'd been fascinated at what Boolean had been telling her. The man had always been very chatty, but Dorion had trouble following this story and all its references, even though Charley apparently knew what he meant. All those references, even though they didn't come from the same worlds. Who or what was an Einstein or a Tesla, and what was so wonderful about a Nobel Prize, whatever that was, that it would cause such misery? And what was so unusual about mysterious appearances and disappearances and frog rains and the like? Hell, they happened all the time. . . .

For Charley, the sudden rescue from the continual bottom of the heap she'd been forced into for so long had come first as a shock and now as a joy. She no longer was even all that nervous about falling off the damned saddle, although, tied in as she was and short of aerial saddle fights, there was little chance of that. Being able to talk with someone, even one of great power with a surface personality that was pleasing, masking something she knew she could never really comprehend, and being treated as an equal, at least for social purposes, by that man was something she hadn't really thought she'd ever experience again. It little mattered that he came from a world which had known far more wars and experienced even more tyranny than hers—whose last major war, except a few banana republic ones, was the one against the Germans and Japanese. Or that had apparently successfully somehow torn its way from England in revolution back in the Seventeen Hundreds sometime and as a result had had to fight a bloody civil war over slavery in the middle Eighteen Hundreds instead of being forced to obey the British abolition back in the Thirties, and had something called a Congress instead of a parliament.

But by their common times there were more similarities than differences. She knew Einstein and MIT and Cal Tech, and there were a lot more similarities than differences between them now from her point of view. He was no more out of touch with rock 'n' roll, or TV stars, or fashion than anybody else who'd been stuck here and out of touch for thirty years.

But that did bring up the question of just how *he* had come to be here.

When Lompong had vanished along with all his project and a lot of technicians and army people and the like, there had been consternation. The only man who might decipher Lompong's work and figure it out was Lang.

Lang himself was fascinated with the result when he was told of it by high security people and couldn't resist. However, while there were gigabytes of material in Lompong's computer areas, how it all tied together was a mystery. Worse, thanks to his experience with Lang, some key material, perhaps *the* key material, was encoded in a way even Lompong's bosses didn't know about. Not until they tried to break it and wound up activating an insidious set of computer "viruses" that began to systematically destroy not only all the data but the entire data base series of the Livermore computer system, right down to the payroll information and budget trackers. There were backups, of course, but they had now destroyed two and had only one left. Lang looked but could not touch, even though he pointed out that data that was so highly protected was useless anyway unless the scheme was cracked. No deal. One had to remain—and that was the way it was.

Still, while nobody really knew how Lompong's mind worked, Lang had the closest idea, and he was able to do a lot of work, laboriously, interpolating from papers, conversations from associates not swallowed up in the "incident," and the disparate data bases you *could* use without the data being eaten. It was fascinating; so much so that he was on long leave from MIT and working full time on it. After three years, he thought he'd gotten at least the general idea behind what his old pupil was trying to do, and he was taking a break, driving to Las Vegas for a conference there—Boolean, it appeared, had no trouble with flying saddles but never liked airplanes—and it happened.

"It was late but I was feeling good, and driving always cleared my mind and got out my frustrations," he reminisced. "It happened very suddenly and at about seventy-five miles an hour. One moment I was on the Interstate, the next thing I knew I was surrounded by pitch dark and I had the damnedest feeling I was falling, only slowly. I slowed to a stop, which did nothing, opened the window, and got the dry air of the maelstrom, although I didn't know it then. I opened the door, looked down, and closed it again and just stayed there, scared to death. I don't know what I thought—that maybe I'd crashed and was going to hell in an automobile or something. It went on and on and on, and then I landed, not hard but with a bump that bounced the shocks all to creation and me with it, and suddenly I'm sitting on solid ground surrounded by the damnedest fog you ever saw right up to the door handles. Fog—in Nevada! Well, I knew I wasn't in Nevada and the only way to find out where was to drive there."

"You came down in a null? But I thought changewinds didn't cross nulls."

"They don't, but the weak spots gravitate there before they dissipate, sometimes hours, or even days, later, so you always land *down* in a null, just as you did. It has a lot to do with magnetic fields but I think you'd need a lot more classroom before I could explain it to you. At any rate, I drove a while, and finally I saw the lights of a border crossing and drove right to it, and became the first, and to my knowledge, only individual ever to drive up to the Masalurian or any other entry station. I think the two guys on duty there were more terrified than I was. Naturally, I didn't know Akhbreed and they didn't know English, but they decided that the car had to be the product of a powerful sorcerer, so they treated me nice, gave me some wine and chocolates out of their own lunches, and sent word to the Chief Sorcerer in a hurry. The adepts at least knew there'd been a changewind in the colonies the night before and figured some outplaner had been caught and they were right. Karl was an old Prussian from some world that I was never quite sure about, and my German wasn't great but it was passable, and that's how I started on the road to becoming the great and powerful Wizard of Oz."

"Hold it." Dorion put in. "Even *I* know enough to know that the odds of you just happening on a changewind that far up the outplane is about like the odds of all of us being carried off by giant moths."

"Slimmer. I didn't just 'happen' into it, though. Apparently Roy had an even easier time of it here than I did at the start and he figured out the system in record time. Most important, he knew more about the changewinds than they did here—here they were scared silly of them, since it was the one random event over which the spells had no control or effect. I know that some of his party and most of his equipment was smashed when he got here—and the rest was useless because of a lack of power—but he'd saved his portable computer, and he knew the mathematics of magic better than anybody, having independently reinvented it in what seemed to have been a streamlined and vastly improved version. He went after me, Dorion. Who knows how many nets he cast before he got me? How many disasters and disappearances and freak weather he caused before he finally figured out how to nail me exactly? He wanted me here, with him the master now, and me the cowering subject. It didn't turn out that way, though, first because it's tough to guide the maelstrom in the outplane and have any control over where the weak point drifts, shifts, and gyrates here. You can even shift weak points and come out in the wrong spot. I did that deliberately with Sam and you, Charley; Klittichorn did it by accident with me. And Karl was much too strong for him to take on right then, particularly since Roy hadn't made any friends here, either. Again, too strong too fast."

"He learned, though," Dorion noted.

"Oh, yes. He plays the social and political game better than I ever could now. In fact, he has a much higher tolerance for what passes for intellect here than I do, and no real aversion to the system he sees. He doesn't care, so long as he's on top. Twice he'd been thwarted by mastering the technical and ignoring the social and cultural requirements; he's not about to get stung a third time. Underneath, though, he hates them—he hates all of them who don't acclaim him as a virtual god, as two-bit hacks like Rutanibir do. The Akhbreed system must revolt him; every time he saw it in action he must have flashed back to his own childhood under the terror regime. It finally occurred to him that he survived then by playing the tyrant's games until opportunity presented itself. Now he's played the Akhbreed and sorcerer's Guild like a well-tuned orchestra. There's only one person he really fears in all creation, and that's the man who cheated him twice. To him, I'm the only man who could possibly cheat him a third time—and he's right. But the deck's so stacked I'm not certain, even if everything now goes right, that I can do it. I only know I've got to try."

"Not much chance of an all-out attack on everybody now, is there?" Dorion asked hopefully. "I mean, consider the losses here. A lot of the colonials aren't going to be too thrilled about signing up with him after word of this gets around."

"You mistake him, then," Boolean responded. "He doesn't care about this rebellion, and he's no liberator. He's had to play that game as well to keep them loyal, and get the men and materiel he needed, and to keep the loyalty of the Storm Princess. But that child, when born, will screw him up royally. If he doesn't get Sam, he won't wait, army or no army, position or no position. He'll simply convince his people that all is ready whether it is or not, and if he wants something passionately he can do it. Take out the hubs and the majority of Second Rank sorcerers and let the rebellion come later, that's all. The Akhbreed can never hold the colonies if they don't hold the hubs anyway. He really doesn't care."

"Then—what is his real motive?" Charley wanted to know.

"I've caught up with him, I think, and corrected most or all of my wrong assumptions about his work. I got into his maelstrom and got you out and I managed to trigger the burst early on your world so you'd be sucked down in the center instead of destroyed. I think I know more about how this whole thing works than anybody alive except Roy himself, and that's the trouble. Klittichorn is an ancient Khmer deity from the pre-Buddhist days, one of many but a powerful one. He took the name, I'm convinced, not as a mark of humor, since he has none himself, nor out of nostalgia, either. Countless sorcerers have died or been horribly mutilated and destroyed going for the First Rank. The best have been sucked down through the netherhells to the Seat of Probability itself, where they have been crushed in a universe that could possibly fit in a sand bucket. I think Roy has cracked it. I think he may be the only mind capable of cracking it. I think the destruction of the hubs and the release of massive changewind power, enough power, possibly, to destroy or transform beyond any recognition not only

Akahlar but possibly the outplanes as well, as part of a plan. A careful, premeditated plan. There was always a touch of the Oriental mystic in him. He seemed upset that his own theories seemed to preclude any need for any gods at all.

"I think he wants to rewrite the bottom line. I think he wants to fill in the gap and redo the cosmos to his own designs. I think he's convinced he's found the way to the First Rank and the replacement of pure chaos with a true regulating governor. Having been convinced that there are no gods, he now intends to supply at least one. And if you want to know what kind that would be, well, all I know about Klittichorn the god is what he told us in conversations long ago about his ancient culture, and, as I remember it, Klittichorn was a god of absolutes not easily appeased, and human sacrifice was clearly part of his requirements."

"Jesus!" Charley swore.

"Uh-huh, but if you need more motivation, consider this. It appears that the detachment of Khmer Rouge soldiers, who tortured and murdered his parents in front of him and kept him for over a year in a slave labor battalion, were composed mostly, or entirely, of young women, many if not most mere teenagers. He always exhibited a great deal of hostility towards women, and we weren't sure what was going on inside him. Unless he's mellowed, which I doubt, it must eat his guts out to have to play up to the Storm Princess. The conventional explanation around Princeton was that his experiences had made him a confirmed homosexual, but there were those who saw such hostility in him that they, mused that he had the potential to explode in a different direction. Possibly as a rapist or serial killer of young women or something even more creative. It's a curious pathology, a mixture of hatred and fear. You can understand, I think, what it must mean to him that a young woman is his greatest threat, and yet that fear level is such that it might well explain why you two kept slipping from his grasp. I don't think he's exploded yet. I think he's tried to make himself an automaton, to even believe he's above sex and emotions of any sort. But—imagine if he attains First Rank, Charley. Not a god, but Roy Lompong with the powers of a god. What will keep him from exploding *then*?"

10
Reunions

It was raining out. It was usually raining out, at least half the time, between the jungle and the sea, and it didn't really bother her that much. She really didn't feel much like doing anything these days except lying around; keeping house for the boys was more than enough work for her, and if she really needed help she could shoot a simple flare and have one of the other wives run to her.

The place was as clean and straight as she could make it. She prided herself on doing it all each day, if only to prove to herself and to others that she was still capable of things. You had to keep at it; with the mud and constant dampness, any missed spots would be seized as high ground by mold and fungi and general jungle rot. At least now she understood why the people who were native to jungle areas hadn't ever bothered with much in the way of clothes or the like and had lived in simple huts of grass and bamboo. The forces of the living jungle, fed by the constant heat and humidity, attacked almost anything vulnerable.

And things *were* pretty loose here. The boys had one set of stock clothes apiece which they kept in a sealed trunk and put on just for important visitors, and they'd worn them that first day, but now things had gotten loose again and, frankly, the village was basically a nudist colony, which suited her just fine.

Bugs weren't a real problem so long as you kept the netting on the doors and windows and remembered to rub a potion on the stilts once a month so nothing wanted to crawl up it. The floors were of a rock-hard native wood that insects didn't bother, although it warped a bit and wasn't ideal in its primary use. The walls were of a bamboolike plant, the roof was some kind of woven grasses over a rust-proof metallic webbing, and it was waterproof. Inside ventilation was by a clever series of permanently netted openings that let some light and all the air through but caught most of the rain and all of anything else. It was enough that only a central oil lamp was needed to pretty well illuminate the place.

It had only a single interior, but it was fairly spacious, the only thing blocking free access was a thick pole rising from the ground below, though the floor, and up to the roof center. There were two sets of bunk beds over to one side—handmade affairs of the same wood as the floor, with criss-crossed and tightly bound vines providing the support for thin and well-worn mattresses. She didn't know what the mattresses were made of, but they looked like some kind of soft vinyl, the only plastic stuff she'd seen here and so it probably wasn't, and she had no idea what they were filled with but they held the human body, even her, fairly comfortably. They had ordered her a bed weeks ago, but she didn't care when it arrived. All four were seldom home at the same time and she had whichever lower she wanted.

Other than that, there was a large round table, also of the same irregular wood and looking hand-carved, with four matching chairs and one obviously cobbled from another set somewhere; a large chest with all sorts of clay pots, gourds, and the like, and another with a set of well-worn and dented pots, pans, plates, and utensils. A makeshift cupboard and shelves held some fruit, containers of dried meat, and some jar-sealed delicacies. Without a refrigerator or freezer there wasn't much else you could keep around. Food was caught or picked from the Company common stores which were constantly restocked, the men of the camp taking turns doing the required hunting, fishing, and the like. The women were supposed to plant and tend and pick the gardens and citrus grove, and tend to the *miriks,* a chickenlike bird that thrived here and gave regular fine-tasting eggs. Then they would pick up and deliver what they needed at the end of the day for the next day's food.

Cooking was done on a wood stove on the porch, where the smoke could easily disperse. It was of stone and reminded her of nothing as much as the most elaborate permanent backyard barbecue she'd ever seen. Still, with a little instruction from the other women, she'd had no trouble in mastering it pretty well, and getting to know the seasonings and oils and herbs and spices by eye, as well as how to cook without getting spattered or asphyxiated. She'd gotten real good real fast because she'd been a cook for Boday all that time, and because she was very eager to learn and please.

Over to one side was a partially finished project with the basic tools for the carpenter's job set in a case next to it. She'd always been a fair carpenter and the crib was taking real shape, but she was finding herself too easily frustrated and upset by little things, and she just hadn't been able to keep at it. She knew she'd let the boys finish it, although it bothered her. She was proud that she still did all the same work as the others, that she could be "normal." Of course, she had thought that she would handle the later stages of pregnancy better than she had; what was a little more weight and tummy when she already carried so much? It wasn't like that, though. After a while you hardly thought about the fat, but this was like a bowling ball that didn't move exactly the same as you did. Dead weight that shifted suddenly and wrongly and threw you off balance and made you permanently a little uncomfortable, and you didn't get used to it.

She heaved herself out of the chair, got her cup, and lumbered over to the door where there were two amphoras, each containing a supply of pretty good wine—one white, one red. Covantians seemed to live on wine, and to be able to produce a drinkable product somehow in the damnedest places. They mostly looked kind of American Indian, but she was certain that they must somewhere have had common ancestors with the French or Italians. She didn't like drinking so much alcohol, for the sake of the kid, but these were deliberately fairly weak, and they were here and running water was not.

Central wells provided the water, which was taken in large gourds on the head back to each hut. She'd gotten quite good at carrying fairly heavy burdens on her head, and so each day as needed she'd climb down the ladder after lowering the vine-rope-supported platform that served as a kind of dumb-waiter, get her own food from the stores, and get what water she needed as well. The fact that she managed this while being now so hugely pregnant was a matter of pride to her, and she wanted to do it as long as she was the least able. It was one of her jobs, her duties. At least now, with the boys out on the boat for up to four days at a stretch, it was mostly just getting stuff for her, although she missed them.

It was a very primitive life, with no amenities, full of constant work just to keep in the same place, and yet she was happy and content with it. She did not want to do anything else or be anyone else. She understood her place, what was expected of her and what was not, all her duties and responsibilities, and it was all she wanted, all she could be. She, like the others, was the perfect Covantian wife, and the spell allowed for nothing less than true belief. She wanted nothing else because she could not; she acted and thought as she did because she could think no other way.

That went as well for her sexual nature. Women no longer attracted her; she could not really remember how they once did, although she remembered it. Men, who had never really attracted her before, now seemed attractive, alluring, sexy; their moves, even their mannerisms, fascinated her, and she felt real lust at times with all those naked guys around.

Of course, her now being hugely pregnant had only allowed for so much, and they were more concerned than she was about hurting the kid, but they'd had some fun anyway and she'd managed some oral tricks. Still, she dreamed and fantasized about after the child was born, when they could truly unite with her.

Oddly, those fantasies particularly pleased her, as did the unusual, for her, eroticism brought on by things even vaguely phallic. For the first time, she had feelings like the other girls had; for the first time, she was over on Charley's side with the "normal" folks. For the first time, she felt like she fit in, and it gave her an enormous sense of inner peace and a feeling of belonging. She had approached it at Pasedo's with her memory gone, but her sexual nature had still stood in the way.

Until now, nobody had really understood her, including herself. Even Etanalon's magic mirror had drawn its basics from her, and since she was confused so it could only work with what it had. It wasn't that she was this Storm Princess, or that she wanted to run from responsibility. It was rather that she'd always been an outsider, a totally square peg, even back home, and even more so in this far more structured and restrictive society. Nobody who didn't always feel different and abnormal—and was—could ever understand that, and only now, when she was in all ways as "normal" as the other girls here, or the ones she was likely to meet, did she herself truly understand her own longing.

If anything, she was more "normal" than Charley had ever been. Charley would look down her nose at this kind of life. She never needed or wanted a husband or anything that smacked of convention, that was clear from the way she'd gone and kept going on this world. The funny thing was, Boday was more a model for Charley, love potion or no love potion. Boday had talents, not all of which were of the noblest sort it was true, and she'd carved her way by force of will, brains, and without any magical powers, into a position where she was totally in control of her life, and really needed no one even in this traditional, male-dominated society. Yeah, that's where things had taken a wrong turn at the start. Boday and Charley were kind of natural partners, or at least soulmates; she hadn't even fit in with Boday. Not sexually—Boday had been straight until she'd gulped that potion, as straight as Charley—but even in that they both had the same basic lack of regard for men as anything more than sex partners and certainly no desire for long-term commitments. Not that Boday hadn't married guys—it was practically a hobby with her—but she dumped them just as quick when lust cooled down.

Well, that was the two of them. She'd had another option chosen for her, but it was one that meshed with and quieted her own inner demons. She hadn't even had any of those Storm Princess dreams since, nor did she feel the rain or other storms now any more than ordinary people had. Whatever powers she had were gone with her old life, and she felt freed by that as well.

She sat uncomfortably in a chair at the table and picked up a worn and weathered deck of playing cards. Cards here weren't like the ones back home; for one thing, they had ones to fifteens in five suits and looked more like Tarot cards than regular ones, but by removing the extras she could make a fifty-two card four-suited deck and, by now, she was more than used to the suits and knew the funny squiggles for the proper numbers. She shuffled the cards and dealt them on the table in the familiar pattern of Klondike like her father used to play. She knew and had played a lot of solitaire games from back when she was living with Boday. They were good time-passers when she didn't feel like doing much else, although lately she'd been taking them much too seriously. Somehow she wasn't in full control of her emotions any more, and it didn't seem to be the spell. The other girls said it was a natural part of the last stages of being pregnant, but it was the hardest of all to take.

Any little things that seemed to go wrong, even the most petty little shit, and she'd wind up crying and getting depressed for long periods. She'd bawled more at nothing the last few weeks than she had at any time since she herself was a baby. Sometimes she'd get suddenly feeling real insecure. even paranoid, and she'd huddle there and shake with fear and finally, if she couldn't stand it any more, she'd manage to get down and go over to Putie's as fast as possible just for company and a hug.

Other times, just as suddenly, she would have an enormous need to just be totally alone and get real introspective, like now.

It worked the other way, too. Sometimes with other people she just couldn't stop talking and talking even if she had nothing else really to say, and the littlest things would strike her as enormously funny, and she'd laugh abnormally long and hard to get the giggles and be unable to stop. And all the extremes might come one after the other, like somebody throwing a switch.

It bothered her, but she didn't really want to intrude on the others, particularly since Quisu was just getting over having her own kid, a boy with the lungs of a lumberjack, and had her own hands full, and Putie'd had hers, a daughter, just three days ago and was in pretty poor shape, while Meda was due any day now. All had their men, or most of them, around as well and that made her long for her own husbands, all of whom were out working double duty to fill in for the guys attending their own wives back here.

The fact was, nobody really knew when she was due. She'd not looked at a calendar, let alone a watch, in so long she had no sense of how much time had gone by except that it seemed like years and was definitely less than nine months. For that reason they'd rigged up a bell on the porch so if she suddenly felt the baby coming, she could summon help in a hurry. They'd all offered to take her in while the boys were away, but with all those other men around she felt more comfortable here. It wasn't modesty, just feeling too much like a stranger intruding on somebody else. She'd seen and even helped with the babies, though, and she wanted her own real bad.

Still, she worried. She worried about her old friends and what might have become of them, and she worried about her own eventual safety, since she knew that while *she* might have changed, the child inside had not, as evidenced by the thunder and lightning all around the place when she kicked. Mostly, though, she worried about the impending birth. Not that she wouldn't be more than happy to have it over with, but she'd sat there by Quisu and then Putie, and it didn't look like much romance or fun at all. In fact, it looked awful enough that if she had some way of backing out of it, she certainly would have lost her nerve. Seeing the level of pain and discomfort it brought, and seeing, too, Quisu's almost twenty-two-hour labor, she knew now just why it was called "labor," and she didn't like that one bit.

She heard someone coming up the ladder and turned, curious. It didn't cause any alarm, since she knew all the people there were for a hundred or more miles in any direction, but she was curious as to who would be dropping by. She was quite unprepared for the figure that struggled in, using the doorway to steady himself. He looked like hell, his clothes were in shreds, and the shirt was heavily stained with blood.

"Crim! My God! Is that *you?* What are you doing here? And what happened to you?"

She went over to him and tried to help him to one of the beds, but he shook her off and collapsed in a chair instead. She immediately forgot her own thirst and offered the cup of wine to him, which he drank greedily and then tried to catch his breath.

"Been—protecting you," he managed. "Did a good job for a while, but it was finally too much."

She frowned. "Protecting me—from who?" She suddenly had a fearful thought. "I'm not going back, Crim. You can't make me!"

"I knew the situation, that's why I could only protect, not bring you out," he told her. "I wish I could—that would have prevented this, but that doesn't matter now. Nothing matters right now but the moment. How many people are there in the camp right now, besides you and me?"

She thought a moment. "Sixteen, counting the other girls. Why?" She began fussing with his shirt to see and perhaps help dress the wound, but he again would have none of it.

"Forget me now. If we don't act and soon, it won't make any difference if the wound's bad or not. Can you call the others? Get others here in a hurry?"

"Yeah, I got a bell, but—"

"Then do it! Now! All our lives depend on it! Theirs, too!"

She knew Crim well enough to take him at his word, and she went out and immediately rang the bell loud and long for all it was worth. When she finally decided that even the dead couldn't have missed, she went back inside. "Now—what's this all about?"

"Sam—if *I* could find you, *they* could find you. Klittichorn's already started the war. He attacked and destroyed Masalur. Boolean got away but it's ugly. Now a mercenary bastard I should have killed years ago named Zamofir is riding here hard. They've got repeating guns that can shoot hundreds of rounds a minute and they intend to get you and everybody else and just level this place, just to make sure."

"Zamofir! That son of a bitch from the train who was in with them raiders? Oh, I know him, Crim. How many?"

By that time the first of the camp people had appeared, with several more following. Two of Putie's husbands, Ladar and Somaz, and one of Quisu's, Dabuk, anyway, as well as Putie herself. They initially froze in hostility at the sight of Crim, but his condition told them he wasn't somebody to be feared. Sam told them briefly who the stranger was, and that he was trustworthy, and they listened with growing concern.

Ladar, a big, muscular man, and by agreement of the women the best-looking male body they'd ever seen, nodded. "How many are there?"

"There were twenty when they started, but there are only fourteen now," the Navigator responded with a touch of pride in his voice. "But they're mad as hell and they got nothing but blood in their eyes at this stage. I overheard them saying they were going to kill every living thing here and burn the place. I pulled two of the fancy rifles off the dead ones and got two boxes of ammunition as well. Hauled them on foot the last three leegs. They're simple to operate and you don't have to aim—they'll nail most anything within maybe a thirty-or forty-degree angle of where they're aimed. You have anything else to fight with?"

Ladar turned to Dabuk. "Get back to the still. That stuff's pure grain alcohol. You remember the firebombs Jerbal used back in that raid? Make some. Figure what to do with the rest. Somaz, you and Putie go tell the others and have everybody meet here. This here and the mill across the way are the first two buildings they got to pass. You—Navigator. How much time you figure we got?"

"An hour, maybe a little less. Hard to tell today."

He nodded. "Might be just enough. All right, everybody—*move!*"

They put Putie in charge, getting the other women well back in the jungle they all knew, along with the two babies. They were just to go as far back as they could, far enough back so that the crying of the babies wouldn't attract anybody. Sam was ordered back, too, but she refused. "No, this is my fight, my fault," she told them. "If it wasn't for me, they wouldn't be comin' here. The others'll make out, but I want my crack at the bastards. Besides, if they get us and I'm killed, maybe at least they won't risk stayin' around to find the others, but if I'm not here, they'll stay until they find us." That last was the clincher.

Crim showed Ladar how to work the submachine gun and the big man took it and one box of ammo and set up in the loft above the mill about a hundred yards away across a clearing. Crim himself kept the other one, propping himself up behind the porch stove and cutting a hole in the netting big enough to fire through. Other men took their positions with baskets filled with fire bombs—small gourds filled with nearly pure grain alcohol and plugged with strips of cloth. The rest loaded rifles and pistols, all single-shot legal kinds, and waited in a line behind bales of hay. All seemed almost relieved that they didn't have long to wait.

They rode into the camp slowly, bold as brass, eyeing everything like they were speculators out to see if the place was worth buying. Sam had a feeling of unreality about the scene, as if she had seen it many times before in countless western movies, where Constable Earp faced down the Clanton mob or a hundred old Duke Morrison films on late night TV. The only difference was, most gunfights were at dawn, not sunset. Damn! This was more Charley's style than hers. She couldn't help counting them, and suddenly came up short.

"Crim!" she whispered urgently. *"I only count ten!"*

Crim nodded. "One or two to watch the road just in case, and two more probably coming in on foot to cover them. We'll just have to take the hidden ones as they come. We got the high ground."

A man—one of Famay's boys, Sam saw—got up from behind a hay bale, rifle at the ready. "That's far enough, strangers!" he called out. "What do you want here?"

Zamofir, looking ridiculous and haggard at one and the same time, with his big waxed moustache and riding clothes, came a bit forward, but not too much. "Covanti's under attack," the little man shouted back. "A general uprising by the natives in a ton of colonies. We've been sent here to evacuate all of you to the hub until the crisis has passed."

"That so? We heard of the troubles but there ain't no natives around here, either. This ain't their type of place. And if we was gonna be evacuated, they'd send the army."

"The army's too busy handling the flow of refugees and setting up defenses. There's whole *armies* of rebels converging on the hub border, and massacres of Akhbreed throughout the colonies. They couldn't spare a troop of soldiers for this little outpost, so they sent us, instead."

Zamofir, she thought, was as glib and convincing as ever, and just as much a skunk and a liar.

"That's pretty good, you bastard!" Crim yelled down at him. "Zamofir, if I didn't know you so well, I'd almost swallow that myself!"

Zamofir suddenly went white and somehow slid, horse and all, back into the midst of the gang. "Crim! I—uh! Old friend, I know we haven't seen eye to eye on a lot of this, but . . . *scatter, boys! They're ready for us!"*

At that moment Crim and Ladar opened up a sudden, withering crossfire, and men and horses went down in a bloody mess in the clearing. Some who had bolted at Zamofir's first syllable made for the mill or the house, on the instinct that neither man would fire towards the other's position. It was also clear that they'd gotten more horses than men: machinegun fire was being returned from the midst of the clearing, behind the figures of horses, some still, some thrashing in agony. Bullets whistled through the house and mill and down the main road, and Sam beat a hasty retreat to the rear of the house, where the angle kept direct shots from hitting.

Furniture, pans, you name it, started moving, flying, and shattering all at the same time.

She was ashamed of herself for cowering like this, and she was worried for Crim. It didn't sound like he was firing any more.

The firing at her didn't last long, though; she heard sounds like breaking glass outside and then the sounds of men screaming, and, cautiously, she made her way forward again to see. The men in the trees had started throwing firebombs down on the massed men in the clearing, creating a hellish fire, and individual shots picked off men, some on fire, who ran from the cover into the open.

Suddenly there were sounds on the porch vibrating through the floor, and into the interior lurched a huge, filthy, bearded raider brandishing a pistol. He stood there, staring at her, and gave a laugh and then brought the pistol up, still chuckling. Suddenly someone appeared behind him, and, before he realized that anyone was there, he suddenly stiffened and bent backwards a little, the most incredulous expression on his face, then keeled over and collapsed on the floor, a big Navigator's knife sticking full into his back.

"The sun set just in time," Kira said with satisfaction. "Now, help me get out of Crim's shirt and jacket before I tangle and fall myself!"

Sam was almost too shocked to do anything, but Kira galvanized her into action. There was more shooting outside now, and a lot of yelling.

Kira got the rest of Crim's clothing off and then crouched down and looked at the situation outside. Although the sun had set, it was still very light, but there was little to see. The survivors of the raiders and whoever was still going defending the camp were all under cover now, and it was hard to tell who, what, or where, or even friend from foe.

Kira looked over at Sam and gave her a reassuring smile. "I feel like a native now. Crim couldn't haul much more than he did, so I guess I'm bare-assed and everything else for the duration."

Sam partly recovered her composure. "Crim—I didn't hear. . . ."

"Like I said, nick of time," the pretty woman responded. "That bastard got under the porch, climbed up, and pulled Crim and half the netting down. I guess he thought Crim was dead, and if sunset had been another five minutes, or those guys had waited until dawn, he would be. Now he's sort of suspended, at least 'til dawn." She sighed. "Wish I had something decent to fight with. Any weapons here except this one-shot pistol?"

"Crim had the repeater. The only thing we got is an old set of sabers, Jubi—one of my husbands—kept from his old army days."

"Get them. God, that horse barbecue out there smells awful!"

Sam fumbled and then opened the trunk. Although it was growing pitch dark in the house without the lantern, she knew her way as if it were the back of her hand.

Kira took both sabers, hefted them, then picked one. "This'll do. You take the pistol and shoot anybody who comes through the door."

"What're you gonna do?"

"A little hunt in the dark. This is my element, remember? And I'm fresh as a daisy." She started to duck out, but Sam called after her.

"Kira—what about Crim? Come morning, I mean. And you?"

"If help doesn't come before morning, then Crim will die," she responded calmly, as if referring to someone else. And if Crim dies, I probably will, too. That makes the next few hours real precious, doesn't it?" And, with that, she slipped out.

Sam felt suddenly terribly guilty and panicky at one and the same time. This wasn't the way it was supposed to go, damn it! Would they never leave her alone? Now Crim and Kira were gonna die for her, too, and maybe most or all of the people she loved here! And all she could do was sit there in the dark on the floor with a pistol.

Or could she? Suddenly she smelled smoke, not from outside—that had pretty well died out now—but like it was coming from. . . . *The house was on fire!* The bastards had set fire to it, and maybe to other places in town. The four left behind, and anybody who got away, now working to create light and force the defenders from their own ground out into the open.

And it was a good plan, since there was no question of her staying where she was. She got up and carefully peered out at the porch, or what was left of it. Was the one who set fire to her place hiding under it? Damn it, what could she do? The glow from underneath told her that the place would quickly be engulfed in flames, but she'd also be silhouetted against that glow when she got down. Jumping was out of the question—not in her condition. Taking a deep breath, and holding the pistol tightly, she let herself out over the edge of the porch, turned as best she could, and dropped, landing on her feet for a moment but then falling over. She forgot all her physical limitations, all danger, picked herself up and made for the darkest area she saw nearby, behind some bullet-scarred trees.

She froze for a minute, then peered cautiously around it and back at the house, where flames were now shooting upwards. But—wasn't that somebody on the edge of the porch? Who the hell . . . ?

The dark figure jumped effortlessly to the ground and then began to look around. At that moment, two shots from somewhere crashed into the tree, one just above her head, showering splinters and wood fragments, and she gave an involuntary cry. The figure heard it, turned, and advanced towards her, holding something in his hand.

Sam looked frantically around but couldn't see where to run. There was shooting in back of her and this character in front. Damn it. she couldn't outrun them—she couldn't *waddle* more than ten feet at a stretch.

"Come, come, Susama!" cried a familiar and unwelcome voice. "The threads of our destinies have been criss-crossing for a long time now, and then barely missing entanglement. It is time now, my sweet," Zamofir almost sang to her. "Come out and I will make it swift and painless and then get out of this trap. Resist or make any trouble for me and I will carve the child out first so you can watch, and then I will remain until I have hunted down and killed all the other women as well. Your choice. Whatever, it is time."

She took another deep breath, then turned, and stepped out into the fire's glow, facing him. Oddly, she felt calm, even relaxed, at this moment, and the moment seemed to hang stuck in time.

He was there, showing some blood so at least he'd been nicked a few times, and he was holding the other saber! My god! Did the man actually just *twirl* his moustache? Then he said, "You see, my dear, we are both survivors. We survive and triumph against even the most impossible odds. The trouble is, destiny allows only one of us survival at this juncture." He raised the saber in a sort of salute, then took another step forward.

Kira stepped out of the trees nearby, holding the other saber, blood very definitely on it. "Hers is not the only destiny entwined with yours, you pig," she said to him. "First you take me, and then you can have her."

Zamofir froze, turned, and sighed. "I would think you more confident with a rapier," he said calmly, lowering the sword. "This, my dear, is more a man's weapon." And he leaped towards Kira, who blocked, and they were joined in a duel.

Sam knew she couldn't run any more, that all the fight had been drained out of her. She could do nothing now but stand and watch one hell of a duel, between an old-time movie villain and a naked beauty, with swords that looked left over from a pirate epic.

Clang! Clang! Thrust! Parry! Block! Clang!

With stray bullets still whistling occasionally through the trees, and by the eerie glow of the fire, the two of them fought their duel, and they were pretty damned good at it, both of them. Sam expected Kira to have the moves, the grace, the quickness, but not the arm and wrist strength for such heavy weapons. Clearly Kira did a lot of steady working out with weights—that explained some of the stuff in the wagon. Muscles flexed now, she was still gorgeous, but she had the arms of a female body builder.

Zamofir had some experience and more familiarity with the weapon, but Kira was younger, quicker, and had the moves of a ballet dancer. Sensing that Zamofir was tiring, she pressed in, again, again, again. . . . Now a twirl, a twist, and the little man's saber flew from his grasp and landed a few feet away on the ground. He crouched down, warily, and gave a furtive glance to it, as if he were going to try for it, then suddenly he laughed nervously, whirled, and began to run.

Kira ran after him, but not a runner's gait, holding the saber almost like a javelin, and, when only a few feet in back of him, she let it fly. The sword was thrown with such force that it pierced Zamofir's back and came right out his front, so that from his back you could see only the ornate hilt. He cried out, staggered, then managed to turn back to Kira and almost shrug.

"Just as well," he managed, coughing. "Better . . . a more honorable . . . death . . . than I deserved . . . than to face . . . the wrath . . . of Klittichorn. Never . . . underestimate . . . the power of . . . a woman, eh?"

He smiled at that, then collapsed forward, the sword actually popping up a bit from his back as he hit face down and lay still. Kira went over, put a foot on his back, and pulled the sword out, then came over to Sam. "*That* was almost worth dying for!" she proclaimed. "You okay?"

Sam was stupefied. "That was the most amazing thing I ever saw! Like you was Robin Hood or somebody!"

"I told you once I was a female jock, before I got paralyzed. Since coming back to life, more or less, I've done most everything to make up for lost time. He was right, by the way. I fenced a lot in college, but these damned things are heavy and awkward as hell. I think I sprained my wrist at least. If he'd been in his prime, I wouldn't have had a prayer, but I bet that was the first time he'd fought with swords in years. You don't use it, you lose it. Thank heavens."

"*Now* what do we do?" Sam asked her.

Kira sighed and shrugged. "I dunno. I figure your boys wouldn't shoot a naked lady in this place and I knew who the gang was, but as to who's winning and what's what, it's impossible to say. Unless we see something worth going after, I think we find a dark, secluded spot, sit down, and have a good cry."

"But we can't know much of anything until it's light, and when it's light. . . ."

"Yeah, I know. That's why I'll do most of the crying."

The shooting had stopped completely within another hour, but most of the camp was either burning or had already burned, and there wasn't much to see. Nobody dared come out in the open yet, though; in the darkness and with pockets of flame, it would be impossible to tell who was who and make a decent count to see if all the raiders were dead—or if all the camp people were dead.

Slowly, though, one at a time, the surviving men of the camp made contact with one another. It took most of the night to count all the casualties. On the camp side, six dead, including Ladar, damn it, cut down and shot in the back from his loft position by one of the guys who'd snuck in just for that, and three wounded, none critically—although it looked as if Somaz might well lose both legs, and Kruwen, another of Quisu's husbands, appeared paralyzed from the waist down thanks to a wound in the spinal area. The girls and the babies were okay, certainly, but, ironically, it looked as if the only family left intact was Sam's, whose husbands were still out in the boat and blissfully ignorant of all this. That made her feel doubly guilty, almost unbearably so. It wasn't right that she'd been the cause of this, however unwillingly, and that she alone should survive with her family intact.

By now she was cried out and felt drained and sick, yet her mind was going 'round and 'round. There was no end to it. If Crim and Zamofir had found her, then others would, and that horned bastard would never stop, never, until he killed her and maybe saved the baby to raise, to try again with a Storm Princess raised from the cradle to do his bidding. Now, too, they wouldn't just send mercenary gunmen, they'd send sorcerers and demons.

The wedding spell inherent in the ring was a simple spell, meant for simple folk and for common situations. It was designed to eliminate all complications, not cause them, but cause them it now did. Her duties as a Covantian wife were to love, honor, and obey her husbands, to keep house, relieve the burden of their chores, do whatever was in their best interest, at whatever sacrifice. Her duty to her child was to bear and raise and protect it, and allow it to grow up healthy and strong.

But if she remained here, remained loyal and faithful, she would bring down more terror on this place, and certainly death or worse upon her own husbands. If she tried to pick up and go on, they would find her, and her child would either die or be taken to an evil monster to raise.

But she couldn't run. Not any more. Not physically, not emotionally. She'd be found out anyway. The only solution was to face and defeat the threat, and to do that she would have to be her old self, the surrogate Storm Princess. Had she still had those powers she could have brought lightning down to fry all those bastards, and rain to quench the fires. Had she been the Storm Princess, those men wouldn't be crippled, or dead, and Crim and Kira wouldn't be facing certain death at dawn having given everything to protect her.

But then the ultimate act of love, of sacrifice for her husbands and child-to-be, was to give all this up. The ring and its spell was preventing her from doing what its own logic compelled her to do. She felt its grip on her weaken, felt waves of dizziness and confusion, and sensed somehow that it was locked in a logic loop from which it could not escape. The conflicting demands it was making on her were sending waves of nausea and making her feverish, her emotions running the entire range, her mind beset with complete confusion as to what she could do and should do, until she couldn't stand it any more. It pushed her over the edge, and the only thing she could do to stop it, she did without even thinking about it. She pulled the ring violently from her finger, tearing the skin, and threw it away, and then she collapsed and passed out.

Sam awoke with vivid memories of all that had been until she'd looped out or gone nuts or whatever had happened. She reached over to her ring finger and felt it. There was a bandage on it, but no ring. She had sensed it more than remembered it, but that in itself was strange. She didn't really feel much different. Oh, she knew now what she had to do, if at last she was allowed to do it, but she still felt real affection for those four men and for the others as well, and still thought of the camp as home. Short of Boday's place, it was the closest to a real home she'd had since being dragged to Akahlar.

But there was a difference, and it was again something she sensed, felt, rather than directly experienced.

The power was back. It was raining now, outside wherever she was, and she could sense, feel the storm, join with it if she wished.

She suddenly opened her eyes full and looked around with a start. It was the cottage! *Her* house! And she was in her own bed, and nothing was burned and nothing was out of place! God—had it all been a terrible nightmare? But—no, what about her finger? The return of the powers, of self-control? Had she somehow had the ring torn from her or taken from her and hallucinated the rest as a result?

It *had* to be, because it was day, and there was Crim, coming in the door, and he looked okay! Even his buckskins were clean!

He grinned when he saw her staring at him like she was seeing a ghost.

"Not dead yet," he assured her. "But it was a near thing."

"But—but—Did I dream it? Didn't it happen?"

"It happened," he assured her. "All of it. This is a clean set, by the way—in spite of what you've often accused me of, I *do* have more than one set of clothes. They just had to be retrieved."

"Never mind the clothes! You had a couple of holes in you big enough to run through, you had maybe half your blood, you fell off the porch, and who knows what else. You were a dead man at dawn!"

"That happened as well. It all happened, Sam. I can show you where the dead bodies are stacked, including Zamofir's. I was proud of Kira, even though I had always hoped I could do the slimy bastard in myself." The smile faded. "Also six very brave men are laid out over on the floor of the mill, awaiting a proper funeral. Their wives insisted on doing it all themselves, along with the six who survived. Strong sorcery can rebuild a town that burned and repair the worst of wounds, but it can't raise the dead no matter what the legends say."

She sat up straight. "Sorcery! Boolean!"

"Yes. He got here two hours before dawn—thank the fates. Kira damn near had a heart attack when he showed up. Not alone, either."

She suddenly felt a shock. "God! I must look awful! My hair. . . ."

"You look fine, or at least normal. Relax."

"I—Boday?"

He nodded. "And Charley, too, and a very odd fellow named Dorion, and Boolean's familiar whose name is Cromil and who looks like a green monkey and likes to insult people."

"I—I'm not so sure I'm ready for Boday yet."

"Relax. She's on guard duty overlooking the road right now and she can't come back here until I relieve her. But you'll have to face her sooner or later. How do you feel about it?"

She sighed. "I—I really don't know. I haven't been able to get my head screwed back on right yet. I just need a little time, that's all." She paused a moment. "Can I first see the other women here? I—I sort of feel responsible. Maybe I can help."

Crim nodded. "But be quick. Boolean wants us out of here as fast as is practical. Even now Klittichorn dispatches Sudogs to see what has been happening here, and he must know that as of now the child still lives. Boolean is powerful—even I hadn't realized how powerful until I saw what he did here—but that power has limits. He's not the only one with power, and they can and will gang up on him if they think they have him cornered."

She nodded. "I can take care of the Sudogs," she assured him, "but you're right. I've brought enough misery down on this place. All right—let's go."

The place was so fully restored that it made it all the more jarring to see the corpses laid out in the mill. At least Boolean's healing powers had extended to the wounded; there would be no amputations or paralysis. It did not, however, end the sadness of the men who died bravely defending what was theirs.

Sam had come there mainly to comfort the others, but as she looked at Ladar and the others she'd come to know so well, bloody and still, she suddenly found herself filled not with sadness nor even guilt but with anger. All that time, until she'd finally faced up to that changewind back in Covanti, she'd been running away. Running away from herself, running away from duties, responsibilities, burdens. She hadn't asked for them, of course, but they were hers none the less.

These guys hadn't run. They'd stood and bravely defended all that was important to them, even to paying the ultimate price. It wasn't fair that she had all this dumped on her, but it wasn't fair that she'd brought death on them, either. They hadn't questioned fairness; they'd done what they had to do to save her and their wives and their camp and all that meant anything to them.

She walked back out to where Crim was waiting and looked up at him. "All right, let's see this big-shot wizard," she said determinedly.

Seeing Charley again was something of a shock, too. Not just the brown skin-deep dye job, but Charley was so thin she looked almost emaciated, and she seemed, well, a whole lot *older,* somehow. Well, Sam reflected, maybe *she* was a whole lot older now where it counted, too.

She kind of liked Dorion on first impression. True, he wasn't much on physique, with pot belly and thinning hair, but there was a certain kindness and gentleness in him that came through right from the start, and the way he doted on Charley was more than the slave ring thing. Anybody could see he was in love with her; anybody, that is, but Charley.

Boolean was a different sort of shock. A man of medium height and build, with a gray-black neatly trimmed beard and deep-set, heavily lined blue eyes, he looked so, well, *ordinary*. Even Charley, who couldn't see the man as he was, had come up with the right impression at the start. The guy looked like a high school science teacher, and sounded much that way, too.

At his suggestion, they went back to her place and sat down, just the two of them, to discuss what happened next. She offered, as host, to make him some tea or coffee, but he just chuckled, snapped his fingers, and they both had just what they wanted right in front of them.

"The man who could do miracles," he chuckled. "Child's play, really. Once you determined the rules and the math and approached magic here as you approach any other scientific discipline, it just all sort of comes naturally. I've never tired of it, and it's as much fun, and just as fascinating as it was the first time. The only thing is, the more you can do, the more godlike your powers become, the more frustrated you become by those things you can't do. Those dead men out there. I could animate their corpses, but I couldn't bring *them* back or restore *their* bodies. They're gone. It's what keeps driving us to push the limits, and what destroys most of us in the end."

She nodded. "But what's next for us, on the practical level?" she asked him. "I mean, let's be realistic here. I can't be positive here, but I think I'm in my eighth month. I can't seem to keep my emotions in check, I haven't got the stamina, and I can't run or fight worth a damn, and as near as I can figure out, the only way to end this madness is to literally walk into the lion's den and face them down. *She'll* be in peak condition and totally in control, and she has Klittichorn for protection. I won't be able to get near enough to lay a glove on her and you know it. On top of that, she can sense the kid. I can't even hide out in a group. I'm willing to do whatever is necessary, but I can't see how I can do it, all things considered. Not until after the baby's born."

"I understand the problem," he replied seriously. "Our related problem is that we can't wait for the birth. He's going to jump the gun at almost any time from right now to no more than a week or two at best. His timetable was already upset by the problems involved in the attack on me. His generals are amateurs and they're now seeing the results of their mistakes. You can train armies of specific worlds rather well, but when you have to simulate conditions, and then mix various races with their own tribal chiefs and loyalties you get a mess. I think the effect on him would be to accentuate the positive and ignore the negatives. He did destroy a hub civilization and break the hold of a sorcerer. He's desperate now. If the child is born, the Storm Princess's powers may be weakened to the point where she couldn't handle multiple changewinds, or perhaps not put them and keep them where they're supposed to be. He can't do it one at a time. His power is limited, the same as mine. The next time he's got to do it, if not simultaneously, at least continuously. Speed and accuracy are at a premium for him right now. Everything he's built all these years, and all his dreams, face ruin unless he acts now."

"But how can I do anything?"

He sighed. "You've heard from Charley and Dorion what the battle and its aftermath was like, what a mess this all is, what horror it is bringing. I don't know whether we can stop the process now. As soon as he feels we're after him he'll jump the gun and do it, and we can't wait because he could jump the gun anyway, thanks to your own biological clock. There is a way out of this, though. Wait a moment."

He got up and went outside and looked down at the clearing. "Charley, will you come up here?" he called. "Dorion, help her out and come up, too. I may need some assistance here."

Charley got up and in, with Dorion's help, and was taken to a chair. She was puzzled, but willing to listen.

Boolean took a deep breath. "Charley, you know the problem. We have to hit them before they hit everybody and make us irrelevant. I'm sure Klittichorn would have done it all as soon as he got the data from Masalur, if he didn't also have to play some politics with the Storm Princess and others. We have to hit him and get him the first time. There will be no second chances. And we have to do it soon."

"You know where he is?" Charley asked him.

Boolean nodded. "I know. I didn't know, exactly, until he hit Masalur, but I was able to identify and follow his threads back. That's what I was doing, and it is the gain we got from Masalur's suffering. It's not close, which is why, even using the flying spells, we must leave immediately. Even with Sam and I in the best of shape, it's a question whether we can do it alone, or with just the forces that we have, even if we make it in time. As it stands, we have less chance. Sam hasn't the mobility or the control she should have, and the child is a dead giveaway. Sam needs a way out."

She nodded. "So?" At the moment she had no idea where he was going with this or what it had to do with her.

"I can't snap my fingers and make her into a peak Amazonian warrior. Well, actually, I could, but not without destroying the child. I'm just now beginning to realize why there *is* such a thing as a Storm Princess, why she comes up in other worlds as well, and why Klittichorn just didn't preempt this threat and have his own knocked up. Too much deduction with too much hunch, but I think I'm on the right track. The Storm Princesses are the only true 'naturals' in magic, and the only ones with influence over and immunity from the changewinds. I think, somehow, they're safety valves—natural regulators—essential to keeping some kind of order. How and why it evolved this way is something we may never know, but, like gravity, it's still there. There's some evidence to show that the death of any of the Storm Princesses anywhere, even on the outplane, is followed by a long period of natural disasters, cataclysms, wars, you name it—until a new one is born. By killing so many in the outplane, Klittichorn has provided the evidence and pattern that this is true—at the cost of who knows how many lives or even civilizations. What will happen when he looses so many changewinds at once on a weakened outplane is something I can't imagine, nor can he. The difference is, I care and he doesn't."

"I'm with you so far," she told him. "I just can't see what it has to do with me."

"Both of you think back, to that first time, in the Tubikosan caves, when we first had a talk. When I transmitted, through the icon, a blood-mixing and sealing spell that turned you, Charley, into a physical twin of Sam's."

They both nodded. "I remember," said Sam. "It seems a hundred years ago."

"It wasn't a mere appearance spell. I had to fool not just someone who knew what the Storm Princess looked like, I had to fool magicians, Sudogs, ones with the ability to see through mere appearances. Anyone short of the highest levels of the Second Rank, who could recognize the spell for what it was. It did more than make you physical twins on the outside; it made you true twins, genetically identical. You still are. The difference in appearance between the two of you may seem great now, but it's a difference in weight—and how long you've been like that and adjusted to it—and experience and, of course, in Charley's case, Boday's alchemy made a stunning difference. But, you see, I had to guard against spells and alchemy, so I had to make those with the power be confused, and they see people differently than the average person does."

"Wait a minute," Sam interrupted him. "If she's actually me down to that level, why isn't she a Storm Princess, too?"

"Good question. There are two answers to that, both relevant. The first is that no one can create a Storm Princess by sorcery. It can not be done, or Klittichorn would have dispensed with his right off and things would be a lot more complicated. Second, there is more than the physical involved here, there is an entire pattern. Notice how the common peasant marriage spell removed your powers yet it didn't change you physically one bit, Sam. It is physical, mental, and psychic, and all must have certain elements exactly right or the balance is destroyed and the rest is ignored. Charley is physically you, no matter how dramatic the difference seems sitting here, but she is nothing like you either mentally or psychically in the areas that seem to count. One of them, quite clearly and unexpectedly, is sexual in nature, something I have been puzzling about since that was shown. There's got to be a reason for that. In many ways, it seems to be part of the key to this overall puzzle, a key that I am afraid Klittichorn has worked out ahead of me, as usual. But that's beside the point for now. The bottom line remains that Sam's current physiology can't be touched for fear of harming her child, yet it places her at great risk and extreme disadvantages in any showdown. We can't just transfer the needed elements to Charley, who's better suited for it, since one can not give away magical gifts of that sort."

"Yeah, well, Sam wouldn't be much use blind, either," Charley noted.

"She wouldn't be blind. Her psychic self has the power. That's why she's been exposed to much magical energy herself and yet never suffered from the problem."

Charley suddenly pushed back a bit from the table. "Oh, no! I think I see now where you're going with this and I don't like the route one bit."

Sam looked at Charley, frowning, then at Boolean. "Well, I don't," she said. "Somebody want to let me in on this?"

"From a magical viewpoint," Boolean patiently explained, "the two of you appear identical. The differences, psychic and mental, are, therefore, easy to factor out completely when you two can be compared side by side like this. Were you not physically the same, all the differences could never be so clearly identified. Since they can in this case, I could transfer those differences."

"Differences? What the hell do you mean?"

"He means," Charley said softly, "that he can take your mind and soul and whatever and put it in my body, and mine in yours. And I get to carry the kid and keep their eyes off you two sneaking up on them while you get in my body. Isn't that about right?"

"I couldn't have said it better myself," the sorcerer replied. "It's an ideal solution shaped by the threads of destiny. And it's best for both of you. Sam gets the mobility and loses a telltale marker; you get out from being a blind, dependent woman without status whose body is good for only one thing. Sam's body also has other attributes. Thanks to the demon of the Jewel of Omak, wherever he now is, she doesn't get sick. No hostile organism can live inside her. Fleas, ticks, mosquitoes and other parasites die when they bite her. In spite of her weight, her blood pressure is perfect, her heart strong, her veins and arteries cleaner than a newborn's. Wounds heal quickly, damaged tissue regenerates."

"So *that's* why I was able to run like that, build those muscles, lift those weights!" Sam exclaimed.

"Well, it didn't hurt," the sorcerer replied. "So where is the problem, Charley? Are you afraid of the process itself?"

"No, no. Not after what you've pulled off so far. I believe you. But—to be fat without even having had the pleasure of eating my way up to it, and pregnant at the point where it's all work and the fun's long past—I'm not so sure I can handle that. Yeah, I'm frustrated here, and it seems like I always have a cold or I'm scratching little bites, but—jeez, Sam. What do you weigh now?"

"Last time I checked it was about two hundred and sixty pounds," she responded. "At least I think I got that from figurin' the halg and stuff."

"Two . . . And when you add the kid and the water weight. . . ."

Sam was astonished. "Jesus, Charley—I can't *believe* you! Ever since you got the way you are you been paranoid about weight. You always were, but it got to be a mania. I got to tell ya, Charley, you don't look real glamorous to me right now. You look fucking anorexic! I ain't no more thrilled about having that body of yours than you are havin' mine. I never liked bein' fat but I kind'a got used to it. The only real hangups I kept were about my health, and now I find out that's no problem at all! I'd be givin' up shit, too, you know." She grabbed her breasts. "I'm at least a forty-four D and I love 'em. Most of all, I'd be givin' up havin' the kid, and I want this kid bad."

"Yeah, but it's *your* kid, not mine. And it's the only one between us!"

"Not necessarily," Boolean cut in. "There's nothing physically wrong with Sam's system. It's Storm Princesses who are prevented from having but the one child—related in some way to that regulatory function I mentioned. You wouldn't be a Storm Princess. There's no reason to believe you would not remain fertile."

"You mean," Sam asked him, "if that spell here had stuck and I wasn't a Storm Princess, I could'a had more kids?"

Boolean shrugged. "Who knows? If you were taken out and stuck here, though, I doubt if it would have been a long or happy life once Klittichorn won. Here—or in Albuquerque, for that matter."

"Yeah, but who would screw somebody that fat without magic?" Charley asked acidly.

Behind her, Dorion said, too low for her to hear, "I would." To him, the resemblance was more marked than could be seen by each of them, and the idea of Charley in Sam's body was, somehow, something of a turn-on.

"So, this is the great Charley Sharkin," Sam retorted. "Bright, ambitious, liberated, and all that. The new woman, right? So what's she do? Finds out when she's turned into a whore and a bimbo that she *loves* being a whore and a bimbo, sellin' herself and actin' cute and dumb and all that. Shit, Charley, I thought I was given a raw deal here, but you're actually *happy* with the deal you got. You just want it improved so you can go on bein' Little Miss Fuckalot until you're big enough to become a madam and sucker in more poor kids. Another Boday, maybe. And to think I always looked up to you—"

"Hold on! Hold on! It's not that *simple,*" Charley protested, then took a moment to compose herself. "Sam—*it's all I have.*"

Sam sighed and looked at Boolean. "Well, if we're really twins now, and you got the power to rebuild the town and heal the wounded overnight, couldn't you just take off the spells that kept me fat and make her thin and pretty?"

"I could," the sorcerer admitted, "but not right off. I don't dare mess with any of those without risking messing up the biochemistry and possibly harming or even killing the kid. I'm not *that* good. Afterwards, if any of us survive this, and the child's born, well—then anything is possible."

That put a different face on it for Charley. "You really mean that? If I keep like that for another month or two, and bear her kid, then the weight and all can be taken away? I mean, if you fail after all this, it won't make any difference anyway, I guess, so otherwise I pay the price of a couple of months like that and then wind up better than I am now." She shrugged. "Well, I guess we'd better do it, then, huh?"

"Jeez," Sam sighed. "This is gonna confuse the hell out of Boday. . . ."

11
Allies, Answers, and Questions

"When do you want to do this?" Sam asked Boolean, a bit nervous in spite of it all.

"Ordinarily I'd have to set up a lab," he replied. "Prepare primer potions to ease the transfer, do a lot of provisional spells, all that. But because you two are true twins, created in the lab for this purpose, so to speak, I think I can do it on the fly, right here and now. It'll save time and ease the stress. Just lie down there, side by side, heads towards me," he instructed. "Dorion, you assist as needed. Sam, I know it's uncomfortable, but bear with it."

"*Everything's* uncomfortable at this stage," she responded, but managed to lie down with some help from Dorion. The magician then guided Charley to the right spot and positioned her as well, then stepped back. He felt oddly mixed emotions at this, but while Boolean had removed the ring from Charley's nose he'd made no move to remove Dorion's. Dorion was stuck if Charley went along, and probably even if she didn't—Boolean's power was far greater than the simple spell that bound the former magician.

He also couldn't avoid a little straight professional curiosity in spite of the personal involvement. The fact was, this wasn't one of the spells they ever taught or talked about in magician school.

Boolean went over to them and stretched out his arms, hands palm down, over each of their faces, and concentrated.

"Now, each of you just close your eyes and go to sleep," he told them softly. "In a nice, deep, pleasant sleep, with no thoughts, no worries, no cares. Just a nice, deep sleep."

They were both out, with soft smiles on their faces, and, oddly, like this and so relaxed, they really *did* look a lot alike.

Boolean turned towards Dorion and said, "I *hope* it's this easy with twinned people and I don't require the prep. Otherwise we could have some very hairy results." And then he winked, and turned back to the two sleeping women. He knelt down behind their heads and placed one hand on the face of each of them. Neither moved or seemed to notice, their breathing heavy and regular.

Dorion felt suddenly uneasy about this, thanks to Boolean's comment. Up to now he'd had so much confidence in the man's power he hadn't doubted, but Boolean was right. Doing this by spell and sheer force of will, with no intermediate medium for the soul except himself, was damned dangerous. He would have to draw both souls, both consciousnesses, even memories, from the bodies into his own as the medium and then switch them with no losses—and pretty damned fast, too—without mixing them or letting them touch in any way, either each other or his own.

The sorcerer took a deep breath, let it out, took a second, let out a bit, closed his eyes tightly, and began.

His body began to tremble slightly, and gobs of sweat broke out on his forehead; his teeth were tightly clenched together and his face contorted into a terrible grimace.

To normal human eyes nothing else was happening, but to Dorion's magically attuned eyes, the great juggling act was clear.

Both women's bodies took on a sudden pale reddish glow. It was all over, except for the different colored mass in Sam's abdomen which had a few slender psychic tendrils to her.

The two large masses coalesced, growing smaller and smaller and yet more intense. and the tendrils from the fetus grew long and wispy, like a few strands of spider's web trying not to let go in the wind.

Now came the tricky part for Boolean, as the two centers of bright energy, now burning with an intense red-white fire, egg-shaped and compact, were drawn into the sorcerer's two hands, then up the arms and into Boolean's own body. He was going to pass them very close—too close for any eye to follow—and Dorion watched as they drew closer and closer, the thin webs from the fetus seeming too tiny and tenuous now to possibly hold.

Now, carefully, the orb from Charley slid just atop the one from Sam, so that Charley's gently brushed by and made ever so gentle contact with the thin tendrils from the fetus and continued on to the other arm.

There! The wispy links had transferred! They were now contracting, getting a bit stronger and thicker as Charley's orb flowed now past the shoulder and down the arms towards Sam's body, while Sam's orb, now free of the contact, went towards Charley.

He'd done it! *The hell with Klittichorn!* Dorion thought in intense admiration and wonder. *That's the greatest feat of unaided sorcery anyone has ever seen!*

Now the orbs passed through the heads, out of Boolean's body, and began to lose their distinctive shapes and some of their intensity, flowing into first the head and then through the rest of the two bodies, fading, fading, until they were finally mere auras such as everyone had.

Boolean suddenly expelled his breath, which he'd been holding for at least the couple of minutes that seemed to have passed, and gasped for air, then removed his hands and fell back.

Dorion was to him in an instant. "Master Boolean! Are you all right?"

Boolean's eyes opened. "For a brief moment, right there in the transfer, my soul, which was still diffuse, intermixed with Sam's," he managed, still a bit out of breath. "I am afraid, Dorion, that I am now cursed to sexually prefer only women." And then he grinned and sat up.

"I have just witnessed perhaps the greatest feat of mind control in all history," Dorion growled. "Why is it, then, that I still want to wring your neck at this point?"

Boolean's grin remained, and he managed to stand up, then make his way back to the pair who still reclined there sleeping. He examined his handiwork and nodded to himself. "It *was* tough, a lot tougher than I figured on," he admitted. "The transfer's complete and successful, but I don't think I want to do that again without the full paraphernalia and a lot of time and prep. I had some mild chest pains at the transfer point and I almost lost my concentration wondering if I was going to have a heart attack or a stroke. One more like that and it'd kill me."

Dorion stared at him and saw how suddenly old and tired he looked and realized that this wasn't a put-on. "Are you certain that you are still up to Klittichorn? Or that *she* is?"

"I can't ever know that until we try it, Dorion. There will be enough time between now and when we get there for me to do some self-repair and reconditioning, though. As to Sam—yes, I think she is, now."

"How long are you going to keep them in the trance?"

"The longer the better so it settles in," the sorcerer responded, "Anything from Crim or Boday yet?"

"I'll check." Dorion stepped outside and looked around, but it was still quiet. He went back in and reported, "Nothing yet. Want me to go check?"

Boolean nodded. "Do that." He turned back to the two sleeping forms, looked down at them, and gave a soft chuckle. "I really feel sorry for those four husbands," he muttered to himself. "Not that she'd enjoy herself like she did, moving back from oral to anal. I'd sure like to leave Charley here if I could. Be good for her, too, to find not just one but many men still wanting her no matter what her weight or condition." He sighed. "Well, can't solve everybody's problems, I guess."

He didn't dare leave her anywhere near here or anywhere that anyone from the rebel camp was likely to spot her. The four guys would just have to suffer, but he made a mental note to make it up to them, if he could, at some point in the future. Decisions, decisions—that's all great power ever really brought you. Decisions without irreversible consequences or accountability.

It was fun to be a sorcerer.

Charley awoke slowly from a very erotic dream and turned slowly to one side. Suddenly she felt a shifting down in her abdomen and it unnerved her and she woke up. Somebody else—Sam—was waking up next to her. She looked over and was startled first to realize that she could see again, in the normal, colorful way, and that excited her. What she was seeing, though, bothered her a lot.

She had never really seen herself properly and in full color with the chocolate brown skin and blue-black hair, and it didn't look right. In fact, Sam was right—God! She'd been skin and bones! Funny it hadn't felt like that. . . .

With a shock she suddenly realized that she was seeing her own body in full living color and three dimensions, yet as third party. Somehow, deep down, she hadn't really believed it was possible, and certainly not like this. Hell. it was still *light* out!

She shifted uncomfortably and ran her hands over her own body as it now was. She remembered how fat Sam had been, but it seemed even more gross, if anything, now.

She tried to get to her feet and found that it took something of a balancing act to do so. Dorion came over, put out his arms, and she took them and let herself be pulled unsteadily to her feet. Christ! It felt like she had a goddamned bowling ball in her stomach, and something in it shifted slowly when she did, but not in the right ways or at the right speed. She let go of Dorion and tried walking a few steps and it, too, felt awkward and weird.

The weight and feel of the breasts also surprised her. They felt like they weighed a ton of dead weight each, shifting when she walked but complicating the balancing act required to maintain equilibrium with the bowling ball in her belly. and the extra padding wasn't any real help, either. Her thighs rubbed together tightly every time she took a step, and produced motion in her ass as well. God, she was *gross!*

"God!" This feels *weird,*" she heard Sam say. "Jeez! I feel so light it's like I was eleven years old again! It just don't feel like I'm all here no more. I guess I got more used to that body than I thought I had. Wow! This is *strange!* I'm actually inside your body, just like it was mine! Uh—how you feelin' Charley?"

"Like a beached whale. I think these tits are more like fifties than forty-fours. Jeez—when did you weigh yourself last?"

"Back in Tishbaal. It was the last scale I saw. I could a done it on the mill scales here, but with bein' pregnant and all it didn't seem worth it. Boy, that's strange, seein' yourself like this, from a different pair of eyes or whatever it is I'm seein' with at the moment. It's different than a mirror. It's real and not backwards."

"You went like this and didn't have screaming fits?"

"Aw, you get used to it pretty fast. Not the kid—you always know that's there. But like Boolean said, you don't get sick, and you don't get clogged. Bigger lungs carryin' more oxygen, so you can't exactly do things fast but you can do 'em, pretty good."

"I gain three times my weight at least and I don't even have the fun of eating my way up to it. It's not fair!"

"Yeah, well, at least you can eat whatever you want and all you want now," Sam noted. "Huh! These eyes are kind'a odd. You see like this when you was in this body?"

"Unless it was something of magic or another plane all I saw was gray, unless I used Shadowcat," Charley told her. "Why? What do you see?"

"Everything, but not quite. The colors are funny. Things look sorta' fuzzy and all, and all the colors are pastels or something, and there's a glow to most everything. Real strong from you and your buddy, there." She stared hard at Charley. "Hey! If I concentrate real hard I can see your insides! Wow! X-ray vision!" She hesitated and looked at Dorion. "Would it hurt the kid if I checked her out?"

"No," Dorion told her. "You're not really using your eyes to see in the old pattern or old ways. You're not really seeing just with them at all. In fact, if you concentrate hard enough, you can see what's in back of you, too. It has a lot to say for it, but it's also limited in vital areas. Those of us with The Sight can't read ordinary books—takes a special kind of ink and paper to see right—and there's a lot of color shift, and a lot of blurring with much motion. You can see things others can't, but there are tradeoffs. You'll learn them. The glows are the auras or spiritual components of people and things. You get pretty good at recognizing specific things by their auras alone."

Charley looked at Dorion. "Then why couldn't *I* see like that?"

"You have to have the power as well. Just three percent of the Akhbreed have it, and they're born with it. You either have it or you don't, and, even then, you never find out unless you're subjected to the intense radiation from dealing with the netherhells. Only ones with really strong natural power see it from the start."

Sam looked now at Charley's distended abdomen and concentrated and, to her immense surprise, she *could* see the fetus in the womb. "Gee—looks just like the films in sex ed, only in three-D and living color," she commented. "This is neat! Kind'a gross in parts, though. And it *glows* real bright." She felt a sudden shiver run through her. "What the hell?"

Boolean reentered the hut and saw what she was doing. "You felt it, huh? That's what the enemy feels as well every time some random part of the power is given off by the child, even though unborn. She can feel you, too, looking at her, and is reacting. I'd stop it for now." He turned to Charley. "And how are you making out?"

"Awful," Charley moaned. "Like a ton of bagged water is inside me all shifting around, dead shifting weight below, slow and awkward. I can't even see my own feet."

Boolean passed a hand in front of her eyes and suddenly Charley's face went blank, staring forward.

"The more you move, the more you will learn about and compensate for the body's limitations and these will be automatically and subconsciously incorporated into your normal movements until, within your limitations, you feel totally confident and can walk, sit, stand, or lie without even thinking about it. When you reach that point you will think of it as your body, your child, and accept it as normal and not think much about it, accepting it and its limitations."

"Jeez! Where were you, when I needed you?" Sam muttered.

He turned to her. "Just a simple spell, like hypnosis, only it won't wear off so rapidly, and by the time it does it'll seem natural to her. It's no panacea, but anyone who can adjust so well to blindness should have little trouble with this. More gradually, the biochemistry of pregnancy will begin to influence her thinking as well. Of course, I could cast a really fine spell so she'd be perfectly happy and all that and do all sorts of other things, but casting individual spells on human beings is kind of like making pacts with the devil.

You never can be sure you've covered all the loopholes and the ones you don't are often doozies." He turned back to Charley, did another wave of his hand, and she came back to full consciousness and frowned.

"Huh! Had a little dizziness there for a moment. It's okay now. Let me move around and do a few things and get the real feel of this. I'm not going to be much help, but if I'm going to survive the next couple of months, I want to be as self-sufficient as possible."

While Boolean and Sam huddled over what was going to be done next, Charley was active, trying out all sorts of things, the ever-concerned Dorion at her side should she need assistance. She even went out and managed to climb the ladder down and back up again, although not without some difficulty. At the end of an hour or so she reported, "You know, this isn't as bad as I thought at first. I guess my hormones are flowing or something, but I'm starting to get the hang of this. It's not like pregnancy is an abnormal condition or something—women's bodies are designed for it. It's just that I suddenly had to take it on in full bloom rather than grow into it gradual like."

"Don't push yourself," Sam told her. "We don't want to lose the kid."

Charley shrugged. "If we were really that delicate, then we'd never have gotten out of caveman days. I'll manage. I'm actually less dependent now than when I couldn't see, by a long shot, and I just picked up and moved that heavy chair over there without thinking about it. You got real muscles under all this fat. I couldn't have moved it before."

Sam nodded. "I kept working out as best I could using weights. There's nobody else around here half the time to move the heavy stuff and do the lifting. I got pretty good around this place carryin' heavy stuff around on my head, but first I had to lift it up there. I'm havin' the opposite problem now discoverin' how weak I suddenly am for anything. When I was with Crim I practiced with swords; now I don't think I could lift one."

"Compare notes later," Boolean told them. "Now we have to plot our move. It's already late afternoon and we can't dawdle here any longer or we'll begin to attract some visitors with real power."

She nodded. "Nothing personal, Sam, but I think I want to be gone before your four husbands get back. I don't think I could explain this to them—or maybe it wouldn't make much difference to 'em. But where are we going? And how? You think it's safe for me in one of those—saddles?"

"You'll be fine in the saddle, and I'll be watching out for you," the sorcerer assured her. "In fact, Sam's the one we'll have to watch for a bit. As to where, we are going to go briefly to a small town in Covanti hub where I need to contact some people and update them and see if there's anybody left out there with both brains and guts. After that I'm going to put you in some safe hands well out of the field of battle, and Sam and I are going north for a while."

"Hey! Wait a minute!" Charley objected, suddenly hesitant. "First of all, I haven't any clothes! If we're going someplace where strangers are, I don't want to be like *this!* And, second, what about Boday? She's technically married to Sam but she'll think *I'm* Sam! This is bad enough without having to deal with *that!*

"Yes, and what about the other people here, and my own husbands?" Sam added worriedly. "They're good people. The boys may be a little rough but they're not really bad."

Boolean thought for a moment. "Well, Charley, we'll get you some clothes when we need them. You didn't seem to mind being undressed before."

"Yeah, well, I didn't have this body before."

He ignored the comment. "As for Boday—well, Cromil has informed her of what we did, although I'm not sure she'll believe it until she sees it for herself. I can probably ease belief by simply separating out that simplistic marriage spell that caused so much trouble late in the game and transferring it over to Sam. Here—I'll do that now." It took maybe ten seconds and a bit of odd gesturing, and Sam actually watched as he reached out and grabbed the slender red thread of a spell she'd never seen before as if it were a real thread and attached it to her. "There. Uh—Sam, I hope you're ready for Boday now."

"Yeah," she sighed. "If she'll accept me this way, sure, why not? I hate to admit it, but I actually missed her."

"As for the locals here," he continued, "well, that's going to have to leave a void, that's all. There are, after all, suddenly far fewer men than women. They might miss you, but I don't think they'd understand how complicated the problem was. It's best you just, well, vanish. I wish I could do more, but time's wasting away."

"But, won't Klittichorn eventually send other forces here? I really do care about them, you see. All of them. I don't think they should suffer any more."

"Don't worry about them. They'll be okay—unless Klittichorn wins. Then I wouldn't give a plugged nickel for anybody. You see, there's not much chance they'll send anything but supernatural forces the next time, and those will be looking for impulses from the child. They won't find them, and they will move on. Right now, they can't afford mindless vengeance with you again on the loose and in full power—the Storm Princess will know that, probably already does. They haven't the time."

Sam wanted to believe it—hell, she *had* to believe it. She took one last look around the place, sighed, and walked out onto the porch, opened the netting, and climbed down the ladder. Odd how easy it was to do that all of a sudden. She was tending to overcompensate and almost turned her ankle at the bottom. *Hav'ta get Boolean to do one of those adjustments on me,* she thought. She had never been this thin or this weak. She felt *tiny,* and she wasn't sure she liked the feeling.

She turned and saw Boday standing there a bit uncertainly. The artist sure looked different without the neck to toe tattoos, but, in a way, she almost looked, well, *normal.* No, better than normal. She was still tall and thin, but she was tight as a drum and look at those *muscles!*

"Hello, Boday," she said, feeling a bit awkward.

"Charley? You are seeing? Or is it. . . has he. . . ?" She grinned. "*Susama!*" And then there was a rush to her and Sam was picked up and hugged and darn near killed by Boday, who'd picked up real muscles herself and damn near crushed the now tiny Sam.

"All right, all right! We've got to go!" Boolean called to them. "Dorion, you help Charley down and go over to the saddles where we parked them. Boday, you and Sam will ride together—you'll both fit very nicely in one of the saddles now, I think—and can renew old times then. I've already mentally summoned Cromil and he'll bring Crim in. Probably Kira instead by the time we're ready to go. That may simplify matters. . . . Hmmm. . . ."

"He always does that—thinks aloud on the practical level," Dorion told them. "He can formulate a spell in his head that it would take a good magician a day just to read, but unless he does that he can't remember to put on his own boots."

The saddles looked both more and less intimidating to Charley when she could see them. Just ordinary saddles, although when Boolean nodded towards one it rose into the air. It was clear right off that no matter what her and Dorion's preferences were, there was no way even Cromil, who was a foot high and weighed maybe twelve pounds, could fit on one with her as she was. Boolean lowered one to the ground, she got on and got as comfortable as possible, and then it rose maybe three feet in the air. She had some initial trouble with balance but managed to stay on and finally decided that she could handle it.

Charley turned and was surprised to see a very pretty young woman, dressed in a tight black stretch pants outfit and pistol belt, walk in as Cromil scampered up, jumped, and perched on Boolean's shoulder. Boday, too, seemed startled by the strange woman's sudden appearance.

"Oh, I forgot about Kira," Boolean said apologetically. "This is the master swordswoman who did in three of the raiders and dueled Zamofir to the death last night."

Charley frowned. "Where'd *she* come from? And what about the guy with the sexy deep voice?"

It was Kira's turn to look confused, and Boolean had to explain, "I had to make a switch in the interest of all concerned. *That's* Sam and *that's* her friend Charley. Probably the only two people in the cosmos who even share the same fingerprints. And that's Boday, about whom you've probably heard much over the past months."

Kira gave a wan smile. "And people have problems with *me* sometimes. Well, glad to meet you. And—Charley—Oh! this is going to be very difficult for me! I'm so used to one being the other. . . ."

"*You* are!" Charley muttered.

"Well, you'll meet Crim in the morning in the flesh. Right now you might say he's with us in spirit. Don't bother to figure it out. I am certain that if someone wants to explain, they will."

Now that's *the kind of body I would kill for,* Charley thought, looking at Kira. She made Sam—or Sam in Charley's body—look positively plain. That woman would be glamorous in a pigsty. Seeing the way even Dorion was looking at this Kira suddenly made her self-conscious and jealous. Worse when Boolean said, "Dorion, you'll double up with Kira for now so I have one less saddle to juggle. Use hers over there—we're donating the horse, Kira. Hope you don't mind."

"No, these people need all they can get. Well! I can't think of any time I had a ride with a naked man. You want front or back?"

Charley fumed inside but couldn't really say or do anything. Any order she gave Dorion would be nullified by Boolean anyway, so what was the use? But he better damn well not get so much as a hard-on or he was gonna regret it later!

All set, they rose high into the air, giving Charley some really bad moments, then set off in a line. After the first hours. Charley had the hang of it, but she sure wished Dorion and that woman were in front rather than in back of her!

She was actually somewhat surprised at her feelings seeing Dorion with the woman. She tried to dismiss it as simple jealousy based on what she looked like now as opposed to what she had looked like, or thought she had looked like. Good lord—was she really *that* thin? Somehow she always felt just a little fat, a little not right, no matter what. Maybe Sam was right—maybe she *had* gone overboard. Well, Sam could fatten up that body now. At least she didn't have to worry about it in *this* body, with that spell that would make any diet useless. Maybe, at least, she could enjoy the next two months pigging out, if she was anyplace she could pig out. Ice cream . . . chocolate. She hadn't had those since, well, since she'd been back home on her own world. If they lost, well, hell, why diet? And if they won, Boolean would eventually make her look great again with no strain. It was a no-lose period.

But Dorion. . . . Well, he *was* kind'a cute, really. Overweight, yeah, but still with the tightest, cutest little ass. . . . He had a crush on her, sure, but in all that time he'd never taken advantage of her. In his own way, he was kind of sweet and a little shy. If that slave spell of his came off, with her looking like this, though, what would be his feelings then? Maybe that was it. The insecurity of being this way. That's what it had been, she knew, all along. Being blind and dependent but beautiful and sexy had given her some measure of power and security. They could be appalled at her liking the old way to this, but in her old society, as well as in Akhbreed culture, looks outweighed anything else most every time. Nobody ever seemed to look beyond, look inside. That was even this hangup the Akhbreed had with the changewind victims. Those Masalurians, at least according to Boolean, still had the same minds, personalities, souls, whatever. They just looked really bizarre now, but no more bizarre than the native colonials had looked, nor than the Akhbreed looked to the colonials.

But something in the back of her mind wondered if maybe she wasn't just as guilty of that. She'd never once put the make on Dorion, who was no worse-looking and better-looking than some or most of her old "clients" back on Tubikosa, but she'd fallen overboard for the handsome, sexy, romantic Halagar, Mister Macho, and look at what he'd been inside. Could that train of thought be right? Could she be just as guilty of what she condemned others for behaving? It was a troubling thought.

They passed over the border once more, this time far easier than going the opposite way. Even the magic sight was gone; the null just glowed in the same way it had when she'd first seen it, but enough so she could see the rebel emplacements. There seemed a *lot* more of them.

The Covantian side seemed, paradoxically, smaller than she'd remembered it, although admittedly her memories were colored by her limited sight and condition at the time. It had just seemed that there had been wall to wall guys down there when they'd crossed the first time, and now it was the kind of makeshift, thin line like the rebels had back then. But the hub ahead was so dark that for a moment she thought she was going blind again.

For Sam, the whole place was alive with a glorious glow, and when they crossed into the hub itself the countryside was not dark, but lit with a dim but beautiful spectral glow. Everything, it seemed, had some kind of aura, and each was unique, both by class and by shape within that class. It was beautiful—but where were the lights? There were vineyards and farms and whole towns down there. Even though it was growing late, there should be lights. Was it a limitation of this new vision, or was something very strange down there?

"I think they're getting smarter than Klittichorn gave them credit for," Boolean's voice came to them. "At least, it seems so. Maybe, just maybe, somebody's gotten paranoid about changewinds in the hub. There's only a few people and some animals down there. Probably civil guards making sure nobody gets any bright ideas about looting. Either Grotag got the shakes after all, or the kings and nobles did."

"But—you mean it's been evacuated?" Charley asked him. "If so, where would they go? And how?"

"Well, it's just a hunch, but the rebels didn't have enough to mass on every border and left only token forces on one before hitting Masalur. If the one opposite is uncovered, as it might well be, then we'll find they've moved the mass of people to the outer ring and into a safe and secure colony, a bit dispersed and with the bulk of the army to protect them. It's smart. If anybody hits Covanti they're going to cream the best vineyards in the cosmos. If it isn't hit, they'll eventually move back in only a little worse for wear. But to hit 'em in the colonies with precision like they used on my hub, they'd need a Second Rank man of their own on sight to aid in spotting, and they don't have enough to go around at all, let alone spare. If everybody's doing this, he's going to have a real empty victory. Of course, everybody won't, but it looks like the smart ones may get through this. Well, we have to pass very near the center of the city. If Grotag's still holding down the fort we'll know who's scared and who's stupid, and it's the loyal Second Rankers he's really after anyway."

The center city showed lights, but the population was far less dense than it should have been. Clearly a fairly large number of people had decided not to move, or to take the chance, or that the risk was in somebody's head, but, still, there couldn't have been more than ten or fifteen percent of the people left. The exception was the big castle in the center, which, to Sam, Dorion, and Boolean, blazed with a light so bright it was almost impossible to look at.

"So Grotag's still at home and holding fast," Boolean noted. "Well, thank the Lord for civilian government and some common sense. It goes to show how useless power is without brains. A few top adepts could hold that shield convincingly and Grotag could protect himself and his people at their side. What a jerk!"

Once beyond the city, there seemed to be far more activity and a lot more life, and it increased as they closed in close to the border. Clearly the evacuation was still in progress and this was the side possibly left undefended by the rebels. They weren't going quite there, though, but angled off to the north, skirting the border, and came upon a town that looked very normal and undisturbed and still with some life in it. The border towns *would* be the last to go in any event, of course, and might not, since they wouldn't be at Ground Zero or near it. The country areas of Masalur hadn't been touched by the changewind except for one narrow swath towards the exit point. These people were just as safe at home.

Down now, not quite to the town, but to a small house on top of a hill overlooking that town, settling down right in the front yard, as it were. Sam and Kira recognized it at once, but it was strange to the others.

Boolean got off, and Dorion slid off his and came over and helped Charley up off hers. She made almost a tearing sound when she did rise, as if she'd been glued to or stuck to the thing.

There was a light on in the front window, and before anyone could approach the front door, it opened, and a pleasant, sweet-looking gray-haired little old lady toddled out and looked at them, then smiled sweetly.

"I've been expecting you," said Etanalon.

Etanalon looked around quizzically at the group. She nodded to Kira and said, "Her I know, but you—" pointing to Charley, "you look like the one who was here but you are not. And you," she went on, pointing to Sam, "you I know as well. Oh, dear. Has the mirror erred? Have you starved yourself for months to get to that state?"

Sam laughed. "No, it's Boolean's tricks. We're kind'a twins, and Boolean switched our bodies around."

Etanalon sighed and nodded. "Ah, yes, that explains it. You, skinny one, should eat something. Anything. I have some fine food and snacks in the kitchen." She looked again at Charley. "But you, my dear . . . I sense great conflict and unhappiness in you. Perhaps we might do something for you." She turned to Dorion. "And you, young man, should get some pants on!"

"No time now for all that should be done," Boolean told her. "I want to be out of Covanti entirely before a good search is launched. Anybody else?"

"Yobi will meet us en route," she told him. "It is cutting it close, but what can Klittichorn have up there? We know the rogues and mental midgets he employs in the field, so what sort of competition can he have on hand?"

"Probably adepts he elevated himself without going through the niceties," the sorceror replied. "That makes them unknowns and thus more dangerous. The best guess I have is that he uses three of them on some kind of mock-up of Akahlar to triangulate and hold the position, then he opens the weak point and the Storm Princess captures and guides the storm. But that still leaves their four Second Rank against our three. Not good odds when one is Klittichorn and the other three are Klittichorn hand-picked and trained."

"Bosh. What kind of experience can they have? Those three have most certainly been concentrated in their training on the single goal of making this work. You have a mental hang-up on Klittichorn, though, which could prove our undoing. Are you certain you wouldn't like to face the mirror?"

Boolean gave a dry chuckle. "I'll handle him, don't worry."

Sam looked at Etanalon wide-eyed. "You are going to help us? I thought you were above this sort of thing."

"No one should be above crushing evil, dear," the sorceress responded. "I have been sitting here treating the individual ills of Akahlar so long, I seem to have temporarily lost my perspective. Just as I could no longer work for the system I found oppressive, so can I not sit idly by while whole masses of people are destroyed or driven mad. Some madnesses are such that they do not know they are mad and so will never seek treatment. Klittichorn is the sort of insanity that visits its madness on the innocent. The man is suffering but he is taking it out on everyone else. I can not sit idly by and let that happen. It was the two of you who made me doubt, but only when Masalur was so brutally assaulted did I realize that Boolean was right."

"I'm going to need to use your lab to get in touch with my people and make certain everything is set up," Boolean told her. "Sam, you come, too. We want to discuss a few things. The rest of you just hang loose; raid the pantry if you want, but I'd suggest sleep."

Etanalon, Boolean, and Sam went into the back and down into the depths of the hill where the sorceress's laboratory was, leaving the rest.

"Yobi, too," Dorion breathed. "I can hardly believe it! She hardly ever moves from her lair for *anything*."

"I think Boolean's right," Kira told them. "I think we should pick some comfortable spots in here and get what rest we can. We don't know just when we'll have to move long, hard, and fast. I don't sleep—nights—so I can keep a sort of watch. I know this place and I'm used to it."

They gave Charley the couch, but she found it too uncomfortable to sleep, and felt a little too keyed up. The others, from Boday to Dorion, had no such problems, and Kira was back snacking in the kitchen. She hauled herself up after a while, feeling a need for fresh air, quietly opened the door, and walked outside.

It was a beautiful night and, with the town below, an almost picture postcard scene. The air was warm, with just enough of a gentle breeze to make it pleasant; the kind of atmosphere and setting that made the troubles seem as distant as home, and allowed you to pretend, if only for a few moments, that nothing was wrong.

A strange, small shape moved nearby, startling her and causing an involuntary cry.

"Sorry," said the strange voice of Cromil. "Didn't mean to make you jump, although sometimes it's fun scaring folks."

She relaxed. "That's all right. I'm surprised you're not down with *them*, though, and that you're talking to me."

The little green familiar spat. "Nothing but boring crap down there. No interest at all to Cromil. Just talking about ways to get themselves killed is all. Got to hand it to him, though. If anybody can pull it all off, Boolean can. Suckered you good, didn't he?"

She frowned and looked at the tiny shape in the darkness. "What do you mean by that?"

"You never figured out how his mind works, have you? So pleasant, so chatty, you'll hand over your jewels and beg him to steal the rest. Gets so complicated sometimes he crosses himself up—

almost did with the two of you. Had all this in mind from the start, he did. Surprised he actually got this far, though. The others all wound up bad."

"Others?"

"Sure. Your friend wasn't the only Storm Princess dupe he managed to snatch from Klittichorn's grasp. Not many, but a few. Took bets on 'em, we did, only neither of us would bet that your friend would be the one to make it this far."

"Bets? What—what happened to the others? Where are they?"

The little green monkey shrugged in very human fashion. "Some dead. That's the easiest state to accomplish in this place. Others trapped, caught by Klittichorn's men, or spells, or whatever. Started you all off pretty equal and pretty low, he did. Wound you all up and let you run. Put the pressure under you when he had to, otherwise just let you run. Set you far away from him and sit there and tell you to find him. Kick you in the ass if you sat down or gave up. A kind of race in the end. First one to reach Boolean wins."

Her jaw dropped a bit. "But—why? You mean he could have pulled us to him at any time? That he *caused* all that we went through?"

"Not specifics. Bailed you out when he could, but mostly you were on your own. See, the winner gets to go up against the Storm Princess, right? Practiced, accomplished, one tough broad, driven by hate. Think of yourself when you got dumped here. Would your friend have been any match for the Storm Princess and sorcerers then? Would she even have understood the dangers or her own self? She'd have been a patsy. Chopped to pieces out of ignorance, hang-ups, you name it. Took education, see? Had to learn about Akahlar, about wizards and spells and all that stuff. All of you were naive, dumb, impractical airheads—typical teenagers. No good to go against them. You had to learn the rules, learn what evil really was, and to separate it from stupidity, which often looks the same. You had to fight some battles, get victimized, even abused. Not planned—we just knew it would happen. Could you cope? Could you survive? Help out when we could and you couldn't, sure, when we could, but that's all. You're the only two that made it."

She sighed. When she saw how close she and Sam had both come to buying the farm, it was even more sobering. Right up to the last minute. . . . She wasn't sure if she was elated or depressed as hell by the news. "I see," she answered. "Both of us had to be degraded, raped, tortured through spells, chased by gunmen, undergo fire and flood —all as a *test?*"

"Not a test—an endurance contest. It wasn't totally random,

either. The more you progressed, the more the destiny threads pointed to your friend. Boolean took something of a chance when he ordered the Demon of the Jewel of Omak to make certain she got pregnant. He had to know it would start a chain reaction that would lead to this point. However, there were indications Klittichorn was attempting to find the proper mate for the Storm Princess—strictly for the one purpose, of course, but satisfying the rebel's own sense of propriety and quieting disturbing rumors about her having a stable of female slave lovers, which was true but politically inconvenient—and your friend, thanks to her weight and her unconventional mate and lifestyle, seemed safest at the time."

"The demon . . . *made* her get pregnant?" Charley was appalled.

"Well, it's not as bad as it sounds. It simply implanted in her mind a natural curiosity about the normal way of doing things and the fact that she could use the hypnotic powers to do it, so, at the point when she dropped an egg, as it were, at the exact prime moment, she did it with one of the wagon train crew. You remember that."

In a way, it was a relief, even though it galled her to think how Sam had been so manipulated. At least the child wasn't a child of one of those gang-raping monsters. It was rape, of course—by Boolean, sort of—but so long as Sam didn't *know* it and thought it was her idea, Sam wouldn't think it so. That didn't really help Charley's own feelings, that Boolean had treated Sam as a thing, a piece of meat, the same way Halagar had treated Charley, but facts were facts, and now *she* had the kid inside *her.* So had she been sort of raped by this third hand? It was too complicated an issue for a night like this.

"But almost immediately after we were all caught in the flood, most of the train was killed, there was the capture, the tortures and rapes, and then we were split up in the Kudaan. Some help Boolean was there in our survival."

"He didn't plan it that way, but who would have expected Sam to use her powers so soon? Or that the mercenaries under the Blue Witch would hit that particular train in their search for Mandan gold cloaks to sell to the rebels? The mess happened, and it took Boolean and Yobi to straighten it out, that's all. When the two of you surfaced at Yobi's without Sam, Crim was contacted to track her down. Until then he'd been tracking you, thinking you were all still together."

"Yeah, but we were only found and rescued because Dorion happened to see us and saw my resemblance to the Storm Princess. Lucked out is what you mean."

"Crim would have tracked you, most likely, in the end. Luck is simply an amateur's term for the threads of destiny that are woven at conception. It's why some people have 'miraculous' escapes and others die in freakish happenings. The threads can be aborted by conflict with others, but Boolean read Sam's and it was a long thread. He and Yobi intervened, got Sam out of Pasedo's, got her mind mostly back, and she'd learned a lot about herself during that period—and so had you."

"So why didn't Boolean just order Crim to take us to Yobi so we'd be together again and then bring us to him, or him to us, right then?"

"Because you weren't ready. You were by now hardened survivors, but you were not ready. Sam was still at war with herself; she was still spending almost all of her time trying to escape her destiny and her obligations rather than facing them willingly. The same went for you, really, so together you would just reinforce each other. You both had grown hard, pragmatic, questioning, but neither of you looked at anyone else, not even each other. You were still turned inward, without a sense of obligation or any willingness to sacrifice for the common cause. It took Halagar to make you see what you'd really become, to see what others perceived you to be, what you thought you wanted or could accept. For Sam, it was easier. She always felt an obligation to others, to her friends, but her lack of ego, of self-esteem, of self-acceptance, and self-worth was driving her mad. In desperation, we had a magician refer her here, to Etanalon. It made her accept herself and resign herself to her duty, but no more. We decided we had to go with what we had, but the unexpected diversion that allowed her to feel normal, turned out to be a blessing even though it panicked us and almost cost us the game."

"Normal? Four husbands in a jungle house in the sticks?"

"Normal to *her*. It gave her something besides a lifetime with Boday to fight for. It showed friends, people she was closed to, dying—and for her, basically. It put *her* in the position of seeing others do what was expected of *her*. It broke the last barrier. She's ready now. In many ways she has far more experience and toughness than her foe. And you were right there, also ready, to play your own part."

Her eyebrows went up, "Me? What part? I was a decoy, maybe. but if it wasn't for my own thinking I'd have drank a potion back in Tubikosa and become permanently a mindless courtesan. I practically did, anyway."

"Well, it was your body, not your mind, that was important in the plan. You were, after all, an add-in, a bonus, there to give Sam the body she needed when the time came, and take on hers and keep the child from harm. We needed only the receptacle, and with only the receptacle the transfer would have been easily done. That you remained mentally alive as well actually complicated matters. Had we not been able to keep an eye on you, so to speak, we might well have had to make other arrangements."

"An eye . . . Dorion, you mean?"

"Of course not. Shadowcat. Like me, your familiar existed both in this plane and in his native one. There distance and even duration are meaningless. He and I discussed everything. We agreed that you should not betray your true self to Halagar lest he beat or possibly kill you. You were far safer when you appeared to have no mind and presented therefore no threat. He truly liked you, which is rare for a familiar. Perhaps too much. He was not supposed to kill Halagar. Boolean would have retrieved you upon his return from seeing what was done to poor Masalur. It caused much consternation that you had vanished, and we overstayed there seeing if we could pick you up on the impulse to come to him. Because of that, Zamofir got there first and all the bloodletting was made necessary. Again, it worked out, as those with true destiny tend to do, but that was the way it was. Because we were late Sam learned duty and sacrifice. Because you finally reached a point where you would rather die, naked, blind, and alone, in a foreign wood than return to being a slave and object in the camp, you learned much, too."

"You make it sound so cold, so calculating, so callous," she said, shaking her head. "Like we were pieces of meat with no rights and no say. Just dolls to make over and play with and never mind the suffering and pain and degradation. Our lives, our *minds*, really meant *nothing* to your master except possible means to his end. And he got just what he wanted, which grates on me. I sit here, fat and ugly and miserable, surrogate mother to somebody else's baby, and Sam's going smiling into maybe worst than death. Somehow, that really pisses me off."

"That's how wars are fought these days. Maybe they have always been fought that way, with the little folks being ordered to charge into the enemy lines. If they don't they get shot as traitors. If they do, they get shot by the enemy, all so their body can be used as a shield and stepstone by the next guy to get another couple of yards. Yours is an interesting race, that climbed from the muck by little murders, and as you grew in power and experience they became bigger murders. Now you have reached the point on many worlds where you can murder your whole species in a matter of a few minutes and that makes you the zenith of human civilization. Here a madman—and there are always madmen in a society built on murders to scale—intends to install himself as master and then as god. My race has sat back and watched, occasionally intervening over the years to get a better view, in utter fascination at this, and some of us spend eternity arguing the points you people raise. You object to being a tool, an object, pushed, shoved, and manipulated by powerful forces beyond your comprehension in the cause of stopping something horrible. Yet if those powers did not do so, would we not be guilty of allowing the greater crime to happen to the greater number? It is a fascinating point. Even your gods reflect this. You are pawns of omnipotent beings. You pray for mercy, for forgiveness, for victory in battle, and the death of your enemies. You sacrifice to them, either really or symbolically, with blood and ritual cannibalism. You are *born* pawns. It is in your nature. It is only when you notice that you are that you object."

She looked over at the tiny figure in the darkness. "Just what *are* you, Cromil?"

"An alternative reality. One from a universe so different that you could not even comprehend it, where the very laws of nature are so different as to be madness to you, as yours are to us. In the long distant past, we learned to use the weak points created by the out-rushing changewind, and, being curious, we lagged along. We need form here, so we take form here; otherwise it is all incomprehensible madness to us. We deal with the powerful, the high priests or sorcerers or whatever. We give some service, they give some things we want. It's worked out pretty well over the years."

"And what *do* creatures like you want from us?" she asked it. "To satisfy curiosity? To explore? More knowledge? Blood? What?"

Cromil's answer stunned her and stung her and she reeled from the impact of its words.

"Amusement," it said.

For a while she said nothing more to the creature because there was nothing more to say. Who was whose god, and who was whose plaything? Who pushed who, and for what motives? Was anybody, even Boolean, even Klittichorn, really free, really a master of fate, really in control?

You going to tell anybody any of this?" Cromil asked curiously.

"Maybe. Maybe not. It's not exactly what Sam needs to know right now, and your own feelings I suspect are pretty well known to the sorcerers."

"Oh, yes"

"Tell me—does Klittichorn have a familiar?"

"Oh, they *all* do. It's kind of necessary to the higher functions of magic. We're very loyal to whichever side we happen to be on, you see, but we tend to stay out of the showdowns. We prefer to watch."

"I'll bet." She yawned in spite of herself. "Well, you've depressed the hell out of me, anyway. I guess, for every body's good, I ought to try to sleep."

"Your role in this, except for mother, is about to end." the familiar told her. "The big show is about to begin now. We are actively wagering on the outcome."

She picked up a rock and threw it at him, but it missed.

To Charley's surprise, they flew next to Masalur, but only Boolean and Cromil went to the hub; the rest, under Etanalon's powers, went east, where she and Dorion had thought of going, and into a colony world that seemed peaceful and virgin. They flew out over a broad, sparkling blue, tropical ocean, landing eventually on a good-sized island, perhaps thirty miles across and twenty miles wide, the largest of a string of isolated volcanic islands. The place looked like those pictures in the magazines of tropical paradise; of coconut palms and virgin sandy beaches, with banana and mango and other tropical fruits—or reasonable cousins thereof—growing wild all over. It was a gorgeous place, the only inhabitants of which appeared to be birds and insects.

There was one structure on the island; a small but comfortable-looking beach house overlooking a picture postcard tropical lagoon. Inside they were surprised to find two bedrooms with big, comfortable, modern beds with spring mattresses, plus a living room and dinette area and something of a den overlooking the lagoon itself, all comfortably furnished if not with the best, then with homey touches appropriate to the setting and decor. Rattan chairs, that sort of thing. The bathroom was an outhouse—somebody had even carved a half-moon in the door—showers were available at a pretty tropical waterfall about a hundred yards into the jungle, in back of the house. There were oil lamps, storage places, and an outdoor covered grill. No electricity or immediate running water, but it looked like somebody's idea of a perfect tropical hideaway.

Boolean arrived about six hours behind them; by then they'd already found the ponds that trapped the fish at low tide, and were feeling quite pleasant. The sorcerer, however, was not alone.

The two creatures were both almost cartoons of extremely erotic girls, but they were not—at least not the way Charley and Sam and the Akhbreed thought of girls. For one thing, they were absolutely identical twins. For another, they had incredibly smooth pea-green skin that seemed almost to lack pores, and glistened a bit in the light, with lips of darkest green and emerald eyes in a sea of pale olive. What appeared to be thick if short dark green hair had the consistency and solidity of brambles, not hiding at all ears like delicate, tiny seashells; and their feet each had three wide, webbed, almost birdlike toes. They had four thin arms that seemed a bit more rigid than human arms and ended in three long identical fingers that closed on things almost clawlike, but were soft and as dexterous as human fingers, and the lower set appeared to be on ball joints, able to reach forward or back equally, and four small but firm breasts, the top pair looking normal but hanging just slightly on the lower pair. And, odder still, they had thin, prehensile tails that did not come out of the spine but out of the point between the vagina and the rectum, about a foot long and ending in a structure that looked like a . . . well, penis.

They were the objects of a lot of attention, and it was good they were not self-conscious about things. Everyone had the same thought: *so these were what the changewind made of the Masalurians. . . .*

"Folks, these are Modar and Sobroa," Boolean told them. "Don't ask me which is which now, but you'll tell when talking to them. Modar used to be six-two and all male, and Sobroa was about this size and the best-looking female adept I ever came across. They were among the small staff who volunteered to maintain the shield and defenses and remain at their posts."

If our form shocks *you,*" said one, in a strange, two-toned kind of voice, "think of what it was for us to suddenly find ourselves this. I hope you will get used to us, because we have not yet gotten used to us and we learn more every day. I fear it will be years before we learn everything."

"What matters," Boolean told them, "is that Sobroa was a trained healer and a midwife. She has no powers now, but she has delivered a *lot* of babies and she knows basic first aid and medicine. Modar was my librarian and something of a romantic and dreamer on the side. He found and mostly designed this place, and there's nothing about it he doesn't know."

"Do you like it?" asked the other one, in a voice that was identical to the first yet somehow different in tone and accent.

"It's *beautiful,*" Sam responded. "Was this a kind of retreat?"

Boolean nodded. "When we had to get away—me or any of the staff—we came here. There's no shipping to speak of on this world, and the population is concentrated in the less tropical climate zones for reasons that would be obvious if you saw them. These islands are a thousand miles from anyone and are likely to stay that way, at least for a number of years. Food, water, all the basics almost fall into your lap. But since it's a Masalurian colony, I highly doubt if anybody would look for you here. Anyone here now is welcome to remain here. Charley, you, and Dorion, of course. Just remember that you are the guests of Sobroa and Modar, they're not your servants. We will be leaving in the morning, and we won't be back until it's done."

It was tempting, really tempting, but first Boday, then Crim, talked to Boolean.

"Boday has not found her Susama to once more give her up. She will go, and if she can be of help to the last she will do so! And if, by miracle of miracles, she survives, she will immortalize the greatest battle in the history of the cosmos!"

"Just not knowing would drive us nuts," Crim told him. "Maybe we can do nothing, and maybe we're crazy, but I want to be there at the end, and I feel inside that Kira does as well. We already almost died for this."

"You both are welcome and may be useful," Boolean told them. "But, remember, if it's you or the enemy, you'll be left to the fates. And if it turns out that you can do nothing, then stay out of the way. Now get some sleep."

The goodbyes were tearful, with Charley doing a lot of hugging and kissing and crying and breaking up Sam and Boday as well, but then it was time. They who would remain watched the others climb on their enchanted saddles, rise up into the burgeoning sunrise, take one last loop around, and then become tiny specks and vanish in the warm light of day.

Dorion looked at Charley. "You wish you were going with them, don't you?" he asked her.

She just smiled and didn't answer.

"Well," he sighed, "so do I. May the gods who brought us all to this point be with them still."

High in the air over the sparkling blue ocean, Sam felt her breakfast remaining lumped in her throat, but she looked ahead, not back. She hadn't slept much, but she felt very wide awake, very keyed up.

My god, it's really happening, she told herself. *Here we go!*

12
The Citadel at the Edge of Chaos

When Klittichorn had dubbed himself the Horned Demon of the Snows he wasn't just doing it to make himself sound colorful.

All her time in Akahlar, Sam had spent in the subtropical or tropical belt, until she'd almost forgotten there was any such thing as winter or that cold meant like the inside of a freezer, not merely a bit of a chill after an intense rain.

Their journey northward had turned steadily if slowly colder by degrees as they passed each border or hub. Boolean was able to put in a perspective she could somewhat understand by asking her to think of Tubikosa as perhaps northern Australia or New Guinea; Masalur would be somewhere around northeast Africa, maybe Egypt, although with a lot better rainfall. Klittichorn, however, had his domain in the equivalent of northern Sweden or perhaps even Iceland or Greenland, up near or on the Arctic Circle.

It was hard for Sam to think of Akahlar as a planet like Earth—in fact, the planet Earth itself. It was too different, too exotic, without the land or sea or other areas to make any comparisons. The intense pull and hold of the Seat of Probability, like a giant sun on a different and lower dimensional plane, held Akahlar where it was, and had also slowly, over the millennia, pulled the other Earths "nearest" to it down so that they intersected for short periods, one atop the other. The hubs and nulls were the only places where, because the worlds were round, the intersection did not take place, and, as such, they were the only parts of the real world of Akahlar that had been able to develop.

Other than the increasing cold, the other thing Sam noticed as they travelled northward was that the intersection points, the parts of the colonies that overlapped Akahlar's reality, grew shorter and more irregular, often much longer on one side of a hub than another. Beyond the Arctic and Antarctic Circles, there was virtually no overlap, just ice and snow and occasional nulls to nowhere in patches here and there. It was for this reason, as well as its hostile environment and remoteness, that Klittichorn had chosen it. Almost no one lived there; just about no one wanted to go there.

But in the region he had picked there were high volcanic ranges providing unexpected warmth among the glacial ice, and the means to tap geothermal heat and power. In a small valley surrounded by glacier-clad volcanic mountain peaks, he had built not just his home and laboratory but a small city, populated by those who were the outcasts of Akhbreed society. Here the political malcontents, the magicians with grudges real or imagined, the disgraced soldiers and criminal classes, could gather with absolute immunity and safety and with a level of comfort and protection that a similar area like the Kudaan Wastes could not provide. Here resided the cream of the outcasts; not merely Akhbreed but colonials as well, picked up by Klittichorn or his agents from their own worlds and brought here to help their master plans.

Klittichorn's great, dull-red castle, with its menorahlike eight towers, dominated the scene. It was not merely his own home and base, but the workplace for many of the people. Below it, on the valley floor, stretched the comfortable and hyper-insulated houses of the people—heated by geothermal steam which also provided their hot water and even their cooking medium—stretching out on either side of the central greenhouses wherein were raised the best food crops adequate for all their needs. Beyond, the massive herds of reindeer and other arctic animals provided the sources of meat as well as the work animals for the society. Just viewing it from the air, as frigid as it was, the region impressed the hell out of all of them. None, not even Boolean, had seen it before.

There were six of them now; all were clad in layer after layer of heavy furs, gloves, you name it, to withstand the bitter cold, but while it was enough to keep them alive and out of harm's way from the elements, it didn't make any of them feel warm or comfortable.

Yobi had joined them in the air over Hanahbak, a thousand miles to the southeast, her great lower bulk covered with a tremendous fur cloak. She looked as if she were just floating there, a being who was her own craft, and if she used a saddle or other conveyance they had not seen it.

"Is that it? Is that where we have to go?" Sam asked, now used to being able to talk through muffled layers and masks and still have the same power of speech as if they were all sitting together comfortably around a fire inside a snug lodge.

"No, I just wanted to take a look at what he'd built," Boolean replied. "I think we're all impressed, although it doesn't really surprise me. He never did anything halfway."

"The scale of it surprises and shocks me," Yobi put in. "I had this picture of a frigid castle redoubt in the middle of wastes, not a somewhat grand city. Didn't you say the fellow was from a *tropical* place?"

"He was, but humans are very adaptable," the sorcerer responded. "He could never have accomplished all this in the south, not with all the people and politics and the Guild snooping about. Besides, look at the steam slowly rising from the ground all around. There's plenty of heat available here for almost anything you need. I bet inside those places, even the castle, it's as warm as Masalur. And if you look at the way the heat shimmers go, the odds are you can get from almost anyplace to anyplace using heated underground tunnels there. Unless you're into skiing or herding reindeer, you might never have to go outside or feel the cold."

"Then where is the man himself?" Crim asked.

"Not far, but better hidden and independent," Boolean told him. "In fact, I think we'll find a reasonable place to make camp here, and then send you and Boday to check it out for us."

"Why not everybody?" Sam asked him.

"I think he knows we're near, or coming," the sorcerer responded, "but I don't want to give him any free shots at us. He has monitoring spells all over here to detect people like us, but he feels he has nothing to fear from ordinary, nonmagical people. Not that there won't be some guards, so care will have to be taken, but to present the three of us to him within sight of his headquarters would be to draw targets on ourselves and give him a few free shots. No, let's keep him guessing as to our strength and location and true nature."

"You don't think he'll panic just by the awareness that we are close?" Yobi asked, concerned.

"Not so long as the Storm Princess knows and feels the presence of the child half a hemisphere away, no. He seeks godlike powers, but there is no way he can have godlike omnipotence. I think our little trick with the switch will fool him because it's too subtle and too unprecedented. I know the way his mind works as well as anyone, at least on the surface level."

They set up a camp back out of the weather in an old lava tube. The outside was freezing and nasty, but heat radiated from the walls within the tube, creating a frozen waterfall where it broke to the outside and some level of comfort within.

Crim surveyed the tube. "Comfortable, but I feel very vulnerable in here," he commented. "If anybody discovers we're here, they could just magically turn the lava back on, or even give us a wall of water, and we'd be through."

"That kind of magic is always telegraphed," Yobi assured him. "We have enough to prevent that sort of thing, so relax. More important is the two of you and whether you can really handle those flying saddles without one or another of us propping you up. You'll have to go in low and be very unobtrusive."

"Will he not see the spell that makes the saddles fly?" Boday asked her worriedly.

"Probably not. It's too minor a spell and there are probably thousands around a place like that. It would be drowned out by the weight of all those already laid on, much as a whisper is drowned by the roar of a crowd. Take care, though. If any of the sentinels that are almost certain to be guarding the place spot you, then all bets are off."

Crim looked a bit nervous. "You sure we can do this and be back before sunset? I don't want Kira to come out under these conditions."

"I fear we will be deprived of poor Kira's company, but for perhaps an hour or so, if that," Boolean told him. "It is late spring here and we're close to the Arctic Circle if not slightly past it. If we are, we won't meet her at all, for this time of year the sun does not set there. Were we in the Antarctic, we wouldn't see you. Cheer up, my friends. We may be in the jaws of death, but at least for now we are absolutely safe from vampires."

Crim and Boday did a bit of practice flying around the peaks and valleys near the cave and both decided that they were pretty confident.

"It'll take you about a half hour to get there," Boolean told them, "and spend only as much time as you absolutely need to get the feel of the place, its tangible defenses, looks, and the like. If you are not back here within three hours we will have to assume that you were seen, possibly captured, and we will go immediately. Understand? Boday, I'll expect you to be able to sketch it when we get back, with Crim's memory as a check. Temporarily, you'll have to be a realist. Accuracy counts. The odds are, when we go in, we'll only get the one shot. Either we go all the way, or that's it."

She shrugged. "Boday is great at all art. She will do what you wish and better that you dream!"

Sam hugged her. "Take care, now. If we're all gonna die in this, don't you be the first."

Boday laughed. "The Gods of Chaos have woven our destinies

too tightly! Boday has suffered too much to die now before she achieves immortality through the works she has yet to create! Come, big man! Let us see this fortress of evil!"

Sam watched them go, feeling nervous for both of them and also for what would come after. She felt guilty realizing that, of all the people here, there was a hierarchy of expendability, and she was the only one absolutely sacred.

Now they could only sit in the volcanic warmth, munch on a few cookies and some strong drink brought along for this, and wait. There was something strangely ridiculous about huddling fur-clad in a cave with these three master sorcerers, who could restore a town overnight, heal the most gravely wounded, make saddles fly, and do all sorts of miracles, all of whom were also huddling here in furs and looking as miserable as she felt.

"It's the fat, dear," Etanalon said to her.

"Huh?"

"You feel colder than you ever have. I can see you shivering like you had a fever even in this relative comfort and warmth. You probably know that most people who are native to cold areas have yellow skins. The yellow is a layer of fat, even on the thin ones, that provides extra insulation, but fat is a premium to them. You have fleshed out a bit on the journey here, but you still eat like a bird because your friend starved that body and shrunk that stomach to the size of a walnut. One wonders about young girls' sense of proportion when they will starve themselves rather than dare be pleasantly and comfortably plump. In hard times, the fat women survived to have babies, the thin ones died out. In many societies a bit of plumpness is considered sexy, but, these days, everyone seems to want to be a skeleton. I believe that if I were a goddess, I'd make a new standard for beauty."

Yobi gave one of her cackles. "Imagine you or *any* of us as gods and goddesses! I suppose I do somewhat resemble some of those monstrous idols some societies worship, but I'm afraid I'd die laughing at prayers to statues of *me*."

"Admit it. You're here because you think our friend out there has found the key," Boolean noted, pointed a finger at her. "For ten thousand years at least sorcerers have tried for that state, and failed, mostly miserably. The lucky ones died. Godhood. The ability to summon and *direct* the forms of order out of what Chaos sends. Not random, like the changewinds, but deliberate. Yet, like the winds, generalized, or as specific as the simplest and most direct spell. The power to right wrongs, change minds, mold and shape civilizations, create."

"And destroy," Cromil commented, peeking out from a fold of Boolean's coat. "You're talking about a man—or woman—having the *power* of a god. There's more to being a god than that. You're afraid Klittichorn's going to get the power. Big deal. Would you really be any better at it—any of you—or just different? Power doesn't confer wisdom, nor make you omnipotent. It just makes an ordinary person with an extraordinary love of power able to exercise it, with all his or her hang-ups and problems."

"The voice of wisdom from the netherhells," Boolean commented dryly.

"Figures. We been talking with people like you for thousands of years and nobody really heard anything from us they didn't want to hear," the familiar retorted.

"I suppose that demons and imps and the like could do better at it, having all that wisdom and a superior civilization," Yobi said sarcastically.

"Of course not. Why do you think they call it the netherhells, anyway, and why's everybody around here always cursing somebody to go to Hell? You know what Hell is? It's *boring*, that's what it is. Deadly dull. That's why we have to come up here to have any fun."

Sam shivered and looked around the cave. "Yeah, ain't we got fun."

"Like, who says this guy would ever be the first one to reach First Rank, anyway?" the familiar went on, ignoring the commentary. "All those universes, all those worlds, and they all got all those gods. Old men in the sky, creatures with wings, creatures that demand sacrifices and have like eight arms, fish gods, horse gods, you name it. Jealous gods, philandering gods, gods who curse men for not being cruel enough in war in their names—who are looked upon as ending war and bringing heaven to earth anyway? We've had our *fill* of gods up here. That's why demons are never on God's side. All the gods are jerks, that's why. So what's one more jerk in the cosmos?"

Boolean looked down at him, frowning. "I wish I knew when you were being cynical and making trouble and when you were telling the truth."

"I think it would be too damn complicated to be a god," Sam commented. "Even if you *were* pure of motive and the power didn't corrupt you, which it almost surely would. I mean, every time I think about somethin' I really would want to change—hate, envy, greed, jealousy, hunger, war—I can't figure out how to do it, unless we make everybody everywhere like, well, the changewind did to

Masalur. They're all absolutely identical, not even sex to cause trouble, in a place you described to me as a swamp that seemed pretty much the same. If it's warm all the time and everybody looks the same there's no need for clothes, or fashion. If they make their own food inside, somehow, and maybe only need to drink water or something, then there's no hunger. Probably no government, neither, since when everybody was the same who would follow somebody when you couldn't even tell who was who?"

"I have a feeling that Masalurian society is going to be more complicated than you think," Boolean noted, "although, I must admit, it'll probably complicate itself because their minds didn't change and they already think differently than ones born and raised like that. Still, the one thing that's not identical is their brains. Their I.Q.s and their aptitudes will be different. In all the colonies and in all the parallel worlds of the outplanes not corrupted by the Akhbreed, we find more cultural similarities than physical ones. Geography, resources, needs of all kind shape competition which heads to the rest, and having only one sex doesn't solve that problem if it still takes two to make a baby. The human need for companionship, closeness, seems overpowering even without the baby thing. Otherwise homosexuals would never feel jealousy. No, I'm afraid you're right. The only way to cure the ills of the human condition, even with godlike powers, is to make people inhuman, either machinelike or perhaps incorporeal beings like the demons and imps, who are so bored they come up here for their entertainment and often meddle just to cause trouble and see what results. Still. . . ."

"Still, you'd like to have the power and find out," Cromil finished smugly. "Only if you can't have it, you sure don't want the good old Horned One to have it, because his vision of insanity is different than *your* vision of insanity."

"Enough, imp! You can be sent back home for a very long time!" Yobi snapped.

Boolean looked over at Sam. "Wouldn't you really take a crack at it, if you could, though? Be honest."

"Only if I had to," she sighed. "Honestly—power like that without the genius to figure out all the angles to using it . . . well, you'd just be some kind of corrupted power monger, or you'd be real careful how or if you used it, 'cause you might not figure all the angles. I think I'm more scared of what it would do to me, or what I might do to lots of others, to want it. I got more sense than that."

Boolean shifted uncomfortably in his furs. "I know I'd always be warm," he muttered. "Still, the puzzle drives me nuts. I've always been able to do anything Roy has, to understand or come up with anything he has, *after* he's worked it out and told me it's possible. The elements are all there, like pieces in a puzzle, but they all don't fit. Okay, we need a Storm Princess because she's immune to the changewind, and we need a sorcerer because the Storm Princess's abilities are natural and couldn't cope with the massive variables involved in actually shaping reality. And we need power—lots of power. Lots of changewinds, not just to knock out or nullify the other Second Rankers but to feed—what? Storm Princesses are some kind of power regulators just by their very existence, temporizers of the changewinds, safety factors on each world. But why in hell are they all lesbians? What can the sex preference have to do with it all? It's insane. Yet you take that sexual preference thing, the least of it all, and the magic goes away. Why?"

Not even the one with all the attributes had the answer. Still, Sam had to wonder. Her? Little Sam Buell? Somehow protecting her world from the major effects of the changewinds depended on her just being alive, living there someplace? Made no sense at all. And whatever it was, it came natural, like breathing. It wasn't something you thought about or even necessarily knew you had.

She had a sudden thought. *Wait a minute—this Storm Princess, the one just over there, wasn't an unconscious regulator. She* had *been, but not now. She drew that changewind right into downtown Masalur hub! She made it march round and round until it covered maybe two thirds of the hub. That's what this was all about, wasn't it? Somebody who could* control *the changewind, deliberate like, not like breathing.*

Like she had done. She'd already done it with regular storms. She'd banished the Sudogs, called lightning down to fry a gunman, summoned a great storm in the Kudaan, and then, in Covanti, she'd stood her ground and actually *deflected* a changewind! She could control the storm like any other, and was immune from its effects other than getting wind-blown and wet. But she couldn't speak to the Maelstrom, which was still just a great storm and not something with thought and deliberateness. Its effects were random, like any storm's; the order that formed from it, bizarre as it might look, held together, made sense, thanks to those laws Boolean talked about. The ones concerning how the universes formed out of one big bang and how snowflakes are so pretty and intricate. A god could somehow talk to those forces, shape those laws, so they formed or did what he or she wanted. It would be like giving a mind, a brain, to a changewind maelstrom.

All these sorcerers spent half their time doing miracles, making magic, and none of them *believed* in magic. It was all natural laws and math and all that. The whole idea that one girl in each world was born with these powers and did this regulation bit, identical girls, they explained simply by noting that regulatory mechanisms always developed in nature, and that the results of the laws of chaos didn't necessarily make sense, they just accomplished what they had to.

"Boolean?" she prompted, and he looked over and raised his eyebrows. "Who are the Storm Princesses in the world that aren't human. Akhbreed types, or whatever you want to call people like you and me? How can there be somebody like *me* in worlds where people breathe water or have horns and tails and all that? Who are *their* regulators?"

"Huh? They don't have them. Or, if there was a common ancestor or thread to the Storm Princess mold, they've been able to mutate or change somehow. That's always been a mystery, of course. Maybe you don't really have to be physically identical. Maybe you only have to be physically identical within the same racial stock. None of the Akhbreed are native to here, after all. They dropped down in the more violent maelstroms of the prehistoric past from up around our area. The others, too, must have regulators of some kind, I suppose—unless there are other factors so that they don't need them and we do. Who knows? One can only study the system that chaos sticks us with, we can't read any master plan into it. I know of a few attempts in the ancient literature to find what regulates the others, but they never came to anything. Still, it's another part of the puzzle, isn't it?"

It was—but not as lightly dismissed as he made it seem. Of course, who was she to think on this, when big brains like him couldn't figure it? Still and all, she doubted that those other universes *had* Storm Princesses, at least not on Earth. Maybe someplace else in each big universe humans like them appeared and with them a Storm Princess. Maybe so. Or maybe all those other Earths had something that only the humans lacked.

The little demon said there were lots of gods. Did he mean it? And, if so, which kind was he talking about? The kind of god she was dragged to church for, or the kind the ancients worshiped that looked like a big Buddha with horns, or what? Or did he see any difference between the worlds of humanity and those who were something else? What if Cromil was telling the truth? What if there really were gods? If those universes had gods, then they wouldn't need Storm Princesses for protection and regulation and all that, right? They'd go from the whims of chance to the control and will of their god.

Fifty million monkeys pounding on typewriters would, given an unlimited amount of time, write the works of Shakespeare.

Her science teacher back in tenth grade had used that as an example of why the Earth was how it was. The universe was so big, it just happened, that's all. Boolean's chaos shit in a nutshell, only her old science teacher hadn't dreamed how big a place it really was.

So fifty million monkeys, given enough time, would write Shakespeare. So the universes, given enough time, would—*develop gods?*

This was getting too heavy for her and she didn't like where it was going, but she couldn't really stop. She didn't have much education, much understanding of things, but maybe all these folks had too much. Suppose, just suppose, in each universe, the system said there'd be a god, or many gods—who knew?—to regulate, to control the changewinds, to stabilize things like they were never stable in Akahlar. But suppose, just suppose, that whatever made gods didn't always work. It worked most of the time but not all the time, particularly when you got way out, where the rest of the humans were. Suppose all the things needed to make a god just never got together, or never got together *right* there? So they just kept floatin' around, never comin' together. . . .

My god! All the holy wars and all the church singin' and all the Hallelujahs and monks and missionaries. . . . All for different gods created out of need or out of some visions from other universes or maybe out of folks' minds 'cause they knew they ought'a have at least one. All for *nothing?* And her mom joining that real fundamentalist sect and even gettin' divorced from Daddy 'cause he thought they was phonies and all that. All for *nothing?* And her science teacher was right that there was no god, just natural laws, but he was wrong, too. *Most people had gods, but we don't!*

It was such an emotionally unnerving concept that she said nothing about it, didn't even want to bring it up to the others. Maybe it wasn't true—exactly. But, somehow, deep down, she thought it had to be at least part of the answer. And old Klittichorn had figured it, and he'd spent all that time getting together all the things needed to make a god of the Akhbreed, and that was what he was planning to do. . . .

Damn! What sacrilege! What a horrible, horrible thing to even *think.* But she couldn't stop thinking it, even though it made her feel sick and empty inside. Did all Akhbreed lack one, or just some? Oh, jeez. . . .

She just *couldn't* be right. Even if she somehow pushed her own emotions and beliefs aside for the sake of argument, she knew she had to be wrong. *I mean, these people here like Boolean—Professor Lng—are all big brains who been studyin' this their whole lives. I never even got to graduate from high school with my C average and I didn't have the brains for college, anyways. This is crazy thinkin', me pretendin' I got more brains than I got, that's all.*

She wouldn't say nothing to the others; no use in getting laughed at.

Crim and Boday were back in a little over two hours, looking frozen to death. The sorcerers risked a bit of magic to warm them and soothe frostbitten areas, and they were soon able to talk about what they had seen—and what they had not.

Boday took the charcoal pencil and paper from her saddle pack and began to sketch. "You see—on a plateau, like so, with downward slopes and then high mountains around. It does not look like much, except for this bulge here in the center, but we think most of it is underground."

"There are fortifications along the downward slope into a V-shaped notch valley before the high mountains begin," Crim elaborated. "Hard to tell just what they were, but they looked dug in and sheltered. There's no question it's the place, though. There's no snow on top of it. Not a bit. You can see the warmth coming from it, and there's almost a little snowstorm where it meets the real cold air, but the stuff that falls never freezes."

"We think the main entry is down here, below the plateau, in the sides," Boday continued, as the sketch took on a remarkably detailed look that seemed almost three-dimensional. "It appears that there is a bridge that can be extended, *so,* making a connection to a fairly wide trail *here,* which is snow-covered but passable if you knew it."

"Except for a few rough edges here and there, it looks kind'a like a flying saucer," Sam commented. "Jeez! How the hell do we get *in* there?"

"We know Klittichorn has very few Second Rank people with him," Yobi remarked, obliquely addressing Sam's question. "The odds are, unless he has one or two spares, they would all be needed to focus the mechanism when they begin their dirty work. I am quite confident that the three of us can take the operators, Klittichorn included, or that we can take whatever spare people—who would be lesser, more inexperienced types—who would be left to guard and run defenses. The trouble is, we can not take both. Their combined power would require at least another three or four as strong as us."

Etanalon nodded. "I agree. From here, even now, I can sense the power level against us. Klittichorn is strong, but so are each of us. The others are mere shadows, but together they are formidable, particularly under their master's direction. If we are to have a chance, they must first be divided."

Boolean nodded, then looked first at Etanalon, then at Yobi. "You know what that means? We have nothing we can draw them out with—they know their strength and time is running out on them. They could go at any moment, but certainly no more than a week to ten days. After that, the child might well be born. They're not going to split themselves up now for any cause at all, or they would have sent some of them after Sam instead of Zamofir. In fact, if we wait for them, they'll have gathered in any of the others they might still have out there and be stronger. We must hit *now!*"

Yobi nodded back to him. "Yes, I think we understand what that means. The only way to have them divided is to have them divide themselves. That means Klittichorn and probably three of his best directing the war, which, once started, they dare not break off, lest they have the whole of the Second Rank up here and on our side regardless of what they do to the hubs. And, I agree as well, we know not how many others might be coming here in preparation for the big attack but surely there are some. We can not wait."

"It's agreed then," Etanalon chimed in, "that the best and only practical method is to provoke them into starting the war now, pulling their strongest to its commission and allowing us to enter dealing only with the second rate."

"Yes, but how do we provoke them?" Boolean asked. "We go in frontally and they'll know it's only we three—they can read the power as much as we. They won't panic—they've been at this too long. They'll just gather together and meet us head on."

Sam's jaw dropped as she couldn't believe what she was hearing. "You mean—after all this, you're gonna let it *happen?* You're gonna actually *make* them do it? Start the war? Kill or transform millions and millions of innocent people? Give him his crack at godhood?"

"We see no alternative, dear," Etanalon responded gently. "Hopefully we can prevent it from covering the whole of Akahlar, depending on how strong his outer defenses prove to be. But without Klittichorn as the will and the glue, it will fall apart in the end, and those of us with great power can aid in picking up the pieces and reregulating the system as we've always done, much as I hate to get back into *that* end of the business. It's either this or we must quit and sit here and wait for him to first win his war and then claim his First Rank status."

"That's what it's always been about, hasn't it?" Sam said accusingly. "You—none of you—really care, deep down, about the lives that will be destroyed, the civilizations and cultures shattered, the people who will be enslaved and all that. It's Klittichorn you've been after all along. Nothing else matters. He's the first one you all are convinced really can make himself a god and you're scared of him. If not you, then nobody. That's it, isn't it?"

Boolean sighed and looked her straight in the eye. "No, Sam, that's not it. Or, rather, that *wasn't* it. I swear it. And it didn't have to be it, either. It didn't have to come down to just us on the edge of a frozen world in the middle of nowhere having to make this decision. There are literally close to a thousand Second Rank sorcerers in Akahlar. A *thousand!* If we had just one percent of them here—just ten—this wouldn't even be a contest. We could shatter that place and fry him and that would be the end of it. One percent! But he's caressed them and cajoled them and fooled them and wined and dined them and fed their prejudices and when all else failed put real, genuine fear into them. He's played to greed, like Grotag getting an empty promise, he believed that his own hub and staff would be spared and that he'd increase his powers and holdings under the new order. He's played to an ancient, corrupt system that so takes its powers for granted that it believes itself invulnerable, and played it like a symphony orchestra. And that leaves three of us—one social pariah, one exile, and one retired researcher—and the three of you to do it."

"But, surely *some* of them . . . !"

"In what I think is our common history, give or take a few years, one fellow went from a laughingstock in a beer hall to ruler of a large and powerful country that prided itself on its intellectuals, its culture, and its sophistication. He turned it into a gangster state that had a relatively weak army and weaker navy and he scared bigger, more powerful countries, or buffaloed them, or lied and agreed to everything they wanted and then did the opposite, in a massive con job that resulted in the most horrible world war we have known. Klittichorn's turned the same neat trick here. And, like his predecessor in my own world, when he eventually must go to war and his power and strength and aims are no longer possible to hide, then he must go for broke. He has to hit them hard and fast before they can organize, figure out who's hitting them and how, and bring down massive concerted force to stop him. To do that at this stage they will all have to admit they were stooges, fools, and dupes, and pretty openly and obviously. That's pretty hard to do when you're used to being a demigod, and, once he starts, that's the only time allowance he has. Sure, we wanted to stop it, but we didn't have the weapon until now and we don't have the allies even now. This is the best we can do. We can't stop him, we can only hope to salvage what wreckage he makes and minimize it."

"But—"

"No buts! The choice has changed from preventing him from wiping out anybody—to preventing him from wiping our *everybody*. Once you're in there, you wrest control from that Storm Princess! You send those things out where they can't do more damage here, and where they will be tempered in the outplanes. You get her and take control and save everybody and everything you can. Now, that's all we can do. The alternative is to do nothing. Is that what you want?"

She sighed and sank back down on the floor of the cave. She wished she had an answer, an instant plan that would solve it all, but there was none. He made too damned good a case. "No, that's not what I want, damn it. I'm just sick and tired of every decision, even life and death, bein' made for me with any choice I got limited to ten seconds or less." She sighed again. "All right—so how are you gonna get him to jump the gun?"

"One thing at a time. Let's first make sure we're rested and well coordinated and know just what we're trying to do."

Crim looked at him. "What about us? Do Boday and I just hang loose and freeze to death, me making sure she lives long enough to do battle sketches?"

"Uh-uh. You wanted in, you're coming. You take those machine guns you got so fond of with you. Now, you stand in front of a Second Rank sorcerer, even a good adept, and empty the clip at them, and they'll laugh and freeze the bullets or turn them to raindrops or something. But if they're taking on me, or Yobi, or Etanalon, they won't even *think* about you. They'll be on magic sight and won't even *notice* you. If that happens and you see us engaging, then you don't hesitate. You blow 'em to Hell."

Crim nodded. "That sounds like my fantasies come true. I always wanted to nail some sorcerers. And if we get in to wherever they're doing their thing? We won't be much use in *there*, I suspect, and they're bound to have a few folks with guns of their own."

"Military stuff, probably. You're better than they are—typically, the average general hasn't shot anything except maybe clay pigeons in years. Keep 'em off us, and if you see the Storm Princess, open up. She doesn't have that kind of magical protection."

"Yeah, but neither do I," Sam noted nervously.

Boolean chuckled. "Uh-huh. Well, you've eavesdropped on your alter ego in there enough. If you were dressed pretty much like her, you might even pass for her. Sure, they might catch on if they put two and two together, but they'll hesitate. They may take no chances at all and divert fire from you—I would in their shoes. If you can act the part, even for a little, you may just throw them for a loop."

"I—I don't know. My dialect's more of a peasant sort than hers, and right now she's fatter, although I suppose with some clothing choices we could fake that. But her hair, that sort of thing."

"Perhaps," suggested Etanalon, "we could minimize that whole confusion. If we knew exactly what she looked like now—right now—it would be a simple matter to adjust your looks to hers. The acting we will leave to you, but I suspect little of it will be required. The *presence,* as it were, is enough."

"Yeah, but how're we gonna know what she looks like? I mean, the last time I tried that mindlink bit she heard me, screamed, shut me out, and sent a changewind after me."

Etanalon smiled sweetly. "Ah, but, my dear, you weren't hypnotized by an expert sorceress, who could subtly guide that link."

"But she'll know I'm close by. They were able to send a changewind after me in Covanti. . . ."

"That's because she was able to turn to Klittichorn right then and there and have *him* trace the link," Etanalon told her. "We will go patiently this time, until she is in the right environment. And we will eventually send her a vision, but with confirmation that you are not close but far away, since the child is far away. Tell me, have you ever attended a live birth?"

"Two. Putie and Quisu. I had nightmares about my own for a week after that. One part of me didn't want to go through that at all, the other wanted it over and done with Why?"

"Perfect. You fantasized based on what you saw. Well, that's all we're going to have you do again, my dear. And we're going to let that young woman in the redoubt there in on that fantasy. Oh, yes, we are. . . ."

The Storm Princess awoke suddenly with a series of very odd sensations, most of them unpleasant. First was the convincing feeling that she had suffered some kind of major menstrual flow and that her bed was now wet with a thin, yet mucousy substance she could still feel draining from within her. Almost immediately, she felt the muscles deep within her contract in spasmodic fashion.

Alida and Botea, her two female slave consorts who generally shared her bed, stirred into wakefulness as she abruptly sat up.

"Alida! Botea! Awaken and switch on the lights!" she commanded, even as she was pulling the covers from the bed and examining the satin sheets for any signs of wetness. She found none, which troubled her even more than if she'd found it, nor did anything seem amiss in and around her vagina. The lights, when they went on, confirmed it.

There was nothing there. Nothing.

A dream? A vision? Or another of those shared things? She felt intermittent short bursts of weakening powers within her, not serious but more frequent than she'd ever known, and that, tied to the nightmare, gave her alarm.

She got up, pushing one of her consorts out of the way, and went immediately to the wall intercom and pushed the red button. Even Klittichorn slept—everyone assured her of it—but he somehow was never asleep when she had to see or talk to him.

"Yes, Princess?" his voice came back, clear and awake.

Quickly she described the vision and the sensations to him, and he was not pleased, but also not easily panicked. "Sense the child, the source of the interference. If your duplicate is close by, then such a thing could be transmitted to force us into hasty action."

"No," she assured him. "It is far away, still distant, remote. The interference I felt there was real, but it was still far away and easily handled."

"Hmmmm. . . . Very well. Get dressed and meet me in the War Room as soon as possible. And, if you feel any more of those muscle spasms down there, let me know and tell me how far apart they might be."

"Lord Klittichorn—if this is no trick, then what might it be?" She was genuinely worried about herself now.

"Silly fool! First the water breaks, and the amniotic fluid drains out. Contractions start either a bit before or almost immediately after that, leading to the birth. Either my guess as to impregnation was wrong or the child is coming early, which is not unprecedented. This is the first time that psychic link has worked to our advantage in warning us. We must seize the initiative now. You may feel no more contractions, but if the link still is sending them, the time between is critical. Once the babe is born and the umbilical cord severed and she takes in her first air and cries out to the world her existence, your power and control is diminished by at least half, and that's far too much. Get dressed and hurry down to the War Room. I will summon the others. Take any of the elixirs I provided depending on your wakefulness and physical strength, but eat nothing."

"I shall do as you ask," she responded, then turned and looked at the two waiting slave girls. "The brown and red saffron ensemble," she told them. "Now!"

She went over to the dresser, sat on the seat, and began to comb her hair and make herself presentable to the world. The slaves came back with the outfit she wanted, which was comfortable yet imposing, the trim on the dress just touching the knee, but with matching leggings and short, comfortable boots. The pair helped her on with it, then one fixed her earrings while the other brushed her long, flowing hair.

She was not fully satisfied, but it would have to do. She got up, examined herself in the dressing mirrors, decided that she could go out like this, slipped the gold ring with the huge ruby on her ring finger, kissed the girls, and walked out, up a short flight of stairs, then down a main hall. She had not touched the elixirs; if she needed any chemical help to do this, then she was not up to it in any case.

She was almost to the main doors of the War Room when she felt another slight twinge down there. She hadn't timed it, but guessed it could be no more than fifteen or twenty minutes from the initial one.

The big red double doors opened before her automatically and she strode into the center of the fortress, the War Room, with its tiered layers leading down to the central circular floor and the great suspended globe of Akahlar in the center. Klittichorn and two of the others, as well as a few slave attendants and the Adjutant, were all there.

She felt curiously awake and excited, as if this was the moment she had waited for and prayed for all her life. *Soon, ghost of my mother, soon,* she thought with some satisfaction. *Now, this very day, the empire of the Akhbreed who killed you and destroyed our beloved people will be no more.*

Etanalon snapped her fingers and Sam came out of it with a start. "Huh? What?" She clearly remembered the vision but not being put under.

"Mission accomplished, I believe," Boolean announced, "although I thought you were taking a big chance going that close in to Klittichorn, Etanalon."

"Well, I wanted to see what the place looked like. It's quite impressive, you know. I'll attend to the makeover of Sam, here. The rest of you be fully prepared to move just as soon as we sense full radiated power from that contraption of his. Once they are committed, we want to move as swiftly as possible. The sooner we get in and get to them, the more hubs and lives we'll save." She turned back to Sam. "Ready?"

"I guess. Won't he sense your use of sorcery, though?"

"I think old Klittichorn's got more on his mind than us right now, dear, and so long as he still thinks you're far away and the power use is slight, what matter now? Stand by. This will tingle for just a wee bit, and then you'll have to depend on me for major warmth until we are inside. It is cozy, but it is not an outdoor outfit."

She felt the tingle, but felt no different—only slightly chillier. She looked down, though, and saw that she now wore the outfit, right down to the cute boots, that the Storm Princess had put on in the vision. She felt her ears and found earrings there, and her hair was longer, softer, and fuller than it had been. She, too, felt a bit fuller, and she noticed that her ring finger now had a duplicate of that mega-ring the Storm Princess had put on. She understood now that Etanalon had somehow shared that vision and manipulated it, and had made her over into as close a double of the real Storm Princess as possible.

Crim and Boday checked their weapons and ammunition belts, and Boday clapped her whip to its strap brace on the side of her belt. To top it all, both had quivers full of crossbow bolts on their backs and very fine-looking crossbows in hand.

"Not the machine guns at the start?" Sam asked Crim.

"Uh-uh. We talked it over. If there are any routine guards out there, we want to take them out silently. Leave the machine guns until the alarms go off."

Boolean looked approvingly at Sam. "A perfect double. Incredible. My genetic spell was right on the money, proving at least that I am a genius. One thing, though—it's unlikely you'll get close enough to get the chance, but by no means should you touch the Storm Princess. Anything else is okay, and, remember, she's as mortal as you are. That goes both ways."

"Huh? Why no touching?"

"Just a feeling. There's an old legend, back home as well as here and elsewhere, about what the Germans in my native world deemed *doppelgangers*. It was said that everyone in the world had, somewhere, an exact duplicate, and if the two ever met and made contact, they would both cease to exist. It's unlikely that there really are many doubles, but people *have* fallen through outplanes to ones below—it's happened many times, enough to be recorded. There's a possibility that there is some kind of difference at the atomic or molecular level that would in fact cause two duplicates from different worlds to cancel one another out. I'm not positive, but why take chances? If we can get that close to her we can nail her a hundred ways. Why sacrifice yourself?"

She nodded. "Well, I'm in favor of that sentiment. Now, how long do we have to wait?"

"Who knows? Not long, I hope. We've started his clock counting down and he wants to attack before the explosion. We all shared the vision of that room, which pretty well confirmed our deductions of what it must look like. I noted the pentagrams, too, Cromil. Some of your buddies are playing in this on his side."

"Aw—he's always had the *prohjjn*—the Stormriders—with him, and their Sudog pets. Probably just gonna use them to confirm his kills, that's all. They can't do much damage now."

Yobi's great, hooded head shook slightly. "I would like to know the importance of the small red dots in the hubs on that globe of his," she commented. "They weren't regular enough to be aim points."

Nobody else had noticed them, including Sam. "Nothing we can do or know about it until we're there," Boolean pointed out. "Still, don't underestimate the bastard. *Whoops!* On your marks, ladies and gentleman! Looks like they switched on the juice!"

"Give it a couple of minutes to make certain it's not a test, or not some ploy to draw out potential attackers," Yobi responded nervously.

"Hey! Don't I get a gun or a sword or something?" Sam asked, more nervous than they were, and maybe a lot more now that she saw these high-power sorcerers were scared, too.

Crim gave a half-smile. "You never could shoot worth a damn. We had you on the rifle coming along, but a rifle wouldn't be much use there and would blow the disguise. And your arm strength now isn't what it used to be. Your looks and the probable ignorance of most of the staff in there as to what's going on inside the War Room is your best defense. If you need a weapon, Boday or I will get you one somehow."

"Yeah, thanks. I think."

"I think it's on for real," Yobi pronounced at last. "That is one hellish amount of power being pumped out of there and in to there as well. Thinking time is done, people. Let us go, and may the gods of Akahlar and the misdirected prayers of its foolish people ride with us!"

This time Sam rode in front of Etanalon, who provided some kind of shield that kept out the wind chill and preserved at least some warmth. Still, it was cold and she was cold and she wasn't sure whether she'd like to freeze to death or go into the jaws of that fortress.

They fanned out; Crim on the left, then Yobi, Boolean in the center and slightly forward, then she and Etanalon on the right, and finally Boday on their right. A sort of V-shaped flying wedge, going over the glaciers and snowy peaks. One more rise, and then it was before them, looking very much as Boday had drawn it only bigger than Sam had imagined it. She had also thought that Boday had exaggerated the smooth, almost plastic-looking appearance, but it really did look unreal, like some humongous giant kid's lost toy.

She, too, felt curiously unreal at this point. From a troubled teenager back in the land of television, cars, rock and roll, and shopping malls, to a fugitive running from storms that chased her and bad dreams that plagued her, to the descent through the maelstrom to Tubikosa, the initial safe haven and then, betrayal by Zenchur, the strange spell of Boolean's, the kidnapping of Charley and her sale to Boday, the love potion that turned Boday into her lover, the strange life they'd led in which she'd grown fat and bored, the demon of the Jewel of Omak, the wagon train, Hude, the great storm and flood, the torture-rape, rescue by Charley and the demon, the fleeing from the mercenaries, Pasedo's and a strange new peasant's life as Misa, then Crim and Kira, Yobi, the great overland journey and her mental breakdown on it, Etanalon and her magic mirrors, then the unexpected life with four husbands and an extended family in a primitive place, the attack by Zamofir, the rescue, the body switching ploy, and all the rest—it all seemed, somehow, like something in a dream, a panorama, that had a few good parts but was mostly nightmare.

All forcing her here, forcing her to this place in this time, going against the cause of her suffering and the suffering of millions. Yet, somehow, even as they closed on the place, she felt curiously distanced, more observer than key participant and guest of honor.

Guest of honor at a funeral, anyway.

Suddenly, just in front of them, there was a great rumble and roar and they halted almost immediately. She knew what was coming, felt it coming, and was the only one among them who did not fear it; in fact, she had to shout to the others to close in and not to break ranks.

The great central maelstrom of the changewind burst through ahead of them, a tremendous, tubular gray-white funnel reaching from the outer perimeter of the "saucer" upwards until it gathered and reached the clouds. The air rumbled and it grew suddenly quite dark, and lightning and thunder began to fill the frozen skies.

Instantly, Sam seemed to know what to do. What was a terrible nightmare to the others was to her a source of power, of strength.

"Etanalon! Let me take the lead and everybody come as close as you can to us!" she shouted above the rising winds and sudden blizzardlike snows stirred up by the great white thing before them. "Boolean! It's okay in the middle, remember? You told me that! They're still there! They're keeping this one right where it is, feeding on it, using its power!"

"Yeah, fine," he responded nervously, "but while I could *project* myself inside, there's no way for us to physically enter now! He's beaten us!"

"The hell with that!" she shot back. "Look at the waves from the changewind radiating outward, warping the very mountains! But they do not touch us because I won't let them! Now, if you all got the guts, let's go in there, and kick their ass!"

"What—how?" Yobi asked, sounding even more panicky than the rest.

"Right through that motherfucker! You asked me to trust you and you forced me all this way—now you put your trust in me and in *my* hands or it was all for nothing! Come on!"

For Boolean, once he'd made the decision to press on, it suddenly became a matter of extreme academic interest to him. *Of course! Of course! That's how he does it! Draws a single great wind up through the netherhells and holds it just below Akahlar with a magnetic repulsor. Keeps it there, building, letting off "steam," as it were, by opening small, mostly random changewinds all over the place. This place—not Greenland, not Iceland! Northwest Territories, by god! It's the damned magnetic north pole!*

The changewind wasn't attracted to this place, it was *repelled* by it, diverting it southward. The inplane angle must be . . . yes, yes. *I see it now! I see how he's doing it! Son of a bitch! What a great mind did I help destroy. . . .*

They approached the maelstrom, tiny specks against the vast and turbulent atmosphere around them, and, as they did, all but Sam and Etanalon closed their eyes, although they would have never admitted to it one another, gritted what teeth they had, and waited for the end.

There was sudden dead silence and calm. "We're through," Etanalon breathed, with obvious amazement. "We're inside the Maelstrom itself! *Physically* inside."

They set down on top of the saucerlike mesa, feeling like ants on a concrete slab, slid off, and looked around. To those with the magic sight, the raised domed shape in the center seemed alive, radiating fingers of blue-white magical energy, fingers that went up and then contacted the edges of the Maelstrom and mated with it.

Boolean dropped to his knees, took out a small pocketknife and scraped a bit at the "saucer."

"Mandan gold," he told them. "The whitish color were oxides and residues. This place just isn't coated with a thin layer of Mandan, it's *all* Mandan—at least the outer shell. Protect the rebel troops my ass! He's been taking what those rebels and gangs bought or stole and melting it down and reforming it!"

"Yeah, it and the Maelstrom protects them from everybody but me," Sam noted. "Uh—I hate to mention this, but while we're safe here, how in hell do we get *in* this thing? The Maelstrom sort'a form fits around it and there's all sorts of flyin' debris down there. I can keep the storm off our backs easy enough, but I sure can't deflect *that* shit. And there don't seem to be no entry up here."

Yobi was still unnerved at being within the one thing she could not control and the only thing she really feared, but she had regained some self-control and this coupled with a desire to get the hell off of here.

"The changewind protects against sorcery," she said a bit unsteadily, "and Mandan gold against the changewind, but Mandan gold is no protection from sorcery." She picked a spot, pointed a long, gnarled finger at it, and a beam of pure white magical energy sprang from it and struck the surface of the "saucer." It began to neatly, almost surgically, burn a neat path right through the top.

"Get ready, everybody!" Boolean warned. "All this energy might disguise us, but the odds are about even that somebody's gonna be down there to find out about the hole in the roof!"

13
War of the Maelstrom

They floated down through the hole, which was wide enough for both Crim and Boday to drop first, Crim with the machine gun ready, Boday with the crossbow, to cover both angles. They appeared to have dropped into a fairly large office, but nobody was home.

Boolean dropped next, then Sam, Etanalon, and, finally, Yobi, whose bulk nearly filled out all the available space. Still, she turned, looked up, and made a series of passes over the roof. The section she had cut out quivered a moment, hanging as it was by only a metallic thread, then went back up into the scaling and reversed the cut. The roof was once again solid and intact.

"Electricity, intercoms—nice place," Boolean noted. "All the comforts of home. But this was never a sorcerer's office. One of the political or military leaders, most likely."

Yobi closed her eyes in concentration, then opened them again. "The door leads to a smaller outer office which also accesses other offices," she told them. All the offices here are vacant, but the hallway outside passes more, and some of those are occupied. I sense no major power as yet within the immediate region. Do any of you?"

"No," Boolean responded. "Crim, Boday—your job. Go!"

Boday's eyes were glazed. "Boday feels like the star of an action epic that will live forever," she said with awe, and, with Crim, they made their way, wall by wall and door by door, out and into the hall and then down. In the first office there were two senior officers in full uniform and a half a dozen lower-ranking military of about as many races, all poring over maps and dispatches and seeming very busy.

"The hell with the crossbow," Crim muttered, back against the wall next to the doorway. He threw the safety off the machine gun, checked the clip, then turned so he was framed in the doorway and let loose a volley. Bodies, chairs, and papers flew everywhere. They both rushed in and while Crim finished two that lay moaning with short bursts, Boday found a fencing sword and ran another through.

The noise attracted others, who were met with a hail of gunfire as they rushed to see what the problem was. When no more people came running, Boolean stepped into the hall, raised his arms, and blue-white lightning snaked from his hands and the bodies shimmered and vanished. Vanished. too, were his furs and buckskins; now he wore the shimmering emerald green robe of his office, and, somehow, he looked both younger and radiant in a powerful sort of way. For the first time, he looked to Sam like the kind of sorcerer she'd expected to meet, and she grew a little more confident. He grinned, turned to her, bowed, and gestured for her to emerge.

"Seems to me if you can do that and look like that, you don't need Crim or Boday or me," she muttered.

"I don't like to waste it. I may need every bit of it and won't have any time to recharge. Onward."

She held her breath and began walking as regally as she could. Boday and Crim emerged and fell in behind her, and none looked to see what the sorcerers were doing. They reached a down stairway, and she didn't hesitate, but paraded down it. When she reached the landing she saw two men, one kind of frog-faced and the other with a turtlelike red- and yellow-spotted head, at the bottom with automatic weapons ready. They almost opened up, but their eyes widened when they saw who was coming down.

"Why do you train weapons on me?" she thundered in her most imperious, spoiled-brat tone. "Have you gone mad?"

They stood and snapped to attention. "Pardon, Highness, but we thought, that is, we heard. . . ."

She strode past them and, behind her, Crim took the one on the left and broke his back and Boday punched in the throat of the one on the right. Even as they both collapsed, Crim muttered, "Too easy so far. Much too easy."

"Perhaps they are as stupidly confident in their own winds defense as the sorcerers of the hubs are with their shields," Boday responded hopefully.

Sam checked the floor and saw that it seemed to lead just to more offices or people's rooms or whatever. No sign of the wide hallway with the double doors. She decided to go down another flight, and they followed. The place *couldn't* be *this* empty, could it?"

"If he's paranoid enough it could be," Boolean said from behind them, reading their thoughts.

Sam reached the next floor and pressed on the big wooden door leading from the stairwell to the floor itself. It opened easily and she thought she recognized it as leading, maybe from the opposite side, to the grand entrance. She strode on, the door closed behind her, and only then did she turn and realize that nobody had followed.

At almost the same moment, from the opposite stairwell, two figures emerged, dressed in black robes. A man and a woman, both young-looking, both clearly adepts of power. She stood there a moment, feeling totally exposed, and wondering what to do, hoping they wouldn't spot her—but they did.

"Highness," said the woman, sounding startled. "We thought you were already in the War Room. We were going in to observe."

"They are still focusing the beam," she responded, hoping what she was saying made any sense. "I took advantage of it to retrieve something I had forgotten."

That seemed to puzzle the adept. "But—your quarters are over *here.* I—" The other, male adept poked her with his elbow and she suddenly realized the way she was sounding. Who were *they,* who called the Storm Princess "Highness," to question her?

"Come, Highness. We are all going the same place," said the male diplomatically, and she had to walk out into the hall while they started walking behind her.

Jesus! Now what? she wondered, trying to figure something out.

At that moment there was a crackling sound behind them, like a massive electrical short, that caused them all to freeze in place. The two adepts and Sam all turned, startled, and saw a resplendent Boolean standing there, flanked by Etanalon in robes of shimmering silver and looking to Sam like the Good Witch of the North.

There was an immediate and near blinding exchange of crackling energy between the adepts and the invading sorcerers, and, slowly, the black robes seemed to catch fire and burn with the intensity of a torch. In less than thirty seconds, both were nothing more than heaps of black ash on the great carpet.

"Oh, dear! Now they're going to have to get that cleaned," Etanalon remarked with seeming sincerity.

"Sorry to leave you like that," Boolean said to Sam. "We had some unexpected and unpleasant company back there and there was a nasty little spell on the door to take care of." There were the sounds of shooting and an explosion behind them in the stairwell, the sound echoing eerily in the stillness of the hall. "It seems, though, that even the defensive spells here can't tell you apart from the real thing."

"No, but we can," said a crackling male voice from just behind her back. Sam turned and saw two robed figures step out from alcoves or side stairs or someplace on either side of the big double doors that had seemed too close before and now seemed an eternity away.

One of the sorcerers wore a yellow robe embroidered with elaborate Oriental-like designs in shimmering red; the other violet, with trim in silver. Both hoods were down, revealing one very old cadaverous man's face, the speaker, and the other, the one in violet—well, it looked more like an animated death's head.

"Nice to see you, John. You're looking quite well," said the yellow-robed sorcerer. "And you, Valentina Ilushya, have never looked more beautiful."

"Sorry I can't say the same for you, Franz. And if that's still Tsao, I double the regret," Boolean responded. "You look dead on your feet, Tsao."

Sam suddenly realized that she was in the midst of the crossfire and carefully edged over to one side. Tsao pointed a skeletal finger in her direction and a bolt shot from it, but Etanalon flicked her own finger and it deflected, allowing Sam to get clear.

Boolean sighed. "Well, this explains some of my political troubles, anyway. I always figured you for treason, Franz, but not to be subordinate to anyone else, least of all Roy. And Tsao, you were never the political type. Not since I beat you out of Masalur. Is that it? It's just revenge against me?"

"For a hundred years I served that old man," Tsao hissed in a voice that sounded more reptilian than human. "A century! And in a mere eight years you became his favorite, you usurped my rightful position. Twenty years I spent in exile because of you!"

"That's because you were an incompetent toady, Tsao. And because it just so happened I had my own portable computer in my trunk when I got here. Took me three years to get the current matched, but after that you didn't have a prayer. Reinventing the three-pronged outlet was a bitch. You don't have a prayer now, either, Tsao. Or do you think Etanalon is more your speed? I never fought you, Franz, but treason always motivates me."

"We do not have to beat you!" Tsao hissed menacingly. "We need only kill your bitch, or perhaps turn her into a toad or something. You may kill us, but you will then not have the power to stop what is going on in there!"

"Oh, I don't know," Boolean responded. "Let's you and him fight and see."

Instantly the entire hall was ablaze in beams of magic energy, not mere lightning as with the adepts, but brilliant, blinding yellow and white light like searchlights, emanating from all four sorcerers. And in the center, where the beams clashed, equidistant from the now darkened, still forms of the sorcerers, figures took shape. Weird, demonic figures, misshapen, horrible, like the gods of some ancient tribes suddenly come to life, and they battled one another with psychic swords and hand-to-hand, or hand to claw or tentacle or whatever contacted what.

For the fighting shapes were constantly changing: wolflike, jaws glistening, spectral heads and snouts closed on dragon necks, and many forms were too nightmarish and too bizarre to figure out.

Rather quickly it seemed that two were getting the upper hand, smashing and then hacking at the other two almost at will, more and more, over and over, until it almost was like kicking a guy after he was down. The figures of the losers began to shrink, first to dog size, then cat, then mouse, until heavy psychic feet stomped on them and crushed them into pulp. Sam could only watch, terrified, unable to move out of the alcove, and wondering who was what.

As quickly as it had begun, it was over, and for a moment all Sam could see was the same four figures standing there, looking exactly the same, but unmoving. To Sam's astonishment, Boday suddenly walked between Boolean and Etanalon and right up to the enemy pair standing there. She looked at one quizzically, then the other, shrugged, and pushed the yellow-robed one over. He fell and shattered, like porcelain, on the floor. The other she also pushed, and he fell and shattered as well, only into a foul-smelling black dust.

Boolean sighed and turned to Etanalon. "Well, that wasn't bad, was it?"

"I was out of practice," she responded. "It took more out of me than I would have liked. Where in the world is Yobi?"

"She comes," Boday assured them. "She had to take on another one in the fine robes of the masters along with two adepts. Crim, by the way, found some *wonderful* little bombs on the soldiers we took out down there. You pull this thing and throw and a few seconds later they blow up and shoot little tiny pieces of metal all over the place. We thought they might form a nice introduction to the room down there."

"Grenades, huh? Worth a try," Boolean said, thinking. "Sam, you okay?"

"All but my heart. I think that's in my mouth," she said shakily. "Are we gonna hav'ta go through more of that in there?"

"No, it'll probably be a lot harder. Ah—here's Crim. Boday said you found grenades—throw bombs."

He nodded. "Four of them, anyway. Say, Yobi was having a tough time with those guys back there. If I hadn't been able to take one of 'em out while they were all concentrating on her she'd have had it. Why didn't you. . . . "He suddenly saw the remains of the two sorcerers. "Oh. Never mind."

Yobi came thundering through the door, partly shattering it, looking winded. Of the trio of sorcerers, she was the only one who looked as bad as ever, but, of course, she could never be accused of looking ordinary.

"You know who that slimy little twerp was?" she thundered. "Bolaquar! Vice Chairman of the Guild itself! No *wonder* nobody'd listen to us!"

"Well, that was Franz—Golimafar," Boolean responded, pointing. "And that thing over there was once Hocheen—you remember him. You sense any more big shots on our back?"

"No, but lots of adepts are about. You were right about the soldiers—mostly headquarters types. Couldn't shoot straight even at a target *my* size. Not too many folks here, unless the rest are all in there. I guess somebody rushed 'em into action before they were ready."

"Yeah, well, speaking of rushed. . . . You feel up to the rest? Yobi? Etanalon?"

They both nodded. "Let's get it over with while I'm still sharp," said the silver-robed sorceress. She looked at the great doors. "That's a mean set of spells on there, though. Could take some real effort breaking through and set off all sorts of alarms to whoever's in there."

Boolean turned to Sam. "Well, I guess that's your job, then, Sam. This time, *don't* close the damned door behind you. Leave it open for us to come in."

"You think they're not layin' for us after all *that?*" she asked him. "Damn, you two would'a woke the dead with that fight. In fact, lookin' at the one guy, you probably did."

"No, that's insulated in there," Etanalon told her. "If they knew, reinforcements would have come out—if there's anyone in there to reinforce. We can't get any sense of who's in there or what's happening, and if we can't, they can't."

"Crim, Boday—you roll in to the right and left as soon as Sam's through," Boolean told them. "Crim, give Boday two of those grenades. Yeah. Fresh clips. Okay, Sam, you open that door, get behind it, and stay behind it until you hear four explosions or we tell you to come out. That should protect you from them, and maybe the surprise and shock will nail a few or take a couple of sorcerers' eyes from that globe in there back here, screwing up the system. The two of you roll in as soon as the things explode and you blast anything blastable. I doubt if you'll be able to nail anybody actually in the area around the globe. They're bound to be shielded. You just keep the slaves and military boys and whatever off our backs, and when your ammunition runs out, head for cover and stay there—understand?"

They both nodded. Sam looked at the pair and shook her head. Crim was really grim and serious about this, but Boday was having the time of her life.

The alchemical artist looked over at Boolean and asked, "That shield any barrier to us or just to magic types?"

"Everybody inside, as far as shooting or the like goes. Anybody who steps outside is dead, though."

"Even the Storm Princess?" she asked.

"Hmmm. . . . No, you're right. If the Storm Princess emerges from that well down there, she's all yours. Sam—stay back and unobtrusive if you can. The odds are once we've joined they won't be able to tell you and the real Storm Princess apart on the magic level, so you'll be relatively safe. If we can break that shield, or the Storm Princess comes out, you get in. Send those changewinds elsewhere. Understand?"

Sam nodded, not quite certain what she could do or how but willing to play it by ear. This was the big one, and her major job right now was to open that damned door. She went over to it, took a deep breath, and pushed.

It didn't open.

"Try pulling, dear," Etanalon suggested. "That also leaves you out here, where it's safer."

Sam felt foolish, pulled the door open full, and then stood behind it in the hall. Boday and Crim rushed in, threw the grenades, and came right back out again. Sam almost slammed the door and inside she could hear four muffled reports. Then she opened it wide again and they went back in, shooting anything they saw.

Boolean led, then Etanalon, and finally Yobi, they strode past the bodies of the dead sorcerers and into the great hall. Sam, feeling suddenly alone and more vulnerable out in the hall than in the eye of the storm, came in after.

The surprise conventional grenades and subsequent machinegun spraying had been far more effective than they'd dreamed it could be. Not prepared for trouble, watching the show blow and fascinated by it, adepts, some probably quite powerful, as well as a number of rebel officers in fully festooned uniforms, lay dead or dying all around. No amount of armor will protect someone who didn't put it on, as the bloody remains of black-robed men and women attested.

The place looked like a miniature of the Roman Coliseum with a roof on, but the main floor was untouched by any of the carnage, any of the action above or outside. There they stood in their pentagrams, staring at that huge globe representing Akahlar, the hubs brightly glowing against the gray, semi-transparent skin of the rest, and something was happening.

Almost a third of the globe's hubs, from Arctic to Antarctic, were blackened, their lights out, as if crossed off on somebody's battle map, in a great and ugly crescent that was widening even as the globe was slowly turning.

Sam watched from the top row of seats, spellbound, sickened by what the sight entailed. And then she looked down and saw *them.* There they were—the man in the crimson robes with the horns on his head and *her,* standing there, eyes calmly fixed on that spinning globe.

She looked back at Klittichorn, feared Horned Demon of the Snows, most powerful and evil of sorcerers, and all she could marvel at was that, even in her visions and nightmares, he'd looked as huge and imposing, and now—hell, he wasn't much if any bigger than *she* was. A little, tiny man, which even the horns didn't help get much bigger.

She could see, too, for the first time, the magical shield that protected them even at this stage; clear, almost totally transparent, but present sort of in a shimmery effect produced by the lights and the fact that it wasn't still but in motion.

"He's got a spin on it somehow," Yobi noted. "Makes it hard to bum a hole through."

"It's got to be going on its own momentum," Etanalon noted. "If we can speed it up a bit rather than slow it down, we might be able to present the same face if we can match its revolutions per minute. What do you say, Boolean?"

"Well, if we can't brake it somehow, maybe we can get it going so fast it'll burn a hole in the floor. Let's give it a go."

"Wait a minute!" Sam almost shouted. "Look at them! They don't even know this all happened, or that we're here! Just gimme one of the machine guns and I'll go down there and blow their fucking brains out."

"They know, dear," Etanalon assured her. "They just don't consider us relevant right now. We are about to make ourselves relevant. Hold on."

The shield seemed to pick up speed until the reflections were just tiny lines of light apparently suspended in the nothingness above the floor. Beams of red-hot energy shot from all three, converging on a single spot, and it began to create a black streak that widened more and more.

The three sorcerers on the other side broke off their concentration, came out as a group, ducked under the black streak, and lined up against the trio in the seats. This time there was no introductory chatter, no insults, no nothing. The battle was immediately joined, and it nearly filled a quarter of the hall. Crim just barely got out of the way of the field of fire, and Sam walked around the top to the opposite side, away from them, and tried to think.

Boday crept up to her. "So, Susama, how do you think it is going?"

"Who the hell knows?" she muttered. "At least they've had to temporarily break off from the looks of it. *Holy shit, Boday!* That means—"

At that moment the walls supporting the entire War Room seemed to collapse in a roar, knocking her briefly forward and tumbling Boday most of the way down to the pit. She rolled, turned, and saw that those walls, perhaps the whole building, no longer existed.

The Maelstrom was contracting onto them!

She rolled, concentrated, and began to push it back. *Oh, no you don't, bitch! I beat you once, I'll beat you again!*

On the opposite side where the sorcerer's battle was taking place, the strategy of the defenders was clear. They had their backs to the stage, as it were; Yobi, Etanalon, and Boolean all had their backs to the wall. Contract the Maelstrom down into them while pressing them or holding them in place and you engulfed them in a power they couldn't resist, couldn't change, and couldn't keep from being subject to.

Sam could help them, immunize them, but that would put them on the outside once more with her, undefended, on the inside. And where in hell was Klittichorn?

Damn it all, this wasn't right! *Feel the storm, become the storm, control the damned storm!*

Now she was there, inside the storm, as the heart of it, but not alone. She felt and sensed the other's presence, the only other in this, *her* domain, who dared to be there, where even Klittichorn dared not intrude.

"*You can not win this time!*" the Storm Princess taunted her. "*The last time it was I who was remote from the storm attacking you at your center! Now it is you who are remote and the storm is here, around me, where I can squeeze your friends!*"

With a shock, Sam realized that, while they certainly had seen her, they *still* thought that she was back in Masalur or someplace like that because of the child's impulses. They—even the Storm Princess—thought she, on scene, was Charley!

She flicked her vision around to where the sorcerers were joined. Still three to three; Klittichorn seemed off to one side, fiddling with something but not joining the fight, depending on the Maelstrom to finish them off. What was he fiddling with? Some kind of portable computer! He was running his shit through to see how to keep the thing up until he could get back to ruining the world!

Once started, he can't stop until he's done it through, the words came to her. He didn't *dare* shut it down, so now—my God, the winds were still coming, only running wild!

Still, first things first. She turned her attention back to where her opposite number had never deviated attention from—the wizard's war.

Yobi in particular was only inches from the slowly tightening wall. For a moment Sam wondered why she didn't just contract quickly, but then she realized that there was only so much you could do and keep control without overrunning your own people. First things first; the Storm Princess was right.

Sam reached out to the storm wall and pulled a segment out. It seemed to her like taffy, and she made it a mentally formed fist aimed straight across from one side of the closing circle to the other, right through the defending sorcerers.

The Storm Princess saw it and tried to block, but so unexpected was the action that she deflected the changewind segment only slightly, so that it sliced right through the middle where the sorcerers' psychic selves were battling! There were screams and some or most were affected in some way, but it was impossible to tell who or how many.

"*Damn it!*" she screamed to the Storm Princess. "*Stop it! This is madness! Madness! They didn't kill your mother or your people, you stupid little bitch! Klittichorn ordered it to get your dumbass support for this! He suckered you like he suckered everybody else!*

Can't you see he's getting you to slaughter your own people in order to become a god?"

The plea didn't work, but it took the Storm Princess's mind off the attack, and somebody over there was still clearly fighting somebody now that the changewind element had passed and dissipated, and now even the Storm Princess would be hard-pressed to tell who was who—they were fighting at an angle to the winds, on the same level!

"Quiet, whore! slut! Usurper! Do you think I am stupid? I am a Princess, daughter of a god and the Storm Queen, my mother. You are but a reflection, a distorted, ugly shadow of my own godhood! I alone am anointed by the gods and by my mother, who is now a goddess above us all, to rule an Akahlar I remake because it pleases me! What is even Klittichorn to me now? I need only close the Maelstrom completely, and then there will be only one, no other!"

Jesus! What a stupid, demented asshole! Sam thought. incredulous. And yet, and yet—something in what she said. If Klittichorn was the big brain, the guy who figured all the angles, he must also have figured that she'd nail him at the end of this as well. How could he stop her? Unless. . . .

The hell with this. Where was this mad princess? There—still on the floor, maybe ten feet from Klittichorn. And—somebody else? Who? The battle over there seemed to be over. Who the hell was that?

Klittichorn turned away from the portable computer, got up, and looked straight at Boolean. The green sorcerer looked terribly old and near exhaustion, his formerly dark hair and beard now white, but, the fact was, while Klittichorn had fought no battles, he didn't exactly look in peak condition himself.

"Hello, Roy," Boolean said softly. "You came very close to pulling it off."

"Well, Doctor Lang, I would not have had this turn out any other way, assuming that we had to meet at all," the little man in crimson responded. "It is fitting that you should be here for the end."

Boolean looked up at the spinning globe. "Impressive gadget, Roy, but I make only a quarter of the hubs gone. Your three sorcerers are gone, and even I can't tell which Storm Princess is which at the moment."

Klittichorn chuckled. "You are weak, Doctor Lang. Too much has gone out of you. All you have done by this is murder about a hundred million people instead of letting them be transformed into something different. And that will be sufficient for me. I did not want to murder them, but you forced me to do so. Then I will dispose of the pitiful wreck that is all that remains of you, then I will achieve First Rank, and bring logic and order to this chaos as my destiny commands."

"What do you mean, murder?"

"You see those red dots up there? Each one represents a bomb, each scientifically worked out as to its placement, geography, and kilotonnage to completely eradicate all life within each of the hubs. The timers began the moment we activated the full system. Naturally, any that we were able to cover in the more merciful Changewind manner were transformed along with the lands and people and are no more. The rest—they will begin going off any time now. The signal has been given, was given, the moment I had to shut down the progression. You can not believe how long I have planned this, covering every eventuality, even this. Nor do I care which little bitch is which. Either one will do."

Boolean blanched. "Roy—have you gone mad? *I* dishonored *you*. I admit that. Perhaps in a few minutes I will pay the price for it. I don't think I deserve it, but at least I can understand how it would be justice to you. But—you're talking about *genocide*, Roy! My God, would you dishonor your own parents? Have you looked at yourself, Roy? I no longer see the face of the victim, I see the face of the Khmer Rouge there, murdering, slaughtering millions of their own. How can you become like *them*, Roy? How can you give those who murdered your family and enslaved you for so long the final victory?"

"I reject your pitiful moralizing!" Klittichorn snapped back. "The man you knew is no more! *I* have replaced him! *I*, in human form, have become the incarnation of Siva, the Destroyer of Universes! What is done here is nothing compared to what I do merely for sport! The girl, can you not recognize her by her mastery of such energy as Durga, the Goddess of Death? And your girl her other aspect, Kali? Soon we shall combine, we two, in the Dance that Heralds the End of the World, and lose our Earthly aspects, having done our duty, and resume our rightful place at the left hand of Isvara Brahman, there to witness the timeless recreation of a better world! You see everything only with the blind eyes and arrogant ignorance of the westerner! You who so polluted and defiled poor Cambodia that I had to send the dark children to wipe them out, to purge them of the west and its evil! Come! Let us do our little dance, corrupter of souls, so that I may get on and do mine!"

My god! He is totally mad! was the only thought Boolean could make before the onslaught of sheer, brutal power struck him, and the battle was joined. It was, right off, a battle he knew he must lose, for he faced fanaticism and madness along with brilliance and power, while he defended weakly and from a position of guilt. *No! Purge the guilt! Don't think of Roy Lompong! Think of those bombs, those millions of people . . . !*

The Storm Princess tightened the ring some more, although she could sense no life forms within the Maelstrom not inside the stage circle. Klittichorn was locked in battle; the others seemed weak, irrelevant, and not near enough to her. Her battle was not with the likes of them, but with the Usurper battling quite strongly from afar. No—suddenly there was one, quite close, just opposite her. For a moment she took her mind off the Maelstrom and looked with her eyes.

It was like looking into a mirror, and she was startled at the sight in spite of herself. Sam was not at all startled; she saw just what she expected to see, and she didn't like it one bit.

"So, little decoy, they send you at last as if to frighten me," the Storm Princess muttered between clenched teeth. "In a way I almost feel sorry for you, as insignificant as you are."

Sam smiled grimly at her and began walking slowly towards her. Their eyes met, and there was something in Sam's eyes that suddenly caused doubt, even fear, inside the thoughts of the Storm Princess. She took a step back as Sam continued to advance, oblivious of the Maelstrom around them.

"Mother protect me!" the Storm Princess muttered. "*You're not the decoy! You're. . . .*"

Back around the side of the great spinning globe, Sam pressed on and the Storm Princess retreated. They made a quarter of the circuit, and then the Princess found her back to the wizard's battle and stopped, with no way out except through the storm, and that would be no out. The storm and its most terrifying effects were as nothing to either of them. But what lay beyond now? Not the building, certainly, and possibly not the mountains, either. Cold, no matter what, for that would require changing the whole planet's position and tilt to alter, but what? A chasm hundreds of feet deep? A glacier? Some alien horror?

Sam knew now what she had to do. "We must touch, sister. You know what that does? It cancels us both out. We cease to exist, to the betterment of this and many other worlds, maybe. I ain't afraid no more. 'cause it'll mean something. Nothin' I ever done or hoped to do ever really meant somethin' before." She stepped forward, and the Storm Princess looked panicky for a way out.

Suddenly something snakelike seemed to come out of nowhere

and wrap itself around the Storm Princess's throat. It wasn't hard enough to strangle her, having partly caught the collar, but it surprised and held her, and she was pulled with some force to a strangely familiar dark shape just beyond.

So sudden was the whole action that it startled Sam and stopped her dead in her tracks, only a few feet from the Princess. She stared, confused, and then saw who it was.

"Boday! What the hell . . . ?"

Boday had slipped the whip off the confused woman's neck but held her now in a sort of wrestling grip, forcing the Storm Princess's mouth open and her head back, and then stuffing a small vial into her mouth. The Princess swallowed it involuntarily, then cried out and sank, unconscious, to the cement floor of the stage area. Boday bent down, picked her up, and grinned at Sam.

"Don't you worry about her," Boday said with a smile. "She'll never do anybody any harm again. Let me past and you go help out Boolean. I think he's losing bad. Just remember when it's done to leave me a way out of here!"

She stepped back and let Boday go by to the far side of the globe, confused as hell but not questioning it.

She was at Khttichorn's back, but she could easily tell that he knew she was there and also that he was winning. In fact, the magical sight was a sea of crimson, with only a small glow of green left that was even now contracting more and more.

"Soon he'll be smaller than me," she heard Cromil's amused voice near her. She turned, furious, and a wisp of changewind lashed out from the Maelstrom like Boday's whip and caught the little creature dead on. He screamed and then vanished into the storm, whether dead or simply banished back to his own strange universe she couldn't know.

Still, her fury had caused that, and without even thinking about it. She turned again and brought just the nearest side of the Maelstrom wall inwards, touching but not harming her, and engulfing the brightly shining orange mass.

Klittichorn, an inch from victory, seemed to sense it and suddenly whirled. "No! Not yet!" he screamed, and it was on him. She held it there, just where it was, then rolled it back to see if she had caught anything but the sorcerer in the mess. Where Klittichorn had stood was now a mass of solid ice. Pink ice. If it was random, it was certainly appropriate. Just beyond was the little left of the stage area, and on it lay a green robe, collapsed like an old rag doll.

She rushed over to him, heedless of the cold, almost slipping on the ice, and bent down. He looked horrible, more like that walking skeleton he'd faced down outside than anything like the man he'd been. Still, as she could see by the very tiny glow still within him, he was not dead yet, but he was dying and he knew it. Still, somehow, he saw her or sensed her, and he tried to speak.

"A-bombs," he gasped, sounding like a voice from beyond the grave. "He put A-bombs in all the hubs he didn't change!"

She looked up at the globe, still incredibly spinning around on its theoretical axis. "Is there any way I can get rid of them? There's still a lot of changewind energy here."

"Not focused," he managed. "Need the others. No way out. Yobi . . . gone. Etanalon . . . gone. I go now myself. Millions will die. . . . Horrible nuclear waste. . . . He thought . . . he was . . . already . . . a god."

"Oh, my god!" she breathed, and then something snapped inside her. "No, damn it! Don't you die on me now, you bastard! Join me! Join me in the Wind!"

She let it wash over them as she clung tightly to him, but this time she didn't ward off its force. "Join with it," she told him softly. "Join me and join with it. Mate with me and the Wind!" And she kissed his skull of a face and picked his brittle body up and clung tightly to it.

She held his pitiful shell in passionate embrace, a passion she did not feel but knew somehow was not really necessary, and let the wind take them both, melding them together within the Maelstrom. She felt the clothing dissolve, their very bodies seem to melt and meld into new forms, and she felt him understand and accept her and she accept him, and together they merged with each other and with the wind.

Her mind and his mind exploded and joined, creating something new, something unique, something great, but something only her half could shape. It was all so clear to her now! Everything!

And the irony was that Klittichorn's pitiful, mad dream of godhood would not have been his to claim, but that of the Storm Princess, who alone was the Shaper of What Was. It was the feminine who gave birth, even to gods.

In Sam's own, simplistic way, she had guessed the key. Chaos created gods and goddesses like snowflakes, each different, each unique, each the protector as well as the ultimate ruler of their worlds. But even that was a random process, the fifty million monkeys creating into infinity produced not the works of Shakespeare but a system by which the man and the works might be created. But not every snowflake was perfect, and not every copy of Shakespeare was, either. In some worlds, perhaps for physical reasons—

perhaps for no particular reason but chance—the process had stopped short of the final creation. Stability had been achieved, regulation established, short of local godhood.

There the elements had not merged, the opposites that created. The being with the power to call the Winds had to mate with the being who could command them, and the two had to merge with the wind and become something newer and greater than any of the three. How early had it been, in the other planes? In the trees or in the oceans, perhaps? Simpler gods for simpler times and more rational development.

But not just any god would do. It had to be a fusion of opposites, the cerebral and emotional, the male and the female, the old and the young, and countless other variables and elements had to merge. This did not necessarily make a perfect local god, nor even a great or wise one, but the patterns created by the order formed from the creation out of Chaos did not mandate that.

Akahlar had been created out of that first great explosion, but not as it was now, nor even the way the others had been formed at the time. It had been a vast, empty place upon which the other realities, the other universes close at hand, had fallen, compressed by the pull of the Seat of Probability after the great explosion's force had passed. Its compressed and compacted state had ground out the nulls and created the overlaps with countless worlds around the few untouched areas, the hubs, and it had been populated from the outplanes long after things had settled and developed for billions of years.

The ironic thing was that those who became its masters had come from worlds where the gods were created by the minds of men, not the patterns of Chaos. Violent, fierce people unregulated and untempered by anything above them. In them, the elements to form the gods did not truly exist, although the need for them did and took form in ancestral yearnings for such beings. In their worlds, and perhaps only in their worlds, the prototypes for the gods continued to be fashioned and born as the patterns dictated, but never to understand, never to unite, never to form the whole that was required. And there was a reason for this.

They were from the far outplanes, the last of Creation, where the changewinds weakened into shadows of themselves and their power was greatly diminished. Humankind multiplied and occupied their Earths, further separating and making unlikely that the elements, any of the elements, would ever meet, unite, or comprehend what the patterns urged. For it was always the female element who sought out and chose her lovers, and the pattern had gone slightly awry; for the women always took their lovers from their complements, not their opposites, rarely uniting with a male at all and even rarer with the changewind.

Yet there was a kind of stability imposed, as even apart the separate elements maintained an automatic, unconscious regulation, keeping the worst of the Winds at bay, and only when they died or were removed before the patterns forced another element to be born, somewhere, in their world, did the Winds have true free reign, producing the improbable elements that might give the world an Alexander, a Caesar, a Napoleon, or a Hitler, or, conversely, a Buddha, a Jesus, or a Gandhi.

Only here, in Akahlar, where the magic was real and accepted and taken for granted, had the line of the female become institutionalized, mother choosing mate for all the wrong reasons and bearing another and yet another version of herself, and using the powers of the Winds while ignorant of her own place or the meaning of things, believing themselves goddesses while actually being but an element of the divine.

She looked down upon the ruins of Klittichorn's fortress and saw that there were in fact survivors down there, survivors whom She recognized and identified. She reached out a spectral hand to them and created for them an avenue and an ice bridge to safety beyond. She was about to do more but She felt a sharp and painful disturbance within Her, one She did not fully comprehend, being above pain now, or so She had thought. The survivors would get out; She would have to come back to them later.

At the speed of light She was at its source, a great, horrible explosion sending horrible thunder and searing fire outwards over a vast radius, obliterating, even atomizing, much of what its blast touched, She dampened it, pulled it upward, kept it from doing further harm, but now there was a second, and She knew what She was facing.

Too late on the first, She froze the second as it was forming its mushroom shape, suspending it there, then went methodically from hub to hub, pulling the power of the Winds to render the other bombs useless junk. Only then did She return to the first, and discover that there were in fact limits to Her powers. Even this universe was vast, and She was but the Goddess of Akahlar. She could not roll back time, but She could undo much of its effects.

Frightened people, frightened armies, frozen in the vision of that second bomb, were now unfrozen; the great, irregular mushroom shape stopped billowing upwards and instead seemed to them to solidify. On a shaky, bent foundation stem the structure could not stand; it toppled over and fragmented as it hit the ground over hundreds of square miles, burying the hub and its defenders and attackers knee-deep in chunks of true mushroom.

For the first hub there was less hope; it was already a blackened plane, with the bare charred remnants of what had once been a great kingdom and great seat of empire. There She could do some things; within limits even raise the dead, as little was truly impossible now, but She could not spin it back, could not take that explosion back, and far too much of it had gone. Better now to simply contain the damage and limit its effects to what had already occurred, spinning the dust and radiation outward into the netherhells between the outplanes where they would hardly be noticed. Let this burned, dead hub become then a place of pilgrimage, a grim reminder to the millions who survived through the bravery of a few as to what great power can really do, and what price might be paid for turning one's back on evil.

For they could have stopped this; the high and mighty Akhbreed sorcerers in their towers and in their lairs, but they had chosen to believe what they wanted to believe and to compromise with evil, succumb to evil, or turn their eyes, ears, and brains away from it, and ignore it until it was too late. They had shown how weak and fallible their power was, how they misunderstood the fullness of their charge to protect their people. They had let their sense of power replace their common sense, and so had failed both their people and themselves, and now they sat smug and fat in their castles, congratulating themselves that all was now well and that someone had done for them at great sacrifice what just a few of them could have done with no sacrifice required at all.

She reached down to them, as they sat in their towers as before, ignorant of just what horrors they and their people had been spared, and touched them with the breeze they could not control, the one power to which they were subject. The office of Chief Sorcerer was herein abolished; now they were revealed by their loss of power as just the pitiful old men and women, frail and scared and very ordinary, as they always were, but now stripped of their cloaks of invincibility and forced to appear with their minute souls bared to their people.

The shield came down. There would never again be shields to keep subject populations separate and in check, coordinated by the masters of the hubs. She knew that this would cause much death and suffering, that the wars would now rage for a while, and that the Akhbreed and the most militant of the colonials would be a long time finding a peace, but they would be forced eventually to an accommodation, for they needed each other, and the vast majority of colonial races understood that as well. If the Akhbreed would let them, some of those races would fight at its side in the defense of a broader, freer organization, less kingdom than interdependent commonwealth. The Akhbreed who refused alliance would die, or be overthrown by those who saw survival and the future as overwhelming prejudice.

She cried for those who would die and those who would never learn, and most of all for the innocents caught between, but this was the sort of hard decision that her other half could make and the only long-term solution. She would be able to help, to guide them, to perhaps minimize the appalling losses, but the War of the Maelstrom might take a generation to sort out the world of Akahlar.

When She had time to learn all Her powers and Her limits, to study what could be done and how best to do it, some provision might be made for the innocents. Nor was She still naive enough to believe that the system She envisioned for Akahlar would evolve on its own. Something would have to be done to give them a guide, a nudge in the right direction. Prophets and teachers might be quite useful to develop here, and perhaps a book to guide them and give them the plan.

For a moment, She wondered if this was the way it always worked out, that others suddenly thrust into Her position had not done much the same.

But there had to be one place of safety, one point of shining sanity upon Akahlar, if only as an example. A holy city within a centralized hub, perhaps, to train those not only of the Akhbreed but also of the natives to carry the message and the plan, safe from wars and revolutions and barbarism, so that no matter how ugly things got there was one source for putting it right.

Masalur! Astride the equator, near the center of the greatest kingdoms. Masalur, who had known both the horrors of war and subjugation and the wrench of the winds; who had an almost unique core population that remained intact, a bridge between the opposites, between the changelings and the whole, between the rebels and the Akhbreed, between the male and the female, and whose old government had allowed, however reluctantly, the experiments with native self-government and self-sufficiency and whose colonial populations as a result had, in the main, eschewed the fight and caused Klittichorn to have to import dissident armies to help.

Its magically charged hub, with its swampy core and its large and strange population, surrounded by a ring of Akhbreed, would be a holy place. In this hub, the weapons would not work, the spells would not hold, and judgments might be rendered directly by Her until such time as a new form of government could evolve, a multiracial government, to teach and give example to the world.

This kind of responsibility had been the sort that Her feminine half had been fearful of and had not wanted; that her male half had wanted above all else but with no clear direction as to what he wanted that power for. Now he would provide the drive, the joy of power, and She, through whom it must be filtered and accommodation reached, would temporize and shape and guide it. Together, the three in one, the male, the female, and the Wind, might well make something worthwhile, something great. And if She could not banish the horrors of the world and the darkest parts of the human soul, then at least She might provide justice.

Lonely figures, like tiny dots against a sea of white, crawling, clawing their way forward, yet freezing, without a place to go. . . .

Other creatures, strange and hideous yet impervious to the cold, clawing around the edges of what remained of Klittichorn's redoubt.

Two in particular drew Her interest; the others could claw and mew and stalk each other through eternity on that ice for all She cared, and dream only of what might have been.

She reached psychic fingers down to them, to the two strange figures back on the ice and to the tiny dots fighting their losing battle against the elements, knowing, at least, what to do with them. But she held them suspended, for a brief moment, in the netherworld between the ticks of the clock. She had something else to do first, one last obligation, one last, personal bit of housekeeping, before She withdrew to oversee her grand design, knowing that in the times to come She could no longer afford such personal attachments, that the greater good would come first.

There was a sound, like the gentle tinkling of bells in the breeze, that woke Charley up. She sat up in the bed, frowning, for it was quite dark and the snores around told her that she alone had heard what it was and come awake.

For a moment she thought it was just the child, now perhaps only days from being born—and that would be a relief! She hadn't slept too well these past couple of weeks as it was because of that.

Something formed in front of her bed, out of the darkness; a shimmering mass, and two strange figures, semi-transparent, superimposed over a seething mass of clouds formed there. The vision made no intellectual sense; the smaller figure superimposed on the larger seemed paradoxically to be the greater. A small, yet increasingly familiar feminine form atop a larger, more imposing, father figure.

"We had to come back, for just this once," the female figure said.

She frowned, unsure whether she was dreaming this or what. The others apparently heard nothing and slept on. "Sam?" she said, hesitantly, "Is that *you?*"

"It is and it isn't," the figure replied. "Once I was Sam, and he was Boolean, but it is becoming harder and harder with each passing moment to tell one from the other. Our time is short, and full integration of my three parts proceeds at a pace even I can barely comprehend, so this is the last time this will be possible."

"Sam—what happened to you? Up there . . .?"

"I can't explain. The results will be apparent to you all in the days and years to come. Let it suffice that Klittichorn is dead, and while there may well be others like him in the ages to come, none will ever again pose the kind of threat he did. The others will be returned here shortly; they can give you as much as any person can about what happened. This last visit is for me alone, for the sake of what has gone before."

There was a sudden blurring of the images, and the figure struggled to come back and retain full focus and form.

"The time is shorter than I thought," the Sam figure told her. "We must go."

"Go? Go where? Sam—where are you? What happened to you? Will I see you again?" *And where'd you get that vocabulary?*

"I can't explain and it makes no difference anyway. You were always bright; you will be able to figure out a little of it. The rest you will simply not believe. It doesn't matter. Only false gods are dependent upon belief. That's none of your concern. I came here just to see you this last time, and to tell you a few things about your own self."

"What? What's this all about, Sam?"

"The child is no longer a Storm Princess, just a beautiful little baby girl who will need love. The position of Storm Princess has been abolished. It is redundant. Love her, Charley. Think of her as your own."

"Uh—yeah, okay, Sam. But. . . ."

"You have a lot of potential, Charley, that you either threw away or had thrown away. You have a second chance now. Tell me, would you rather go home, now? Have the baby in a real hospital, live in the world you grew up in?"

Charley had thought about that for a long time but had never expected to be asked the question when it meant something. "No, Sam, I don't think so. I don't think I could just pick up, not as somebody else, which I am now, after all this here."

"Then remain in Masalur, Charley. Here there will be no more war, no more slavery. Trust me on this. The rest of Akahlar will be in foment for many years, perhaps a generation or more, but not here. And here, as the creation of Boolean the Great, surrogate of Sam, you'll have additional position, power, and prestige. Nor will you be alone. What wealth you need you will find; what you do with your life and how you spend it is your own affair, as it should be. But you'll make your own choices from here on in; they will not be imposed. Farewell, Charley. Remember us fondly. And if our daughter ever asks about Sam Buell—lie."

"Sam—you should know. . . . Cromil told me. All that hell we went through, all that shit they put us through—most of it was deliberate. Sam! They *used* us!"

"We know, Charley. We have a far better understanding of it and source of information than Cromil. Charley—just, well, don't waste yourself as a bimbo any more. Make some right choices for a change. Live your life and enjoy it. For our sake—and for our daughter. Don't stay blind to everything, now you can see. Farewell, Charley. We didn't ask for this, didn't want it, but we couldn't avoid it. Live a life like Sam still dreams of living, and know, curiously, that she envies you."

The vision flickered again, this time worse, the white smoky background seeming to reach out and swallow them up.

"Sam! Wait!" But the vision had vanished, gone into the darkness.

"Damn you, Sam!" she grumbled. "I'm still *fat!*"

14
Aftermaths and Beginnings

They were scattered along the beach like bits of flotsam and jetsam washed in from a storm, although the sky was sunny with just a few fleecy clouds and had been for many days.

It was Dorion who found them, while out walking along the shores of the lagoon and trying to decide on the meaning of things. Charley had had a vision, or so she said; Sam had come, sort of with Boolean, almost as ghosts, to announce both a victory and a farewell, yet the promise of Charley's weight loss had not been fulfilled. A dream? Perhaps, but why had Charley, who had never been able to master the language, awakened now speaking flawless Akhbreed? And acquired a voice that was still her voice, but a bit higher, softer, definitely in the feminine register, and kind of sexy? A dream? A new spell? Or, in fact, had things truly changed, and, if so, how?

And what about him? Sometime yesterday, he was suddenly aware that the spell binding him as her slave had simply vanished; the ring was not inert, just a piece of jewelry, and in a very silly place for jewelry. She hadn't known, and he hadn't told her, although their relationship remained ambivalent. She was so hung up on her looks she couldn't seem to think of anything else; so long as that was so, the fact that she *thought* the ring bound him was sufficient to keep him there and on hand, not allowing her reason to dismiss him.

Suddenly he stopped dead on the beach and stared. By the gods—the beach was littered with *bodies!* He broke free of his shock and ran to the closest one and stared down at it.

This one was familiar, although a bit different-looking; Etanalon had never looked so radiant, and the silver robe did wonders for her. He bent down, fearing she was dead, but she stirred, frowned, then opened her eyes and saw him, and then she smiled.

"Help me up, Dorion, if you please," she asked him kindly, and he did so. She looked around. "The others?"

"I see more over there. You were just the first."

She nodded. "Let us check them." She yawned, stretched, and stamped her feet to get herself going. "Not bad for an old ice monster," she muttered to herself, and followed him.

Next, bundled in furs and sweating like a stuck pig in them under the tropical sun, was Crim, looking like he needed a bath, shave, and a very long rest. Etanalon checked him out while Dorion went to the next figure down. Crim opened his eyes and did an imitation of Etanalon waking up. "Huh? What? Where . . . ?"

"Hey! There's a real pretty naked lady over there!" Dorion shouted, and Etanalon left Crim to manage and rushed over to the next patient. Dorion turned over the nude form and gasped; the sight also startled Etanalon, even though she might have expected it.

"It's *Kira?*" Dorion breathed, then looked back at Crim, just making it as far as sitting up. "But—I thought—" His head went back and forth between the pair. "How . . . ?"

"Their curse is ended, undone to the core," Etanalon told him. "Yet she as well as he are whole, and in the prime of their half-spent best years." She chuckled. "If you think *you* are shocked, imagine what it's going to be like when they see each other!"

They heard a familiar voice cursing and rushed to the next figure, who was even now getting up on her own. Boday groaned, stretched, then looked around, saw where she was and saw the others, and grinned, then immediately began shedding her own fur clothing and boots. "Hey! You two! Victory is sweetness and Boday has become legend!" she shouted exuberantly. She looked around. "Have you seen someone who looks a lot like my darling Susama?"

Etanalon came over to her. "Uh, Boday, I'm afraid you won't be seeing Susama any more. You see—"

"Ah! Boday knows that! She understands! The fates never intended that her Susama should be limited to being the wife and love-slave of Boday! No, I said somebody who *looks like* her."

"No, I—wait a minute!"

The fancy clothing was unmistakable now, and before either Dorion or Etanalon could reach the unconscious form, Boday was there, turning her over, brushing the woman's hair back and the sand from her face. She twitched, then sighed, then opened her eyes and looked at Boday.

"I love you," sighed the girl who looked like Sam, eyeing Boday as if the alchemical artist were a true goddess.

Boday smiled. "Boday knows you do, her little Princess! Ah, never again will Boday have to worry about who will cook her meals, mend her clothes, clean the place, or assist and provide whatever Boday needs. That's all you want to do now, isn't it, my Princess? Now and forevermore!"

"Yes, my darling," the girl who looked like Sam responded.

Both Etanalon and Dorion stood there, staring. Finally it was Dorion who said, "That's not—*is* it?"

Boday looked up at them and grinned broadly. "Once, yes, she was called the Storm Princess and filled with hate and madness, but no more. Never more. Now she is filled only with joy and devotion for Boday!"

"But—how?" Etanalon wanted to know.

Boday shrugged. "A little taste of the whip, a bit of a choke hold, and an entire phial of Boday's own special ultra-powerful, quick-acting love potion, which she fixed up in your own lab over the evening we spent there. It was not intended for this, but there they were, face to face, my Susama and the Princess, and then the fates placed Boday, at just the right angle, with all the means at hand! So Boday saved Susama and the Princess, which allowed Susama to save Boolean, which allowed them both to save the world and make of Klittichorn some kind of ice sculpture or whatever. Boday has claimed her own rewards; no thanks are necessary, even if, in the end, *it is Boday who saved the world!*"

The alchemical artist paused, looked back at the princess, then at them, and shrugged. "After all, what else is she good for? Her powers are gone, and she's not well equipped to go to work for a living. This way at least she is useful, and happy."

Dorion was about to say something, thought better of it, then averted his eyes and caught sight of something, or someone else, still further along. "Who can *that* be?"

There was an enormous cloak of familiar brown cloth, but the figure filling it was almost lost within the vastness of its folds. The cloak was familiar to them—clearly it was Yobi's—but the woman inside was not. Although middle-aged she was still something of a beauty, stately and statuesque, not at all grandmotherly or matronly like Etanalon.

"Who is *that*?" Dorion asked. "And where's Yobi?"

"That *is* Yobi, dear," Etanalon replied. "That is the Yobi who attained the Second Rank, before she paid the price of her researches and her battles and went places and did things that so terribly changed her. It is Yobi before she paid her terrible price, now given a second chance at it. I believe she will need a smaller, grander cloak of rank now."

Dorion shook his head in wonder, then got up, leaving Yobi's recovery to Etanalon, turned, and looked back up the beach. "I had wondered what would happen when they saw each other in the light of day," he said, smiling. "Look."

Etanalon turned and saw, back up the beach, the figure of a tall, handsome man in a long embrace with a young, naked woman, each holding the other as if they were afraid to let go.

"That's sweet," the sorceress commented. "I was so afraid that after all this time they'd be sick of each other."

"I'll go tell Charley and the others," Dorion shouted, starting to turn for the house halfway around the lagoon. "Boy, we're gonna have one *hell* of a party!"

Yobi groaned, opened her eyes, saw Etanalon, and went through the whole routine. The old sorceress allowed herself to be helped up, and only then did she look at herself and realize the change that had been wrought. "Oh, my!" she muttered. "Oh *my!*"

"Yes, dear, but I'd think very seriously about playing those demon games any more," Etanalon cautioned. "I seriously doubt if anybody will give you a third crack at it."

"We still—we have our powers back?"

"About like before, it seems to me. Neither magic nor the rest were abolished, only limited in their range and scope, which is reasonable. Akahlar depends too much upon people like us to wipe us out now, and I get the distinct impression that there are far fewer of us in the Second Rank than there were yesterday. Don't you?"

"Indeed. But not everything works. The boy, Dorion—he still had the ring in his nose but it was just a ring. No power. No enslavement."

"That's not permitted in Masalur, I think. We'll have to divine the rules once again, but that's a fascinating chore. You know, I doubted right up to the end whether or not we weren't stupid suicidal idiots for going against all that, but it seems to have worked out nicely that we did. Except for that brief horrid transformation on the ice, we—you and I—came out of this pretty well. In fact, I'd say that we are probably right now the *de facto* heads of the Guild, whatever's left of it."

"Just as well," Yobi noted. "Otherwise we'd be stuck forever in this island paradise."

They joined Boday and her new escort, which amused Yobi no end, and continued on up the beach towards the house. They passed Crim and Kira, who didn't seem to be aware that anyone else was there, and decided not to disturb them.

Etanalon looked over at Boday and her fawning lovesick princess and said, "You know, something's been bothering me since I heard your version of events, Boday. Why did you go down in my lab and spend so much time mixing your love concoction at that point? Not for this end, surely. You can't see the future. Might it have been in the back of your head to secure the love of Susama once and for all?"

"Oh, no! Boday understood the special position of her Susama. Why do you think she never slipped Susama the potion during all that time in Tubikosa? Boday did not come on this journey, give up everything, for *her*. It was to renew herself, to fill her emptied soul, and that it has done. No. she spent months in the company of that pair up at the house, and hours in talking sense to that silly girl there who had no sense of what was truly important. It was the idea that, if the opportunity presented itself, a few drops, perhaps, in a farewell toast, to cement a deserving relationship, as it were. It was concentrate, by the way. My princess here probably swallowed enough of it to make love-slaves out of the whole of center city Tubikosa, but that's all right. She had a lot of hate to smother."

Etanalon looked at the house. "And did you manage it?"

"No, there was no opportunity, which is why it was still in the belt." She reached down and pulled a small phial out of her leather belt, held it up and looked at it. "There are still a few drops in there. Probably more than enough. Perhaps it will be done yet."

"No, hold off," Yobi interrupted. "Ever since she got here people have been making most of her decisions for her, so that the few she could make couldn't help but be a bit wrong. It will be sad if she keeps to that pattern, but it is her choice to make. At least she's earned *that* right."

Charley shared the shock, surprises, and joy at having them back, and did not let them alone until each of their stories was drawn out and compared. Boday was already sketching, and dreaming one day of an entire panorama in oils, perhaps a diorama depicting the epic fight against the forces of evil that had saved Akahlar.

During one of Charley's frequent trips to the outhouse—it seemed like she had to pee every ten minutes these days—Etanalon followed her in conversation, and during the course of it let slip that Dorion's slave spell was nullified, gone. Apparently, although he had to know, he had neither told her nor acted any differently.

She shook her head in wonder. "Why'? Why would he do that? Pretend to still be my slave?"

"He loves you, dear. You know that. He gave up what little he had for you. Surely that must be obvious."

"Yeah, I guess so, but . . . , well, he could do a lot better than me if he was just a little more assertive. He *is* kind of cute, you know. I mean, I'm *fat*, and any moment now I'm gonna be a *mother* to a kid by a father long dead now. Either one would be bad enough, but both together is a hell of a burden to stick a guy with. I mean, he's not really in love with me; he's in *love* with some little slip of a courtesan who could charm the balls off a pawnbroker's sign. That girl's gone. The closest to her is the one Boday's got, and she's kind'a out of circulation. You yourself examined me and told me the spells were still there, so I'm not gonna change. Who the hell would want a five-foot-two-inch 50-42-50 butterball, never mind one with a kid?"

What she said was true, as far as it went, but it wasn't because of the Omak demon's curse. Someone had undone all that and rewoven an elegant new spell, one so fine and so carefully tuned that it was beyond even the best of Second Rank sorcerers. Without harming the child in any way, or affecting her, Charley had been carefully redesigned, reengineered from the inside. Nothing showed, but her bone structure, muscle tone, everything, had been finely tuned so that her current weight and stature was her normal condition. When not pregnant she would be exceptionally strong, unnaturally healthy, free of all the diseases and maladies that plagued all but the best magicians, able to climb, lift, run, and lots of other things—without feeling any more winded than someone in peak condition. But she was also exceptionally fertile, able to bear many children, if she chose to do so. without stressing the body the way it did many women. She was under no spells or charms: a skillful weaver of the winds had changed her as surely as the inhabitants of Masalur hub had been changed, yet she was still Akhbreed. Someone, who thought Charley had learned every lesson except the most important one, had wanted her to look that way.

And that was why, in spite of the fact that a skilled sorcerer like Etanalon could in fact have granted Charley's wish, she neither did so nor suggested the possibility. There was something potentially great in Charley that everyone seemed to sense when she was being herself: Charley alone could not see it because she was too busy looking in the mirror to look within herself. Sam had been helped by mirrors; to Charley they were her curse. Why begin questioning the judgment of the First Rank now?

"Is it really so terrible being fat?" Etanalon asked her. "Why do you want to be thin? Not for health, surely. That is a good reason for some but not for you. Do you feel so terrible this way?"

"Yes, No. Well. . . . It's the way other people see you, react to you. Other women, guys. I mean, what kind of man would be interested in me looking like this'? And I think other women might be worse yet. I know how I used to feel when I looked at some fat girl. Sure, I love not constantly dieting and not worrying if I want some bonbons, but it's just not me."

"And you really believe that Dorion is in love with an idealized vision of your outside, that he is not in love more with your inside? With what he sees inside you?"

"Now, maybe, he thinks so, 'cause he's been so cloistered and shy and all, but I saw the way he looked at that Kira."

"Happily married men have been looking like that at bodies like Kira's since there were women and men to look at each other," the sorceress responded. "And women like you look at bodies like Crim's in that manner as well. Or bodies like that Halagar's, never considering what's inside. But they rarely want to settle down with one like that. They just look. like one appreciates fine works of art or the beauties of nature."

"You really think I should give it a try with him, then?"

"It's your decision, and you've known him longer and more intimately than I. If you are that unsure, get Boday to mix you up a love potion, but I don't think you'd want to do that to anyone else, and I don't think you'd be happy that way. But, if I were you. I might give it a shot. You could do worse, with a nearly instant newborn around, you are very quickly going to find his measure and his commitment.

"I—I'll have to think about it, that's all."

"That's all one can ask another to do in these matters, dear," Etanalon replied with a smile.

"I can't believe it! They're all over the place!" Dorion was both excited and stunned beyond belief at the discovery. "I mean, I never saw 'em before, but you just kick a rock and there's a diamond the size of a child's rubber ball, or a ruby fit for an idol's navel, or an emerald the size of a small melon! The island's *crawling* with big gem-quality stones!"

Charley nodded and smiled. "Well, at least now I know what she was talking about when she said we would have all the wealth we needed." Gold and silver were common in Akahlar—any competent alchemist could make them from common lead—but gem-quality stones, flawless, with perfect luster, almost ready for the cutter, were very rare indeed.

This had followed on the heels of Yobi and Etanalon's visit to Masalur hub to check things out, their sorcery protection against anything they might be likely to find. What they had found, though, was far different than what they had left. The slavery spells on the Akhbreed survivors, who numbered more than three hundred thousand people, were all broken and ineffective. They had then risen up collectively against the remaining skeletal force of Hedum and the other nurbreed conquerors, joined unexpectedly by forces from the transformed millions of the inner hub who had once been their brethren, and overcome them, only to be joined by forces from no less than eleven colonial worlds, accompanied by Akhbreed who lived there—the very worlds where Boolean's experiment in self-government had been permitted and encouraged. More races were coming out now and, after testing the political and social winds, were blowing the way of the colonies, and tremendous pressure was being exerted even now on the nine unconnected Masalurian rebel worlds.

They had not waited for peace. A compact had been drawn up by the pragmatists and those horrified by what had occurred. Masalur was being reconstituted as a republic, a form of government known in some remote areas of the colonial worlds but never among the Akhbreed, with each race of Masalur who signed brought on as an equal partner with equal voice and representation in a kind of parliamentary assembly still mostly on paper. The entrepreneurs, the Navigator's Guild people in the region, and others were already starting to redevelop commercial ventures, often in partnership now with locally owned, and in a few cases hastily formed, native corporations. A combined army, for defense of the republic rather than for subjugating it internally, was being assembled under former officers, and was having to be talked out of carrying their "revolution" to other kingdoms while their own was still being born.

Revolution by example was being preached instead. Without shields and Chief Sorcerers, and with the Akhbreed's vulnerability exposed by the wars and revolutions, such an arrangement could be offered as the only viable alternative to civil war and the breakdown of services and authority. The rebels, in the main, didn't want to revert to primitive ways and tribalism; they wanted what the Akhbreed had, and the smartest among them understood that the

Akhbreed alone knew how to harness the power of water for electricity and engineer sewage systems, running water, and the rest. Much blood would be spilled, and centuries of hatred and oppression could not be overcome in a night by high-sounding principles and promises, but it was a start.

It wasn't perfect, and not everybody went along right now, nor was everybody satisfied, but it seemed a damn sight better to those on the island who heard about it than anything else in all Akahlar. Those without sorcery had a meeting to discuss just what they wanted to do in this new world.

Boday pointed to Charley. "Boday still remembers the brilliant undergarment you and Susama created which more than financed our journey. Surely there are other such ideas that can be found, developed, licensed. Whole new vistas are opening up! Imagine, if you will, if we could just convince the four-breasted Masalurians that these 'bras' were good! And think not only of the Akhbreed and Masalurians but of all the races that products can now be developed for!"

The project interested everyone. Crim, for example, was a member of the Navigator's Guild, and could arrange for coordinated transport. Kira could wine and dine and charm the pants off the most hard-hearted businessmen and politicians. Dorion had no powers, not that he'd lost that much to begin with, but he had his Guild membership and lots of contacts there.

"But you're going at it all wrong," Charley told them. "Sure, we might actually manage it, but then we'd become Akahlar's greatest corporation, with an economic hold on it. Our company would become a pseudo-empire, stronger and possibly with less heart in the end than the old ones and more powerful. No, what we want to do is to start with some ideas that show the way, and provide a center, perhaps in Masalur hub itself, in the remaining outer circle, where everyone with creativity could come, both to share ideas, learn, and to test and market their own new products and ideas. Making money gets boring after a while. Becoming the intellectual and artistic center of the whole world, though—*that's* exciting!"

Kira, Dorion, Boday, even the two Masalurians, were fascinated by the concept but still not clear about the details of her vision.

"Isn't that what the great University hub is for?" Boday asked her.

"No, no! I'm not talking about education and I'm not talking about theory, both of which that probably does fine. I'm talking about a forum and an outlet for the ones who graduated from there, and those who never got the chance to go but still have great ideas."

"Can you picture it for us?" Kira asked her. "Show us, somehow, what you mean?"

Charley smiled. "I'm not the artist you are, Boday, but gimme that pad and I'll show you what I have in mind. And it's only the start of it. Surely, sometime, hopefully soon, *somebody* in Akahlar will invent air conditioning. . . ."

The Mother of Invention was pregnant again, but she didn't mind even if some other people thought she was overdoing it. Misa, now eleven and in the process of turning from adorable to sexy and dangerous, had been partly responsible for it, teaching and giving to her mother as much or more than her mother was giving her, and being an unexpected joy. That had been compounded by the arrival of Jonkuk, now nine and the spitting image of his father at that age although with a highly extroverted personality, but, damn it, who would have suspected that Dorion would be so phenomenal in bed?

Not that he really believed it yet; after all, if your wife's had a little prior experience with, maybe, two or three hundred other guys, you would tend to think you were being flattered, but there was something to be said for the fact that she had been absolutely faithful now for eleven years, and why she had Joni, age six now, and Petor, age three, afterwards, and they probably wouldn't stop with the one on the way, either. They both loved kids, particularly theirs, and, hell, they could afford them.

Not that it had slowed Charley down. The concept of day-care and an equal spot for women in the policy-making body that controlled the entity known throughout Akahlar simply as The Mall had been laid down from the start. After all, three of its seven-member board were females, and two more were sort of all of the above.

Stepping into the Grand Promenade, with its large grass and tree-lined park going down the middle between the two long rows of multilevel shops, galleries, and boutiques, she stopped to look into the windows of some of the fashion galleries. They were catching on quickly to the potential business here; the traditional chadoorlike garb of even the most conservative kingdoms was giving way to modernity with the collapse of the Chief Sorcerer's authority and the failure of the old religions to keep pace with the revolutionary new conditions present on Akahlar.

It had started with just this section, but even now it seemed to go on and on in all directions, less a collection of shops and stores than a small city in its own right, with its own electric power and its own population just to staff the place and keep it clean and perfect. Fashion and cosmetics tailored to a thousand races, but even if you foreswore clothes altogether where you were from, there was something here for you. Inventors here had created a kind of escalator system previously unheard of; others were trying different methods of cooling and compression, even electricity from solar energy. There were toys galore, and shops selling everything from sports stuff to commercial fishing gear. They liked to brag that there was nothing you could not buy at The Mall, and two-thirds of it could be bought nowhere else, although the best and cleverest products were now being copied and imitated.

There were playgrounds for the kids as well, and separate day-care for the employees and those guests who had them. All the staff was multiracial, and it was surprising how easy it was for even the most hidebound old Akhbreeds to accept that when they were here shopping for a new creation or a stunning coat or the latest in jewelry creations. And going up now were the resort hotels that would make this a true destination community, and they were listening right now to proposals for creating a water park and to another fellow who appeared to have independently reinvented the amusement park.

She walked by two young Akhbreed women, skinny and slinky in obviously newly bought tropical fashions including sandals and the latest inventive rage, sunglasses, and they gave her a look that could only mean, *Hey, you fat, barefoot slob of a baby factory, how dare you be in a place like this?* It no longer particularly bothered her. In fact, her one fond wish was that someday one of them would actually make a comment like that and she could reply, *"Hey, skin and bones! While you're still trying to score in bars, I got a great marriage, great kids, and, on top of that, I own this fucking place!"* Nobody ever had, but there was always hope.

The fact was, she *was* comfortable with herself. True, she'd still like to be 36-24-36 and not worry about it, but not if she had to trade what she had to get it. Not if she had to trade *any* of it.

Kira shouted her name and waved, then came and joined her. She was still what Charley would want to look like, what *any* woman with any taste would want to look like, although she was starting to show just a little wear and tear. Kids, even with house-keepers and day-care, will still do that to you, although Kira hadn't been quite as gung-ho as Charley on that score, having been a bit gun-shy having her first baby just a few days past nine months after seeing her first sunshine in years.

Kira, in fact, was just back after a couple of months on the road with Crim and the kids setting up some new delivery contracts, and she was just seeing some of the new projects after being away.

"Am I going crazy, or is that building-sized mural of Boday's on the North Wall being redone again?" she asked, shaking her head.

Charley chuckled. "Yeah, our big attraction. *War of the Maelstrom.* I don't think she'll ever actually finish it, but it keeps getting more grandiose and, I suspect, less realistic as she goes along."

"Well, I remember the initial one had her as just a tiny figure down in the corner, and now it seems like Boday is the star of the entire painting. Before we're through we'll have an entire building side that's nothing but Boday in a reclining position, whip in hand."

Charley laughed. "Well, the rest of the Board will have something to say about that. Still, her gallery's going great guns, even if I can't figure out a damned thing in it—I mistook a fire box for one of their creations the other day. And I'm somewhat afraid that her body painting studio is going to catch on and become the next real fad."

"Well, not for me it isn't. How's Dorion and the kids?"

"Except in one department, I think Dory was born the wrong sex. He absolutely adores the kids, loves cooking and keeping house, and seems perfectly content to let me run the business end while he stays home. Of course, he keeps writing those epic first-person accounts of him and the great sorcerers that nobody will publish, but it keeps him occupied. It's the only blessing to my failure to ever learn to read Akhbreed, although he's pestered me to teach him how to read and write English. And, of course, he's created a whole range of ingenious children's toys and games for our kids that have wound up being successfully marketed. I think that's his true secret—he's never wanted to grow up, and now he doesn't have to."

"Not Crim. He's getting sick of being on the road half the year, coming home and having his own children ask for his identification. That's why we all went along on this last one—and I think it will be the *last* one. Lately he's been talking about building a new chain of world-specific malls in the provincial capitals and other hubs. We have to go that route soon, I think, or the Masalurians will run out of places to live."

Charley leaned back in the chair and sighed, looking around at it all. "You know, sometimes I really can't believe that such a nightmare as I was cast into turned out like this. God! You know, this place, this life—me, my family, all of it—is more than I ever dreamed of achieving when I was a kid. I keep living in fear that one day I'm gonna wake up or be awakened and find this was all a dream or some hypnotic trickery. So far, though, it and you have all still been here. And it just keeps getting better."

"Well, at least nobody's come up with television yet. I have hopes that it won't happen in our lifetime but you never know."

"Oh, I dunno. The idea of a Hedum variety show fascinates me. Still, I look around and I wonder what Sam is doing now. If she's finally happy, or if she still exists as we understand it, and if at least she knows what we've done here. I think she'd love this place."

"You know there's actually a large cult movement growing around her, complete with prophets and visions and holy books?"

"No! In the other lands?"

"Uh-huh. And creeping this way, I'm afraid. Masalur's holy ground to them."

"Jeez! Well, I hope they don't expect me to be their high priestess and interpreter, or decide that all this is profaning holy ground or something. You know, that vision I had, all those years ago—it was kind'a like she was gonna become a goddess, more or less against her will. There was some sadness in her, like she always just slightly missed the boat her whole life. Be kind'a weird if she was, huh? If that cult really was worshiping a live one? A god created from a teenage girl who never wanted anything but a normal life in absolute obscurity and a half-baked old physics professor? Hell, you always think of being a goddess as having no troubles at all, no pain, no worries, and anything you want. I'd like to do it, just for a little bit. Point my astral finger and say, '*From this point on, the more chocolate you eat the more weight you will lose.*'"

Kira laughed, and then remarked, "You know, it *is* something to think about. Between the two of you, *you* might have had fun as a goddess, while the one who might well have gotten it, would carry it as a burden." She sighed, "I don't know, though. Maybe, if you must have a god, that's the kind of attitude you want your Supreme Being to have."

Charley shrugged. "Yeah, well, maybe I *am* living the life she so much wanted, but I love it and if Sam's up there in the great beyond looking down at me with jealous eyes she can just eat her heart out."

The sky, which only a moment before had been a clear blue one, suddenly went dark, and storm clouds suddenly rumbled overhead, and there was the feeling of the barometer dropping and the distant sounds of thunder.

"Only kidding, Sam!" Charley said loudly to the sky. "Only kidding!"